# The Elson Readers

# Book Eight

(Revision of Elson Grammar School Reader, Book Four)

by

## William H. Elson
Author of Good English Series

AND

## Christine M. Keck
Head Union Junior High School English, Grand Rapids, Michigan

# Publisher's Note

Recognizing the need to return to more traditional principles in education, Lost Classics Book Company is republishing forgotten late 19th and early 20th century literature and textbooks to aid parents in the education of their children.

This edition of *The Elson Readers—Book Eight* was reprinted from the 1921 copyright edition. The text has been updated and edited only where necessary. Spelling and punctuation have been updated in works of prose, but not in poetry—these things being the prerogative of the poet.

We have included a glossary and pronunciation guide of more than 1746 terms at the end of the book to encourage children to look up words they don't know.

*The Elson Readers—Book Eight* has been assigned a reading level of 1120L. More information concerning this reading level assessment may be attained by visiting www.lexile.com.

© Copyright 2005
Lost Classics Book Company
Library of Congress Catalog Card Number: 2001091014
ISBN 978-1-890623-22-7
Part of
*The Elson Readers*
Nine Volumes: *Primer* through *Book Eight*
ISBN 978-1-890623-23-4

On the Cover:
Titania, Queen of the Fairies. Costume design for "A Midsummer Night's Dream" produced by Robert Courtneidge at the Princes Theatre, Manchester by C. Wilhelm (1858-1925)
**Victoria & Albert Museum, London, UK/Bridgeman Art Library**

# William H. Elson

———•———

In the early 1930s, William Harris Elson capped off a successful career as an educator and author of textbook readers by creating the "Fun with Dick and Jane" pre-primer readers with co-author William Scott Gray. Dick and Jane, their families, friends, and pets entered the popular culture as symbols of childhood, and the books themselves became synonymous with the first steps in learning to read.

In 1909, *The Elson Grammar School Reader*, the first in a nine-volume series of school readers, appeared to immediate success. *The Elson Readers*, which Lost Classics Book Company is reprinting, were among Elson's earliest creations and go well beyond the scope of the "Dick and Jane" books. Following a carefully planned model that stresses both improving comprehension and developing appreciation for literature, Elson organized the books in a way that built on the understanding and skills taught in earlier volumes.

Assisting Elson on the series were publishing house writers Lura Runkel and Christine Keck. Runkel helped on the primer and the first and second volume, while Keck worked on the fifth through the eighth volume. Obviously both writers were schooled well in Elson's methodology, as the series displays remarkable consistency and accuracy throughout the entire set of books.

Through the eighth grade, or age 13 to 14, each succeeding book in the *Elson Readers* series introduces students to increasingly complex genres and better writers. The result of using the series as intended is better reading skills and comprehension as well as a growing appreciation for good writing. But the books are so thorough that they may be used individually and still advance a student's understanding and appreciation for the types of writing in a particular volume.

Born on November 22, 1854 in Carroll County, Ohio, Elson lived through a tumultuous period, becoming an educator who helped usher in numerous innovations. Although he did not receive his A.B. degree from Indiana University until 1895, he was active as a schoolteacher and as a school administrator for many years before, beginning with his first teaching assignment in 1881. By 1907 he had established the first technical high school in the nation in Cleveland, Ohio, where he served as school superintendent from 1906-12.

Elson's contributions to teaching children to read and appreciate literature included not only the Elson Readers but many other series for which he served as primary author or editor, including *Good English* (3 vols., 1916); *Child-Library Readers* (9 vols., 1923-34); and *Elson Junior Literature* (2 vols., 1932). By the time of his death on February 2, 1935, his books had sold over fifty million copies and were in use in 34 countries on every continent.

Besides helping to create the engaging "Fun with Dick and Jane" books, William Harris Elson implemented a developmental approach to learning reading skills that still works extremely well. Lost Classics Book Company's republication of this volume from the *Elson Readers* provides access to a book that will provide children with a delightful and effective learning experience.

David E. Vancil, Ph.D.
Indiana State University

*Biographical Dictionary of American Educators.* 3 Vols. Edited by John F. Ohles. Westport, CT: Greenwood Press, 1978. Alphabetical entry.
*The National Cyclopaedia of American Biography.* Volume 26. New York: James T. White & Co., 1937. Pp. 367-68.

# Preface

—✝—

This book is based on the belief that an efficient reader for the eighth grade must score high when tested on five fundamental features: *quality* of literature, *variety* of literature, *organization* of literature, *quantity* of literature, and *definite helps* sufficient to make the text a genuine tool for classroom use.

First among these features is the essential that the foundation of the book must be the acknowledged masterpieces of American and British authors. American boys and girls may be depended upon to read current magazines and newspapers, but if they are ever to have their taste and judgment of literary values enriched by familiarity with the classics of our literature, the schools must provide the opportunity. This ideal does not mean the exclusion of well-established present-day writers, but it does mean that the core of the school reader should be the rich literary heritage that has won recognition for its enduring value. Moreover, these masterpieces must come to the pupil in complete units, not in mere excerpts or garbled "cross-sections," for the pupil in his school life should gain some real literary possessions.

**Quality of Literature**

A study of the contents of *The Elson Readers, Book Eight,* will show how consistently its authors have based the book on this sound test of quality. The works of the acknowledged "makers" of our literature have been abundantly drawn upon to furnish a foundation of great stories and poems, gripping in interest and well within the powers of pupil appreciation in this grade.

Variety is fundamental to a well-rounded course of reading. If the school reader is to provide for all the purposes that a collection of literature for this grade should serve, it must contain material covering at least the following types: (1) literature representing both British and American authors; (2) some of the best contemporary poetry and prose as well as the great literature of the past; (3) patriotic

**Variety of Literature**

literature, rich in ideals of home and country, loyalty and service, industry and thrift, cooperation, and citizenship—ideals of which, during World War One, American children gained a new conception that the school reader should perpetuate; (4) literature suited to festival occasions, particularly those celebrated in the schools; (5) literature of the seasons, nature, and out-of-door life; (6) literature of humor that will enliven the reading and cultivate the power to discriminate between *wholesome* humor—an essential part of life—and crude humor, so prevalent in the pupil's outside reading; (7) adventure stories both imaginative and real; (8) literature that portrays the romance of industry; (9) literature suited to dramatization, providing real project material.

This book offers a well-rounded course of reading covering all the types mentioned above. Especially by means of groups of stories and poems *that portray love of our free country and its flag, and unselfish service to others, this book makes a stirring appeal to the true spirit of good citizenship.* Moreover, wholesome ethical ideals pervade the literature throughout.

The literature of a school reader, if it is to do effective work, must be purposefully organized. Sound organization groups into **Organization of Literature** related units the various selections that center about a common theme. *This arrangement enables the pupil to see the larger dominant ideas of the book as a whole, instead of looking upon it as a confused scrapbook of miscellaneous selections.* Such arrangement also fosters literary comparison by bringing together selections having a common theme or authorship.

This book has been so organized as to fulfill these purposes. There are four main parts, each distinguished by unity of theme. "Part I" aims to develop a wholesome appreciation of nature; "Part II" deals with the magic world of adventure; "Part III" makes clear the basic principles of our "Great American Experiment" in self-government and points out the way to the right kind of citizenship; and "Part IV" presents certain phases of life in our homeland that will make America more significant to boys and girls. Through these grouped selections, fundamental ideals in the development of personal character and good citizenship are established.

*Five unique features* keep the plan of the book and the dominant theme of each part clearly in the foreground: (1) A pupils' introduction called "Literature and Life" that emphasizes the joy and value of reading and makes clear the plan of the book, showing the pupil what to look for in each main part; (2) Visual "guideposts"—large-type headings, half-title pages, and pictures typifying the theme of each unit; (3) A special "Introduction" to each main part, that gives the pupil a graphic but simple forecast of the main ideal dominating the group; (4) "Notes and Questions" that stress the contribution each story or poem makes to the main idea of the group; (5) A "Review" following each main division that serves, *first*, to crystallize into permanent form the various impressions left in the pupil's mind by the selections within each unit, and, *second*, to call into play the pupil's initiative, leading him to apply the ideas that dominate the group either through parallel readings or through his own experience.

Obviously, a book that is to supply the pupil with a year's course in literature must be a generous volume. Variety is impossible without quantity, especially where literary wholes rather than mere fragmentary excerpts are offered. Particularly is this true when complete units are included not only for intensive study, but also for extensive reading—longer units to be read mainly for the story element. *In bulk such units should be as large as the pupil can control readily in rapid silent reading, a kind of reading that increases the power to enjoy with intelligence a magazine or a book.*

**Quantity of Literature**

*The Elson Readers, Book Eight,* which is a condensation of *Junior High School Literature, Book Two,* is a generous volume that provides for these needs. Its inclusiveness makes possible a proper balance between prose and poetry, between long and short selections, and between material for intensive and extensive reading.

If the pupil is to gain the full benefit from reading, certain definite helps must be provided. An efficient reader must **Definite Helps** score a high test not only on the *fundamentals* of *quality, variety, organization,* and *quantity* of literature, but also on its *fitness as a tool for classroom use.*

The effectiveness of this reader as such a tool may be indicated by the following distinguishing features:

(1) A distinctive introduction, "Literature and Life" (see page 17), shows what literature is and gives the plan of the book.

(2) Definite provisions are made for developing speed and concentration in silent reading. (See pages 13, 29, 41, etc.)

(3) A comprehensive glossary contains the words and phrases that offer valuable vocabulary training, either of pronunciation or meaning. The teacher is free to use the glossary according to the needs of his or her particular class, but suggested type words and phrases are listed under "Notes and Questions."

(4) A complete program of study, "How to Gain the Full Benefit from Your Reading" (pages 37-39), gives a concise explanation of the various helps found in the book.

(5) The helps to study are more than mere notes; they aid in making significant the larger purposes of the selections. These "Notes and Questions" include:

(a) Biographies of the authors that supply data for interpreting the stories and poems.

(b) Historical settings, wherever they are necessary to the intelligent understanding of the selection (see pages 143, 262, etc.).

(c) Questions and suggestions that present clearly the main idea, stimulate original discussion and comparison, and bring out modern parallels to the situations found in the selections.

(d) Words of common use frequently mispronounced, listed for study under "Discussion" (see page 38, etc.).

(e) Phrases that offer idiomatic difficulty; for convenience in locating these phrases the page and line number is indicated.

(f) Problems, individual and social (see pages 91, 237, etc.).

# Contents

CITIZENSHIP AND SERVICE

### PART IV. LITERATURE AND LIFE IN THE HOMELAND

AMERICAN SCENES AND LEGENDS

AMERICAN LITERATURE OF LIGHTER VEIN

AMERICAN WORKERS AND THEIR WORK

## Suggestions for an Order of Reading

In the *Elson Readers* selections are grouped according to theme or authorship. Such an arrangement enables the pupil to see the dominant ideas of the book as a whole. This purpose is further aided by an "Introduction" and a "Review" for each main group. The book, therefore, emphasizes certain fundamental ideals, making them stand out clearly in the mind of the pupil. This result can best be accomplished by reading the selections in the order given.

It goes without saying that selections particularly suited to the celebration of special days will be read in connection with such festival occasions. For example, "A Christmas Carol," page 151, will be read immediately before the Christmas holidays, even if the class at that particular time is in the midst of some other main part of the reader. Before assigning a selection out of order, however, the teacher should scrutinize the notes and questions, to make certain that no references are made within these notes to a discussion in an introduction or to other selections in the group that pupils have not yet read. In case such references are found the teacher may well conduct a brief class discussion to make these questions significant to the pupils.

It is the belief of the authors that many of the longer prose stories should be read silently and reported on in class. In this way the monotony incident to the reading of such selections aloud in class will be avoided. However, the class will wish to read aloud certain passages from these longer units because of their beauty, their dramatic quality, or the forceful way in which the author has expressed his thoughts. Class readings are suggested for this purpose. In this way reading aloud is given purposefulness.

## Suggestions for Silent and Oral Reading

**Silent Reading.** This book includes abundant material for both silent and oral reading. Some stories and poems must be read thoughtfully in order to gain the author's full meaning; such reading cannot be done rapidly. In other selections the meaning can be grasped easily, and the reading can be rapid; in such cases you read mainly for the central thought, for the story element.

Ability in silent reading is of great importance for two reasons. First, you read silently much more often than you read aloud to others. Second, investigations prove that pupils who have learned to read silently with speed generally gain and retain from their reading more facts than the slow readers do. You should, therefore, train yourself in rapid silent reading, concentrating your mind on the thought of the selection. You will soon discover that as you give closer attention to a story you will not only understand it better but you will also remember more of it. In the early grades your training in silent reading has enabled you to gather facts from individual paragraphs and to hold in mind the thread of the narrative in shorter selections. But you are to extend this power steadily until you can gather facts and follow the unfolding plot in selections of considerable length. A number of stories in this book are long enough to train you to read with intelligence a newspaper, a magazine article, or a book. And this is precisely the ability you most need, not only in preparing lessons in history and other school subjects, but in all your reading throughout life. As you train yourself to grasp swiftly and accurately the meaning of a page, you increase your capacity to enjoy books—one of the most pleasurable things in life. Theodore Roosevelt trained himself to be such a rapid reader that he was able to grasp the central thought of a page almost as quickly as he could turn the leaves of the book.

You read silently both for the story element and for fact-gathering. In preparing lessons in geography and history and in the use of geographical and historical stories, you have the best possible opportunity

13

to increase your ability to gather facts quickly from the printed page. These informational studies, however, do not take the place of the reading lesson in literature. Some selections, such as Audubon's "The Mockingbird," are informational, and you read them mainly for the facts they contain. In others, such as "Coaly-Bay, the Outlaw Horse," the story element is the important thing, and fact-gathering is subordinate. Still others, such as "You Are the Hope of the World," have inspirational value, and you read them for their stimulating influence on your life.

Notice that you read more rapidly when you are looking for the answer to some particular question or looking for a certain passage than you do when you read merely to follow the thread of the story. Moving your lips or pointing to the words with your finger retards your speed.

In the selections in this book suggested for silent reading you may test your ability in thought-gathering in any of the following ways:

1. By using a list of questions covering the most important ideas of the selection (for example, see "Questions for Testing Silent Reading," p. 40).

2. By telling the story from a given outline (for example, see "Outline for Testing Silent Reading," p. 41).

3. By making a list of questions yourself for some classmate to use in testing his thought-gathering ability, while you make similar use of questions that he has prepared.

4. By telling the story from an outline that you have made. Telling the substance of the story from your own outline is an excellent kind of test because you test not only your understanding of the story, but also your memory and your power to express the thought of what you have read.

In testing for comprehension, the plan followed should be suited to the kind of selection to which the test is applied. In testing for facts, questions that bring out the main thoughts should be used. In testing for plot structure the outline is particularly helpful, though questions that deal with the steps in the development of the narrative may be equally effective.

In all your reading, both at home and at school, you should read as rapidly as you can, but not so fast that you fail to gain the thought. In preparing your lessons on selections in this book, test your comprehension by seeing how many of the questions under "Discussion," which develop the most important thoughts of the story, you can answer after one reading. You may have to read parts of the story more than once in order to gain the full meaning. If you record your reading speed and your thought-gathering ability, comparing your standing with that of your classmates and with the standard for eighth-grade pupils, you will be able to see whether or not you are making satisfactory progress. *The standard for eighth-grade boys and girls is 280 words per minute, with the ability to reproduce after one reading 50% of the ideas in a 400-word passage.* The following forms will suggest a way to record your results:

### INDIVIDUAL RECORD

| DATE | TITLES | SPEED | | COMPREHENSION |
|------|--------|-------|---|---------------|
| | | No. of minutes required to read story | No. words per minute | Ten points for each of ten test questions* |
| | Coaly-Bay.............. | | | |
| | Total No. Words, 2930 | | | |
| | The Ransom of Red Chief. | | | |
| | Total No. Words, 4130 | | | |

*Questions to be selected by the teacher.

### CLASS RECORD

| DATE | SPEED | | | COMPREHENSION | | | |
|------|-------|---|---|---------------|---|---|---|
| | No. words per minute | | | Ten points for each of ten test questions | | | |
| | Lowest | Highest | Median | Lowest | Highest | Median | |
| | | | | | | | |

You may wish occasionally, perhaps once a term, to find out your rating in a more accurate and scientific way by the use of one of the many standardized silent-reading tests. Such a test will give you an opportunity to compare your ability with that of boys and girls of similar grade throughout the country.

**Oral Reading.** In the prose selections suggested for silent reading, you will wish to read aloud certain passages because of their beauty, their dramatic quality, or the forceful way in which the author has expressed his thoughts. In these prose selections, *Class Readings* are suggested for this purpose. Sometimes these readings are intended for individual pupils; sometimes, particularly in dialogue, they are intended for groups. *Class Reading* also includes supplementary poems and stories suggested for oral presentation.

Narrative poems such as "Evangeline" and "The Building of the Ship," together with poems consisting of descriptive scenes such as "Snow-Bound," may well be treated as silent reading, provided adequate provision is made for reading aloud those units that are conspicuous for their beauty of thought or expression.

In general, however, poetry should be read aloud, for much of the beauty of poetry lies in its rhythm. The voice, with its infinite possibilities of change, is an important factor in interpreting a poem. As you listen to your teacher or some other good reader, you will appreciate how much pleasure one who has learned the art of reading aloud is able to give others. Through oral reading the ear of the listener becomes sensitive to a pleasing voice, to correct pronunciation, and to distinct articulation. The sympathetic reading of many of the poems in this book will reveal to you the beauty of the language that we speak. Longfellow says, "Of equal honor with him who writes a grand poem is he who reads it grandly."

## LITERATURE AND LIFE

### THE THREE JOYS OF READING

Reading, as you have already come to know, brings you a threefold joy. First, it gives you the joy of sharing in the adventures of men in bygone times and in far-distant lands. Already, in your imagination, you have been comrades in the enchanting lives of Robinson Crusoe and Gulliver and Hiawatha. You have lived again in the magic realm where ruled the King of the Golden River and in that other land of romance where good King Arthur held his knightly court. This book that you hold in your hand will lead you still further in quest of stirring deeds, making you the companion of rollicking old John Gilpin and of Evangeline in her romantic wanderings and of many others. Always, whether in school years or in later life, there will be this joy of reading that can transport you to other times and places full of mystery and adventure.

Second, reading brings you the joy of gaining your full portion of the wisdom that mankind has stored up through the ages. Through literature you have already shared some of the shrewd advice of Franklin and Lincoln on the subject of thrift, timely enough in America today, and have learned what good citizenship meant to patriots, from the colonial ideals shown in *Grandfather's Chair* to the vigorous Americanism of Theodore Roosevelt. Through literature, also, you have learned how brave men have fought for freedom. The stories of great leaders—Leonidas and Robert Bruce and our own George Washington—have given you an understanding of what liberty means. In this book you will learn the views of Daniel Webster on the duties that our country, as the model of self-government, owes the world—wisdom as useful today as it was two genera- tions ago—and many other bits of knowledge that you may well treasure as guides to lead you through life. All your years this second joy of reading will give you the power to ripen your judgment by the accumulated wisdom left as an inheritance by the world's greatest minds.

And the third joy that reading brings you is the awakening of your feelings to the wonders that lie all about you in the great outdoor world. Already the poets have enriched your lives by revealing the charms of nature when viewed through "seeing eyes." If you have read with an understanding mind the poem by Robert Burns, "To a Mountain Daisy," even the commonest flowers of the field will have their message for you. And such lovers of nature as Audubon and Roosevelt and Baynes have shown you how a trip through the woods may bring stirring adventure, or the quieter joy of close kinship with birds and beasts. In this book, Bryant, Wordsworth, Ernest Thompson Seton, and many others will reveal to you new pictures of the beauty of the world in which we live.

### What Is Literature?

Through reading, then, you gain happiness and power. But all about you there is so much to read—thousands of books and magazines and papers—that it may be well to pause long enough to answer the question, "What kind of reading will bring these rewards? What is literature?"

In one sense, anything written or printed, anything expressed in permanent or semipermanent form, as distinguished from that which is merely spoken, is literature. The ballad, a songstory, was repeated from generation to generation by word of mouth, changing in details of language and incident in the process; when it was written down and then printed, it became fixed, became literature. So also the traveler may tell you of his adventures, may tell audiences in many cities of his adventures; when he writes his story and it is published as a book, it becomes literature, in this sense of the word.

In a truer sense, however, the word "literature" is more strictly limited. You have seen that it is *permanence* of form that distinguishes the book or the printed story from mere tradition. But thousands of books are printed that find a few readers for a time and then are as completely forgotten as if they had been merely words spoken in casual conversation. Many things are printed, also, which are not intended to have permanence, such as newspaper stories of daily happenings in the city or throughout the world. The newspaper, to be sure, adds greatly to our power of partaking in the important events of the day, wherever they may occur. One knows about battles half a world away, almost as soon as they are fought, or about a new remedy for disease, or the triumph of a great man. But these records are of a day; true literature is for all time. It has a different permanence from that of mere printed paper. Literature, in this truer sense, means not merely that which is printed, in contrast to that which is spoken. It means the expression of the *facts* of life, or of the *interpretation* of life, or of the *beauty* of life, in *language of such enduring charm that men treasure it and will not let it die.*

In your reading you have already become acquainted with literature that sets forth the "facts of life." When Parkman wrote his account of the American buffalo in *The Oregon Trail*, he was making a permanent record of wildlife on the Western Plains in pioneer days. When Hamlin Garland wrote sketches of his boyhood on the prairie, he was recording the primitive life of midwestern farmers so vividly that the pictures will enable future generations to understand the hardships, as well as the simple joys, of the thrifty, toiling folk who built our "inland empire." When Sir Walter Scott gave us his *Tales of a Grandfather* he was preserving for all time the thrilling "facts of life" that centered around Scotland's brave struggle for freedom centuries ago. And in our own day the poet Noyes in his "Song of the Trawlers" records the heroism of English seamen, offering their lives in the same great cause. The book you hold in your hand will give you still other examples of literature that deals with the "facts of life." Daniel Webster, in "The American Experiment," will set forth for you the ideals of our great democracy; the poet Whittier will paint for you in "Snow-Bound" a picture that will give you a clear understanding of life in rural New England; Herschel Hall through his story "Pete of the Steel-Mills" will give you a glimpse of the romance that may be found amidst the toil of huge industrial centers. These and many others of the makers of literature will help you to gain an acquaintance with some of the "facts of life." Many of these facts, it is true, you may learn from your geography or your history text or from an encyclopedia, but all through life you will find pleasure and increased understanding if you will supplement books of this latter kind by the literature of great authors who have recorded their observation of events and peoples *in language of such enduring charm that men treasure it and will not let it die.*

Literature that *interprets* life has also been a part of your reading course. Lowell in his poem "To a Dandelion" has shown the little flower as a symbol of the riches that lie all about us in the commonest of things; so also Robert Burns has touched the mountain daisy with his poetic fancy and made of it a token of life's uncertainties. Hawthorne in "The Great Stone Face" and Ruskin in "The King of the Golden River" have interpreted for us the great ideal of service to others. And in this book, Bryant through his poem "To a Waterfowl" breathes a message of hope and faith to all mankind, while Dickens in "A Christmas Carol" interprets the spirit of human brotherhood that makes life worthwhile. And last, there is the literature that makes evident to us the beauty that our more prosaic eyes might fail to note. Wordsworth writes a poem about daffodils, and ever after, if you have read it with an understanding mind, you see new beauty in the flower life that lies about you. When you have read in this book Browning's "Home-Thoughts from Abroad," springtime will come to you filled with new delights.

Facts, interpretation, beauty—these form the body of real literature. And when master writers clothe this body *in language of such enduring charm that men treasure it and will not let it die*, true literature comes into being. Thus the experiences, the meaning, the emotions of life are given permanent form to enrich mankind throughout the centuries.

### The Plan of this Book

This book offers you a generous body of literature that will provide all three of the "Joys of Reading." The literature is divided into four main groups. The first of these, called "The World of Nature," is largely made up of poems, such as Wordsworth's song "To a Skylark," that appeal to the sense of beauty, or interpret for you some of nature's charms. But you will find, also, selections by such writers as Audubon and Garland and Ernest Thompson Seton that set forth the "facts of life" in the outdoor world. For literature of whatever theme—whether it be of nature or adventure or patriotism—is not confined to any one appeal, but is blended of all three elements—fact, interpretation, beauty. Animals, birds, flowers, trees, the changing seasons—all these are the themes of various selections in this part of your book. As you read you will begin to see that the writer of true literature makes his poem or story out of what he sees in life that is worth expressing in words of such power and beauty that "the world will not let it die."

A second part of your book contains a group of stories and poems called "The World of Adventure." Some of these are hundreds of years old, others were written just the other day, but all of them will grip you with the vital interest you feel in reading about "doers of great deeds," or will give you the joy of reading that comes when you are transported in imagination to realms of mystery.

A little later in your book appears a group of selections under the title "The Great American Experiment" that you will find very different from the stories and poems of the preceding groups. How mankind has struggled through the centuries for liberty, how our country has organized its hard-won freedom in what Daniel Webster called a "Great Experiment," how American boys and girls can do their part in making this experiment a success—these are some of the themes that make "Part III" perhaps the most important section in your book; for one of the purposes of literature is to set forth great ideals, and young Americans can find no subject of greater value than the right kind of citizenship.

And last, you will read a long section called "Literature and Life in the Homeland." Through it you will catch a few glimpses of the complex life that makes up this America of ours. The more intimately you come to know the many phases of our country, the better citizen you will be. This understanding you may gain through reading, for literature expresses the soul of a people. Literature and life—after all, this sums up the whole matter. They are not separate things, but united. Literature is not worth much unless it comes from the life of the people, and life is not worth much if it means just working for a living or for pleasure or in order to heap up a pile of money. If we are able to widen our experiences, to see facts for ourselves and to be able to interpret their meaning, to see beauty in all the world about us, life gains in richness. And it is literature that helps us to gain these riches.

# Part I

## The World of Nature

*God made all the creatures and gave them our love and our fear,*
*To give sign we and they are his children, one family here.*

—Robert Browning

AUTUMN

# THE WORLD OF NATURE

## An Introduction

As long as man has lived on this earth, he has been powerfully influenced by the world of nature. To tribesmen in very early times, fire seemed a mysterious spirit, willing to help man where rightly used, capable of destroying him and his property when enraged. One people had a legend that Prometheus, a friend of man, stole fire from heaven so that men might equal gods. The same mystery surrounded the movements of the heavenly bodies. Many ancient peoples worshiped the sun as a god—the source of light and life. The moon was a pale goddess, exerting wide influence on men and their fortunes. Through many centuries the stars were supposed to bring fortune or disaster. Indeed, the word "disaster" itself refers to evil stars. We still say, sometimes, "My stars!" or "My lucky star." Shakespeare speaks often of this influence of the stars upon men; and Napoleon, who lived only two centuries ago, believed implicitly in the influence of the stars upon his fortunes. Savage tribes, and ignorant men even of today, see in the appearance of comets portents of disaster. Panics are still known to occur in certain parts of the earth when there is an eclipse of the sun. The Teutonic tribes of northern Europe believed that thunder was caused by the hammer of Thor, one of their divinities; the ancient Greeks thought it was the voice of Jove; many Christian peoples, even, have regarded great storms as signs of God's anger.

In large part, these ideas and many others like them have been due to ignorance about nature. Fire, lightning, eclipses, storms, earthquakes, the mystery of the sea—these were not understood and therefore were thought to be caused by the gods. Many peoples have believed that even the kindly aspects of nature were influenced by supernatural powers. There were divinities of the harvest, of the rain, of the months and seasons. The wood and the water were inhabited by deities of less importance. The origin of the flowers was explained by this religion of nature. Thus men in all ages have felt the influence of nature upon them and have sought to explain it, in art and song and story, as well as in religion.

We have won from nature many of her secrets now. We have chained the lightning so that it pulls long trains of cars, puts the complicated machinery of a great factory in motion, performs more services in our daily lives than ever the genius called forth by Aladdin's lamp. We have learned the secrets of the air, so that we can project our thoughts through innumerable leagues, even without the use of wires. The deeds that the forces of Nature perform at man's bidding are so astounding that the stories of what ancient peoples thought their nature gods could do seem small and insignificant. Even the imagination of man has been surpassed by the wonders he has learned to perform.

Yet the influence of nature upon our lives is none the less real, nor are her secrets all discovered. Part of our business in this life is to *establish relations* with the world in which we live—that is, to appreciate and learn how to enjoy the things that surround us. If we move into a big house set in the midst of a large plot of ground, we get acquainted with the rooms of this house, with the furniture, with its conveniences and inconveniences, with every part of the ground that surrounds the house, with the trees and flowers and birds and animals that are near us. The great world, into which we come when we are born, is such a house. It is not just a place for eating and sleeping and working and playing. There are people to get acquainted with. There is the body which is our personal house to get acquainted with. We must learn to find our way around. As we look out through the windows of our eyes we seek to find our place in the world of nature outside. If we look attentively we shall soon come to see that this world of nature is full of many wonders. We shall see, for example, that animals have personalities like human beings. One may learn secrets of nature from the brook, from the forest, from the birds. We use the conveniences that science has brought to us; we should also realize the wonder and magic of the world. Always there are the passing days with sunrise and high noon and the evening star. Always there is the magic of spring or of the day in June or of the first snowfall. And always there are living creatures about us, insects, and birds and animals and inhabitants of lake and sea. The world of nature is full of life and mystery. Through science, and through what poets and other keen observers have set down for us in books, we shall be able to make our way about and to add beauty and interest to our lives.

The selections that follow are given to you as guides to this exploration. First, there is a little group of stories which will prove to you the truth of the statement that "animals have personalities like human beings." After that you will find selections about birds, giving some thoughts on the influence these children of Nature have upon the lives of men. For example, you will learn how an American poet, at a moment of great discouragement in his own life, was given new courage by the sight of a waterfowl following its sure course through the trackless air. This part of your book will also show you how the flowers and the trees and the changing seasons add to the charm and magic of nature.

Some of these poems and stories interpret life, others merely express the beauty of our outdoor surroundings. As you read them, see if you can understand why it is that men "treasure" the poems of such writers as Bryant and Wordsworth and Tennyson.

In many of the selections in this part of the book you are dealing not with science, the knowledge of the facts of nature as you get these facts from geography or botany or chemistry, but with facts as interpreted through the imagination of the poets. In others you have examples of what men of scientific training have observed in their studies of nature.  You need both; one study supplements the other; both are the means by which you establish relations between the soul that is you and the outside world which is to be your home for all the years of your life.

# ANIMALS

## COALY-BAY, THE OUTLAW HORSE*

### ERNEST THOMPSON SETON

### THE WILLFUL BEAUTY

Five years ago in the Bitterroot Mountains of Idaho there was a beautiful little foal.  His coat was bright bay; his legs, mane, and tail were glossy black—coal black and bright bay—so they named him Coaly-Bay.

5    "Coaly-Bay" sounds like "Kolibey," which is an Arab title of nobility, and those who saw the handsome colt, and did not know how he came by the name, thought he must be of Arab blood.  No doubt he was, in a far-away sense; just as all our best horses have Arab blood, and once in a while it seems to come 10 out strong and show in every part of the creature, in his frame, his power, and his wild, free, roving spirit.

Coaly-Bay loved to race like the wind; he gloried in his speed and his tireless legs; when he was careering with the herd of colts, if they met a fence or ditch, it was as natural for Coaly-Bay 15 to overleap it as it was for the others to sheer off.

---

*See Silent and Oral Reading, page 13.

So he grew up strong of limb, restless of spirit, and rebellious at any thought of restraint. Even the kindly curb of the hay yard or the stable was unwelcome, and he soon showed that he would rather stand out all night in a driving storm than be
5 locked in a comfortable stall where he had no vestige of the liberty he loved so well.

He became very clever at dodging the horse wrangler whose job it was to bring the horse herd to the corral. The very sight of that man set Coaly-Bay going. He became what is known as
10 a "quit-the-bunch"—that is, a horse of such independent mind that he will go his own way the moment he does not like the way of the herd.

So each month the colt became more set on living free, and more cunning in the means he took to win his way. Far down
15 in his soul, too, there must have been a streak of cruelty, for he stuck at nothing and spared no one that seemed to stand between him and his one desire.

When he was three years of age, just in the perfection of his young strength and beauty, his real troubles began, for now
20 his owner undertook to break him to ride. He was as tricky and vicious as he was handsome, and the first day's experience was a terrible battle between the horse trainer and the beautiful colt. But the man was skillful. He knew how to apply his power, and all the wild plunging, bucking, rearing, and rolling of the
25 wild one had no desirable result. With all his strength the horse was hopelessly helpless in the hands of the skillful horseman, and Coaly-Bay was so far mastered at length that a good rider could use him. But each time the saddle went on, he made a new fight. After a few months of this the colt seemed to realize
30 that it was useless to resist; it simply won for him lashings and spurrings, so he pretended to reform. For a week he was ridden each day, and not once did he buck, but on the last day he came home lame.

His owner turned him out to pasture. Three days later he
35 seemed all right; he was caught and saddled. He did not buck,

but within five minutes he went lame as before. Again he was turned out to pasture, and after a week, saddled, only to go lame again.

His owner did not know what to think, whether the horse
5 really had a lame leg or was only shamming, but he took the first chance to get rid of him, and though Coaly-Bay was easily worth fifty dollars, he sold him for twenty-five. The new owner felt he had a bargain, but after being ridden half a mile Coaly-Bay went lame. The rider got off to examine the foot, whereupon Coaly-Bay
10 broke away and galloped back to his old pasture. Here he was caught, and the new owner, being neither gentle nor sweet, applied spur without mercy, so that the next twenty miles was covered in less than two hours, and no sign of lameness appeared.

Now they were at the ranch of this new owner. Coaly-Bay
15 was led from the door of the house to the pasture, limping all the way, and then turned out. He limped over to the other horses. On one side of the pasture was the garden of a neighbor. This man was very proud of his fine vegetables and had put a six-foot fence around the place. Yet the very night after Coaly-Bay
20 arrived, certain of the horses got into the garden somehow and did a great deal of damage. But they leaped out before daylight and no one saw them.

The gardener was furious, but the ranchman stoutly maintained that it must have been some other horses, since his were
25 behind a six-foot fence.

Next night it happened again. The ranchman went out very early and saw all his horses in the pasture, with Coaly-Bay behind them. His lameness seemed worse now instead of better. In a few days, however, the horse was seen walking all right,
30 so the ranchman's son caught him and tried to ride him. But this seemed too good a chance to lose; all his old wickedness returned to the horse; the boy was bucked off at once and hurt. The ranchman himself now leaped into the saddle; Coaly-Bay bucked for ten minutes, but finding he could not throw the man,
35 he tried to crush his leg against a post, but the rider guarded

himself well. Coaly-Bay reared and threw himself backward;
the rider slipped off, the horse fell, jarring heavily, and before
he could rise the man was in the saddle again. The horse now
ran away, plunging and bucking; he stopped short, but the rider
5 did not go over his head, so Coaly-Bay turned, seized the man's
boot in his teeth, and but for heavy blows on the nose would
have torn him dreadfully. It was quite clear now that Coaly-Bay
was an "outlaw"—that is, an incurably vicious horse.

The saddle was jerked off, and he was driven, limping, into
10 the pasture.

The raids on the garden continued, and the two men began
to quarrel over them. But to prove that his horses were not
guilty the ranchman asked the gardener to sit up with him and
watch. That night as the moon was brightly shining they saw,
15 not all the horses, but Coaly-Bay, walk straight up to the garden
fence—no sign of a limp now—easily leap over it, and proceed
to gobble the finest things he could find. After they had made
sure of his identity, the men ran forward. Coaly-Bay cleared
the fence like a deer, lightly raced over the pasture to mix with
20 the horse herd, and when the men came near him he had—oh,
such an awful limp.

"That settles it," said the rancher. "He's a fraud, but he's a
beauty, and good stuff, too."

"Yes, but it settles who took my garden truck," said the
25 other.

"Wal, I suppose so," was the answer; "but luk a here, neighbor,
you haven't lost more'n ten dollars in truck. That horse is easily
worth—a hundred. Give me twenty-five dollars, take the horse,
an' call it square."

30 "Not much I will," said the gardener. "I'm out twenty-five
dollars' worth of truck; the horse isn't worth a cent more. I'll
take him and call it even."

And so the thing was settled. The ranchman said nothing
about Coaly-Bay being vicious as well as cunning, but the
35 gardener found out the very first time he tried to ride him that

the horse was as bad as he was beautiful.

Next day a sign appeared on the gardener's gate:

> ### FOR SALE
>
> First-class horse, sound
> and gentle, $10.00

5

### THE BEAR BAIT

Now at this time a band of hunters came riding by. There were three mountaineers, two men from the city, and the writer of this story. The city men were going to hunt bear. They had
10 guns and everything needed for bear hunting, except bait. It is usual to buy some worthless horse or cow, drive it into the mountains where the bears are, and kill it there. So, seeing the sign, the hunters called to the gardener: "Haven't you got a cheaper horse?"

15    The gardener replied: "Look at him there, ain't he a beauty? You won't find a cheaper horse if you travel a thousand miles."

"We are looking for an old bear bait, and five dollars is our limit," replied the hunter.

Horses were cheap and plentiful in that country; buyers
20 were scarce. The gardener feared that Coaly-Bay would escape. "Wal, if that's the best you can do, he's yourn."

The hunter handed him five dollars, then said: "Now stranger, the bargain's settled. Will you tell me why you sell this fine horse for five dollars?"

25    "Mighty simple. He can't be rode. He's dead lame when he's going your way and sound as a dollar going his own; no fence in the country can hold him; he's a dangerous outlaw. He's wickeder nor old Nick."

"Well, he's an almighty handsome bear bait," and the hunters
30 rode on.

Coaly-Bay was driven with the pack horses and limped dreadfully on the trail. Once or twice he tried to go back, but he was easily turned by the men behind him. His limp grew worse, and toward night it was painful to see him.

5 The leading guide remarked: "That thar limp is no fake. He's got some deep-seated trouble."

Day after day the hunters rode farther into the mountains, driving the horses along and hobbling them at night. Coaly-Bay went with the rest, limping along, tossing his 10 head and his long splendid mane at every step. One of the hunters tried to ride him and nearly lost his life, for the horse seemed possessed of a demon as soon as the man was on his back.

The road grew harder as it rose. A very bad bog had to be 15 crossed one day. Several horses were mired in it, and as the men rushed to the rescue, Coaly-Bay saw his chance of escape. He wheeled in a moment and turned himself from a limping, towheaded, sorry, bad-eyed creature into a high-spirited horse. Head and tail aloft now, shaking their black streamers in the 20 wind, he gave a joyous neigh, and, without a trace of lameness, dashed for his home one hundred miles away, threading each narrow trail with perfect certainty, though he had seen it but once before, and in a few minutes he had steamed away from their sight.

25 The men were furious, but one of them, saying not a word, leaped on his horse—to do what? Follow that free-ranging racer? Sheer folly. Oh, no!—he knew a better plan. He knew the country. Two miles around by the trail, half a mile by the rough cut-off that he took, was Panther Gap. The runaway must 30 pass through that, and Coaly-Bay raced down the trail to find the guide below awaiting him. Tossing his head with anger, he wheeled on up the trail again, and within a few yards recovered his monotonous limp and his evil expression. He was driven into camp, and there he vented his rage by kicking in the ribs 35 of a harmless little pack horse.

### HIS DESTINED END

This was bear country, and the hunters resolved to end his dangerous pranks and make him useful for once. They dared not catch him; it was not really safe to go near him, but two of the guides drove him to a distant glade where bears abounded.
5 A thrill of pity came over me as I saw that beautiful untamable creature going away with his imitation limp.

"Aren't you coming along?" called the guide.

"No, I don't want to see him die," was the answer. Then as the tossing head was disappearing I called: "Say, fellows, I wish you
10 would bring me that mane and tail when you come back!"

Fifteen minutes later a distant rifle crack was heard, and in my mind's eye I saw that proud head and those superb limbs, robbed of their sustaining indomitable spirit, falling flat and limp—to suffer the unsightly end of fleshly things. Poor
15 Coaly-Bay; he would not bear the yoke. Rebellious to the end, he had fought against the fate of all his kind. It seemed to me the spirit of an eagle or a wolf it was that dwelt behind those full, bright eyes that ordered all his wayward life.

I tried to put the tragic finish out of mind and had not long
20 to battle with the thought, not even one short hour, for the men came back.

Down the long trail to the west they had driven him; there was no chance for him to turn aside. He must go on, and the men behind felt safe in that.

25 Farther away from his old home on the Bitterroot River he had gone each time he journeyed. And now he had passed the high divide and was keeping the narrow trail that leads to the valley of bears and on to Salmon River, and still away to the open, wild Columbian Plains, limping sadly as though he knew.
30 His glossy hide flashed back the golden sunlight still richer than it fell, and the men behind followed like hangmen in the death train of a nobleman condemned—down the narrow trail till it opened into a little meadow, with rank, rich grass, a lovely

mountain stream, and winding bear paths up and down the waterside.

"Guess this'll do," said the older man. "Well, here goes for a sure death or a clean miss," said the other confidently, and, 5 waiting till the limper was out in the middle of the meadow, he gave a short, sharp whistle. Instantly Coaly-Bay was alert. He swung and faced his tormentors, his noble head erect, his nostrils flaring; a picture of horse beauty—yes, of horse perfection.

The rifle was leveled, the very brain its mark, just on the 10 cross line of the eyes and ears, that meant sure, sudden, painless death. The rifle cracked. The great horse wheeled and dashed away. It was sudden death or miss—and the marksman missed.

Away went the wild horse at his famous best, not for his eastern home, but down the unknown western trail, away and away; 15 the pine woods hid him from view, and left behind was the rifleman vainly trying to force the empty cartridge from his gun.

Down that trail with an inborn certainty he went, and on through the pines, then leaped a great bog, and splashed an hour later through the limpid Clearwater, and on, responsive to some 20 unknown guide that subtly called him from the farther west. And so he went till the dwindling pines gave place to scrubby cedars and these in turn were mixed with sage, and onward still, till the far-away flat plains of Salmon River were about him, and ever on, tireless, as it seemed, he went, and crossed the canyon 25 of the mighty Snake, and up again to the high, wild plains where the wire fence still is not, and on, beyond the Buffalo Hump, till moving specks on the far horizon caught his eager eyes, and coming on and near, they moved and rushed aside to wheel and face about. He lifted up his voice and called to them, the long 30 shrill neigh of his kindred when they bugled to each other on the far Chaldean plain; and back their answer came. This way and that they wheeled and sped and caracoled, and Coaly-Bay drew nearer, called, and gave the countersigns his kindred know, till this they were assured—he was their kind, he was of the wild, 35 free blood that man had never tamed. And when the night came

down on the purpling plain his place was in the herd as one who after many a long hard journey in the dark had found his home. There you may see him yet, for still his strength endures, and his beauty is not less. The riders tell me they have seen
5 him many times by Cedra. He is swift and strong among the swift ones, but it is that flowing mane and tail that mark him chiefly from afar.

There on the wild free plains of sage he lives; the stormwind smites his glossy coat at night and the winter snows are driven
10 hard on him at times; the wolves are there to harry all the weak ones of the herd, and in the spring the mighty grizzly, too, may come to claim his toll. There are no luscious pastures made by man, no grain foods; nothing but the wild, hard hay, the wind and the open plains, but here at last he found the thing he
15 craved—the one worth all the rest. Long may he roam—this is my wish, and this—that I may see him once again in all the glory of his speed with his black mane on the wind, the spur-galls gone from his flanks, and in his eyes the blazing light that grew in his far-off forebears' eyes as they spurned Arabian plains to leave
20 behind the racing wild beast and the fleet gazelle—yes, too, the driving sandstorm that o'erwhelmed the rest, but strove in vain on the dusty wake of the desert's highest born.

---

### How to Gain the Full Benefit from Your Reading

The reading of "Coaly-Bay, the Outlaw Horse," besides giving you pleasure, has no doubt given you a new idea of the unbreakable spirit of a horse chafing under restraint and an insight into the nature of animals that has set you to thinking. But if you are to get the full benefit from the story, or in fact from any story or poem in this book, you will need to pause long enough to notice certain facts. These will help you to enjoy more keenly and to understand more clearly what you read and at the same time to train yourself in good habits of reading.

**Introductions and Reviews.** First, you should read and discuss in class "Literature and Life" (pp. 17-22) and examine the "Table of Contents" to gain a general understanding of the aims and purposes of the book as a whole. As you study the contents, you will notice that each story and poem is a part of a special group that centers about some one big idea, such as nature, adventure, etc. Each selection will have a fuller meaning for you and will leave a more lasting impression if you understand how it, united with others in teamwork, helps to bring out the central thought of the unit. Before reading the selections in any group, you are asked to read and discuss in class the "Introduction" that precedes it, in order that you may know in a general way what to expect. As a preparation for a full appreciation of "Coaly-Bay," read the introduction to "The World of Nature," page 25. And after you have read all the selections in a group, you will enjoy a pleasant class period discussing the "Review" found at the close of each unit—taking stock, as it were, of the joy and benefit gained from your reading.

In addition to the introductions and the reviews, this book furnishes other aids to your reading, in the form of helpful "Notes and Questions" that contain some or all of the following features:

**Biography.** It is always desirable to know something about the author. When you learn, for example, on page 39, that Ernest Thompson Seton has written many famous books about animals and that he was appointed official naturalist for the government of Manitoba, Canada, you feel that he writes with authority in his chosen field.

**Discussion.** After you have read the story through, in preparation for the class period, you will find under the topic "Discussion," questions and notes that will help you gain the full meaning. For example, see question 2, page 39. Other questions, such as 3 and 4, will call your attention to the methods authors employ to get their effects, and to the beauty of the language. Others call attention to the connection between the thought of the selection and the central idea of the unit, as question 7. Still others bring out the effect the story has upon the reader, as question 6.

**Glossary.** One of the benefits that you should gain from reading is the learning of new words and the ability to use them. At the end of the "Discussion" on page 40 you will find a list of words, the meaning of which you are to look up in the glossary (p. 523), and a second list that you should find out how to pronounce by using the glossary. Many of these words you may think you know how to pronounce correctly; but perhaps you have been mispronouncing some of them. Look in the glossary for the words listed under question 10, and you may find that you have been mispronouncing Arab or Salmon. When you are looking up words in the pronunciation lists, be sure that you also understand their meaning. In addition to the words in these lists the glossary includes many other words. Whenever a selection contains a word that you are not sure you understand, form the habit of looking it up in the glossary or the dictionary.

Besides the individual words you do not understand, you will sometimes find a phrase, or a group of words, used in some special sense. The most striking of these are listed under the topic "Phrases for Study." Look them up in the glossary, for you will often find the hardest passage of the reading lesson made easy by the explanation of a single phrase.

## NOTES AND QUESTIONS

**Biography.** Ernest Thompson Seton (1860-1946), the artist and author, was born in England, but spent most of his life in America. He was educated at the Toronto Collegiate Institute and at the Royal Academy, London. He was always interested in the study of birds and animals as he found them in their natural haunts in the backwoods of Canada and on the western plains of the United States, where he lived for a number of years. For several years he served as official naturalist to the government of Manitoba, Canada. Mr. Seton was well-known as an artist and illustrated many of his own books on birds and animals; he was also one of the chief illustrators of the *Century Dictionary*. He wrote many books about birds and animals, among which are: *The Biography of a Grizzly*; *Wild Animals at Home*; and *Wild Animal Ways*, from which "Coaly-Bay, the Outlaw Horse" is taken.

**Discussion.** 1. Which one of the four owners that Coaly-Bay had at different times made the best bargain? Which one seemed to get the worst of it? Which one made short work of his ownership? Did any of them show a sympathy with Coaly-Bay's spirit? 2. Arabian horses are noted for graceful form, speed, intelligence, and spirit; can you tell why those who saw Coaly-Bay thought he must be of Arabian blood? 3. How does the leading guide's remark about Coaly-Bay's lameness show that it was a skillful imitation? 4. Notice the beauty of the author's description of Coaly-Bay's joining his kindred. With this in mind, prepare to read aloud the last three paragraphs of the story; which sentences do you like particularly well? 5. Compare the information on the sign with that given by the gardener to the hunters after the bargain was settled; how do you account for the difference? 6. How do you explain your sympathy for the horse in spite of his viciousness? 7. In the "Introduction" on pages 25 and 26 you read that some selections present the facts of nature as "interpreted through the imagination of the poets," while others show "what men of scientific training have observed"; to which of these kinds does this story belong? 8. On page 27 you read that "animals have personalities like human beings"; how does the story of Coaly-Bay prove the truth of this statement? 9. Find in the glossary the meaning of: foal; careering; vestige; bucking; hobbling; superb; limpid; caracoled; harry. 10. *Pronounce:* Arab; corral; indomitable; Salmon; subtly.

### Phrases for Study

*(Numbers in heavy type refer to pages; numbers in light type to lines.)*

| | |
|---|---|
| possessed of a demon, **34**, 12 | Chaldean plain, **36**, 31 |
| high divide, **35**, 27 | purpling plain, **37**, 1 |
| at his famous best, **36**, 13 | claim his toll, **37**, 12 |
| inborn certainty, **36**, 17 | spurned Arabian plains, **37**, 19 |
| wire fence still is not, **36**, 26 | desert's highest born, **37**, 22 |

**Questions for Testing Silent Reading**. *The Willful Beauty*. 1. Where is the scene of this story laid? 2. How did Coaly-Bay get his name? 3. Tell about his nature. 4. What is a "quit-the-bunch" horse? 5. Tell of the horse trainer's experience trying to break Coaly-Bay for riding. 6. What was the horse's trick? 7. For how much did the owner sell him? 8. How did the new owner feel about the sale? 9. What happened in the neighbor's vegetable garden? 10. Why was Coaly-Bay called an "outlaw" horse? 11. How did the gardener come into possession of the horse? 12. How did the gardener advertise?

*The Bear Bait*. 1. Who composed the band of hunters? 2. What did they do when they saw the sign? 3. What was the bait used for bear hunting? 4. How much did the hunters pay for Coaly-Bay? 5. What was the gardener's explanation of the low price? 6. Describe Coaly-Bay as he was driven along with the packhorses. 7. Tell of his attempt to escape. 8. How was he outwitted? 9. How did he vent his rage?

*His Destined End*. 1. What did the hunters resolve to do? 2. How did Ernest Thompson Seton feel when Coaly-Bay was driven away for bear bait? 3. How did the horse look as he faced his tormentors? 4. What happened when the rifle cracked? 5. In what direction did Coaly-Bay flee? 6. Tell about his flight.  7. Tell about Coaly-Bay's joining his wild kindred.  8. How are hunters able to recognize him?  9. Tell about his life on the free plains. 10. What is the author's wish for him?

**Outline for Testing Silent Reading**. *The Willful Beauty.*  (a) The scene of the story.  (b) Coaly-Bay, his appearance and his nature.  (c) The owner's experience in breaking him for riding.  (d) Coaly-Bay's trick.  (e) The ranchman's bargain.  (f) The new owner's experience with Coaly-Bay and his neighbor's vegetable garden.  (g) Settling with the gardener.  (h) The sign at the gate.

*The Bear Bait.*  (a) The band of hunters.  (b) Coaly-Bay sold for bear bait.  (c) The horse's attempt to escape and his capture.

*His Destined End.*  (a) Coaly-Bay being driven to the bear glade. (b) Ernest Thompson Seton's feeling for the horse.  (c) The crack of the rifle.  (d) Coaly-Bay's escape.  (e) Joining his wild kindred.  (f) Life upon the free plains.  (g) The author's wish.

---

## Satan, the War Dog That Saved a Town*

### Ernest Harold Baynes

"Somewhere in France," and not far from Verdun, a little village occupied a very important position in the Allies' line. It was held by a garrison consisting of a few hundred French soldiers, who had orders to hold on until they were relieved.

5 The enemy had succeeded in cutting them off from their friends in the rear, but they fought on bravely alone.  For days they had hindered the German advance, answering the enemy batteries with a steady stream of shells.

But now their ammunition was giving out, and there was no 10 way of getting more, for the enemy was in possession of every road.  Worst of all, the Germans had managed to plant a battery on the left in a position from which it could pour a deadly fire into the French town.  Owing to the shortage of shells, only a

---

*See Silent and Oral Reading, page 13.

weak reply could be made by the garrison.  If the latter could
only let the French army know the position of that battery, it
might yet be silenced in time.  But there was no way of letting it
know.  The telephone and telegraph wires had been cut, the last
5 homing pigeons had been killed by a bursting shell, and every
other means of communication was destroyed.

With the French garrison was a famous dog trainer named
Duval, from the war dog school at Satory.  He had been sent to
the front with two dogs, Rip and Satan, both in the messenger
10 service of the French army.  Rip, a soft-eyed Irish setter, was
killed in action soon after his arrival, and Satan had been left
with the French troops two miles in the rear of the now isolated
town where his master was stationed.

Satan was an ideal messenger dog, swift-limbed, intelligent,
15 and absolutely fearless under fire.  He was black as night, a
mongrel by birth, but a thoroughbred by nature.  His father was
a champion English greyhound, and from him he inherited his
speed.  His mother was a working Scotch collie that had won
more than one silver cup at the sheepdog trials in Scotland.

20      Satan loved just one man in all the world, and that man
was Duval.  Together they had walked several times over the
ground which now stretched between them, and Duval knew
that if their friends in the rear had any message to send, Satan
would bring it if it could be brought.  So every little while he
25 would raise his head cautiously and look out over the shell-torn
ground, hoping to see his dog.

At last he started forward with a great cry, "Voila!  Satan!
Satan!"  At first his companions could see nothing but a black
speck moving toward them from the distance.  But presently
30 the black speck took the form of a dog—a black dog wearing
a gas mask and skimming the earth as he came.  As he raced
over the rough ground and leaped the shell holes, some of the
men declared that he was flying—that they even saw his wings.
But the ground was fairly smoking under the enemy fire, and no
35 one but Duval believed that even this great speed and courage

would save him from death. Perhaps they were right, for down he went as a German bullet found its mark.

Duval saw him as he fell and saw him stagger to his feet again, confused and faltering. Taking his life in his hands the
5 man leaped to the top of the trench wall in full view of the enemy, and heedless of the bullets which sang around him, shouted at the top of his voice: "Satan! Satan! Come, *mon ami!* For France! For—!" A bullet cut him down.

But Satan had seen and heard, and with a frantic yelp—of
10 pain or joy, no one could tell—once more he was into his stride. On three legs now, and with the fourth swinging loose at the hip, he moved swiftly toward his goal. As he swept into the town a dozen hands caught him, and from a metal tube on his collar they took a message which read: "For God's sake, hold on. Will
15 send troops to relieve you tomorrow." It was signed by a well-known officer whose word could be relied on, and a cheer went up from the weary men. But how could they hold on? How was it possible with that German battery withering them with its fire? But the metal tube containing the message was not all that Satan
20 had brought them. What some of the men had mistaken for wings on his shoulders were two little baskets, and in each basket there was a homing pigeon frightened almost to death.

An officer took a message pad of tissue paper and wrote upon it: "Silence the battery on our left." Then he added some
25 figures showing the exact position of the battery. The message was folded and placed in a small aluminum capsule, and that was attached to the leg of a pigeon. A copy of the message was entrusted to the other bird, and both were tossed into the air. Away they went as if they knew the importance of their work,
30 and the men in the town watched them as they sped toward the French lines far away. Then a score of German rifles cracked, and one of the little messengers fell earthward with a mist of blue-gray feathers in his wake.

But the other pigeon passed through the hail of bullets
35 unhurt and flew straight to his loft, where an alert young officer

caught him up. The anxious men of the garrison did not see their message read, nor could they hear the sharp, terse order given to the waiting gunners. But they heard the deep roar of the big French guns which smothered with bursting shells
5 the German battery on their left, and they knew that the town was saved.

### NOTES AND QUESTIONS

**Biography.** Ernest Harold Baynes (1868-1925), the naturalist-author, lived in Meriden, New Hampshire. He was an authority on the service of birds and animals in World War One, having been sent overseas to the front to make a permanent history of the war work done by animals. Because of this, his story, "Satan, the War Dog," has peculiar interest. Mr. Baynes was a member of the American Bison Society and the National Association of Audubon Societies and was president of the Meriden Humane Society. He organized the Meriden Bird Club, which has made his town a refuge spot for birds, and the Bird Club of Long Island, of which Theodore Roosevelt was president. Mr. Baynes's book, *Wild Bird Guests,* was written to interest people in protecting birds. It has a preface by Colonel Roosevelt, in which he says, "The Meriden Club has furnished a model for all similar experiments in preserving bird life, and Mr. Baynes writes in advocacy of a cause which by practical achievement he has shown to be entitled to the support of every sensible man, woman, and child in the country."

**Discussion.** 1. In what war did the incident related in this story occur? 2. What made the situation of the French garrison unbearable? 3. How did Satan save the town? 4. What did Satan bring besides the message? 5. What happened to the homing pigeons? 6. How does this story prove that "animals have personalities like human beings"? Commit to memory Browning's lines on page 23, that express this same thought. 7. Read again what is said in "Literature and Life," pages 17 and 18, about the three joys of reading; which of these joys has the reading of this story given you? 8. Find in the glossary the meaning of: garrison; mongrel; *voilà mon ami;* terse. 9. *Pronounce:* isolated; aluminum.

**Class Reading.** (See page 16.) The description of Satan, page 42, line 14, to page 43, line 12; the rest of the story, page 43, line 12, to the end.

**Outline for Testing Silent Reading.** (a) The condition of the French garrison; (b) Satan and his message; (c) The homing pigeon and the silencing of the German battery.

**Library Reading.** (Read, below, the discussion under "Library Reading.") *Pierrot, Dog of Belgium*, Dyer; "What We Two Dogs Did" (in *The Ladies' Home Journal*, September, 1919); "Autobiographic Sketch of the Most Famous War Dog" (in *The Literary Digest*, April, 1919); *Bob, Son of Battle*, Ollivant; *The Call of the Wild*, London; *Stickeen*, Muir; *A Wilderness Dog*, Hawkes.

---

### Library Reading

Your interest in the various authors, aroused by reading their stories or poems in this volume, may make you wish to know more of their work; or your interest in the subjects they discuss may make you wish to extend your knowledge along these lines through directed library reading. For example, your interest in "Satan, the War Dog" may lead you to read other animal stories, particularly about dogs, or other stories by Baynes, such as "Our Animal Allies in the World War" (in *Harper's Magazine*, January, 1921). Or your interest in "Coaly-Bay, the Outlaw Horse" may lead you to read other stories about horses, such as "The Pacing Mustang," Seton (in *Wild Animals I Have Known*); *Ben, the Battle Horse*, Dyer; *Piebald, King of Broncos*, Hawkes; "The Bronco That Would Not Be Broken," Lindsay (in *The Chinese Nightingale and Other Poems*); "Bucephalus," Baldwin (in *The Wonder-Book of Horses*).

You will do your class and yourself a real service by planning an orderly oral or written report, giving all the boys and girls the benefit of your individual reading. Your classmates will enjoy hearing you review a favorite book or a particular story in a book or magazine, giving the title, the author, the time and scene, the principal characters, and a brief outline of the story, reading such selected passages from it as you think will give your classmates the most pleasure.

The public library is the source to which you will go for additional reading and reference material. In order to learn how to use, intelligently and effectively, the public library, or your school library, ask the librarian to explain to you the card catalogue system and the arrangement of the books on the shelves. Locate in your library *Who's Who in America, Who's Who* (British), the sets of encyclopedias, and the dictionaries, so that you may be independent in looking up biographical and historical facts, or other information.

# The Thundering Herd*

## Clarence Hawkes

### The Journey Across the Prairie

Bennie Anderson sat on the lee side of the prairie schooner, watching the dancing camp fire and listening to the howling of the coyotes. Four months before, the Anderson family, consisting of Mr. and Mrs. Anderson, Thomas, a boy of nine years, and
5 the solitary watcher by the camp fire, named Benjamin, aged eleven years, had said good-bye to Indiana.

Ill luck had always followed the Andersons in that state, and Bennie's father had said that perhaps a change of scene would also change their luck. So nearly all their belongings had been
10 packed into the canvas-covered wagon; two dilapidated mules hitched to it, the old cow tied behind, and with the dog following beneath the wagon, they had left the tumble-down cabin and the Indiana homestead, and had started for the frontier beyond the Mississippi.

15 Mr. Anderson was an old hunter, and as there were two rifles in the wagon, not to mention an old shotgun, there was usually plenty of fresh duck or prairie chicken to eat. Among the most cherished possessions was a very good field glass, which had been the property of an uncle who had used it in the Civil
20 War. This glass proved to be their best ally upon the great plains, where the stretches of smooth land are so vast, and the distances so great, that the naked eye is wholly inadequate to the demands made upon it, especially if one wants to see all the wildlife upon the plains as Bennie did.

25 The modest Anderson caravan had not journeyed far into the Missouri Bad Lands, at right angles to the old Oregon Trail,

---

*See Silent and Oral Reading, page 13.

which so many adventurers had followed before and have since, before the signs of buffaloes became plentiful, although the boys did not at first recognize them. It was not until late September or early October, however, that the Andersons saw buffaloes 5 in any numbers. Hitherto, there had been an occasional lonely bison feeding in some coulee, but they now began to see them in larger numbers.

The jolting wagon by this time had pounded its weary way over the plains and through the Bad Lands and the desert-like 10 portions of the prairies, where there was nothing but sagebrush and sprawling cactus, until they had reached a point near the northwest corner of Missouri.

It was not an infrequent sight to see upon the slope of a distant swell a dozen buffaloes peacefully grazing, like domestic 15 cattle. They usually made off at a slow trot whenever the wagon got within a few hundred yards of them. Not knowing much of the habits or disposition of the bison, Mr. Anderson said that they would not attempt to kill any at present even for meat, as deer and other game were plentiful.

20 So they journeyed along without molesting the bison that they saw, satisfied to leave them alone, if they were in turn left alone. This amicable arrangement might have held good until they reached their journey's end, in the heart of Kansas, had not something happened that made the killing of a few bison 25 the price of safety to the party. This was an event that no one of the emigrants ever forgot as long as he lived, and an incident that filled one night with excitement and peril.

They had been traveling for two days over a nearly unbroken stretch of slightly undulating prairie. The summer sun had 30 baked the earth till it was hard and lifeless. Every tuft of grass was burned to a crisp. Even the sagebrush that grew in all the sandy spots seemed parched by the shimmering heat. The sky was a bright, intense blue, and each night the sunset was red and the afterglow partially obscured by a cloud of dust.

35 The watercourses and the cottonwoods were half a day's journey

apart, and an intolerable thirst was over all the landscape.

The second day of this trying desert-like prairie stretch of their journey was just drawing to a close when they noted upon the northern horizon what at first seemed to be a cloud of smoke.

5  At the thought of a prairie fire upon such a parched area as these plains, a horrible fear seized upon the little party, and Mr. Anderson hurried to the top of the nearest swell to learn if their worst fears were true. On mounting the eminence, he discovered that the cloud extended from the east to the west as
10 far as the eye could reach. It certainly was not smoke, but each minute it grew in density and volume, like a menace, something dark and foreboding that would engulf them.

Presently as he watched, he thought he heard a low rumbling, like the first indistinct sounds of thunder, and putting his ear to
15 the ground in Indian fashion, he could hear the rumbling plainly. It was like the approach of a mighty earthquake, only it traveled much more slowly; like the rumbling of the surf; like the voice of the sea, or the hurricane, heard at a distance.

Again the anxious man scanned the dark, ominous-looking
20 cloud that now belted half the horizon, and this time he thought that he discerned dark particles like tiny dancing motes in the cloud. Then as he gazed, the specks grew larger, like gnats or small flies, close to where the horizon line should have been. Here and there were clouds of the dark specks, like swarms of
25 busy insects. But what a myriad there was. In some places they fairly darkened the cloud.

### THE AVALANCHE OF BUFFALOES

Then in a flash the truth dawned upon the incredulous man, leaving him gasping with astonishment and quaking with fear. All these tiny specks upon the horizon line were buffaloes.
30 A mighty host stretching from east to west as far as the eye could reach, and to the north an unknown distance. Like an avalanche that rushes upon its way, unmindful of human life, the Thundering Herd was rolling down upon them.

For a few seconds he gazed, fascinated and held to the spot by his very fear and the wonder of it all. Darker and darker grew the cloud. Plainer and plainer the headlong rush of the countless host was seen, while the rumbling of their thousands of hoofs,
5 which at first had been like distant thunder, now swelled to the volume of a rapidly approaching hurricane. The solid earth was felt to vibrate and rock, to tremble and quake.

Mr. Anderson waited to see no more, but fled back to his family, whose escape from this sea of hoofs now seemed to him
10 almost hopeless. The boys hurried to meet him, their faces pale with fright, for even the rest of the family now realized that some great danger was swooping down upon them.

Mr. Anderson made his plan of escape as he ran. To think of fleeing was out of the question. Their slow moving schooner
15 would be overtaken in almost no time. There was no canyon, no coulee in which to take refuge; no butte to which they might flee; not even a tree or a rock behind which they might crouch, and thus be partly shielded. Out in the open the danger must be met, with nothing but the shelter of the wagon
20 to keep off the grinding hoofs, and only the muzzles of their three guns to stand between them and annihilation when the crash came.

Hastily they turned the wagon about, with its hind end toward the herd. The mules were unhitched from the pole
25 and each hitched to the front wheel. A rope was also passed through the side strap of the harness of each mule, and he was fastened to the hind wheel of the wagon, so that he could not swing about and be across the tide when this sea of buffaloes should strike them. This kept the mules with their heels toward
30 the herd, thus securing the additional aid of a mule's heels on guard at each side of the wagon. Old Brindle was secured to the pole of the wagon, where the mules had been. The wheels were blocked. What furniture the wagon contained was piled up behind to help make a barricade. When all had been made
35 as snug as possible, the family crawled under the wagon and

awaited results. The muzzles of the two rifles were held in readiness for an emergency at either side of the wagon, while Mrs. Anderson had the shotgun in readiness to reinforce the garrison should they need more loaded weapons at a moment's
5 notice.

Nearer and nearer came the Thundering Herd, while the vibrations in the solid earth grew with each passing second. The clouds of dust shut out the light of the setting sun, and made a dark pall over all the landscape, which was like the descending
10 of the mantle of death.

Bennie gritted his teeth together and tried hard not to let the muzzle of his rifle shake as he pointed it out between the spokes of the hind wheel on his side of the wagon.

On came the terrible battalions of galloping hoofs, the mas-
15 sive heads and black beards of mighty bulls glowering through the clouds of dust. Each second the pounding of their hoofs swelled in volume, and each second the vibrations of the solid earth became more pronounced. Like the smoke of a great conflagration, the dust clouds settled over the prairies until the
20 crouching, trembling human beings, so impotent in this vast mad rush of wild beasts, could see the frontlets of the bulls but a few rods away. But almost before they had time to realize it, the mad, galloping, pushing, steaming, snorting herd was all about them, pounding by so close that the coats of the nearest
25 bulls brushed the sides of the mules.

At first they seemed to turn out a bit for the wagon, but presently a bunch of buffaloes, more compact than the rest of the herd, was seen bearing down upon them as though they were charging the schooner, although they probably did not
30 even notice it.

"Ready with your rifle, Bennie," called Mr. Anderson, and father and son both cocked their guns. When the bunch was almost upon them, both fired, and a mighty bull fell kicking against the back of the wagon, but his kicks were not of long
35 duration, for at this short range the rifles did fearful execution.

There was no respite, however, for close behind the fallen bull came more, and Mr. Anderson reached for the shotgun, and piled another bull upon the first, although he had to finish him with a Colt's revolver, which was destined to stand them in much
5 better stead than the guns.

It was with difficulty that the muzzle-loading rifles could be loaded while lying down in the cramped position under the wagon, but the Colt's revolver, which was a forty-four and just as effective at this short range as a rifle, could be readily reloaded,
10 and Mrs. Anderson kept its five chambers full.

Old Abe, the mule upon the right side of the wagon, now took his turn in the fray, for a bull galloped too close to him, raking Abe's flank with his sharp horn. The mule let both heels fly, striking another bull fairly in the forehead, and felling him to
15 the ground. But a buffalo's skull is as thick as a board, and the bull jumped up and galloped on with his fellows.

For a few minutes the two dead bulls at the rear of the wagon seemed to act as a buffer, and the others parted just enough to graze the wagon. The mules, which brayed and
20 kicked whenever the buffaloes came too close, also helped, but presently another bunch was seen bearing down upon them. They were close together and crowding, and did not seem likely to give way for the crouching fugitives under the wagon.

Although Bennie and his father both fired, and Mr. Anderson
25 followed up the rifle shots with both barrels from the shotgun and three shots from the Colt's, yet they struck the wagon with a terrific shock.

There was frantic kicking and frenzied braying from both Abe and Ulysses and a violent kicking and pounding in the wagon
30 that seemed to be immediately over their heads.

It was plain that instantaneous action of some kind was necessary if their domicile was to be saved, for one of the crowding bulls had been carried immediately into the wagon. He had become entangled in the top, and was pawing and kicking to
35 free himself. His great head just protruded over the seat.

Mr. Anderson reached up quickly with the Colt's, and put an end to his kicking with two well directed shots.

There were now four dead bulls piled up behind the wagon and one inside of it, and soon the blood from their last victim
5 came trickling through upon the helpless family. It was a gruesome position, but they could not escape it, and all were so glad that the blood was not their own that they did not mind.

"We are pretty well barricaded now, Bennie," shouted Mr. Anderson, just making himself heard above the thunder of gal-
10 loping hoofs. "I think we are safe. They cannot get at us over all that beef, and they cannot get through the side, so I do not see but we are secure."

"Thank God!" exclaimed Mrs. Anderson fervently; "but I shan't feel safe until the last buffalo has passed."

15 She had barely ceased speaking when old Abe uttered a piercing bray, in which were both terror and pain. He accompanied the outcry with a vicious kick, but almost immediately sank to the earth, kicking and pawing. It was then seen that a bull had ripped open the mule's left side, giving him a mortal
20 wound. His frantic kicking so endangered the cowering fugitives under the wagon that Mr. Anderson was obliged to shoot him. His loss was irreparable, and the boys whimpered softly to themselves as they saw their old friend stretched out dead beside the wagon.

25 Old Brindle at this point became unmanageable, breaking her rope, so that the seething black mass swallowed her. "There goes Brindle, too," sobbed Tommy. "I guess we'll starve now."

Poor Shep, who had been securely tied at the forward end of the wagon, cowered and whimpered as though he too thought
30 the judgment day had come, and it was his and Tommy's lot to comfort each other—the dog licking the boy's hands, and he in turn patting the dog's head.

The loss of old Brindle and Abe proved to be the turning point in the misfortunes of the Andersons, for the herd now
35 parted at the barricade made by the dead buffalo, the mule, and

the wagon, so that although every few minutes it seemed as though they would be engulfed, yet the danger veered to one side and passed by.

Half an hour and then an hour went by, and still there was
5 no diminution of the herd. The second hour and the third passed, and still they came, crowding and pushing, blowing and snorting, steaming and reeking.

"Won't they ever go by, Father?" asked Bennie. "I should think there were a million of them."

10 "It is the most wonderful thing that I ever saw," replied Mr. Anderson. "I have often heard old hunters tell about the countless herds of buffaloes, but I had always supposed that they were lying. In the future I will believe anything about their numbers."

15 At last seeing that they were in no immediate danger, Mr. Anderson told the boys to go to sleep if they could, and he would watch. If there was any need of their help, he would call them. Accordingly, all the firearms were loaded and placed by Mr. Anderson, and the boys and Shep curled up near the forward
20 wheels to rest. They were terribly tired, for the excitement and the hard work had told upon their young nerves and muscles.

The last thing Bennie remembered was the thunder of the myriad hoofs, and the rocking and trembling of the earth under him. But even these sounds soon ceased for him, and he and
25 his brother slept.

When he again opened his eyes, the sun was shining brightly, and the clouds of dust that had obscured the moon when he fell asleep had been partly dissipated. Here and there he could see an occasional buffalo galloping southward, but the mighty herd,
30 whose numbers had seemed like the stars, was gone.

"It's the tail end of the procession, boy," called Bennie's father. "The last installment went by about fifteen minutes ago. I did not dream that bison could be found in such numbers in western Missouri at the present time. I had supposed the few scattering
35 head that we saw were all that were left in the state."

This conclusion of Mr. Anderson's was quite right, but that autumn, for some unaccountable reason, the great herd had come down for a part of the way on the Missouri River on its southern migration, following the old trail of two decades before
5 instead of crossing western Nebraska and Kansas. It had been a costly experiment, however, for all the way hunters had swarmed upon their flanks and they had lost thousands of head. But what did that matter? Their number was legion.

## NOTES AND QUESTIONS

**Biography.** Clarence Hawkes (1869-1954), the naturalist-author, was a native of Massachusetts. He was a member of the American Bison Society, which has for its purpose the conservation of American buffaloes. When he was fourteen years of age, he was made totally blind by an accidental shot in the eyes. In 1893 he began writing and giving public lectures. Among his many books are: *Little Foresters*; *Shaggy Coat*; *Tenants of the Trees*; *Black Bruin*; *The Wilderness Dog*; and *King of the Thundering Herd,* from which "The Thundering Herd" is taken.

**Discussion.** 1. The events narrated in this story took place, it is said, in 1871. Describe the caravan and tell where the family was going. 2. How long had they been traveling when the incident of the thundering herd occurred? 3. Where did the event occur, and under what conditions? 4. What does this story tell you of the number of buffaloes on the plains at that time? 5. Find in the glossary the meaning of: dilapidated; inadequate; coulee; eminence; incredulous; butte; annihilation; frontlet; buffer; domicile; veered; diminution; dissipated. 6. *Pronounce*: coyote; ally; amicable; undulating; pall; impotent; respite; irreparable.

### Phrases for Study

prairie schooner, **46**, 1                    belted half the horizon, **48**, 20
Missouri Bad Lands, **46**, 26

**Class Reading**. The plan of escape, page 49, line 13, to page 50, line 5; the description of the approach of the herd, page 48, lines 4 to 27; the passing of the herd, page 50, line 26, to the end.

**Outline for Testing Silent Reading.** Make an outline to guide you in telling the story.

**Library Reading.** The other chapters of *King of the Thundering*

*Herd* (an interesting social exercise may be made by assigning the various chapters to different members, to be read silently and reported on in class); another story by this author: "Passing of the Buffalo" (in *Overland Monthly*, May, 1915).

## Magazine Reading

The author of "The Thundering Herd" contributed stories, articles, and verse to many magazines and newspapers. In like manner Lowell, Holmes, Longfellow, Emerson, Whittier, and Poe were all contributors to the magazines of their time. Many of the masterpieces of American literature were first published in magazines, and doubtless some of the poems and prose stories of today will also be considered masterpieces in the future.

More and more the average American is coming to depend upon current periodicals for his general reading; from the large number of magazines now published he chooses one that suits his particular interest and taste. Examine the magazines in the library and ask the librarian's advice as to which you will be likely to find most useful and enjoyable. You are probably familiar with some or all of the following: *The Junior Red Cross News, St. Nicholas, The Youth's Companion, The Saturday Evening Post, The National Geographic Magazine, Popular Mechanics, The Outlook, Good Housekeeping, The World's Work, The Literary Digest.* What others do you sometimes read?

Valuable suggestions for magazine reading will be gained if each member of the class chooses some one magazine, agreeing to examine the current numbers as they appear, and to inform the class of the most interesting articles, stories, and poems. In this way the individual reading of each member is placed at the service of the entire class.

Perhaps you have had the experience of reading a story in some magazine, and later, when you wished to refer to it, of being unable to recall in which number or in which magazine you had read it. *The Readers' Guide to Periodical Literature* will help you to locate a story, poem, or article by title, author, or subject. It will also be helpful in showing you what has appeared in current magazines by certain authors or on certain subjects. Ask your teacher or the librarian to show you how to use *The Readers' Guide.*

# BIRDS

## To a Waterfowl

### William Cullen Bryant

Whither, midst falling dew,
While glow the heavens with the last steps of day,
Far through their rosy depths dost thou pursue
    Thy solitary way?

5    Vainly the fowler's eye
Might mark thy distant flight to do thee wrong,
As, darkly painted on the crimson sky,
    Thy figure floats along.

    Seek'st thou the plashy brink
10 Of weedy lake, or marge of river wide,
Or where the rocking billows rise and sink
    On the chafed ocean-side?

There is a Power whose care
Teaches thy way along that pathless coast—
The desert and illimitable air—
    Lone wandering, but not lost.

5   All day thy wings have fanned,
At that far height, the cold, thin atmosphere;
Yet stoop not, weary, to the welcome land,
    Though the dark night is near.

And soon that toil shall end;
10 Soon shalt thou find a summer home, and rest,
And scream among thy fellows; reeds shall bend
    Soon o'er thy sheltered nest.

Thou'rt gone; the abyss of heaven
Hath swallowed up thy form; yet on my heart
15 Deeply hath sunk the lesson thou hast given,
    And shall not soon depart.

He who from zone to zone
Guides through the boundless sky thy certain flight,
In the long way that I must tread alone
20   Will lead my steps aright.

## NOTES AND QUESTIONS

**Biography.** William Cullen Bryant (1794-1878), the first great American poet, was born in western Massachusetts and educated in the district school. At home he had the use of his father's library, an exceptionally fine one, and he made the most of its advantages. In 1816 he journeyed on foot to Plainfield, Massachusetts, to look for a place to open a law office. He felt forlorn and desolate, and the world seemed big and cold. On his way he paused, impressed by the beauty of the sunset, and saw a solitary wild fowl wing its way along the horizon until it was lost in the distance. He went on with new courage, and when he stopped for the night, he sat down and wrote this beautiful poem of faith and hope, "To a Waterfowl." Many of his best poems were inspired by nature or one of nature's creatures.

Bryant soon gave up the study of law to devote himself to his literary work. In addition to writing poetry, he was editor of the *New York Evening Post*, one of America's greatest newspapers. His long life was full of usefulness and happiness. Bryant had the gift of seeing that the commonest things about him were interesting and worthwhile. He died in 1878, one of the most loved of American poets.

**The Lyric.** "To a Waterfowl" is a lyric poem, that is, a musical poem appropriate for song—"suited to be sung to the lyre." Nature is a favorite theme for lyric poets. In a lyric, the poet expresses his own observations and emotions—his love, his joy, his grief. A great lyric not only expresses the poet's feeling, but it has the power to make us feel. We learn through it to feel tenderness, or pity, or sorrow, or happiness. What feeling caused Bryant to write "To a Waterfowl"? Other well-known lyrics by Bryant are "Robert of Lincoln," a poem in which he gives us a glimpse of his quiet humor; "March," "The Gladness of Nature," and "The Yellow Violet," poems in which he expresses joy at the return of spring; "The Death of the Flowers," a poem that commemorates the death of the poet's sister; and "To a Fringed Gentian," a poem of hope. Note lyrics by other authors in this book.

**Discussion.** 1. After a good reader has read this entire poem in class, tell under what circumstances it was written. 2. How does the poet speak of the sunset? 3. What characteristics did Bryant show in stopping to enjoy the sunset and to watch the bird? 4. What was the appearance of the bird against the sky? 5. What words used in the fourth stanza emphasize the thought that there is no path or road for the bird to follow through the air? 6. Find the lines that tell what toil is referred to in the sixth stanza. When will the bird's toil end? What will follow toil? 7. How does the thought that the bird is guided help the poet? 8. What comparison does he make between his life and the flight of the bird? 9. What did you learn in "Literature and Life," page 20 about literature that *interprets* life? Can you show that this poem is such a piece of literature? 10. Find in the glossary the meaning of: plashy; marge; desert. 11. *Pronounce:* illimitable; abyss.

### Phrases for Study

| | |
|---|---|
| chafed ocean-side, **56**, 12 | from zone to zone, **57**, 17 |
| thin atmosphere, **57**, 6 | certain flight, **57**, 18 |

**Class Reading.** Bring to class and read other lyrics by Bryant.

## Newspaper Reading

William Cullen Bryant, as editor of the *New York Evening Post*, influenced the thinking of a large circle of readers. Since that time the newspaper has constantly grown in power, until today [1921] it is one of the important factors in American life and education.

The first newspaper in the United States, *Public Occurrences*, was started in 1690. The oldest existing newspaper in the country is the *New Hampshire Gazette*, founded in 1756. Since the days of Benjamin Franklin, and later of William Cullen Bryant, there have been many influential journalists in America, notably: Horace Greeley, editor of the *New York Tribune*; Charles A. Dana, editor of the *New York Sun*; and Henry Watterson, editor of the Louisville *Courier Journal*. Who is the editor of the newspaper with which you are most familiar?

Bring to class copies of some local newspaper and show that there is a regular place for general news, editorials, society news, sports, market reports, jokes, cartoons, and advertisements; of what advantage to the busy reader is a definite place in the paper for each of these? *Headlines* in large type call attention to the story, and *leads* in smaller type directly under the headlines give a brief summary of the story. How do these, also, help to save the reader's time?

When was the first newspaper started in your community? Have you seen copies of newspapers printed one hundred years ago or printed during the Civil War? If you can, bring to class copies of old-time newspapers and compare them with those of today.

Keep a class scrapbook for current events and for interesting newspaper mention of literary men and women and their works. Note especially accounts of local visits by authors. A committee of pupils may be chosen to be responsible for pasting the clippings as they are handed in from time to time by members of the class. Do you have a regular time in your school for reporting on current events? Bring to class clippings from current newspapers that relate to stories, authors, or characters found in your text—Rip Van Winkle, Evangeline, Kipling, Roosevelt, etc.

Read again the discussion of "What Is Literature?" pages 18 to 20. Is a newspaper article a true example of literature? What is the chief value of newspapers?

# The Skylark

### James Hogg

Bird of the wilderness,
Blithesome, and cumberless,
Sweet be thy matin o'er moorland and lea!
Emblem of happiness,
5    Blest is thy dwelling place—
O to abide in the desert with thee!
Wild is thy lay and loud,
Far in the downy cloud;
Love gives it energy, love gave it birth.

10    Where on thy dewy wing,
Where art thou journeying?
Thy lay is in heaven, thy love is on earth,
O'er fell and fountain sheen,
O'er moor and mountain green,
15 O'er the red streamer that heralds the day,
Over the cloudlet dim,
Over the rainbow's rim,
Musical cherub, soar, singing, away!
Then, when the gloaming comes,
20    Low in the heather blooms,
Sweet will thy welcome and bed of love be!

## NOTES AND QUESTIONS

**Biography.** James Hogg (1770-1835) was born in Ettrick, Scotland. He is called "The Ettrick Shepherd" because he came from a family of shepherds and worked in his youth as a cowherd and sheep tender. He spent many of his evening hours listening to old ballads and legends, which his mother recited to him. By the time he was twenty, Hogg was known as a song writer. Ten years later he assisted Walter Scott in the collection of old ballads for the *Border Minstrelsy* and shortly afterwards published a small volume of his own poetry. The publication of *The Queen's Wake* in 1831, a collection of tales and ballads supposed to have been sung to Mary, Queen of Scots, by native bards of Scotland, established his reputation as an author.

**Discussion.** 1. To whom is the poem addressed? 2. What different names does the poet give to the bird? 3. What claim has the skylark to the first of these names? 4. What word refers to the lark's morning song? 5. What line in the second stanza tells you that it is early morning? 6. Find a line that tells how high the lark flies while singing. 7. Where does the lark make its nest? 8. What word used by the poet in describing the lark's nest tells his country? 9. Where do you think the shepherd poet was when he heard the lark? Could other shepherds have received happiness or strength from the song of the lark, even though they could not express their thoughts in poetry? 10. What must you have in yourself in order to enjoy the song of a bird as the poet enjoyed it? 11. Read again the discussion of Lyrics on page 58, and tell why you think this is a lyric poem. 12. Find in the glossary the meaning of: lay; fell; heather.

## To a Skylark

### William Wordsworth

Ethereal minstrel! Pilgrim of the sky!
Dost thou despise the earth where cares abound?
Or, while the wings aspire, are heart and eye
Both with thy nest upon the dewy ground?
5 Thy nest which thou canst drop into at will,
Those quivering wings composed, that music still!

Leave to the nightingale her shady wood;
A privacy of glorious light is thine,
Whence thou dost pour upon the world a flood
10 Of harmony, with instinct more divine;
Type of the wise, who soar but never roam,
True to the kindred points of Heaven and Home!

## NOTES AND QUESTIONS

**Biography.** William Wordsworth (1770-1850) was born in the Cumberland Highlands of northern England. The beauty of this country had a great influence on him and his poetry. In 1799 he retired to the beautiful Lake Country, not far from his boyhood home, and there lived a simple life, depending almost entirely on nature for companionship and inspiration. Wordsworth was devoted to the cause of liberty, and he believed firmly in the beauty and charm of the humble life. The simplicity and sincerity of his nature are revealed in his poems on birds and flowers. Although most of Wordsworth's poems are about everyday, prosaic events and subjects, they often contain profound truths and an intense emotional strain.

**Discussion.** 1. How did Wordsworth feel toward the skylark, according to line 1? 2. In what two ways was he thinking of the bird? 3. What claim has the skylark to the title "ethereal minstrel"? To the title "pilgrim of the sky"? 4. What questions does the poet ask the skylark? How did James Hogg answer these questions in the first stanza of his poem? 5. Find a line of Wordsworth's poem that tells where the nest is made. What words used by James Hogg show that he thought of the "dewy ground"? 6. The darkness of night hides the nightingale; what does Wordsworth say hides the skylark? 7. What habit makes the lark "true to Heaven"? What habit makes him "true to Home"? Which habit is a type of our longing to do good and great things? Which habit is a type of the faithful performance of common duties? 8. What feeling led Wordsworth to write this lyric? 9. You will enjoy hearing these lines read in class by a good reader. 10. Read again what is said in "Literature and Life" on page 20 about literature that interprets life; can you show that this poem is such a piece of literature? 11. Wordsworth's life was enriched by an appreciation of nature. What did you learn on page 27 of the "Introduction" about the wonders of nature? 12. What are some of the wonders that "add beauty and interest to our lives"? 13. Find in the glossary the meaning of: aspire; composed; instinct.

### Phrases for Study

privacy of glorious light is thine, **61**, 8

soar but never roam, **61**, 11

kindred points, **61**, 12

## To a Skylark

### Percy Bysshe Shelley

Hail to thee, blithe Spirit!
   Bird thou never wert,
That from heaven, or near it,
   Pourest thy full heart
5 In profuse strains of unpremeditated art.


   Higher still and higher
      From the earth thou springest
Like a cloud of fire;
      The blue deep thou wingest
10 And singing still dost soar, and soaring ever singest.


   In the golden lightning
      Of the sunken sun,
O'er which clouds are bright'ning,
      Thou dost float and run
15 Like an unbodied joy whose race is just begun.


   The pale purple even
      Melts around thy flight;
Like a star of heaven,
      In the broad daylight
20 Thou art unseen—but yet I hear thy shrill delight,


   Keen as are the arrows
      Of that silver sphere
Whose intense lamp narrows
      In the white dawn clear,
25 Until we hardly see—we feel that it is there.

All the earth and air
  With thy voice is loud,
As, when night, is bare,
  From one lonely cloud
5 The moon rains out her beams, and heaven is overflowed.

What thou art we know not:
  What is most like thee?
From rainbow clouds there flow not
  Drops so bright to see
10 As from thy presence showers a rain of melody.

Like a Poet hidden
  In the light of thought,
Singing hymns unbidden
  Till the world is wrought
15 To sympathy with hopes and fears it heeded not;

Like a high-born maiden
  In a palace tower,
Soothing her love-laden
  Soul in secret hour
20 With music sweet as love—which overflows her bower;

Like a glow-worm golden
  In a dell of dew,
Scattering unbeholden
  Its aerial hue
25 Among the flowers and grass which screen it from the view;

Like a rose embowered
  In its own green leaves,
By warm winds deflowered,
  Till the scent it gives
30 Makes faint with too much sweet those heavy-wingéd thieves;

Sound of vernal showers
   On the twinkling grass,
Rain-awakened flowers,
   All that ever was
5 Joyous and clear and fresh, thy music doth surpass.

Teach us, Sprite or Bird,
   What sweet thoughts are thine;
I have never heard
   Praise of love or wine
10 That panted forth a flood of rapture so divine.

Chorus Hymeneal,
   Or triumphal chaunt,
Matched with thine would be all
   But an empty vaunt,
15 A thing wherein we feel there is some hidden want.

What objects are the fountains
   Of thy happy strain?
What fields or waves or mountains?
   What shapes of sky or plain?
20 What love of thine own kind?  What ignorance of pain?

With thy clear, keen joyance
   Languor cannot be;
Shadow of annoyance
   Never came near thee;
25 Thou lovest—but ne'er knew love's sad satiety.

Waking or asleep
   Thou of death must deem
Things more true and deep
   Than we mortals dream—
30 Or how could thy notes flow in such a crystal stream?

We look before and after,
    And pine for what is not;
Our sincerest laughter
    With some pain is fraught;
5 Our sweetest songs are those that tell of saddest thought.

Yet if we could scorn
    Hate and pride and fear;
If we were things born
    Not to shed a tear,
10 I know not how thy joy we ever should come near.

Better than all measures
    Of delightful sound,
Better than all treasures
    That in books are found,
15 Thy skill to poet were, thou scorner of the ground!

Teach me half the gladness
    That thy brain must know
Such harmonious madness
    From my lips would flow,
20 The world should listen then—as I am listening now.

## NOTES AND QUESTIONS

**Biography.** Percy Bysshe Shelley (1792-1822) was an English poet, born at Field Place, Essex. He studied at Eton, one of England's famous boarding schools for boys, and at Oxford University. Some years later he went to live in Italy, and it was there that his best-known poems were written. Although he wrote a number of long poems, his fame rests upon his shorter pieces and lyrics. Shelley had a very sensitive and sympathetic nature, a lively and charming imagination, and a rather unruly and unconventional personality. He was always generous and indulgent with others and fearless in his pursuit of what he thought was right. When only thirty, on a pleasure cruise off the coast of Italy, he was drowned.

**Discussion.** 1. By what name is the skylark addressed in the first line? 2. What characteristics of the lark's song and flight made the poet say, "Bird thou never wert"? 3. Find a line in the second stanza that shows the energy and enthusiasm with which the lark begins its flight; why should this sudden spring of the bird make the poet think of fire? 4. What question does the poet ask in the seventh stanza? In what stanzas does he try to answer the question? 5. Is he satisfied with any of the comparisons he has made? Find the lines which tell us that the song of the lark is sweeter and more joyous than any of these things. 6. In which stanzas does the poet compare music produced by man with the music of the lark's song? How does our music seem when compared to the song of the lark? 7. What question is asked in lines 16 and 17, on page 65? 8. In the questions that follow, the poet suggests what the lark may be singing about; what things does he suggest? 9. From what does the poet say the lark has never suffered? 10. How are we affected by "hate and pride and fear"? 11. The poet tries to imagine how we would feel if we were not affected by hate or pride or fear and knew no sorrow; does he think we would then feel joy as great as the lark's? Find the line in which he tells us. 12. What does the poet ask of the bird in the last stanza? Why does he want to know this gladness? 13. Compare this poem on the skylark with those of Wordsworth and Hogg. What impressed each poet most in the skylark? 14. What did you learn in "Literature and Life" on page 19, about true literature? This poem was written more than one hundred years ago; can you tell why men "treasure it and will not let it die"? 15. Find in the glossary the meaning of: even; wrought; unbeholden; deflowered; vernal; chaunt; languor; fraught. 16. *Pronounce:* aerial; Hymeneal; satiety.

## Phrases for Study

unpremeditated art, **63**, 5

unbodied joy, **63**, 15

silver sphere, **63**, 22

harmonious madness, **66**, 18

# Hark, Hark! The Lark

### William Shakespeare

Hark, hark! the lark at heaven's gate sings;
  And Phoebus 'gins arise,
His steeds to water at those springs
  On chaliced flowers that lies;
5 And winking Mary-buds begin
  To ope their golden eyes.
With every thing that pretty is,
  My lady sweet, arise,
  Arise, arise.

## NOTES AND QUESTIONS

**Biography.** William Shakespeare (1564-1616), a famous English poet and the greatest dramatist the world has produced, was born at Stratford-on-Avon, England. At the age of twenty-two, after his marriage with Anne Hathaway, he moved to London, where for twenty-five years he wrote poems and plays, was an actor, and later became a shareholder in a theater. This was the time of Queen Elizabeth and is known as the Elizabethan Age. It was a period rich in genius of many kinds, but especially in the creation of dramatic literature. In 1612 Shakespeare retired to Stratford, where he spent the last few years of his life.

**Discussion.** 1. At what time of day does the lark sing "at heaven's gate"? What lines tell you that it is morning? 2. By what other name is Phoebus known? 3. For what was the watering of the steeds a preparation? 4. The use of "lies" in the song is old English idiom; what does it add to the poem? 5. What is added to the picture by the poet's choice of marigolds as the opening flowers? 6. Which lines do you think are the most beautiful in this little song? 7. Which lines sing themselves to you? The Schubert music of this lyric is particularly pleasing. 8. Have you heard this lyric rendered by a good singer? You would enjoy listening to the recordings of it by Gluck, Williams, and others. 9. Who can memorize these lines in the shortest time? 10. Find in the glossary the meaning of: chaliced.

# THE MOCKINGBIRD*

### JOHN JAMES AUDUBON

It is where the great magnolia shoots up its majestic trunk,
crowned with evergreen leaves and decorated with a thousand
beautiful flowers that perfume the air around; where the forests
and fields are adorned with blossoms of every hue; where the
5 golden orange ornaments the gardens and the groves; where
bignonias of various kinds interlace their climbing stems around
the white-flowered stuartia, and mounting still higher, cover the
summits of the lofty trees around, accompanied with innumerable vines that here and there festoon the dense foliage of the
10 magnificent woods, lending to the vernal breeze a slight portion
of the perfume of their clustered flowers; where a genial warmth
seldom forsakes the atmosphere; where berries and fruits of
all descriptions are met with at every step—in a word, kind
reader, it is where Nature seems to have paused, as she passed
15 over the earth, and opening her stores, to have strewed with
unsparing hand the diversified seeds from which have sprung all
the beautiful and splendid forms which I should in vain attempt
to describe, that the mockingbird should have fixed its abode,
there only that its wondrous song should be heard.
20     But where is that favored land? It is in that great continent,
to whose distant shores Europe has sent forth her adventurous
sons, to wrest for themselves a habitation from the wild inhabitants of the forest and to convert the neglected soil into fields
of exuberant fertility. It is, reader, in Louisiana that these
25 bounties of nature are in the greatest perfection. It is there
that you should listen to the love song of the mockingbird, as
I at this moment do. See how he flies round his mate, with
motions as light as those of the butterfly! His tail is widely
expanded, he mounts in the air to a small distance, describes

---

*See Silent and Oral Reading, page 13.

a circle, and, again alighting, approaches his beloved one, his
eyes gleaming with delight, for she has already promised to
be his and his only. His beautiful wings are gently raised, he
bows to his love, and again bouncing upward, opens his bill,
5 and pours forth his melody, full of exultation at the conquest
which he has made.

They are not the soft sounds of the flute or the hautboy
that I hear, but the sweeter notes of Nature's own music. The
mellowness of the song, the varied modulations and gradations,
10 the extent of its compass, the great brilliancy of execution, are
unrivaled. There is probably no bird in the world that possesses
all the musical qualifications of this king of song, who has derived
all from Nature's self. Yes, reader, all!

No sooner has he again alighted near his mate than, as if
15 his breast were about to be rent with delight, he again pours
forth his notes with more softness and richness than before. He
now soars higher, glancing around with a vigilant eye, to assure
himself that none has witnessed his bliss. When these love
scenes are over, he dances through the air, full of animation and
20 delight, and, as if to convince his lovely mate that to enrich her
hopes he has much more love in store, he that moment begins
anew, and imitates all the notes which Nature has imparted to
the other songsters of the grove.

For a while, each long day and pleasant night are thus spent.
25 A nest is to be prepared, and the choice of a place in which
to lay it is to become a matter of mutual consideration. The
orange, the fig, the pear tree of the gardens are inspected; the
thick brier patches are also visited. They appear all so well
suited for the purpose in view, and so well do the birds know
30 that man is not their most dangerous enemy, that, instead of
retiring from him, they at length fix their abode in his vicinity,
perhaps in the nearest tree to his window. Dried twigs, leaves,
grasses, cotton, flax, and other substances are picked up, carried
to a forked branch, and there arranged. Five eggs are deposited
35 in due time, when the male, having little more to do than to sing

his mate to repose, attunes his pipe anew. Every now and then he spies an insect on the ground, the taste of which he is sure will please his beloved one. He drops upon it, takes it in his bill, beats it against the earth, and flies to the nest to feed and
5 receive the warm thanks of his devoted female.

When a fortnight has elapsed, the young brood demand all their care and attention. No cat, no vile snake, no dreaded hawk is likely to visit their habitation. Indeed the inmates of the next house have by this time become quite attached to the lovely
10 pair of mockingbirds and take pleasure in contributing to their safety. The dewberries from the fields and many kinds of fruit from the gardens, mixed with insects, supply the young as well as the parents with food. The brood is soon seen emerging from the nest, and in another fortnight, being now able to fly with
15 vigor and to provide for themselves, they leave the parent birds, as many other species do.

In winter, nearly all the mockingbirds approach the farm-houses and plantations, living about the gardens or outhouses. They are then frequently seen on the roofs and perched
20 on the chimney tops; yet they always appear full of animation. While searching for food on the ground, their motions are light and elegant, and they frequently open their wings as butterflies do when basking in the sun, moving a step or two and again throwing out their wings. When the weather is mild, the old
25 males are heard singing with as much spirit as during the spring or summer, while the younger birds are busily engaged in practicing, preparatory to the love season. They seldom resort to the interior of the forest either during the day or by night, but usually roost among the foliage of evergreens, in the immediate
30 vicinity of houses in Louisiana, although in the eastern states they prefer low fir trees.

The flight of the mockingbird is performed by short jerks of the body and wings, at every one of which a strong twitching motion of the tail is perceived. This motion is still more
35 apparent while the bird is walking, when it opens its tail like a

fan and instantly closes it again. When traveling, this flight is
only a little prolonged, as the bird goes from tree to tree, or
at most across a field, scarcely, if ever, rising higher than the
top of the forest. During this migration, it generally resorts
5 to the highest parts of the woods near watercourses, utters
its usual mournful note, and roosts in these places. It travels
mostly by day.

Few hawks attack the mockingbirds, as on their approach,
however sudden it may be, they are always ready not only to
10 defend themselves vigorously and with undaunted courage,
but to meet the aggressor half way, and force him to abandon
his intention. The only hawk that occasionally surprises the
mockingbird is the *Falco Starlen,* which flies low with great
swiftness and carries the bird off without any apparent stop.
15 Should it happen that the ruffian misses his prey, the mockingbird
in turn becomes the assailant and pursues the hawk with great
courage, calling in the meantime all the birds of its species to
its assistance; and, although it cannot overtake the marauder,
the alarm created by their cries, which are propagated in suc-
20 cession among all the birds in the vicinity, like the watchwords
of sentinels on duty, prevents him from succeeding in his
attempts.

The musical powers of this bird have often been taken notice
of by European naturalists, and persons who find pleasure in
25 listening to the songs of different birds while in confinement
or at large. Some of these persons have described the notes
of the nightingale as occasionally fully equal to those of our
bird. I have frequently heard both species, in confinement and
in the wild state, and without prejudice have no hesitation in
30 pronouncing the notes of the European philomel equal to those
of a soubrette of taste, which, could she study under a Mozart,
might perhaps in time become very interesting in her way. But
to compare her essays to the finished talent of the mockingbird
is, in my opinion, quite absurd.

## NOTES AND QUESTIONS

**Biography.** John James Audubon (1780-1851) was born near New Orleans. His mother died while he was very young, and his father, who was a Frenchman, took the boy to France. There Audubon grew up and was educated. He studied drawing with some of the celebrated French artists. In 1798 he returned to America, and from then on he spent most of his time in this country. He devoted himself to the study of natural history and especially to birds. His great work, *The Birds of America*, contains life-size pictures of more than a thousand birds. The drawings for these he made himself, and they are artistically excellent as well as true to nature. "The Mockingbird" is taken from the text made by Audubon to accompany the pictures. Because of his interest in birds, the clubs for the care and study of birds, which have been formed throughout the United States, are called "Audubon Societies."

**Discussion**. 1. The first two paragraphs describe the place where the bird lives; how does the description of the second paragraph differ from that of the first? 2. How does the author imply that the richness of the plant life of this region is reproduced in the bird's song? 3. How does Audubon say the musical powers of the mockingbird compare with those of the nightingale? 4. You will enjoy hearing the recordings: "Mockingbird," Gluck, with bird voices by Kellogg; "Bird Chorus" and "Songs of Our Native Birds," Kellogg; "Songs and Calls of Our Native Birds," Gorst; also Columbia record, "Bird Calls," Avis. 5. In the introduction on pages 27 and 28 you read that some selections present the facts of Nature as interpreted through the poets' imagination, while others show what men of scientific training have observed; which does this story represent? 6. Find in the glossary the meaning of: diversified; hautboy; modulations; derived; imparted; resort; essays. 7. *Pronounce:* bignonias; genial; species, foliage; ruffian; Mozart.

### Phrases for Study

exuberant fertility, **69**, 24

extent of its compass, **70**, 10

mutual consideration, **70**, 26

attunes his pipe anew, **71**, 1

propagated in succession, **72**, 19

soubrette of taste, **72**, 31

finished talent, **72**, 33

**Outline for Testing Silent Reading**. Make an outline to guide you in telling the main thoughts of this selection.

**Library Reading.** "A Mockingbird," Bynner, and "The Mockingbird," Stanton (in *Melody of Earth*); "Bob, the Mockingbird," Lanier (in *The Lanier Book*); selections from *Our Humble Helpers,* Fabre.

## Suggestions for Theme Topics

The reading period calls forth many interesting subjects that you will wish to learn more about and discuss with your classmates. You will find it well worthwhile occasionally to make a report to the class on some particular subject connected with your reading lesson that you have become interested in and to which you have given some thought and study. Most of these reports you will doubtless like to give orally, but some of them you may wish to present in written form. Whether your report is oral or written, always make sure that it has a good beginning, tells interesting facts, and ends well. You will add interest to your report if you appeal to the eyes as well as to the ears of your audience by the use of pictures, maps, and blackboard sketches.

You will add to your knowledge of the subject; (a) by firsthand experience; (b) by talking with persons familiar with the subject; (c) or by further reading. Indeed all of these sources should be freely drawn upon in preparing on a theme topic. Here are some suggestions: 1. An incident from your own observation of a mockingbird (or any other song bird). 2. What I know about Audubon's great work, *The Birds of America*. 3. Incidents from the lives of other naturalists (Fabre, Thoreau, Burroughs, etc.). 4. An Audubon society that I know about and what it has accomplished. 5. A review of "Bob, the Story of Our Mockingbird," Lanier (in *The Lanier Book*). 6. What I know about making bird houses, bird baths, and feeding shelves. (*Bird Houses and How to Build Them* and *How to Attract Birds*, sent free by Department of Agriculture, Washington, D.C.)

# FLOWERS AND TREES

### Morning-Glories

#### Madison Cawein

They swing from the garden-trellis
    In Ariel-airy ease;
And their aromatic honey
    Is sought by the earliest bees.

5 The rose, it knows their secret,
    And the jessamine also knows;
And the rose told me the story
    That the jessamine told the rose.

And the jessamine said: "At midnight,
10    Ere the red cock woke and crew,
The fays of Queen Titania
    Came here to bathe in the dew.

"And the yellow moonlight glistened
  On braids of elfin hair;
And fairy feet on the flowers
  Fell softer than any air.

5 "And their petticoats, gay as bubbles,
  They hung up, every one,
On the morning-glory's tendrils,
  Till their moonlight bath was done.

10 "And the red cock crew too early,
  And the fairies fled in fear,
Leaving their petticoats, purple and pink
  Like blossoms hanging here."

## NOTES AND QUESTIONS

**Biography.** Madison Cawein (1865-1915) was born in Louisville, Kentucky and received his education in the public schools. In 1887 he published his first poems in a book called *Blooms of the Berry.* In most of his poems, nature is the theme. He spent his life learning her ways and describing them in poetry full of rich imagery. Cawein is often called "the Keats of Kentucky," because of the resemblance of his verses to those of the great English poet.

**Discussion.** 1. The poet has made a compound word by using the name Shakespeare gave to a fairy or sprite with the word "airy." What do you think was his purpose in doing this? 2. When is the name of the flower first mentioned? 3. What reason do you think the poet had for not telling it earlier? 4. Who told the poet this story? 5. How can you learn to know flowers as this poet knew them? 6. What poems have you read in which the poet talks to a bird or a flower? 7. Why does the poet think of the fairies as fleeing at cockcrow? 8. Compare this poem with Keats's "Sweet Peas" (in *The Elson Readers*, *Book Seven*, page 80). 9. Find in the glossary the meaning of: Ariel-airy; aromatic; fay; elfin. *Pronounce:* jessamine; Titania.

**Class Reading.** Bring to class and read: "The Flowerphone," Brown (in *Melody of Earth*).

## Pine-Trees and the Sky: Evening

### Rupert Brooke

I'd watched the sorrow of the evening sky,
And smelt the sea, and earth, and the warm clover,
And heard the waves, and the sea-gull's mocking cry.

And in them all was only the old cry,
5 That song they always sing—"The best is over!
You may remember now, and think, and sigh,
O silly lover!"
And I was tired and sick that all was over,
And because I,
10 For all my thinking, never could recover
One moment of the good hours that were over.
And I was sorry and sick, and wished to die.

Then from the sad west turning wearily,
I saw the pines against the white north sky,
15 Very beautiful, and still, and bending over
Their sharp black heads against a quiet sky.
And there was peace in them; and I
Was happy, and forgot to play the lover,
And laughed, and did no longer wish to die;
20 Being glad of you, O pine-trees and the sky!

### NOTES AND QUESTIONS

**Biography.** Rupert Brooke (1887-1915) was born in Rugby, England.
When World War One broke out, he gave up his advanced studies at
Cambridge University to become sub-lieutenant in the Royal Navy and
accompanied the Antwerp Expeditionary Force in October, 1914. In
February, 1915, he sailed with the British Mediterranean Force to take
part in the Dardanelles Campaign. Because of an attack of blood poisoning

he was removed from the transport to a French hospital where he died very suddenly on April 23. He lies buried on the Greek island of Skyros. His poems appear under the titles: *1914 and Other Poems* and *Collected Poems.*

**Discussion.** 1. What cause did the poet think the evening sky would have for sorrowing? 2. Why did the setting sun bring the thought that "the best is over"? 3. How did the cry of the sea-gull affect the poet? 4. The changing western sky made the poet think how life had changed for him; the fading color made him think of joys that were gone forever; what did he see when he turned to the north? Can you tell why he was comforted by the sight? 5. Can you tell why he felt brave and strong when he looked at the white sky and the quiet trees? 6. Compare this poem with Bryant's "To a Waterfowl"; what likenesses do you find?

**Class Reading.** Bring to class and read: "The Soldier," Brooke; "The Island of Skyros" (a poem in memory of Brooke), Masefield.

---

## THE RHODORA

### RALPH WALDO EMERSON

In May, when sea winds pierced our solitudes,
I found the fresh rhodora in the woods,
Spreading its leafless blooms in a damp nook,
To please the desert and the sluggish brook.
5 The purple petals fallen in the pool
Made the black water with their beauty gay;
Here might the redbird come his plumes to cool,
And court the flower that cheapens his array.
Rhodora! if the sages ask thee why
10 This charm is wasted on the earth and sky,
Tell them, dear, that if eyes were made for seeing,
Then beauty is its own excuse for being;
Why thou wert there, O rival of the rose,
I never thought to ask; I never knew;
15 But in my simple ignorance suppose
The selfsame power that brought me there brought you.

## NOTES AND QUESTIONS

**Biography.** Ralph Waldo Emerson (1803-1882), a native of Boston, was born not far from Franklin's birthplace, but he lived most of his life in Concord, near Boston. He was the oldest among that brilliant group of New England scholars and writers that developed under the influence of Harvard College. Emerson was a quiet boy, but his high ambitions and sturdy determination were shown by the fact that he worked his way through college. He is best known for his essays, full of noble ideas which won for him the title "Sage of Concord." As a poet, he was not particular about meter, making his lines often purposely rugged; but his verse is always full of thought. His poems of nature are as clear-cut and vivid as snapshots.

**Discussion.** 1. Under what circumstances did the poet find the rhodora? 2. What tells you that the flower grew in a lonely place? 3. What comparison does the poet make between the color of the bird and the color of the flower? 4. Why is the poet not troubled at the thought of the rhodora's wasting its loveliness? 5. Mention ways in which we show that there is a use for beauty in the satisfaction it gives the eye. 6. Who can memorize these lines in the shortest time? 7. Read the fourth and last stanzas of "To a Waterfowl"; compare the thought in these stanzas with the thought in the last line of "The Rhodora." 8. Find in the glossary the meaning of: blooms; cheapens.

---

## FLOWER IN THE CRANNIED WALL

### ALFRED, LORD TENNYSON

Flower in the crannied wall,
I pluck you out of the crannies;
I hold you here, root and all, in my hand,
Little flower—but if I could understand
5 What you are, root and all, and all in all,
I should know what God and man is.

## NOTES AND QUESTIONS

**Biography.** Alfred Tennyson (1809-1892) was one of the greatest English poets. At eight years of age he wrote verses and at fourteen a drama in blank verse. While a student at Cambridge University, he won a medal for his poem, "Timbuctoo." In 1842 he published two notable volumes of poems. After writing *The Princess* and *In Memoriam* he was appointed poet laureate, and from that time on he gradually became one of the most loved and most admired men in England. During his long life of eighty-three years Tennyson wrote a large amount of beautiful verse, contributing to the store of English literature some of its finest poems—*The Idylls of the King*, *In Memoriam*, and *Locksley Hall*.

**Discussion.** 1. What do you find in the first three lines that tells you the flower was small and not firmly rooted? 2. Why does the poet make the insignificance of the flower so plain to us? 3. To whom is the poet talking? 4. What does his use of the words, "little flower," tell you of Tennyson's feeling for flowers? 5. What other poems have you read that show how birds and flowers speak to those who have learned to listen? 6. If Tennyson had known all he wanted to know about that little flower, he would have known what no mortal knows of the great mysteries of life and death. What did you learn on pages 25 and 26 about the belief ancient peoples had concerning the mysteries of life and the origin of flowers? 7. On page 26 it is stated that we "have won from Nature many of her secrets." Mention some of the "secrets" that men of science have recently learned. 8. What great secret does this poem tell us has never been discovered? 9. In "Literature and Life," page 19, you read that there are poems of such enduring charm that people treasure them and "will not let them die"; why do you think that this little poem is one that people will always treasure? 10. Compare with this poem by Tennyson these lines from one of Wordsworth's great poems:

> To me the meanest flower that blows can give
> Thoughts that do often lie too deep for tears.

# SPRING AND AUTUMN

## THE COMING OF SPRING*

### HAMLIN GARLAND

### SPRING WORK AND PLAY

Spring came to the settlers on Sun Prairie with a wonderful message, like a pardon to imprisoned people. For five months they had been shut closely within their cabins. Nothing could be sweeter than the joy they felt when the mild south wind
5 began to blow and the snow began to sink away, leaving warm, brown patches of earth in the snowy fields. It seemed that the sun god had not forsaken them, after all.

The first island to appear in the midst of the ocean of slush and mud around the Stewart house was the chip pile; and there
10 the spring work began. As soon as the slush began to gather, Jack, the hired man, was set to work each morning, digging ditches and chopping canals in the ice so that the barn would not be inundated by the spring rains. During the middle of the day he busied himself at sawing and splitting the pile of

---

*See Silent and Oral Reading, page 13.

logs which Mr. Stewart had been hauling during the open days of winter.

Jack came from far lands and possessed, as Lincoln soon discovered, unusual powers of dancing and playing the fiddle.
5 He brought, also, stirring stories of distant forests, strange people, and many battles; and Lincoln, who had an eye for character, set himself to work to distinguish between what the hired man knew, what he thought he knew, and what he merely lied about.

10    There was plenty of work for the boys. They had cows to milk and the drains to keep open. It was their business also to pile the wood behind the men as they sawed and split the large logs into short lengths. They used a crosscut saw, which made pleasant music in the still, warm air of springtime. Afterwards
15 these pieces, split into small sticks ready for the stove, were thrown into a conical heap, which it was Lincoln's business to repile in shapely ricks.

Boys always insist upon having entertainment, even in their work, and Lincoln found amusement in planning a new ditch
20 and in seeing it remove the puddle before the barn door. There was a certain pleasure also in piling wood neatly and rapidly, and in watching the deft and powerful swing of the shining axes, as they lifted and fell, and rose again in the hands of the strong men. Then, too, the sap began to flow out of the maple logs, and
25 Lincoln and Owen wore their tongues to the quick, licking the trickle from the rough wood. They also stripped out the inner bark of the elm logs and chewed it. It had a sweet, nut-like flavor, and was considered most excellent forage.

It was back-breaking work, piling wood, and the boys could
30 not have endured it had it not been for the companionship of the men and the hope they had of going skating at night.

Every hour of free time was improved by Lincoln and Rance and Milton, for they knew by experience how transitory the skating season was. Early in the crisp spring air, when the trees
35 hung thick with frost, transforming the earth into fairyland, and

the cloudless sky was blue as a plowshare, they clattered away
to the nearest pond, where the jay and the snowbird dashed
amid the glorified willow trees, and the ice outspread like a
burnished share. On such mornings the air was so crisp and still
5 it seemed the whole earth waited for the sun.

At night during the full moon nearly all the boys and girls of
the neighborhood met, to rove up and down the long swales and
to play "gool" or "pom, pom, pull away" upon the frozen ponds.
These games could be played with skates quite as well as in
10 any other way. There was a singular charm in these excursions
across the plain at night, or winding up the swales filled with
imprisoned arid icebound water. Lincoln and Rance often skated
off alone and in silence, far away from the others, and the
majesty of the night fell upon them with a light which silenced
15 and made them afraid.

### THE WONDERS OF SPRING

There was a singular charm about this time of the year.
Travel was quite impossible, for the frost had left the roads
bottomless; and so upon the chip pile the boys sat to watch the
snow disappear from the fields and draw sullenly away from the
20 russet grass to take a final stand at the fence corners and in
the hedges. They watched the ducks as they came straggling
back in long flocks, lighting in the cornfields to find food. They
came in enormous numbers, sometimes so great the sky seemed
darkened with them, and when they alighted on the fields, they
25 covered the ground like some strange, down-dropping storm
from the sky, and when alarmed they rose with a sound like the
rumbling of thunder. At times the lines were so long that those
in the front rank were lost in the northern sky, while those in
the rear were dim clouds beneath the southern sun. Many brant
30 and geese also passed, and it was always a pleasure to Lincoln
to see these noble birds pushing their way boldly into the north.
He could imitate their cries, and often caused them to turn and
waver in their flight by uttering their resounding cries.

One day in late March at the close of a warm sunny day (just as the red disk of the sun was going down in a cloudless sky in the west), down from a low hilltop, and thrilling through the misty, wavering atmosphere, came a singular, soft, joyous,
5 "boom, boom, boom, cutta, cutta, war-whoop!"

"Hooray!" shouted Lincoln. "Spring is here."

"What was that?" asked the hired man.

"That? Why that's the prairie chicken. It means it is spring!"

10    There is no sweeter sound in the ears of a prairie-born man than the splendid morning chorus of these noble birds, for it is an infallible sign that winter has broken at last. The drum of the prairie cock carries with it a thousand associations of warm sun and springing grass, which thrill the heart with massive joy of
15 living. It is almost worth while to live through a long unbroken Western winter just for the exquisite delight which comes with the first exultant phrase of the vernal symphony.

Day by day this note is taken by others, until the whole horizon rings with the jocund call of hundreds of cocks and the
20 whooping cries of thousands of hens, as they flock and dance about on the bare earth of the ridges. Here they battle for their mates, and strut about till the ground is beaten hard and smooth with their little feet.

About this time the banking was taken away from the house,
25 and the windows, which had been sealed up for five months, were opened. It was a beautiful moment to Lincoln, when they sat at dinner in the kitchen, with the windows and doors wide open to the warm wind, and the sunshine floating in upon the floor. The hens caw-cawing, in a mounting ecstasy of greeting to
30 the spring, voiced something he had never felt before.

As the wood pile took shape, Mr. Stewart called upon Lincoln and the hired man to help fan up the seed wheat. This the boys hated because it was a dusty and monotonous job. It was of no use to cry out; the work had to be done, and so, on a bright
35 afternoon, while Jack turned the crank of the mill, Lincoln

dipped wheat from the bin into the hopper or held the sacks for his father to fill. It seemed particularly hard to be confined there in the dust and noise, while out in the splendid sunlight the ducks were flying, the prairie chickens calling, and the ice was
5 cracking and booming under the ring of the skaters' steel.

### The Easter Outing

Another diversion of the boys at this season of the year was the hiding of Easter eggs. The hiding of eggs for Easter was a curious custom, quite common among the children of the settlers from New York and the Middle States. The avowed
10 purpose was to lay up a supply of eggs for Easter Sunday. But as they were always extremely plentiful at this season of the year, and almost worthless, the motive must be sought deeper down. Perhaps it was a survival of some old-world superstitions. Anyhow, Lincoln and his brother Owen began to hide eggs in
15 all sorts of out-of-the-way places for fully three weeks before Easter Sunday.

It was understood by Mr. Stewart that if he could discover their hiding places the eggs might be confiscated, and he made elaborate pretense of searching for them. One of the shrewd
20 ways in which the boys made concealment was by lifting a flake of hay from the stack and making a hole beneath it. Upon letting the flake of weather-beaten thatch fall back into place, all signs of the nest disappeared. As the hens were laying a great many eggs each day, it was very difficult for Mrs. Stewart to tell how
25 many the boys were hiding—she did not greatly care.

In his meetings with Milton and Rance, Lincoln compared notes, as to numbers, and together the four boys planned their Easter outing. Day after day Mr. Stewart, to the great dread of the boys, went poking about, close to the very spot where the
30 eggs were hidden, and twice he found a small "nest." But this only added to the value of those remaining and stimulated the boys to yet other and more skillful devices in concealment.

They were able, in spite of his search, to save up several

dozens of eggs, which they triumphantly brought to light on
Easter morning, with gusty shouts of laughter over the pretended
dismay of their parents.

With these eggs packed in a pail and with a few biscuits and
5 some salt and pepper, Lincoln and Owen started out to meet their
companions, Rance and Milton; together they all set forth toward
the distant belt of forest in which Burr Oak Creek ran.

There, in the warm spring sun, on the grassy bank beside
the stream they built their fire and cooked their eggs for their
10 midday meal. Some they boiled, others they roasted in the
ashes. Rance caught a chub or two from the brook, which added
a wild savor to the meal, but eggs were considered a necessary
order of the day; all else was by the way.

Something primeval and splendid clustered about this unusual
15 camp fire. Around them were bare trees, with buds just beginning
to swell. The grass was green only in the sunny nooks, but the
sky was filled with soft white clouds. For guests they had the
squirrels and the blue jays. It was a celebration of their escape
from the bonds of winter and a greeting to spring. There was no
20 conscious feeling in this feast, as far as the boys were concerned.
But the deep-down explanation was this: they had gone back
to the worship of the Anglo-Saxon divinity of spring; they had
returned to the primitive, to the freedom of the savage, not
knowing that the egg was the symbol of regenerate nature.

25      As a matter of fact, the flavor of these eggs was not good;
the burned shell had a disagreeable odor, and the boys would
have been very sorry if Mrs. Stewart had served up for them
anything so disagreeable of flavor. But the curl of smoke from
the grass with which they started the fire, the scream of the
30 jay, the hawk sweeping by overhead, the touch of ashes on their
tongues, the smell of the growing grass, and the sky above made
it all wonderful and wild and very sweet. When at night they
returned, tired and sleepy, to the warmly lighted kitchen and to
mother, they considered the day well spent, uniting as it did the
35 pleasures of both civilization and barbarism.

## NOTES AND QUESTIONS

**Biography.** Hamlin Garland (1860-1940) was born in Wisconsin. His father was a farmer pioneer, who, lured by the hope of cheaper acres, better soil, and bigger crops, moved from Wisconsin to Minnesota, from Minnesota to Iowa, and from Iowa to South Dakota. When Hamlin Garland turned his attention to literature, he was keen enough to see the literary value of his early experiences. He resolved to interpret truthfully the life of the western farmer and its great hardships and limitations, no less than its hopes, joys, and achievements. This selection is taken from *Boy Life on the Prairie.*

**Discussion.** 1. How did the settlers on Sun Prairie feel at the coming of spring? Why? 2. What was the first outdoor work of the spring? Can you give any reason why this would be the first work done? 3. Would you like to do the boys' part of this work? Give reasons for your answer. 4. Would the maple logs interest you as much as they interested Lincoln? Explain why. 5. What does the fact that Lincoln watched the migrating birds tell you about his interest in nature? 6. What work was the boy called upon to do at this time that he disliked very much? Find the sentence that tells why he did not complain about it. 7. What experiences did Lincoln have that you would enjoy? What experiences that you would not enjoy? 8. What qualities made Lincoln a worthy home member and a good American citizen? 9. Is such a life as his necessary to produce these qualities? 10. What would be the result if all boys and girls would persevere in unpleasant duties as Lincoln did? 11. How would our country be helped if all its citizens worked in this way? 12. On page 86, lines 14 to 25, the author compares the boys' picnic to the ancient celebration of spring by primitive peoples. What did you learn on pages 25 and 26 about the influence of nature upon early peoples? 13. In the "Introduction" on page 26 you were told that an important part of our business in life is "to *establish relations* with the world in which we live." Can you show that the boys of this story had established such relations, and that this added great enjoyment to their lives? 14. What were you told in "Literature and Life," pages 19 and 20, about literature as a source of learning the "facts of life"? How does this selection give you a clearer idea of the "facts of life" on a midwestern farm than you could gain from your history or geography or from an encyclopedia? 15. Find in the glossary the meaning of: inundated; conical; transitory; swales; infallible; ecstasy; confiscated. 16. *Pronounce:* exquisite; horizon; jocund; savor; primeval.

### Phrases for Study

to the quick, **82**, 25

take a final stand, **83**, 20

Anglo-Saxon divinity, **86**, 22

symbol of regenerate nature, **86**, 24

**Class Reading.** Bring to class and read: "The Call of Spring," Noyes (in *High Tide*).

**Outline for Testing Silent Reading.** Make an outline to guide you in telling the story.

**Library Reading.** *A Son of the Middle Border*, Garland.

**Suggested Theme Topic.** Life on a modern farm as compared with the life led by the boys of this story.

---

## HOME-THOUGHTS, FROM ABROAD

### ROBERT BROWNING

Oh, to be in England,
Now that April's there!
And whoever wakes in England
Sees, some morning, unaware,
5 That the lowest boughs and the brushwood sheaf
Round the elm-tree bole are in tiny leaf,
While the chaffinch sings on the orchard bough
In England—now!

And after April, when May follows,
10 And the whitethroat builds, and all the swallows!
Hark, where my blossomed pear-tree in the hedge
Leans to the field and scatters on the clover
Blossoms and dewdrops—at the bent spray's edge
That's the wise thrush; he sings each song twice over,
15 Lest you should think he never could recapture
The first fine, careless rapture!

And though the fields look rough with hoary dew,
All will be gay when noontide wakes anew
The buttercups, the little children's dower,
—Far brighter than this gaudy melon-flower!

## NOTES AND QUESTIONS

**Biography.** Robert Browning (1812-1889) was born in Camberwell, a suburb of London. His four grandparents were respectively of English, German, Scotch, and Creole birth. His father was fond of writing verses, and his mother was very musical. Browning's education was gained from a private school in the neighborhood and from tutors at home. In 1846 he married the poet, Elizabeth Barrett, and they lived for years in the old palace, Casa Guidi, in Florence, Italy. After his wife's death he returned to England, but spent most of his summers abroad. He died in Venice, and is buried in the Poets' Corner of Westminster Abbey.

Much of Browning's poetry is difficult reading. He condenses a great deal of thought into one phrase or word and leaves much to the imagination of the reader. Many of his short poems, however, are comparatively simple.

**Discussion**. 1. Browning wrote this poem while in Italy; read the lines that show his longing for England. 2. What word gives the idea that spring comes suddenly in England? 3. What are the signs that the poet associates especially with early spring? 4. Commit to memory the lovely description of the thrush's song. 5. Notice the beautiful setting given to the thrush; which words add especially to the beauty of the picture? 6. How will "noontide wake anew the buttercups"? 7. Tell why buttercups are "the little children's dower." 8. To what flower in Italy is the buttercup compared? 9. Describe in a few lines what you love best in the springtime at your home. 10. Contest: Who can read the entire poem most effectively? 11. What did you learn in "Literature and Life," page 21, about literature that makes beauty evident to us? Can you show that this poem is such a piece of literature? 12. Find in the glossary the meaning of: bole; whitethroat; rapture; dower. 13. *Pronounce:* elm-tree; chaffinch; dewdrop; anew; gaudy.

**Class Reading.** Bring to class and read: "Go Down to Kew in Lilactime," Noyes (from "The Barrel-Organ" in *Poems*); "Een Napoli," Daly (in *High Tide*); "Apple Blossoms," Martin (in *The Elson Readers, Book Six*). Compare these poems with "Home-Thoughts, from Abroad."

# A VAGABOND SONG

### BLISS CARMAN

There is something in the Autumn that is native to my blood—
Touch of manner, hint of mood;
And my heart is like a rime,
With the yellow and the purple and the crimson keeping time.

5 The scarlet of the maples can shake me like a cry
Of bugles going by.
And my lonely spirit thrills
To see the frosty asters like smoke upon the hills.

There is something in October sets the gypsy blood astir;
10 We must rise and follow her,
When from every hill of flame
She calls and calls each vagabond by name.

### NOTES AND QUESTIONS

**Biography.** Bliss Carman (1861-1929) was born in Fredericton, New Brunswick. After he graduated from New Brunswick University, he studied at Harvard and the University of Edinburgh. Like many other poets, he began his career with journalistic work. He was editor of the *Independent* and later of the *Chap-Book*. Most of his time was devoted to poetry, and he published many books. His first volume was *Low Tide on Grand Pré*. Among his later works are *Echoes from Vagabondia* and *April Airs*.

**Discussion.** 1. To what does the poet say his heart keeps time? 2. Where does he see these colors? 3. How does the color of the maples affect him? 4. What connection do you see between scarlet and the sound of bugles? 5. What color were the asters that appeared like smoke? 6. Whom does the poet say he must follow? 7. What gives the appearance of flame to the hills?

**Class Reading.** Bring to class and read: "Indian Summer," Teasdale (in *Rivers to the Sea*).

## Suggested Problems

You will find in this book suggested problems, some of which are to be worked out by you alone and some with the help of your classmates. The members of most eighth-grade classes represent a wide range of abilities in art, music, reading, composing, folk dancing, dramatizing, printing, manual training, etc. All the talent in the class should be used, and each member should feel responsibility for his share.

Your class may wish to celebrate the harvest days of autumn or the coming of spring with a festival or pageant. These suggestions will be helpful in such a class undertaking: (a) Reading or recitation of one or more appropriate nature poems (See "Part III," "Poems of Nature" in *The Home Book of Verse*, Stevenson); (b) Three-minute talks by class members on harvest or spring celebrations in other lands; (c) Tableaux, antomimes, or dramatizations of nature myths and folk-stories, as, Apollo, Dionysus, Ceres and Persephone, Baucis and Philemon, the dryads, Balder, Siegfried and Brunhild, Sleeping Beauty, Robin Hood, Hiawatha, etc.; (d) Games and dances representing flowers, seeds, trees, birds, butterflies, winds, raindrops, snowflakes, conflict between frost spirits and sunbeams, etc.; (e) Designing and making simple costumes, symbols, and settings for the dances and dramatizations; (f) Appropriate songs and instrumental music by class members; (g) Recordings ("Spring Song," Mendelssohn; "The Heavens Are Telling," Haydn; "Hark, Hark! The Lark," Shakespeare-Schubert; "Papillon," Grieg; "Pastoral Symphony," Beethoven; etc.); (h) A contest to see who can recognize the greatest number of wild flowers, grains, trees, birds, or butterflies, from the objects themselves, slides, or from colored pictures that may be secured from the library or museum; (i) Advertisements of the festival or pageant by means of posters and newspaper announcements prepared by class members. You will find additional suggestions in: *The Victory of the Gardens, A Pageant in Four Episodes* (Bureau of Education, Department of the Interior, Washington, D.C.); *Plays for School Children*, Lütkenhaus; *Harper's Book of Little Plays; Patriotic Plays and Pageants for Young People, Silver Thread and Other Folk-Plays*, Mackay.

A similar festival or pageant might well be made for the celebration of Thanksgiving Day. See *Children's Book of Thanksgiving Stories*, Dickenson.

## THE WORLD OF NATURE

### A Review

Which of the joys described in "Literature and Life" has the reading of the selections in "Part I" given you? Explain what literature is, about which you read on page 19. Point out in "Part I" examples of literature that express (a) the *facts* of life, (b) the *interpretation* of life, (c) the *beauty* of life. You read in the "Introduction," page 26, that "men in all ages have felt the influence of nature"; mention wonderful things that we have learned to perform through our uses of nature's laws.

How has your acquaintance with "Coaly-Bay" and "Satan, the War Dog" enriched your experiences? The authors of these stories have shown qualities in these animals that will make all other horses and dogs more interesting and your treatment of them more sympathetic; explain the feeling you have for Coaly-Bay. What other stories of horses, of dogs, or about the service of animals in war have you read? What interesting animal stories have you found in current magazines? You read in the "Introduction," page 27, that "animals have personalities like human beings"; what evidences of this do you find in Coaly-Bay and in Satan? How were the buffalo herds destroyed? What is the most interesting story about animals that you found in the preceding books of this series?

A poet sees and feels, and with magic words he makes us see and feel what he has experienced. He gives new meaning to common experiences, and expresses this meaning in language of "enduring charm"; which poems in "Part I" interpret life? Three English poets have used the skylark as a subject; which poem pictures the bird most vividly? Which poet has caught in the rhythm of his lines the music of the bird and its swinging flight? Find lines in each of these poems that describe the skylark's song. Read again what is said in "Literature and Life," page 21, and in the "Introduction," page 27, of Bryant's "To a Waterfowl"; does this poem interpret life? What difference do you notice between the poet's treatment of a bird subject and Audubon's?

What lines of "enduring beauty" do you remember in the poems about flowers? Compare "Pine-Trees and the Sky" with "To a Waterfowl"; what likenesses do you find? Show that Rupert Brooke followed the same plan used by Bryant, that is, a fact in the poet's life, the interpretation of the fact, and the poet's sure instinct for beauty of expression. What nature lyrics do you find in "Part I"? Have you heard recordings of any of these? Which lyrics can you repeat from memory? What nature lyrics have you found in current magazines? What acquaintance with contemporary poetry have you made through library reading, other than magazine reading, in connection with "Part I"? What nature lyric in the preceding books of this series was most pleasing to you?

What progress have you made in becoming acquainted with your library—the arrangement of the books, the card catalogue, and the *Readers' Guide to Periodical Literature?* Make a list of selections—titles and authors—showing your library reading under three headings—books, magazines, and newspapers. Make a list of books and stories that have been reviewed in class; which review inspired you to read the book or story? What progress has your class made with its scrapbook for newspaper clippings? Which sections of your local newspaper interest you most? Which of the "Suggestions for Theme Topics" brought out the best oral discussion? Explain the aptness of the quotation from Browning, page 23, and of the picture, page 24, as an introduction to "Part I."

In the "Notes and Questions" throughout this book are a number of suggested problems. Working out these problems will greatly increase your interest in reading and will bring you the added pleasure that cooperation with others in a common project always brings. In many schools the class in English organizes in the form of a club, to give the pupils an opportunity to cooperate in working out suggestions. If your class forms such a club, with regular recitation periods set aside each month for meetings, you can carry out many interesting projects, using the club as a "clearing house" for the various ideas suggested by the individual reading of the club members.

Some of these suggested problems are: (a) "Silent Reading," page 13; (b) "Library Reading," including "Book Reviews," page 45; (c) "Magazine Reading," page 55; (d) "Newspaper Reading," page 59; (e) "Contemporary Writers"—Noting selections by them, reading from their works, comparing their writings in theme and treatment with those of earlier writers, reporting any interesting newspaper or magazine references to them, and preparing a program for Contemporary Writers' Day in your school; (f) Collections—Making a collection of pictures, cartoons, newspaper and magazine references, humorous sayings, songs, and recordings that illustrate particular selections; (g) Dramatization—Planning and presenting scenes from "A Christmas Carol," and from other selections; (h) Public Readings—Readings for entertainment, lyrics, ballads, and passages from short stories, using the club as an audience; (i) Good Citizenship—Making a list of suggestions you find in this book that help you to be a good citizen, and preparing a program for Good Citizenship Day in your school; (j) Conservation and Thrift—Making a list of measures taken to conserve public health, to protect wild birds and animals, to preserve forests, and to encourage thrift; (k) Excursions—Taking a trip through a library under the guidance of the teacher or librarian, locating various departments, or visiting homes, statues, and monuments of writers located in your town.

# PART II

## THE WORLD OF ADVENTURE

*Great deeds cannot die*
*They with sun and moon renew their light*
*Forever blessing those that look on them.*
                              —Tennyson

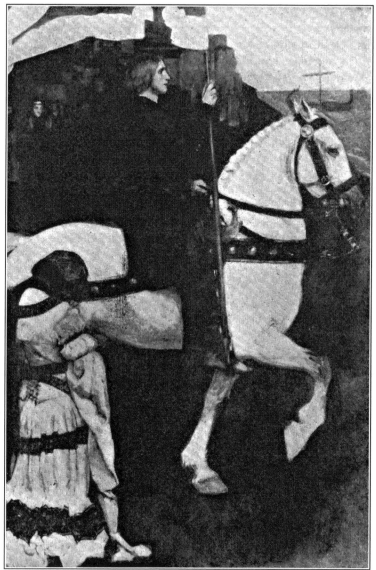

Sir Galahad

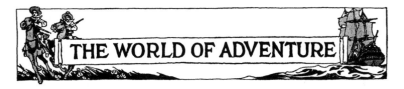

# THE WORLD OF ADVENTURE

## AN INTRODUCTION

The basis of all literature is adventure. A cookbook is not literature, because it merely sets down certain rules for the preparation of food. Of course, a boy or girl who knows nothing about cooking may try to apply the rules for making a chocolate cake and, in the process, may have a very exciting adventure, but the cookbook itself does not contain adventure; it is not literature.

Adventure is an experience out of the ordinary. It need not be thrilling in the sense that an escape from a wild beast is thrilling. When Rupert Brooke became aware of the beauty of the pine trees, and of the effect of this vision upon his sadness, that was an adventure. When Wordsworth heard the lark far above him and fell to wondering about the singer and found in it a symbol of life, that was an adventure.

The records of these adventures give us literature. The necessary element is imagination. If the poet's imagination had been asleep, he never would have given us that poem about the pine trees and the sky. Even daily life is full of adventure if the imagination is active. People who are intensely interested in every form of life have no lack of adventure. For them life is not dull and prosy; it is filled with the spice of imagination.

In this section of your book you will find stories and poems that deal mainly with adventure in the usual sense of the word—a thrilling or exciting experience. Some of them, such as the "Incident of the French Camp," are based on real happenings. The poet did not himself pass through the adventures; yet through his imagination, he was able to picture the scenes so vividly that he seemed to have been present. Other stories of adventure, such as "The Highwayman," are based on old legends dealing with events that have only a partial foundation of fact. A third type of story of adventure is purely imaginary; the events which it narrates never actually took place. The writer sees these imaginary events so vividly, however, that they seem as real as if they were matters of historical fact. An example is Poe's "The Masque of the Red Death," which you will read in this section of your book.

In all of these stories of adventure the element of imagination enters. Whether the author deals with an actual event, or an old legend, or a purely imaginary plot, he *sees* his story in action, just as if he were at the theater looking upon a story told through action. And the author tells it to you in such a way that you, too, see it *in action*, as though you were at the theater by the author's side.

Now in this fact lies an important lesson. You must learn to see these stories, to visualize them as though they were little dramas. Many people do not do this. You may hear someone telling a story about an acquaintance: Mr. Smith did this or that, and then this or that happened, and probably Mr. Smith will do so and so. But these statements of what happened may not bring to your mind any pictures. You may *know* the events of the story, the setting in which it took place, and the names of the characters, without seeing these people in action, doing these things as though they were characters in a play.

You can train your mind to do this *creative reading*, so that your reading becomes as interesting as a play. As you read the following selections, try to cultivate this power by asking yourself, at each point in the story, how the persons of the story look and what the scene is. Try to plan how you would paint them if you were an artist, or to visualize what the pictures would look like if they were made for the movies.

For your reading of stories of adventure is your own private moving picture show, if you wish to have it that way. Such reading is a never-ending source of delight.

# STORIES OF THE SUPERNATURAL

## THE MASQUE OF THE RED DEATH*

### EDGAR ALLAN POE

The "Red Death" had long devastated the country. No pestilence had ever been so fatal, or so hideous. Blood was its avatar and its seal—the redness and the horror of blood. There were sharp pains and sudden dizziness, and then profuse bleeding
5 at the pores, with dissolution. The scarlet stains upon the body, and especially upon the face, of the victim were the pest ban which shut him out from the aid and from the sympathy of his fellow men. And the whole seizure, progress, and termination of the disease were the incidents of half an hour.
10 But the Prince Prospero was happy and dauntless and sagacious. When his dominions were half depopulated, he summoned to his presence a thousand hale and light-hearted friends from among the knights and dames of his court, and with these retired to the deep seclusion of one of his castellated abbeys. This
15 was an extensive and magnificent structure, the creation of the prince's own eccentric yet august taste. A strong and lofty wall

---

*See Silent and Oral Reading, page 13.

girdled it in. This wall had gates of iron. The courtiers, having entered, brought furnaces and massy hammers, and welded the bolts. They resolved to leave means neither of ingress nor egress to the sudden impulses of despair or of frenzy from within.
5 The abbey was amply provisioned. With such precautions the courtiers might bid defiance to contagion. The external world could take care of itself. In the meantime it was folly to grieve, or to think. The prince had provided all the appliances of pleasure. There were buffoons, there were improvisatori, there
10 were ballet dancers, there were musicians, there was beauty, there was wine. All these and security were within. Without was the "Red Death."

It was toward the close of the fifth or sixth month of his seclusion, and while the pestilence raged most furiously abroad,
15 that the Prince Prospero entertained his thousand friends at a masked ball of the most unusual magnificence.

It was a voluptuous scene, that masquerade. But first let me tell of the rooms in which it was held. There were seven—an imperial suite. In many palaces, however, such suites form
20 a long and straight vista, while the folding doors slide back nearly to the walls on either hand, so that the view of the whole extent is scarcely impeded. Here the case was very different, as might have been expected from the prince's love of the bizarre. The apartments were so irregularly disposed that the vision
25 embraced but little more than one at a time. There was a sharp turn at every twenty or thirty yards, and at each turn a novel effect. To the right and left, in the middle of each wall, a tall and narrow Gothic window looked out upon a closed corridor which pursued the windings of the suite. These windows were
30 of stained glass, whose color varied in accordance with the prevailing hue of the decorations of the chamber into which it opened. That at the eastern extremity was hung, for example, in blue—and vividly blue were its windows. The second chamber was purple in its ornaments and tapestries, and here the panes
35 were purple. The third was green throughout, and so were

the casements. The fourth was furnished and lighted with orange, the fifth with white, the sixth with violet. The seventh apartment was closely shrouded in black velvet tapestries that hung all over the ceiling and down the walls, falling in heavy
5 folds upon a carpet of the same material and hue. But, in this chamber only, the color of the windows failed to correspond with the decorations. The panes here were scarlet—a deep blood-color. Now in no one of the seven apartments was there any lamp or candelabrum, amid the profusion of golden orna-
10 ments that lay scattered to and fro or depended from the roof. There was no light of any kind emanating from lamp or candle within the suite of chambers. But in the corridors that followed the suite there stood, opposite to each window, a heavy tripod, bearing a brazier of fire, that projected its rays through the
15 tinted glass and, so, glaringly illumined the room. And thus were produced a multitude of gaudy and fantastic appearances. But in the western or black chamber the effect of the firelight that streamed upon the dark hangings through the blood-tinted panes was ghastly in the extreme, and produced so wild a look
20 upon the countenances of those who entered that there were few of the company bold enough to set foot within its precincts at all.

It was in this apartment, also, that there stood against the western wall a gigantic clock of ebony. Its pendulum swung
25 to and fro with a dull, heavy, monotonous clang; and when the minute hand made the circuit of the face, and the hour was to be stricken, there came from the brazen lungs of the clock a sound which was clear and loud and deep and exceedingly musical, but of so peculiar a note and emphasis that, at each lapse of an
30 hour, the musicians of the orchestra were constrained to pause, momentarily, in their performance, to hearken to the sound; and thus the waltzers perforce ceased their evolutions; and there was a brief disconcert of the whole gay company; and, while the chimes of the clock yet rang, it was observed that the giddiest
35 grew pale, and the more aged and sedate passed their hands over

their brows as if in confused revery or meditation. But when
the echoes had fully ceased, a light laughter at once pervaded
the assembly; the musicians looked at each other and smiled as
if at their own nervousness and folly, and made whispering
5 vows, each to the other, that the next chiming of the clock
should produce in them no similar emotion; and then, after a
lapse of sixty minutes (which embrace three thousand and six
hundred seconds of the Time that flies), there came yet another
chiming of the clock, and then were the same disconcert and
10 tremulousness and meditation as before.

But, in spite of these things, it was a gay and magnificent
revel. The tastes of the prince were peculiar. He had a fine eye
for colors and effects. He disregarded the *decora* of mere fashion.
His plans were bold and fiery, and his conceptions glowed with
15 barbaric luster. There were some who would have thought him
mad. His followers felt that he was not. It was necessary to hear
and see and touch him to be sure that he was not.

He had directed, in great part, the movable embellishments
of the seven chambers, upon occasion of this great *fête*; and
20 it was his own guiding taste which had given character to the
masqueraders. Be sure they were grotesque. There were much
glare and glitter and piquancy and phantasm—much of what
has been since seen in *Hernani*. There were arabesque figures
with unsuited limbs and appointments. There were delirious
25 fancies such as the madman fashions. There was much of the
beautiful, much of the wanton, much of the bizarre, something
of the terrible, and not a little of that which might have excited
disgust. To and fro in the seven chambers there stalked, in fact,
a multitude of dreams. And these—the dreams—writhed in and
30 about, taking hue from the rooms, and causing the wild music
of the orchestra to seem as the echo of their steps. And, anon,
there strikes the ebony clock which stands in the hall of the
velvet. And then, for a moment, all is still, and all is silent save
the voice of the clock. The dreams are stiff-frozen as they stand.
35 But the echoes of the chime die away—they have endured but

an instant—and a light, half-subdued laughter floats after them
as they depart. And now again the music swells, and the dreams
live, and writhe to and fro more merrily than ever, taking hue
from the many-tinted windows through which stream the rays
5 from the tripods. But to the chamber which lies most westwardly
of the seven there are now none of the maskers who venture; for
the night is waning away, and there flows a ruddier light through
the blood-colored panes; and the blackness of the sable drapery
appalls; and to him whose foot falls upon the sable carpet, there
10 comes from the near clock of ebony a muted peal more solemnly
emphatic than any which reaches their ears who indulge in the
more remote gayeties of the other apartments.

But these other apartments were densely crowded, and
in them beat feverishly the heart of life. And the revel went
15 whirlingly on, until at length there commenced the sounding of
midnight upon the clock. And then the music ceased, as I have
told, and the evolutions of the waltzers were quieted; and there
was an uneasy cessation of all things as before. But now there
were twelve strokes to be sounded by the bell of the clock; and
20 thus it happened, perhaps, that more of thought crept, with
more of time, into the meditations of the thoughtful among those
who reveled. And thus, too, it happened, perhaps, that before
the last echoes of the last chime had utterly sunk into silence,
there were many individuals in the crowd who had found leisure
25 to become aware of the presence of a masked figure which had
arrested the attention of no single individual before. And the
rumor of this new presence having spread itself whisperingly
around, there arose at length from the whole company a buzz,
or murmur, expressive of disapprobation and surprise—then,
30 finally, of terror, of horror, and of disgust.

In an assembly of phantasms such as I have painted, it
may well be supposed that no ordinary appearance could have
excited such sensation. In truth the masquerade license of
the night was nearly unlimited; but the figure in question had
35 out-Heroded Herod, and gone beyond the bounds of even the

prince's indefinite decorum. There are chords in the hearts of the most reckless which cannot be touched without emotion. Even with the utterly lost, to whom life and death are equally jests, there are matters of which no jest can be made. The whole
5 company, indeed, seemed now deeply to feel that in the costume and bearing of the stranger neither wit nor propriety existed. The figure was tall and gaunt, and shrouded from head to foot in the habiliments of the grave. The mask which concealed the visage was made so nearly to resemble the countenance of a
10 stiffened corpse that the closest scrutiny must have had difficulty in detecting the cheat. And yet all this might have been endured, if not approved, by the mad revelers around. But the mummer had gone so far as to assume the type of the Red Death. His vesture was dabbled in blood—and his broad brow, with all the
15 features of the face, was besprinkled with the scarlet horror.

When the eyes of Prince Prospero fell upon this spectral image (which with a slow and solemn movement, as if more fully to sustain its role, stalked to and fro among the waltzers), he was seen to be convulsed, in the first moment, with a strong
20 shudder either of terror or distaste; but, in the next, his brow reddened with rage.

"Who dares?" he demanded hoarsely of the courtiers who stood near him—"who dares insult us with this blasphemous mockery? Seize him and unmask him—that we may know whom
25 we have to hang at sunrise, from the battlements!"

It was in the eastern or blue chamber in which stood the Prince Prospero as he uttered these words. They rang throughout the seven rooms loudly and clearly—for the prince was a bold and robust man, and the music had become hushed at the
30 waving of his hand.

It was in the blue room where stood the prince, with a group of pale courtiers by his side. At first, as he spoke, there was a slight, rushing movement of this group in the direction of the intruder, who at the moment was also near at hand, and now
35 with deliberate and stately step, made closer approach to the

speaker. But from a certain nameless awe with which the mad assumptions of the mummer had inspired the whole party, there were found none who put forth hand to seize him; so that, unimpeded, he passed within a yard of the prince's person;
5 and while the vast assembly, as if with one impulse, shrank from the centers of the rooms to the walls, he made his way uninterruptedly, but with the same solemn and measured step which had distinguished him from the first, through the blue chamber to the purple through the purple to the green—through
10 the green to the orange through this again to the white—and even thence to the violet, ere a decided movement had been made to arrest him. It was then, however, that the Prince Prospero, maddening with rage and the shame of his own momentary cowardice, rushed hurriedly through the six chambers, while
15 none followed him, on account of a deadly terror that had seized upon all. He bore aloft a drawn dagger, and had approached, in rapid impetuosity, to within three or four feet of the retreating figure, when the latter, having attained the extremity of the velvet apartment, turned suddenly and confronted his pursuer.
20 There was a sharp cry—and the dagger dropped gleaming upon the sable carpet, upon which, instantly afterwards, fell prostrate in death the Prince Prospero. Then, summoning the wild courage of despair, a throng of the revelers at once threw themselves into the black apartment, and, seizing the mummer,
25 whose tall figure stood erect and motionless within the shadow of the ebony clock, gasped in unutterable horror at finding the grave cerements and corpse-like mask, which they handled with so violent a rudeness, untenanted by any tangible form.

And now was acknowledged the presence of the Red Death.
30 He had come like a thief in the night. And one by one dropped the revelers in the blood-bedewed halls of their revel, and died each in the despairing posture of his fall. And the life of the ebony clock went out with that of the last of the gay. And the flames of the tripods expired. And Darkness and Decay and the
35 Red Death held illimitable dominion over all.

## NOTES AND QUESTIONS

**Biography.** Edgar Allan Poe (1809-1849) was one of the great American poets and short story writers. Born in Boston, he was left an orphan at an early age and was adopted by a wealthy citizen of Richmond, Virginia. Poe went to school in England and later attended the University of Virginia, and the Military Academy at West Point, but he was little interested in any subject except literature. Before he was twenty, Poe had published a volume of poetry. During the brief twenty remaining years of his life he was constantly publishing poems and tales, contributing to newspapers and magazines and doing editorial work. His writings are weird and mysterious, and his poetry is perhaps the most purely musical of any in our language. His prose tales of mystery and adventure have served as models for many well-known writers. Poe was the originator of the modern short story.

**The Short Story.** In "The Masque of the Red Death," a typical short story, Poe aimed to make a single, vivid effect. To get this he planned a story of four parts: an introduction (paragraphs 1 and 2) that suggests the effect he wished to produce; a main incident (paragraphs 3-12) that develops the suggested effect; a powerful climax (paragraph 13) that indelibly impresses this effect on the reader; and a conclusion (paragraph 14)—all these to include no unnecessary character, incident, or detail. Poe aimed to suggest from the beginning a fear that should increase until it ended in a climax of awful terror.

Poe chose, as the cause of the terror, the fear of death by a plague; can you tell why the fear of the plague was so great? Poe desired to describe a more terrible plague than any of which he had ever read—it should be a red death; to whom would the thought of this death, which no one could prevent, be most terrible? Explain why he chose a prince for the principal character. A masque is a revel in which all wear masks; whose revel did this prove to be? Is this what the title suggests?

The introduction gives the situation at the beginning of the main incident and introduces all the characters but one; tell in a few words what this situation is. How many characters are mentioned by name? How many are described? How do the thousand friends that are only figures add to the effect of terror? Coming directly after the description of the awful plague, what effect upon you has the statement "But the Prince Prospero was happy and dauntless and sagacious"? What is really suggested by the fact that they welded the gate? By the determination to let the "external world take care of itself"? By the thought that it was "folly to grieve, or to think"? What was the prince's real object in providing "all the appliances of pleasure"? Does the introduction leave you confident that "security was within"? From this beginning would you expect the ending to be happy or tragic?

Notice how Poe develops the main incident: Prince Prospero entertains his friends at a masked ball, to which comes an intruder masked as a victim of the Red Death. Prospero, enraged, commands that the intruder be unmasked. At what stage in the progress of the pestilence was this ball given? Do you think such a revelry at such a time showed a "happy and dauntless and sagacious" mind? Try to make a mental picture of the scene Poe has so wonderfully described. Make a list of the adjectives Poe uses to aid him in picturing it, such as "novel," page 100, line 26. As you read this description of the rooms, the color, and the fantastic moving figures, do you feel it to be a joyful scene? Poe uses this description of the ball to aid him in making the reader feel this terror; note that he uses three means to produce this effect.

Show that Poe has prepared in the introduction for the use of color as one of these means. With what color was the fear of the dancers associated? How was this color used in the seventh room, and what effect did it have upon the dancers?

Poe wished to suggest still more subtly the fear of the Red Death that filled every heart; could he have chosen anything more suited to this purpose than the "clock of ebony," with its stroke "of so peculiar a note" that the whole gay company had to stop to hear the striking of each hour? What was the reason that this particular sound so disconcerted the dancers? What made the thought of passing time so terrible to them?

Where is the first hint given of the approach of the masked figure that is so terrible? At what hour did the "new presence" come? With what does superstition associate this hour? How does Poe show us the falseness of Prospero's claim to be considered "happy and dauntless and sagacious"? In what way did Prospero betray the fear he really felt? What was the one thing about this figure that could not be endured?

Poe, in approaching the climax, creates suspense by describing the masked figure's slow progress through each room. Notice how well the slow movement of the narrative here imitates this "solemn and measured step"; what causes this "nameless awe"? Note the final rush toward the climax—the prince's rage, his pursuit and threatening dagger, the stranger's sudden stand, Prospero's death, and (full climax) the seizure of the terrible figure and the "unutterable horror."

Poe's swift conclusion of the story shows his wonderful art. Having reached the climax, the full effect of horror, a few sentences give the result: "Now was acknowledged the presence of the Red Death. . . . And Darkness and Decay and the Red Death held illimitable dominion over all." Point out ways by which Poe makes this conclusion more terrible, such for example as "the deaths, one by one." Has Poe secured the effect at which he aimed? Has he pictured Prospero's character in such a way as to make you feel this terrible ending certain to come, and not unjust? Fear of so terrible a plague is natural; what was there in Prospero's fear that takes away our sympathy?

**Discussion.** 1. What is said in the introduction on page 98 about purely imaginary stories of adventure? How does Poe make the events of this story seem as if they had really happened? 2. What two kinds of adventure are mentioned on page 97? Which of these kinds is narrated in "The Masque of the Red Death"? 3. Name several stories dealing with this kind of adventure that you read in "Part I." 4. What other imaginative stories by Poe have you read? 5. Look up in the glossary the meaning of: sagacious; depopulated; bizarre; perforce; grotesque; decorum; habiliments; tangible. 6. *Pronounce:* eccentric; august; courtiers; ballet-dancer; suite; disconcert; fête; piquancy; robust; illimitable.

### Phrases for Study

bid defiance to contagion, **100**, 6

decora of mere fashion, **102**, 13

masquerade license, **103**, 33

out-Heroded Herod, **103**, 35

sustain its role, **104**, 18

attained the extremity, **105**, 18

**Class Reading.** Read aloud the paragraphs of the introduction, trying to suggest by your reading Poe's purpose in writing them; the paragraphs that contain the development of the main incident, trying to suggest what Poe has so powerfully suggested in his story—the terrible fear under all the seeming gayety, and its final outburst; the paragraph that gives the climax, striving to suggest by your reading the increasing fear and final horror; selected sentences that exemplify Poe's imaginative and poetic style, such as in the descriptions of the clock and of the dancers, and in the last paragraph, particularly the last sentence; selected descriptions that give you the most vivid pictures, noting especially the sentence in each that is most poetically expressed; examples showing the careful selection of words especially fitted to express the thought.

**Outline for Testing Silent Reading.** Make an outline to guide you in telling the story.

**Library Reading.** "A Descent into the Maelstrom," Poe.

**Suggestions for Theme Topics.** (Two-Minute Talks.) 1. A great plague of which I know or have read. 2. The Black Death in the fourteenth century. (Use encyclopedias or other library sources.) 3. Contrast the behavior of Prospero with that of Surgeon-General William C. Gorgas, who fought yellow fever in Panama and who rescued Cuba from disease. (*The Mentor*, November, 1920; use *The Readers' Guide* to find other material.) 4. Father Damien and his work among the lepers on the Island of Molokai. (*A Treasury of Heroes and Heroines*, Edwards.) 5. Experiences of Dr. Wilfred C. Grenfell as a medical missionary, from his autobiography, *A Labrador Doctor*. (*Who's Who in America* will tell you simple facts of the author's life.)

---

## THE RAVEN

### EDGAR ALLAN POE

Once upon a midnight dreary, while I pondered, weak and weary,
Over many a quaint and curious volume of forgotten lore—
While I nodded, nearly napping, suddenly there came a tapping,
As of someone gently rapping, rapping at my chamber door.
5 "'Tis some visitor," I muttered, "tapping at my chamber door
     Only this and nothing more."

Ah, distinctly I remember it was in the bleak December,
And each separate dying ember wrought its ghost upon the floor.
Eagerly I wished the morrow; vainly I had sought to borrow
10 From my books surcease of sorrow—sorrow for the lost Lenore.
For the rare and radiant maiden whom the angels name Lenore:
     Nameless here forevermore.

And the silken, sad, uncertain rustling of each purple curtain
Thrilled me—filled me with fantastic terrors never felt before;
15 So that now, to still the beating of my heart, I stood repeating:
"'Tis some visitor entreating entrance at my chamber door,
Some late visitor entreating entrance at my chamber door—
     This it is and nothing more."

Presently my soul grew stronger; hesitating then no longer,
"Sir," said I, "or Madam, truly your forgiveness I implore;
But the fact is I was napping, and so gently you came rapping,
And so faintly you came tapping, tapping at my chamber door,
5 That I scarce was sure I heard you"—here I opened wide the
        door—
Darkness there and nothing more.


Deep into that darkness peering, long I stood there wondering,
        fearing,
Doubting, dreaming dreams no mortal ever dared to dream
        before;
But the silence was unbroken, and the stillness gave no token,
10 And the only word there spoken was the whispered word,
        "Lenore?"
This I whispered; and an echo murmured back the word,
        "Lenore"—
        Merely this and nothing more.


Back into the chamber turning, all my soul within me burning,
Soon again I heard a tapping somewhat louder than before.
15 "Surely," said I, "surely that is something at my window lattice;
Let me see, then, what thereat is, and this mystery explore;
Let my heart be still a moment and this mystery explore—
        Tis the wind and nothing more."


Open here I flung the shutter, when, with many a flirt and flutter,
20 In there stepped a stately Raven of the saintly days of yore.
Not the least obeisance made he; not a minute stopped or stayed
        he;
But, with mien of lord or lady, perched above my chamber door,
Perched upon a bust of Pallas just above my chamber door
        Perched, and sat, and nothing more.

Then this ebony bird beguiling my sad fancy into smiling
By the grave and stern decorum of the countenance it wore—
"Though thy crest be shorn and shaven, thou," I said, "art sure
    no craven,
Ghastly grim and ancient Raven wandering from the Nightly
    shore;
5 Tell me what thy lordly name is on the Night's Plutonian shore!"
    Quoth the Raven, "Nevermore."

Much I marveled this ungainly fowl to hear discourse so plainly,
Though its answer little meaning—little relevancy bore;
For we cannot help agreeing that no living human being
10 Ever yet was blessed with seeing bird above his chamber door,
Bird or beast upon the sculptured bust above his chamber door,
    With such name as "Nevermore."

But the Raven, sitting lonely on the placid bust, spoke only
That one word, as if his soul in that one word he did outpour;
15 Nothing further then he uttered; not a feather then he fluttered,
Till I scarcely more than muttered, "Other friends have flown
    before;
On the morrow he will leave me, as my Hopes have flown before."
    Then the bird said, "Nevermore."

Startled at the stillness broken by reply so aptly spoken,
20 "Doubtless," said I "what it utters is its only stock and store,
Caught from some unhappy master whom unmerciful Disaster
Followed fast and followed faster till his songs one burden bore;
Till the dirges of his Hope that melancholy burden bore
    Of 'Never—nevermore.'"

25 But the Raven still beguiling all my fancy into smiling,
Straight I wheeled a cushioned seat in front of bird and bust
    and door;
Then, upon the Velvet sinking, I betook myself to linking

Fancy unto fancy, thinking what this ominous bird of yore,
What this grim, ungainly, ghastly, gaunt, and ominous bird of
    yore,
      Meant in croaking "Nevermore."

This I sat engaged in guessing, but no syllable expressing
5 To the fowl whose fiery eyes now burned into my bosom's core;
This and more I sat divining, with my head at ease reclining
On the cushion's velvet lining that the lamplight gloated o'er,
But whose velvet violet lining with the lamplight gloating o'er
    She shall press, ah, nevermore!

10 Then, methought, the air grew denser, perfumed from an
    unseen censer
Swung by seraphim whose footfalls tinkled on the tufted floor.
"Wretch," I cried, "thy God hath lent thee—by these angels he
    hath sent thee
Respite—respite and nepenthe from thy memories of Lenore!
Quaff, oh, quaff this kind nepenthe, and forget this lost Lenore!"
15     Quoth the Raven, "Nevermore."

"Prophet!" said I, "thing of evil! prophet still, if bird or devil!
Whether Tempter sent, or whether tempest tossed thee here
    ashore,
Desolate yet all undaunted, on this desert land enchanted
On this home by Horror haunted—tell me truly, I implore:
20 Is there—is there balm in Gilead?—tell me—tell me, I implore!"
    Quoth the Raven, "Nevermore."

"Prophet!" said I, "thing of evil—prophet still, if bird or devil!
By that Heaven that bends above us, by that God we both adore,
Tell this soul with sorrow laden if, within the distant Aidenn,
25 It shall clasp a sainted maiden whom the angels name Lenore
Clasp a rare and radiant maiden whom the angels name Lenore!"
    Quoth the Raven, "Nevermore."

"Be that word our sign of parting, bird or fiend!" I shrieked,
    upstarting;
"Get thee back into the tempest and the Night's Plutonian shore!
Leave no black plume as a token of that lie thy soul hath spoken
Leave my loneliness unbroken! quit the bust above my door!
5 Take thy beak from out my heart, and take thy form from off
    my door!"
        Quoth the Raven, "Nevermore."

And the Raven, never flitting, still is sitting, still is sitting
On the pallid bust of Pallas just above my chamber door;
And his eyes have all the seeming of a demon's that is dreaming;
10 And the lamplight o'er him streaming throws his shadow on
    the floor;
And my soul from out that shadow that lies floating on the floor
        Shall be lifted—nevermore!

### NOTES AND QUESTIONS

For **Biography** see page 106.

**Discussion.** 1. Do you think this poem was written to tell a story or to give expression to feeling? 2. Tell the incidents of the story contained in the poem. 3. What does the poet say he had hoped to find in his books that December night? 4. What sound aroused him? 5. What reasons can you give for the terror that seized him at the sound? 6. Why does the raven seem to bring more gloom and sorrow into the room? 7. What do you think the "never flitting" raven symbolizes or represents? 8. What other poems or stories have you read that show Poe's love of the mysterious and terrible? 9. Have you ever enjoyed reading something you could not understand? Did you enjoy it because your imagination was excited or because you liked the sound of the words? 10. Find lines of this poem that you like although you cannot explain them; can you tell why you like them? 11. Find examples of alliteration in the poem, that is, the repetition of the same letter or sound at the beginning of two or more words in close succession, as "nodded, nearly napping." 12. Find words that give or suggest the sound described. 13. What lines in the first stanza rhyme? What are the end words of these lines? 14. What lines in the second stanza rhyme? What are the end words of these lines? 15. Study each stanza to find the lines that rhyme and the end words in each. 16. What have you learned about these end words? 17. What rhyme do you find in the first line of the first stanza? In the third line? 18. Find a word in the fourth line that rhymes with the last word in the third line. 19. Study each of the stanzas in this way to find the rhymes in the lines. 20. With which of the two kinds of adventure mentioned in the "Introduction" on page 97 does this poem deal? 21. Is it an imaginative story, or has it some basis of fact or legend? 22. "Lenore" represents Poe's young wife, who, it was certain, could not live long. In this poem, written two years before her death, Poe imagined what his feelings would be at her death. Point out lines that express these feelings. 23. What were you told in the introduction on page 98 about the value of creative reading, or reading in such a way as to see the story in action through your imagination? 24. Which of these narratives by Poe can you see the more clearly? 25. Find in the glossary the meaning of: surcease; beguiling; craven; divining; censer, nepenthe. 26. *Pronounce:* obeisance; decorum; placid; ominous; respite.

## Phrases for Study

**Class Reading**.  Bring to class and read "Annabel Lee" and "The

wrought its ghost, **109**, 8

Night's Plutonian shore, **111**, 5

little relevancy bore, **111**, 8

stock and store, **111**, 20

one burden bore, **111**, 22

dirges of his Hope, **111**, 23

linking fancy unto fancy, **111**, 27

balm in Gilead, **112**, 20

Bells," Poe.

**Magazine Reading.**  Bring to class and read, or make a brief oral report on, the best story of mystery that you have read in a magazine.

# NARRATIVES IN VERSE

## Bonnie George Campbell

### Folk Ballad

High upon Highlands,
    and low upon Tay,
Bonnie George Campbell
    rade out on a day.

5 Saddled and bridled,
    and gallant rade he;
Hame cam his guid horse,
    but never cam he.

Out cam his auld mither
10     greeting fu' sair,[1]
And out came his bonnie bride
    riving[2] her hair.

---

[1]greeting fu' sair, weeping bitterly        [2]riving, tearing

"The meadow lies green,
  the corn is unshorn,
But Bonnie George Campbell
  will never return."

5 Saddled and bridled
    and booted rade he;
  A plume in his helmet,
    a sword at his knee.

  Saddled and bridled
10    and booted rade he;
  Toom[3] hame cam the saddle,
    but never cam he!

## NOTES AND QUESTIONS

**The Ballad.** The folk ballads, of which "Bonnie George Campbell" is an excellent example, have come down to us from the far-off past. Such ballads are not the work of any one author, but, like the stories of King Arthur, were preserved mainly in the memories of men. Some of them were sung or recited to the music of the harp or lute by minstrels who wandered from village to village, and from castle to castle, entertaining their hearers in return for food and lodging; or by the bards and minstrels who were maintained by kings and nobles to entertain them and to celebrate their deeds and honors. Often these ballads were made by the people, not by professional singers, and were expressions of the folk love of adventure. Indeed, the best definition of a popular, or folk, ballad is "a tale telling itself in song." This means that it always tells a story; that it has no known author, being composed by several people or by a community and then handed down orally, without ever being put into writing, from generation to generation; and finally, that it is sung, not recited. In this way such folk ballads as "Sir Patrick Spens" and "Bonnie George Campbell" were transmitted for generations, in different versions, before they were written down and became a part of what we call *literature*. When the invention of the printing press made it possible to put these old ballads into a permanent form, they were collected from the recitations of old men and women

---

[3] toom, empty

who knew them, and printed. Thus they have become a precious literary possession, telling us something of the life, the history, and the standards, superstitions, and beliefs of distant times and thrilling us with their stirring stories. The beauty of these old ballads lies in the stories they tell, and in their directness and simplicity. They merely tell the main facts of the story, leaving details to the imagination of the reader. They are almost wholly without literary ornament; their language is the language of the people, not of the king's court.

Many modern poets have written stories in verse which are also called ballads. Some of these imitate the old ballads not only in form and simple, unadorned language, but also in the use of old-fashioned words and expressions. Other modern ballads are simple narratives in verse—short stories dealing with stirring subjects, with battle, adventure, etc. But while the true old ballad directs the attention to the story only, the modern ballads often introduce descriptions of the characters.

**Discussion.** 1. Who can read this poem so well that the listeners may gain the thought of the story? 2. Who is the hero? 3. Note that this ballad suggests an emotion, but not the poet's; whose emotion is suggested? 4. Their grief is told by the effects of the hero's failure to return home; what are these effects? 5. Notice that the details of the hero's death are left to the reader's imagination. 6. Who is speaking in the fourth stanza? 7. Make a list of the Scotch words that you could understand from the context; of those that it was necessary for you to look up. 8. What characteristics of the folk ballad does this poem have? How have the old ballads come down to us? 9. What other old ballad have you read? 16. You will enjoy hearing recordings of modern ballads such as Kipling's "Fuzzy-Wuzzy," "Gypsy Trail," "On the Road to Mandalay," etc.

## John Gilpin

### William Cowper

John Gilpin was a citizen
  Of credit and renown,
A trainband captain eke was he
  Of famous London town.

5 John Gilpin's spouse said to her dear:
  "Though wedded we have been
These twice ten tedious years, yet we
  No holiday have seen.

"Tomorrow is our wedding-day,
10   And we will then repair
Unto the Bell at Edmonton,
  All in a chaise and pair.

"My sister, and my sister's child,
  Myself, and children three
15 Will fill the chaise; so you must ride
  On horseback after we."

He soon replied—"I do admire
  Of womankind but one,
And you are she, my dearest dear;
20   Therefore it shall be done.

"I am a linendraper bold,
  As all the world doth know;
And my good friend the calender
  Will lend his horse to go."

Quoth Mistress Gilpin—"That's well said;
    And for that wine is dear,
We will be furnished with our own,
    Which is both bright and clear."

5 John Gilpin kissed his loving wife;
    O'erjoyed was he to find
That, though on pleasure she was bent,
    She had a frugal mind.

The morning came, the chaise was brought,
10    But yet was not allowed
To drive up to the door, lest all
    Should say that she was proud.

So three doors off the chaise was stayed,
    Where they did all get in,
15 Six precious souls and all agog
    To dash through thick and thin.

Smack went the whip, round went the wheels;
    Were never folks so glad;
The stones did rattle underneath,
20    As if Cheapside were mad.

John Gilpin at his horse's side
    Seized fast the flowing mane;
And up he got, in haste to ride,
    But soon came down again;

25 For saddletree scarce reached had he,
    His journey to begin,
When, turning round his head, he saw
    Three customers come in.

So down he came; for loss of time,
  Although it grieved him sore,
Yet loss of pence, full well he knew,
  Would trouble him much more.

5 'Twas long before the customers
  Were suited to their mind,
When Betty screaming came downstairs,
  "The wine is left behind!"

"Good lack!" quoth he, "yet bring it me,
10  My leathern belt likewise,
In which I bear my trusty sword
  When I do exercise."

Now Mistress Gilpin (careful soul!)
  Had two stone bottles found,
15 To hold the liquor that she loved,
  And keep it safe and sound.

Each bottle had a curling ear,
  Through which the belt he drew,
And hung a bottle on each side
20  To make his balance true.

Then over all, that he might be
  Equipped from top to toe,
His long red cloak, well brushed and neat,
  He manfully did throw.

25 Now see him mounted once again
  Upon his nimble steed,
Full slowly pacing o'er the stones,
  With caution and good heed.

But finding soon a smoother road
    Beneath his well-shod feet,
The snorting beast began to trot,
    Which galled him in his seat.

5 So "Fair and softly," John he cried;
    But John he cried in vain;
That trot became a gallop soon,
    In spite of curb and rein.

So stooping down, as needs he must
10    Who cannot sit upright,
He grasped the mane with both his hands
    And eke with all his might.

His horse, who never in that sort
    Had handled been before,
15 What thing upon his back had got
    Did wonder more and more.

Away went Gilpin, neck or naught;
    Away went hat and wig;
He little dreamt, when he set out,
20    Of running such a rig.

The wind did blow, the cloak did fly,
    Like streamer long and gay,
Till, loop and button failing both,
    At last it flew away.

25 Then might all people well discern
    The bottles he had slung;
A bottle swinging at each side,
    As hath been said or sung.

The dogs did bark, the children screamed;
    Up flew the windows all;
And every soul cried out, "Well done!"
    As loud as he could bawl.

5 Away went Gilpin—who but he?
    His fame soon spread around;
"He carries weight!" "He rides a race!"
    "'Tis for a thousand pound!"

And still as fast as he drew near,
10    'Twas wonderful to view
How in a trice the turnpike men
    Their gates wide open threw.

And now, as he went bowing down
    His reeking head full low,
15 The bottles twain behind his back
    Were shattered at a blow.

Down ran the wine into the road,
    Most piteous to be seen;
Which made his horse's flanks to smoke
20    As they had basted been.

But still he seemed to carry weight,
    With leathern girdle braced;
For all might see the bottle-necks
    Still dangling at his waist.

25 Thus all through merry Islington,
    These gambols he did play,
Until he came unto the Wash
    Of Edmonton so gay;

And there he threw the Wash about,
    On both sides of the way,
Just like unto a trundling mop,
    Or a wild goose at play.

5 At Edmonton, his loving wife
    From the balcony spied
Her tender husband, wondering much
    To see how he did ride.

"Stop, stop, John Gilpin!—Here's the house!"
10     They all at once did cry;
"The dinner waits, and we are tired."
    Said Gilpin—"So am I."

But yet his horse was not a whit
    Inclined to tarry there;
15 For why? His owner had a house
    Full ten miles off, at Ware.

So like an arrow swift he flew,
    Shot by an archer strong;
So did he fly—which brings me to
20     The middle of my song.

Away went Gilpin, out of breath,
    And sore against his will,
Till, at his friend the calender's,
    His horse at last stood still.

25 The calender, amazed to see
    His neighbor in such trim,
Laid down his pipe, flew to the gate,
    And thus accosted him:

"What news? what news? your tidings tell;
   Tell me you must and shall—
Say why bareheaded you are come,
   Or why you come at all?"

5 Now Gilpin had a pleasant wit,
   And loved a timely joke;
And thus unto the calender,
   In merry guise, he spoke:

"I came because your horse would come;
10    And, if I well forbode,
My hat and wig will soon be here—
   They are upon the road."

The calender, right glad to find
   His friend in merry pin,
15 Returned him not a single word.
   But to the house went in;

When straight he came, with hat and wig—
   A wig that flowed behind,
A hat not much the worse for wear,
20    Each comely in its kind.

He held them up, and in his turn,
   Thus showed his ready wit:
"My head is twice as big as yours,
   They therefore needs must fit.

25 "But let me scrape the dirt away
   That hangs upon your face;
And stop and eat, for well you may
   Be in a hungry case."

Said John—"It is my wedding-day,
   And all the world would stare,
If wife should dine at Edmonton
   And I should dine at Ware."

5 So turning to his horse, he said,
   "I am in haste to dine;
'Twas for your pleasure you came here;
   You shall go back for mine."

Ah! luckless speech and bootless boast,
10   For which he paid full dear;
For while he spake, a braying ass
   Did sing most loud and clear;

Whereat his horse did snort, as he
   Had heard a lion roar,
15 And galloped off with all his might,
   As he had done before.

Away went Gilpin, and away
   Went Gilpin's hat and wig;
He lost them sooner than at first,
20   For why? They were too big.

Now Mistress Gilpin, when she saw
   Her husband posting down
Into the country far away,
   She pulled out half-a-crown;

25 And thus unto the youth she said,
   That drove them to the Bell,
"This shall be yours, when you bring back
   My husband safe and well."

The youth did ride, and soon did meet
  John coming back amain;
Whom in a trice he tried to stop
  By catching at his rein;

5 But not performing what he meant,
  And gladly would have done,
The frightened steed he frighted more
  And made him faster run.

Away went Gilpin, and away
10  Went postboy at his heels;
The postboy's horse right glad to miss
  The lumbering of the wheels.

Six gentlemen upon the road,
  Thus seeing Gilpin fly,
15 With postboy scampering in the rear,
  They raised a hue and cry:

"Stop thief! stop thief!—a highwayman!"
  Not one of them was mute;
And all and each that passed that way
20  Did join in the pursuit.

And now the turnpike-gates again
  Flew open in short space,
The toll-men thinking, as before,
  That Gilpin rode a race.

25 And so he did, and won it too,
  For he got first to town;
Nor stopped till where he had got up
  He did again get down.

Now let us sing, Long live the King,
And Gilpin, long live he;
And when he next doth ride abroad,
May I be there to see!

## NOTES AND QUESTIONS

**Biography.** William Cowper (1731-1800) was born at Great Berkhamstead, England. He attended Westminster School and later was admitted to the bar. He wrote a number of long poems, of which "The Task" is probably the best known. "John Gilpin" is undoubtedly his most popular short poem. Cowper suffered greatly from melancholy; one day when he was feeling depressed, a friend told him the story of John Gilpin. He was so much amused that he determined to share his enjoyment with others, and the next day he wrote the ballad.

**Discussion.** 1. How does the poet's language add to the humor of the poem? 2. Find stanzas in which the humor is furnished entirely by the poet's manner of telling something. 3. What expression in line 12, page 118, shows that this is not a very modern poem? 4. What do you think was the poet's purpose in writing this ballad? 5. Have you read any other poems that amuse and entertain you as this ballad does? 6. Can you name an American poet who has written humorous poems? 7. What good does such a poem as this do? 8. The story of this poem is a good one to test your power of visualizing incidents and scenes, as you were advised to do in the "Introduction" on page 98. Make a list of the pictures that would be contained in your "private moving picture show" for this story. Where in this series would you place the picture on page 115? 9. Find in the glossary the meaning of: trainband; calender; agog; trice; gambol; guise; bootless; posting; amain. 10. *Pronounce:* tedious; comely.

### Phrases for Study

of credit and renown, **118**, 2

chaise and pair, **118**, 12

for that, **119**, 2

neck or naught, **121**, 17

running such a rig, **121**, 20

he carries weight., **122**, 7

basted been, **122**, 20

in merry pin, **124**, 14

**Magazine Reading.** Bring to class and read, or make a brief report on, the most interesting narrative in verse that you have read in a magazine.

## The Highwayman

### Alfred Noyes

#### Part One

The wind was a torrent of darkness among the gusty trees;
The moon was a ghostly galleon tossed upon cloudy seas;
The road was a ribbon of moonlight over the purple moor;
And the highwayman came riding—
5     Riding—riding—
The highwayman came riding, up to the old inn door.

He'd a French cocked hat on his forehead, a bunch of lace at
    his chin,
A coat of the claret velvet, and breeches of brown doeskin;
They fitted with never a wrinkle; his boots were up to the
    thigh!
10 And he rode with a jeweled twinkle,
    His pistol butts a-twinkle,
His rapier hilt a-twinkle, under the jeweled sky.

Over the cobbles he clattered and clashed in the dark inn yard
And he tapped with his whip on the shutters, but all was locked
    and barred;
15 He whistled a tune to the window, and who should be waiting
    there
But the landlord's black-eyed daughter,
    Bess, the landlord's daughter,
Plaiting a dark red love knot into her long black hair.

And dark in the dark old inn yard a stable-wicket creaked
20 Where Tim the ostler listened; his face was white and peaked;
His eyes were hollows of madness, his hair like moldy hay,
But he loved the landlord's daughter,
    The landlord's red-lipped daughter;
Dumb as a dog he listened, and he heard the robber say—

"One kiss, my bonny sweetheart; I'm after a prize tonight;
But I shall be back with the yellow gold before the morning
      light;
Yet, if they press me sharply, and harry me through the day,
Then look for me by moonlight;
5     Watch for me by moonlight;
I'll come to thee by moonlight, though hell should bar the way."


He rose upright in the stirrups; he scarce could reach her hand,
But she loosened her hair i' the casement! His face burned like
      a brand
As the black cascade of perfume came tumbling over his breast;
10 And he kissed its waves in the moonlight
      (Oh, sweet black waves in the moonlight!) ;
Then he tugged at his rein in the moonlight, and galloped away
      to the West.


### Part Two

He did not come in the dawning; he did not come at noon;
And out o' the tawny sunset, before the rise o' the moon,
15 When the road was a gypsy's ribbon, looping the purple moor,
A redcoat troop came marching—
      Marching—marching—
King George's men came marching, up to the old inn door.


They said no word to the landlord; they drank his ale instead;
20 But they gagged his daughter and bound her to the foot of her
      narrow bed;
Two of them knelt at her casement, with muskets at their side!
There was death at every window;
      And hell at one dark window;
For Bess could see, through her casement, the road that he
      would ride.

They had tied her up to attention, with many a sniggering jest
They had bound a musket beside her, with the barrel beneath
      her breast!
"Now keep good watch!" and they kissed her.
She heard the dead man say:
5 *Look for me by moonlight;*
    *Watch for me by moonlight;*
*I'll come to thee by moonlight, though hell should bar the way!*


She twisted her hands behind her; but all the knots held good!
She writhed her hands till her fingers were wet with sweat or
      blood!
10 They stretched and strained in the darkness, and the hour
      crawled by like years,
Till, now, on the stroke of midnight,
    Cold on the stroke of midnight,
The tip of one finger touched it!  The trigger at least was hers!

15 The tip of one finger touched it; she strove no more for the rest!
Up, she stood to attention, with the barrel beneath her breast.
She would not risk their hearing; she would not strive again;
For the road lay bare in the moonlight,
    Blank and bare in the moonlight;
And the blood of her veins in the moonlight throbbed to her
    love's refrain.

20 *Tlot-tlot; tlot-tlot!* Had they heard it?  The horse-hoof's ringing
     clear;
*Tlot-tlot, tlot-tlot,* in the distance! Were they deaf that they did
    not hear?
Down the ribbon of moonlight, over the brow of the hill,
The highwayman came riding,
    Riding—riding—
25 The redcoats looked to their priming! She stood up, straight
    and still!

*Tlot-tlot*, in the frosty silence! *Tlot-tlot*, in the echoing night!
Nearer he came and nearer! Her face was like a light!
Her eyes grew wide for a moment; she drew one last deep breath;
Then her finger moved in the moonlight;
5      Her musket shattered the moonlight;
Shattered her breast in the moonlight and warned him—with
     her death.

He turned; he spurred to the westward; he did not know who
     stood
Bowed, with her head o'er the musket, drenched with her own
     red blood!
Not till the dawn he heard it, and slowly blanched to hear
10 How Bess, the landlord's daughter,
     The landlord's black-eyed daughter,
Had watched for her love in the moonlight, and died in the
     darkness there.

Back he spurred like a madman, shrieking a curse to the sky,
With the white road smoking behind him, and his rapier
     brandished high!
15 Blood red were his spurs i' the golden noon; wine-red was his
     velvet coat,
When they shot him down on the highway,
     Down like a dog on the highway;
And he lay in his blood on the highway, with the bunch of lace
     at his throat.

*And still of a winter's night, they say, when the wind is*
     *in the trees,*
20 *When the moon is a ghostly galleon tossed upon cloudy seas,*
*When the road is a ribbon of moonlight over the purple moor,*
*A highwayman comes riding*
     *Riding—riding—*
*A highwayman comes riding, up to the old inn door.*

*Over the cobbles he clatters and clangs in the dark inn yard;*
*And he taps with his whip on the shutters, but all is locked*
    *and barred;*
*He whistles a tune to the window, and who should be*
    *waiting there*
*But the landlord's black-eyed daughter,*
5     *Bess, the landlord's daughter,*
*Plaiting a dark red love knot into her long black hair.*

## NOTES AND QUESTIONS

**Biography.** Alfred Noyes (1880-1950), an English poet, lived in London. He was educated at Oxford University and devoted himself to literature, contributing to many English magazines. During World War One he wrote many stirring poems, one of the best of which is "Kilmeny." In 1918-1919 Mr. Noyes lectured in the United States and taught literature at Princeton University.

**Discussion.** 1. Where is the scene of this story laid? At what time? How can you tell? 2. How did people travel at that time? 3. How do you think the highwayman expected to get his "prize"? 4. Whom does he mean when he says, "If they press me sharply"? 5. What are we to imagine that Tim, the ostler, did? 6. How does the poet want you to feel toward Tim? 7. What did the troopers expect the highwayman to do? 8. How was he warned? 9. Why did he not remain in hiding after his escape? 10. Does it seem fitting that the highwayman should meet a violent death? Why? 11. What comparisons are made in the first stanza? Which of these can you picture most clearly? 12. How does the poet suggest the movement of the horse? How does he suggest the movement of the troopers? 13. What is added to the story by the last two stanzas of the poem? 14. Read again what is said of this poem in the introduction on page 97; mention other poems you have read that were based on an old legend. 15. Compare your "private moving picture show" of this story with that of "John Gilpin"; which do you see the more clearly? 16. Find in the glossary the meaning of: plaiting; harry; casement; looping: priming. 17. *Pronounce:* moor; breeches; rapier; ostler.

**Class Reading.** Bring to class and read aloud "Kilmeny" (in *The Elson, Readers, Book Seven*), and other narrative poems by Noyes.

# LOCHINVAR

### SIR WALTER SCOTT

Oh, young Lochinvar is come out of the West;
Through all the wide Border his steed was the best;
And save his good broadsword he weapons had none.
He rode all unarmed, and he rode all alone.
5 So faithful in love, and so dauntless in war,
There never was knight like the young Lochinvar.

He stayed not for brake, and he stopped not for stone;
He swam the Eske river where ford there was none;
But ere he alighted at Netherby gate,
10 The bride had consented; the gallant came late;
For a laggard in love, and a dastard in war,
Was to wed the fair Ellen of brave Lochinvar.

So, boldly he entered the Netherby hall,
'Mong bridesmen and kinsmen and brothers and all;
15 Then spoke the bride's father, his hand on his sword
(For the poor craven bridegroom said never a word),
"Oh, come ye in peace here, or come ye in war,
Or to dance at our bridal, young Lord Lochinvar?"

"I long wooed your daughter; my suit you denied—
20 Love swells like the Solway; but ebbs like its tide;
And now I am come, with this lost love of mine
To lead but one measure, drink one cup of wine.
There are maidens in Scotland more lovely by far
That would gladly be bride to the young Lochinvar."

25 The bride kissed the goblet; the knight took it up;
He quaffed off the wine, and he threw down the cup,

She looked down to blush, and she looked up to sigh,
With a smile on her lips and a tear in her eye.
He took her soft hand ere her mother could bar—
"Now tread we a measure!" said young Lochinvar.

5 So stately his form, and so lovely her face,
That never a hall such a galliard did grace;
While her mother did fret, and her father did fume,
And the bridegroom stood dangling his bonnet and plume;
And the bride-maidens whispered, "'Twere better by far
10 To have matched our fair cousin with young Lochinvar."

One touch to her hand, and one word in her ear,
When they reached the hall door and the charger stood near;
So light to the croup the fair lady he swung,
So light to the saddle before her he sprung!
15 "She is won! We are gone, over bank, bush, and scar!
They'll have fleet steeds that follow!" quoth young Lochinvar

There was mounting 'mong Graemes of the Netherby clan;
Forsters, Fenwicks, and Musgraves, they rode and they ran;
There was racing and chasing on Cannobie Lee;
20 But the lost bride of Netherby ne'er did they see.
So daring in love, and so dauntless in war,
'Have ye e'er heard of gallant like young Lochinvar?

NOTES AND QUESTIONS

**Biography.** Walter Scott (1771-1832) was born in Edinburgh, Scotland. Even in his childhood he loved nothing better than to wander through Scotland, looking up castles and ruins and listening to the stories connected with them as told by the old people of the villages. He became familiar with all the ballads and legends of his locality, and these, with Bishop Percy's collection of ballads, which he read later, exerted a strong influence on his life. He loved the history and romance of Scotland and made them known to all the world through his many poems and novels.

In his long poem, "Marmion," Scott represents Lady Heron as singing the ballad, "Lochinvar," to the accompaniment of the harp. "Lochinvar" is based on the old ballad "Katharine Janfarie."

**Discussion.** 1. What geographical references tell you that the scene of this story is laid in Scotland? 2. What names mentioned do you recognize as Scotch names? 3. Find a line in the first stanza that sums up the character of Lochinvar. 4. Find a line in the second stanza that describes the character of the bridegroom. 5. Find a line in the third stanza that adds to the picture of the bridegroom given in the second stanza. 6. How is the reader affected by the contrast between the two men? 7. Find the question asked by the bride's father. Why was his hand on his sword as he asked it? 8. What impression did Lochinvar give the bride's father by his answer? 9. Do you think Lochinvar was sincere in his response? 10. Describe the picture the sixth stanza makes you see. 11. What did Lochinvar accomplish by means of the dance? 12. What were we told in the first stanza that explains Lochinvar's escape? 13. Who are mentioned as the pursuers? 14. What do you know of the methods of travel and communication before 1800? 15. What two kinds of adventure are mentioned in the "Introduction" on page 97? Which of these kinds does this story narrate? 16. In this poem Scott has imitated the old ballad style; point out some of the passages that show this. 17. Find in the glossary the meaning of: border; brake; measure; bar; galliard; bonnet; croup; scar. 18. *Pronounce:* Lochinvar; dauntless; gallant.

**Class Reading.** Bring to class and read Longfellow's ballad "The Skeleton in Armor" (in *The Elson Readers, Book Seven*), noting the similarity of theme.

---

## THE LEAP OF ROUSHAN BEG

### HENRY WADSWORTH LONGFELLOW

Mounted on Kyrat strong and fleet,
His chestnut steed with four white feet,
Roushan Beg, called Kurroglou,
Son of the road and bandit chief,
5 Seeking refuge and relief,
Up the mountain pathway flew.

Such was the Kyrat's wondrous speed,
Never yet could any steed
   Reach the dust-cloud in his course.
More than maiden, more than wife,
5 More than gold, and next to life
   Roushan the Robber loved his horse.

In the land that lies beyond
Erzeroum and Trebizond,
   Garden-girt, his fortress stood;
10 Plundered khan, or caravan
Journeying north from Koordistan,
   Gave him wealth and wine and food.

Seven hundred and fourscore
Men at arms his livery wore;
15    Did his bidding night and day.
Now, through regions all unknown,
He was wandering, lost, alone,
   Seeking, without guide, his way.

Suddenly the pathway ends;
20 Sheer the precipice descends;
   Loud the torrent roars unseen;
Thirty feet from side to side
Yawns the chasm; on air must ride
   He who crosses this ravine.

25 Following close in his pursuit,
At the precipice's foot
   Reyhan the Arab of Orfah
Halted with his hundred men,
Shouting upward from the glen,
30    "La Illah illa Allah!"

Gently Roushan Beg caressed
Kyrat's forehead, neck, and breast;
   Kissed him upon both his eyes;
Sang to him in his wild way,
5 As upon the topmost spray
   Sings a bird before it flies:

"O my Kyrat, O my steed,
Round and slender as a reed,
   Carry me this peril through!
10 Satin housings shall be thine,
Shoes of gold, O Kyrat mine,
   O thou soul of Kurroglou!

"Soft thy skin as silken skein;
Soft as woman's hair thy mane;
15    Tender are thine eyes and true;
All thy hoofs like ivory shine,
Polished bright; O life of mine,
   Leap, and rescue Kurroglou!"

Kyrat, then, the strong and fleet,
20 Drew together his four white feet,
   Paused a moment on the verge,
Measured with his eye the space,
And into the air's embrace
   Leaped as leaps the ocean surge.

25 As the ocean surge o'er sand
Bears a swimmer safe to land,
   Kyrat safe his rider bore;
Rattling down the deep abyss
Fragments of the precipice
30    Rolled like pebbles on a shore.

Roushan's tasseled cap of red
Trembled not upon his head;
   Careless sat he and upright;
Neither hand nor bridle shook;
5 Nor his head he turned to look,
   As he galloped out of sight.

Flash of harness in the air,
Seen a moment, like the glare
   Of a sword drawn from its sheath;
10 Thus the phantom horseman passed,
And the shadow that he cast
   Leaped the cataract underneath.

Reyhan the Arab held his breath
While this vision of life and death
15    Passed above him. "Allahu!"
Cried he. "In all Koordistan
Lives there not so brave a man
   As this Robber Kurroglou!"

## NOTES AND QUESTIONS

**Biography.** Henry Wadsworth Longfellow (1807-1882), one of the greatest of American poets, was born in Portland, Maine. He was graduated from Bowdoin College in 1825, in the same class with Nathaniel Hawthorne. While in college Longfellow developed a great interest in foreign languages and also showed marked ability in verse making. He spent three years in Europe and upon his return became professor of modern languages at Bowdoin. *Outre Mer*, his first book, is in prose and gives an account of his life in Europe.

From Bowdoin, Longfellow went to Harvard University to teach, but in 1854 he gave up his college work and devoted himself to the writing of poetry. By his many translations from foreign tongues Longfellow has greatly enriched our literature; but in his own poems he remained thoroughly American. The titles, "poet of culture," "poet of peace, of the home, and history," and "the children's poet," which have been bestowed upon him show the nature of his work and the esteem in which he is held.

Longfellow won recognition from the lovers of poetry in England as well as in America, and after his death his bust was placed in the "Poets' Corner" in Westminster Abbey, where stand memorials to Shakespeare and others who have won imperishable fame.

**Discussion.** 1. Describe in your own words Roushan Beg's perilous position before the leap. 2. What do you think had brought him to this peril? 3. Find lines that show his love for his horse. 4. Find lines that tell how he gained his wealth. 5. What shows Kyrat's intelligence? 6. To what does the poet compare the leap of the horse? 7. To which one of the two, Roushan Beg or Kyrat, does the greater part of the credit belong for the leap? Why? 8. To whom did the watching Arab give the credit? 9. How did the bearing of Roushan Beg after the leap influence the Arab? 10. Describe the appearance of Kyrat. 11. Compare Kyrat with Coaly-Bay; what likenesses do you find? 12. Why would you call this poem a ballad? 13. What other ballads by Longfellow have you read? 14. Find in the glossary the meaning of: fourscore; livery; housings; verge. 15. *Pronounce:* Roushan; khan; chasm; forehead.

### Phrases for Study

son of the road, **135**, 4

reach the dust-cloud, **136**, 3

into the air's embrace, **137**, 23

vision of life and death, **138**, 14

**Class Reading.** Bring to class and read "Muléykeh," Browning.

---

## "How They Brought the Good News From Ghent to Aix"

### Robert Browning

I sprang to the stirrup, and Joris, and he;
I galloped, Dirck galloped, we galloped all three;
"Good speed!" cried the watch, as the gatebolts undrew;
"Speed!" echoed the wall to us galloping through;
5 Behind shut the postern; the lights sank to rest;
And into the midnight we galloped abreast.

Not a word to each other; we kept the great pace
Neck by neck, stride by stride; never changing our place;
I turned in my saddle and made its girths tight,
Then shortened each stirrup, and set the pique right
5 Rebuckled the cheek-strap, chained slacker the bit,
Nor galloped less steadily Roland a whit.

'Twas moonset at starting; but while we drew near
Lokeren, the cocks crew, and twilight dawned clear;
At Boom, a great yellow star came out to see;
10 At Düffeld 'twas morning as plain as could be;
And from Mecheln church-steeple we heard the half-chime,
So Joris broke silence with, "Yet there is time!"

At Aershot, up leaped of a sudden the sun,
And against him the cattle stood black every one,
15 To stare through the mist at us galloping past;
And I saw my stout galloper Roland at last,
With resolute shoulders, each butting away
The haze, as some bluff river headland its spray;

And his low head and crest, just one sharp ear bent back
20 For my voice, and the other pricked out on his track;
And one eye's black intelligence—ever that glance
O'er its white edge at me, his own master, askance!
And the thick, heavy spume-flakes which aye and anon
His fierce lips shook upward in galloping on.

25 By Hasselt, Dirck groaned; and cried Joris, "Stay spur!
Your Roos galloped bravely—the fault's not in her;
We'll remember at Aix"—for one heard the quick wheeze
Of her chest, saw the stretched neck and staggering knees,
And sunk tail, and horrible heave of the flank,
30 As down on her haunches she shuddered and sank.

So we were left galloping, Joris and I;
Past Looz and past Tongres, no cloud in the sky;
The broad sun above laughed a pitiless laugh;
'Neath our feet broke the brittle bright stubble like chaff;
5  Till over by Dalhem a dome-spire sprang white,
And "Gallop," gasped Joris, "for Aix is in sight!"

"How they'll greet us!"—and all in a moment his roan
Rolled neck and croup over, lay dead as a stone;
And there was my Roland to bear the whole weight
10 Of the news which alone could save Aix from her fate,
With his nostrils like pits full of blood to the brim,
And with circles of red for his eye-sockets' rim.

Then I cast loose my buffcoat, each holster let fall,
Shook off both my jack-boots, let go belt and all,
15 Stood up in the stirrup, leaned, patted his ear,
Called my Roland his pet name, my horse without peer;
Clapped my hands, laughed and sang, any noise, bad or good,
Till at length into Aix Roland galloped and stood.

And all I remember is—friends flocking round
20 As I sat with his head 'twixt my knees on the ground;
And no voice but was praising this Roland of mine,
As I poured down his throat our last measure of wine,
Which (the burgesses voted by common consent)
Was no more than his due who brought good news from Ghent.

## NOTES AND QUESTIONS

For **Biography** see page 89.

**Discussion.** 1. This poem is without historical basis; the ride occurred only in the mind of the poet; what does this tell you of Browning's power of imagination? 2. Does he tell what he imagined the good news was? 3. Why do you think three riders started to carry this news? 4. How does the beginning of the poem give you the impression of haste? 5. At what time did the messengers start? 6. How is the passing of time noted by the riders? 7. When did the rider see his horse for the first time during the ride? Why had he not seen him before? 8. Would the news which you imagine the messengers were carrying require such haste as is described in the poem? 9. Which stanza gives the most vivid impression of haste? Which gives the impression of endurance? Which is the expression of desperation? 10. To whom does the rider give the credit for carrying the message? To whom would you give it? Why? 11. Find in the glossary the meaning of: abreast; slacker; butting; bluff; askance; peer; burgess. 12. *Pronounce:* Ghent; Aix; pique.

### Phrases for Study

aye and anon, **140**, 23
stay spur, **140**, 25

laughed a pitiless laugh, **141**, 3
by common consent, **141**, 23

## Incident of the French Camp

### Robert Browning

You know, we French stormed Ratisbon;
   A mile or so away,
On a little mound, Napoleon
   Stood on our storming-day;
5 With neck out-thrust, you fancy how,
   Legs wide, arms locked behind,
As if to balance the prone brow
   Oppressive with its mind.

Just as perhaps he mused, "My plans
10    That soar, to earth may fall,
Let once my army-leader Lannes
   Waver at yonder wall"—
Out 'twixt, the battery-smokes there flew
   A rider, bound on bound
15 Full-galloping; nor bridle drew
   Until he reached the mound.

Then off there flung in smiling joy,
    And held himself erect
By just his horse's mane, a boy;
    You hardly could suspect
5 (So tight he kept his lips compressed,
    Scarce any blood came through)—
You looked twice e'er you saw his breast
    Was all but shot in two.

"Well," cried he, "Emperor, by God's grace
10    We've got you Ratisbon!
The Marshal's in the market-place,
    And you'll be there anon
To see your flag-bird flap his vans
    Where I, to heart's desire,
15 Perched him!" The chief's eye flashed; his plans
    Soared up again like fire.

The chief's eye flashed; but presently
    Softened itself, as sheathes
A film the mother-eagle's eye
20    When her bruised eaglet breathes;
"You're wounded!" "Nay," his soldier's pride
    Touched to the quick, he said:
"I'm killed, Sire!" And his chief beside,
    Smiling, the boy fell dead.

## NOTES AND QUESTIONS

For **Biography** see page 89.

**Historical Note.** Ratisbon, a walled city of Bavaria, was besieged in 1809 by Napoleon. The Bavarians made such a vigorous defense for five days that Napoleon's victory was no small achievement. The poem, based on this incident, shows the beauty of a devotion to duty that forgets self. It also shows the admiration of soldiers for such a leader as Napoleon.

**Discussion.** 1. Find lines that verify the statements made in the "Introduction" on page 97 about this poem. 2. What does the expression, "we French," tell you about the speaker? 3. Where was Napoleon at the time Ratisbon was " stormed"? 4. Describe in your own words the position in which he stood. 5. What were Napoleon's thoughts as he stood on the mound? 6. Why is his sentence not finished? 7. What would Napoleon think when he saw a horse galloping toward him? 8. At what was he surprised? 9. What lines make us feel his shock of horror? 10. What was the boy's message? 11. Had he reason for his "smiling joy"? 12. Why does the poet repeat the words, "The chief's eye flashed"? What did the flashing of the eye show? 13. What different thought caused his eye to soften? 14. To what does the poet compare the softening of Napoleon's eye? 15. Why does the thought of the eagle seem appropriate in connection with Napoleon? 16. Who is the hero of this story? 17. What thought gave him power to smile in spite of his terrible pain? 18. Read the lines from Tennyson on page 95. Why are they especially fitting to introduce a group of selections that includes many stories of heroic adventure? 19. Find in the glossary the meaning of: prone; oppressive; flag-bird; van.

**Suggestions for Theme Topics.** (Two-Minute Talks.) 1. A true war incident, preferably of World War One. 2. A story illustrating devotion to a leader and a cause. 3. A description of Napoleon's personal appearance.

---

## A BALLAD OF JOHN SILVER

### JOHN MASEFIELD

We were schooner-rigged and rakish, with a long and lissome
    hull,
And we flew the pretty colors of the cross-bones and the skull;
We'd a big black Jolly Roger flapping grimly at the fore,
And we sailed the Spanish Water in the happy days of yore.

5 We'd a long brass gun amidship, like a well-conducted ship;
We had each a brace of pistols and a cutlass at the hip;
It's a point which tells against us, and a fact to be deplored,
But we chased the goodly merchant-men and laid their ships
    aboard.

Then the dead men fouled the scuppers, and the wounded
    filled the chains,
And the paint-work all was spatter-dashed with other people's
    brains;
She was boarded, she was looted, she was scuttled till she sank
And the pale survivors left us by the medium of the plank.

5 Oh! then it was (while standing by the taffrail on the poop)
We could hear the drowning folk lament the absent chicken
    coop;
Then, having washed the blood away, we'd little else to do
Than to dance a quiet hornpipe as the old salts taught us to.

Oh! the fiddle on the fo'c's'le, and the slapping naked soles,
10 And the genial "Down the middle, Jake, and curtsey when she
    rolls!"
With the silver seas around us and the pale moon overhead,
And the lookout not a-looking and his pipe-bowl glowing red

Ah! the pig-tailed, quidding pirates and the pretty pranks we
    played
All have since been put a stop to by the naughty Board of Trade
15 The schooners and the merry crews are laid away to rest,
A little south the sunset in the Islands of the Blest.

## NOTES AND QUESTIONS

**Biography.** John Masefield (1875-1967) was an English poet. At an early age he took to sea and for several years was a sailor. This experience furnished the basis for *Salt-Water Ballads* and a collection of short sea tales. During World War One, Masefield made a study for the English government of the campaign on the Gallipoli Peninsula, having taken part in the engagement there, and served in France in Red Cross work. In 1916 the poet lectured in America, arousing great interest in his poetry.

**Discussion.** 1. To whom does "We" refer? 2. What do the skull and cross-bones signify? 3. What was the black Jolly Roger? 4. What body of water was known as the Spanish Water, or Spanish Main? 5. How was the ship armored? 6. How were the sailors armed? For what purpose? 7. What did they do to the merchant ships? What did they do to the crews? 8. How did the pirates amuse themselves? 9. Mention several modern inventions which have forced the pirate to give up his business. 10. The character John Silver is found in the greatest of pirate stories, *Treasure Island;* have you read the book? 11. Find in the glossary the meaning of: lissome; brace; aboard; scuttled; salts.

### Phrases for Study

fouled the scuppers, **145,** 1          medium of the plank, **145,** 4
filled the chains, **145,** 1          Board of Trade, **145,** 14

**Class Reading.** Bring to class and read "The Tarry Buccaneer," Masefield (in *Salt-Water Ballads*).

**Suggested Theme Topic.** How the American navy put an end to the Tripolitan piracy.

---

## Fleurette*

### *(The Wounded Canadian Speaks)*

#### Robert W. Service

My leg? It's off at the knee.
Do I miss it? Well, some. You see
I've had it since I was born;
5 And lately a devilish corn.
(I rather chuckle with glee
To think how I've fooled that corn.)

But I'll hobble around all right.
It isn't that, it's my face.
10 Oh, I know I'm a hideous sight,
Hardly a thing in place;
Sort of gargoyle, you'd say.

---

*From *Rhymes of a Red Cross Man,* by Robert W. Service.

Nurse won't give me a glass,
But I see the folks as they pass
Shudder and turn away;
Turn away in distress . . .
5 Mirror enough, I guess.
I'm gay! You bet I am gay;
But I wasn't a while ago.
If you'd seen me even today,
The darndest picture of woe,
10 With this Caliban mug of mine,
So ravaged and raw and red,
Turned to the wall—in fine
Wishing that I was dead . . .
What has happened since then,
15 Since I lay with my face to the wall,
The most despairing of men?
Listen! I'll tell you all.
That *poilu* across the way,
With the shrapnel wound on his head,
20 Has a sister; she came today
To sit a while by his bed.
All morning I heard him fret:
"Oh, when will she come, Fleurette?"

Then sudden, a joyous cry;
25 The tripping of little feet;
The softest, tenderest sigh;
A voice so fresh and sweet,
Clear as a silver bell,
Fresh as the morning dews:
30 *"C'est toi, c'est toi, Marcel!*
*Mon frere, comme je suis heureuse!"*

So over the blanket's rim
I raised my terrible face,

And I saw—how I envied him—
A girl of such delicate grace;
Sixteen, all laughter and love;
As gay as a linnet, and yet
5 As tenderly sweet as a dove:
Half woman, half child—Fleurette.

Then I turned to the wall again
(I was awfully blue, you see),
And I thought with a bitter pain:
10 "Such visions are not for me."
So there like a log I lay,
All hidden, I thought from view,
When sudden I heard her say:
"Ah! Who is that malheureux?"
15 Then briefly I heard him tell
(However he came to know)
How I'd smothered a bomb that fell
Into the trench, and so
None of my men were hit,
20 Though it busted me up a bit.
Well, I didn't quiver an eye,
And he chattered, and there she sat;
And I fancied I heard her sigh
But I wouldn't just swear to that.
25 And maybe she wasn't so bright,
Though she talked in a merry strain,
And I closed my eyes ever so tight,
Yet I saw her ever so plain:
Her dear little tilted nose,
30 Her delicate, dimpled chin,
Her mouth like a budding rose,
And the glistening pearls within;
Her eyes like the violet:
Such a rare little queen—Fleurette.

And at last when she rose to go,
The light was a little dim,
And I ventured to peep, and so
I saw her graceful and slim,
5 And she kissed him and kissed him, and, oh,
How I envied and envied him!

So when she was gone I said
In rather a dreary voice
To him of the opposite bed:
10 "Ah, friend, how you must rejoice!
But me, I'm a thing of dread.
For me nevermore the bliss,
The thrill of a woman's kiss."

Then I stopped, for lo! she was there,
15 And a great light shone in her eyes.
And me! I could only stare,
I was taken so by surprise,
When gently she bent her head:
"May I kiss you, sergeant?" she said.
20 Then she kissed my burning lips,
With her mouth like a scented flower,
And I thrilled to the finger-tips,
And I hadn't even the power
To say: "God bless you, dear!"
25 And I felt such a precious tear
Fall on my withered cheek,
And darn it! I couldn't speak.

And so she went sadly away,
And, I know that my eyes were wet.
30 Ah, not to my dying day
Will I forget, forget!
Can you wonder now I am gay?
God bless her, that little Fleurette!

## NOTES AND QUESTIONS

**Biography.** Robert W. Service (1874-1958), a Canadian poet, has been called "the Kipling of the Arctic World." His earlier poetry, which is full of the grandeur and the lure of the Yukon, established his fame as a poet. His experiences during World War One as an ambulance driver in France are set forth in *The Rhymes of a Red Cross Man*, from which "Fleurette" is taken. This poem is considered by many of his admirers as his masterpiece. The humorous poem, "The Cremation of Sam McGee," in *The Spell of the Yukon*, gives a good idea of his prewar poetry.

**Discussion.** 1. Who is speaking in this poem? 2. Why does he speak so lightly of the loss of his leg? 3. Why does the nurse refuse to give him a mirror? 4. Who was Caliban? 5. What comparison could there be between the soldier's face and Caliban's? 6. What did the French soldier tell his sister about the Canadian? What shows that she was impressed by the story? 7. What feeling must a story of self-sacrifice inspire? 8. What caused the great light that shone in the girl's eyes? 9. How did she show him that he was not "a thing of dread"? 10. The French sentence, page 147, lines 30 and 31, means

> "It is you, it is you, Marcel!
> My brother, how happy I am!"

Find in the glossary the meaning of other French words in the poem, and of: gargoyle; linnet. 11. *Pronounce:* Fleurette.

**Class Reading.** Bring to class and read "Grand Pere" (another war poem), Service.

**Newspaper Reading.** Not all heroic deeds of adventure occur on the battlefield. Bring to class and read an item from your daily newspaper, telling of a brave action by someone.

**Suggested Theme Topic.** How crippled and disfigured soldiers of the World Wars were marvelously helped by surgery, and fitted with artificial legs, arms, etc., so that they could carry on useful occupations.

# A STORY OF CHRISTMAS

## A Christmas Carol*

### Charles Dickens

*Stave One*

### Marley's Ghost

Marley was dead, to begin with. There is no doubt whatever about that. The register of his burial was signed by the clergyman, the clerk, the undertaker, and the chief mourner. Scrooge signed it; and Scrooge's name was good upon 'Change, for
5 anything he chose to put his hand to. Old Marley was as dead as a doornail.

Mind! I don't mean to say that I know, of my own knowledge, what there is particularly dead about a doornail. I might have been inclined, myself, to regard a coffin nail as the deadest piece
10 of ironmongery in the trade. But the wisdom of our ancestors is in the simile; and my unhallowed hands shall not disturb it, or the country's done for. You will therefore permit me to repeat, emphatically, that Marley was as dead as a doornail.

---

*See Silent and Oral Reading, page 13.

Scrooge knew he was dead? Of course he did. How could it be otherwise? Scrooge and he were partners for I don't know how many years. Scrooge was his sole executor, his sole administrator, his sole assign, his sole residuary legatee, his
5 sole friend, and sole mourner. And even Scrooge was not so dreadfully cut up by the sad event but that he was an excellent man of business on the very day of the funeral, and solemnized it with an undoubted bargain.

The mention of Marley's funeral brings me back to the point
10 I started from. There is no doubt that Marley was dead. This must be distinctly understood or nothing wonderful can come of the story I am going to relate. If we were not perfectly convinced that Hamlet's father died before the play began, there would be nothing more remarkable in his taking a stroll
15 at night in an easterly wind upon his own ramparts, than there would be in any other middle aged gentleman rashly turning out after dark in a breezy spot—say Saint Paul's Churchyard for instance—literally to astonish his son's weak mind.

Scrooge never painted out old Marley's name. There it stood,
20 years afterwards, above the warehouse door: Scrooge and Marley. The firm was known as Scrooge and Marley. Sometimes people new to the business called Scrooge Scrooge and sometimes Marley, but he answered to both names; it was all the same to him.
25    Oh! But he was a tight fisted hand at the grindstone, Scrooge! A squeezing, wrenching, grasping, scraping, clutching, covetous old sinner! Hard and sharp as flint from which no steel had ever struck out generous fire; secret and self-contained, and solitary as an oyster. The cold within him froze his old
30 features, nipped his pointed nose, shriveled his cheek, stiffened his gait; made his eyes red, his thin lips blue; and spoke out shrewdly in his grating voice. A frosty rime was on his head, and on his eyebrows, and his wiry chin. He carried his own low temperature always about with him; he iced his office in the dog
35 days and didn't thaw it one degree at Christmas.

External heat and cold had little influence on Scrooge. No
warmth could warm, or wintry weather chill him. No wind that
blew was bitterer than he; no falling snow was more intent upon
its purpose; no pelting rain less open to entreaty. Foul weather
5 didn't know where to have him. The heaviest rain, and snow,
and hail, and sleet could boast of the advantage over him in
only one respect. They often "came down" handsomely, and
Scrooge never did.

Nobody ever stopped him in the street to say, with glad-
10 some looks, "My dear Scrooge, how are you? When will you
come to see me?" No beggars implored him to bestow a trifle;
no children asked him what it was o'clock; no man or woman
ever once in all his life inquired the way to such and such
a place of Scrooge. Even the blind men's dogs appeared to
15 know him; and when they saw him coming on, would tug their
owners into doorways and up courts; and then would wag their
tails as though they said, "No eye at all is better than an evil
eye, dark master!"

But what did Scrooge care? It was the very thing he liked.
20 To edge his way along the crowded paths of life, warning all
human sympathy to keep its distance, was what the knowing
ones call "nuts" to Scrooge.

Once upon a time—of all the good days in the year, on
Christmas Eve—old Scrooge sat busy in his countinghouse.
25 It was cold, bleak, biting weather, foggy withal; and he could
hear the people in the court outside go wheezing up and down,
beating their hands upon their breasts, and stamping their feet
upon the pavement stones to warm them. The city clocks had
only just gone three, but it was quite dark already; it had not
30 been light all day; and candles were flaring in the windows of
the neighboring offices, like ruddy smears upon the palpable
brown air. The fog came pouring in at every chink and keyhole,
and was so dense without, that although the court was of the
narrowest, the houses opposite were mere phantoms. To see
35 the dingy cloud come drooping down, obscuring everything, one

might have thought that Nature lived hard by, and was brewing on a large scale.

The door of Scrooge's countinghouse was open that he might keep his eye upon his clerk, who in a dismal little cell beyond, a
5 sort of tank, was copying letters. Scrooge had a very small fire, but the clerk's fire was so very much smaller that it looked like one coal. But he couldn't replenish it, for Scrooge kept the coal box in his own room; and so surely as the clerk came in with the shovel, the master predicted that it would be necessary for
10 them to part. Wherefore the clerk put on his white comforter, and tried to warm himself at the candle, in which effort, not being a man of a strong imagination, he failed.

"A Merry Christmas, Uncle! God save you!" cried a cheerful voice. It was the voice of Scrooge's nephew, who came upon
15 him so quickly that this was the first intimation he had of his approach.

"Bah!" said Scrooge, "Humbug!"

He had so heated himself with rapid walking in the fog and frost, this nephew of Scrooge's, that he was all in a glow; his
20 face was ruddy and handsome; his eyes sparkled, and his breath smoked again.

"Christmas a humbug, Uncle!" said Scrooge's nephew. "You don't mean that, I am sure."

"I do," said Scrooge. "Merry Christmas! What right have
25 you to be merry? What reason have you to be merry? You're poor enough."

"Come, then," returned the nephew, gaily. "What right have you to be dismal? What reason have you to be morose? You're rich enough."

30      Scrooge having no better answer ready on the spur of the moment, said, "Bah!" again and followed it up with "Humbug."

"Don't be cross, Uncle," said the nephew.

"What else can I be," returned the uncle, "when I live in such a world of fools as this? Merry Christmas! Out upon merry
35 Christmas! What's Christmas time to you but a time for paying

bills without money; a time for finding yourself a year older, but not an hour richer; a time for balancing your books and having every item in 'em through a round dozen of months presented dead against you? If I could work my will," said
5 Scrooge, indignantly, "every idiot who goes about with 'Merry Christmas' on his lips, should be boiled with his own pudding, and buried with a stake of holly through his heart. He should!"

"Uncle!" pleaded the nephew.

"Nephew!" returned the uncle, sternly, "keep Christmas in
10 your own way, and let me keep it in mine."

"Keep it!" repeated Scrooge's nephew. "But you don't keep it."

"Let me leave it alone, then," said Scrooge. "Much good may it do you! Much good it has ever done you!"

15    "There are many things from which I might have derived good, by which I have not profited, I dare say," returned the nephew, "Christmas among the rest. But I am sure I have always thought of Christmas time, when it has come round—apart from the veneration due to its sacred name and origin, if anything
20 belonging to it can be apart from that—as a good time; a kind, forgiving, charitable, pleasant time; the only time I know of, in the long calendar of the year, when men and women seem by one consent to open their shut-up hearts freely, and to think of people below them as if they really were fellow passengers
25 to the grave, and not another race of creatures bound on other journeys. And therefore, Uncle, though it has never put a scrap of gold or silver in my pocket, I believe that it has done me good, and will do me good; and I say, God bless it!"

The clerk in the tank involuntarily applauded; becoming
30 immediately sensible of the impropriety, he poked the fire, and extinguished the last frail spark forever.

"Let me hear another sound from you," said Scrooge, "and you'll keep your Christmas by losing your situation. You're quite a powerful speaker, sir," he added, turning to his nephew. "I
35 wonder you don't go into Parliament."

"Don't be angry, Uncle. Come! Dine with us tomorrow."
Scrooge said that he would see him—yes, indeed he did. He
went the whole length of the expression, and said that he would
see him in that extremity first.

5      "But why?" cried Scrooge's nephew. "Why?"

"Why did you get married?" said Scrooge.

"Because I fell in love."

"Because you fell in love!" growled Scrooge, as if that were
the only one thing in the world more ridiculous than a merry
10 Christmas. "Good afternoon!"

"Nay, Uncle, but you never came to see me before that
happened. Why give it as a reason for not coming now?"

"Good afternoon," said Scrooge.

"I want nothing from you; I ask nothing of you; why cannot
15 we be friends?"

"Good afternoon," said Scrooge.

"I am sorry, with all my heart, to find you so resolute. We
have never had any quarrel to which I have been a party. But
I have made the trial in homage to Christmas, and I'll keep my
20 Christmas humor to the last. So a Merry Christmas, Uncle!"

"Good afternoon!" said Scrooge.

"And a Happy New Year!"

"Good afternoon!" said Scrooge.

His nephew left the room without an angry word, notwith-
25 standing. He stopped at the outer door to bestow the greetings
of the season on the clerk, who, cold as he was, was warmer
than Scrooge; for he returned them cordially.

"There's another fellow," muttered Scrooge, who overheard
him, "my clerk, with fifteen shillings a week, and a wife and
30 family, talking about a merry Christmas. I'll retire to Bedlam."

This lunatic, in letting Scrooge's nephew out, had let two
other people in. They were portly gentlemen, pleasant to behold,
and now stood, with their hats off, in Scrooge's office. They had
books and papers in their hands, and bowed to him.

35      "Scrooge and Marley's, I believe," said one of the gentlemen,

referring to his list. "Have I the pleasure of addressing Mr. Scrooge or Mr. Marley?"

"Mr. Marley has been dead these seven years," Scrooge replied. "He died seven years ago this very night."

5    "We have no doubt his liberality is well represented by his surviving partner," said the gentleman, presenting his credentials.

It certainly was; for they had been two kindred spirits. At the ominous word "liberality," Scrooge frowned, and shook his 10 head, and handed the credentials back.

"At this festive season of the year, Mr. Scrooge," said the gentleman, taking up a pen, "it is more than usually desirable that we should make some slight provision for the poor and destitute, who suffer greatly at the present time. Many thousands are in 15 want of common necessaries; hundreds of thousands are in want of common comforts, sir."

"Are there no prisons?" asked Scrooge.

"Plenty of prisons," said the gentleman, laying down the pen again.

20    "And the union workhouses?" demanded Scrooge. "Are they still in operation?"

"They are, still," returned the gentleman. "I wish I could say they were not."

"The Treadmill and the Poor Law are in full vigor, then?" 25 said Scrooge.

"Both very busy, sir."

"Oh! I was afraid, from what you said at first, that something had occurred to stop them in their useful course," said Scrooge. "I'm very glad to hear it."

30    "Under the impression that they scarcely furnish Christian cheer of mind or body to the multitude," returned the gentleman, "a few of us are endeavoring to raise a fund to buy the poor some meat and drink, and means of warmth. We choose this time, because it is a time, of all others, when want is keenly felt, and 35 abundance rejoices. What shall I put you down for?"

"Nothing!" Scrooge replied.

"You wish to be anonymous?"

"I wish to be left alone," said Scrooge. "Since you ask me what I wish, gentlemen, that is my answer. I don't make merry
5 myself at Christmas, and I can't afford to make idle people merry. I help to support the establishments I have mentioned; they cost enough; and those who are badly off must go there."

"Many can't go there; and many would rather die."

"If they would rather die," said Scrooge, "they had better
10 do it, and decrease the surplus population. Besides—excuse me—I don't know that."

"But you might know it," observed the gentleman.

"It's not my business," Scrooge returned. "It's enough for a man to understand his own business, and not to interfere with
15 other people's. Mine occupies me constantly. Good afternoon, gentlemen!"

Seeing clearly that it would be useless to pursue their point, the gentlemen withdrew. Scrooge resumed his labors with an improved opinion of himself, and in a more facetious temper
20 than was usual with him.

Meanwhile the fog and darkness thickened so that people ran about with flaring links, proffering their services to go before horses in carriages, and conduct them on their way. The ancient tower of a church, whose gruff old bell was always peeping slyly
25 down at Scrooge out of a Gothic window in the wall, became invisible, and struck the hours and quarters in the clouds, with tremulous vibrations afterwards as if its teeth were chattering in its frozen head up there. The cold became intense. In the main street at the corner of the court, some laborers were repairing the
30 gas pipes, and had lighted a great fire in a brazier, round which a party of ragged men and boys were gathered, warming their hands and winking their eyes before the blaze in rapture.

The waterplug, being left in solitude, its overflowings sullenly congealed, and turned to misanthropic ice. The brightness of the
35 shops where holly sprigs and berries crackled in the lamp heat of

the windows made pale faces ruddy as they passed. Poulterers' and grocers' trades became a splendid joke, a glorious pageant, with which it was next to impossible to believe that such dull principles as bargain and sale had anything to do. The Lord
5 Mayor, in the stronghold of the mighty Mansion House, gave orders to his fifty cooks and butlers to keep Christmas as a Lord Mayor's household should; and even the little tailor, whom he had fined five shillings on the previous Monday for being drunk and bloodthirsty in the streets, stirred up tomorrow's
10 pudding in his garret, while his lean wife and the baby sallied out to buy the beef.

Foggier yet, and colder! Piercing, searching, biting cold. If the good Saint Dunstan had but nipped the Evil Spirit's nose with a touch of such weather as that, instead of using his familiar
15 weapons, then indeed he would have roared to lusty purpose. The owner of one scant young nose, gnawed and mumbled by the hungry cold as bones are gnawed by dogs, stooped down at Scrooge's keyhole to regale him with a Christmas carol; but at the first sound of

20        God bless you, merry gentleman!
         May nothing you dismay!

Scrooge seized the ruler with such energy of action that the singer fled in terror, leaving the keyhole to the fog and even more congenial frost.
25   At length the hour of shutting up the countinghouse arrived. With an ill will Scrooge dismounted from his stool and tacitly admitted the fact to the expectant clerk in the tank, who instantly snuffed his candle out and put on his hat.

"You'll want all day tomorrow, I suppose?" said Scrooge.
30   "If quite convenient, sir."

"It's not convenient," said Scrooge, "and it's not fair. If I was to stop half a crown for it, you'd think yourself ill-used, I'll be bound?"

The clerk smiled faintly.

"And yet," said Scrooge, "you don't think me ill-used when I pay a day's wages for no work."

The clerk observed that it was only once a year.

5 "A poor excuse for picking a man's pocket every twenty-fifth of December!" said Scrooge, buttoning his greatcoat to the chin. "But I suppose you must have the whole day. Be here all the earlier next morning!"

The clerk promised that he would; and Scrooge walked out 10 with a growl. The office was closed in a twinkling, and the clerk, with the long ends of his white comforter dangling below his waist (for he boasted no greatcoat), went down a slide on Cornhill, at the end of a lane of boys, twenty times, in honor of its being Christmas Eve, and then ran home to Camden Town as 15 hard as he could pelt, to play at blindman's buff.

Scrooge took his melancholy dinner in his usual melancholy tavern; and having read all the newspapers, and beguiled the rest of the evening with his banker's book, went home to bed. He lived in chambers which had once belonged to his deceased 20 partner. They were a gloomy suite of rooms, in a lowering pile of building up a yard, where it had so little business to be that one could scarcely help fancying it must have run there when it was a young house, playing at hide and seek with other houses, and have forgotten the way out again. It was old enough now, 25 and dreary enough, for nobody lived in it but Scrooge, the other rooms being all let out as offices. The yard was so dark that even Scrooge, who knew its every stone, was fain to grope with his hands. The fog and frost so hung about the black old gateway of the house that it seemed as if the Genius of the Weather sat 30 in mournful meditation on the threshold.

Now it is a fact that there was nothing at all particular about the knocker on the door except that it was very large. It is also a fact that Scrooge had seen it, night and morning, during his whole residence in that place; also that Scrooge had as little 35 of what is called fancy about him as any man in the city of

London, even including—which is a bold word—the corporation, aldermen, and livery. Let it also be borne in mind that Scrooge had not bestowed one thought on Marley since his last mention of his seven years' dead partner that afternoon. And then let
5 any man explain to me, if he can, how it happened that Scrooge, having his key in the lock of the door, saw in the knocker, without its undergoing any intermediate process of change—not a knocker, but Marley's face.

Marley's face. It was not in impenetrable shadow as the
10 other objects in the yard were, but had a dismal light about it like a bad lobster in a dark cellar. It was not angry or ferocious, but looked at Scrooge as Marley used to look—with ghostly spectacles turned up on its ghostly forehead. The hair was curiously stirred, as if by breath or hot air; and, though the
15 eyes were wide open, they were perfectly motionless. That, and its livid color, made it horrible; but its horror seemed to be in spite of the face and beyond its control rather than a part of its own expression.

As Scrooge looked fixedly at this phenomenon, it was a
20 knocker again.

To say that he was not startled, or that his blood was not conscious of a terrible sensation to which it had been a stranger from infancy, would be untrue. But he put his hand upon the key he had relinquished, turned it sturdily, walked in, and lighted
25 his candle.

He did pause, with a moment's irresolution, before he shut the door; and he did look cautiously behind it first, as if he half expected to be terrified with the sight of Marley's pigtail sticking out into the hall. But there was nothing on the back of the door
30 except the screws and nuts that held the knocker on; so he said "Pooh, pooh!" and closed it with a bang.

The sound resounded through the house like thunder. Every room above, and every cask in the wine merchant's cellars below, appeared to have a separate peal of echoes of its own. Scrooge
35 was not a man to be frightened by echoes. He fastened the

door, and walked across the hall, and up the stairs, slowly too, trimming his candle as he went.

You may talk vaguely about driving a coach and six up a good old flight of stairs, or through a bad young Act of Parliament; but
5 I mean to say you might have got a hearse up that staircase, and taken it broadwise, with the splinter bar toward the wall, and the door toward the balustrades, and done it easy. There was plenty of width for that, and room to spare; which is perhaps the reason why Scrooge thought he saw a locomotive hearse
10 going on before him in the gloom. Half a dozen gas lamps out of the street wouldn't have lighted the entry too well, so you may suppose that it was pretty dark with Scrooge's dip.

Up Scrooge went, not caring a button for that; darkness is cheap, and Scrooge liked it. But before he shut his heavy door,
15 he walked through his rooms to see that all was right. He had just enough recollection of the face to desire to do that.

Sitting room, bedroom, lumber room. All as they should be. Nobody under the table; nobody under the sofa; a small fire in the grate; spoon and basin ready; and the little saucepan of
20 gruel (Scrooge had a cold in his head) upon the hob. Nobody under the bed; nobody in the closet; nobody in his dressing gown, which was hanging up in a suspicious attitude against the wall. Lumber room as usual. Old fireguard, old shoes, two fish baskets, washing stand on three legs, and a poker.

25      Quite satisfied, he closed his door, and locked himself in—double-locked himself in—which was not his custom. Thus secured against surprise, he took off his cravat; put on his dressing gown and slippers, and his nightcap; and sat down before the fire to take his gruel.

30      It was a very low fire indeed; nothing on such a bitter night. He was obliged to sit close to it, and brood over it, before he could extract the least sensation of warmth from such a handful of fuel. The fireplace was an old one, built by some Dutch merchant long ago, and paved all round with quaint
35 Dutch tiles, designed to illustrate the Scriptures. There were

Cains and Abels, Pharaoh's daughters, Queens of Sheba, angelic messengers descending through the air on clouds like feather beds, Abrahams, Belshazzars, Apostles putting off to sea in butter boats, hundreds of figures, to attract his thoughts; and
5 yet that face of Marley, seven years dead, came like the ancient prophet's rod, and swallowed up the whole. If each smooth tile had been a blank at first, with power to shape some picture on its surface from the disjointed fragments of his thoughts, there would have been a copy of old Marley's head on every one.
10 "Humbug!" said Scrooge, and walked across the room.

After several turns, he sat down again. As he threw his head back in the chair, his glance happened to rest upon a bell, a disused bell, that hung in the room, and communicated for some purpose now forgotten with a chamber in the highest story of
15 the building. It was with great astonishment, and with a strange, inexplicable dread, that as he looked, he saw this bell begin to swing. It swung so softly in the outset that it scarcely made a sound; but soon it rang out loudly, and so did every bell in the house.

20 This might have lasted half a minute, or a minute, but it seemed an hour. The bells ceased as they had begun, together. They were succeeded by a clanking noise, deep down below; as if some person were dragging a heavy chain over the casks in the wine merchant's cellar. Scrooge then remembered to
25 have heard that ghosts in haunted houses were described as dragging chains.

The cellar door flew open with a booming sound, and then he heard the noise much louder, on the floors below; then coming up the stairs; then coming straight toward his door.

30 "It's humbug still!" said Scrooge. "I won't believe it."

His color changed though, when, without a pause, it came on through the heavy door, and passed into the room before his eyes. Upon its coming in, the dying flame leaped up, as though it cried, "I know him! Marley's Ghost!" and fell again.

35 The same face; the very same. Marley in his pigtail, usual

waistcoat, tights, and boots; the tassels on the latter bristling, like his pigtail, and his coat skirts, and the hair upon his head. The chain he drew was clasped about his middle. It was long, and wound about him like a tail; and it was made (for Scrooge
5 observed it closely) of cash boxes, keys, padlocks, ledgers, deeds, and heavy purses wrought in steel. His body was transparent, so that Scrooge, observing him, and looking through his waistcoat, could see the two buttons on his coat behind.

Scrooge had often heard it said that Marley had no bowels,
10 but he had never believed it until now.

No, nor did he believe it even now. Though he looked the phantom through and through, and saw it standing before him; though he felt the chilling influence of its death-cold eyes; and marked the very texture of the folded kerchief bound about its
15 head and chin, which wrapper he had not observed before; he was still incredulous, and fought against his senses.

"How now!" said Scrooge, caustic and cold as ever. "What do you want with me?"

"Much!" Marley's voice, no doubt about it.

20     "Who are you?"

"Ask me who I was."

"Who were you then?" said Scrooge, raising his voice. "You're particular for a shade." He was going to say "to a shade," but substituted this, as more appropriate.

25     "In life I was your partner, Jacob Marley."

"Can you—can you sit down?" asked Scrooge, looking doubt-fully at him.

"I can."

"Do it then."

30     Scrooge asked the question, because he didn't know whether a ghost so transparent might find himself in a condition to take a chair; and felt that in the event of its being impossible, it might involve the necessity of an embarrassing explanation. But the ghost sat down on the opposite side of the fireplace, as if he
35 were quite used to it.

"You don't believe in me," observed the ghost.

"I don't," said Scrooge.

"What evidence would you have of my reality beyond that of your senses?"

5     "I don't know," said Scrooge.

"Why do you doubt your senses?"

"Because," said Scrooge, "a little thing affects them. A slight disorder of the stomach makes them cheats. You may be an undigested bit of beef, a blot of mustard, a crumb of cheese, a
10 fragment of an underdone potato. There's more of gravy than of grave about you, whatever you are!"

Scrooge was not much in the habit of cracking jokes, nor did he feel, in his heart, by any means waggish then. The truth is, that he tried to be smart, as a means of distracting his own
15 attention and keeping down his terror; for the specter's voice disturbed the very marrow in his bones.

To sit, staring at those fixed, glazed eyes in silence for a moment, would play, Scrooge felt, the very deuce with him. There was something very awful, too, in the specter's being
20 provided with an infernal atmosphere of its own. Scrooge could not feel it himself, but this was clearly the case; for though the ghost sat perfectly motionless, its hair, and skirts, and tassels were still agitated as by the hot vapor from an oven.

"You see this toothpick?" said Scrooge, returning quickly to
25 the charge, for the reason just assigned, and wishing, though it were only for a second, to divert the vision's stony gaze from himself.

"I do," replied the ghost.

"You are not looking at it," said Scrooge.

30     "But I see it," said the ghost, "notwithstanding."

"Well!" returned Scrooge. "I have but to swallow this, and be for the rest of my days persecuted by a legion of goblins, all of my own creation. Humbug, I tell you—humbug!"

At this the spirit raised a frightful cry, and shook its chain
35 with such a dismal and appalling noise that Scrooge held on tight

to his chair to save himself from falling in a swoon. But how much greater was his horror when the phantom, taking off the bandage round its head, as if it were too warm to wear indoors, its lower jaw dropped down upon its breast!

5    Scrooge fell upon his knees, and clasped his hands before his face.

"Mercy!" he said. "Dreadful Apparition, why do you trouble me?"

"Man of the worldly mind!" replied the ghost, "do you believe 10 in me or not?"

"I do," said Scrooge. "I must. But why do spirits walk the earth, and why do they come to me?"

"It is required of every man," the ghost returned, "that the spirit within him should walk abroad among his fellow men, and 15 travel far and wide; and if that spirit goes not forth in life, it is condemned to do so after death. It is doomed to wander through the world—oh, woe is me!—and witness what it cannot share, but might have shared on earth, and turned to happiness!"

Again the specter raised a cry and shook its chain, and 20 wrung its shadowy hands.

"You are fettered," said Scrooge, trembling. "Tell me why."

"I wear the chain I forged in life," replied the ghost. "I made it link by link, and yard by yard; I girded it on of my own free will, and of my own free will I wore it. Is its pattern strange 25 to you?"

Scrooge trembled more and more.

"Or would you know," pursued the ghost, "the weight and length of the strong coil you bear yourself? It was full as heavy and as long as this, seven Christmas Eves ago. You have labored 30 on it since. It is a ponderous chain!"

Scrooge glanced about him on the floor, in the expectation of finding himself surrounded by some fifty or sixty fathoms of iron cable; but he could see nothing.

"Jacob," he said imploringly. "Old Jacob Marley, tell me more. 35 Speak comfort to me, Jacob."

"I have none to give," the Ghost replied. "It comes from other regions, Ebenezer Scrooge, and is conveyed by other ministers, to other kinds of men. Nor can I tell you what I would. A very little more is all permitted to me. I cannot rest, I cannot
5 stay, I cannot linger anywhere. My spirit never walked beyond our countinghouse—mark me!—in life my spirit never roved beyond the narrow limits of our money-changing hole; and weary journeys lie before me!"

It was a habit with Scrooge, whenever he became thoughtful,
10 to put his hands in his breeches pockets. Pondering on what the ghost had said, he did so now, but without lifting up his eyes or getting off his knees.

"You must have been very slow about it, Jacob," Scrooge observed, in a businesslike manner, though with humility and
15 deference.

"Slow!" the ghost repeated.

"Seven years dead," mused Scrooge. "And traveling all the time!"

"The whole time," said the ghost. "No rest, no peace. Inces-
20 sant torture of remorse."

"You travel fast?" said Scrooge.

"On the wings of the wind," replied the ghost.

"You might have got over a great quantity of ground in seven years," said Scrooge.
25    The ghost, on hearing this, set up another cry, and clanked its chain so hideously in the dead silence of the night that the ward would have been justified in indicting it for a nuisance.

"Oh! captive, bound and double-ironed," cried the phantom, "not to know that ages of incessant labor, by immortal creatures,
30 for this earth, must pass into eternity before the good of which it is susceptible is all developed. Not to know that any Christian spirit working kindly in its little sphere, whatever it may be, will find its mortal life too short for its vast means of usefulness. Not to know that no space of regret can make amends for one life's
35 opportunity misused! Yet such was I! Oh! such was I!"

"But you were always a good man of business, Jacob," faltered Scrooge, who now began to apply this to himself.

"Business!" cried the ghost, wringing its hands again. "Mankind was my business. The common welfare was my business;
5 charity, mercy, forbearance, and benevolence were all my business. The dealings of my trade were but a drop of water in the comprehensive ocean of my business!"

It held up its chain at arm's length, as if that were the cause of all its unavailing grief, and flung it heavily upon the ground
10 again.

"At this time of the rolling year," the specter said, "I suffer most. Why did I walk through crowds of fellow beings with my eyes turned down, and never raise them to that blessed star which led the Wise Men to a poor abode! Were there no poor
15 homes to which its light would have conducted me!"

Scrooge was very much dismayed to hear the specter going on at this rate, and began to quake exceedingly.

"Hear me!" cried the ghost. "My time is nearly gone."

"I will," said Scrooge. "But don't be hard upon me! Don't
20 be flowery, Jacob! Pray!"

"How it is that I appear before you in a shape that you can see, I may not tell. I have sat invisible beside you many and many a day."

It was not an agreeable idea. Scrooge shivered, and wiped
25 the perspiration from his brow.

"That is no light part of my penance," pursued the ghost. "I am here tonight to warn you that you have yet a chance and hope of escaping my fate. A chance and hope of my procuring, Ebenezer."

30    "You were always a good friend to me," said Scrooge. "Thank'ee."

"You will be haunted," resumed the Ghost, "by three spirits."

Scrooge's countenance fell almost as low as the ghost's had done. "Is that the chance and hope you mentioned, Jacob?" he
35 demanded, in a faltering voice.

"It is."

"I—I think I'd rather not," said Scrooge.

"Without their visits," said the ghost, "you cannot hope to shun the path I tread. Expect the first tomorrow when the
5 bell tolls one."

"Couldn't I take 'em all at once, and have it over, Jacob?" hinted Scrooge.

"Expect the second on the next night at the same hour. The third upon the next night when the last stroke of twelve has
10 ceased to vibrate. Look to see me no more; and look that, for your own sake, you remember what has passed between us!"

When it had said these words, the specter took its wrapper from the table, and bound it round its head, as before. Scrooge knew this by the smart sound its teeth made when the jaws were
15 brought together by the bandage. He ventured to raise his eyes again; and found his supernatural visitor confronting him in an erect attitude, with its chain wound over and about its arm.

The apparition walked backward from him; and at every step it took, the window raised itself a little, so that when the specter
20 reached it, it was wide open. It beckoned Scrooge to approach, which he did. When they were within two paces of each other, Marley's ghost held up its hand, warning him to come no nearer. Scrooge stopped.

Not so much in obedience as in surprise and fear; for on the
25 raising of the hand, he became sensible of confused noises in the air; incoherent sounds of lamentation and regret; wailings inexpressibly sorrowful and self-accusatory. The specter, after listening for a moment, joined in the mournful dirge, and floated out upon the bleak, dark night.

30 Scrooge followed to the window, desperate in his curiosity. He looked out.

The air was filled with phantoms, wandering hither and thither in restless haste, and moaning as they went. Every one of them wore chains like Marley's Ghost; some few (they might be guilty
35 governments) were linked together; none were free. Many had

been personally known to Scrooge in their lives. He had been quite familiar with the one old ghost, in a white waistcoat, with a monstrous iron safe attached to its ankle, who cried piteously at being unable to assist a wretched woman with an infant, whom
5 it saw below, upon a doorstep. The misery with them all was, clearly, that they sought to interfere, for good, in human matters, and had lost the power forever.

Whether these creatures faded into mist, or mist enshrouded them, he could not tell. But they and their spirit voices faded
10 together; and the night became as it had been when he walked home.

Scrooge closed the window, and examined the door by which the ghost had entered. It was double-locked, as he had locked it with his own hands, and the bolts were undisturbed. He tried
15 to say "Humbug!" but stopped at the first syllable. And being from the emotion he had undergone, or the fatigue of the day, or his glimpse of the invisible world, or the dull conversation of the ghost, or the lateness of the hour, much in need of repose, he went straight to bed, without undressing, and fell asleep upon
20 the instant.


## *Stave Two*

### The First of the Three Spirits

When Scrooge awoke, it was so dark that, looking out of bed, he could scarcely distinguish the transparent window from the opaque walls of his chamber. He was endeavoring to pierce the darkness with his ferret eyes, when the chimes of a neighboring
25 church struck the four quarters. So he listened for the hour.

To his great astonishment the heavy bell went on from six to seven, and from seven to eight, and regularly up to twelve, then stopped. Twelve! It was past two when he went to bed. The clock was wrong. An icicle must have got into the works.
30 Twelve!

He touched the spring of his repeater to correct this most

preposterous clock. Its rapid little pulse beat twelve, and stopped. "Why, it isn't possible," said Scrooge, "that I can have slept through a whole day and far into another night. It isn't possible that anything has happened to the sun, and this is
5 twelve at noon!"

The idea being an alarming one, he scrambled out of bed and groped his way to the window. He was obliged to rub the frost off with the sleeve of his dressing gown before he could see anything, and could see very little then. All he could make
10 out was that it was still very foggy and extremely cold and that there was no noise of people running to and fro, and making a great stir, as there unquestionably would have been if night had beaten off bright day and taken possession of the world. This was a great relief, because "three days after sight of this First
15 of Exchange pay to Mr. Ebenezer Scrooge or his order" and so forth, would have become a mere United States' security if there were no days to count by.

Scrooge went to bed again, and thought, and thought, and thought it over and over and over, and could make nothing of
20 it. The more he thought, the more perplexed he was; and the more he endeavored not to think, the more he thought. Marley's ghost bothered him exceedingly. Every time he resolved within himself, after mature inquiry, that it was all a dream, his mind flew back again, like a strong spring released, to its first position,
25 and presented the same problem to be worked all through, "Was it a dream or not?"

Scrooge lay in this state until the chimes had gone three quarters more, when he remembered on a sudden, that the ghost had warned him of a visitation when the bell tolled one. He
30 resolved to lie awake until the hour was passed; and, considering that he could no more go to sleep than go to heaven, this was perhaps the wisest resolution in his power.

The quarter was so long that he was more than once convinced he must have sunk into a doze unconsciously, and missed
35 the clock. At length it broke upon his listening ear.

"Ding, dong!"

"A quarter past," said Scrooge, counting.

"Ding, dong!"

"Half-past!" said Scrooge.

5  "Ding, dong!"

"A quarter to it," said Scrooge.

"Ding, dong!"

"The hour itself," said Scrooge, triumphantly, "and nothing else!"

10    He spoke before the hour bell sounded, which it now did with a deep, dull, hollow, melancholy ONE. Light flashed up in the room upon the instant, and the curtains of his bed were drawn.

The curtains of his bed were drawn aside, I tell you, by a hand. Not the curtains at his feet, nor the curtains at his
15 back, but those to which his face was addressed. The curtains of his bed were drawn aside; and Scrooge, starting up into a half-recumbent attitude, found himself face to face with the unearthly visitor, who drew them, as close to it as I am now to you, and I am standing in the spirit at your elbow.

20    It was a strange figure—like a child; yet not so like a child as like an old man viewed through some supernatural medium which gave him the appearance of having receded from the view, and being diminished to a child's proportions. Its hair, which hung about its neck and down its back, was white as
25 if with age; and yet the face had not a wrinkle in it, and the tenderest bloom was on the skin. The arms were very long and muscular; the hands the same, as if its hold were of uncommon strength. Its legs and feet, most delicately formed, were, like those upper members, bare. It wore a tunic of the purest
30 white; and round its waist was bound a lustrous belt, the sheen of which was beautiful. It held a branch of fresh green holly in its hand; and, in singular contradiction of that wintry emblem, had its dress trimmed with summer flowers. But the strangest thing about it was that from the crown of its head there sprang
35 a bright, clear jet of light, by which all this was visible, and

which was doubtless the occasion of its using, in its duller moments, a great extinguisher for a cap, which it now held under its arm.

Even this, though, when Scrooge looked at it with increasing
5 steadiness, was not its strangest quality. For, as its belt sparkled and glittered now in one part and now in another, and what as light one instant at another time was dark, so the figure itself fluctuated in its distinctness, being now a thing with one arm, now with one leg, now with twenty legs, now a pair of legs
10 without a head, now a head without a body, of which dissolving parts no outline would be visible in the dense gloom wherein they melted away. And in the very wonder of this, it would be itself again, distinct, and clear as ever.

"Are you the spirit, sir, whose coming was foretold to me?"
15 asked Scrooge.

"I am!"

The voice was soft and gentle. Singularly low, as if instead of being so close behind him, it were at a distance.

"Who and what are you?" Scrooge demanded.
20 "I am the Ghost of Christmas Past."

"Long past?" inquired Scrooge, observant of its dwarfish stature.

"No. Your past."

Perhaps Scrooge could not have told anybody why, if anybody
25 could have asked him; but he had a special desire to see the spirit in his cap, and begged him to be covered.

"What!" exclaimed the ghost, "would you so soon put out, with worldly hands, the light I give? Is it not enough that you are one of these whose passions made this cap, and force me
30 through whole trains of years to wear it low upon my brow?"

Scrooge reverently disclaimed all intention to offend, or any knowledge of having willfully "bonneted" the spirit at any period of his life. He then made bold to inquire what business brought him there.

35 "Your welfare!" said the ghost.

Scrooge expressed himself much obliged, but could not help thinking that a night of unbroken rest would have been more conducive to that end. The spirit must have heard him thinking, for it said immediately:

5     "Your reclamation, then. Take heed!"

It put out its strong hand as it spoke, and clasped him gently by the arm.

"Rise! and walk with me!"

It would have been in vain for Scrooge to plead that the
10 weather and the hour were not adapted to pedestrian purposes; that bed was warm, and the thermometer a long way below freezing; that he was clad but lightly in his slippers, dressing gown, and nightcap; and that he had a cold upon him at that time. The grasp, though gentle as a woman's hand, was not to
15 be resisted. He rose; but finding that the spirit made toward the window, clasped its robe in supplication.

"I am a mortal," Scrooge remonstrated, "and liable to fall."

"Bear but a touch of my hand there," said the spirit, laying it upon his heart, "and you shall be upheld in more than this!"

20     As the words were spoken, they passed through the wall, and stood upon an open country road, with fields on either hand. The city had entirely vanished. Not a vestige of it was to be seen. The darkness and the mist had vanished with it, for it was a clear, cold, winter day, with snow upon the ground.

25     "Good Heaven!" said Scrooge, clasping his hands together, as he looked about him. "I was bred in this place. I was a boy here!"

The spirit gazed upon him mildly. Its gentle touch, though it had been light and instantaneous, appeared still present to the
30 old man's sense of feeling. He was conscious of a thousand odors floating in the air, each one connected with a thousand thoughts, and hopes, and joys, and cares, long, long forgotten!

"Your lip is trembling," said the ghost. "And what is that upon your cheek?"

35     Scrooge muttered, with an unusual catching in his voice,

that it was a pimple, and begged the ghost to lead him where he would.

"You recollect the way?" inquired the spirit.

"Remember it!" cried Scrooge with fervor—"I could walk
5 it blindfold."

"Strange to have forgotten it for so many years!" observed the ghost. "Let us go on."

They walked along the road; Scrooge recognizing every gate, and post, and tree; until a little market town appeared in the
10 distance, with its bridge, its church, and winding river. Some shaggy ponies now were seen trotting toward them with boys upon their backs, who called to other boys in country gigs and carts, driven by farmers. All these boys were in great spirits, and shouted to each other, until the broad fields were so full of
15 merry music that the crisp air laughed to hear it.

"These are but shadows of the things that have been," said the ghost. "They have no consciousness of us."

The jocund travelers came on; and as they came, Scrooge knew and named them every one. Why was he rejoiced beyond
20 all bounds to see them! Why did his cold eye glisten, and his heart leap up as they went past! Why was he filled with gladness when he heard them give each other Merry Christmas, as they parted at crossroads and byways for their several homes! What was Merry Christmas to Scrooge? Out upon Merry Christmas!
25 What good had it ever done to him?

"The school is not quite deserted," said the ghost. "A solitary child, neglected by his friends, is left there still."

Scrooge said he knew it. And he sobbed.

They left the highroad, by a well-remembered lane, and
30 soon approached a mansion of dull red brick, with a little weathercock surmounted cupola on the roof, and a bell hanging in it. It was a large house, but one of broken fortunes; for the spacious offices were little used, their walls were damp and mossy, their windows broken, and their gates decayed. Fowls
35 clucked and strutted in the stables, and the coach-houses and

sheds were overrun with grass. Nor was it more retentive of its ancient state within, for entering the dreary hall and glancing through the open doors of many rooms, they found them poorly furnished, cold and vast. There was an earthy
5 savor in the air, a chilly bareness in the place, which associated itself somehow with too much getting up by candlelight, and not too much to eat.

They went, the ghost and Scrooge, across the hall, to a door at the back of the house. It opened before them and disclosed
10 a long, bare, melancholy room, made barer still by lines of plain deal forms and desks. At one of these a lonely boy was reading near a feeble fire; and Scrooge sat down upon a form, and wept to see his poor, forgotten self as he had used to be.

Not a latent echo in the house, not a squeak and scuffle from
15 the mice behind the paneling, not a drip from the half-thawed waterspout in the dull yard behind, not a sigh among the leafless boughs of one despondent poplar, not the idle swinging of an empty storehouse door, no, not a clicking in the fire, but fell upon the heart of Scrooge with softening influence, and gave a
20 freer passage to his tears.

The spirit touched him on the arm, and pointed to his younger self, intent upon his reading. Suddenly a man, in foreign garment, wonderfully real and distinct to look at, stood outside the window, with an ax stuck in his belt, and leading an ass
25 laden with wood, by the bridle.

"Why, it's Ali Baba!" Scrooge exclaimed in ecstasy. "It's dear old honest Ali Baba! Yes, yes, I know! One Christmas time, when yonder solitary child was left here all alone, he did come, for the first time, just like that. Poor boy! And Valentine," said
30 Scrooge, "and his wild brother, Orson; there they go! And what's his name, who was put down in his drawers, asleep, at the Gate of Damascus; don't you see him! And the sultan's groom turned upside down by the genii; there he is upon his head! Serve him right. I'm glad of it. What business had he to be married
35 to the princess!"

To hear Scrooge expending all the earnestness of his nature on such subjects, in a most extraordinary voice between laughing and crying, and to see his heightened and excited face would have been a surprise to his business friends in the city, indeed.

5     "There's the parrot!" cried Scrooge. "Green body and yellow tail, with a thing like a lettuce growing out of the top of his head; there he is! Poor Robin Crusoe, he called him, when he came home again after sailing round the island. 'Poor Robin Crusoe, where have you been, Robin Crusoe?' The man thought
10 he was dreaming, but he wasn't. It was the parrot, you know. There goes Friday, running for his life to the little creek! Halloa! Whoop! Halloo!"

Then, with a rapidity of transition very foreign to his usual character, he said, in pity for his former self, "Poor boy!" and
15 cried again.

"I wish—" Scrooge muttered, putting his hand in his pocket, and looking about him, after drying his eyes with his cuff, "but it's too late now."

"What is the matter?" asked the spirit.

20     "Nothing," said Scrooge. "Nothing. There was a boy singing a Christmas carol at my door last night. I should like to have given him something; that's all."

The ghost smiled thoughtfully, and waved its hand, saying as it did so, "Let us see another Christmas!"

25     Scrooge's former self grew larger at the words, and the room became a little darker and more dirty. The panels shrank, the windows cracked; fragments of plaster fell out of the ceiling, and the naked laths were shown instead; but how all this was brought about, Scrooge knew no more than you do. He only
30 knew that it was quite correct; that everything had happened so; that there he was, alone again, when all the other boys had gone home for the jolly holidays.

He was not reading now, but walking up and down despairingly. Scrooge looked at the ghost, and with a mournful shaking
35 of his head, glanced anxiously toward the door.

It opened; and a little girl, much younger than the boy, came darting in, and putting her arms about his neck and often kissing him, addressed him as her "Dear, dear brother."

"I have come to bring you home, dear brother!" said the child,
5 clapping her tiny hands, and bending down to laugh. "To bring you home, home, home!"

"Home, little Fan?" returned the boy.

"Yes!" said the child, brimful of glee. "Home, for good and all. Home, for ever and ever. Father is so much kinder than
10 he used to be that home's like Heaven! He spoke so gently to me one dear night when I was going to bed that I was not afraid to ask him once more if you might come home; and he said yes, you should; and sent me in a coach to bring you. And you're to be a man!" said the child, opening her eyes, "and are never to
15 come back here; but first, we're to be together all the Christmas long, and have the merriest time in all the world."

"You are quite a woman, little Fan!" exclaimed the boy.

She clapped her hands and laughed, and tried to touch his head, but being too little, laughed again, and stood on
20 tiptoe to embrace him. Then she began to drag him, in her childish eagerness, toward the door; and he, nothing loath to go, accompanied her.

A terrible voice in the hall cried, "Bring down Master Scrooge's box, there!" and in the hall appeared the schoolmaster
25 himself, who glared on Master Scrooge with a ferocious conde-scension, and threw him into a dreadful state of mind by shaking hands with him. He then conveyed him and his sister into the veriest old well of a shivering best-parlor that ever was seen, where the maps upon the wall and the celestial and terrestrial
30 globes in the windows were waxy with cold. Here he produced a decanter of curiously light wine and a block of curiously heavy cake, and administered installments of those dainties to the young people, at the same time sending out a meager servant to offer a glass of "something" to the postboy, who answered that
35 he thanked the gentleman, but if it was the same tap as he

had tasted before, he had rather not.  Master Scrooge's trunk being by this time tied on to the top of the chaise, the children bade the schoolmaster good-bye right willingly, and getting into it, drove gaily down the garden-sweep, the quick wheels
5 dashing the hoarfrost and snow from off the dark leaves of the evergreens like spray.

"Always a delicate creature whom a breath might have withered," said the ghost. "But she had a large heart!"

"So she had," cried Scrooge. "You're right. I'll not gainsay
10 it, Spirit. God forbid!"

"She died a woman," said the ghost, "and had, as I think, children."

"One child," Scrooge returned.

"True," said the ghost. "Your nephew!"
15     Scrooge seemed uneasy in his mind and answered briefly, "Yes."

Although they had but that moment left the school behind them, they were now in the busy thoroughfares of a city, where shadowy passengers passed and repassed, where shadowy carts
20 and coaches battled for the way, and all the strife and tumult of a real city were.  It was made plain enough, by the dressing of the shops, that here, too, it was Christmas time again; but it was evening, and the streets were lighted up.

The ghost stopped at a certain warehouse door and asked
25 Scrooge if he knew it.

"Know it!" said Scrooge. "Was I apprenticed here?"

They went in.  At sight of an old gentleman in a Welsh wig, sitting behind such a high desk that if he had been two inches taller he must have knocked his head against the ceiling, Scrooge
30 cried in great excitement:

"Why, it's old Fezziwig!  Bless his heart; it's Fezziwig alive again!"

Old Fezziwig laid down his pen, and looked up at the clock, which pointed to the hour of seven.  He rubbed his hands,
35 adjusted his capacious waistcoat, laughed all over himself,

from his shoes to his organ of benevolence and called out in a comfortable, oily, rich, fat, jovial voice:

"Yo ho, there! Ebenezer! Dick!"

Scrooge's former self, now grown a young man, came briskly 5 in, accompanied by his fellow 'prentice.

"Dick Wilkins, to be sure!" said Scrooge to the ghost. "Bless me, yes. There he is. He was very much attached to me, was Dick. Poor Dick! Dear, dear!"

"Yo ho, my boys!" said Fezziwig. "No more work tonight. 10 Christmas Eve, Dick. Christmas, Ebenezer! Let's have the shutters up," cried old Fezziwig with a sharp clap of his hands, "before a man can say Jack Robinson!"

You wouldn't believe how those two fellows went at it! They charged into the street with the shutters—one, two, three—had 15 'em up in their places—four, five, six—barred 'em and pinned 'em—seven, eight, nine—and came back before you could have got to twelve, panting like race horses.

"Hilli-ho!" cried old Fezziwig, skipping down from the high desk with wonderful agility. "Clear away, my lads, and let's have 20 lots of room here! Hilli-ho, Dick! Chirrup, Ebenezer!"

Clear away! There was nothing they wouldn't have cleared away, or couldn't have cleared away, with old Fezziwig looking on. It was done in a minute. Every movable was packed off as if it were dismissed from public life forevermore; the floor was 25 swept and watered; the lamps were trimmed; fuel was heaped upon the fire; and the warehouse was as snug, and warm, and dry, and bright a ballroom as you would desire to see upon a winter's night.

In came a fiddler with a music book, and went up to the 30 lofty desk, and made an orchestra of it, and tuned like fifty stomachaches. In came Mrs. Fezziwig, one vast substantial smile. In came the three Miss Fezziwigs, beaming and lovable. In came the six young followers whose hearts they broke. In came all the young men and women employed in the business. 35 In came the housemaid, with her cousin, the baker. In came the

cook, with her brother's particular friend, the milkman.  In came the boy from over the way, who was suspected of not having board enough from his master, trying to hide himself behind the girl from next door but one, who was proved to have had her
5 ears pulled by her mistress.  In they all came, one after another; some shyly, some boldly, some gracefully, some awkwardly, some pushing, some pulling; in they all came, anyhow and everyhow. Away they all went, twenty couples at once, hands half round and back again the other way; down the middle and up again;
10 round and round in various stages of affectionate grouping; old top couple always turning up in the wrong place; new top couple starting off again, as soon as they got there; all top couples at last, and not a bottom one to help them.  When this result was brought about, old Fezziwig, clapping his hands to stop the
15 dance, cried out, "Well done!" and the fiddler plunged his hot face into a pot of porter, especially provided for that purpose. But scorning rest upon his reappearance, he instantly began again, though there were no dancers yet, as if the other fiddler had been carried home, exhausted, on a shutter, and he were a
20 brand new man resolved to beat him out of sight, or perish.

There were more dances, and there were forfeits, and more dances, and there was cake, and there was negus, and there was a great piece of cold roast, and there was a great piece of cold boiled, and there were mince pies, and plenty of beer.  But the
25 great effect of the evening came after the roast and boiled, when the fiddler (an artful dog, mind!  the sort of man who knew his business better than you or I could have told it him!) struck up "Sir Roger de Coverley."  Then old Fezziwig stood out to dance with Mrs. Fezziwig.  Top couple, too, with a good stiff piece of
30 work cut out for them; three or four and twenty pair of partners; people who were not to be trifled with; people who would dance, and had no notion of walking.

But if they had been twice as many, ah, four times, old Fezziwig would have been a match for them, and so would Mrs.
35 Fezziwig.  As to her, she was worthy to be his partner in every

sense of the term. If that's not high praise, tell me higher, and I'll use it. A positive light appeared to issue from Fezziwig's calves. They shone in every part of the dance like moons. You couldn't have predicted, at any given time, what would become
5 of 'em next. And when old Fezziwig and Mrs. Fezziwig had gone all through the dance; advance and retire; hold hands with your partner; bow and curtsy; corkscrew; thread-the-needle; and back again to your place; Fezziwig "cut"—cut so deftly that he appeared to wink with his legs, and came up on his feet again
10 without a stagger.

When the clock struck eleven, this domestic ball broke up. Mr. and Mrs. Fezziwig took their stations, one on either side the door, and shaking hands with every person individually as he or she went out, wished him or her a Merry Christmas.
15 When everybody had retired but the two 'prentices, they did the same to them; and thus the cheerful voices died away, and the lads were left to their beds, which were under a counter in the back-shop.

During the whole of this time Scrooge had acted like a man
20 out of his wits. His heart and soul were in the scene, and with his former self. He corroborated everything, remembered everything, enjoyed everything, and underwent the strangest agitation. It was not until now, when the bright faces of his former self and Dick were turned from them, that he remembered the ghost
25 and became conscious that it was looking full upon him, while the light upon its head burned very clear.

"A small matter," said the ghost, "to make these silly folks so full of gratitude."

"Small!" echoed Scrooge.

30    The spirit signed to him to listen to the two apprentices, who were pouring out their hearts in praise of Fezziwig, and when he had done so, said:

"Why! Is it not? He has spent but a few pounds of your mortal money, three or four, perhaps. Is that so much that he
35 deserves this praise?"

"It isn't that," said Scrooge, heated by the remark, and speaking unconsciously like his former, not his latter, self. "It isn't that, Spirit. He has the power to render us happy or unhappy; to make our service light or burdensome, a pleasure or a toil.
5 Say that his power lies in words and looks, in things so slight and insignificant that it is impossible to add and count 'em up, what then? The happiness he gives is quite as great as if it cost a fortune."

He felt the spirit's glance and stopped.

10 "What is the matter?" asked the ghost.

"Nothing particular," said Scrooge.

"Something, I think?" the ghost insisted.

"No," said Scrooge. "No. I should like to be able to say a word or two to my clerk just now! That's all."

15 His former self turned down the lamps as he gave utterance to the wish, and Scrooge and the ghost again stood side by side in the open air.

"My time grows short," observed the spirit. "Quick!"

This was not addressed to Scrooge or to anyone whom he
20 could see, but it produced an immediate effect. For again Scrooge saw himself. He was older now, a man in the prime of life. His face had not the harsh and rigid lines of later years, but it had begun to wear the signs of care and avarice. There was an eager, greedy, restless motion in the eye, which showed
25 the passion that had taken root, and where the shadow of the growing tree would fall.

He was not alone, but sat by the side of a fair young girl in a mourning-dress, in whose eyes there were tears, which sparkled in the light that shone out of the Ghost of Christmas Past.

30 "It matters little," she said, softly. "To you, very little. Another idol has displaced me; and if it can cheer and comfort you in time to come, as I would have tried to do, I have no just cause to grieve."

"What idol has displaced you?" he rejoined.

35 "A golden one."

"This is the evenhanded dealing of the world!" he said. "There is nothing on which it is so hard as poverty; and there is nothing it professes to condemn with such severity as the pursuit of wealth!"

5    "You fear the world too much," she answered gently. "All your other hopes have merged into the hope of being beyond the chance of its sordid reproach. I have seen your nobler aspirations fall off one by one, until the master passion, Gain, engrosses you. Have I not?"

10   "What then?" he retorted. "Even if I have grown so much wiser, what then? I am not changed toward you."

She shook her head.

"Am I?"

"Our contract is an old one. It was made when we were 15 both poor and content to be so, until, in good season, we could improve our worldly fortune by our patient industry. You are changed. When it was made, you were another man."

"I was a boy," he said impatiently.

"Your own feeling tells you that you were not what you are," 20 she returned. "I am. That which promised happiness when we were one in heart is fraught with misery now that we are two. How often and how keenly I have thought of this I will not say. It is enough that I have thought of it and can release you."

"Have I ever sought release?"

25   "In words? No. Never."

"In what, then?"

"In a changed nature, in an altered spirit, in another atmosphere of life, another hope as its great end. In everything that made my love of any worth or value in your sight. If this had 30 never been between us," said the girl, looking mildly, but with steadiness, upon him, "tell me, would you seek me out and try to win me now? Ah, no!"

He seemed to yield to the justice of this supposition, in spite of himself. But he said with a struggle, "You think not."

35   "I would gladly think otherwise if I could," she answered,

"Heaven knows! When I have learned a truth like this, I know
how strong and irresistible it must be. But if you were free
today, tomorrow, yesterday, can even I believe that you would
choose a dowerless girl—you who, in your very confidence with
5 her, weigh everything by gain; or, choosing her, if for a moment
you were false enough to your one guiding principle to do so,
do I not know that your repentance and regret would surely
follow? I do, and I release you. With a full heart, for the love
of him you once were."

10    He was about to speak, but with her head turned from him,
she resumed:

"You may—the memory of what is past half makes me hope
you will—have pain in this. A very, very brief time, and you will
dismiss the recollection of it, gladly, as an unprofitable dream,
15 from which it happened well that you awoke. May you be happy
in the life you have chosen!"

She left him, and they parted.

"Spirit!" said Scrooge, "show me no more! Conduct me home.
Why do you delight to torture me?"

20    "One shadow more!" exclaimed the ghost.

"No more!" cried Scrooge. "No more. I don't wish to see
it. Show me no more!"

But the relentless ghost pinioned him in both his arms, and
forced him to observe what happened next.

25    They were in another scene and place, a room, not very
large or handsome, but full of comfort. Near to the winter fire
sat a beautiful young girl, so like the last that Scrooge believed
it was the same, until he saw her, now a comely matron, sitting
opposite her daughter. The noise in this room was perfectly
30 tumultuous, for there were more children there than Scrooge in
his agitated state of mind could count; and, unlike the celebrated
herd in the poem, they were not forty children conducting
themselves like one, but every child was conducting itself like
forty. The consequences were uproarious beyond belief, but no
35 one seemed to care; on the contrary, the mother and daughter

laughed heartily, and enjoyed it very much; and the latter, soon
beginning to mingle in the sports, got pillaged by the young
brigands most ruthlessly. What would I not have given to be
one of them! Though I never could have been so rude, no, no!
5 I wouldn't for the wealth of all the world have crushed that
braided hair, and torn it down; and for the precious little shoe, I
wouldn't have plucked it off, God bless my soul! to save my life.
As to measuring her waist in sport, as they did, bold young brood,
I couldn't have done it; I should have expected my arm to have
10 grown round it for a punishment, and never come straight again.
And yet I should have dearly liked, I own, to have touched her
lips; to have questioned her, that she might have opened them;
to have looked upon the lashes of her downcast eyes, and never
raised a blush; to have let loose waves of hair, an inch of which
15 would be a keepsake beyond price; in short, I should have liked,
I do confess, to have had the lightest license of a child, and yet
been man enough to know its value.

But now a knocking at the door was heard, and such a rush
immediately ensued that she with laughing face and plundered
20 dress was borne toward it, the center of a flushed and boisterous
group just in time to greet the father, who came home attended
by a man laden with Christmas toys and presents. Then the
shouting and the struggling, and the onslaught that was made on
the defenseless porter. The scaling him with chairs for ladders
25 to dive into his pockets, despoil him of brown-paper parcels,
hold on tight by his cravat, hug him round the neck, pommel
his back, and kick his legs in irrepressible affection! The shouts
of wonder and delight with which the development of every
package was received! The terrible announcement that the baby
30 had been taken in the act of putting a doll's frying pan into his
mouth, and was more than suspected of having swallowed a
fictitious turkey, glued on a wooden platter! The immense relief
of finding this a false alarm! The joy, and gratitude, and ecstasy!
They are all indescribable alike. It is enough that by degrees
35 the children and their emotions got out of the parlor and by one

stair at a time up to the top of the house, where they went to bed, and so subsided.

And now Scrooge looked on more attentively than ever, when the master of the house, having his daughter leaning fondly on
5 him, sat down with her and her mother at his own fireside; and when he thought that such another creature, quite as graceful and as full of promise, might have called him father, and been a springtime in the haggard winter of his life, his sight grew very dim indeed.

10 "Belle," said the husband, turning to his wife with a smile, "I saw an old friend of yours this afternoon."

"Who was it?"

"Guess!"

"How can I? Tut, don't I know?" she added in the same
15 breath, laughing as he laughed. "Mr. Scrooge."

"Mr. Scrooge it was. I passed his office window; and as it was not shut up, and he had a candle inside, I could scarcely help seeing him. His partner lies upon the point of death, I hear; and there he sat alone. Quite alone in the world, I do believe."

20 "Spirit!" said Scrooge in a broken voice, "remove me from this place."

"I told you these were shadows of the things that have been," said the ghost. "That they are what they are, do not blame me!"

25 "Remove me!" Scrooge exclaimed; "I cannot bear it!"

He turned upon the ghost, and seeing that it looked upon him with a face in which in some strange way there were fragments of all the faces it had shown him, wrestled with it.

"Leave me! Take me back. Haunt me no longer!"

30 In the struggle, if that can be called a struggle in which the ghost with no visible resistance on its own part was undisturbed by any effort of its adversary, Scrooge observed that its light was burning high and bright; and dimly connecting that with its influence over him, he seized the extinguisher cap, and by a
35 sudden action pressed it down upon his head.

The spirit dropped beneath it, so that the extinguisher covered its whole form; but though Scrooge pressed it down with all his force, he could not hide the light which streamed from under it in an unbroken flood upon the ground.

5    He was conscious of being exhausted and overcome by an irresistible drowsiness, and further, of being in his own bedroom. He gave the cap a parting squeeze, in which his hand relaxed, and had barely time to reel to bed before he sank into a heavy slumber.

## Stave Three

### The Second of the Three Spirits

10    Awaking in the middle of a prodigiously tough snore, and sitting up in bed to get his thoughts together, Scrooge had no occasion to be told that the bell was again upon the stroke of one. He felt that he was restored to consciousness in the right nick of time, for the especial purpose of holding a conference
15 with the second messenger dispatched to him through Jacob Marley's intervention. But, finding that he turned uncomfortably cold when he began to wonder which of his curtains this new specter would draw back, he put them every one aside with his own hands, and lying down again, established a sharp lookout
20 all round the bed. For he wished to challenge the spirit on the moment of its appearance, and did not wish to be taken by surprise and made nervous.

Gentlemen of the free-and-easy sort who plume themselves on being acquainted with a move or two, and being usually equal
25 to the time of day, express the wide range of their capacity for adventure by observing that they are good for anything from pitch-and-toss to manslaughter, between which opposite extremes, no doubt, there lies a tolerably wide and comprehensive range of subjects. Without venturing for Scrooge quite as
30 hardily as this, I don't mind calling on you to believe that he was ready for a good broad field of strange appearances, and that

nothing between a baby and rhinoceros would have astonished him very much.

Now, being prepared for almost anything, he was not by any means prepared for nothing; and, consequently, when the bell
5 struck one, and no shape appeared, he was taken with a violent fit of trembling. Five minutes, ten minutes, a quarter of an hour went by, yet nothing came. All this time he lay upon his bed, the very core and center of a blaze of ruddy light which streamed upon it when the clock proclaimed the hour; and which, being
10 only light, was more alarming than a dozen ghosts, as he was powerless to make out what it meant, or would be at; and was sometimes apprehensive that he might be at that very moment an interesting case of spontaneous combustion, without having the consolation of knowing it. At last, however, he began to
15 think—as you or I would have thought at first, for it is always the person not in the predicament who knows what ought to have been done in it and would unquestionably have done it, too—at last, I say, he began to think that the source and secret of this ghostly light might be in the adjoining room, from whence,
20 on further tracing it, it seemed to shine. This idea taking full possession of his mind, he got up softly and shuffled in his slippers to the door.

The moment Scrooge's hand was on the lock, a strange voice called him by name and bade him enter. He obeyed.
25 It was his own room. There was no doubt about that. But it had undergone a surprising transformation. The walls and ceiling were so hung with living green that it looked a perfect grove, from every part of which bright gleaming berries glistened. The crisp leaves of holly, mistletoe, and ivy reflected back the
30 light, as if so many little mirrors had been scattered there; and such a mighty blaze went roaring up the chimney as that dull petrification of a hearth had never known in Scrooge's time, or Marley's, or for many and many a winter season gone. Heaped up on the floor, to form a kind of throne, were turkeys, geese,
35 game, poultry, brawn, great joints of meat, sucking pigs, long

wreaths of sausages, mince pies, plum puddings, barrels of oysters, red-hot chestnuts, cherry-cheeked apples, juicy oranges, luscious pears, immense twelfth-cakes, and seething bowls of punch, that made the chamber dim with their delicious steam.
5 In easy state upon this couch there sat a jolly giant, glorious to see, who bore a glowing torch, in shape not unlike Plenty's horn, and held it up, high up, to shed its light on Scrooge, as he came peeping round the door.

"Come in!" exclaimed the ghost. "Come in! and know me 10 better, man!"

Scrooge entered timidly, and hung his head before this spirit. He was not the dogged Scrooge he had been; and though the spirit's eyes were clear and kind, he did not like to meet them.

"I am the Ghost of Christmas Present," said the spirit. "Look 15 upon me!"

Scrooge reverently did so. It was clothed in one simple deep green robe, or mantle, bordered with white fur. This garment hung so loosely on the figure that its capacious breast was bare, as if disdaining to be warded or concealed by any artifice. Its 20 feet, observable beneath the ample folds of the garment, were also bare, and on its head it wore no other covering than a holly wreath set here and there with shining icicles. Its dark brown curls were long and free; free as its genial face, its sparkling eye, its open hand, its cheery voice, its unconstrained demeanor, and 25 its joyful air. Girded round its middle was an antique scabbard; but no sword was in it, and the ancient sheath was eaten up with rust.

"You have never seen the like of me before!" exclaimed the spirit.
30    "Never," Scrooge made answer to it.

"Have never walked forth with the younger members of my family, meaning (for I am very young) my elder brothers born in these later years?" pursued the phantom.

"I don't think I have," said Scrooge. "I am afraid I have not. 35 Have you had many brothers, Spirit?"

"More than eighteen hundred," said the ghost.

"A tremendous family to provide for!" muttered Scrooge.

The Ghost of Christmas Present rose.

5 "Spirit," said Scrooge, submissively, "conduct me where you will. I went forth last night on compulsion, and I learned a lesson which is working now. Tonight, if you have aught to teach me, let me profit by it."

"Touch my robe!"

Scrooge did as he was told, and held it fast.

10 Holly, mistletoe, red berries, ivy, turkeys, geese, game, poultry, brawn, meat, pigs, sausages, oysters, pies, puddings, fruit, and punch all vanished instantly. So did the room, the fire, the ruddy glow, the hour of night, and they stood in the city streets on Christmas morning, where (for the weather was severe) 15 the people made a rough, but brisk and not unpleasant kind of music, in scraping the snow from the pavement in front of their dwellings and from the tops of their houses; whence it was mad delight to the boys to see it come plumping down into the road below, and splitting into artificial little snow storms.

20 The house fronts looked black enough, and the windows blacker, contrasting with the smooth white sheet of snow upon the roofs, and with the dirtier snow upon the ground, which last deposit had been plowed up in deep furrows by the heavy wheels of carts and wagons, furrows that crossed and recrossed 25 each other hundreds of times where the great streets branched off and made intricate channels, hard to trace, in the thick yellow mud and icy water. The sky was gloomy, and the shortest streets were choked up with a dingy mist, half-thawed, half-frozen, whose heavier particles descended in a shower 30 of sooty atoms, as if all the chimneys in Great Britain had, by one consent, caught fire, and were blazing away to their dear hearts' content. There was nothing very cheerful in the climate or the town, and yet was there an air of cheerfulness abroad that the clearest summer air and brightest summer sun 35 might have endeavored to diffuse in vain.

For the people who were shoveling away on the housetops
were jovial and full of glee, calling out to one another from the
parapets, and now and then exchanging a facetious snowball—
better-natured missile far than many a wordy jest—laughing
5 heartily if it went right and not less heartily if it went wrong.
The poulterers' shops were still half open, and the fruiterers'
were radiant in their glory. There were great, round, pot-bellied
baskets of chestnuts, shaped like the waistcoats of jolly old
gentlemen, lolling at the doors, and tumbling out into the street
10 in their apoplectic opulence. There were ruddy, brown-faced,
broad-birthed Spanish onions, winking from their shelves
in wanton slyness at the girls as they went by and glanced
demurely at the hung up mistletoe. There were pears and
apples, clustered high in blooming pyramids; there were bunches
15 of grapes, made, in the shopkeepers' benevolence, to dangle
from conspicuous hooks, that people's mouths might water
gratis as they passed; there were piles of filberts, mossy and
brown, recalling, in their fragrance, ancient walks among the
woods, and pleasant shufflings ankle deep through withered
20 leaves; there were Norfolk Biffins, squab and swarthy, setting off
the yellow of the oranges and lemons, and in the great compact-
ness of their juicy persons, urgently entreating and beseeching
to be carried home in paper bags and eaten after dinner. The
very gold and silver fish, set forth among these choice fruits in
25 a bowl, though members of a dull and stagnant-blooded race,
appeared to know that there was something going on; and, to
a fish, went gasping round and round their little world in slow
and passionless excitement.

The grocers'! oh, the grocers'! nearly closed, with perhaps
30 two shutters down, or one; but through those gaps such glimpses!
It was not alone that the scales descending on the counter made
a merry sound, or that the twine and roller parted company
so briskly, or that the canisters were rattled up and down like
juggling tricks, or even that the blended scents of tea and coffee
35 were so grateful to the nose, or even that the raisins were so

plentiful and rare, the almonds so extremely white, the sticks
of cinnamon so long and straight, the other spices so delicious,
the candied fruits so caked and spotted with molten sugar as to
make the coldest lookers-on feel faint and subsequently bilious.
5 Nor was it that the figs were moist and pulpy, or that the French
plums blushed in modest tartness from their highly decorated
boxes, or that everything was good to eat and in its Christmas
dress; but the customers were all so hurried and so eager in the
hopeful promise of the day that they tumbled up against each
10 other at the door, clashing their wicker baskets wildly, and left
their purchases upon the counter, and came running back to
fetch them, and committed hundreds of the like mistakes in
the best humor possible; while the grocer and his people were
so frank and fresh that the polished hearts with which they
15 fastened their aprons behind might have been their own, worn
outside for general inspection and for Christmas daws to peck
at if they chose.

But soon the steeples called good people all to church and
chapel, and away they came, flocking through the streets in their
20 best clothes, and with their gayest faces. And at the same time
there emerged from scores of by-streets, lanes, and nameless
turnings, innumerable people, carrying their dinners to the
bakers' shops. The sight of these poor revelers appeared to
interest the spirit very much, for he stood with Scrooge beside
25 him in a baker's doorway, and taking off the covers as their
bearers passed, sprinkled incense on their dinners from his torch.
And it was a very uncommon kind of torch, for once or twice
when there were angry words between some dinner carriers
who had jostled with each other, he shed a few drops of water
30 on them from it, and their good humor was restored directly.
For, they said, it was a shame to quarrel upon Christmas Day.
And so it was! God love it, so it was!

In time the bells ceased, and the bakers' were shut up; and
yet there was a genial shadowing forth of all these dinners and
35 the progress of their cooking, in the thawed blotch of wet above

each baker's oven; where the pavement smoked as if its stones were cooking too.

"Is there a peculiar flavor in what you sprinkle from your torch?" asked Scrooge.

5    "There is. My own."

"Would it apply to any kind of dinner on this day?" asked Scrooge.

"To any kindly given. To a poor one most."

"Why to a poor one most?" asked Scrooge.

10    "Because it needs it most."

"Spirit," said Scrooge, after a moment's thought, "I wonder you, of all the beings in the many worlds about us, should desire to cramp these people's opportunities of innocent enjoyment."

15    "I!" cried the spirit.

"You would deprive them of their means of dining every seventh day, often the only day on which they can be said to dine at all," said Scrooge. "Wouldn't you?"

"I!" cried the Spirit.

20    "You seek to close these places on the Seventh Day?" said Scrooge. "And it comes to the same thing."

"I seek!" exclaimed the Spirit.

"Forgive me if I am wrong. It has been done in your name, or at least in that of your family," said Scrooge.

25    "There are some upon this earth of yours," returned the Spirit, "who lay claim to know us, and who do their deeds of passion, pride, ill-will, hatred, envy, bigotry, and selfishness in our name, who are strange to us and all our kith and kin, as if they had never lived. Remember that, and charge their doings
30 on themselves, not us."

Scrooge promised that he would; and they went on, invisible, as they had been before, into the suburbs of the town. It was a remarkable quality of the ghost (which Scrooge had observed at the baker's), that notwithstanding his gigantic size, he could
35 accommodate himself to any place with ease, and that he stood

beneath a low roof quite as gracefully and like a supernatural creature, as it was possible he could have done in any lofty hall.

And perhaps it was the pleasure the good spirit had in show-
5 ing off this power of his, or else it was his own kind, generous, hearty nature, and his sympathy with all poor men, that led him straight to Scrooge's clerk's; for there he went and took Scrooge with him, holding to his robe; and on the threshold of the door the Spirit smiled, and stopped to bless Bob Cratchit's
10 dwelling with the sprinklings of his torch. Think of that! Bob had but fifteen "bob" a week himself; he pocketed on Saturdays but fifteen copies of his Christian name, and yet the Ghost of Christmas Present blessed his four-roomed house!

Then up rose Mrs. Cratchit, Cratchit's wife, dressed out but
15 poorly in a twice-turned gown, but brave in ribbons, which are cheap and make a goodly show for sixpence; and she laid the cloth, assisted by Belinda Cratchit, second of her daughters, also brave in ribbons, while Master Peter Cratchit plunged a fork into the saucepan of potatoes, and getting the corners of
20 his monstrous shirt collar (Bob's private property, conferred upon his son and heir in honor of the day) into his mouth, rejoiced to find himself so gallantly attired and yearned to show his linen in the fashionable parks. And now two smaller Cratchits, boy and girl, came tearing in, screaming that outside
25 the baker's they had smelt the goose and known it for their own; and, basking in luxurious thoughts of sage-and-onion, these young Cratchits danced about the table, and exalted Master Peter Cratchit to the skies, while he (not proud, although his collars nearly choked him) blew the fire, until the slow
30 potatoes bubbling up, knocked loudly at the saucepan lid to be let out and peeled.

"What has ever got your precious father, then?" said Mrs. Cratchit. "And your brother, Tiny Tim! And Martha warn't as late last Christmas Day by half-an-hour!"

35     "Here's Martha, Mother!" said a girl, appearing as she spoke.

"Here's Martha, Mother!" cried the two young Cratchits. "Hurrah! There's *such* a goose, Martha!"

"Why, bless your heart alive, my dear, how late you are!" said Mrs. Cratchit, kissing her a dozen times and taking off her shawl
5 and bonnet for her with officious zeal.

"We'd a deal of work to finish up last night," replied the girl, "and had to clear away this morning, Mother!"

"Well! Never mind so long as you are come," said Mrs. Cratchit. "Sit ye down before the fire, my dear, and have a
10 warm, Lord bless ye!"

"No, no! There's Father coming," cried the two young Cratchits, who were everywhere at once. "Hide, Martha, hide!"

So Martha hid herself, and in came little Bob, the father, with at least three feet of comforter exclusive of the fringe,
15 hanging down before him; and his threadbare clothes darned up and brushed to look seasonable; and Tiny Tim upon his shoulder. Alas for Tiny Tim, he bore a little crutch, and had his limbs supported by an iron frame!

"Why, where's our Martha?" cried Bob Cratchit, looking round.
20 "Not coming," said Mrs. Cratchit.

"Not coming!" said Bob, with a sudden declension in his high spirits, for he had been Tim's blood horse all the way from church and had come home rampant. "Not coming upon Christmas Day!"

25      Martha didn't like to see him disappointed, if it were only in joke, so she came out prematurely from behind the closet door and ran into his arms, while the two young Cratchits hustled Tiny Tim and bore him off into the wash house, that he might hear the pudding singing in the copper.

30      "And how did little Tim behave?" asked Mrs. Cratchit, when she had rallied Bob on his credulity, and Bob had hugged his daughter to his heart's content.

"As good as gold," said Bob, "and better. Somehow he gets thoughtful, sitting by himself so much, and thinks the strangest
35 things you ever heard. He told me, coming home, that he hoped

the people saw him in the church, because he was a cripple, and it might be pleasant to them to remember upon Christmas Day who made lame beggars walk and blind men see." Bob's voice was tremulous when he told them this, and trembled more when 5 he said that Tiny Tim was growing strong and hearty.

His active little crutch was heard upon the floor, and back came Tiny Tim before another word was spoken, escorted by his brother and sister to his stool before the fire; and while Bob, turning up his cuffs—as if, poor fellow, they were capable of 10 being made more shabby—compounded some hot mixture in a jug with gin and lemons, and stirred it round and round and put it on the hob to simmer, Master Peter and the two ubiquitous young Cratchits went to fetch the goose, with which they soon returned in high procession.

15 Such a bustle ensued that you might have thought a goose the rarest of all birds, a feathered phenomenon, to which a black swan was a matter of course—and in truth it was something very like it in that house. Mrs. Cratchit made the gravy (ready beforehand in a little saucepan) hissing hot; Master Peter mashed 20 the potatoes with incredible vigor; Miss Belinda sweetened up the apple sauce; Martha dusted the hot plates; Bob took Tiny Tim beside him in a tiny corner at the table; the two young Cratchits set chairs for everybody, not forgetting themselves, and mounting guard upon their posts, crammed spoons into their 25 mouths, lest they should shriek for goose before their turn came to be helped. At last the dishes were set on, and grace was said. It was succeeded by a breathless pause, as Mrs. Cratchit, looking slowly all along the carving knife, prepared to plunge it in the breast; but when she did, and when the long expected 30 gush of stuffing issued forth, one murmur of delight arose all around the board, and even Tiny Tim, excited by the two young Cratchits, beat on the table with the handle of his knife, and feebly cried Hurrah!

There never was such a goose. Bob said he didn't believe 35 there ever was such a goose cooked. Its tenderness and flavor,

size and cheapness, were the themes of universal admiration.
Eked out by the apple sauce and mashed potatoes, it was a
sufficient dinner for the whole family; indeed, as Mrs. Cratchit
said with great delight (surveying one small atom of a bone upon
5 the dish), they hadn't ate it all at last! Yet everyone had had
enough, and the youngest Cratchits in particular were steeped
in sage-and-onion to the eyebrows! But now, the plates being
changed by Miss Belinda, Mrs. Cratchit left the room alone—
too nervous to bear witnesses—to take the pudding up and
10 bring it in.

Suppose it should not be done enough! Suppose it should
break in turning out! Suppose somebody should have got over
the wall of the backyard, and stolen it while they were merry
with the goose—a supposition at which the two young Cratchits
15 became livid! All sorts of horrors were supposed.

Hallo! A great deal of steam! The pudding was out of the
copper. A smell like a washing day! That was the cloth. A smell
like an eating house and a pastry cook's next door to each other,
with a laundress's next door to that! That was the pudding!
20 In half a minute Mrs. Cratchit entered—flushed, but smiling
proudly—with the pudding, like a speckled cannonball, so hard
and firm, blazing in half of half-a-quartern of ignited brandy, and
bedight with Christmas holly stuck into the top.

Oh, a wonderful pudding! Bob Cratchit said, and calmly
25 too, that he regarded it as the greatest success achieved by
Mrs. Cratchit since their marriage. Mrs. Cratchit said that now
the weight was off her mind she would confess she had had her
doubts about the quantity of flour. Everybody had something
to say about it, but nobody said or thought it was at all a small
30 pudding for a large family. It would have been flat heresy to do
so. Any Cratchit would have blushed to hint at such a thing.

At last the dinner was all done, the cloth was cleared, the
hearth swept, and the fire made up. The compound in the jug
being tasted, and considered perfect, apples and oranges were
35 put upon the table, and a shovel full of chestnuts on the fire.

Then all the Cratchit family drew around the hearth, in what Bob Cratchit called a circle, meaning half a one; and at Bob Cratchit's elbow stood the family display of glass—two tumblers and a custard cup without a handle.

5 These held the hot stuff from the jug, however, as well as golden goblets would have done; and Bob served it out with beaming looks, while the chestnuts on the fire sputtered and cracked noisily. Then Bob proposed:

"A Merry Christmas to us all, my dears. God bless us!"

10 Which all the family reechoed.

"God bless us every one!" said Tiny Tim, the last of all.

He sat very close to his father's side upon his little stool. Bob held his withered little hand in his, as if he loved the child and wished to keep him by his side and dreaded that he might

15 be taken from him.

"Spirit," said Scrooge, with an interest he had never felt before, "tell me if Tiny Tim will live."

"I see a vacant seat," replied the ghost, "in the poor chimney corner, and a crutch without an owner, carefully preserved. If

20 these shadows remain unaltered by the future, the child will die."

"No, no," said Scrooge. "Oh, no, kind Spirit! say he will be spared."

"If these shadows remain unaltered by the future, none other

25 of my race," returned the ghost, "will find him here. What then? If he be like to die, he had better do it and decrease the surplus population."

Scrooge hung his head to hear his own words quoted by the spirit and was overcome with penitence and grief.

30 "Man," said the ghost, "if man you be in heart, not adamant, forbear that wicked cant until you have discovered what the surplus is, and where it is. Will you decide what men shall live, what men shall die? It may be that in the sight of Heaven you are more worthless and less fit to live than millions like

35 this poor man's child. Oh, God! to hear the insect on the leaf

pronouncing on the too much life among his hungry brothers in the dust!"

Scrooge bent before the ghost's rebuke, and trembling cast his eyes upon the ground. But he raised them speedily on
5 hearing his own name.

"Mr. Scrooge!" said Bob, "I'll give you Mr. Scrooge, the Founder of the Feast!"

"The Founder of the Feast, indeed!" cried Mrs. Cratchit, reddening. "I wish I had him here. I'd give him a piece of my mind
10 to feast upon, and I hope he'd have a good appetite for it."

"My dear," said Bob, "the children! Christmas Day."

"It should be Christmas Day, I am sure," said she, "on which one drinks the health of such an odious, stingy, hard, unfeeling man as Mr. Scrooge. You know he is, Robert! Nobody knows it
15 better than you do, poor fellow!"

"My dear," was Bob's mild answer, "Christmas Day."

"I'll drink his health for your sake and the Day's," said Mrs. Cratchit, "not for his. Long life to him! A Merry Christmas and a Happy New Year! He'll be very merry and happy, I have
20 no doubt!"

The children drank the toast after her. It was the first of their proceedings which had no heartiness in it. Tiny Tim drank it last of all, but he didn't care two-pence for it. Scrooge was the ogre of the family. The mention of his name cast a
25 dark shadow on the party, which was not dispelled for full five minutes.

After it had passed away, they were ten times merrier than before from the mere relief of Scrooge the Baleful being done with. Bob Cratchit told them how he had a situation in his
30 eye for Master Peter, which would bring in, if obtained, full five-and-sixpence weekly. The two young Cratchits laughed tremendously at the idea of Peter's being a man of business; and Peter himself looked thoughtfully at the fire from between his collars, as if he were deliberating what particular investments he
35 should favor when he came into the receipt of that bewildering

income. Martha, who was a poor apprentice at a milliner's, then told them what kind of work she had to do, and how many hours she worked at a stretch, and how she meant to lie abed tomorrow morning for a good long rest, tomorrow being a holiday 5 she passed at home. Also how she had seen a countess and a lord some days before, and how the lord "was much about as tall as Peter," at which Peter pulled up his collars so high that you couldn't have seen his head if you had been there. All this time the chestnuts and the jug went round and round; and by 10 and by they had a song about a lost child traveling in the snow from Tiny Tim, who had a plaintive little voice and sang it very well indeed.

There was nothing of high mark in this. They were not a handsome family; they were not well dressed; their shoes 15 were far from being waterproof; their clothes were scanty; and Peter might have known, and very likely did, the inside of a pawnbroker's. But, they were happy, grateful, pleased with one another, and contented with the time; and when they faded, and looked happier yet in the bright sprinklings of the spirit's torch 20 at parting, Scrooge had his eye upon them, and especially on Tiny Tim, until the last.

By this time it was getting dark and snowing pretty heavily; and as Scrooge and the spirit went along the streets, the brightness of the roaring fires in kitchens, parlors, and all sorts of 25 rooms was wonderful. Here, the flickering of the blaze showed preparations for a cozy dinner, with hot plates baking through and through before the fire and deep red curtains ready to be drawn to shut out cold and darkness. There, all the children of the house were running out into the snow to meet their married 30 sisters, brothers, cousins, uncles, aunts, and be the first to greet them. Here, again, were shadows on the window blind of guests assembling; and there a group of handsome girls, all hooded and fur-booted, and all chattering at once, tripped lightly off to some near neighbor's house, where woe upon the single man who saw 35 them enter—artful witches! well they knew it—in a glow!

But if you had judged from the numbers of people on their
way to friendly gatherings, you might have thought that no one
was at home to give them welcome when they got there, instead
of every house expecting company and piling up its fires half-
5 chimney high. Blessings on it, how the ghost exulted! How
it bared its breadth of breast, and opened its capacious palm,
and floated on, outpouring, with a generous hand, its bright and
harmless mirth, on everything within its reach! The very lamplighter, who ran on before, dotting the dusky street with specks
10 of light, and who was dressed to spend the evening somewhere,
laughed out loudly as the spirit passed, though little kenned the
lamplighter that he had any company but Christmas!

And now, without a word of warning from the ghost, they
stood upon a bleak and desert moor, where monstrous masses
15 of rude stone were cast about, as though it were the burial
place of giants; and water spread itself wheresoever it listed,
or would have done so but for the frost that held it prisoner;
and nothing grew but moss and furze, and coarse, rank grass.
Down in the west the setting sun had left a streak of fiery red,
20 which glared upon the desolation for an instant, like a sullen
eye, and frowning lower, lower, lower yet, was lost in the thick
gloom of darkest night.

"What place is this?" asked Scrooge.

"A place where miners live, who labor in the bowels of the
25 earth," returned the spirit. "But they know me. See!"

A light shone from the window of a hut, and swiftly they
advanced toward it. Passing through the wall of mud and stone,
they found a cheerful company assembled round a glowing
fire. An old, old man and woman, with their children and their
30 children's children, and another generation beyond that, all
decked out gaily in their holiday attire. The old man in a voice
that seldom rose above the howling of the wind upon the barren
waste was singing them a Christmas song; it had been a very old
song when he was a boy, and from time to time they all joined
35 in the chorus. So surely as they raised their voices, the old

man got quite blithe and loud; and so surely as they stopped, his vigor sank again.

The spirit did not tarry here, but bade Scrooge hold his robe, and passing on above the moor, sped whither? Not to sea? To
5 sea. To Scrooge's horror, looking back, he saw the last of the land, a frightful range of rocks, behind them; and his ears were deafened by the thundering of water as it rolled, and roared, and raged among the dreadful caverns it had worn and fiercely tried to undermine the earth.

10 Built upon a dismal reef of sunken rocks, some league or so from shore, on which the waters chafed and dashed the wild year through, there stood a solitary lighthouse. Great heaps of seaweed clung to its base, and storm birds—born of the wind one might suppose as seaweed of the water—rose and fell about
15 it, like the waves they skimmed.

But even here, two men who watched the light had made a fire that through the loophole in the thick stone wall shed out a ray of brightness on the awful sea. Joining their horny hands over the rough table at which they sat, they wished each other
20 Merry Christmas in their can of grog; and one of them—the elder, too—with his face all damaged and scarred with hard weather, as the figurehead of an old ship might be—struck up a sturdy song that was like a gale in itself.

Again the ghost sped on, above the black and heaving sea—on,
25 on—until being far away, as he told Scrooge, from any shore, they lighted on a ship. They stood beside the helmsman at the wheel, the lookout in the bow, the officers who had the watch; dark, ghostly figures in their several stations; but every man among them hummed a Christmas tune, or had a Christmas thought, or spoke
30 below his breath to his companion of some bygone Christmas Day with homeward hopes belonging to it. And every man on board, waking or sleeping, good or bad, had had a kinder word for another on that day than on any day in the year; and had shared to some extent in its festivities; and had remembered those he cared for at a
35 distance and had known that they delighted to remember him.

It was a great surprise to Scrooge, while listening to the moaning of the wind and thinking what a solemn thing it was to move on through the lonely darkness over an unknown abyss, whose depths were secrets as profound as death—it was a great
5 surprise to Scrooge, while thus engaged, to hear a hearty laugh. It was a much greater surprise to Scrooge to recognize it as his own nephew's and to find himself in a bright, dry, gleaming room, with the spirit standing smiling by his side and looking at the same nephew with approving affability.

10      "Ha, ha!" laughed Scrooge's nephew. "Ha, ha, ha!"

If you should happen, by any unlikely chance, to know a man more blest in a laugh than Scrooge's nephew, all I can say is I should like to know him, too. Introduce him to me, and I'll cultivate his acquaintance.

15      It is a fair, even-handed, noble adjustment of things, that while there is infection in disease and sorrow, there is nothing in the world so irresistibly contagious as laughter and good humor. When Scrooge's nephew laughed in this way—holding his sides, rolling his head, and twisting his face into the most extravagant
20 contortions—Scrooge's niece, by marriage, laughed as heartily as he. And their assembled friends, being not a bit behindhand, roared out lustily. "Ha, ha! Ha, ha, ha!"

"He said that Christmas was a humbug, as I live!" cried Scrooge's nephew. "He believed it, too!"

25      "More shame for him, Fred!" said Scrooge's niece indignantly. Bless those women; they never do anything by halves. They are always in earnest.

She was very pretty, exceedingly pretty. With a dimpled, surprised-looking, capital face; a ripe little mouth that seemed
30 made to be kissed—as no doubt it was; all kinds of good little dots about her chin that melted into one another when she laughed; and the sunniest pair of eyes you ever saw in any little creature's head. Altogether she was what you would have called provoking, you know, but satisfactory, too. Oh, perfectly
35 satisfactory.

"He's a comical old fellow," said Scrooge's nephew, "that's the truth, and not so pleasant as he might be. However, his offenses carry their own punishment, and I have nothing to say against him."

5 "I'm sure he is very rich, Fred," hinted Scrooge's niece. "At least you always tell me so."

"What of that, my dear!" said Scrooge's nephew. "His wealth is of no use to him. He doesn't do any good with it. He doesn't make himself comfortable with it. He hasn't the satisfaction
10 of thinking—ha, ha, ha!—that he is ever going to benefit us with it."

"I have no patience with him," observed Scrooge's niece. Scrooge's niece's sisters, and all of the other ladies, expressed the same opinion.

15 "Oh, I have!" said Scrooge's nephew. "I am sorry for him; I couldn't be angry with him if I tried. Who suffers by his ill whims? Himself, always. Here, he takes it into his head to dislike us, and he won't come and dine with us. What's the consequence? He doesn't lose much of a dinner."

20 "Indeed, I think he loses a very good dinner," interrupted Scrooge's niece. Everybody else said the same; and they must be allowed to have been competent judges, because they had just had dinner, and, with the dessert upon the table, were clustered round the fire, by lamplight.

25 "Well! I'm very glad to hear it," said Scrooge's nephew, "because I haven't any great faith in these young housekeepers. What do you say, Topper?"

Topper had clearly got his eye upon one of Scrooge's niece's sisters, for he answered that a bachelor was a wretched outcast
30 who had no right to express an opinion on the subject. Whereat Scrooge's niece's sister—the plump one with the lace tucker, not the one with the roses—blushed.

"Do go on, Fred," said Scrooge's niece, clapping her hands. "He never finishes what he begins to say! He is such a ridiculous
35 fellow!"

Scrooge's nephew reveled in another laugh, and as it was impossible to keep the infection off, though the plump sister tried hard to do it with aromatic vinegar, his example was unanimously followed.

5  "I was only going to say," said Scrooge's nephew, "that the consequence of his taking a dislike to us and not making merry with us, is, as I think, that he loses some pleasant moments, which could do him no harm. I am sure he loses pleasanter companions than he can find in his own thoughts, either in his
10  moldy old office or his dusty chambers. I mean to give him the same chance every year, whether he likes it or not, for I pity him. He may rail at Christmas till he dies, but he can't help thinking better of it—I defy him—if he finds me going there, in good temper, year after year, and saying, 'Uncle Scrooge,
15  how are you?' If it only puts him in the vein to leave his poor clerk fifty pounds, that's something; and I think I shook him yesterday."

It was their turn to laugh now at the notion of his shaking Scrooge. But being thoroughly good-natured, and not much
20  caring what they laughed at, so that they laughed at any rate, he encouraged them in their merriment, and passed the bottle joyously.

After tea, they had some music. For they were a musical family and knew what they were about when they sang a glee
25  or catch, I can assure you, especially Topper, who could growl away in the bass like a good one and never swell the large veins in his forehead or get red in the face over it. Scrooge's niece played well upon the harp, and played among other tunes a simple little air (a mere nothing; you might learn to whistle it in
30  two minutes) which had been familiar to the child who fetched Scrooge from the boarding school, as he had been reminded by the Ghost of Christmas Past. When this strain of music sounded, all the things the ghost had shown him came upon his mind; he softened more and more, and thought that if he could have
35  listened to it often, years ago, he might have cultivated the kind-

nesses of life for his own happiness with his own hands, without resorting to the sexton's spade that buried Jacob Marley.

But they didn't devote the whole evening to music. After a while they played at forfeits; for it is good to be children 5 sometimes, and never better than at Christmas, when its mighty founder was a child himself. Stop! There was first a game at blindman's buff. Of course there was. And I no more believe Topper was really blind than I believe he had eyes in his boots. My opinion is that it was a done thing between him and Scrooge's 10 nephew, and that the Ghost of Christmas Present knew it. The way he went after that plump sister in the lace tucker was an outrage on the credulity of human nature. Knocking down the fire irons, tumbling over the chairs, bumping up against the piano, smothering himself among the curtains; wherever she went, 15 there went he. He always knew where the plump sister was. He wouldn't catch anybody else. If you had fallen up against him, as some of them did, and stood there, he would leave made a feint of endeavoring to seize you, which would have been an affront to your understanding, and would instantly have sidled off in the 20 direction of the plump sister. She often cried out that it wasn't fair, and it really was not. But when at last he caught her; when, in spite of all her silken rustlings, and her rapid flutterings past him, he got her into a corner whence there was no escape, then his conduct was the most execrable. For his pretending 25 not to know her, his pretending that it was necessary to touch her headdress, and further to assure himself of her identity by pressing a certain ring upon her finger and a certain chain about her neck, was vile, monstrous! No doubt she told him her opinion of it, when, another blind man being in office, they were so very 30 confidential together behind the curtains.

Scrooge's niece was not one of the blindman's buff party, but was made comfortable with a large chair and a footstool, in a snug corner, where the ghost and Scrooge were close behind her. But she joined in the forfeits and loved her love to admiration 35 with all the letters of the alphabet. Likewise at the game of

How, When, and Where, she was very great, and to the secret
joy of Scrooge's nephew, beat her sisters hollow; though they
were sharp girls, too, as Topper could have told you. There
might have been twenty people there, young and old, but they
5 all played, and so did Scrooge; for, wholly forgetting, in the
interest he had in what was going on, that his voice made no
sound in their ears, he sometimes came out with his guess quite
loud, and very often guessed quite right, too, for the sharpest
needle, best Whitechapel, warranted not to cut in the eye, was
10 not sharper than Scrooge, blunt as he took it in his head to be.

The ghost was greatly pleased to find him in this mood and
looked upon him with such favor that he begged like a boy to
be allowed to stay until the guests departed. But this the spirit
said could not be done.

15 "Here is a new game," said Scrooge. "One half-hour, spirit,
only one!"

It was a game called Yes and No, where Scrooge's nephew
had to think of something and the rest must find out what, he
only answering to their questions yes or no, as the case was.
20 The brisk fire of questioning to which he was exposed elicited
from him that he was thinking of an animal, a live animal, rather
a disagreeable animal, a savage animal, an animal that growled
and grunted sometimes, and talked sometimes, and lived in
London, and walked about the streets, and wasn't made a show
25 of, and wasn't led by anybody, and didn't live in a menagerie,
and was never killed in a market, and was not a horse, or an ass,
or a cow, or a bull, or a tiger, or a dog, or a pig, or a cat, or a bear.
At every fresh question that was put to him, this nephew burst
into a fresh roar of laughter, and was so inexpressibly tickled
30 that he was obliged to get up off the sofa and stamp. At last the
plump sister, falling into a similar state, cried out:

"I have found it out! I know what it is, Fred! I know what
it is!"

"What is it?" cried Fred.

35     "It's your Uncle Scro-o-o-o-oge!"

Which it certainly was. Admiration was the universal sentiment, though some objected that the reply to "Is it a bear?"
ought to have been "Yes," inasmuch as an answer in the negative
was sufficient to have diverted their thoughts from Mr. Scrooge,
5 supposing they had ever had any tendency that way.

"He has given us plenty of merriment, I am sure," said Fred,
"and it would be ungrateful not to drink his health. Here is a
glass of mulled wine ready to our hand at the moment, and I
say, 'Uncle Scrooge!'"

10      "Well! Uncle Scrooge!" they cried.

"A Merry Christmas and a Happy New Year to the old man,
whatever he is!" said Scrooge's nephew. "He wouldn't take it
from me, but may he have it, nevertheless. Uncle Scrooge!"

Uncle Scrooge had imperceptibly become so gay and light of
15 heart that he would have pledged the unconscious company in
return and thanked them in an inaudible speech, if the ghost had
given him time. But the whole scene passed off in the breath of
the last word spoken by his nephew, and he and the Spirit were
again upon their travels.

20      Much they saw, and far they went, and many homes they
visited, but always with a happy end. The spirit stood beside
sick beds, and they were cheerful; on foreign lands, and they
were close at home; by struggling men, and they were patient
in their greater hope; by poverty, and it was rich. In almshouse,
25 hospital, and jail, in misery's every refuge, where vain man
in his little brief authority had not made fast the door and
barred the spirit out, he left his blessing and taught Scrooge
his precepts.

It was a long night, if it were only a night; but Scrooge had
30 his doubts of this, because the Christmas holidays appeared
to be condensed into the space of time they passed together.
It was strange, too, that while Scrooge remained unaltered in
his outward form, the ghost grew older, clearly older. Scrooge
had observed this change, but never spoke of it until they left
35 a children's Twelfth-night party, when, looking at the spirit as

they stood together in an open place, he noticed that its hair was gray.

"Are spirits' lives so short?" asked Scrooge.

"My life upon this globe is very brief," replied the ghost. "It
5 ends tonight."

"Tonight!" cried Scrooge.

"Tonight at midnight. Hark! The time is drawing near."

The chimes were ringing the three quarters past eleven at that moment.

10 "Forgive me if I am not justified in what I ask," said Scrooge, looking intently at the spirit's robe, "but I see something strange, and not belonging to yourself, protruding from your skirts. Is it a foot or a claw?"

"It might be a claw, for the flesh there is upon it," was the
15 spirit's sorrowful reply. "Look here."

From the foldings of its robe it brought two children, wretched, abject, frightful, hideous, miserable. They knelt down at its feet, and clung upon the outside of its garment.

"Oh, Man! look here. Look, look, down here!" exclaimed
20 the ghost.

They were a boy and girl. Yellow, meager, ragged, scowling, wolfish; but prostrate, too, in their humility. Where graceful youth should have filled their features out and touched them with its freshest tints, a stale and shriveled hand, like that of
25 age, had pinched and twisted them and pulled them into shreds. Where angels might have sat enthroned, devils lurked and glared out menacing. No change, no degradation, no perversion of humanity, in any grade, through all the mysteries of wonderful creation, has monsters half so horrible and dread.

30 Scrooge started back, appalled. Having them shown to him in this way, he tried to say they were fine children, but the words choked themselves, rather than be parties to a lie of such enormous magnitude.

"Spirit! are they yours?" Scrooge could say no more.

35 "They are Man's," said the spirit, looking down upon them.

"And they cling to me, appealing from their fathers. This boy is Ignorance. This girl is Want. Beware them both, and all of their degree, but most of all beware this boy, for on his brow I see written that which is doom, unless the writing be erased.
5 Deny it!" cried the spirit, stretching out its hand toward the city. "Slander those who tell it ye! Admit it for your factious purposes and make it worse! And bide the end!"

"Have they no refuge or resource?" cried Scrooge.

"Are there no prisons?" said the spirit, turning on him for the
10 last time with his own words. "Are there no workhouses?"

The bell struck twelve.

Scrooge looked about him for the ghost, and saw it not. As the last stroke ceased to vibrate, he remembered the prediction of old Jacob Marley, and lifting up his eyes, beheld a solemn
15 phantom, draped and hooded, coming, like a mist along the ground, toward him.

### *Stave Four*

#### The Last of the Spirits

The phantom slowly, gravely, silently approached. When it came near him, Scrooge bent down upon his knee; for in the very air through which this spirit moved, it seemed to scatter
20 gloom and mystery.

It was shrouded in a deep black garment, which concealed its head, its face, its form, and left nothing of it visible save one outstretched hand. But for this it would have been difficult to detach its figure from the night, and separate it from the
25 darkness by which it was surrounded.

He felt that it was tall and stately, when it came beside him, and that its mysterious presence filled him with a solemn dread. He knew no more, for the spirit neither spoke nor moved.

"I am in the presence of the Ghost of Christmas Yet To
30 Come?" said Scrooge.

The spirit answered not, but pointed downward with its hand.

"You are about to show me shadows of the things that have not happened, but will happen in the time before us," Scrooge pursued. "Is that so, Spirit?"

5 The upper portion of the garment was contracted for an instant in its folds, as if the spirit had inclined its head. That was the only answer he received.

Although well used to ghostly company by this time, Scrooge feared the silent shape so much that his legs trembled beneath him, and he found that he could hardly stand when he prepared

10 to follow it. The spirit paused a moment, as observing his condition and giving him time to recover.

But Scrooge was all the worse for this. It thrilled him with a vague, uncertain horror, to know that behind the dusky shroud there were ghostly eyes intently fixed upon him, while he,

15 though he stretched his own to the utmost, could see nothing but a spectral hand and one great heap of black.

"Ghost of the Future!" he exclaimed. "I fear you more than any specter I have seen. But, as I know your purpose is to do me good, and as I hope to live to be another man from what I was,

20 I am prepared to bear you company and do it with a thankful heart. Will you not speak to me?"

It gave him no reply. The hand was pointed straight before them.

"Lead on!" said Scrooge. "Lead on! The night is waning fast,

25 and it is precious time to me, I know. Lead on, Spirit!"

The phantom moved away as it had come toward him. Scrooge followed in the shadow of its dress, which bore him up, he thought, and carried him along.

They scarcely seemed to enter the city, for the city rather

30 seemed to spring up about them and encompass them of its own act. But there they were, in the heart of it; on 'Change, amongst the merchants, who hurried up and down, and chinked the money in their pockets, and conversed in groups, and looked at their watches, and trifled thoughtfully with their great gold

35 seals, and so forth, as Scrooge had seen them often.

The spirit stopped beside one little knot of business men. Observing that the hand was pointed to them, Scrooge advanced to listen to their talk.

"No," said a great fat man with a monstrous chin, "I don't
5 know much about it, either way. I only know he's dead."

"When did he die?" inquired another.

"Last night, I believe."

"Why, what was the matter with him?" asked a third, taking a vast quantity of snuff out of a very large snuffbox. "I thought
10 he'd never die."

"God knows," said the first, with a yawn.

"What has he done with his money?" asked a red-faced gentleman with a pendulous excrescence on the end of his nose that shook like the gills of a turkey cock.
15 "I haven't heard," said the man with the large chin, yawning again. "Left it to his company, perhaps. He hasn't left it to me. That's all I know."

This pleasantry was received with a general laugh.

"It's likely to be a very cheap funeral," said the same speaker,
20 "for upon my life I don't know of anybody to go to it. Suppose we make up a party and volunteer?"

"I don't mind going if a lunch is provided," observed the gentleman with the excrescence on his nose. "But I must be fed if I make one."
25 Another laugh.

"Well, I am the most disinterested among you, after all," said the first speaker, "for I never wear black gloves, and I never eat lunch. But I'll offer to go, if anybody else will. When I come to think of it, I'm not at all sure that I wasn't his most
30 particular friend, for we used to stop and speak whenever we met. Bye-bye!"

Speakers and listeners strolled away and mixed with other groups. Scrooge knew the men and looked toward the spirit for an explanation.
35 The phantom glided on into a street. Its finger pointed to

two persons meeting.  Scrooge listened again thinking that the explanation might lie here.

He knew these men, also, perfectly.  They were men of business, very wealthy and of great importance.  He had made a
5 point of always standing well in their esteem, in a business point of view, that is, strictly in a business point of view.

"How are you?" said one.

"How are you?" returned the other.

"Well!" said the first.  "Old Scratch has got his own at last,
10 hey?"

"So I am told," returned the second.  "Cold, isn't it?"

"Seasonable for Christmas time.  You're not a skater, I suppose?"

"No.  No.  Something else to think of.  Good morning!"

15     Not another word.  That was their greeting, their conversation, and their parting.

Scrooge was at first inclined to be surprised that the spirit should attach importance to conversations apparently so trivial, but feeling assured that they must have some hidden purpose,
20 he set himself to consider what it was likely to be.  They could scarcely be supposed to have any bearing on the death of Jacob, his old partner, for that was past, and this ghost's province was the future.  Nor could he think of anyone immediately connected with himself, to whom he could apply them.  But nothing doubting
25 that to whomsoever they applied they had some latent moral for his own improvement, he resolved to treasure up every word he heard and everything he saw, and especially to observe the shadow of himself when it appeared.  For he had an expectation that the conduct of his future self would give him the clue he missed and
30 would render the solution of these riddles easy.

He looked about in that very place for his own image; but another man stood in his accustomed corner, and though the clock pointed to his usual time of day for being there, he saw no likeness of himself among the multitudes that poured in through
35 the porch.  It gave him little surprise, however, for he had been

revolving in his mind a change of life, and thought and hoped he saw his new-born resolutions carried out in this.

Quiet and dark beside him stood the phantom, with its outstretched hand. When he aroused himself from his thoughtful quest, he fancied from the turn of the hand and its situation in reference to himself that the unseen eyes were looking at him keenly. It made him shudder and feel very cold.

They left the busy scene, and went into an obscure part of the town where Scrooge had never penetrated before, although he recognized its situation and its bad repute. The ways were foul and narrow; the shops and houses wretched; the people half-naked, drunken, slipshod, ugly. Alleys and archways, like so many cesspools, disgorged their offenses of smell and dirt and life upon the straggling streets; and the whole quarter reeked with crime, with filth, and misery.

Far in this den of infamous resort there was a low-browed, beetling shop, below a penthouse roof, where iron, old rags, bottles, bones, and greasy offal were bought. Upon the floor within were piled up heaps of rusty keys, nails, chains, hinges, files, scales, weights, and refuse iron of all kinds. Secrets that few would like to scrutinize were bred and hidden in mountains of unseemly rags, masses of corrupt fat, and sepulchers of bones. Sitting in among the wares he dealt in, by a charcoal stove made of old bricks, was a gray-haired rascal, nearly seventy years of age, who had screened himself from the cold air without by a frowzy curtaining of miscellaneous tatters hung upon a line and smoked his pipe in all the luxury of calm retirement.

Scrooge and the phantom came into the presence of this man just as a woman with a heavy bundle slunk into the shop. But she had scarcely entered, when another woman, similarly laden, came in too; and she was closely followed by a man in faded black, who was no less startled by the sight of them than they had been upon the recognition of each other. After a short period of blank astonishment, in which the old man with the pipe had joined them, they all three burst into a laugh.

"Let the charwoman alone to be the first!" cried she who had entered first. "Let the laundress alone to be the second, and let the undertaker's man alone to be the third. Look here, old Joe, here's a chance! If we haven't all three met here without
5 meaning it!"

"You couldn't have met in a better place," said old Joe, removing his pipe from his mouth. "Come into the parlor. You were made free of it long ago, you know; and the other two an't strangers. Stop till I shut the door of the shop. Ah! How it
10 skreeks! There an't such a rusty bit of metal in the place as its own hinges, I believe; and I'm sure there's no such old bones here as mine. Ha, ha! We're all suitable to our calling; we're well matched. Come into the parlor. Come into the parlor."

The parlor was the space behind the screen of rags. The
15 old man raked the fire together with an old stair rod, and having trimmed his smoky lamp (for it was night) with the stem of his pipe, put it in his mouth again.

While he did this, the woman who had already spoken, threw her bundle on the floor and sat down in a flaunting manner on a
20 stool, crossing her elbows on her knees and looking with a bold defiance at the other two.

"What odds then! What odds, Mrs. Dilber?" said the woman. "Every person has a right to take care of themselves. He always did!"

25     "That's true, indeed!" said the laundress. "No man more so."

"Why, then, don't stand staring as if you was afraid, woman! Who's the wiser? We're not going to pick holes in each other's coats, I suppose?"

30     "No, indeed!" said Mrs. Dilber and the man together. "We should hope not."

"Very well, then!" cried the woman. "That's enough. Who's the worse for the loss of a few things like these? Not a dead man, I suppose."

35     "No, indeed," said Mrs. Dilber, laughing.

"If he wanted to keep 'em after he was dead, a wicked old screw," pursued the woman, "why wasn't he natural in his lifetime? If he had been, he'd have had somebody to look after him when he was struck with death, instead of lying gasping out

5 his last there, alone by himself."

"It's the truest word that was ever spoke," said Mrs. Dilber. "It's a judgment on him."

"I wish it was a little heavier one," replied the woman, "and it should have been, you may depend upon it, if I could have

10 laid my hands on anything else. Open that bundle, old Joe, and let me know the value of it. Speak out plain. I'm not afraid to be the first, nor afraid for them to see it. We knew pretty well that we were helping ourselves before we met here, I believe. It's no sin. Open the bundle, Joe."

15 But the gallantry of her friends would not allow of this; and the man in faded black, mounting the breach first, produced his plunder. It was not extensive. A seal or two, a pencil case, a pair of sleeve buttons, and a brooch of no great value were all. They were severally examined and appraised by Old Joe,

20 who chalked the sums he was disposed to give for each upon the wall, and added them up into a total when he found there was nothing more to come.

"That's your account," said Joe, "and I wouldn't give another sixpence, if I was to be boiled for not doing it. Who's next?"

25 Mrs. Dilber was next. Sheets and towels, a little wearing apparel, two old-fashioned silver teaspoons, a pair of sugar tongs, and a few boots. Her account was stated on the wall in the same manner.

"I always give too much to ladies. It's a weakness of mine,

30 and that's the way I ruin myself," said old Joe. "That's your account. If you asked me for another penny and made it an open question, I'd repent of being so liberal and knock off half a crown."

"And now undo my bundle, Joe," said the first woman.

35 Joe went down on his knees for the greater convenience of

opening it, and having unfastened a great many knots, dragged
out a large and heavy roll of some dark stuff.

"What do you call this?" said Joe. "Bed curtains!"

"Ah!" returned the woman, laughing and leaning forward on
5 her crossed arms. "Bed curtains!"

"You don't mean to say you took 'em down, rings and all, with
him lying there?" said Joe.

"Yes, I do," replied the woman. "Why not?"

"You were born to make your fortune," said Joe, "and you'll
10 certainly do it."

"I certainly shan't hold my hand when I can get anything in
it by reaching it out, for the sake of such a man as he was, I
promise you, Joe," returned the woman coolly. "Don't drop that
oil upon the blankets, now."

15     "His blankets?" asked Joe.

"Whose else's do you think?" replied the woman. "He isn't
likely to take cold without 'em, I dare say."

"I hope he didn't die of anything catching? Eh?" said Old
Joe, stopping in his work and looking up.

20     "Don't you be afraid of that," returned the woman. "I ain't
so fond of his company that I'd loiter about him for such things,
if he did. Ah! you may look through that shirt till your eyes
ache, but you won't find a hole in it, nor a threadbare place. It's
the best he had, and a fine one, too. They'd have wasted it if
25 it hadn't been for me."

"What do you call wasting of it?" asked Old Joe.

"Putting it on him to be buried in, to be sure," replied the
woman with a laugh. "Somebody was fool enough to do it,
but I took it off again. If calico ain't good enough for such
30 a purpose, it isn't good enough for anything. It's quite as
becoming to the body. He can't look uglier than he did in
that one."

Scrooge listened to this dialogue in horror. As they sat
grouped about their spoil in the scanty light afforded by the
35 old man's lamp, he viewed them with a detestation and disgust

which could hardly have been greater, though they had been obscene demons marketing the corpse itself.

"Ha, ha!" laughed the same woman when Old Joe, producing a flannel bag with money in it, told out their several gains upon
5 the ground. "This is the end of it, you see! He frightened everyone away from him when he was alive to profit us when he was dead! Ha, ha, ha!"

"Spirit!" said Scrooge, shuddering from head to foot. "I see, I see. The case of this unhappy man might be my own. My life
10 tends that way, now. Merciful Heaven, what is this!"

He recoiled in terror, for the scene had changed, and now he almost touched a bed, a bare, uncurtained bed on which, beneath a ragged sheet, there lay a something covered up, which, though it was dumb, announced itself in awful language.

15 The room was very dark, too dark to be observed with any accuracy, though Scrooge glanced round it in obedience to a secret impulse, anxious to know what kind of room it was. A pale light, rising in the outer air, fell straight upon the bed, and on it, plundered and bereft, unwatched, unwept, uncared for,
20 was the body of this man.

Scrooge glanced toward the phantom. Its steady hand was pointed to the head. The cover was so carelessly adjusted that the slightest raising of it, the motion of a finger upon Scrooge's part, would have disclosed the face. He thought of it, felt how
25 easy it would be to do, and longed to do it, but had no more power to withdraw the veil than to dismiss the spectre at his side.

O, cold, cold, rigid, dreadful Death, set up thine altar here, and dress it with such terrors as thou hast at thy command; for
30 this is thy dominion! But of the loved, revered, and honored head, thou canst not turn one hair to thy dread purposes or make one feature odious. It is not that the hand is heavy and will fall down when released; it is not that the heart and pulse are still; but that the hand was open, generous, and true; the
35 heart brave, warm, and tender; and the pulse a man's. Strike,

Shadow, strike! And see his good deeds springing from the wound to sow the world with life immortal!

No voice pronounced these words in Scrooge's ears, and yet he heard them when he looked upon the bed. He thought, if
5 this man could be raised up now, what would be his foremost thoughts? Avarice, hard dealing, griping cares? They have brought him to a rich end, truly!

He lay in the dark, empty house, with not a man, a woman, or a child to say that he was kind to me in this or that, and
10 for the memory of one kind word I will be kind to him. A cat was tearing at the door, and there was a sound of gnawing rats beneath the hearthstone. What they wanted in the room of death, and why they were so restless and disturbed, Scrooge did not dare to think.

15 "Spirit!" he said, "this is a fearful place. In leaving it, I shall not leave its lesson, trust me. Let us go!"

Still the ghost pointed with an unmoved finger to the head.

"I understand you," Scrooge returned, "and I would do it, if I could. But I have not the power, Spirit. I have not the
20 power."

Again it seemed to look upon him.

"If there is any person in the town who feels emotion caused by this man's death," said Scrooge quite agonized, "show that person to me, Spirit, I beseech you!"

25 The phantom spread its dark robe before him for a moment, like a wing, and withdrawing it, revealed a room by daylight, where a mother and her children were.

She was expecting someone, and with anxious eagerness; for she walked up and down the room; started at every sound;
30 looked out from the window; glanced at the clock; tried, but in vain, to work with her needle; and could hardly bear the voices of the children in their play.

At length the long expected knock was heard. She hurried to the door and met her husband, a man whose face was careworn
35 and depressed, though he was young. There was a remarkable

expression in it now, a kind of serious delight of which he felt ashamed and which he struggled to repress.

He sat down to the dinner that had been hoarding for him by the fire, and when she asked him faintly what news (which
5 was not until after a long silence), he appeared embarrassed how to answer.

"Is it good," she said, "or bad?"—to help him.

"Bad," he answered.

"We are quite ruined?"

10 "No. There is hope yet, Caroline."

"If he relents," she said, amazed, "there is! Nothing is past hope, if such a miracle has happened."

"He is past relenting," said her husband. "He is dead."

She was a mild and patient creature if her face spoke truth,
15 but she was thankful in her soul to hear it, and she said so, with clasped hands. She prayed forgiveness the next moment and was sorry, but the first was the emotion of the heart.

"What the half-drunken woman whom I told you of last night said to me when I tried to see him and obtain a week's delay,
20 and what I thought was a mere excuse to avoid me turns out to have been quite true. He was not only very ill, but dying, then."

"To whom will our debt be transferred?"

"I don't know. But before that time we shall be ready with
25 the money, and even though we were not, it would be bad fortune indeed to find so merciless a creditor in his successor. We may sleep tonight with light hearts, Caroline!"

Yes. Soften it as they would, their hearts were lighter. The children's faces, hushed and clustered round to hear what they
30 so little understood, were brighter, and it was a happier house for this man's death! The only emotion that the ghost could show him, caused by the event, was one of pleasure.

"Let me see some tenderness connected with a death," said Scrooge, "or that dark chamber, Spirit, which we left just now,
35 will be forever present to me."

The ghost conducted him through several streets familiar to his feet, and as they went along, Scrooge looked here and there to find himself, but nowhere was he to be seen. They entered poor Bob Cratchit's house, the dwelling he had visited before, and
5 found the mother and the children seated round the fire.

Quiet. Very quiet. The noisy little Cratchits were as still as statues in one corner and sat looking up at Peter, who had a book before him. The mother and her daughters were engaged in sewing. But surely they were very quiet!

10     "'And He took a child, and set him in the midst of them.'"

Where had Scrooge heard those words? He had not dreamed them. The boy must have read them out, as he and the spirit crossed the threshold. Why did he not go on?

The mother laid her work upon the table and put her hand
15 up to her face.

"The color hurts my eyes," she said.

The color? Ah, poor Tiny Tim!

"They're better now again," said Cratchit's wife. "It makes them weak by candlelight, and I wouldn't show weak eyes to
20 your father when he comes home, for the world. It must be near his time."

"Past it, rather," Peter answered, shutting up his book. "But I think he's walked a little slower than he used, these few last evenings, Mother."

25     They were very quiet again. At last she said, and in a steady, cheerful voice that only faltered once:

"I have known him walk with—I have known him walk with Tiny Tim upon his shoulder, very fast indeed."

"And so have I," cried Peter. "Often."

30     "And so have I," exclaimed another. So had all.

"But he was so very light to carry," she resumed, intent upon her work, "and his father loved him so that it was no trouble—no trouble. And there is your father at the door!"

She hurried out to meet him, and little Bob in his com-
35 forter—he had need of it, poor fellow—came in. His tea was

ready for him on the hob, and they all tried who should help him to it most. Then the two young Cratchits got upon his knees and laid, each child, a little cheek against his face, as if they said, "Don't mind it Father. Don't be grieved!"

5 Bob was very cheerful with them and spoke pleasantly to all the family. He looked at the work upon the table and praised the industry and speed of Mrs. Cratchit and the girls. They would be done long before Sunday, he said.

"Sunday! You went today, then, Robert?" said his wife.

10 "Yes, my dear," returned Bob. "I wish you could have gone. It would have done you good to see how green a place it is. But you'll see it often. I promised him that I would walk there on a Sunday. My little, little child!" cried Bob. "My little child!"

He broke down all at once. He couldn't help it. If he could 15 have helped it, he and his child would have been farther apart perhaps than they were.

He left the room and went upstairs into the room above, which was lighted cheerfully and hung with Christmas. There was a chair set close beside the child, and there were signs of 20 someone having been there lately. Poor Bob sat down in it, and when he had thought a little and composed himself, he kissed the little face. He was reconciled to what had happened and went down again quite happy.

They drew about the fire and talked; the girls and mother 25 working still. Bob told them of the extraordinary kindness of Mr. Scrooge's nephew, whom he had scarcely seen but once, and who, meeting him in the street that day and seeing that he looked a little—"just a little down, you know," said Bob, inquired what had happened to distress him. "On which," said Bob, "for 30 he is the pleasantest spoken gentleman you ever heard, I told him. 'I am heartily sorry for it, Mr. Cratchit,' he said, 'and heartily sorry for your good wife.' By the bye, how he ever knew *that*, I don't know."

"Knew what, my dear?"

35 "Why, that you were a good wife," replied Bob.

"Everybody knows that!" said Peter.

"Very well observed, my boy!" cried Bob. "I hope they
do. 'Heartily sorry,' he said, 'for your good wife. If I can
be of service to you in any way,' he said, giving me his card,
5 'that's where I live. Pray come to me.' Now, it wasn't," cried
Bob, "for the sake of anything he might be able to do for us
so much as for his kind way that this was quite delightful.
It really seemed as if he had known our Tiny Tim and felt
with us."

10    "I'm sure he's a good soul!" said Mrs. Cratchit.

"You would be surer of it, my dear," returned Bob, "if you
saw and spoke to him. I shouldn't be at all surprised, mark what
I say, if he got Peter a better situation."

"Only hear that, Peter," said Mrs. Cratchit.

15    "And then," cried one of the girls, "Peter will be keeping
company with someone and setting up for himself."

"Get along with you!" retorted Peter, grinning.

"It's just as likely as not," said Bob, "one of these days,
though there's plenty of time for that, my dear. But however
20 and whenever we part from one another, I am sure we shall
none of us forget poor Tiny Tim—shall we—or this first parting
that there was among us?"

"Never, Father!" cried they all.

"And I know," said Bob, "I know, my dears, that when we
25 recollect how patient and how mild he was—although he was a
little, little child—we shall not quarrel easily among ourselves
and forget poor Tiny Tim in doing it."

"No, never, Father!" they all cried again.

"I am very happy," said little Bob, "I am very happy!"

30    Mrs. Cratchit kissed him, his daughters kissed him, the two
young Cratchits kissed him, and Peter and himself shook hands.
Spirit of Tiny Tim, thy childish essence was from God!

"Spectre," said Scrooge, "something informs me that our
parting moment is at hand. I know it, but I know not how. Tell
35 me what man that was whom we saw lying dead?"

The Ghost of Christmas Yet To Come conveyed him as before—though at a different time, he thought; indeed, there seemed no order in these latter visions save that they were in the future—into the resorts of business men, but showed him
5 not himself. Indeed, the spirit did not stay for anything, but went straight on, as to the end just now desired, until besought by Scrooge to tarry for a moment.

"This court," said Scrooge, "through which we hurry now is where my place of occupation is, and has been for a length
10 of time. I see the house. Let me behold what I shall be in days to come!"

The spirit stopped; the hand was pointed elsewhere.

"The house is yonder," Scrooge exclaimed. "Why do you point away?"

15 The inexorable finger underwent no change.

Scrooge hastened to the window of his office and looked in. It was an office still, but not his. The furniture was not the same, and the figure in the chair was not himself. The phantom pointed as before.

20 He joined it once again, and wondering why and whither he had gone, accompanied it until they reached an iron gate. He paused to look around before entering.

A churchyard. Here, then, the wretched man whose name he had now to learn, lay underneath the ground. It was a worthy
25 place. Walled in by houses; overrun by grass and weeds, the growth of vegetation's death, not life; choked up with too much burying, fat with repleted appetite. A worthy place!

The spirit stood among the graves and pointed down to one. He advanced toward it trembling. The phantom was exactly
30 as it had been, but he dreaded that he saw new meaning in its solemn shape.

"Before I draw nearer to that stone to which you point," said Scrooge, "answer me one question. Are these the shadows of the things that will be, or are they shadows of things that
35 may be, only?"

Still the ghost pointed downward to the grave by which it stood.

"Men's courses will foreshadow certain ends, to which, if persevered in, they must lead," said Scrooge. "But if the courses
5 be departed from, the ends will change. Say it is thus with what you show me!"

The spirit was immovable as ever.

Scrooge crept toward it, trembling as he went, and following the finger, read upon the stone of the neglected grave his own
10 name: EBENEZER SCROOGE.

"Am I that man who lay upon the bed?" he cried upon his knees.

The finger pointed from the grave to him and back again.

"No, Spirit! Oh, no, no!"

15     The finger still was there.

"Spirit!" he cried, tight clutching at its robe. "Hear me! I am not the man I was. I will not be the man I must have been but for this intercourse. Why show me this if I am past all hope!"

For the first time the hand appeared to shake.

20     "Good Spirit," he pursued, as down upon the ground he fell before it, "your nature intercedes for me and pities me. Assure me that I yet may change these shadows you have shown me by an altered life!"

The kind hand trembled.

25     "I will honor Christmas in my heart and try to keep it all the year. I will live in the past, the present, and the future. The spirits of all three shall strive within me. I will not shut out the lessons that they teach. Oh, tell me I may sponge away the writing on this stone!"

30     In his agony, he caught the spectral hand. It sought to free itself, but he was strong in his entreaty and detained it. The spirit, stronger yet, repulsed him.

Holding up his hands in one last prayer to have his fate reversed, he saw an alteration in the phantom's hood and dress.
35 It shrank, collapsed, and dwindled down to a bedpost.

## Stave Five

### The End of It

Yes! and the bedpost was his own. The bed was his own, the room was his own. Best and happiest of all, the time before him was his own to make amends in!

"I will live in the past, the present, and the future!" Scrooge
5 repeated, as he scrambled out of bed. "The spirits of all three shall strive within me. Oh, Jacob Marley! Heaven and the Christmas time be praised for this! I say it on my knees, old Jacob, on my knees!"

He was so fluttered and so glowing with his good intentions
10 that his broken voice would scarcely answer to his call. He had been sobbing violently in his conflict with the spirit, and his face was wet with tears.

"They are not torn down," cried Scrooge, folding one of his bed curtains in his arms, "they are not torn down, rings and all.
15 They are here; I am here; the shadows of the things that would have been may be dispelled. They will be. I know they will!"

His hands were busy with his garments all this time, turning them inside out, putting them on upside down, tearing them, mislaying them, making them parties to every kind of
20 extravagance.

"I don't know what to do!" cried Scrooge, laughing and crying in the same breath and making a perfect Laocoön of himself with his stockings. "I am as light as a feather; I am as happy as an angel; I am as merry as a schoolboy; I am as giddy as a drunken
25 man. A Merry Christmas to everybody! A Happy New Year to all the world. Hallo here! Whoop! Hallo!"

He had frisked into the sitting room and was now standing there perfectly winded.

"There's the saucepan that the gruel was in!" cried Scrooge,
30 starting off again and frisking round the fireplace. "There's the door by which the ghost of Jacob Marley entered! There's the

corner where the Ghost of Christmas Present sat! There's the window where I saw the wandering spirits! It's all right; it's all true; it all happened. Ha, ha, ha!"

Really, for a man who had been out of practice for so many 5 years, it was a splendid laugh, a most illustrious laugh. The father of a long, long line of brilliant laughs!

"I don't know what day of the month it is!" said Scrooge. "I don't know how long I've been among the spirits. I don't know anything. I'm quite a baby. Never mind. I don't care. I'd rather 10 be a baby. Hallo! Whoop! Hallo here!"

He was checked in his transports by the churches ringing out the lustiest peals he had ever heard. Clash, clang, hammer, ding, dong, bell. Bell, dong, ding, hammer, clang, clash! Oh, glorious, glorious!

15        Running to the window, he opened it and put out his head. No fog, no mist; clear, bright, jovial, stirring, cold; cold, piping for the blood to dance to; golden sunlight; heavenly sky; sweet fresh air; merry bells. Oh, glorious. Glorious!

"What's today!" cried Scrooge, calling downward to a boy in 20 Sunday clothes, who perhaps had loitered in to look about him.

"Eh?" returned the boy with all his might of wonder.

"What's today, my fine fellow?" said Scrooge.

"Today!" replied the boy. "Why, CHRISTMAS DAY."

"It's Christmas Day!" said Scrooge to himself. "I haven't 25 missed it. The spirits have done it all in one night. They can do anything they like. Of course they can. Of course they can. Hallo, my fine fellow?"

"Hallo!" returned the boy.

"Do you know the poulterer's, in the next street but one, at 30 the corner?" Scrooge inquired.

"I should hope I did," replied the lad.

"An intelligent boy!" said Scrooge. "A remarkable boy! Do you know whether they've sold the prize turkey that was hanging up there? Not the little prize turkey, the big one?"

35        "What, the one as big as me?" returned the boy.

"What a delightful boy!" said Scrooge. "It's a pleasure to talk to him. Yes, my buck!"

"It's hanging there now," replied the boy.

"Is it?" said Scrooge. "Go and buy it."

5  "Walk-ER!" exclaimed the boy.

"No, no," said Scrooge, "I am in earnest. Go and buy it and tell 'em to bring it here, that I may give them the direction where to take it. Come back with the man, and I'll give you a shilling. Come back with him in less than five minutes, and I'll
10 give you half a crown!"

The boy was off like a shot. He must have had a steady hand at a trigger who could have got a shot off half so fast.

"I'll send it to Bob Cratchit's!" whispered Scrooge, rubbing his hands and splitting with a laugh. "He shan't know who sends
15 it. It's twice the size of Tiny Tim. Joe Miller never made such a joke as sending it to Bob's will be!"

The hand in which he wrote the address was not a steady one, but write it he did, somehow, and went downstairs to open the street door, ready for the coming of the poulterer's man.
20 As he stood there, waiting his arrival, the knocker caught his eye.

"I shall love it as long as I live!" cried Scrooge, patting it with his hand. "I scarcely ever looked at it before. What an honest expression it has in its face! It's a wonderful knocker! Here's the
25 turkey. Hallo! Whoop! How are you? Merry Christmas!"

It *was* a turkey! He could never have stood upon his legs, that bird. He would have snapped 'em off short in a minute, like sticks of sealing wax.

"Why, it's impossible to carry that to Camden Town," said
30 Scrooge. "You must have a cab."

The chuckle with which he said this, and the chuckle with which he paid for the turkey, and the chuckle with which he paid for the cab, and the chuckle with which he recompensed the boy were only to be exceeded by the chuckle with which he sat down
35 breathless in his chair again and chuckled till he cried.

Shaving was not an easy task, for his hand continued to shake very much, and shaving requires attention, even when you don't dance while you are at it. But if he had cut the end of his nose off, he would have put a piece of sticking plaster over 5 it and been quite satisfied.

He dressed himself "all in his best," and at last got out into the streets. The people were by this time pouring forth, as he had seen them with the Ghost of Christmas Present, and walking with his hands behind him, Scrooge regarded everyone 10 with a delighted smile. He looked so irresistibly pleasant, in a word, that three or four good-humored fellows said, "Good morning, sir! A Merry Christmas to you!" And Scrooge said often, afterwards, that of all the blithe sounds he had ever heard, those were the blithest in his ears.

15 He had not gone far when coming on toward him he beheld the portly gentleman who had walked into his countinghouse the day before and said, "Scrooge and Marley's, I believe?" It sent a pang across his heart to think how this old gentleman would look upon him when they met, but he knew what path lay 20 straight before him, and he took it.

"My dear sir," said Scrooge, quickening his pace and taking the old gentleman by both his hands. "How do you do? I hope you succeeded yesterday. It was very kind of you. A Merry Christmas to you, sir!"

25 "Mr. Scrooge?"

"Yes," said Scrooge. "That is my name, and I fear it may not be pleasant to you. Allow me to ask your pardon. And will you have the goodness"—here Scrooge whispered in his ear.

"Lord bless me!" cried the gentleman, as if his breath were 30 gone. "My dear Mr. Scrooge, are you serious?"

"If you please," said Mr. Scrooge. "Not a farthing less. A great many back payments are included in it, I assure you. Will you do me that favor?"

"My dear sir," said the other, shaking hands with him, "I don't 35 know what to say to such munifi—"

"Don't say anything, please," retorted Scrooge. "Come and see me. Will you come and see me?"

"I will!" cried the old gentleman. And it was clear he meant to do it.

5 "Thank'ee," said Scrooge. "I am much obliged to you. I thank you fifty times. Bless you!"

He went to church, and walked about the streets, and watched the people hurrying to and fro, and patted children on the head, and questioned beggars, and looked down into 10 the kitchens of houses, and up to the windows; and found that everything could yield him pleasure. He had never dreamed that any walk—that anything—could give him so much happiness. In the afternoon, he turned his steps toward his nephew's house.

He passed the door a dozen times before he had the courage 15 to go up and knock. But he made a dash and did it.

"Is your master at home, my dear?" said Scrooge to the girl. Nice girl! Very.

"Yes, sir."

"Where is he, my love?" said Scrooge.

20 "He's in the dining room, sir, along with mistress. I'll show you upstairs, if you please."

"Thank'ee. He knows me," said Scrooge, with his hand already on the dining room lock. "I'll go in here, my dear."

He turned it gently and sidled his face in round the door. 25 They were looking at the table (which was spread out in great array), for these young housekeepers are always nervous on such points and like to see that everything is right.

"Fred!" said Scrooge.

Dear heart alive, how his niece by marriage started! Scrooge 30 had forgotten, for the moment, about her sitting in the corner with the footstool, or he wouldn't have done it on any account.

"Why, bless my soul!" cried Fred, "who's that?"

"It's I. Your Uncle Scrooge. I have come to dinner. Will you let me in, Fred?"

35 Let him in! It is a mercy he didn't shake his arm off. He was

at home in five minutes. Nothing could be heartier. His niece looked just the same. So did Topper when he came. So did the plump sister when she came. So did everyone when they came. Wonderful party, wonderful games, wonderful unanimity, 5 won-der-ful happiness!

But he was early at the office next morning. Oh, he was early there. If he could only be there first and catch Bob Cratchit coming late! That was the thing he had set his heart upon.

And he did it; yes, he did! The clock struck nine. No Bob. 10 A quarter past. No Bob. He was full eighteen minutes and a half behind his time. Scrooge sat with his door wide open that he might see him come into the tank.

His hat was off before he opened the door, his comforter too. He was on his stool in a jiffy, driving away with his pen as 15 if he were trying to overtake nine o'clock.

"Hallo!" growled Scrooge in his accustomed voice as near as he could feign it. "What do you mean by coming here at this time of day?"

"I am very sorry, sir," said Bob. "I am behind my time."

20   "You are?" repeated Scrooge. "Yes, I think you are. Step this way, sir, if you please."

"It's only once a year, sir," pleaded Bob, appearing from the tank. "It shall not be repeated. I was making rather merry yesterday, sir."

25   "Now, I'll tell you what, my friend," said Scrooge, "I am not going to stand this sort of thing any longer. And therefore," he continued, leaping from his stool and giving Bob such a dig in the waistcoat that he staggered back into the tank again, "and therefore I am about to raise your salary!"

30   Bob trembled and got a little nearer to the ruler. He had a momentary idea of knocking Scrooge down with it, holding him, and calling to the people in the court for help and a strait waistcoat.

"A Merry Christmas, Bob!" said Scrooge, with an earnestness 35 that could not be mistaken, as he clapped him on the back.

"A merrier Christmas, Bob, my good fellow, than I have given
you for many a year! I'll raise your salary and endeavor to assist
your struggling family, and we will discuss your affairs this very
afternoon over a Christmas bowl of smoking bishop, Bob! Make
5 up the fires and buy another coal scuttle before you dot another
i, Bob Cratchit!"

Scrooge was better than his word. He did it all, and infinitely
more, and to Tiny Tim, who did not die, he was a second father.
He became as good a friend, as good a master, and as good a man
10 as the good old city knew, or any other good old city, town, or
borough in the good old world. Some people laughed to see the
alteration in him, but he let them laugh and little heeded them;
for he was wise enough to know that nothing ever happened on
this globe, for good, at which some people did not have their
15 fill of laughter in the outset; and knowing that such as these
would be blind anyway, he thought it quite as well that they
should wrinkle up their eyes in grins as have the malady in less
attractive forms. His own heart laughed, and that was quite
enough for him.

20    He had no further intercourse with spirits, but lived upon
the Total Abstinence Principle, ever afterwards; and it was
always said of him that he knew how to keep Christmas well,
if any man alive possessed the knowledge. May that be truly
said of us, and all of us! And so, as Tiny Tim observed, God
25 Bless Us, Every One!

## NOTES AND QUESTIONS

**Biography.** Charles Dickens (1812-1870), the greatest writer of fiction
who had appeared since Scott, was born at Portsmouth, England. When
he was eleven years old, the Dickens family moved to London, and the
young boy began earning his own living. At nineteen he started his literary
career as a reporter on a newspaper. Then, under the pen name, "Boz," he
produced a series of sketches, "illustrative of everyday life and everyday
people." These sketches and *The Pickwick Papers*, a masterpiece of
humorous literature, which soon followed, made the author famous. From

this time until his death Dickens enjoyed a popularity greater than that of any other living writer. Some of Dickens's novels were a direct aid to social reform. Daniel Webster said that he had done more to improve the condition of the English poor than all the statesmen Great Britain had sent into Parliament. From a literary standpoint, *A Tale of Two Cities*, a story of the time of the French Revolution, is considered by many to be Dickens's best novel.

**Discussion.** Stave One. 1. What is the central idea or purpose of this story? 2. What does the author tell us about Scrooge's character at the beginning of the story? 3. If Dickens had not told us anything before, what would we learn of Scrooge from his conversation with his nephew? 4. What would we learn from the visit of the gentleman who asked for a contribution? 5. What does his treatment of the carol singer tell us? 6. What does his treatment of his clerk tell us? 7. Has the author any reason for making the weather so unpleasant? 8. What reason do you think the author had for making Scrooge's rooms so gloomy? 9. In what respect do we feel that Scrooge needs to change? 10. What is the author's plan for reforming him? 11. Find in the glossary the meaning of: stave; 'Change; palpable; Bedlam; Poor Law; Saint Dunstan; corporation; Belshazzar; ward. 12. *Pronounce:* ironmongery; simile; homage; Parliament; inexplicable. (For "Phrases" see p. 236.)

**Class Reading.** Description of Scrooge, page 152, line 25, to page 153, line 22; the nephew defending Christmas, page 155, lines 15 to 28; the clerk leaving the countinghouse, page 159, line 25, to page 160, line 15; description of Marley, page 163, line 35, to page 164, line 8; Marley and Scrooge, page 164, line 17, to page 169, line 29.

**Discussion**. Stave Two. 1. Describe the Ghost of Christmas Past. 2. What did the ghost say was its purpose in visiting Scrooge? 3. What did it first show Scrooge? 4. How soon did Scrooge show that he was affected by what he saw? 5. What stories was the boy, Ebenezer Scrooge, reading? How do you know? 6. Of what did this vision of himself when a boy make Scrooge think? Of whom did the vision of his little sister remind Scrooge? 7. How did the vision of the happy Christmas Eve at Mr. Fezziwig's affect Scrooge? Of whom did this make him think? 8. Which of all the "shadows" made him feel most keenly what he had missed in life? 9. Find in the glossary the meaning of: ferret; visitation; supplication; remonstrated; sweep; apprenticed; aspiration; dowerless; pinioned; brigand. 10. *Pronounce:* opaque; vestige; jocund; Genii; gainsay; corroborated. (For "Phrases" see p. 236.)

**Class Reading.** Description of the spirit, page 172, line 20; to page 173, line 13; the Fezziwigs, page 179, line 27, to page 182, line 18: Scrooge and his former sweetheart, page 183, line 20, to page 185, line 17.

**Discussion.** Stave Three. 1. Describe the Ghost of Christmas Present. 2. Describe its throne. 3. Where did it take Scrooge; where did they stay longest? 4. Which of these visits did you enjoy most? Why? 5. What feelings were awakened in Scrooge by these sights? 6. What effect did the spirit have upon those whom it visited? 7. Select passages that made you smile as you read them. 8. Give instances which show that the Cratchits were a contented family and pleased with each other. 9. Why did the spirit show Ignorance and Want to Scrooge? 10. Find in the glossary the meaning of: intervention; brawn; twelfth-cakes; intricate; broad-girthed; squab; "bob"; threadbare; steeped; copper; cant; baleful; furze; capital; catch. 11. *Pronounce:* manslaughter; predicament; lolling; bedight; bow; elicited; almshouse. (For "Phrases" see page 236.)

**Class Reading.** The Cratchits, page 195, line 14, to page 201, line 21; at the home of Scrooge's nephew, page 204, line 5, to page 209, line 19.

**Discussion.** Stave Four. 1. Describe the last of the spirits. 2. What did this spirit show Scrooge? 3. What was its "hidden purpose" in having Scrooge overhear the conversation of former business associates? 4. What was the effect upon Scrooge of seeing people carry away his goods and of listening to the dialogue of Joe, the laundress, the charwoman, and the undertaker's man? 5. What did the visit to Caroline's home and to Bob Cratchit's show Scrooge? 6. When the spirit took him to the churchyard, why was Scrooge so anxious to know whether what he had seen were things that *will* be or that *may* be? 7. Did he receive any answer to his pleading? 8. What promises did he make? 9. Did Scrooge need the visit of this last spirit? Why? 10. Find in the glossary the meaning of: charwoman; repleted. 11. *Pronounce:* gills; disgorged; brooch; inexorable. (For "Phrases" see p. 236.)

**Class Reading.** Thoughts on death, page 219, line 28, to page 220, line 2; in the churchyard, page 225, line 23, to page 226, line 35.

**Discussion.** Stave Five. 1. How did Scrooge know he was alive? 2. What tells you that he had really suffered in the night? 3. How did he express his joy at being alive? 4. Who received his first attention? 5. How do you account for the "wonderful happiness" at the nephew's? 6. How did Scrooge show that his repentance was real? 7. Turn again to the picture on page 96. Why is this picture appropriate in connection with the lesson that Scrooge learned? 8. What did you learn in "Literature and Life," on pages 18 and 19 about literature that *interprets* life? What does this story interpret? 9. Find in the glossary the meaning of: Laocoön; piping; malady. 10. *Pronounce:* unanimity; feign; borough; abstinence.

## Phrases for Study

where to have him, **153**, 5

"came down" handsomely, **153**, 7

what the knowing ones, **153** 21

brewing on a large scale, **154**, 1

United States' security, **171**, 16

nothing loath, **178**, 21

celebrated herd, **185**, 31

gentleman of the free, **188**, 23

a move or two, **188**, 24

the time of day, **188**, 25

half-a-quartern of, **198**, 22

of high mark, **201**, 13

loved her love, **207**, 34

be parties to, **210**, 32

what odds, **216**, 22

mounting the breach, **217**, 16

sow the world with, **220**, 2

merciless a creditor, **221**, 26

ends will change, **226**, 5

Total Abstinence Principle, **233**, 21

**Class Reading.** The next morning, page 227, line 1, to page 230, line 5; Scrooge and the portly gentleman, page 230, line 15, to page 231, line 6; Scrooge and his nephew, page 231, line 13, to page 232, line 5; Scrooge and Bob Cratchit, page 232, line 6, to page 233, line 8.

**Outline for Testing Silent Reading.** Read the story through silently at one sitting if possible. For testing your understanding of the story, you may use, as an outline, the scenes given in the dramatization on page 237; or, you may make an outline, using the subtitles of the five staves as topics, adding subtopics for each. An interesting social exercise may be made by dividing the class into five groups, and assigning to each group one stave of the story. Each group will prepare an outline and select one member to tell the substance of the stave to the class, following the outline.

**Library Reading.** "Solomon Crow's Christmas Pockets," "The Freys' Christmas Party," and "Duke's Christmas," Stuart (in *Solomon Crow's Christmas Pockets and Other Tales*); *Ten Boys from Dickens* and *Ten Girls from Dickens*, Sweetser; *Short Plays from Dickens*, Browne; *The Birds' Christmas Carol*, Wiggin.

**Magazine Reading.** Bring to class, or make a brief report on, the best Christmas story that you have read in a magazine.

**Suggestions for Theme Topics.** 1. Compare the condition of workers in this story with working conditions at the present time. 2. Compare the loyalty of Bob Cratchit to his employer with that of some modern worker of whom you have heard or read. 3. In your study of civics you have learned of laws that your state has enacted for the improvement of working conditions in industry; make a list of these and report upon them to the class. 4. Make a report on Cruikshank's illustrations of Dickens's characters and of Arthur Rackham's illustrations for *A Christmas Carol*, showing the class some of these pictures.

**A Suggested Problem.** Dickens called this story "a Christmas carol in prose"; compare its message with that of the original Christmas carol, "Peace on earth, good will toward men." Why did Dickens divide the story into "staves" instead of chapters? After you have read *A Christmas Carol* through silently and have enjoyed the class readings and discussions, you will find pleasure in dramatizing it for a Christmas program. The conversation in the story will furnish you ideas for the dialogue. Use the words of Dickens whenever possible. The descriptions and the story itself offer suggestions for costumes and for acting. The scenes indicated below afford a large number of pupils an opportunity to take part; the different scenes may be assigned to groups and worked out independently of each other.

Act I. Scrooge on Christmas Eve.
    Scene 1. In Scrooge's countinghouse. A visit from the nephew.
    Scene 2. In Scrooge's room. Appearance of Marley's ghost.

Act II. The Spirit of Christmas Past, showing Scrooge "shadows of the things that have been."
    Scene 1. The school of Scrooge's childhood.
    Scene 2. Christmas at the Fezziwigs'.

Act III. The Spirit of Christmas Present, showing Scrooge the universal happiness at Christmas time.
    Scene 1. Christmas at Bob Cratchit's.
    Scene 2. Christmas at the nephew's.

Act IV. The Spirit of Christmas Yet To Come, showing Scrooge the horrors attending the death of an unloved man.
    Scene 1. In Joe's shop.
    Scene 2. In the churchyard.

Act V. Scrooge awakes transformed on Christmas morning.
    Scene 1. In his room giving orders for Christmas cheer.
    Scene 2. At his nephew's.
    Scene 3. Next morning at the countinghouse.

# A TALE FROM SHAKESPEARE

## A Midsummer Night's Dream*

### Charles and Mary Lamb

There was a law in the city of Athens which gave to its citizens the power of compelling their daughters to marry whomsoever they pleased, for upon a daughter's refusing to marry the man her father had chosen to be her husband, the
5 father was empowered by this law to cause her to be put to death; but as fathers do not often desire the death of their own daughters, even though they do happen to prove a little refractory, this law was seldom or never put in execution, though perhaps the young ladies of that city were not infrequently
10 threatened by their parents with the terrors of it.

There was one instance, however, of an old man, whose name was Egeus, who actually did come before Theseus (at that time the reigning Duke of Athens) to complain that his daughter Hermia, whom he had commanded to marry Demetrius, a young man of
15 a noble Athenian family, refused to obey him because she loved

---

*See Silent and Oral Reading, page 13.

another young Athenian, named Lysander. Egeus demanded justice of Theseus and desired that this cruel law might be put in force against his daughter.

Hermia pleaded, in excuse for her disobedience, that Deme-
5 trius had formerly professed love for her dear friend Helena, and that Helena loved Demetrius to distraction; but this honorable reason, which Hermia gave for not obeying her father's command, moved not the stern Egeus. Theseus, though a great and merciful prince, had no power to alter the laws of his country;
10 therefore, he could only give Hermia four days to consider of it, and at the end of that time, if she still refused to marry Demetrius, she was to be put to death.

When Hermia was dismissed, she went to her lover Lysander and told him the peril she was in and that she must either give
15 him up and marry Demetrius or lose her life in four days.

Lysander was in great affliction at hearing these evil tidings, but recollecting that he had an aunt who lived at some distance from Athens, and that at the place where she lived the cruel law could not be put in force against Hermia (this law not extending
20 beyond the boundaries of the city), he proposed to Hermia that she should steal out of her father's house that night and go with him to his aunt's house, where he would marry her. "I will meet you," said Lysander, "in the wood a few miles without the city, in that delightful wood where we have so often walked with Helena
25 in the pleasant month of May."

To this proposal Hermia joyfully agreed, and she told no one of her intended flight but her friend Helena. Helena (as maidens will do foolish things for love) very ungenerously resolved to go and tell this to Demetrius, though she could hope no benefit
30 from betraying her friend's secret, but the poor pleasure of following her faithless lover to the wood, for she well knew that Demetrius would go thither in pursuit of Hermia.

The wood in which Lysander and Hermia proposed to meet was the favorite haunt of those little beings known by the name
35 of *Fairies*. Oberon the king, and Titania the queen of the fairies,

with all their tiny train of followers, in this wood held their midnight revels.

Between this little king and queen of sprites there happened, at this time, a sad disagreement; they never met by moonlight
5 in the shady walks of this pleasant wood but they were quarreling, till all their fairy elves would creep into acorn cups and hide themselves for fear.

The cause of this unhappy disagreement was Titania's refusing to give Oberon a little changeling boy, whose mother had
10 been Titania's friend, and upon her death the fairy queen stole the child from its nurse and brought him up in the woods.

The night on which the lovers were to meet in this wood, as Titania was walking with some of her maids of honor, she met Oberon attended by his train of fairy courtiers.

15 "Ill met by moonlight, proud Titania," said the fairy king. The queen replied, "What, jealous Oberon, is it you? Fairies, skip hence; I have forsworn his company." "Tarry, rash fairy," said Oberon; "am not I thy lord? Why does Titania cross her Oberon? Give me your little changeling boy to be my page."

20 "Set your heart at rest," answered the queen; "your whole fairy kingdom buys not the boy of me." She then left her lord in great anger. "Well, go your way," said Oberon; "before the morning dawns I will torment you for this injury."

Oberon then sent for Puck, his chief favorite and counselor.
25 Puck (or as he was sometimes called, Robin Goodfellow) was a shrewd and knavish sprite that used to play comical pranks in the neighboring villages, sometimes getting into the dairies and skimming the milk, sometimes plunging his light and airy form into the butter churn, and while he was dancing his fantastic
30 shape in the churn, in vain the dairy-maid would labor to change her cream into butter. Nor had the village swains any better success; whenever Puck chose to play his freaks in the brewing copper, the ale was sure to be spoiled. When a few good neighbors were met to drink some comfortable ale together, Puck would
35 jump into the bowl of ale in the likeness of a roasted crab, and

when some old goody was going to drink he would bob against her lips, and spill the ale over her withered chin, and presently after, when the same old dame was gravely seating herself to tell her neighbors a sad and melancholy story, Puck would slip her
5 three-legged stool from under her, and down would topple the poor old woman, and then the old gossips would laugh at her and swear they never wasted a merrier hour.

"Come hither, Puck," said Oberon to this little merry wanderer of the night; "fetch me the flower which maids call
10 love-in-idleness; the juice of that little purple flower, laid on the eyelids of those who sleep, will make them, when they awake, dote on the first thing they see. Some of the juice of that flower I will drop on the eyelids of my Titania when she is asleep, and the first thing she looks upon when she opens her eyes she will
15 fall in love with, even though it be a lion or a bear, a meddling monkey, or a busy ape, and before I will take this charm from off her sight, which I can do with another charm I know of, I will make her give me that boy to be my page."

Puck, who loved mischief to his heart, was highly diverted
20 with this intended frolic of his master and ran to seek the flower, and while Oberon was awaiting the return of Puck, he observed Demetrius and Helena enter the wood. He overheard Demetrius reproaching Helena for following him, and after many unkind words on his part, and gentle expostulations from Helena
25 reminding him of his former love and professions of true faith to her, he left her (as he said) to the mercy of the wild beasts, and she ran after him as swiftly as she could.

The fairy king, who was always friendly to true lovers, felt great compassion for Helena and, perhaps, as Lysander said they
30 used to walk by moonlight in this pleasant wood, Oberon might have seen Helena in those happy times when she was beloved by Demetrius. However that might be, when Puck returned with the little purple flower, Oberon said to his favorite, "Take a part of this flower; there has been a sweet Athenian lady here, who
35 is in love with a disdainful youth; if you find him sleeping, drop

some of the love juice in his eyes, but contrive to do it when she is near him, that the first thing he sees when he awakes may be this despised lady. You will know the man by the Athenian garments which he wears." Puck promised to manage this matter
5 very dexterously, and then Oberon went, unperceived by Titania, to her bower, where she was preparing to go to rest. Her fairy bower was a bank, where grew wild thyme, cowslips, and sweet violets, under a canopy of woodbine, mink roses, and eglantine. There Titania always slept some part of the night, her coverlet
10 the enameled skin of a snake, which, though a small mantle, was wide enough to wrap a fairy in.

He found Titania giving orders to her fairies, how they were to employ themselves while she slept. "Some of you," said Her Majesty, "must kill cankers in the musk rose buds and some wage
15 war with the bats for their leathern wings, to make my small elves coats; and some of you keep watch that the clamorous owl, that nightly hoots, come not near me; but first sing me to sleep." Then they began to sing this song:

> You spotted snakes with double tongue,
20 > Thorny hedgehogs, be not seen;
> Newts and blindworms do no wrong,
> Come not near our Fairy Queen.
> Philomel, with melody,
> Sing in our sweet lullaby,
25 > Lulla, lulla, lullaby; lulla, lulla, lullaby;
> Never harm, nor spell, nor charm,
> Come our lovely lady nigh;
> So good night with lullaby.

When the fairies had sung their queen asleep with this pretty
30 lullaby, they left her to perform the important services she had enjoined them. Oberon then softly drew near his Titania and dropped some of the love juice on her eyelids, saying,

> What then seest when thee dost wake,
> Do it for thy true-love take.

But to return to Hermia, who made her escape out of her father's house that night to avoid the death she was doomed to for refusing to marry Demetrius. When she entered the wood, she found her dear Lysander waiting for her, to conduct her to
5 his aunt's house; but before they had passed half through the wood, Hermia was so much fatigued that Lysander, who was very careful of this dear lady, who had proved her affection for him even by hazarding her life for his sake, persuaded her to rest till morning on a bank of soft moss, and lying down himself on the
10 ground at some little distance, they soon fell fast asleep. Here they were found by Puck, who, seeing a handsome young man asleep, and perceiving that his clothes were made in the Athenian fashion, and that a pretty lady was sleeping near him, concluded that this must be the Athenian maid and her disdainful lover
15 whom Oberon had sent him to seek; and he naturally enough conjectured that, as they were alone together, she must be the first thing he would see when he awoke; so, without more ado, he proceeded to pour some of the juice of the little purple flower into his eyes. But it so fell out that Helena came that way and,
20 instead of Hermia, was the first object Lysander beheld when he opened his eyes; and strange to relate, so powerful was the love charm, all his love for Hermia vanished away, and Lysander fell in love with Helena.

Had he first seen Hermia when he awoke, the blunder Puck
25 committed would have been of no consequence, for he could not love that faithful lady too well; but for poor Lysander to be forced by a fairy love charm to forget his own true Hermia and to run after another lady and leave Hermia asleep quite alone in a wood at midnight was a sad chance indeed.

30     Thus this misfortune happened. Helena, as has been before related, endeavored to keep pace with Demetrius when he ran away so rudely from her; but she could not continue this unequal race long, men being always better runners in a long race than ladies. Helena soon lost sight of Demetrius; and as she was
35 wandering about, dejected and forlorn, she arrived at the place

where Lysander was sleeping. "Ah!" said she, "this is Lysander lying on the ground; is he dead or asleep?" Then, gently touching him, she said, "Good sir, if you are alive, awake." Upon this, Lysander opened his eyes and (the love charm beginning to work)
5 immediately addressed her in terms of extravagant love and admiration, telling her she as much excelled Hermia in beauty as a dove does a raven, and that he would run through fire for her sweet sake, and many more such lover-like speeches. Helena, knowing Lysander was her friend Hermia's lover and that he was
10 solemnly engaged to marry her, was in the utmost rage when she heard herself addressed in this manner, for she thought, as well she might, that Lysander was making a jest of her. "Oh!" said she, "why was I born to be mocked and scorned by everyone? Is it not enough, is it not enough, young man, that I can never get a sweet
15 look or a kind word from Demetrius; but you, sir, must pretend in this disdainful manner to court me? I thought, Lysander, you were a lord of more true gentleness." Saying these words in great anger, she ran away, and Lysander followed her, quite forgetful of his own Hermia, who was still asleep.
20      When Hermia awoke, she was in a sad fright at finding herself alone. She wandered about the wood, not knowing what was become of Lysander or which way to go to seek for him. In the meantime, Demetrius, not being able to find Hermia and his rival Lysander, and fatigued with his fruitless search, was observed by
25 Oberon fast asleep. Oberon had learned by some questions he had asked of Puck that he had applied the love charm to the wrong person's eyes; and now having found the person first intended, he touched the eyelids of the sleeping Demetrius with the love juice, and he instantly awoke; and the first thing he saw being
30 Helena, he, as Lysander had done before, began to address love speeches to her; and just at that moment Lysander, followed by Hermia (for through Puck's unlucky mistake it was now become Hermia's turn to run after her lover), made his appearance; and then Lysander and Demetrius, both speaking together, made
35 love to Helena, they being each one under the influence of the

same potent charm.

The astonished Helena thought that Demetrius, Lysander, and her once dear friend Hermia were all in a plot together to make a jest of her.

5    Hermia was as much surprised as Helena; she knew not why Lysander and Demetrius, who both before loved her, were now become the lovers of Helena. And to Hermia the matter seemed to be no jest. The ladies, who before had always been the dearest of friends, now fell to high words together.

10    "Unkind Hermia," said Helena, "it is you have set Lysander on to vex me with mock praises, and your other lover, Demetrius, who used almost to spurn me with his foot, have you not bid him call me goddess, nymph, rare, precious, and celestial? He would not speak thus to me, whom he hates, if you did not set 15 him on to make a jest of me. Unkind Hermia, to join with men in scorning your poor friend. Have you forgotten our school-day friendship? How often, Hermia, have we two, sitting on one cushion, both singing one song, with our needles working the same flower, both on the same sampler wrought; growing up 20 together in fashion of a double cherry, scarcely seeming parted! Hermia, it is not friendly in you, it is not maidenly to join with men in scorning your poor friend."

"I am amazed at your passionate words," said Hermia. "I scorn you not; it seems you scorn me." "Aye, do," returned 25 Helena, "persevere, counterfeit serious looks, and make mouths at me when I turn my back; then wink at each other and hold the sweet jest up. If you had any pity, grace, or manners you would not use me thus."

While Helena and Hermia were speaking these angry words 30 to each other, Demetrius and Lysander left them to fight together in the wood for the love of Helena.

When they found the gentlemen had left them, they departed, and once more wandered, weary in the wood, in search of their lovers.

35    As soon as they were gone, the fairy king, who with little Puck

had been listening to their quarrels, said to him, "This is your negligence, Puck, or did you do this willfully?" "Believe me, king of shadows," answered Puck, "it was a mistake; did not you tell me I should know the man by his Athenian garments? However,
5 I am not sorry this has happened, for I think their jangling makes excellent sport." "You heard," said Oberon, "that Demetrius and Lysander are gone to seek a convenient place to fight in. I command you to overhang the night with a thick fog and lead these quarrelsome lovers so astray in the dark that they shall not be
10 able to find each other. Counterfeit each of their voices to the other, and with bitter taunts provoke them to follow you, while they think it is their rival's tongue they hear. See you do this till they are so weary they can go no farther, and when you find they are asleep, drop the juice of this other flower into Lysander's eyes,
15 and when he awakes he will forget his new love for Helena and return to his old passion for Hermia, and then the two fair ladies may each one be happy with the man she loves, and they will think all that has passed a vexatious dream. About this quickly, Puck, and I will go and see what sweet love my Titania has found."

20      Titania was still sleeping, and Oberon seeing a clown near her, who had lost his way in the wood and was likewise asleep, "This fellow," said he, "shall be my Titania's true love," and clapping an ass's head over the clown's, it seemed to fit him as well as if it had grown upon his own shoulders. Though
25 Oberon fixed the ass's head on very gently, it awakened him, and rising up, unconscious of what Oberon had done to him, he went toward the bower where the fairy queen slept.

"Ah! what angel is that I see?" said Titania, opening her eyes, and the juice of the little purple flower beginning to take effect.
30 "Are you as wise as you are beautiful?"

"Why, mistress," said the foolish clown, "if I have wit enough to find the way out of this wood, I have enough to serve my turn."

"Out of the wood do not desire to go," said the enamored queen. "I am a spirit of no common rate. I love you. Go with
35 me, and I will give you fairies to attend upon you."

She then called four of her fairies; their names were Pease-blossom, Cobweb, Moth, and Mustardseed.

"Attend," said the queen, "upon this sweet gentleman; hop in his walks, and gambol in his sight; feed him with grapes and
5 apricots, and steal for him the honey bags from the bees. Come, sit with me," said she to the clown, "and let me play with your amiable hairy cheeks, my beautiful ass! and kiss your fair large ears, my gentle joy!"

"Where is Peaseblossom?" said the ass-headed clown, not
10 much regarding the fairy queen's courtship, but very proud of his new attendants.

"Here, sir," said little Peaseblossom.

"Scratch my head," said the clown. "Where is Cobweb?"

"Here, sir," said Cobweb.

15 "Good Mr. Cobweb," said the foolish clown, "kill me the red bumble bee on the top of that thistle yonder; and, good Mr. Cobweb, bring me the honey bag. Do not fret yourself too much in the action, Mr. Cobweb, and take care the honey bag break not; I should be sorry to have you overflown with a honeybag.
20 Where is Mustardseed?"

"Here, sir," said Mustardseed; "what is your will?"

"Nothing," said the clown, "good Mr. Mustardseed, but to help Mr. Peaseblossom to scratch; I must go to a barber's, Mr. Mustardseed, for methinks I am marvelous hairy about the face."

25 "My sweet love," said the queen, "what will you have to eat? I have a venturous fairy shall seek the squirrel's hoard and fetch you some new nuts."

"I had rather have a handful of dried peas," said the clown, who with his ass's head had got an ass's appetite. "But, I pray, let
30 none of your people disturb me, for I have a mind to sleep."

"Sleep, then," said the queen, "and I will wind you in my arms. O how I love you! how I dote upon you!"

When the fairy king saw the clown sleeping in the arms of his queen, he advanced within her sight and reproached her
35 with having lavished her favors upon an ass.

This she could not deny, as the clown was then sleeping within her arms, with his ass's head crowned by her with flowers.

When Oberon had teased her for some time, he again demanded the changeling boy, which she, ashamed of being discovered by her
5 lord with her new favorite, did not dare to refuse him.

Oberon, having thus obtained the little boy he had so long wished for to be his page, took pity on the disgraceful situation into which, by his merry contrivance, he had brought his Titania, and threw some of the juice of the other flower into her eyes;
10 and the fairy queen immediately recovered her senses and wondered at her late dotage, saying she now loathed the sight of the strange monster.

Oberon likewise took the ass's head from off the clown and left him to finish his nap with his own fool's head upon his
15 shoulders.

Oberon and his Titania being now perfectly reconciled, he related to her the history of the lovers and their midnight quarrels, and she agreed to go with him and see the end of their adventures.

20     The fairy king and queen found the lovers and their fair ladies, at no great distance from each other, sleeping on a grassplot; for Puck, to make amends for his former mistake, had contrived with the utmost diligence to bring them all to the same spot, unknown to each other; and he had carefully removed
25 the charm from off the eyes of Lysander with the antidote the fairy king gave to him.

Hermia first awoke, and finding her lost Lysander asleep so near her, was looking at him and wondering at his strange inconstancy. Lysander presently opening his eyes, and seeing
30 his dear Hermia, recovered his reason, which the fairy charm had before clouded, and with his reason, his love for Hermia; and they began to talk over the adventures of the night, doubting if these things had really happened, or if they had both been dreaming the same bewildering dream.

35     Helena and Demetrius were by this time awake; and a sweet

sleep having quieted Helena's disturbed and angry spirits, she listened with delight to the professions of love which Demetrius still made to her, and which, to her surprise as well as pleasure, she began to perceive were sincere.

5     These fair, night-wandering ladies, now no longer rivals, became once more true friends; all the unkind words which had passed were forgiven, and they calmly consulted together what was best to be done in their present situation. It was soon agreed that as Demetrius had given up his pretensions to Hermia he
10 should endeavor to prevail upon her father to revoke the cruel sentence of death which had been passed against her. Demetrius was preparing to return to Athens for this friendly purpose when they were surprised with the sight of Egeus, Hermia's father, who came to the wood in pursuit of his runaway daughter.

15     When Egeus understood that Demetrius would not now marry his daughter, he no longer opposed her marriage with Lysander but gave his consent that they should be wedded on the fourth day from that time, being the same day on which Hermia had been condemned to lose her life; and on that same day Helena joyfully
20 agreed to marry her beloved and now faithful Demetrius.

    The fairy king and queen, who were invisible spectators of this reconciliation, and now saw the happy ending of the lovers' history, brought about through the good offices of Oberon, received so much pleasure that these kind spirits resolved
25 to celebrate the approaching nuptials with sports and revels throughout their fairy kingdom.

    And now, if any are offended with this story of fairies and their pranks, as judging it incredible and strange, they have only to think that they have been asleep and dreaming and that all
30 these adventures were visions which they saw in their sleep, and I hope none of my readers will be so unreasonable as to be offended with a pretty, harmless Midsummer Night's Dream.

## NOTES AND QUESTIONS

35     **Biography.** Charles Lamb (1775-1834), an English writer, spent his

entire life in London. His father was a clerk in a lawyer's office, and Charles was an accountant until he was fifty years of age. He was, however, a great reader and spent his hours of leisure at the bookstores and printshops, or at home reading with his sister Mary. He and Mary wrote _Tales from Shakespeare_, giving in simple prose the stories of many of Shakespeare's plays. In a letter to a friend, Lamb said of his sister: "She is doing for Godwin's bookseller twenty of Shakespeare's plays, to be made into children's tales. Six are already done by her: _The Tempest, Winter's Tale, Midsummer Night, Much Ado, Two Gentlemen of Verona_, and _Cymbeline_; and the _Merchant of Venice_ is in forwardness. I have done _Othello_ and _Macbeth_, and mean to do all the tragedies. I think it will be popular among the little people, besides money. It is to bring in sixty guineas. Mary has done them capitally, I think you'd think."

**Discussion.** 1. Make a list of the characters mentioned in the story. 2. Which are the principal characters? 3. What complaint did Hermia's father make to the duke? What was the duke's decision? 4. What plan for the safety of Hermia and himself did Lysander make? To whom was this plan told? 5. Tell who Oberon, Titania, and Puck are. 6. What flower did Oberon send Puck to find? What magic was in it? 7. What did Oberon tell Puck to do with the juice of the flower? 8. Who is the Athenian youth that Oberon asks Puck to find? 9. Who is the youth that Puck finds? 10. What happens when Lysander awakes? 11. What does Oberon do with the juice of the flower? Account for the presence in the woods of Helena and Demetrius. 12. By what means did Oberon try to gain possession of the boy? How did he succeed? 13. How did Puck make amends for his mistake? 14. What did Lysander and Hermia say about "the adventures of the night"? 15. What did Egeus consent that Demetrius should do? 16. To whom were the four lovers indebted for their peace and happiness? 17. Find in the glossary the meaning of: refractory; forsworn; swain; potent; enamored; amiable; antidote; pretensions; nuptials. 18. _Pronounce:_ revels; courtier; dexterously; thyme; hazarding; counterfeit; dotage.

**Outline for Testing Silent Beading.** Make an outline to guide you in telling the story.

**Library Reading.** Other stories in _Tales from Shakespeare_, Lamb.

## THE WORLD OF ADVENTURE

### A Review

In the "Introduction," page 97, you learned that the basis of all literature is adventure and that adventures when treated with imagination give us literature; what three types of adventure stories are mentioned? Robert W. Service in "Fleurette" tells of an event such as he himself might have witnessed; what other selections in this group are based upon a real happening that the writer himself experienced or about which he had heard or read? Sir Walter Scott took an incident from an old border ballad and gave us the poem "Lochinvar"; what other poem or story in "Part II" is based upon a legend? A third type of adventure story is one in which the events are purely imaginary. Such a story Shakespeare created in *A Midsummer Night's Dream;* what other stories in "Part II" narrate events that never actually happened?

No doubt you are training your imagination to picture the events until you can see the stories *in action,* as if they were little dramas being enacted by players before your eyes; which selections in "Part II" were you able to visualize most vividly? Discuss in class the advantages and disadvantages of "your own private movie," about which you read in the "Introduction" on page 98, as compared with a regular movie.

What did you learn in "Part II" about ballads? How does a folk ballad differ from a ballad like "The Highwayman"? Which of the ballads in "Part II" would you select as best suited for a public reading? What ballads have you heard on recordings? What ballads have you heard sung by a good singer?

What did you learn about the short story that will increase your pleasure in reading short stories? What library reading have you done in connection with "Part II"? In your current magazine reading what ballads and adventure stories have you read? What newspaper item have you read recently that would furnish the plot for an interesting short story? Mention some especially interesting stories of adventure that you read in the preceding books of this series. Mention some of the ballads. What progress have you made in the use of the library catalogue and of *The Readers' Guide to Periodical Literature*? Do you find your interest in magazines and newspapers increasing? Which book review gave you the most pleasure? Which one gave you the most interesting information? What did you learn about public health from book reviews in connection with "The Masque of the Red Death"? Which of the "Suggestions for Theme Topics" in "Part II" was most helpful in information? Which one was made interesting by illustrative material, such as pictures, sketches, and objects?

What progress in silent reading have you made since you began this book? Compare your record for speed and comprehension with the standard for eighth-grade pupils. What material did you find in "Part II" suitable for an interesting Christmas entertainment? Which "Suggested Problem" gave you the greatest pleasure in working out its details? What country claims each poet as a citizen? What newspaper or magazine references to them have you read? What other poems by these writers have you read?

# PART III

## THE GREAT AMERICAN EXPERIMENT

*America! America!*
*God shed his grace on thee,*
*And crown thy good with brotherhood*
*From sea to shining sea.*
—Katherine Lee Bates

THE MINUTEMAN OF CONCORD

# THE GREAT AMERICAN EXPERIMENT

### An Introduction

Perhaps you have sometimes felt the thrill that goes through one in the presence of a noble action or of a deep emotion. Someone may have shown strength of character in a crisis or may have done a big and generous thing, and you have said, "what a hero." Or the sight of the flag or of our soldiers returning from war has thrilled you with love of our country. Or someone has said something that has set you on fire with ambition to do things—to be a great lawyer or doctor or manufacturer or to build a great business. These impulses to render patriotic service, this ambition to make your life count—all take you out of your usual self and awaken the best traits of your character. You could sing for joy. If you could express your feelings in words, you would be a poet, for out of sincere and deep emotion poetry is born.

Among all the emotions that men feel in their best moments, none are deeper and more filled with good than those connected with love of home and country and with those ideals of service and cooperation without which no country can long endure. The growth, through many centuries, of this love of country and freedom that has made self-government possible is the most important fact in modern history. The growth has been slow—discouragingly slow. But there have been great moments in the history of the nations when vast multitudes of people have been swept by powerful emotions drawing them out of themselves and on to some new advance toward freedom. Out of these emotions, at these dramatic moments in history, have come poems and prose that have inspired people to deeds of patriotism and service for others.

It is, then, with literature as a means of expressing the loftiest ideals of liberty and service that the selections in this part of our book have to do. There are three groups. In the first are some records of the growth of the "Eternal Spirit of Freedom." This spirit of freedom is born of the feeling that people have the right, as our Declaration of Independence states it, to "life, liberty, and the pursuit of happiness." There have always been ambitious people who have wished to ensure their own power by keeping the masses of their fellows in subjection. Often they have succeeded. But through all the centuries there have come moments, now in one part of the world and now in another, that have shown how firmly imbedded in the human heart is the conviction that people ought to be free, free to shape their lives according to their desires and their abilities and not according to the commands of emperor or king. The literature in this first section refers to different times and peoples, but it all bears witness to this fire of liberty that sometimes smolders under oppression but is never destroyed. As you read these selections, remember that they are only a few out of many such stories and poems that express this eternal spirit of freedom; you can easily find many others, and thus you will come to realize how much of what we are and have today has grown out of the passionate desire for liberty that never dies.

The next unit in this part of your book, called "America's Experiment in Free Government," shows you something of America's service to the spirit of freedom. Many times in the past the spirit of liberty, awakened in people because of the oppression of some tyrant, has led only to temporary relief, by the overthrow of the particular tyrant, without providing permanent freedom through the overthrow of the oppressive system of government. Indeed, many Americans during the Revolution had no idea of setting up a new and independent form of government; they intended only to put an end to the oppression of George III. But others, more far-sighted, saw that at last there had come the opportunity to set up a government in which the people themselves should be the rulers.

The foundations for such a form of government had already been laid. In England, for a thousand years, people had been developing the idea of a limited representation of the citizens through a parliament. In 1688, the English people rebelled against their king and established the supremacy of this Parliament over the monarch. Thus the people, in theory at least, gained control of their government. English freedom was not complete, however, because the Parliament was not yet fully representative of all the people. In fact a century later it became as tyrannical as the king. Meantime, in the colonial assemblies of America, the principle of representative government was pushed farther. The colonists were mainly descendants of liberty-loving Englishmen, and the ideals of free government were born in them. Remote from England, they governed themselves as they thought best. When at last the ties binding them to the mother country were cut loose, the "Great American Experiment," far more important to the future of all people everywhere than any mere question of gaining temporary relief from a tyrannical British king, came into being. It was an "experiment," because it was based on the idea that a nation made up of people from all parts of the world, living in a territory of vast extent and under very different conditions of climate, occupation, and degree of wealth, might, through representatives chosen by all its citizens, determine its own plan of government. Nowhere else had the idea that people should govern themselves been tried out on such a vast scale. The older governments of Europe thought such an experiment would surely fail. They wanted it to fail, for with its success no throne would be secure.

Read, then, in this light the selections which show something of the nature of this experiment in self-government and of the principles on which it was founded. It is an experiment that has met every test, thus far. It has brought about more liberal government even in the older European countries. It has become a beacon for the inspiration of the oppressed, wherever they live. It is destined to become the model and the influence by which all people shall one day govern themselves and find liberty and happiness.

The last section, called "Citizenship and Service," rounds out the story of freedom and patriotism. First is the *passionate desire for liberty*, growing up in the Old World and in America in times past and once more blazing forth in the crisis of World War One. Next is the *American idea of free government*—that is, the idea of a government controlled by all the people and obeyed by all the people, because they realize that unrestrained liberty is anarchy and that free government means "a liberty connected with order." And last is the *spirit of service*, of brotherhood, of cooperation of all for the good of all, without which no free government can endure.

There is no more important subject than this for you to study. It is something to be studied that you may know that free government is not merely or even mainly a mode of electing presidents and legislatures. It is something for you to see in imagination that you may realize what it has cost and through how many centuries it has developed and that you may know, also, that we must guard it and carry it on farther in each generation. And it is something that you must *feel*—ideals and emotions that will so control you that you will swear to do your part to preserve what people have won of the right to rule themselves. For unless this study and imagination and feeling pass into action, unless you are willing to take the lessons of service that the selections in the last part of this group teach you as a motive force in your own life, tyranny in one form or another will gain control of a nation grown cold to the ideals of liberty and service, and free government will be no more. Which God forbid! The responsibility rests on you, you boys and girls who are now preparing not merely for happy and successful lives in free America, but for carrying out the great tradition of liberty and service.

# THE ETERNAL SPIRIT OF FREEDOM

## Spartacus to the Gladiators

### Elijah Kellogg

It had been a day of triumph in Capua. Lentulus returning
with victorious eagles had amused the populace with the sports
of the amphitheater to an extent hitherto unknown even in
that luxurious city. The shouts of revelry had died away; the
5 roar of the lion had ceased; the last loiterer had retired from
the banquet; and the lights in the palace of the victor were
extinguished. The moon, piercing the tissue of fleecy clouds,
silvered the dewdrop on the corselet of the Roman sentinel and
tipped the dark waters of Volturnus with wavy, tremulous light.
10 It was a night of holy calm, when the zephyr sways the young
spring leaves and whispers among the hollow reeds its dreamy
music. No sound was heard but the last sob of some weary wave,
telling its story to the smooth pebbles of the beach, and then all
was still as the breast when the spirit has departed.

15    In the deep recesses of the amphitheater a band of gladiators

were crowded together—their muscles still knotted with the
agony of conflict, the foam upon their lips, and the scowl of
battle yet lingering upon their brows—when Spartacus, rising in
the midst of that grim assemblage, thus addressed them:

5      "Ye call me chief, and ye do well to call him chief who, for
twelve long years, has met upon the arena every shape of man
or beast that the broad empire of Rome could furnish and yet
never has lowered his arm.  And if there be one among you who
can say that, ever, in public fight or private brawl, my actions
10 did belie my tongue, let him step forth and say it.  If there be
three in all your throng dare face me on the bloody sand, let
them come on!

"Yet, I was not always thus, a hired butcher, a savage chief
of savage men.  My father was a reverent man who feared great
15 Jupiter and brought to the rural deities his offerings of fruits and
flowers.  He dwelt among the vine-clad rocks and olive groves
at the foot of Helicon.  My early life ran quiet as the brook by
which I sported.  I was taught to prune the vine, to tend the
flock, and then, at noon, I gathered my sheep beneath the shade
20 and played upon the shepherd's flute.  I had a friend, the son of
our neighbor; we led our flocks to the same pasture and shared
together our rustic meal.

"One evening, after the sheep were folded and we were all
seated beneath the myrtle that shaded our cottage, my grandsire,
25 an old man, was telling of Marathon and Leuctra and how, in
ancient times, a little band of Spartans, in a defile of the mountains, withstood a whole army.  I did not then know what war
meant, but my cheeks burned—I knew not why—and I clasped
the knees of that venerable man till my mother, parting the hair
30 from off my brow, kissed my throbbing temples and bade me go
to rest and think no more of those old tales and savage wars.

"That very night the Romans landed on our shore, and the
clash of steel was heard within our quiet vale.  I saw the breast
that had nourished me trampled by the iron hoof of the warhorse;
35 the bleeding body of my father flung amid the blazing rafters

of our dwelling. Today I killed a man in the arena, and when I broke his helmet clasps, behold! he was my friend! He knew me—smiled faintly—gasped—and died; the same sweet smile that I had marked upon his face when, in adventurous boyhood,
5 we scaled some lofty cliff to pluck the first ripe grapes and bear them home in childish triumph. I told the praetor he was my friend, noble and brave, and I begged his body that I might burn it upon the funeral pile and mourn over him. Aye, on my knees, amid the dust and blood of the arena, I begged that boon, while
10 all the Roman maids and matrons, and those holy virgins they call vestal, and the rabble, shouted in mockery, deeming it rare sport, forsooth, to see Rome's fiercest gladiator turn pale and tremble like a very child before that piece of bleeding clay, but the praetor drew back as if I were pollution and sternly said, 'Let
15 the carrion rot! There are no noble men but Romans!' And he, deprived of funeral rites, must wander, a hapless ghost, beside the waters of that sluggish river, and look—and look—and look in vain to the bright Elysian Fields where dwell his ancestors and noble kindred. And so must you, and so must I, die like
20 dogs!

"O Rome! Rome! thou hast been a tender nurse to me! Aye, thou hast given to that poor, gentle, timid shepherd lad, who never knew a harsher sound than a flute-note, muscles of iron and a heart of flint; taught him to drive the sword through
25 rugged brass and plaited mail and warm it in the marrow of his foe! to gaze into the glaring eyeballs of the fierce Numidian lion, even as a smooth-cheeked boy upon a laughing girl. And he shall pay thee back till thy yellow Tiber is red as frothing wine, and in its deepest ooze thy lifeblood lies curdled!

30 "Ye stand here now like giants, as ye are! The strength of brass is in your toughened sinews, but tomorrow some Roman Adonis, breathing sweet odors from his curly locks, shall come and with his lily fingers pat your brawny shoulders and bet his sesterces upon your blood! Hark! Hear ye yon lion roaring in
35 his den? 'Tis three days since he tasted meat, but tomorrow

he shall break his fast upon your flesh, and ye shall be a dainty meal for him.

"If ye are brutes, then stand here like fat oxen waiting for the butcher's knife; if ye are men, follow me! strike down yon
5 sentinel and gain the mountain passes and there do bloody work as did your sires at old Thermopylae! Is Sparta dead? Is the old Grecian spirit frozen in your veins that you do crouch and cower like baseborn slaves beneath your master's lash? O comrades! warriors! Thracians! if we must fight, let us fight for ourselves;
10 if we must slaughter, let us slaughter our oppressors; if we must die, let us die under the open sky, by the bright waters, in noble, honorable battle."

## NOTES AND QUESTIONS

**Biographical and Historical Note.** This is a supposed speech of Spartacus written by Elijah Kellogg, a New England clergyman. Spartacus was a Thracian who served in the Roman army. Having deserted, he was taken prisoner, sold as a slave, and trained as a gladiator at Capua, a Roman city, containing an amphitheater famous for its gladiatorial contests and combats of wild beasts. In 73 B.C. Spartacus escaped and gathered about him a large army of slaves and gladiators with whom he intended to push northward until they were all able to return to their homes. After attacking many towns, however, they were finally overcome. Spartacus died in battle, and six thousand of his followers were crucified.

**Discussion.** 1. Who was Spartacus, and what was the occasion of his speech? 2. To whom was he talking? 3. Of what battles did his grandsire tell one evening? How did these tales of battle affect the young Spartacus? 4. In *The Elson Readers, Book Seven*, you read of "a little band of Spartans" at Thermopylae; can you tell what these brave Spartans did for the freedom of their people? 5. Tell the story of Spartacus and his boyhood friend whom he killed. 6. What appeal does Spartacus make to his comrades in the last paragraph? 7. Find a statement in the "Introduction" on page 256 that is particularly appropriate to the thought of this selection. 8. Find in the glossary the meaning of: zephyr; arena; belie; Jupiter; venerable; Adonis. 9. *Pronounce:* recesses; sinews.

### Phrases for Study

victorious eagles, **259**, 2           must wander, **261**, 16
rural deities, **260**, 15              Yellow Tiber, **261**, 28

# THE ISLES OF GREECE

### LORD BYRON

The isles of Greece, the isles of Greece!
   Where burning Sappho loved and sung,
Where grew the arts of war and peace,
   Where Delos rose, and Phoebus sprung!
5 Eternal summer gilds them yet;
But all, except their sun, is set.

.   .   .   .   .   .   .   .   .

The mountains look on Marathon
   And Marathon looks on the sea;
And musing there an hour alone,
10   I dreamed that Greece might still be free;
For, standing on the Persian's grave,
I could not deem myself a slave.

A king sat on the rocky brow
   Which looks o'er sea-born Salamis;
15 And ships by thousands lay below,
   And men in nations—all were his!
He counted them at break of day—
And when the sun set, where were they?

And where are they? and where art thou,
20   My country? On thy voiceless shore
The heroic lay is tuneless now—
   The heroic bosom beats no more.
And must thy lyre, so long divine,
Degenerate into hands like mine?

'Tis something, in the dearth of fame,
    Though linked among a fettered race,
To feel at least a patriot's shame,
    Even as I sing, suffuse my face;
5 For what is left the poet here?
For Greeks a blush—for Greece a tear.

Must we but weep o'er days more blest?
    Must we but blush?—Our fathers bled.
Earth, render back from out thy breast
10    A remnant of our Spartan dead
Of the three hundred grant but three,
To make a new Thermopylae!

What, silent still? and silent all?
    Ah, no; the voices of the dead
15 Sound like a distant torrent's fall,
    And answer, "Let one living head,
But one, arise—we come, we come!"
'    Tis but the living who are dumb.

In vain—in vain; strike other chords.
20    Fill high the cup with Saurian wine!
Leave battles to the Turkish hordes,
    And shed the blood of Scio's vine!
Hark! rising to the ignoble call
How answers each bold bacchanal!

     ·   ·   ·   ·   ·   ·   ·

25 The tyrant of the Chersonese
    Was freedom's best and bravest friend;
That tyrant was Miltiades!
    O that the present hour would lend
Another despot of the kind!
30 Such chains as his were sure to bind.

Trust not for freedom to the Franks—
    They have a king who buys and sells;
In native swords and native ranks
    The only hope of courage dwells;
5 But Turkish force and Latin fraud
Would break your shield, however broad.

Place me on Sunium's marbled steep,
    Where nothing save the waves and I
May hear our mutual murmurs sweep;
10    There, swan-like, let me sing and die;
A land of slaves shall ne'er be mine—
Dash down yon cup of Samian wine!

## NOTES AND QUESTIONS

**Biography.** George Gordon, Lord Byron (1788-1824), was born in London. He was educated at Harrow, a famous English school, and at Cambridge University. He began to write at an early age, and before he was twenty had published a small volume of poems. Byron's poetry was greatly admired in his lifetime, and he remains in the first rank of English poets. His best known long poems, *Childe Harold, Don Juan, Manfred,* and *The Bride of Abydos,* were translated into most of the European languages and had a great influence on the literature of the continent. These romantic tales brought to his countrymen the life of "the gorgeous East." He also wrote some passionate short poems on liberty. In 1820, when the Greeks revolted against Turkey, Byron became aroused and finally went to their aid, but died at Missolonghi, in Greece, before he had an opportunity to engage in battle.

**Historical Note.** Ancient Greece, consisting of the peninsula and the numerous islands around it, was the leader of the civilized world in the time before Christ. Not only were Grecian art and literature developed to a degree that has not been surpassed, but the Greeks of the ancient world were famous for their love of liberty and their patriotism. About 500 B.C. the Persians invaded Greece and made repeated attempts to conquer the country. Three famous battles were fought. At Marathon, under the great general, Miltiades, the Greeks defeated a vast Persian army; at Thermopylae, under Leonidas, a little band of three hundred Spartans gave their lives in defense of a mountain pass; and at Salamis the Greek navy defeated a much larger fleet of the invaders while Xerxes, the Persian king, as described in the third stanza, watched in dismay from a "rocky brow" that overlooked the battle. Thus the Greeks in ancient times won glory.

But in the last century B.C. and in succeeding centuries, ambitious countries made attacks on Greece, and her patriotism and courage were not sufficient to throw off the foreign yokes. Her last conqueror was Turkey, under whose dominion she still was when Byron wrote *Don Juan*, from which "The Isles of Greece" is taken. In these stanzas the poet contrasts the glorious history of ancient Greece with the pitiable condition the country was in at the beginning of the nineteenth century—when the Greeks were still a race conquered and "fettered" by the Turks. The deep strain of sorrow throughout "The Isles of Greece" is due, however, not so much to the fact that Greece was enslaved as to the feeling in the heart of the poet that the people of Greece had no longer the old-time spirit of their ancestors and their determination to resist the oppressor.

**Discussion.** 1. What object do you think Byron hoped to gain by bringing the glories of the past so vividly before the modern Greek? 2. This is an English poet's idea of how a Greek poet might have sung; what line in the first stanza expresses a thought that a Greek poet would hardly admit? 3. What do the names Marathon, Salamis, Thermopylae suggest? 4. What "ignoble call" does the poet imply the modern Greek would answer? 5. Wherein does the poet say the hope of modern Greece lies? 6. What event in Byron's life makes you know he felt the position of Greece keenly? (It is interesting to note that in December, 1823, Daniel Webster introduced a resolution in Congress which is believed to be the first official expression favorable to the independence of Greece uttered by any government of Christendom.) 7. What did you read in the "Introduction" on page 256 about "ambitious men" who try to keep freedom down? Who were oppressing Greece at the time this poem was written? 8. What do you know about Greece's part in World War One that tells you how that country regards freedom at the present time? 9. How does a poem such as this aid in the growth of the spirit of freedom? 10. The music of the poem makes it a pleasure to read it aloud; notice how naturally the emphasis of the rhythm accents the important words. 11. Find in the glossary the meaning of: voiceless; lay; degenerate; fettered. 12. *Pronounce:* dearth; bacchanal.

### Phrases for Study

burning Sappho, **263,** 2

but all, except their sun, **263,** 6

Persian's grave, **263,** 11

men in nations, **263,** 16

Latin fraud, **265,** 5

swan-like, let me sing, **265,** 10

**Class Reading.** Bring to class and read "Marco Bozzaris," Halleck. (Marco Bozzaris, the leader of the Greek Revolution, was killed August 20,

1823, in an attack upon the Turks near Missolonghi. His last words were: "To die for liberty is a pleasure, not a pain.")

**Suggestions for Theme Topics.** (Two-Minute Talks.) 1. The Battle of Salamis. 2. Miltiades and the Battle of Marathon. 3. The Pass of Thermopylae. (Use encyclopedias and other library sources; see "Leonidas, the Spartan" in *The Elson Readers, Book Seven.*)

## Paul Revere's Ride

### Henry Wadsworth Longfellow

Listen, my children, and you shall hear
Of the midnight ride of Paul Revere,
On the eighteenth of April, in Seventy-five
Hardly a man is now alive
5 Who remembers that famous day and year.

He said to his friend: "If the British march
By land or sea from the town tonight,
Hang a lantern aloft in the belfry arch
Of the North Church tower, as a signal light—
10 One if by land, and two if by sea;
And I on the opposite shore will be
Ready to ride and spread the alarm
Through every Middlesex village and farm
For the country-folk to be up and to arm."
15 Then he said "Good night," and with muffled oar
Silently rowed to the Charlestown shore,
Just as the moon rose over the bay,
Where, swinging wide at her moorings, lay
The Somerset, British man-of-war—
20 A phantom ship, with each mast and spar
Across the moon, like a prison bar,

And a huge black hulk, that was magnified
By its own reflection in the tide.

Meanwhile, his friend through alley and street
Wanders and watches with eager ears,
5 Till in the silence around him he hears
The muster of men at the barrack door,
The sound of arms, and the tramp of feet,
And the measured tread of the grenadiers
Marching down to their boats on the shore.

10 Then he climbed to the tower of the church,
Up the wooden stairs, with stealthy tread,
To the belfry-chamber overhead,
And startled the pigeons from their perch
On the somber rafters, that round him made
15 Masses and moving shapes of shade—
Up the trembling ladder, steep and tall,
To the highest window in the wall,
Where he paused to listen and look down
A moment on the roofs of the town,
20 And the moonlight flowing over all.

Beneath, in the churchyard, lay the dead
In their night-encampment on the hill,
Wrapped in silence so deep and still
That he could hear, like a sentinel's tread,
25 The watchful night-wind, as it went
Creeping along from tent to tent,
And seeming to whisper, "All is well!"
A moment only he feels the spell
Of the place and the hour, the secret dread
30 Of the lonely belfry and the dead;
For suddenly all his thoughts are bent
On a shadowy something far away,

Where the river widens to meet the bay—
A line of black, that bends and floats
On the rising tide, like a bridge of boats.

Meanwhile, impatient to mount and ride,
5 Booted and spurred, with a heavy stride,
On the opposite shore walked Paul Revere.
Now he patted his horse's side;
Now gazed at the landscape far and near;
Then impetuous stamped the earth,
10 And turned and tightened his saddle-girth;
But mostly he watched with eager search
The belfry-tower of the old North Church
As it rose above the graves on the hill,
Lonely, and spectral, and somber, and still.
15 And lo! as he looks, on the belfry's height,
A glimmer, and then a gleam of light!
He springs to the saddle, the bridle he turns,
But lingers and gazes, till full on his sight
A second lamp in the belfry burns!

20 The hurry of hoofs in a village street,
A shape in the moonlight, a bulk in the dark,
And beneath from the pebbles, in passing, a spark
Struck out by a steed flying fearless and fleet—
That was all! And yet, through the gloom and the light,
25 The fate of a nation was riding that night;
And the spark struck out by that steed, in his flight,
Kindled the land into flame with its heat.
He has left the village and mounted the steep,
And beneath him, tranquil and broad and deep,
30 Is the Mystic, meeting the ocean tides;
And under the alders, that skirt its edge,
Now soft on the sand, now loud on the ledge,
Is heard the tramp of the steed as he rides.

It was twelve by the village clock
When he crossed the bridge into Medford town.
He heard the crowing of the cock,
And the barking of the farmer's dog,
5 And felt the damp of the river-fog
That rises after the sun goes down.

It was one by the village clock
When he galloped into Lexington.
He saw the gilded weathercock
10 Swim in the moonlight as he passed,
And the meeting-house windows, blank and bare,
Gaze at him with a spectral glare,
As if they already stood aghast
At the bloody work they would look upon.

15 It was two by the village clock
When he came to the bridge in Concord town.
He heard the bleating of the flock
And the twitter of birds among the trees
And felt the breath of the morning breeze
20 Blowing over the meadows brown.
And one was safe and asleep in his bed
Who at the bridge would be first to fall,
Who that day would be lying dead,
Pierced by a British musket-ball.

25 You know the rest. In the books you have read,
How the British-regulars fired and fled,
How the farmers gave them ball for ball,
From behind each fence and farmyard wall,
Chasing the redcoats down the lane;
30 Then crossing the fields to emerge again
Under the trees at the turn of the road,
And only pausing to fire and load.
So through the night rode Paul Revere;

And so through the night went his cry of alarm
To every Middlesex village and farm—
A cry of defiance, and not of fear,
A voice in the darkness, a knock at the door,
5 And a word that shall echo forevermore!
For, borne on the night-wind of the Past,
Through all our history, to the last,
In the hour of darkness and peril and need,
The people will waken and listen to hear
10 The hurrying hoof-beats of that steed,
And the midnight message of Paul Revere.

## NOTES AND QUESTIONS

For **Biography** see page 138.

**Discussion.** 1. Read the poem through thoughtfully and be able to tell the story from this outline: (a) Understanding as to signals between Paul Revere and his friend; (b) The friend in Boston; (c) Paul Revere on the Charlestown side of the river; (d) The ride. 2. What was Paul Revere's message? 3. Find the lines that describe the churchyard. 4. How does Longfellow make you feel the hurry of the rider? 5. What to you is the most expressive line in the poem? 6. Read again what is said on page 20 about the value of supplementing history books with literature. How is the story "in the books you have read" of the battle of Lexington enriched by the story in the poem? 7. How did Longfellow's prophecy at the end of the poem apply to our country in the World Wars? 8. What statement in the first paragraph of the "Introduction" on page 255 shows you the motive that caused Longfellow to write this poem? 9. Draw a map showing the relative positions of Boston, Charlestown, Medford, Lexington, Concord. 10. Suggest a series of pictures that would tell the story of this famous historic ride; where in your series would you place the picture on page 259? 11. Find in the glossary the meaning of: grenadier; impetuous; spectral; tranquil; emerge. 12. *Pronounce:* barrack; alder.

### Phrases for Study

night-encampment, **268**, 22
from tent to tent, **268**, 26

fate of a nation, **269**, 25
night-wind of the Past, **271**, 6

**Class Reading.** Bring to class and read "The Reveille," Harte; "A Troop of the Guard," Hagedorn (in *The Home Book of Verse*).

## Concord Hymn

### Ralph Waldo Emerson

By the rude bridge that arched the flood,
  Their flag to April's breeze unfurled,
Here once the embattled farmers stood,
  And fired the shot heard round the world.

5 The foe long since in silence slept;
  Alike the conqueror silent sleeps;
And time the ruined bridge has swept
  Down the dark stream which seaward creeps.

On this green bank, by this soft stream,
10   We set today a votive stone,
That memory may their deed redeem,
  When, like our sires, our sons are gone.

Spirit, that made those freemen dare
  To die, and leave their children free,
15 Bid time and Nature gently spare
  The shaft we raise to them and Thee.

### NOTES AND QUESTIONS

For **Biography** see page 79.

**Historical Note.** Emerson wrote this poem to celebrate the completion of the monument which marks the spot on which the battle of Concord was fought, April 19, 1775. This monument is the work of the American sculptor, Daniel C. French. The "Concord Hymn" was sung at the celebration, April 19, 1836.

**Discussion.** 1. In what sense was the shot "heard round the world"? 2. What did this battle mean to the world? 3. For what purpose does the poet say this "votive stone" is set? 4. How does this poem help memory "to redeem the deed"? 5. In what different ways does "memory redeem the deeds" of the World War heroes? 6. Why do we observe Memorial Day? 7. In the prayer in the last stanza the poet tells us to whom the shaft is raised; which of these is greater, the "freemen" or the "spirit"? 8. Find in the glossary the meaning of: arched; embattled; votive.

**Class Reading.** Bring to class and read some newspaper item which shows that the spirit of freedom still lives.

---

# I Have a Rendezvous With Death*

### Alan Seeger

I have a rendezvous with Death
At some disputed barricade,
When Spring comes back with rustling shade
And apple-blossoms fill the air—
5 I have a rendezvous with Death
When Spring brings back blue days and fair.

It may be he shall take my hand
And lead me into his dark land
And close my eyes and quench my breath—
10 It may be I shall pass him still.
I have a rendezvous with Death
On some scarred slope of battered hill,
When Spring comes round again this year,
And the first meadow-flowers appear.

15 God knows 'twere better to be deep
Pillowed in silk and scented down,
Where love throbs out in blissful sleep,
Pulse nigh to pulse, and breath to breath,

---

*From *Poems*, by Alan Seeger

Where hushed awakenings are dear . . . .
But I've a rendezvous with Death
At midnight in some flaming town,
When Spring trips north again this year;
5 And I to my pledged word am true—
I shall not fail that rendezvous.

## NOTES AND QUESTIONS

**Biography.** Alan Seeger (1888-1916) was an American poet who greatly admired French art and literature. In 1912 he went to Paris to study and write. He was visiting in London when World War One broke out, but returned to Paris immediately and joined the Foreign Legion to fight for France. This poem was written from the trenches during the winter, while Seeger was waiting for the renewal of active warfare in the spring. The poet took part in the battle of Champagne and was killed in action, July 4, 1916, in the attack on the village of Bello-en-Santerre. During the war he formed a great friendship with an Egyptian, Rif Baer, who thus describes his last charge: "After the first bound forward, we lay flat on the ground. I caught sight of Seeger and made a sign to him with my hand. He answered with a smile. How pale he was! His tall silhouette stood out on the green of the cornfields. He was the tallest man in his section. His head was erect, and pride was in his eye. I saw him running forward, with bayonet fixed. Soon he disappeared, and that was the last time I saw my friend."

**Discussion.** 1. Notice how the beautiful descriptions of nature, contrasted with the grim determination to keep the rendezvous, emphasize the joy of life and of living and make the keeping of the pledge the more heroic; find lines that bring out sharply this contrast. 2. This poem expresses a young man's generous consecration of himself to death while love of life is keen; which lines bring out this thought most beautifully? 3. What other soldier-poets have you learned to know in this book? Do you know of any others? 4. How does this poem show that the spirit of liberty was the same in World War One as it was in the days of Paul Revere? 5. *Pronounce:* rendezvous.

**Library Reading.** Other poems by the same author (in *Poems*).

## Rouge Bouquet

### Joyce Kilmer

In a wood they call the Rouge Bouquet
There is a new-made grave today,
Built by never a spade nor pick,
Yet covered with earth ten meters thick.
5 There lie many fighting men,
    Dead in their youthful prime;
Never to laugh nor love again
    Nor taste the Summertime.
For Death came flying through the air
10 And stopped his flight at the dugout stair,
Touched his prey and left them there,
    Clay to clay.
He hid their bodies stealthily
In the soil of the land they sought to free,
15     And fled away.
Now over the grave abrupt and clear
    Three volleys ring;
And perhaps their brave young spirits hear
    The bugle sing:
20 "Go to sleep!
Go to sleep!
Slumber well where the shell screamed and fell.
Let your rifles rest on the muddy floor;
You will not need them any more.
25 Danger's past;
Now at last,
Go to sleep!"

There is on earth no worthier grave
To hold the bodies of the brave

Than this place of pain and pride
Where they nobly fought and nobly died.
Never fear but in the skies
    Saints and angels stand
5 Smiling with their holy eyes
    On this new-come band.
St. Michael's sword darts through the air
And touches the aureole on his hair,
As he sees them stand saluting there,
10    His stalwart sons;
And Patrick, Brigid, Columkill
Rejoice that in veins of warriors still
    The Gael's blood runs.
And up to Heaven's doorway floats,
15    From the wood called Rouge Bouquet,
A delicate cloud of bugle-notes
    That softly say:
"Farewell!
Farewell!
20 Comrades true, born anew, peace to you!
Your souls shall be where the heroes are;
And your memory shine like the morning-star.
Brave and dear,
Shield us here.
25 Farewell!"

## NOTES AND QUESTIONS

**Biography.** Joyce Kilmer (1886-1918), born in New Brunswick, NJ, crowded much into the brief thirty-two years of his life. Before he was twenty-two he had graduated from Rutgers College and Columbia University. He was literary critic for the *New York Times* and the *Literary Digest*. His life was a particularly happy one, both in his chosen field of work and in his home with his wife and four children. Joyce Kilmer was soldier as well as poet, like David of old, of whom it was said, he "smote now his harp and now the hostile horde." When the United States entered

World War One, he was among the first to enlist and insisted upon going as a private. "Naturally I'm expecting to go, being of appropriate age and sex," he wrote to a friend. After serving nearly a year, he died in the eager carrying out of a particularly dangerous piece of work. When the men of his own "Sixty-ninth" found him, his attitude was so like his keen, living self that they did not at first think him dead, for he lay as if scouting, seeking out the hidden battery which he was trying to locate. He lies buried on the trampled hillside where he fell, close to the river Ourcq. "Rouge Bouquet" was written in a dugout, and the poet called it "probably the best verse I have written."

**Discussion.** 1. Where did these fighting men meet death? 2. How does the refrain resemble "taps"? 3. Notice how painstakingly the poet worked out exactly the same rhyme scheme in the two stanzas; what interesting fact do you note in the twenty-second line of each stanza? 4. What part of "taps" do these lines imitate? 5. Why does the poet say "There is no worthier grave"? 6. Notice that this group of selections is called "The Eternal Spirit of Freedom"; what famous struggles for liberty are mentioned? 7. Find in the glossary the meaning of: meter; aureole; Gael. 8. *Pronounce:* Rouge Bouquet; stalwart.

**Class Reading.** Bring to class and read "Main Street"; "Roofs"; "The Snowman in the Yard"; "Trees"; "To a Blackbird and His Mate Who Died in the Spring"; "Dave Lilly"; Joyce Kilmer (in *Poems, Essays, and Letters,* Vol. 1). *The Bookman,* October, 1918, has a portrait of Joyce Kilmer; try to get a copy to show your classmates.

**A Suggested Problem.** In the "Introduction" on page 256 you read that the selections in this group "are only a few out of many such stories and poems that express this eternal spirit of freedom." Be prepared to contribute to a program of additional selections found in outside reading.

# AMERICA'S EXPERIMENT IN
# FREE GOVERNMENT

## Supposed Speech of John Adams

### Daniel Webster

Sink or swim, live or die, survive or perish, I give my hand and my heart to this vote. It is true, indeed, that in the beginning we aimed not at independence. But there is a divinity which shapes our ends. The injustice of England has driven us to
5 arms; and, blinded to her own interest, she has obstinately persisted, till independence is now within our grasp. We have but to reach forth to it, and it is ours. Why, then, should we defer the declaration?

If we postpone independence, do we mean to carry on or
10 to give up the war? Do we mean to submit, and consent that we shall be ground to powder, and our country and its rights trodden down in the dust? I know we do not mean to submit. We never shall submit!

The war, then, must go on; we must fight it through. And if

the war must go on, why put off the declaration of independence? That measure will strengthen us. It will give us character abroad. Nations will then treat with us, which they never can do while we acknowledge ourselves subjects in arms against
5 our sovereign.

If we fail, it can be no worse for us. But we shall not fail. The cause will raise up armies; the cause will create navies. The people—the people, if we are true to them, will carry us, and will carry themselves, gloriously through this struggle. I care not how
10 fickle other people have been found. I know the people of these colonies; and I know that resistance to British aggression is deep and settled in their hearts and cannot be eradicated.

Sir, the declaration of independence will inspire the people with increased courage. Instead of a long and bloody war for
15 the restoration of privileges, for redress of grievances, set before them the glorious object of entire independence, and it will breathe into them anew the spirit of life.

Read this declaration at the head of the army; every sword will be drawn, and the solemn vow uttered to maintain it or perish on
20 the bed of honor. Publish it from the pulpit; religion will approve it, and the love of religious liberty will cling around it, resolved to stand with it or fall with it. Send it to the public halls; proclaim it there; let them see it who saw their brothers and their sons fall on the field of Bunker Hill and in the streets of Lexington and
25 Concord, and the very walls will cry out in its support.

Sir, I know the uncertainty of human affairs, but I see, I see clearly through this day's business. You and I, indeed, may rue it. We may not live to see the time this declaration shall be made good. We may die; die colonists; die slaves; die, it may be,
30 ignominiously, and on the scaffold. Be it so; be it so. If it be the pleasure of Heaven that my country shall require the poor offering of my life, the victim shall be ready at the appointed hour of sacrifice come when that hour may. But while I do live, let me have a country, or at least the hope of a country, and
35 that a free country.

But whatever may be our fate, be assured—be assured that this declaration will stand. It may cost treasure, and it may cost blood; but it will stand, and it will richly compensate for both. Through the thick gloom of the present I see the brightness of 5 the future, as the sun in heaven. We shall make this a glorious, an immortal day. When we are in our graves, our children will honor it. They will celebrate it with thanksgiving, with festivity, with bonfires, and illuminations. On its annual return they will shed tears, copious tears, gushing tears; not of subjection and 10 slavery, not of agony and distress, but of exultation, of gratitude, and of joy.

Sir, before God, I believe the hour is come. My judgment approves the measure, and my whole heart is in it. All that I have, and all that I am, and all that I hope in this life, I am now 15 ready here to stake upon it; and I leave off as I began, that, live or die, survive or perish, I am for the declaration. It is my living sentiment, and, by the blessing of God, it shall be my dying sentiment; independence now, independence forever.

## NOTES AND QUESTIONS

**Biography.** Daniel Webster (1782-1852) stands out as America's foremost orator. His eloquence, his clear thinking, and the force of his personality made him equally great, whether answering an opponent in the Senate or delivering less passionate orations on anniversary occasions. He was the champion of the idea of complete union among the states. His service in the Senate, representing not only the people of Massachusetts but all who believed with him in "Liberty and Union, now and forever, one and inseparable," and his service as secretary of state in President Tyler's cabinet, make him one of America's great statesmen.

**Historical Note.** John Adams, the second president of the United States, died in Boston on July 4, 1826. just fifty years after the signing of the Declaration of Independence. He was not only conscious, before his death, of the significance of the day, but spoke of his colleague, Thomas Jefferson, and the fact that Jefferson would survive him. A few days later, news came from Virginia that Jefferson had died on the same day, a few hours earlier than Adams. The whole country was deeply affected by the remarkable coincidence of the passing away at the same time of these two great men, each of whom had signed the Declaration of Independence and served as president of the United States. On the second of August a public memorial meeting was held in Faneuil Hall, Boston, at which Daniel Webster delivered an oration on "Adams and Jefferson." In this selection, which is merely a part of the oration, Webster represents what Adams might have said in the debate about the Declaration of Independence in the Continental Congress.

**Discussion.** 1. What was the vote under discussion at the time of this supposed speech? 2. Why, in the opinion of the speaker, must the colonists carry on the war? 3. What advantages does he say they will gain by the Declaration of Independence? 4. Whom does he address as "Sir"? 5. What plan does he suggest for making the declaration known to the people? 6. What results does he expect will come from this action? 7. Show that the speaker has considered the possible consequences of signing the declaration. 8. What prophecy does he make concerning the day on which the declaration was signed? Has this prophecy been fulfilled? 9. Point out lines in the speech that seem to you to be the most stirring. 10. The signing of the Declaration of Independence was the first great step in America's experiment in free government; why was it of great moment? 11. Find in the glossary the meaning of: eradicated; ignominiously; copious.

---

## Liberty and Union

### (From Washington's Farewell Address)

### George Washington

Friends and Fellow Citizens:

The period for a new election of a citizen, to administer the executive government of the United States, being not far distant, and the time actually arrived when your thoughts must
5 be employed in designating the person who is to be clothed with that important trust, it appears to me proper, especially as it may conduce to a more distinct expression of the public voice, that I should now apprise you of the resolution I have formed, to decline being considered among the number of those out of
10 whom a choice is to be made. . . .

The unity of government, which constitutes you one people, is also now dear to you. It is justly so, for it is a main pillar in the edifice of your real independence—the support of your tranquility at home and your peace abroad, of your safety, of
5 your prosperity, of that very liberty which you so highly prize.

But it is easy to foresee that from different causes and from different quarters, much pains will be taken, many artifices employed to weaken in your minds the conviction of this truth; as this is the point in your political fortress against which the
10 batteries of internal and external enemies will be most constantly and actively, though often covertly and insidiously, directed—it is of infinite moment that you should properly estimate the immense value of your national union to your collective and individual happiness; that you should cherish a cordial, habitual,
15 and immovable attachment to it; accustoming yourself to think and speak of it as of the palladium of your political safety and prosperity; watching for its preservation with jealous anxiety; discountenancing whatever may suggest even a suspicion that it can, in any event, be abandoned; and indignantly frowning upon
20 the first dawning of every attempt to alienate any portion of our country from the rest, or to enfeeble the sacred ties which now link together the various parts.

For this you have every inducement of sympathy and interest. Citizens, by birth or choice, of a common country, that
25 country has a right to concentrate your affections. The name of American, which belongs to you, in your national capacity, must always exalt the just pride of patriotism more than any appellation derived from local discriminations. You have in a common cause fought and triumphed together; the independence
30 and liberty you possess are the work of joint counsels and joint efforts, of common dangers, sufferings, and successes.

To the efficacy and permanency of your union a government for the whole is indispensable. No alliances, however strict, between the parts can be an adequate substitute; they must
35 inevitably experience the infractions and interruptions which

all alliances in all times have experienced. Sensible of this momentous truth, you have improved upon your first essay by the adoption of a constitution of government better calculated than your former for an intimate union and for the efficacious
5 management of your common concerns.

This government, the offspring of our own choice, uninfluenced and unawed, adopted upon full investigation and mature deliberation, completely free in its principles, in the distribution of its powers, uniting security with energy, and containing within
10 itself a provision for its own amendment, has a just claim to your confidence and your support. Respect for its authority, compliance with its laws, acquiescence in its measures are duties enjoined by the fundamental maxims of true liberty. The basis of our political systems is the right of the people to make and to
15 alter their constitution of government; but the constitution which at any time exists, till changed by an explicit and authentic act of the whole people, is sacredly obligatory upon all. The very idea of the power and the right of the people to establish government presupposes the duty of every individual to obey
20 the established government. . . .

In all the changes to which you may be invited, remember that time and habit are at least as necessary to fix the true character of governments as of other human institutions—that experience is the surest standard by which to test the real
25 tendency of the existing constitution of a country; that facility in changes, upon the credit of mere hypothesis and opinion, exposes to perpetual change, from the endless variety of hypothesis and opinion. And remember especially that for the efficient management of your common interest, in a country so extensive
30 as ours, a government of as much vigor as is consistent with the perfect security of liberty is indispensable. Liberty itself will find in such a government, with powers properly distributed and adjusted, its surest guardian. It is, indeed, little else than a name where the government is too feeble to withstand the enterprises
35 of faction, to confine each member of society within the limits

prescribed by the laws, and to maintain all in the secure and tranquil enjoyment of the rights of person and property. . . .

If, in the opinion of the people, the distribution or modification of the constitutional powers be in any particular wrong, let
5 it be corrected by an amendment in the way which the constitution designates. But let there be no change by usurpation, for, though this, in one instance, may be the instrument of good, it is the customary weapon by which free governments are destroyed. The precedent must always greatly overbalance in
10 permanent evil any partial or transient benefit which the use can at any time yield.

Of all the dispositions and habits which lead to political prosperity, religion and morality are indispensable supports. In vain would that man claim the tribute of patriotism, who
15 should labor to subvert these great pillars of human happiness, these firmest props of the duties of men and citizens. The mere politician, equally with the pious man, ought to respect and to cherish them. A volume could not trace all their connections with private and public felicity. . . .
20     Promote then, as an object of primary importance, institutions for the general diffusion of knowledge. In proportion as the structure of a government gives force to public opinion, it is essential that public opinion should be enlightened. . . .

Observe good faith and justice toward all nations; cultivate
25 peace and harmony with all: religion and morality enjoin this conduct; and can it be that good policy does not equally enjoin it? It will be worthy of a free, enlightened, and, at no distant period, a great nation to give to mankind the magnanimous and too novel example of a people always guided by an exalted
30 justice and benevolence. . . .

In the execution of such a plan, nothing is more essential than that permanent, inveterate antipathies against particular nations, and passionate attachments for others, should be excluded; and that, in place of them, just and amicable feelings
35 toward all should be cultivated. The nation which indulges

toward another an habitual hatred, or an habitual fondness, is in some degrees a slave. . . . .

In offering to you, my countrymen, these counsels of an old and affectionate friend, I dare not hope they will make the
5 strong and lasting impression I could wish; that they will control the usual current of the passions, or prevent our nation from running the course which has hitherto marked the destiny of nations. But, if I may even flatter myself that they may be productive of some partial benefit, some occasional good; that
10 they may now and then recur to moderate the fury of party spirit, to warn against the mischiefs of foreign intrigue, to guard against the impostures of pretended patriotism; this hope will be a full recompense for the solicitude for your welfare, by which they have been dictated.

## NOTES AND QUESTIONS

**Biographical and Historical Note.** George Washington (1732-1799) took the oath of office as first president of the United States in 1789, having been unanimously chosen, under the new Constitution, to fill that office. He was reelected and served until 1797. Though urged to accept the nomination for a third term, he declined and retired from public life to Mount Vernon, his estate in Virginia. In his "Farewell Address to the People of the United States," he impresses upon the nation the political principles which he regarded as fundamental and which had governed the policy of his administration. In Washington's day the Atlantic Ocean was a barrier between the Old World and the New, and America was practically isolated, but the steamship, the cable, and the wireless have annihilated distance, and whether we wish it or not, we are forced to play our part in world affairs.

**Discussion.** 1. Picture to yourself our country in Washington's time with reference to the extent of territory, the cities, and the means of transportation and communication; why is our unity of government even more remarkable today than it was in 1797? 2. What means of changing the constitution have we? 3. What changes have been made by amendments? 4. In line 10, page 282, Washington warns against "external" enemies. What reason is mentioned in the "Introduction" on page 257 for the hostility of some European governments? 5. In the "Introduction" on page 258 you read a definition of the *American idea of free government*. What advice on page

283 shows that Washington had the same view of a successful democracy? 6. What are the "pillars of human happiness" according to Washington? 7. Why did Washington think education so necessary in a democracy? 8. How did our course in World War One prove that we were guided "by an exalted justice"? 9. In "Literature and Life" on page 18 you read that the "second joy of reading will give you the power to ripen your judgment by the accumulated wisdom left as an inheritance by the world's greatest minds." What wise advice have you gained from this selection? 10. Find in the glossary the meaning of: apprise; covertly; insidiously; palladium; alienate; local; efficacious; acquiescence; maxim; hypothesis; usurpation; subvert; felicity; impostures. 11. *Pronounce:* address; artifice; essay; precedent; inveterate; amicable; solicitude.

**Suggestions for Theme Topics.** 1. The relations of the United States to Cuba. 2. Our relations to Puerto Rico. 3. Our relations to Hawaii. 4. Our relations to the Philippines.

---

## The American Experiment

### Daniel Webster

It was the extraordinary fortune of Washington that having been intrusted in revolutionary times with the supreme military command, and having fulfilled that trust with equal renown for wisdom and for valor, he should be placed at the head of
5 the first government in which an attempt was to be made on a large scale to rear the fabric of social order on the basis of a written constitution and of a pure representative principle. A government was to be established, without a throne, without an aristocracy, without castes, orders, or privileges—and this
10 government, instead of being a democracy existing and acting within the walls of a single city, was to be extended over a vast country of different climates, interests, and habits, and of various communions of our common Christian faith. The experiment certainly was entirely new. A popular government of this extent, it was evident, could be framed only by carrying

into full effect the principle of representation or of delegated power, and the world was to see whether society could, by the strength of this principle, maintain its own peace and good government, carry forward its own great interests, and conduct
5 itself to political renown and glory.

At the period of the birth of Washington, there existed in Europe no political liberty in large communities except in the provinces of Holland, and except that England herself had set a great example, so far as it went, by her glorious revolution of
10 1688. Everywhere else despotic power was predominant, and the feudal or military principle held the mass of mankind in hopeless bondage. One half of Europe was crushed beneath the Bourbon scepter, and no conception of political liberty, no hope even of religious toleration, existed among that nation which
15 was America's first ally. The king was the state, the king was the country, the king was all. There was one king, with power not derived from his people, and too high to be questioned, and the rest were all subjects with no political right but obedience. All above was intangible power; all below was quiet subjection. A
20 recent occurrence in the French chamber shows us how public opinion on these subjects is changed. A minister had spoken of the "king's subjects." "There are no subjects," exclaimed hundreds of voices at once, "in a country where the people make the king!"

Gentlemen, the spirit of human liberty and of free govern-
25 ment, nurtured and grown into strength and beauty in America, has stretched its course into the midst of the nations. Like an emanation from Heaven, it has gone forth, and it will not return void. It must change, it is fast changing, the face of the earth. Our great, our high duty is to show in our own example that this
30 spirit is a spirit of health as well as a spirit of power; that its benignity is as great as its strength; that its efficiency to secure individual rights, social relations, and moral order, is equal to the irresistible force with which it prostrates principalities and powers. The world, at this moment, is regarding us with a
35 willing, but something of a fearful, admiration. Its deep and

awful anxiety is to learn whether free states may be stable
as well as free; whether popular power may be trusted as
well as feared; in short, whether wise, regular, and virtuous
self-government is a vision for the contemplation of theorists,
5 or a truth established, illustrated, and brought into practice in
the country of Washington.

### NOTES AND QUESTIONS

For **Biography** see page 280.

**Discussion.** 1. This selection is taken from an address, "The Character
of Washington," delivered at a public dinner in Washington on February 22,
1832, the centennial of George Washington's birthday; why was a discussion
of the "American experiment" especially appropriate on such an occasion?
2. How does Daniel Webster in the first paragraph define this experiment?
3. Explain the two distinctive features of this experiment. 4. Why was the
use of "the principle of representation or delegated power" so necessary in
the American experiment in free government? 5. In the second paragraph
Webster reviews the situation with reference to political liberty in Europe;
what change in France within the century does he note? 6. Can you
mention any like changes that have occurred in Europe since Webster's
time? 7. In the last paragraph what prophecy does Webster make? 8. To
what extent has this prophecy come true? 9. Read again what is said in the
first paragraph in the "Introduction" on page 257 about the "Great American
Experiment." What similar ideas do you get from the first paragraphs of
Webster's speech? 10. Find in the last paragraph lines that you think aptly
express America's situation in the world today. 11. Find in the glossary the
meaning of: conception; void; stable. 12. *Pronounce:* ally; benignity.

### Phrases for Study

| | |
|---|---|
| fabric of social order, **286**, 6 | feudal or military, **287**, 11 |
| various communions, **286**, 13 | Bourbon scepter, **287**, 13 |
| delegated power, **287**, 2 | prostrates principalities, **287** 33 |
| glorious revolution, **287**, 9 | contemplation of theorists, **288**, 4 |

# The Poor Voter on Election Day

### John Greenleaf Whittier

The proudest now is but my peer,
    The highest not more high;
Today, of all the weary year,
    A king of men am I.
5 Today, alike are great and small,
    The nameless and the known.
My palace is the people's hall;
    The ballot box my throne!

Who serves today upon the list
10    Beside the served shall stand;
Alike the brown and wrinkled fist
    The gloved and dainty hand
The rich is level with the poor;
    The weak is strong today;
15 And sleekest broadcloth counts no more
    Than homespun frock of gray.

Today let pomp and vain pretense
    My stubborn right abide;
I set a plain man's common sense
20    Against the pedant's pride.
Today shall simple manhood try
    The strength of gold and land;
The wide world has not wealth to buy
    The power in my right hand!

25 While there's a grief to seek redress,
    Or balance to adjust,
Where weighs our living manhood less
    Than Mammon's vilest dust—

> While there's a right to need my vote,
>    A wrong to sweep away,
> Up! clouted knee and ragged coat!
>    A man's a man today!

## NOTES AND QUESTIONS

**Biography.** John Greenleaf Whittier (1807-1892) was born near Haverhill, Massachusetts, in the same county as Salem, the birthplace of Hawthorne. The old farmhouse in which Whittier lived as a child was built by the poet's great-great-grandfather and is still standing. His family were Quakers, sturdy of character as of stature. Whittier's boyhood was that of a typical New England farm boy, consisting of hard work, no luxuries, and few pleasures. Unlike Lowell and Longfellow, he did not go to college, but worked his way through an academy. As a boy his one book was the family Bible. When the district schoolmaster lent him a copy of Burns's *Poems*, his interest in poetry was awakened and he began writing verses of his own. Whittier is often compared with Burns in the simple naturalness of his style, his patriotism, his fiery indignation at wrong, and his sympathy with the humble and the oppressed. He is considered one of the greatest American poets.

**Discussion.** 1. What does the poor voter mean when he says, "Today a king of men am I"? 2. What sentence in the Declaration of Independence does this poem help make clear? 3. What are some of the "griefs that seek redress" and "rights to need my vote" at the present time? 4. What progress along these lines has been made by legislation since Whittier's time? 5. Why is it so important in a democracy that there be no "slackers" among the citizens who have the qualifications to vote? 6. In some communities voters are "tagged" at the polls in order to make those who have not voted conspicuous and ashamed; what is the situation in an ideal community? 7. What are some of the advantages of living in a democracy where one voter counts for the same as another? 8. In a democracy, why is voting on election day a citizen's duty? 9. Find in the glossary the meaning of: pedant; clouted. 10. *Pronounce:* pretense; redress.

### Phrases for Study

| | |
|---|---|
| weary year, **289**, 3 | try the strength of gold, **289**, 22 |
| stubborn right abide, **289**, 18 | Mammon's vilest dust, **289**, 28 |

**Newspaper Reading.** Bring to class editorials that urge reforms in some of the things that Whittier calls "wrongs to sweep away."

# Gettysburg Address

## Abraham Lincoln

Fourscore and seven years ago our fathers brought forth on this continent a new nation, conceived in liberty and dedicated to the proposition that all men are created equal.

Now we are engaged in a great civil war; testing whether
5 that nation, or any nation so conceived and so dedicated, can long endure. We are met on a great battlefield of that war. We have come to dedicate a portion of that field as a final resting place for those who here gave their lives that that nation might live. It is altogether fitting and proper that we should do this.

10 But, in a larger sense, we cannot dedicate—we cannot consecrate—we cannot hallow—this ground. The brave men, living and dead, who struggled here have consecrated it far above our poor power to add or detract. The world will little note, nor long remember, what we say here, but it can never
15 forget what they did here. It is for us the living, rather, to be dedicated here to the unfinished work which they who fought here have thus far so nobly advanced. It is rather for us to be here dedicated to the great task remaining before us—that from these honored dead we take increased devotion to that cause
20 for which they gave the last full measure of devotion—that we here highly resolve that these dead shall not have died in vain—that this nation, under God, shall have a new birth of freedom—and that government of the people, by the people, for the people, shall not perish from the earth.

## NOTES AND QUESTIONS

**Biographical and Historical Note.** Abraham Lincoln (1809-1865), the sixteenth president of the United States, was born on a farm near Hodgensville, Kentucky. When he was seven years old, the Lincoln family moved to Indiana, and in 1830 to Illinois. Lincoln's boyhood was full of hardships and privation. He was able to attend school only a few months altogether, but he had a small number of good books, which he read again and again. By hard struggles he educated himself, became a lawyer, a member of Congress, and in 1860 was elected president. He was assassinated by John Wilkes Booth on April 14, 1865. There are many memorials to Lincoln: the farm where he was born was presented to the nation in 1916; the Abraham Lincoln Memorial in Washington, D.C., stands in Potomac Park, near the shore of the Potomac River; there is a beautiful monument in Springfield, Illinois, where he is buried; a national highway crossing the continent from east to west has been named the Lincoln Highway; one of the most famous statues of Lincoln is the one by Saint Gaudens which stands in Lincoln Park, Chicago.

Lincoln was asked to be present and say a few words at the dedication of the national cemetery at Gettysburg, November 19, 1863. Contrary to his prediction, the world *has* noted and remembered what he said on that occasion. Like all his writings, the address shows intense thought and feeling expressed in simple words. Edward Everett, who delivered the oration of the day, wrote to Mr. Lincoln, "I should be glad if I could flatter myself that I came as near the central idea of the occasion in two hours as you did in two minutes."

**Discussion.** 1. In a speech delivered in Independence Hall in 1861, just before he became president, Lincoln said, "I have never had a feeling, politically, that did not spring from the sentiments embodied in the Declaration of Independence...It was not the mere matter of the separation of the colonies from the motherland, but that sentiment in the Declaration of Independence which gave liberty, not alone to the people of this country but, I hope, to the world, for all future time"; what is the sentence in the Declaration of Independence to which Lincoln refers? 2. Is there anything in this address that you can apply to the World Wars? 3. Memorize the address. 4. Find in the glossary the meaning of: conceived; proposition; hallow; detract; measure.

**Class Reading.** Bring to class and read "O Captain! My Captain," Whitman (in *The Elson Readers, Book Seven*).

**Library Reading.** "The Perfect Tribute," Andrews.

**Magazine Reading.** You will be interested in seeing the established version of the "Gettysburg Address." Draw from the library and bring to class "Lincoln's Gettysburg Address," *The Century*, for February, 1894; note Lincoln's handwriting; compare the three versions of the address: Lincoln's first draft, the Associated Press report, and Lincoln's revised autograph copy. Show the accepted version to the class.

---

## ABRAHAM LINCOLN

### WOODROW WILSON

No more significant memorial could have been presented to the nation than this. It expresses so much of what is singular and noteworthy in the history of the country; it suggests so many of the things that we prize most highly in our life and in
5 our system of government. How eloquent this little house within this shrine is of the vigor of democracy! There is nowhere in the land any home so remote, so humble, that it may not contain the power of mind and heart and conscience to which nations yield and history submits its processes. Nature pays no tribute
10 to aristocracy, subscribes to no creed of caste, renders fealty to no monarch or master of any name or kind. Genius is no snob. It does not run after titles or seek by preference the high circles of society. It affects humble company as well as great. It pays no special tribute to universities or learned societies or
15 conventional standards of greatness, but serenely chooses its own comrades, its own haunts, its own cradle even, and its own life of adventure and of training. Here is proof of it. This little hut was the cradle of one of the great sons of men, a man of singular, delightful, vital genius who presently emerged upon
20 the great stage of the nation's history, gaunt, shy, ungainly, but dominant and majestic, a natural ruler of men, himself inevitably the central figure of the great plot. No man can explain this, but

every man can see how it demonstrates the vigor of democracy, where every door is open, in every hamlet and countryside, in city and wilderness alike, for the ruler to emerge when he will and claim his leadership in the free life. Such are the authentic
5 proofs of the validity and vitality of democracy.

Here, no less, hides the mystery of democracy. Who shall guess this secret of nature and providence and a free polity? Whatever the vigor and vitality of the stock from which he sprang, its mere vigor and soundness do not explain where this man got
10 his great heart that seemed to comprehend all mankind in its catholic and benignant sympathy, the mind that sat enthroned behind those brooding, melancholy eyes, whose vision swept many an horizon which those about him dreamed not of—that mind that comprehended what it had never seen, and understood
15 the language of affairs with the ready ease of one to the manner born—or that nature which seemed in its varied richness to be the familiar of men of every way of life. This is the sacred mystery of democracy; that its richest fruits spring up out of soils which no man has prepared and in circumstances amidst
20 which they are the least expected. This is a place alike of mystery and of reassurance.

It is likely that in a society ordered otherwise than our own Lincoln could not have found himself or the path of fame and power upon which he walked serenely to his death. In this
25 place it is right that we should remind ourselves of the solid and striking facts upon which our faith in democracy is founded. Many another man besides Lincoln has served the nation in its highest places of counsel and of action whose origins were as humble as his. Though the greatest example of the universal
30 energy, richness, stimulation, and force of democracy, he is only one example among many. The permeating and all-pervasive virtue of the freedom which challenges us in America to make the most of every gift and power we possess, every page of our history serves to emphasize and illustrate. Standing here in this
35 place, it seems almost the whole of the stirring story.

Here Lincoln had his beginnings. Here the end and consummation of that great life seem remote and a bit incredible. And yet there was no break anywhere between beginning and end, no lack of natural sequence anywhere. Nothing really incredible
5 happened. Lincoln was unaffectedly as much at home in the White House as he was here. Do you share with me the feeling, I wonder, that he was permanently at home nowhere? It seems to me that in the case of a man—I would rather say of a spirit—like Lincoln, the question where he was is of little significance, that
10 it is always what he was that really arrests our thought and takes hold of our imagination. It is the spirit always that is sovereign. Lincoln, like the rest of us, was put through the discipline of the world—a very rough and exacting discipline for him, an indispensable discipline for every man who would know what he
15 is about in the midst of the world's affairs, but his spirit got only its schooling there. It did not derive its character or its vision from the experiences which brought it to its full revelation. The test of every American must always be, not where he is, but what he is. That, also, is of the essence of democracy and is the
20 moral of which this place is most gravely expressive.

We would like to think of men like Lincoln and Washington as typical Americans, but no man can be typical who is so unusual as these great men were. It was typical of American life that it should produce such men with supreme indifference as to the
25 manner in which it produced them, and as readily here in this hut as amidst the little circle of cultivated gentlemen to whom Virginia owed so much in leadership and example. And Lincoln and Washington were typical Americans in the use they made of their genius. But there will be few such men at best, and
30 we will not look into the mystery of how and why they come. We will only keep the door open for them always, and a hearty welcome—after we have recognized them.

I have read many biographies of Lincoln; I have sought out with the greatest interest the many intimate stories that are told
35 of him, the narratives of nearby friends, the sketches at close

quarters, in which those who had the privilege of being associated
with him have tried to depict for us the very man himself "in
his habit as he lived," but I have nowhere found a real intimate
of Lincoln's. I nowhere get the impression in any narrative or
5 reminiscence that the writer had in fact penetrated to the heart
of his mystery, or that any man could penetrate to the heart of it.
That brooding spirit had no real familiars. I get the impression
that it never spoke out in complete self-revelation and that it
could not reveal itself completely to anyone. It was a very lonely
10 spirit that looked out from underneath those shaggy brows and
comprehended men without fully communing with them, as if,
in spite of all its genial efforts at comradeship, it dwelt apart,
saw its visions of duty where no man looked on. There is a very
holy and very terrible isolation for the conscience of every man
15 who seeks to read the destiny in affairs for others as well as for
himself, for a nation as well as for individuals. That privacy no
man can intrude upon. The lonely search of the spirit for the right
perhaps no man can assist. This strange child of the cabin kept
company with invisible things, was born into no intimacy but that
20 of his own silently assembling and deploying thoughts.

I have come here today, not to utter a eulogy on Lincoln; he
stands in need of none, but to endeavor to interpret the meaning
of this gift to the nation of the place of his birth and origin.
Is not this an altar upon which we may forever keep alive the
25 vestal fire of democracy as upon a shrine at which some of the
deepest and most sacred hopes of mankind may from age to age
be rekindled? For these hopes must constantly be rekindled
and only those who live can rekindle them. The only stuff that
can retain the life-giving heat is the stuff of living hearts. And
30 the hopes of mankind cannot be kept alive by words merely, by
constitutions and doctrines of right and codes of liberty. The
object of democracy is to transmute these into the life and action
of society, the self-denial and self-sacrifice of heroic men and
women willing to make their lives an embodiment of right and
35 service and enlightened purpose. The commands of democracy

are as imperative as its privileges and opportunities are wide and generous. Its compulsion is upon us. It will be great and lift a great light for the guidance of the nations only if we are great and carry that light high for the guidance of our own feet. We 5 are not worthy to stand here unless we ourselves be in deed and in truth real democrats and servants of mankind, ready to give our very lives for the freedom and justice and spiritual exaltation of the great nation which shelters and nurtures us.

## NOTES AND QUESTIONS

**Biographical and Historical Note.** Woodrow Wilson (1856-1924), twenty-eighth president of the United States, was a native of Virginia. He was educated at Princeton University and later became president of that institution. He was for some years a teacher of history, and he has written many books on history and government, which are models of good English. In 1911 he became governor of New Jersey, and in 1913 he entered upon his duties as president of the United States, serving throughout the difficult period of World War One.

This address was delivered September 4, 1916, by Mr. Wilson when the Lincoln birthplace farm near Hodgensville, Kentucky was presented to the nation and accepted by the War Department. By popular subscription the log cabin itself was inclosed in an imposing granite memorial building.

**Discussion.** 1. How does Lincoln's life demonstrate "the vigor of democracy"? 2. Discuss "Genius is no snob." 3. What sentence in the second paragraph describes Lincoln? What do you think of this sentence as an example of saying much in a few words? 4. What are some of the "mysteries of democracy" which Lincoln's life expressed? 5. How do your school and other democratic institutions help you "to make the most of every gift and power you possess"? 6. How does Mr. Wilson explain his feeling that Lincoln was "permanently at home nowhere"? 7. What is the "test of every American"? 8. In what way were Washington and Lincoln typical Americans? 9. Why does Mr. Wilson feel that Lincoln was "a lonely spirit"? 10. In what way might "this cabin" keep alive the hopes of mankind even better than "constitution, doctrines of right, and codes of liberty"? 11. What is your opinion of people who are willing to enjoy the privileges but are not willing to share the duties of the society to which they belong? 12. What is expected of "real democrats"? 13. Which sentence best visualizes for you the occasion—the cabin and the crowds listening to the president?

14. Be prepared to read to the class a sentence selected because it seemed especially significant to you. 15. Find in the glossary the meaning of: significant; democracy; aristocracy; fealty; catholic; consummation; depict; familiars; communing; vestal; transmute. 16. *Pronounce:* haunts; dominant; validity; benignant; reassurance; permeating; sovereign.

### Phrases for Study

submits its processes, **293**, 9
creed of caste, **293**, 10
conventional standards, **293**, 15
great plot, **293**, 22

to the manner born, **294**, 16
familiar of men, **294**, 17
natural sequence, **295**, 4
read the destiny, **296**,15

**Library Reading.** *He Knew Lincoln,* Tarbell; *Boys' Life of Lincoln,* Nicolay.

**Magazine Reading.** See *Collier's* for September 9, 1916, for an illustrated description of the acceptance of the memorial.

**Suggestions for Theme Topics.** 1. Other great Americans of humble origin. 2. The best "intimate" story I know about Lincoln.

---

## HOME AND COUNTRY

### HENRY W. GRADY

The germ of the best patriotism is in the love that a man has for the home he inhabits, for the soil he tills, for the trees that give him shade, and the hills that stand in his pathway.

I teach my son to love Georgia—to love the soil that he
5 stands on—the broad acres that hold her substance, the dimpling valleys in which her beauty rests, the forests that sing her songs of lullaby and of praise, and the brooks that run with her rippling laughter. The love of home—deep-rooted and abiding—that blurs the eyes of the dying soldier with the vision of an old

homestead amid green fields and clustering trees—that follows the busy man through the clamoring world, and at last draws his tired feet from the highway and leads him through shady lanes and well-remembered paths until he gathers up the broken
5 threads of his life—this, lodged in the heart of the citizen, is the saving principle of our government.

We note the barracks of our standing army with their rolling drums and their fluttering flags as points of strength and protection. But the citizen standing in the doorway of his
10 home, contented on his threshold, his family gathered about his hearthstone while the evening of a well-spent day closes in scenes and sounds that are dearest—he shall save the Republic when the drumtap is futile and the barracks are exhausted.

This love shall not be pent up or provincial. The home
15 should be consecrated to humanity, and from its rooftree should fly the flag of the Republic. Every simple fruit gathered there, every sacrifice endured, and every victory won should bring better joy and inspiration in the knowledge that it will deepen the glory of our Republic and widen the harvest of humanity.

20 Exalt the citizen. As the state is the unit of the government, he is the unit of the state. Teach him that his home is his castle, and his sovereignty rests beneath his hat. Make him self-respecting, self-reliant, and responsible. Let him lean on the state for nothing that his own arm can do and on the
25 government for nothing that his state can do. Let him cultivate independence to the point of sacrifice and learn that humble things with unbartered liberty are better than splendors bought with its price. Let him neither surrender his individuality to government nor merge it with the mob. Let him stand upright
30 and fearless, a freeman born of freemen, sturdy in his own strength, dowering his family in the sweat of his brow, loving to his state, loyal to his Republic, earnest in his allegiance wherever it rests, but building his altar in the midst of his household gods and shrining in his own heart the uttermost temple of
35 its liberty.

## NOTES AND QUESTIONS

**Biography.** Henry W. Grady (1851-1889) was born in Athens, Georgia. He graduated from the University of Georgia and studied at the University of Virginia. At an early age he became editor of the Rome *Courier* and later established the Atlanta *Herald*. In 1882 he became part owner and managing editor of the *Atlanta Constitution*, one of the great newspapers of the South. He was an eloquent speaker and was widely known and admired for his broad sympathies and kindliness.

**Discussion.** 1. What does the author consider "the germ of the best patriotism"? 2. The love of home forms the basis for the love of the homeland; why does the author regard this as "the saving principle of our government"? 3. Which is the greater in saving the Republic, the patriotic citizen, or the drumbeat, the flag, and the barracks? 4. Can you tell how every sacrifice endured and every service rendered in the home "will deepen the glory of the Republic"? 5. What ways to exalt the citizen are suggested in the last paragraph? 6. The author defines the relation in America between the home and the homeland; why is this a suitable conclusion to a group of selections dealing with America's experiment in free government? 7. Find in the glossary the meaning of: dimpling; provincial; unbartered; allegiance.

# CITIZENSHIP AND SERVICE

## You Are the Hope of the World*

### Hermann Hagedorn

Girls and boys of America you are the hope of the world. Why?

Because the world is sick to death of war, and the world kings favor war, and democracies abhor war, and because the
5 United States is the most powerful democracy in the world, and because, when Europe's present leaders are dead, you girls and boys of ten, twelve, fourteen, fifteen, sixteen, seventeen, will be governing the United States, and, therefore, if you wish, leading the world! Be clear about this. The world looks to you in hope
10 because you are the logical heirs of the present generation of leaders. If you have the gumption and the go, the knowledge, the vision, and the largeness of hearts to accept that inheritance, you will have it in your power to determine the course of the world's history for centuries to come!

---

*See Silent and Oral Reading, page 13.

The world asks you to think.  It doesn't ask you to stand on a street corner and wave the flag; it doesn't ask you to enlist.  The world asks you to sit down and think about your country.

5    Democracy isn't a success, Young America.  Not yet.  But it isn't a failure, either.  Not yet.  It's just a gorgeous experiment that you and I and Tom and Mary and Jane and Betty and Larry and Jack and Susan and Bill could make a success that would shake the world, if we'd only make up our minds to take

10 democracy as seriously as we take, say, baseball—or crêpe de Chine.

We know what America stands for; we know what America is.  Golden girls and boys, have you ever thought what America might be?

15   We're wasteful—look at our forests, look at the youth in our slums

We're materialistic—look at the faces in our cities, look how hard we are to arouse in defense of a principle, look how quickly, after our moment of exaltation and sacrifice, we drop back into

20 the sordid round of getting and spending.

We're improvident, blindly careless of everything beyond the present hour—we never prepare!

As citizens we are indifferent—we will endure in our government every form of extravagance, inefficiency, and corruption

25 conceivable rather than jump into the midst of the mess and help to clean it up.

"We know all these things," you say a little wearily.  "But what can we do?"

You?  You can do everything.  Your elders are busy, and

30 many of them are stodgy, and they are accustomed to waste and corruption and muddling, and many are afraid of change, any change, and resent as an imposition any attempt to make them think.  Thinking is more laborious than digging trenches after you're forty, especially when you're out of training,

35 and many of our elders are.  But you, Young America, are

not.  Thinking to you isn't a chore; it is an adventure!  Your minds are like a fresh horse, crazy to take six bars.  You are the hope of the world because you have enthusiasm and ginger, because you feel, and you haven't yet forgotten how
5 to think.

What can you do?

You know what the men and women of your country did to defend American principles abroad.  Let it be your part to find out what your city, your state, your nation are doing for
10 the welfare of their citizens and the upholding of American principles at home.

You can do more.  You must do more.  You, the girls and boys of America, must create a new standard of values for your generation.  For a century, men the world over, but especially
15 here in our United States, have bowed to material success as to the greatest god they knew.  We have exalted the man with money as we have exalted no other type in American life.  We have praised his virtues and ignored his vices; we have listened to him, as we never would to a saint in glory, when he told us
20 the stages of his progress toward success; we have pointed to him as a shining example of the best to which a youth might aspire.

He who has dollars, we said, has success; he who has not dollars, has not success.  It is the first duty of man to be
25 successful, we said.  Therefore, get dollars!

The youth of America has obeyed that insistent mandate, generation after generation; and in countless hearts, aspirations for something higher than dollar-chasing have been sternly crushed in order that the golden quest should be unimpeded;
30 and men have made unbelievable fortunes; and the glamour of their achievement has made other men everywhere a little greedier, a little more ruthless, a little more jealous of their own, a little more envious of others, impatient of law, intolerant of opposition, scornful of all things that cannot be clutched
35 with hands.

We have been taught that success can be written only in figures, and a few men have gathered in the dollars of the many, and, in consequence, we have slums and child labor and strikes and starvation and bomb outrages and the rumblings 5 of revolution. No reform that social theorists can devise can sweep those offspring of our god, Success, for long out of our national life. As long as the gathering of dollars is regarded as the highest form of victorious effort, we shall have inequality, injustice, bitterness, and class strife. If we are ever to be free 10 of them, we must have a new standard of success. We must learn that success consists not in what we have but in what we are, not in what we hold in our pockets but in what we hold in our heads and our hearts, not in our skill to buy low and sell high, but in our ability greatly to dream, to build, to battle, to 15 kindle, to serve.

Young America, it must be your business in these years to raise this new standard before the eyes of your fellow citizens, your aim to give them a new ideal of what constitutes success, for without such a new standard, without such a new ideal, 20 all that you do for citizenship and democracy will be only a stopgap that will hold the floods of corruption back here or there for a year or for ten years, only to release them at last in increased volume.

Our present ideal of success is based on selfish, individualistic 25 enterprise and greed.

How can that harmonize with democracy, whose essence is service?

The answer is simple. It cannot harmonize with it; it never has; it never will. In every village, town, and state, greed 30 and selfish enterprise—the qualities that make for "success" as we know it—are the inveterate enemies of democratic institutions.

If you want dollars above all, do not talk of citizenship and democracy.

35    But if you want democracy above all, know that success

in life lies not in the accumulation of unnecessary bonds and houses, but in service, in knowledge, and in the appreciation of beauty.

If you want honestly to help your country, set about now to 5 give her a notion of what makes real success.

## NOTES AND QUESTIONS

**Biography.** Hermann Hagedorn (1882-1964), a native of New York and a graduate of Harvard University, was an author and social worker. For several years he taught English at Harvard University. He wrote a number of books and plays; his shorter articles and poems appeared from time to time in magazines. This selection is taken from his book for American boys and girls, *You Are the Hope of the World.*

**Discussion.** 1. Why do you think boys and girls take "baseball or crêpe de Chine" more seriously than the "gorgeous experiment" of democracy? 2. What practical training in taking active part in a democracy does your school offer? 3. How do boys and girls respond when responsibility for order in the halls or care of equipment, for instance, is placed upon them? 4. In your opinion, what does America stand for? 5. Which of the shortcomings listed by the author have you noticed in your community? 6. What efforts are you or your school making to remedy some of these things now? 7. Hermann Hagedorn seems hard on the "elders"; what purpose may he have in his remarks? 8. What are the standards of success in your school and community? 9. What characters in history or in your circle of acquaintances do you know who have had other aspirations than dollars? 10. What is the new standard of success? 11. How can boys and girls put into practice in school these high ideals—"greatly to dream, to build, to battle, to kindle, to serve"? 12. What can you do, because you love American democracy, to make these ideals the standards by which the popularity of boys and girls in your school is ,judged? 13. Read again what is said in the "Introduction" on page 258 about "the spirit of service" that every good citizen must have; why is this spirit so necessary in a free government? 14. Find in the glossary the meaning of: materialistic; sordid; corruption; stodgy; mandate. 15. *Pronounce:* abhor; exaltation; individualistic.

### Phrases for Study

world kings, **301**, 3

logical heirs, **301**, 10

take six bars, **303**, 2

standard of values, **303**, 13

golden quest, **303**, 29

social theorists, **304**, 5

**Outline for Testing Silent Reading.** Make an outline to guide you in telling the main thoughts of this selection.

**Library Reading.** Other chapters from *You Are the Hope of the World.*

**Newspaper Reading.** Bring to class and read the best editorial you can find urging some needed improvement in citizenship.

**Suggestions for theme topics.** 1. A school experiment in self-government. 2. Things in my school that tend to make pupils social, that is, to develop in them a spirit of cooperation (teamwork) and service (helpfulness to others). 3. How a school by its organization and discipline may help to realize a true democracy. 4. A report on the George *Junior Republic* (*The Junior Republic,* George). 5. How a school composed of many nationalities typifies our Republic. 6. How the presence of different nationalities in a school helps the students to become more intelligent, more sympathetic, more tolerant, and more democratic. 7. How the Boy Scouts, the Camp Fire Girls, the Girl Scouts, and similar organizations promote the spirit of democracy. 8. Book reviews of *The Promised Land,* Antin; *How the Other Half Lives*, Riis; *From Alien to Citizen*, Steiner.

**A Suggested Problem.** Write out a list of things you can do to make your town or neighborhood a better community. (*The Delineator* for March, 1920, contains suggestions for community improvements.) Keep a record for a week of the particular thing you have done each day, such as helping to beautify your school grounds or your home, picking up waste paper, etc. Or make a program for a "Good Health Day" discussion.

---

# THE HERITAGE OF NOBLE LIVES

### THEODORE ROOSEVELT

The Americans who stand highest on the list of the world's worthies are Washington, who fought to found the country which he afterwards governed, and Lincoln, who saved it through the blood of the best and bravest in the land; Washington, the soldier
5 and statesman, the man of cool head, dauntless heart, and iron will, the greatest of good men and the best of great men, and Lincoln, sad, patient, kindly Lincoln, who for four years toiled

and suffered for the people, and when his work was done, laid down his life that the flag which had been rent in sunder might once more be made whole and without a seam.

It would be difficult to exaggerate the material effects
5 of the careers of Washington and Lincoln upon the United States. Without Washington we should probably never have won our independence of the British crown, and we should almost certainly have failed to become a great nation, remaining instead a cluster of jangling little communities, drifting toward the type
10 of government prevalent in Spanish America. Without Lincoln we might perhaps have failed to keep the political unity we had won, and even if, as is possible, we had kept it, both the struggle by which it was kept and the results of this struggle would have been so different that the effect upon our national history could
15 not have failed to be profound.

Yet the nation's debt to these men is not confined to what it owes them for its material well-being, incalculable though this debt is. Beyond the fact that we are an independent and united people, with half a continent as our heritage, lies the
20 fact that every American is richer by the heritage of the noble deeds and noble words of Washington and of Lincoln. Each of us who reads the Gettysburg speech or the second inaugural address of the greatest American of the nineteenth century, or who studies the long campaigns and lofty statesmanship of that
25 other American who was even greater, cannot but feel within him that lift toward things higher and nobler which can never be bestowed by the enjoyment of mere material prosperity.

It is not only the country which these men helped to make and helped to save that is ours by inheritance; we inherit also all
30 that is best and highest in their characters and in their lives.

In the same way that we are the better for the deeds of our mighty men who have served the nation well, so we are the worse for the deeds and the words of those who have striven to bring evil on the land. We have examples enough and to spare
35 that tend to evil; nevertheless, for our good fortune, the men

who have most impressed themselves upon the thought of the
nation have left behind them careers the influence of which
must tell for good.  The unscrupulous speculator who rises
to enormous wealth by swindling his neighbor; the capitalist
5 who oppresses the workingman; the agitator who wrongs the
workingman yet more deeply by trying to teach him to rely, not
upon himself, but partly upon the charity of individuals or of the
state and partly upon mob violence; the man in public life who
is a demagogue or corrupt, and the newspaper writer who fails
10 to attack him because of his corruption, or who slanderously
assails him when he is honest; the political leader who, cursed
by some obliquity of moral or mental vision, seeks to produce
sectional or social strife—all these, though important in their
day, have hitherto failed to leave any lasting impress upon the
15 life of the nation.

The men who have profoundly influenced the growth of
our national character have been in most cases precisely those
men whose influence was for the best and was strongly felt as
antagonistic to the worst tendency of the age.  The great writers,
20 who have written in prose or verse, have done much for us.  The
great orators whose burning words on behalf of liberty, of union,
of honest government have rung through our legislative halls,
have done even more.  Most of all has been done by the men
who have spoken to us through deeds and not words, or whose
25 words have gathered their especial charm and significance
because they came from men who did speak in deeds.  A nation's
greatness lies in its possibility of achievement in the present, and
nothing helps it more than the consciousness of achievement
in the past.

## NOTES AND QUESTIONS

**Biography.**  Theodore Roosevelt (1858-1919), twenty-sixth president
of the United States, was born in New York City.  As a boy he was of frail
physique, but overcame this handicap by systematic exercise and outdoor
life.  Roosevelt graduated from Harvard University in 1880, was elected to
the legislature of New York the same year, and served three terms.  In 1884

ill-health led him to go to the far West, where for two years he lived the life of a cowboy. Returning to New York in 1886, Roosevelt wrote in four volumes the history of the development of the great West, *The Winning of the West*. In 1897 President McKinley appointed him assistant secretary of the navy; this position he gave up to enter the Spanish-American War. He raised a regiment of volunteer cavalry in the West, called "Rough Riders," of which he was made lieutenant colonel. In 1898 he was elected governor of New York, and in 1900 vice president of the United States. Upon the death of McKinley a few months later, Roosevelt became president, and in 1904 he was elected to the presidency. He was always a vigorous American, basing his theory of politics on honesty, courage, hard work, and fair play. This selection is taken from his book, *American Ideals and Other Essays*.

**Discussion.** 1. Give the topic of each paragraph. 2. Arrange these topics in the form of an outline and listen while six pupils give the substance of the selection, each giving the thought of one paragraph in his own words. 3. Give another title to the selection. 4. Why is the influence of men who speak in deeds greater than that of those who speak only in words? 5. In what ways have the lives of Washington and Lincoln influenced the nation? 6. What debt do all citizens owe these men for their noble examples of service? 7. Find in the glossary the meaning of: worthies; sunder; material; jangling; prevalent; unscrupulous; sectional; consciousness. 8. *Pronounce:* dauntless; incalculable; demagogue.

## Phrases for Study

political unity, **307**, 11

mob violence, **308**, 8

obliquity of moral or mental vision, **308**, 12

**Library Reading.** *The Boys' Life of Theodore Roosevelt*, Hagedorn.

## Letter to Mrs. Bixby

Executive Mansion, Washington
November 21, 1864

Mrs. Bixby
   Boston, Mass.
5 Dear Madam:
   I have been shown in the files of the War Department a statement of the Adjutant General of Massachusetts that you are
the mother of five sons who have died gloriously on the field of
battle. I feel how weak and fruitless must be any words of mine
10 which should attempt to beguile you from the grief of a loss so
overwhelming, but I cannot refrain from tendering to you the
consolation that may be found in the thanks of the Republic
that they died to save. I pray that the Heavenly Father may
assuage the anguish of your bereavement, and leave you only
15 the cherished memory of the loved and lost, and the solemn
pride that must be yours to have laid so costly a sacrifice upon
the altar of freedom.
   Yours very sincerely and respectfully,

Abraham Lincoln

### NOTES AND QUESTIONS

For **Biography** see page 292.

**Discussion.** 1. Of what fine qualities in President Lincoln does this
letter give evidence? 2. Memorize these words from Lincoln's second
inaugural address: "With malice toward none, with charity for all, with
firmness in the right, as God gives us to see the right, let us strive on to
finish the work we are in; to bind up the nation's wounds; to care for him
who shall have borne the battle, and for his widow and his orphan—to do
all which may achieve a just and lasting peace among ourselves, and with
all nations." 3. Do these words from Lincoln's inaugural address support
Roosevelt's characterization of him in the first paragraph of "The Heritage of
Noble Lives"? 4. Find in the glossary the meaning of: beguile; bereavement.
5. *Pronounce:* adjutant; sacrifice:

# Yussouf

### James Russell Lowell

A stranger came one night to Yussouf's tent,
Saying, "Behold one outcast and in dread,
Against whose life the bow of power is bent,
Who flies, and hath not where to lay his head;
5 I come to thee for shelter and for food—
To Yussouf, called through all our tribes, 'The Good.'"

"This tent is mine," said Yussouf, "but no more
Than it is God's; come in, and be at peace
Freely shalt thou partake of all my store
10 As I of His who buildeth over these
Our tents His glorious roof of night and day,
And at whose door none ever yet heard 'Nay.'"

So Yussouf entertained his guest that night,
And, waking him ere day, said: "Here is gold;
15 My swiftest horse is saddled for thy flight;
Depart before the prying day grow bold."
As one lamp lights another, nor grows less,
So nobleness enkindleth nobleness.

That inward light the stranger's face made grand,
20 Which shines from all self-conquest; kneeling low,
He bowed his forehead upon Yussouf's hand,
Sobbing: "O Sheik, I cannot leave thee so;
I will repay thee; all this thou hast done
Unto that Ibrahim who slew thy son!"

25 "Take thrice the gold," said Yussouf, "for with thee
Into the desert, never to return,

My one black thought shall ride away from me.
First-born, for whom by day and night I yearn,
Balanced and just are all of God's decrees;
Thou art avenged, my first-born sleep in peace!"

## NOTES AND QUESTIONS

**Biography.** James Russell Lowell (1819-1891) came from an old and influential New England family. Born in an atmosphere of learning in Cambridge, he enjoyed every advantage for culture that inherited taste, ample means, and convenient opportunity could offer. Besides the facilities of Harvard College nearby, he had his father's library—one of the richest in the country. It is not strange, then, that Lowell grew fo be one of the most scholarly Americans of his time. After leaving college he became deeply interested in political problems and was thus stirred to his first serious efforts in literature. In 1848 appeared his *Vision of Sir Launfal*, a narrative poem with a beautiful meaning. Few patriotic poems surpass his *Commemoration Ode*, a poem which Lowell read at Harvard College on July 21, 1865, at a commemoration held in memory of the sons of the college who had fallen during the Civil War. Besides his poetical works, he wrote many books of travel and essays about literature. He succeeded Longfellow in his professorship at Harvard and was the first editor of the *Atlantic Monthly*.

**Discussion.** 1. Where do you think the scene of this poem is laid? Give the reason for your answer. 2. What do you know of the habits of people who live in tents? 3. What virtues would men living in this way most admire? Why? 4. How do you think Yussouf had won his title of "The Good"? 5. To what does the stranger compare himself? 6. What does the bending of the bow signify? 7. To what tribes does the stranger refer? 8. What did the stranger expect? What more than he expected did Yussouf do? How did this affect the stranger? 9. What was the struggle going on in the stranger's mind and heart that is called "self-conquest"? 10. What emotions made the stranger's face "grand"? 11. What do you suppose Yussouf's "one black thought" had been? 12. How did he avenge his son? 13. When does Yussouf show himself most noble? 14. Which lines in the last stanza are addressed to the stranger and which to the dead son? 15. Into which two lines is the thought of the poem condensed? 16. Find in the glossary the meaning of: prying; enkindleth; sheik.

**Class Reading.** Bring to class and read "The Shepherd of King Admetus;" "The Finding of the Lyre," Lowell.

# A Man's a Man For A'[1] That

### Robert Burns

Is there[2] for honest poverty
    That hings[3] his head, an' a' that?
The coward slave, we pass him by
    We dare be poor for a' that!
5 For a' that, an' a' that,
    Our toils obscure, an' a' that,
The rank is but the guinea's stamp,
    The man's the gowd[4] for a' that.

What though on hamely fare we dine,
10    Wear hoddin[5] gray, an' a' that?
Gie[6] fools their silks, and knaves their wine
    A man's a man for a' that.
For a' that, an' a' that,
    Their tinsel show, an' a' that,
15 The honest man, the' e'er sae[7] poor,
    Is king o' men for a' that.

Ye see yon birkie ca'd[8] a lord,
    Wha struts, an' stares, an' a' that;
Tho' hundreds worship at his word,
20    He's but a coof[9] for a' that.
For a' that, an' a' that,
    His ribband, star, an' a' that,
The man o' independent mind,
    He looks an' laughs at a' that.

[1] *a'*, all
[2] *is there,* is there a man
[3] *hings,* hangs
[4] *gowd,* gold
[5] *hoddin,* coarse, woolen cloth
[6] *gie,* give
[7] *sae,* so
[8] *birkie ca'd,* fellow called
[9] *coof,* fool

A prince can mak a belted knight,
　　A marquis, duke, an' a' that;
But an honest man's aboon[10] his might—
　　Guid[11] faith, he manna fa'[12] that!
5 For a' that, an' a' that,
　　Their dignities, an' a' that,
The pith o' sense an' pride o' worth
　　Are higher rank than a' that.

Then let us pray that come it may
10　　(As come it will for a' that),
That sense and worth, o'er a' the earth,
　　Shall bear the gree,[13] an' a' that.
For a' that, an' a' that,
　　It's coming yet for a' that,
15 That man to man, the world o'er,
　　Shall brothers be for a' that.

## NOTES AND QUESTIONS

**Biography.** Robert Burns (1759-1796), who was born near Ayr, Scotland, is one of the world's best loved and most famous poets. From his early youth he worked hard on his father's small, unproductive farm, and later he struggled with an unsuccessful farm of his own. Though his short life was filled with poverty and hardship, he saw the beauty in common things, and his heart was full of sympathy. These qualities are well illustrated by the familiar poems, "To a Mountain Daisy" and "To a Mouse." He was a strong believer in equal rights for everyone. He felt no envy of those who were accounted great, but gloried in the privilege of being independent. His poem, "A Man's a Man for A' That," expresses the same idea of equality that we find in the Declaration of Independence.

**Discussion.** 1. The first two lines are contracted; what is left out? What does Burns call the person "that hangs his head" because of "honest poverty"? 3. Explain the comparison of a person to a coin in lines 7 and 8, page 313. 4. How may we help to realize the poet's prayer expressed in the last stanza? 5. Learn this stanza by heart. 6. Burns, the humble

---

[10] *aboon,* above
[11] *guid, good*

[12] *mauna fa',* must not claim
[13] *gree,* prize

poet, made the world happier and better through his poems of brotherhood and love; how does he exemplify the spirit of democracy? 7. Why do you think men treasure this poem and will not let it die? 8. Compare "A Man's a Man for A' That" with Whittier's "The Poor Voter on Election Day"; what resemblances do you find? 9. *Pronounce:* guinea; marquis.

**Class Reading.** Bring to class and read "A Consecration," Masefield (in *Collected Poems*).

---

## IF

### RUDYARD KIPLING

If you can keep your head when all about you
    Are losing theirs and blaming it on you;
If you can trust yourself when all men doubt you,
    But make allowance for their doubting, too;
5 If you can wait and not be tired by waiting;
    Or, being lied about, don't deal in lies;
Or, being hated, don't give way to hating;
    And yet don't look too good, nor talk too wise;

If you can dream—and not make dreams your master;
10   If you can think—and not make thoughts your aim;
If you can meet with Triumph and Disaster,
    And treat these two impostors just the same;
If you can bear to hear the truth you've spoken
    Twisted by knaves to make a trap for fools;
15 Or watch the things you gave your life to, broken,
    And stoop and build them up with worn-out tools;

If you can make one heap of all your winnings
    And risk it on the turn of pitch-and-toss,
And lose, and start again at your beginnings
20   And never breathe a word about your loss;

If you can force your heart and nerve and sinew
  To serve your turn long after they are gone,
And so hold on when there is nothing in you
  Except the will which says to them: "Hold on";

5 If you can talk with crowds and keep your virtue,
  Or walk with kings—nor lose the common touch;
If neither foes nor loving friends can hurt you;
  If all men count with you, but none too much;
If you can fill the unforgiving minute
10   With sixty seconds' worth of distance run,
YOURS is the Earth and everything that's in it,
  And—which is more—you'll be a Man, my son.

### NOTES AND QUESTIONS

**Biography.** Rudyard Kipling (1865-1936) was born in Bombay, India, of British parents. He was sent to England to be educated, but returned to India at the age of seventeen to work as a journalist. Very soon he began to write tales of the life about him, as well as poems dealing with British civil officials and soldiers in India. By the time he was twenty-four he had won fame with his *Plain Tales from the Hills* and other short stories; and when he published *Barrack Room Ballads*, in 1892, he became widely recognized as a great poet. From 1892 to 1896 he lived in the United States. Perhaps he is best known to boys and girls as the author of the *Jungle Books.* He was a master of the art of telling stories, either in prose or verse. His ballads about the British soldier, "Tommy Atkins," and about his experiences on the frontiers of civilization, have a ring and a movement that suggest the old days when the ballad-maker was a man of action, living the adventures that he celebrated in song.

**Discussion.** 1. Which of these "Ifs" seems to you especially difficult to practice? 2. Notice how in the first two examples the conditions are made doubly difficult by the additions, "and blaming it on you" and "But make allowance for their doubting, too." 3. What is better than looking good and talking wise? 4. What does Kipling imply should be the aim of dreaming and of thinking? 5. How does he regard triumph and disaster? Can you cite an instance where victory proved disastrous, or one where disaster was turned into triumph? 6. Which "If" embodies advice especially good for athletes? 7. Which one makes a fine motto when a difficult task is before you that you must see through to the end?  8. How might "loving friends" hurt one?  9. Which "If" suggests making good use of one's time? 10. Is the reward worth striving for?  11. Find in the glossary the meaning of: impostor; knave.

**Library Reading.**  *The Iron Trail*, Beach.  (Compare the hero with that of Kipling's "If.")

## COLUMBUS

### JOAQUIN MILLER

Behind him lay the gray Azores,
    Behind, the Gates of Hercules;
Before him not the ghosts of shores,
    Before him only shoreless seas.
5 The good mate said: "Now must we pray,
    For lo! the very stars are gone.
Brave Admiral, speak, what shall I say?"
    "Why, say 'Sail on! sail on! and on!'"

"My men grow mutinous day by day;
10    My men grow ghastly wan and weak."
The stout mate thought of home; a spray
    Of salt wave washed his swarthy cheek,
"What shall I say, brave Admiral, say,
    If we sight naught but seas at dawn?"
15 "Why, you shall say at break of day,
    'Sail on! sail on! and on!'"

They sailed and sailed, as winds might blow
    Until at last the blanched mate said:
"Why, now not even God would know
20    Should I and all my men fall dead.

These very winds forget their way,
 For God from these dread seas is gone;
Now speak, brave Admiral, speak and say"
 He said: "Sail on! sail on! and on!"

5 They sailed. They sailed. Then spake the mate:
 "This mad sea shows his teeth tonight.
He curls his lips, he lies in wait,
 With lifted teeth, as if to bite!
Brave Admiral, say but one good word;
10 What shall we do when hope is gone?"
The words leaped like a leaping sword:
 "Sail on! sail on! and on!"

Then, pale and worn, he kept his deck,
 And peered through darkness. All, that night
15 Of all dark nights! And then a speck
 A light! A light! A light! A light!
It grew, a starlit flag unfurled!
 It grew to be Time's burst of dawn.
He gained a world; he gave that world
20 Its grandest lesson: "On! sail on!"

## NOTES AND QUESTIONS

**Biography.** Cincinnatus Heine Miller (1841-1913) was born in Wabash District, Indiana, but moved with his family when he was about thirteen years of age to the Willamette Valley, Oregon. Here he studied law and was admitted to the bar. His spare time while practicing his profession was spent in verse making. He wrote a defense of the Mexican brigand, Joaquin Murietta, and adopted his first name as a pseudonym. After traveling in Europe, he published his first volume of poems, *Songs of the Sierras*.

**Discussion.** 1. Do you like the way this poem opens? 2. Why did the poet not start his narrative with the beginning of the voyage? 3. What are the Gates of Hercules? 4. To whom did the mate expect to repeat what

Columbus said? 5. How had a crew been secured for this voyage? 6. How did the men stand the test of the voyage? 7. What report of them did the mate give to Columbus? 8. What did he want Columbus to do if they should "sight naught but seas at dawn"? 9. What made the mate think that God had gone from those seas? 10. When did the events narrated in the fourth stanza take place? 11. What is the last question asked by the mate? How did Columbus answer the question? 12. What thought does the "leaping sword" give you? 13. Does the description of Columbus with which the last stanza opens seem in contrast with the "leaping sword"? 14. What did Columbus see that night? 15. What did that light tell him? 16. What does the poet mean when he says "It grew"? 17. What is the "starlit flag"? 18. What lesson did Columbus teach that world? 19. How has the poet made us feel the wonder, the triumph, and the thankfulness of Columbus when the light appeared? 20. Why does the poet stop at this point? 21. What "grandest lesson" did Columbus give to the world? 22. How do you value perseverance and courage such as Columbus exemplified? 23. Compare the lesson this poem teaches with that of Kipling's "If"; with that of Burns's "A Man's a Man for A' That"; with that of Lowell's "Yussouf." 24. Find in the glossary: blanched; very; dread. 25. *Pronounce:* Joaquin.

### Phrases for Study

gray Azores, **317**, 1
ghosts of shores, **317**, 3

ghastly wan, **317**, 10
Time's burst of dawn, **318**, 18

---

## The Bugle Song

### Alfred, Lord Tennyson

The splendor falls on castle walls
    And snowy summits, old in story;
The long light shakes across the lakes;
    And the wild cataract leaps in glory.
5 Blow, bugle, blow; set the wild echoes flying;
  Blow, bugle; answer, echoes, dying, dying, dying.

O hark! O hear! how thin and clear,
   And thinner, clearer, farther going!
O sweet and far from cliff and scar,
   The horns of Elfland, faintly blowing!
5 Blow—let us hear the purple glens replying;
Blow, bugle; answer, echoes, dying, dying, dying.

O love, they die in yon rich sky;
   They faint on hill or field or river.
Our echoes roll from soul to soul,
10      And grow forever and forever.
Blow, bugle, blow; set the wild echoes flying;
And answer, echoes, answer, dying, dying, dying.


NOTES AND QUESTIONS

For **Biography** see page 80.

**Discussion.** 1. Find the two lines in the last stanza that express the heart of the poem. 2. The echoes of the bugle die; what becomes of the echoes of our words and actions? 3. What lines in Lowell's poem "Yussouf" (page 311) express the same thought? 4. Can you give an illustration from your school experience of the fact that a good example is contagious? How about selfish conduct? What opinion does Roosevelt express on this point in "The Heritage of Noble Lives" (page 306)? 5. Notice that the first stanza describes a beautiful setting for the blowing of the bugle; the second stanza is a poetic description of the echoes of the bugle; and the third is the poet's interpretation of the echoes, which he expresses to one whom he loves and who perhaps is with him at the moment. 6. Does the poet succeed in making you see a beautiful picture in the first four lines of the poem? 7. To what does the poet compare the echoes in the second stanza? 8. What words in the poem are particularly expressive? 9. Notice how the choice of words, the varied and interesting rhymes, and the alliteration all contribute to the music of the poem. 10. Read again the note about lyric poetry on page 58, and then tell why this poem is called a lyric. Have you heard a recording of it? 11. It is interesting to notice that Rupert Brooke in

"Pine-Trees and the Sky," Bryant in "To a Waterfowl," and Tennyson in this poem follow the same plan—first stating a fact and then following with an interpretation of it, beautifully expressed. 12. You will enjoy listening to a good reader in your class who is able to bring out the beauty of the imagery, the music of the lyric, and the contrast between "our echoes" and those of the bugle. 13. Memorize the poem.

## THE CHAMBERED NAUTILUS

### OLIVER WENDELL HOLMES

This is the ship of pearl, which, poets feign,
    Sails the unshadowed main
    The venturous bark that flings
On the sweet summer wind its purpled wings
5 In gulfs enchanted, where the siren sings,
    And coral reefs lie bare,
Where the cold sea-maids rise to sun their streaming hair.

Its webs of living gauze no more unfurl;
    Wrecked is the ship of pearl!
10    And every chambered cell,
Where its dim dreaming life was wont to dwell,
As the frail tenant shaped his growing shell,
    Before thee lies revealed—
Its irised ceiling rent, its sunless crypt unsealed!

15 Year after year beheld the silent toil
    That spread his lustrous coil;
    Still, as the spiral grew,
He left the past year's dwelling for the new,

Stole with soft step its shining archway through,
   Built up its idle door,
Stretched in his last-found home, and knew the old no more.

Thanks for the heavenly message brought by thee,
5   Child of the wandering sea,
   Cast from her lap, forlorn!
From thy dead lips a clearer note is born
Than ever Triton blew from wreathéd horn!
   While on mine ear it rings,
10 Through the deep caves of thought I hear a voice that sings:

Build thee more stately mansions, O my soul,
   As the swift seasons roll!
   Leave thy low-vaulted past!
Let each new temple, nobler than the last,
15 Shut thee from heaven with a dome more vast,
   Till thou at length art free,
Leaving thine outgrown shell by life's unresting sea!


## NOTES AND QUESTIONS

**Biography.** Oliver Wendell Holmes (1809-1894) was born in Cambridge, Massachusetts, the son of a Congregational minister. He attended Phillips Andover Academy and graduated from Harvard College in 1829. After studying medicine and anatomy in Paris, he began practicing in Boston. In 1847 he was made professor of physiology and anatomy at Harvard University, in which position he continued for thirty-five years. Holmes became famous when only twenty-one through the stirring stanzas of "Old Ironsides," a poem which he wrote as a protest against the dismantling of the historic battleship *Constitution.*

When Lowell was offered the editorship of the *Atlantic Monthly*, he made it a condition of his acceptance that Holmes should be a contributor. The result was a series of articles entitled *The Autocrat of the Breakfast Table.* Among his best-known poems are "The Chambered Nautilus" and "The Deacon's Masterpiece."

**Note.** "The Chambered Nautilus" appeared in the *Atlantic Monthly* in 1858. The poet makes the "wrecked" shell that lies before him a symbol of life. The nautilus builds each year a new and larger cell or compartment, into which it moves, closing up the cell that it previously occupied. If you have seen a nautilus shell, you will understand how well it symbolizes progress and growth and how well the poet has described both the form and the color of the shell.

**Discussion.** 1. In what stanzas does the poet talk to us about the nautilus? 2. In what stanza does he address the shell? 3. Which stanza tells the message brought by the shell? 4. Why was it necessary for the poet to tell us the history of the shell before he interpreted its message? 5. What made it possible for the poet to hear the message brought by the shell? 6. Does this help you understand what kind of boy Oliver Wendell Holmes must have been? 7. To what old belief concerning the nautilus does the poet refer in the first stanza? 8. What things mentioned show that the poet is thinking of the warm waters in which the nautilus lives? 9. Do you like the use of the word "wrecked" in connection with the nautilus? Why? 10. Who was the "frail tenant"? 11. What does the broken shell reveal? 12. Find lines in the third stanza which tell how the cells are formed and why they were "sunless" as long as the shell was unbroken? 13. How may the soul build more lofty mansions? What thoughts will help? What actions will help? 14. What does the poet mean by the "outgrown shell" of the soul? 15. Compare the lesson of this poem with that of "The Bugle Song"; with that of "If." 16. Find in the glossary the meaning of: siren; irised; rent; crypt; lustrous; Triton. 17. *Pronounce:* coral; wont.

## Phrases for Study

unshadowed main, **321**, 2  
chambered cell, **321**, 10  

wreathed horn, **322**, 8  
low-vaulted past, **322**, 13

## A DEFINITION OF A GENTLEMAN

### CARDINAL NEWMAN

It is almost a definition of a gentleman to say he is one who never inflicts pain. This description is both refined and, as far as it goes, accurate. He is mainly occupied in merely removing the obstacles which hinder the free and unembarrassed action
5 of those about him, and he concurs with their movements rather than takes the initiative himself. His benefits may be considered as parallel to what are called comforts or conveniences in arrangements of a personal nature—like an easy-chair or a good fire, which do their part in dispelling cold and fatigue, though
10 nature provides both means of rest and animal heat without them. The true gentleman in like manner carefully avoids whatever may cause a jar or a jolt in the minds of those with whom he is cast—all clashing of opinion, or collision of feeling, all restraint, or suspicion, or gloom, or resentment; his great
15 concern being to make everyone at his ease and at home. He has his eyes on all his company; he is tender toward the bashful, gentle toward the distant, and merciful toward the absurd; he can recollect to whom he is speaking; he guards against unseasonable allusions or topics which may irritate; he is seldom
20 prominent in conversation and never wearisome. He makes light of favors while he does them and seems to be receiving when he is conferring. He never speaks of himself except when compelled; never defends himself by a mere retort. He has no ears for slander or gossip; is scrupulous in imputing motives
25 to those who interfere with him; and interprets everything for the best. He is never mean or little in his disputes; never takes unfair advantage; never mistakes personalities or sharp sayings for arguments; or insinuates evil which he dare not say out. From a long-sighted prudence he observes the maxim of the
30 ancient sage that we should ever conduct ourselves toward our

enemy as if he were one day to be our friend.  He has too much
good sense to be affronted at insults; he is too well employed
to remember injuries; and too indolent to bear malice.  He is
patient, forbearing, and resigned on philosophical principles; he
5 submits to pain because it is inevitable, to bereavement because
it is irreparable, and to death because it is his destiny.  If he
engages in controversy of any kind, his disciplined intellect
preserves him from the blundering discourtesy of better, perhaps,
but less educated minds; who, like blunt weapons, tear and hack
10 instead of cutting clean, who mistake the point in argument,
waste their strength on trifles, misconceive their adversary, and
leave the question more involved than they find it.  He may be
right or wrong in his opinion, but he is too clear-headed to be
unjust; he is as simple as he is forcible, and as brief as he is
15 decisive.  Nowhere shall we find greater candor, consideration,
indulgence.  He throws himself into the minds of his opponents;
he accounts for their mistakes.  He knows the weakness of human
reason as well as its strength, its province, and its limits.

## NOTES AND QUESTIONS

**Biography.**  John Henry Newman (1801-1890), a distinguished
clergyman, was born in London.  He graduated from Trinity College,
Oxford, and became noted as a scholar and a preacher.  In 1879 he was
made a cardinal.  This selection is taken from his book, *The Idea of a
University*.  Cardinal Newman is well known as the author of the familiar
hymn, "Lead, Kindly Light," which he wrote while on a voyage in the
Mediterranean Sea.

**Discussion.**  1. What undesirable qualities does Cardinal Newman
mention that you have perhaps discovered in yourself—or in others—and
that you have determined to overcome?  2. What useful hints have you
learned for making and preserving friendships and for the treatment of
enemies?  3. Memorize and apply Tennyson's lines about manners:

> For manners are not idle, but the fruit
> Of loyal nature and of noble mind.

4. Have you observed in your school social affairs that everyone has a good
time when all the boys and girls "have eyes on all the company," instead

of separating into cliques? 5. What does this selection add to your idea of service? 6. Why is this selection a fitting summary of the poems that precede it in this group? 7. Find in the glossary the meaning of: initiative; retort; insinuate; indolent; resigned; candor. 8. *Pronounce:* affronted; irreparable; misconceive; province.

### Phrases for Study

concurs with their movements, **324**, 5

unseasonable allusions, **324**, 19

scrupulous in imputing, **324**, 24

philosophical principles, **325**, 4

disciplined intellect, **325**, 7

**A Suggested Problem.** Make a list of five suggestions learned from Cardinal Newman which you resolve to put into practice, choosing the ones that apply especially to you; keep the list before you and check up on yourself. (Like means were used by Washington and Franklin to improve their conduct.)

---

## Abraham Lincoln Walks at Midnight

### (In Springfield, Illinois)

#### Vachel Lindsay

It is portentous, and a thing of state,
That here at midnight, in our little town,
A mourning figure walks, and will not rest,
Near the old courthouse pacing up and down.

5 Or by his homestead, or in shadowed yards,
He lingers where his children used to play;
Or through the market, on the well-worn stones,
He stalks until the dawn-stars burn away.

A bronzed, lank man! His suit of ancient black,
10 A famous high top hat, and plain worn shawl
Make him the quaint great figure that men love,
The prairie-lawyer, master of us all.

He cannot sleep upon his hillside now.
He is among us—as in times before!
And we who toss and lie awake for long
Breathe deep, and start, to see him pass the door.

5 His head is bowed. He thinks on men and kings.
Yea, when the sick world cries, how can he sleep?
Too many peasants fight, they know not why;
Too many homesteads in black terror weep.

The sins of all the war-lords burn his heart.
10 He sees the dreadnaughts scouring every main.
He carries on his shawl-wrapped shoulders now
The bitterness, the folly, and the pain.

He cannot rest until a spirit-dawn
Shall come—the shining hope of Europe free;
15 The league of sober folk, the Worker's Earth,
Bringing long peace to Cornland, Alp, and Sea.

It breaks his heart that kings must murder still,
That all his hours of travail here for men
Seem yet in vain. And who will bring white peace
20 That he may sleep upon his hill again?

## NOTES AND QUESTIONS

**Biography.** Vachel Lindsay (1879-1931) was one of America's best known modern poets. He recited his poems in many cities of the United States. In the summer of 1912 he walked from Illinois to New Mexico, distributing his rhymes and speaking in behalf of the "gospel of beauty." *A Handy Guide for Beggars* is his story of a similar journey through Georgia, and in it he tells how everywhere, like the minstrels of old, he received hospitality in exchange for his songs. His poetry breathes a spirit of human brotherhood that reminds one of Lincoln and Emerson and Walt Whitman. *General William Booth Enters Heaven and Other*

*Poems, The Congo and Other Poems,* and *The Chinese Nightingale and Other Poems* are titles of his collections of poetry. The poet's home was in Springfield, Illinois, the former home and the burial place of Abraham Lincoln.

**Discussion.** 1. Abraham Lincoln typifies the life and yearnings of the common people, and for this reason he has appealed to the poets who help interpret life for us; mention some other poets who have made Lincoln the subject of poems. 2. Why does this poet feel that Lincoln cannot "sleep upon the hill"? 3. What will bring rest to him again? 4. What is being done today to bring about the "spirit-dawn"? 5. What answer would you like to make to the poet's question? 6. What lines do you like especially well? 7. Another modern poet, Arthur Guiterman, in "He Leads Us Still," has also expressed the idea that Lincoln's spirit lives today. The poem closes—

> He leads us still! O'er chasms yet unspanned
> Our pathway lies; the work is but begun.
> But we shall do our part and leave our land
> The mightier for noble battles won.
> Here truth must triumph, honor must prevail;
> The nation Lincoln died for cannot fail.

8. Find in the glossary the meaning of: portentous; state; scouring; main; Cornland; Alp; travail.

---

## CLOSE UP THE RANKS!

### EDWARD SIMS VAN ZILE

Gently Death came and bent to him asleep;
His spirit passed, and, lo, his lovers weep,
But not for him, for him the unafraid—
In tears, we ask, "Who'll lead the great crusade?

5 "Who'll hearten us to carry on the war
For those ideals our fathers battled for;
To give our hearts to one dear flag alone,
The flag he loved whose splendid soul has flown?"

With his last breath he gave a clarion cry:
"They only serve who do not fear to die;
He only lives who's worthy of our dead
Beware the peril of the seed that's spread

5 "By them who'll reap a harvest of despair;
By them whose dreams unstable are as air;
By them who see the rainbow in the sky,
But not the storm that threatens by and by."

Our leader rests, his voice forever still;
10 But let us vow to do our leader's will!
Close up the ranks! Our Captain is not dead!
His soul shall live, and by his soul we're led;

Led forward fighting for the real, the true,
Not turned aside by what the dreamers do.
15 If he could speak he would not have us weep;
But souls awake whose Captain lies asleep.

## NOTES AND QUESTIONS

**Biography.** Edward Sims Van Zile (1863-1931), a native of Troy, New York, was an editorial writer and author. He was editor of *Current Literature*.

**Discussion.** 1. What thought in "Close Up the Ranks!" is similar to that expressed in "Abraham Lincoln Walks at Midnight" and in "He Leads Us Still"? 2. What ideals that Roosevelt stood for are expressed in this poem? 3. What is the significance of the title? 4. Lines 4-8, above, utter a warning against certain types of men who spread "seed" that will result in "a harvest of despair." What types of such men does Roosevelt warn us against in "The Heritage of Noble Lives," on page 306? 5. Find in the glossary the meaning of: crusade; clarion.

**Magazine Reading.** In the *Review of Reviews* for July, 1919, there is a collection of poems written on the death of Theodore Roosevelt, among them "Great-Heart," by Kipling, who was an admirer of Roosevelt. Be prepared to read to the class the poem in this collection that appeals most strongly to you.

## THE GREAT AMERICAN EXPERIMENT

### A REVIEW

You have learned in your study of history that the spirit of freedom is eternal and that ever since the world began, liberty-loving people have fought to win freedom for themselves and for those that come after them. You have traced with particular interest the development of freedom in our own country from the time the Pilgrims landed at Plymouth Rock to our participation in World War One. You have discovered that history, which deals with a record of facts, appeals to your understanding, while literature, which takes the facts of history as a basis and treats them with imagination, appeals particularly to your feelings. What are the historic facts—the "dramatic moments in history" about which you read in the "Introduction," page 255—upon which the various poems in the group called "The Eternal Spirit of Freedom" are based? Compare the poet's treatment of Paul Revere's ride with the historian's treatment, as found in your history textbooks. Discuss in class which method of treatment, the literary or the historic, is the more likely to inspire noble conduct. To the poets represented in this group the love of freedom was a strong conviction, not an idle sentiment; which of them sacrificed their lives to maintain this principle? Give the circumstances in each case. Read again what is said on page 58 about lyrics and note that patriotism, like nature, is a favorite theme for lyric poets; what lyrics do you find in this group? Which of these were inspired by World War One?

The three groups of selections in "Part III" illustrate how the spirit of freedom and patriotism has manifested itself, about which you read in the "Introduction," page 258; with what idea of free government do the selections in the second group deal?

At the time of the American Revolution what was the situation in Europe as to free government? What distinctly new feature characterized the American experiment in free government? What foundations for such a form of government had already been laid in England, about which you read in the "Introduction," page 257? What arguments for adoption of the Declaration of Independence does Webster make in his "Supposed Speech of John Adams"? What did you learn from Washington of America's place in the world? In what respects were the ideas of the British poet Burns and the American poet Whittier alike? What famous definition of our government did Abraham Lincoln make? America is called the land of opportunity; how does Woodrow Wilson show that Abraham Lincoln's life proves the truth of this claim? What do you learn from Henry W. Grady about the relationship between love of home and good citizenship?

But even the best system of government cannot succeed unless people everywhere feel the bond of human brotherhood and are willing to work for the common welfare. What title is given the third group of selections in "Part III"? Hermann Hagedorn calls the boys and girls of America "the hope of the world"; do you think he expects too much from them or do you think they are ready to take up responsibility? What can you do in your home and school and neighborhood to help put into practice the "glorious experiment of democracy"? What great service of Washington and Lincoln does Roosevelt point out? What fine expression of his feeling for a great service did Lincoln make? How was Yussouf's feeling for "the brotherhood of man" tested? American boys and girls have daily opportunities to render individual service; what opportunities for organized service does the Junior Red Cross offer? The Camp Fire Girls? The Boy Scouts and the Girl Scouts? What part does your school take in these national organizations? Discuss in class (two-minute talks) the purposes of each of these organizations as expressed in their laws, pledges, mottoes, and emblems. Read again the last paragraph of the "Introduction," page 258, and think how you, as an individual and as a member of one of these national organizations, may help to carry on "the great tradition" of liberty and service. What ideals of life and service are exemplified in the poems "Columbus," "The Bugle Song," and "The Chambered Nautilus"? What ideals of conduct did you gain from Cardinal Newman?

What progress have you made in silent reading? Compare your record for speed and comprehension with that of your classmates and with the eighth-grade standard. What library reading have you done in connection with your study of "Part III"? Was any oral discussion growing out of "Suggestions for Theme Topics" in "Part III" so stimulating that it resulted in a worthwhile class activity? Which "Suggested Problem" was most helpful? Plan a program for a "Service Day" or a "Good Citizenship Day," from material found or suggested in this book, with the help of the library and the department of music. How do you think "A Code of Morals," Hutchins (in *American Magazine*, April, 1918), may be used to help American boys and girls realize their ideals of good citizenship? Bring to class any newspaper or magazine article that points out ways for improving the neighborhood or the city.

# Part IV

## Literature and Life in the Homeland

*Look to the work the times reveal!*
*Give thanks with all thy flaming heart,*
*Crave but to have in it a part.*
*Give thanks and clasp thy heritage—*
*To be alive in such an age!*

—Angela Morgan

GEORGE WASHINGTON

LITERATURE AND LIFE IN THE HOMELAND

## An Introduction

From one point of view, literature knows neither place nor time. The succession of the seasons, the relation of people to the forces of nature, the mysteries of life and death are the same to all peoples and in all times. Plato wrote in ancient Greece about love, justice, and ideal government, and what he wrote has value for us more than twenty centuries after his death. Shakespeare wrote dramas for his countrymen three hundred and more years ago; we still see his plays performed in our theaters, study them in our schools, read them in our homes; they have been translated into other languages and have become a part of the literature of many peoples. English daffodils were lovely in the seventeenth century, and an English poet named Robert Herrick wrote some charming lines about them. Daffodils were lovely a century ago, and an English poet named William Wordsworth made them also the subject of a song. Both of these poems we read here in America when the first spring flowers come, and we find them as fresh and new as the flowers themselves. Through translations, great novels and poems and dramas, at first written in German, French, Russian, and other foreign languages, have become part of English literature. Literature knows no bounds of nationality or of the centuries. It has an immortality of life here on earth and speaks to us, if we so desire, as if it had been written in our own language only yesterday.

But in another sense, literature is a form of the history of a race and of a definite period of time. People do certain things, make and unmake governments or win prosperity for their nations. The record of their achievements and failures is set down in history. But we find the reasons for these deeds not in the chronicles of events but in letters, speeches, poems, dramas—in literature. Literature reveals the soul of a people. It shows what were the ideals of justice, brotherhood, love, religion, government, in any period. It is one thing to know the facts about the Boston Tea Party: the date, the men who took part, and the value of the tea destroyed. But to understand why men who were by nature law-abiding and loyal should have done these things, we need to read poems and speeches and pamphlets of that period. Thomas Paine, a writer, not a soldier, expressed in burning words the spirit that filled American patriots with courage during the darkest hours of the Revolution, and Washington ordered that some things he wrote should be read to every company of soldiers, knowing that such words were of more value for inspiring courage in the hearts of discouraged men than the addition of a regiment to their forces. "We hold these truths to be self-evident"—do you remember where these words occur and what follows? "Rights to life, liberty, and the pursuit of happiness." Now compare with these words the verses written by a Scottish plowboy, Robert Burns—"A Man's a Man for A' That." The poem shows clearly the thoughts that were moving men's minds at that revolutionary period, in Great Britain as well as in America, so that the poem becomes a way of understanding the soul of a past time.

Literature, then, has a twofold province: one that has nothing to do with space and time; the other presenting a form of history of a people. From the one point of view you have your fairy tales, which belong to no one language or century but to the children of every race and color. You have Ulysses, a Greek hero of ancient times, and Beowulf, a hero of the early Germanic tribes along the North Sea, whose story was first written down in English, though in a language that we hardly recognize as English today. Both of these you add to your group of heroes who are independent of time and nationality. You have Shakespeare's lovely fairy play, "A Midsummer Night's Dream," written in England more than four centuries ago, but the world to which the fairy drama leads you is of no special place or time—it comes into being, as by a magic wand, whenever you take your book and give yourself up to its power.

On the other hand, when you wish to understand the period of American colonization, you may supplement your history by reading in literature poems and stories that will help you to realize what were the hardships, the manner of life, the types of manhood and womanhood that produced the colonies. You have your history of the Revolution; you may fill in the records of men and battles by reading what literature offers you. A historical account of Concord and Lexington finds fuller meaning when you read Hawthorne's story, "The Gray Champion," and Emerson's poem about the Concord Monument, and Whittier's poem about Lexington. In your history reading you learn about the great westward movement by which the millions of acres in the Louisiana Purchase were settled—the date and price paid and the seller and the constitutional questions involved, and the dates of the admission of Missouri and Kansas as members of the sisterhood of states. But these historical facts take on new meaning when in literature you read also Cooper's tales of Indian life, or Parkman's accounts of pioneer travel, or Longfellow's story of Evangeline, or Eggleston's *Hoosier Schoolmaster,* and many, many others.

In this section of your book some materials are given for acquiring an understanding of what America means and how her present grows out of the past. First you will find a group of poems and stories that will picture for you some typical American scenes or unfold for you some of the famous legends that have come down from early colonial times. Next you will read a section called "American Literature of Lighter Vein," illustrating one of our national traits that has played no small part in our success as a people. For the conquest of this vast continent has been a task demanding ceaseless toil, and it has been the spirit of laughter and good humor that has helped Americans to keep life sweet, despite its tenseness. Last, you will come to a group of selections—"American Workers and Their Work"—that makes a fitting close to a study of our country through its literature. For the secret of our national prosperity is summed up in the ideal of faithful, honest labor. The work of the world calls out many different kinds of skill—the vision of the "dreamer" of great projects, the complicated planning and organizing of the leader, the skillful labor of the doer, but the one supreme essential for success is a loyal spirit of cooperation among all who join to carry on the vast industries on which our national progress is founded. And as you look at America today, busy and prosperous, you find in stories of American workers and their work a means for understanding the scenes in which you will soon be an actor—a farmer or a mechanic or a governor or a captain of industry in the America of tomorrow.

The selections in this part of your book are only examples of a sort of study that you may carry as far as you wish. There is no lack of material. The more you read, the better you will understand America, so that you may give loyal service to America when you grow up. And then, when you are older, you may study England, or France, or any other great people in this way, so that you may know their ideals and what they have added to civilization. So doing, the danger of wars shall be decreased, for we do not easily hate people when we know their best instincts and desires, and the instincts and desires of a people are recorded in their songs, their stories, their expression of the meaning of life.

# AMERICAN SCENES AND LEGENDS

## SONG OF THE CHATTAHOOCHEE*

### SIDNEY LANIER

Out of the hills of Habersham,
    Down the valleys of Hall,
I hurry amain to reach the plain,
Run the rapid and leap the fall,
5 Split at the rock and together again,
Accept my bed, or narrow or wide,
And flee from folly on every side
With a lover's pain to attain the plain
    Far from the hills of Habersham,
10     Far from the valleys of Hall.

All down the hills of Habersham,
    All through the valleys of Hall,
The rushes cried, "Abide, abide";
The willful water-weeds held me thrall;

---

* From *Poems of Sidney Lanier*

The laving laurel turned my tide;
The ferns and the fondling grass said, "Stay";
The dewberry dipped for to work delay;
And the little reeds sighed, "Abide, abide,
5          Here in the hills of Habersham,
          Here in the valleys of Hall."

High o'er the hills of Habersham,
Veiling the valleys of Hall,
The hickory told me manifold
10 Fair tales of shade; the poplar tall
Wrought me her shadowy self to hold;
The chestnut, the oak, the walnut, the pine,
Overleaning, with flickering meaning and sign,
Said: "Pass not so cold, these manifold
15          Deep shades of the hills of Habersham,
          These glades in the valleys of Hall."

And oft in the hills of Habersham,
And oft in the valleys of Hall,
The white quartz shone, and the smooth brook stone
20 Did bar me of passage with friendly brawl;
And many a luminous jewel lone
(Crystals clear or a-cloud with mist,
Ruby, garnet, or amethyst)
Made lures with the lights of streaming stone
25          In the clefts of the hills of Habersham,
          In the beds of the valleys of Hall.

But oh! not the hills of Habersham,
And oh! not the valleys of Hall
Avail; I am fain for to water the plain.
30 Downward the voices of Duty call—
Downward, to toil and be mixed with the main,
The dry fields burn and the mills are to turn,
And a myriad flowers mortally yearn,

And the lordly main from beyond the plain
Calls o'er the hills of Habersham,
Calls through the valleys of Hall.

## NOTES AND QUESTIONS

**Biography.** Sidney Lanier (1842-1881) was a native of Georgia. When he was a mere lad he entered the Confederate army and devoted the most precious years of his life to that service. He was a talented musician and often found it necessary to add to the earnings of his pen by playing in an orchestra. During his last years he lectured on English literature in Johns Hopkins University at Baltimore. Lanier has often been compared with Poe in the exquisite melody of his verse, while in unaffected simplicity and truthfulness to nature he is not surpassed by Bryant or Whittier. His prose as well as his poetry breathes the very spirit of his loved Southland. In the "Song of the Chattahoochee" and "On a Florida River," we scent the balsam of the Georgia pines among which he lived and the fragrance of magnolia groves, jessamine, and wild honeysuckle.

**Discussion.** 1. Who is represented as talking in this poem? 2. Find a line in the first stanza that tells the purpose of the river. 3. Find a line in the last stanza that tells why the river holds to this purpose. 4. What temptations to loiter does the second stanza mention? The third? The fourth? 5. Find lines in the last stanza which show that the river was not turned aside from its duty by anything it met. 6. Find the lines which show that the river expected to give itself in service to others when it reached the plain. 7. Do you feel that the poet is drawing a parallel between the Chattahoochee and life? Which method do you prefer—to let the reader make his own application to life, as in this poem, or to have the poet make it for him, as in Bryant's "To a Waterfowl"? 8. If the poet, in the second stanza, may have had in mind the small delights that make for contentment in life, what may he have had in mind in the third stanza? In the fourth? 9. Find examples of alliteration. 10. What do you notice in the structure of the third and the eighth lines of the first stanza? 11. Find other lines in the poem which have the same rhyme-scheme. 12. Find in the glossary the meaning of: amain; thrall; laving; manifold; lures; avail.

**Class Reading.** Bring to class and read Tennyson's "The Brook."

**Library Reading.** "Little Rivers," van Dyke.

# SNOW-BOUND

## A WINTER IDYL

### JOHN G. WHITTIER

The sun that brief December day
Rose cheerless over hills of gray,
And, darkly circled, gave at noon
A sadder light than waning moon.
5 Slow tracing down the thickening sky
Its mute and ominous prophecy,
A portent seeming less than threat,
It sank from sight before it set.
A chill no coat, however stout,
10 Of homespun stuff could quite shut out,
A hard, dull bitterness of cold,
That checked, mid-vein, the circling race
Of lifeblood in the sharpened face,
The coming of the snowstorm told.
15 The wind blew east; we heard the roar
Of Ocean on his wintry shore,
And felt the strong pulse throbbing there
Beat with low rhythm our inland air.

Meanwhile we did our nightly chores—
20 Brought in the wood from out of doors,
Littered the stalls, and from the mows
Raked down the herd's-grass for the cows;
Heard the horse whinnying for his corn;
And, sharply clashing horn on horn,
25 Impatient down the stanchion rows
The cattle shake their walnut bows;
While, peering from his early perch
Upon the scaffold's pole of birch,

The cock his crested helmet bent
And down his querulous challenge sent.

Unwarned by any sunset light
The gray day darkened into night,
5 A night made hoary with the swarm
And whirl-dance of the blinding storm,
As zigzag wavering to and fro
Crossed and recrossed the wingéd snow;
And ere the early bedtime came,
10 The white drift piled the window frame,
And through the glass the clothesline posts
Looked in like tall and sheeted ghosts.
So all night long the storm roared on;
The morning broke without a sun;
15 In tiny spherule traced with lines
Of Nature's geometric signs,
In starry flake and pellicle,
All day the hoary meteor fell;
And, when the second morning shone,
20 We looked upon a world unknown,
On nothing we could call our own.
Around the glistening wonder bent
The blue walls of the firmament,
No cloud above, no earth below—
25 A universe of sky and snow!
The old familiar sights of ours
Took marvelous shapes; strange domes and towers
Rose up where sty or corncrib stood,
Or garden-wall or belt of wood;
30 A smooth white mound the brush-pile showed,
A fenceless drift what once was road;
The bridle-post an old man sat
With loose-flung coat and high cocked hat;
The well-curb had a Chinese roof;

And even the long sweep, high aloof,
In its slant splendor, seemed to tell
Of Pisa's leaning miracle.

A prompt, decisive man, no breath
5 Our father wasted: "Boys, a path!"
Well pleased (for when did farmer boy
Count such a summons less than joy?),
Our buskins on our feet we drew;
With mittened hands, and caps drawn low
10 To guard our necks and ears from snow,
We cut the solid whiteness through;
And, where the drift was deepest, made
A tunnel walled and overlaid
With dazzling crystal; we had read
15 Of rare Aladdin's wondrous cave,
And to our own his name we gave,
With many a wish the luck were ours
To test his lamp's supernal powers.
We reached the barn with merry din,
20 And roused the prisoned brutes within.
The old horse thrust his long head out,
And grave with wonder gazed about;
The cock his lusty greeting said,
And forth his speckled harem led;
25 The oxen lashed their tails, and hooked,
And mild reproach of hunger looked;
The horned patriarch of the sheep,
Like Egypt's Amun roused from sleep,
Shook his sage head with gesture mute,
30 And emphasized with stamp of foot.

All day the gusty north-wind bore
The loosened drift its breath before;
Low circling round its southern zone,

The sun through dazzling snow-mist shone.
No church-bell lent its Christian tone
To the savage air; no social smoke
Curled over woods of snow-hung oak.
5 A solitude made more intense
By dreary-voiced elements,
The shrieking of the mindless wind,
The moaning tree-boughs swaying blind,
Beyond the circle of our hearth
10 And on the glass the unmeaning beat
Of ghostly finger-tips of sleet.
No welcome sound of toil or mirth
Unbound the spell, and testified
Of human life and thought outside.
15 We minded that the sharpest ear
The buried brooklet could not hear,
The music of whose liquid lip
Had been to us companionship,
And, in our lonely life, had grown
20 To have an almost human tone.

As night drew on, and, from the crest
Of wooded knolls that ridged the west,
The sun, a snow-blown traveler, sank
From sight beneath the smothering bank,
25 We piled with care our nightly stack
Of wood against the chimney-back—
The oaken log, green, huge, and thick,
And on its top the stout backstick;
The knotty forestick laid apart,
30 And filled between with curious art
The ragged brush; then, hovering near,
We watched the first red blaze appear,
Heard the sharp crackle, caught the gleam
On whitewashed wall and sagging beam,

Until the old, rude-furnished room
Burst, flower-like, into rosy bloom;
While radiant with a mimic flame
Outside the sparkling drift became;
5 And through the bare-boughed lilac-tree
Our own warm hearth seemed blazing free.
The crane and pendent trammels showed;
The Turks' heads on the andirons glowed;
While childish fancy, prompt to tell
10 The meaning of the miracle,
Whispered the old rime: *"Under the tree,*
*When fire outdoors burns merrily,*
*There the witches are making tea."*

The moon above the eastern wood
15 Shone at its full; the hill-range stood
Transfigured in the silver flood,
Its blown snows flashing cold and keen,
Dead white, save where some sharp ravine
Took shadow, or the somber green
20 Of hemlocks turned to pitchy black
Against the whiteness at their back.
For such a world and such a night
Most fitting that unwarming light,
Which only seemed where'er it fell
25 To make the coldness visible.

Shut in from all the world without,
We sat the clean-winged hearth about,
Content to let the north-wind roar
In baffled rage at pane and door,
30 While the red logs before us beat
The frost-line back with tropic heat;
And ever, when a louder blast
Shook beam and rafter as it passed,

The merrier up its roaring draught
The great throat of the chimney laughed;
The house-dog on his paws outspread
Laid to the fire his drowsy head;
5 The cat's dark silhouette on the wall
A couchant tiger's seemed to fall;
And, for the winter fireside meet,
Between the andirons' straddling feet,
The mug of cider simmered slow;
10 The apples sputtered in a row;
And, close at hand, the basket stood
With nuts from brown October's wood.

What matter how the night behaved?
What matter how the north-wind raved?
15 Blow high, blow low, not all its snow
Could quench our hearth-fire's ruddy glow.
O Time and Change!—with hair as gray
As was my sire's that winter day,
How strange it seems, with so much gone
20 Of life and love, to still live on!
Ah, brother! only I and thou
Are left of all that circle now—
The dear home faces whereupon
That fitful firelight paled and shone.
25 Henceforward, listen as we will,
The voices of that hearth are still;
Look where we may, the wide earth o'er,
Those lighted faces smile no more.
We tread the paths their feet have worn;
30   We sit beneath their orchard trees;
   We hear, like them, the hum of bees
And rustle of the bladed corn;
We turn the pages that they read;
   Their written words we linger o'er;

But in the sun they cast no shade,
No voice is heard, no sign is made;
  No step is on the conscious floor!
Yet Love will dream and Faith will trust
5 (Since He who knows our need is just)
That somehow, somewhere, meet we must.
Alas for him who never sees
  The stars shine through his cypress-trees!
Who, hopeless, lays his dead away,
10 Nor looks to see the breaking day
Across the mournful marbles play!
Who hath not learned, in hours of faith,
  The truth to flesh and sense unknown,
That Life is ever lord of Death,
15   And Love can never lose its own!

We sped the time with stories old;
Wrought puzzles out, and riddles told;
Or stammered from our schoolbook lore
"The Chief of Gambia's Golden Shore."
20 Our father rode again his ride
On Memphremagog's wooded side;
Sat down again to moose and samp
In trapper's hut and Indian camp;
Lived o'er the old idyllic ease
25 Beneath St. François' hemlock trees;
Again for him the moonlight shone
On Norman cap and bodiced zone;
Again he heard the violin play
Which led the village dance away,
30 And mingled in its merry whirl
The grandam and the laughing girl.
Or, nearer home, our steps he led
Where Salisbury's level marshes spread
  Mile-wide as flies the laden bee;

Where merry mowers, hale and strong,
Swept, scythe on scythe, their swaths along
   The low green prairies of the sea.
We shared the fishing off Boar's Head,
5  And round the rocky Isles of Shoals
   The hake-broil on the driftwood coals;
The chowder on the sand-beach made,
Dipped by the hungry, steaming hot,
With spoons of clamshell from the pot.
10 We heard the tales of witchcraft old,
And dream and sign and marvel told
To sleepy listeners as they lay
Stretched idly on the salted hay,
Adrift along the winding shores,
15 When favoring breezes deigned to blow
The square sail of the gundalow,
And idle lay the useless oars.

Our mother, while she turned her wheel
Or ran the new-knit stocking-heel,
20 Told how the Indian hordes came down
At midnight on Cochecho town,
And how her own great-uncle bore
His cruel scalp-mark to fourscore.
Recalling, in her fitting phrase,
25  So rich and picturesque and free
   (The common unrimed poetry
Of simple life and country ways),
The story of her early days—
She made us welcome to her home;
30 Old hearths grew wide to give us room;
We stole with her a frightened look
At the gray wizard's conjuring book,
The fame whereof went far and wide
Through all the simple country-side;

We heard the hawks at twilight play
The boat-horn on Piscataqua,
The loon's weird laughter far away;
We fished her little trout-brook; knew
5 What flowers in wood and meadow grew;
What sunny hillsides autumn-brown
She climbed to shake the ripe nuts down;
Saw where in sheltered cove and bay
The duck's black squadron anchored lay;
10 And heard the wild geese calling loud
Beneath the gray November cloud.   .

Then, haply, with a look more grave,
And soberer tone, some tale she gave
From painful Sewel's ancient tome,
15 Beloved in every Quaker home,
Of faith fire-winged by martyrdom,
Or Chalkley's Journal, old and quaint—
Gentlest of skippers, rare sea-saint!—
Who, when the dreary calms prevailed,
20 And water-butt and bread-cask failed,
And cruel, hungry eyes pursued
His portly presence, mad for food,
With dark hints muttered under breath
Of casting lots for life or death,
25 Offered, if Heaven withheld supplies,
To be himself the sacrifice.
Then, suddenly, as if to save
The good man from his living grave,
A ripple on the water grew,
30 A school of porpoise flashed in view.
"Take, eat," he said, "and be content;
These fishes in my stead are sent
By Him who gave the tangled ram
To spare the child of Abraham."

Our uncle, innocent of books,
Was rich in lore of fields and brooks,
The ancient teachers never dumb
Of Nature's unhoused lyceum.
5 In moons and tides and weather wise,
He read the clouds as prophecies;
And foul or fair could well divine
By many an occult hint and sign,
Holding the cunning-warded keys
10 To all the woodcraft mysteries;
Himself to Nature's heart so near
That all her voices in his ear
Of beast or bird had meaning clear,
Like Appolonius of old,
15 Who knew the tales the sparrows told,
Or Hermes, who interpreted
What the sage cranes of Nilus said;
A simple, guileless, childlike man,
Content to live where life began;
20 Strong only on his native grounds,
The little world of sights and sounds
Whose girdle was the parish bounds,
  Whereof his fondly partial pride
The common features magnified,
25 As Surrey hills to mountains grew
In White of Selborne's loving view—
He told how teal and loon he shot,
And how the eagle's eggs he got;
The feats on pond and river done,
30 The prodigies of rod and gun;
Till, warming with the tales he told,
Forgotten was the outside cold;
The bitter wind unheeded blew;
From ripening corn the pigeons flew;
35 The partridge drummed i' the wood; the mink

Went fishing down the river-brink.
In fields with bean or clover gay,
The woodchuck, like a hermit gray,
  Peered from the doorway of his cell;
5 The muskrat plied the mason's trade,
And tier by tier his mud-walls laid:
And from the shagbark overhead
  The grizzled squirrel dropped his shell.

Next, the dear aunt, whose smile of cheer
10 And voice in dreams I see and hear—
The sweetest woman ever Fate
Perverse denied a household mate,
Who, lonely, homeless, not the less
Found peace in love's unselfishness,
15 And welcome whereso'er she went,
  A calm and gracious element,
Whose presence seemed the sweet income
And womanly atmosphere of home—
Called up her girlhood memories,
20 The huskings and the apple-bees,
  The sleigh-rides and the summer sails,
Weaving through all the poor details
And homespun warp of circumstance
A golden woof-thread of romance.
25 For well she kept her genial mood
And simple faith of maidenhood;
Before her still a cloud-land lay;
The mirage loomed across her way;
The morning dew, that dried so soon
30 With others, glistened at her noon;
Through years of toil and soil and care,
From glossy tress to thin gray hair,
All unprofaned she held apart
The virgin fancies of the heart.

Be shame to him of woman born
Who had for such but thought of scorn.

There, too, our elder sister plied
Her evening task the stand beside;
5 A full, rich nature, free to trust,
Truthful and almost sternly just,
Impulsive, earnest, prompt to act,
And make her generous thought a fact,
Keeping with many a light disguise
10 The secret of self-sacrifice.
O heart sore-tried! thou hast the best
That Heaven itself could give thee—rest,
Rest from all bitter thoughts and things!
How many a poor one's blessing went
15   With thee beneath the low green tent
Whose curtain never outward swings!

As one who held herself a part
Of all she saw, and let her heart
Against the household bosom lean,
20 Upon the motley-braided mat
Our youngest and our dearest sat,
Lifting her large, sweet, asking eyes,
Now bathed within the fadeless green
And holy peace of Paradise.
25 Oh, looking from some heavenly hill
Or from the shade of saintly palms,
Or silver reach of river calms,
Do those large eyes behold me still?
With me one little year ago
30 The chill weight of the winter snow
For months upon her grave has lain;
And now when summer south-winds blow,
And brier and harebell bloom again,

I tread the pleasant paths we trod,
I see the violet-sprinkled sod,
Whereon she leaned, too frail and weak
The hillside flowers she loved to seek,
5 Yet following me where'er I went
With dark eyes full of love's content.
The birds are glad; the brier-rose fills
The air with sweetness; all the hills
Stretch green to June's unclouded sky;
10 But still I wait with ear and eye
For something gone which should be nigh,
A loss in all familiar things,
In flower that blooms, and bird that sings.
And yet, dear heart! remembering thee,
15   Am I not richer than of old?
Safe in thy immortality,
    What change can reach the wealth I hold?
    What chance can mar the pearl and gold
Thy love hath left in trust with me?
20 And while in life's late afternoon,
    Where cool and long the shadows grow,
I walk to meet the night that soon
    Shall shape and shadow overflow,
I cannot feel that thou art far,
25 Since near at need the angels are;
And when the sunset gates unbar,
    Shall I not see thee waiting stand,
And, white against the evening star,
    The welcome of thy beckoning hand?


30 Brisk wielder of the birch and rule,
The master of the district school
Held at the fire his favored place;
Its warm glow lit a laughing face,
Fresh-hued and fair, where scarce appeared

The uncertain prophecy of beard.
He teased the mitten-blinded cat,
Played cross-pins on my uncle's hat,
Sang songs, and told us what befalls
5 In classic Dartmouth's college halls.
Born the wild northern hills among,
From whence his yeoman father wrung
By patient toil subsistence scant,
Not competence and yet not want,
10 He early gained the power to pay
His cheerful, self-reliant way;
Could doff at ease his scholar's gown
To peddle wares from town to town;
Or through the long vacation's reach
15 In lonely lowland districts teach,
Where all the droll experience found
At stranger hearths in boarding round,
The moonlit skater's keen delight,
The sleigh-drive through the frosty night,
20 The rustic party, with its rough
Accompaniment of blindman's buff,
And whirling plate, and forfeits paid,
His winter task a pastime made.
Happy the snow-locked homes wherein
25 He tuned his merry violin,
Or played the athlete in the barn,
Or held the good dame's winding yarn,
Or mirth-provoking versions told
Of classic legends rare and old,
30 Wherein the scenes of Greece and Rome
Had all the commonplace of home,
And little seemed at best the odds
'Twixt Yankee peddlers and old gods;
Where Pindus-born Araxes took
35 The guise of any grist-mill brook,

And dread Olympus at his will
Became a huckleberry hill.
A careless boy that night he seemed;
  But at his desk he had the look
5 And air of one who wisely schemed,
  And hostage from the future took
In trained thought and lore of book.

Another guest that winter night
Flashed back from lustrous eyes the light.
10 Unmarked by time, and yet not young,
The honeyed music of her tongue
And words of meekness scarcely told
A nature passionate and bold,
Strong, self-concentered, spurning guide,
15 Its milder features dwarfed beside
Her unbent will's majestic pride.
She sat among us, at the best,
A not unfeared, half-welcome guest,
Rebuking with her cultured phrase
20 Our homeliness of words and ways.
A certain pard-like, treacherous grace
  Swayed the lithe limbs and drooped the lash,
  Lent the white teeth their dazzling flash;
  And under low brows, black with night,
25   Rayed out at times a dangerous light;
The sharp heat-lightnings of her face
Presaging ill to him whom Fate
Condemned to share her love or hate.
A woman tropical, intense
30 In thought and act, in soul and sense,
She blended in a like degree
The vixen and the devotee,
Revealing with each freak or feint
  The temper of Petruchio's Kate,

The raptures of Siena's saint.
Her tapering hand and rounded wrist
Had facile power to form a fist;
The warm, dark languish of her eyes
5 Was never safe from wrath's surprise.
Brows saintly calm and lips devout
Knew every change of scowl and pout,
And the sweet voice had notes more high
And shrill for social battle-cry.

10 Since then what old cathedral town
Has missed her pilgrim staff and gown,
What convent-gate has held its lock
Against the challenge of her knock!
Through Smyrna's plague-hushed thoroughfares,
15 Up sea-set Malta's rocky stairs,
Gray olive slopes of hills that hem
Thy tombs and shrines, Jerusalem,
Or startling on her desert-throne
The crazy Queen of Lebanon
20 With claims fantastic as her own,
Her tireless feet have held their way;
And still, unrestful, bowed, and gray,
She watches under Eastern skies,
With hope each day renewed and fresh,
25 The Lord's quick coming in the flesh,
Whereof she dreams and prophesies!

Where'er her troubled path may be,
The Lord's sweet pity with her go!
The outward wayward life we see,
30 The hidden springs we may not know.
Nor is it given us to discern
What threads the fatal sisters spun,
Through what ancestral years has run

The sorrow with the woman born,
What forged her cruel chain of moods,
What set her feet in solitudes,
    And held the love within her mute,
5 What mingled madness in the blood,
    A lifelong discord and annoy,
    Water of tears with oil of joy,
And hid within the folded bud
    Perversities of flower and fruit.
10 It is not ours to separate
The tangled skein of will and fate,
To show what metes and bounds should stand
Upon the soul's debatable land,
And between choice and Providence
15 Divide the circle of events;
    But He who knows our frame is just,
Merciful, and compassionate,
And full of sweet assurances
And hope for all the language is,
20 That He remembereth we are dust!

At last the great logs, crumbling low,
Sent out a dull and duller glow;
The bull's-eye watch that hung in view,
25 Ticking its weary circuit through,
Pointed with mutely-warning sign
Its black hand to the hour of nine.
That sign the pleasant circle broke;
My uncle ceased his pipe to smoke,
30 Knocked from its bowl the refuse gray,
And laid it tenderly away;
Then roused himself to safely cover
The dull red brands with ashes over.
And while, with care, our mother laid
The work aside, her steps she stayed

One moment, seeking to express
Her grateful sense of happiness
For food and shelter, warmth and health,
5 And love's contentment more than wealth,
With simple wishes (not the weak,
Vain prayers which no fulfillment seek,
But such as warm the generous heart,
O'er-prompt to do with Heaven its part)
10 That none might lack, that bitter night,
For bread and clothing, warmth and light.

Within our beds awhile we heard
The wind that round the gables roared,
15 With now and then a ruder shock,
Which made our very bedsteads rock.
We heard the loosened clapboards tossed,
The board-nails snapping in the frost;
And on us, through the unplastered wall,
20 Felt the light-sifted snowflakes fall;
But sleep stole on, as sleep will do
When hearts are light and life is new;
Faint and more faint the murmurs grew,
Till in the summer-land of dreams
25 They softened to the sound of streams,
Low stir of leaves, and dip of oars,
And lapsing waves on quiet shores.

Next morn we wakened with the shout
30 Of merry voices high and clear;
And saw the teamsters drawing near
To break the drifted highways out.
Down the long hillside treading slow
We saw the half-buried oxen go,
Shaking the snow from heads uptossed,

Their straining nostrils white with frost.
Before our door the straggling train
Drew up, an added team to gain.
The elders thrashed their hands a-cold,
5　　Passed, with the cider-mug, their jokes
　　From lip to lip; the younger folks
Down the loose snow-banks, wrestling, rolled;
Then toiled again the cavalcade
　　O'er windy hill, through clogged ravine,
10　And woodland paths that wound between
Low-drooping pine-boughs winter-weighed.
From every barn a team afoot;
At every house a new recruit;
Where, drawn by Nature's subtlest law,
15　Haply the watchful young men saw
Sweet doorway pictures of the curls
And curious eyes of merry girls,
Lifting their hands in mock defense
Against the snowballs' compliments,
20　And reading in each missive tossed
The charm which Eden never lost.

We heard once more the sleigh-bells' sound;
And, following where the teamsters led,
The wise old Doctor went his round,
25　Just pausing at our door to say,
In the brief, autocratic way
Of one who, prompt at Duty's call,
Was free to urge her claim on all,
　　That some poor neighbor sick abed
30　At night our mother's aid would need.
For, one in generous thought and deed,
　　What mattered in the sufferer's sight
　　The Quaker matron's inward light,
The Doctor's mail of Calvin's creed?

All hearts confess the saints elect
  Who, twain in faith, in love agree,
And melt not in an acid sect
  The Christian pearl of Charity!

5  So days went on; a week had passed
Since the great world was heard from last.
The Almanac we studied o'er;
Read and reread our little store
Of books and pamphlets, scarce a score;
10 One harmless novel, mostly hid
From younger eyes, a book forbid,
And poetry (or good or bad,
A single book was all we had),
Where Ellwood's meek, drab-skirted Muse,
15  A stranger to the heathen Nine,
  Sang, with a somewhat nasal whine,
The wars of David and the Jews.
At last the floundering carrier bore
The village paper to our door.
20 Lo! broadening outward as we read,
To warmer zones the horizon spread;
In panoramic length unrolled
We saw the marvel that it told.
Before us passed the painted Creeks,
25  And daft McGregor on his raids
  In Costa Rica's everglades.
And up Taygetus winding slow
Rode Ypsilanti's Mainote Greeks,
A Turk's head at each saddle bow!
30 Welcome to us its week-old news,
Its corner for the rustic Muse,
Its monthly gauge of snow and rain,
Its record, mingling in a breath
The wedding bell and dirge of death;

Jest, anecdote, and lovelorn tale,
The latest culprit sent to jail;
Its hue and cry of stolen and lost,
Its vendue sales and goods at cost,
5　And traffic calling loud for gain.
We felt the stir of hall and street,
The pulse of life that round us beat;
The chill embargo of the snow
Was melted in the genial glow;
10 Wide swung again our ice-locked door,
And all the world was ours once more!

Clasp, Angel of the backward look
　And folded wings of ashen gray
　And voice of echoes far away,
15 The brazen covers of thy book;
The weird palimpsest old and vast,
Wherein thou hid'st the spectral past;
Where, closely mingling, pale and glow
The characters of joy and woe;
20 The monographs of outlived years,
Or smile-illumed or dim with tears,
　Green hills of life that slope to death,
And haunts of home, whose vistaed trees
Shade off to mournful cypresses
25　With the white amaranths underneath.
Even while I look, I can but heed
　The restless sands' incessant fall,
Importunate hours that hours succeed;
Each clamorous with its own sharp need,
30　And duty keeping pace with all.
Shut down and clasp the heavy lids;
I hear again the voice that bids
The dreamer leave his dream midway
For larger hopes and graver fears—

Life greatens in these later years;
The century's aloe flowers today!

Yet, haply, in some lull of life,
Some Truce of God which breaks its strife,
5 The worldling's eyes shall gather dew,
Dreaming in throngful city ways
Of winter joys his boyhood knew;
And dear and early friends—the few
Who yet remain—shall pause to view
10 These Flemish pictures of old days;
Sit with me by the homestead hearth,
And stretch the hands of memory forth
To warm them at the wood-fire's blaze!
And thanks untraced to lips unknown
15 Shall greet me like the odors blown
From unseen meadows newly mown,
Or lilies floating in some pond,
Wood-fringed, the wayside gaze beyond;
The traveler owns the grateful sense
20 Of sweetness near, he knows not whence,
And, pausing, takes with forehead bare
The benediction of the air.

## NOTES AND QUESTIONS

For **Biography** see page 290.

**Discussion.** 1. Into what parts may this poem be divided? 2. How does the description of the sun "that brief December day" prepare you for what is to follow? 3. Of what was the appearance of the sun a "mute prophecy"? 4. What is the difference between a portent and a threat? 5. What told the coming of the storm? 6. What does the poet mention as being the "nightly chores" at his home? 7. What does the word "meanwhile" tell you as to the time at which they did these chores? 8. Find the lines that tell of the beginning of the snowstorm. 9. In what connection is the word "swarm" commonly used? What picture does it give you of the snowflakes? 10. How does the addition of the word "whirl-dance" change the picture you had made? 11. What other words does the poet use to describe the crossing and recrossing of the snow? 12. Find two lines that tell the changes the snow made in the appearance of familiar objects. 13. Why was the making of a path a necessity? 14. Where is the story of Aladdin told? What were his lamp's "supernal powers"? 15. How does the poet make us feel the solitude of the farmhouse? 16. Try to give in your own words the picture of the moonlight on the snow. 17. Try to give in your own words the picture of the hearth. 18. Of whom did the circle gathered around the fire consist? 19. Select the lines that please you most in each description. 20. How did the members of the family amuse themselves? 21. Who told the stories? 22. Of what did their library consist? 23. Who are meant by the "heathen Nine"? 24. Can you explain how Ellwood's Muse may be called a stranger to the "heathen Nine"? 25. What put the household again in touch with the outside world? 26. Of what did they read in the paper? 27. What was printed in the "corner for the rustic Muse"? 28. What is meant by the "hue and cry"? 29. Find lines that tell the effect of the news upon the snow-bound family. 30. What is the voice that bids the dreamer leave his dreams? 31. What is meant by "Truce of God"? 32. Why does the poet compare the pictures he has shown with Flemish pictures? 33. Memorize the lines you like particularly well. 34. Which scenes described in this poem can you picture most clearly? 35. What were you told in "Literature and Life" on pages 19 and 21 about literature as a source of learning the facts of life? How does this poem give you a clearer idea of "the facts of life" on a New England farm than you could gain from your history or geography or from an encyclopedia? 36. What did you read in the "Introduction" on pages 335 and 336 about literature as a "form of history"? What ideals of justice, brotherhood, industry, and thrift does this poem show were characteristic of the simple folk in this region? 37. Find in the glossary the meaning of: idyl; waning; portent; querulous; spherule; sweep; buskins; clean-winged. 38. *Pronounce:* stanchion; harem; silhouette; mirage; cavalcade.

## Phrases for Study

| | |
|---|---|
| geometric signs, **343**, 16 | shape and shadow, **354**, 23 |
| mimic flame, **346**, 3 | hostage from the future, **356**, 6 |
| stars...cypress-trees, **348**, 8 | fatal sisters, **357**, 32 |
| bodiced zone, **348**, 27 | soul's debatable land, **358**, 13 |
| painful Sewel's, **350**, 14 | inward light, **360**, 33 |
| tangled ram, **350**, 33 | mail of Calvin's creed, **360**, 34 |
| Nature's lyceum, **351**, 4 | Angel of the backward look, **362**, 12 |
| glistened at her noon, **352**, 30 | Flemish pictures, **363**, 10 |

**Class Reading.** Select some scene or incident in the poem for special preparation. Study the passage, using all the helps available until you can visualize the scene and enable your classmates to get a vivid picture from your reading.

**Library Reading.** *The Life of a Pioneer*, Shaw; *A Son of the Middle Border*, Garland.

**Suggestions for Theme Topics.** 1. Contrast a modern farmhouse with which you are familiar with the Whittier house pictured in the poem. 2. Contrast the opportunities for education in rural districts in Whittier's boyhood days with those of the present time. 3. Discuss the influence that the schoolmaster might exert on such a household as Whittier describes, illustrating from Whittier's own life. 4. Modes of cooperation in country life in early days and the necessity for it. 5. The most interesting person about the Whittier fireside. 6. An account of the work of Gilbert White in the English village of Selborne (See *The Natural History of Selborne*, White). 7. Rural customs in old New England, as "village dance," etc.

**A Suggested Problem.** In the "Introduction" on page 338 you were told that the selections in this unit are only examples of glimpses into American life and that the better you understand American life, the better citizen you will be. Prepare a program for a class period devoted to "Little Pictures of Varied American Life." Members of the class who have lived for a time or traveled in some distant part of the country may give three-minute talks about life in these communities (illustrated, if possible, by pictures). Pupils who cannot contribute any firsthand experiences may gain material for their discussion from books similar to those listed above under the topic "Library Reading."

## Rip Van Winkle*

### Washington Irving

Whoever has made a voyage up the Hudson must remember the Kaatskill Mountains. They are a dismembered branch of the great Appalachian family and are seen away to the west of the river, swelling up to a noble height and lording it over the
5 surrounding country. Every change of season, every change of weather, indeed, every hour of the day, produces some changes in the magical hues and shapes of these mountains, and they are regarded by all the good wives, far and near, as perfect barometers. When the weather is fair and settled, they are
10 clothed in blue and purple and print their bold outlines on the clear evening sky, but sometimes when the rest of the landscape is cloudless, they will gather a hood of gray vapors about their summits, which, in the last rays of the setting sun, will glow and light up like a crown of glory.

15     At the foot of these fairy mountains the voyager may have descried the light smoke curling up from a village, whose shingle roofs gleam among the trees, just where the blue tints of the upland melt away into the fresh green of the nearer landscape. It is a little village of great antiquity, having been founded by
20 some of the Dutch colonists in the early time of the province, just about the beginning of the government of the good Peter Stuyvesant (may he rest in peace!), and there were some of the houses of the original settlers standing within a few years, built of small yellow bricks brought from Holland, having latticed
25 windows and gable fronts, surmounted with weathercocks.

    In that same village, and in one of these very houses (which, to tell the precise truth, was sadly timeworn and weather-beaten), there lived many years since, while the country was yet a province of Great Britain, a simple, good-natured fellow, of
30 the name of Rip Van Winkle. He was a descendant of the

---

*See Silent and Oral Reading, page 13.

Van Winkles who figured so gallantly in the chivalrous days of Peter Stuyvesant and accompanied him to the siege of Fort Christina. He inherited, however, but little of the martial character of his ancestors. I have observed that he was a
5 simple, good-natured man; he was, moreover, a kind neighbor and an obedient, henpecked husband. Indeed, to the latter circumstances might be owing that meekness of spirit which gained him such universal popularity, for those men are most apt to be obsequious and conciliating abroad who are under the
10 discipline of shrews at home. Their tempers, doubtless, are rendered pliant and malleable in the fiery furnace of domestic tribulation, and a curtain lecture is worth all the sermons in the world for teaching the virtues of patience and long-suffering. A termagant wife may, therefore, in some respects be considered a
15 tolerable blessing, and, if so, Rip Van Winkle was thrice blessed.

Certain it is that he was a great favorite among all the good wives of the village, who, as usual with the amiable sex, took his part in all family squabbles, and never failed, whenever they talked those matters over in their evening gossipings, to lay all
20 the blame on Dame Van Winkle. The children of the village, too, would shout with joy whenever he approached. He assisted at their sports, made their playthings, taught them to fly kites and shoot marbles, and told them long stories of ghosts, witches, and Indians. Whenever he went dodging about the village, he was
25 surrounded by a troop of them, hanging on his skirts, clambering on his back, and playing a thousand tricks on him with impunity, and not a dog would bark at him throughout the neighborhood.

The great error in Rip's composition was an insuperable aversion to all kinds of profitable labor. It could not be from the
30 want of assiduity or perseverance, for he would sit on a wet rock, with a rod as long and heavy as a Tartar's lance, and fish all day without a murmur, even though he should not be encouraged by a single nibble. He would carry a fowling-piece on his shoulder for hours together, trudging through woods and swamps and
35 up hill and down dale to shoot a few squirrels or wild pigeons.

He would never refuse to assist a neighbor, even in the roughest toil, and was a foremost man at all country frolics for husking Indian corn or building stone fences; the women of the village, too, used to employ him to run their errands and to do such
5 little odd jobs as their less obliging husbands would not do for them. In a word, Rip was ready to attend to anybody's business but his own, but as to doing family duty and keeping his farm in order, he found it impossible.

In fact, he declared it was of no use to work on his farm; it
10 was the most pestilent little piece of ground in the whole country; everything about it went wrong, and would go wrong, in spite of him. His fences were continually falling to pieces; his cow would either go astray or get among the cabbages; weeds were sure to grow quicker in his fields than anywhere else; the rain
15 always made a point of setting in just as he had some outdoor work to do, so that though his patrimonial estate had dwindled away under his management, acre by acre, until there was little more left than a mere patch of Indian corn and potatoes, yet it was the worst-conditioned farm in the neighborhood.

20 His children, too, were as ragged and wild as if they belonged to nobody. His son Rip, an urchin begotten in his own likeness, promised to inherit the habits, with the old clothes, of his father. He was generally seen trooping like a colt at his mother's heels, equipped in a pair of his father's cast-off galligaskins, which
25 he had much ado to hold up with one hand, as a lady does her train in bad weather.

Rip Van Winkle, however, was one of those happy mortals, of foolish, well-oiled dispositions, who take the world easy, eat white bread or brown, whichever can be got with least thought
30 or trouble, and would rather starve on a penny than work for a pound. If left to himself, he would have whistled life away in perfect contentment, but his wife kept continually dinning in his ears about his idleness, his carelessness, and the ruin he was bringing on his family. Morning, noon, and night her tongue
35 was incessantly going, and everything he said or did was sure to

produce a torrent of household eloquence. Rip had but one way
of replying to all lectures of the kind, and that, by frequent use,
had grown into a habit. He shrugged his shoulders, shook his
head, cast up his eyes, but said nothing. This, however, always
5 provoked a fresh volley from his wife, so that he was fain to draw
off his forces and take to the outside of the house—the only side
which, in truth, belongs to a henpecked husband.

Rip's sole domestic adherent was his dog Wolf, who was as
much henpecked as his master, for Dame Van Winkle regarded
10 them as companions in idleness and even looked upon Wolf with
an evil eye as the cause of his master's going so often astray.
True it is, in all points of spirit befitting an honorable dog, he
was as courageous an animal as ever scoured the woods—but
what courage can withstand the ever-during and all-besetting
15 terrors of a woman's tongue? The moment Wolf entered the
house his crest fell, his tail drooped to the ground or curled
between his legs, he sneaked about with a gallows air, casting
many a sidelong glance at Dame Van Winkle, and at the least
flourish of a broomstick or ladle he would fly to the door with
20 yelping precipitation.

Times grew worse and worse with Rip Van Winkle as years of
matrimony rolled on; a tart temper never mellows with age, and
a sharp tongue is the only edged tool that grows keener with
constant use. For a long while he used to console himself, when
25 driven from home, by frequenting a kind of perpetual club of
the sages, philosophers, and other idle personages of the village,
which held its sessions on a bench before a small inn, designated
by a rubicund portrait of His Majesty George the Third. Here they
used to sit in the shade through a long, lazy summer's day talking
30 listlessly over village gossip or telling endless sleepy stories
about nothing. But it would have been worth any statesman's
money to have heard the profound discussions that sometimes
took place when by chance an old newspaper fell into their
hands from some passing traveler. How solemnly they would
35 listen to the contents, as drawled out by Derrick Van Bummel,

the schoolmaster, a dapper, learned little man, who was not to be daunted by the most gigantic word in the dictionary, and how sagely they would deliberate upon public events some months after they had taken place.

5   The opinions of this junto were completely controlled by Nicholas Vedder, a patriarch of the village and landlord of the inn at the door of which he took his seat from morning till night, just moving sufficiently to avoid the sun and keep in the shade of a large tree, so that the neighbors could tell the hour by his 10 movements as accurately as by a sundial. It is true he was rarely heard to speak, but smoked his pipe incessantly. His adherents, however (for every great man has his adherents), perfectly understood him and knew how to gather his opinions. When anything that was read or related displeased him, he was 15 observed to smoke his pipe vehemently and to send forth short, frequent, and angry puffs, but when pleased, he would inhale the smoke slowly and tranquilly and emit it in light and placid clouds, and sometimes, taking the pipe from his mouth and letting the fragrant vapor curl about his nose, would gravely nod 20 his head in token of perfect approbation.

From even this stronghold the unlucky Rip was at length routed by his termagant wife, who would suddenly break in upon the tranquility of the assemblage and call the members all to naught, nor was that august personage, Nicholas Vedder himself, 25 sacred from the daring tongue of this terrible virago, who charged him outright with encouraging her husband in habits of idleness.

Poor Rip was at last reduced almost to despair, and his only alternative, to escape from the labor of the farm and clamor of his wife, was to take gun in hand and stroll away into the 30 woods. Here he would sometimes seat himself at the foot of a tree and share the contents of his wallet with Wolf, with whom he sympathized as a fellow sufferer in persecution. "Poor Wolf," he would say, "thy mistress leads thee a dog's life of it, but never mind, my lad—whilst I live thou shalt never want a friend 35 to stand by thee!" Wolf would wag his tail, look wistfully in his master's face, and if dogs can feel pity I verily believe he reciprocated the sentiment with all his heart.

In a long ramble of the kind on a fine autumnal day Rip had unconsciously scrambled to one of the highest parts of the
5 Kaatskill Mountains. He was after his favorite sport of squirrel shooting, and the still solitudes had echoed and reechoed with the reports of his gun. Panting and fatigued, he threw himself, late in the afternoon, on a green knoll, covered with mountain herbage, that crowned the brow of a precipice. From an opening
10 between the trees he could overlook all the lower country for many a mile of rich woodland. He saw at a distance the lordly Hudson, far, far below him, moving on its silent but majestic course, with the reflection of a purple cloud or the sail of a lagging bark here and there sleeping on its glassy bosom and at
15 last losing itself in the blue highlands.

On the other side he looked down into a deep mountain glen, wild, lonely, and shagged, the bottom filled with fragments from the impending cliffs and scarcely lighted by the reflected rays of the setting sun. For some time Rip lay musing on this scene;
20 evening was gradually advancing; the mountains began to throw their long blue shadows over the valleys; he saw that it would be dark long before he could reach the village; and he heaved a heavy sigh when he thought of encountering the terrors of Dame Van Winkle.

25 As he was about to descend, he heard a voice from a distance hallooing, "Rip Van Winkle! Rip Van Winkle!" He looked round, but could see nothing but a crow winging its solitary flight across the mountain. He thought his fancy must have deceived him and turned again to descend, when he heard the same cry
30 ring through the still evening air: "Rip Van Winkle! Rip Van Winkle!"—at the same time Wolf bristled up his back, and giving a low growl, skulked to his master's side, looking fearfully down into the glen. Rip now felt a vague apprehension stealing over him; he looked anxiously in the same direction and perceived a
35 strange figure slowly toiling up the rocks and bending under the

weight of something he carried on his back. He was surprised
to see any human being in this lonely and unfrequented place,
but supposing it to be someone of the neighborhood in need of
assistance, he hastened down to yield it.

5      On nearer approach he was still more surprised at the singularity of the stranger's appearance. He was a short, square-built
old fellow, with thick, bushy hair and a grizzled beard. His
dress was of the antique Dutch fashion: a cloth jerkin strapped
round the waist, several pair of breeches, the outer one of ample
10 volume, decorated with rows of buttons down the sides and
bunches at the knees. He bore on his shoulder a stout keg that
seemed full of liquor and made signs for Rip to approach and
assist him with the load. Though rather shy and distrustful of
his new acquaintance, Rip complied with his usual alacrity, and
15 mutually relieving one another, they clambered up a narrow
gully, apparently the dry bed of a mountain torrent. As they
ascended, Rip every now and then heard long rolling peals like
distant thunder that seemed to issue out of a deep ravine, or
rather cleft, between lofty rocks, toward which their rugged path
20 conducted. He paused for a moment, but supposing it to be the
muttering of one of those transient thundershowers which often
take place in mountain heights, he proceeded. Passing through
the ravine, they came to a hollow, like a small amphitheater,
surrounded by perpendicular precipices, over the brinks of
25 which impending trees shot their branches, so that you only
caught glimpses of the azure sky and the bright evening cloud.
During the whole time Rip and his companion had labored on in
silence, for though the former marveled greatly what could be
the object of carrying a keg of liquor up this wild mountain, yet
30 there was something strange and incomprehensible about the
unknown that inspired awe and checked familiarity.

On entering the amphitheater, new objects of wonder presented themselves. On a level spot in the center was a company
of odd looking personages playing at ninepins. They were
35 dressed in a quaint, outlandish fashion; some wore short doublets,

others, jerkins, with long knives in their belts, and most of them had enormous breeches of similar style with that of the guide's. Their visages, too, were peculiar; one had a large beard, broad face, and small piggish eyes; the face of another seemed
5 to consist entirely of nose, and was surmounted by a white sugar-loaf hat, set off with a little red cock's tail. They all had beards of various shapes and colors. There was one who seemed to be the commander. He was a stout old gentleman with a weather-beaten countenance; he wore a laced doublet, broad
10 belt and hanger, high-crowned hat and feather, red stockings, and high-heeled shoes with roses in them. The whole group reminded Rip of the figures in an old Flemish painting in the parlor of Dominic Van Shaick, the village parson, which had been brought over from Holland at the time of the settlement.
15 What seemed particularly odd to Rip was that, though these folks were evidently amusing themselves, yet they maintained the gravest faces, the most mysterious silence, and were, withal, the most melancholy party of pleasure he had ever witnessed. Nothing interrupted the stillness of the scene but the noise of
20 the balls, which, whenever they were rolled, echoed along the mountains like rumbling peals of thunder.

As Rip and his companion approached them, they suddenly desisted from their play and stared at him with such fixed, statue-like gaze, and such strange, uncouth, lack-luster counte-
25 nances, that his heart turned within him and his knees smote together. His companion now emptied the contents of the keg into large flagons and made signs to him to wait upon the company. He obeyed with fear and trembling; they quaffed the liquor in profound silence and then returned to their game.
30 By degrees Rip's awe and apprehension subsided. He even ventured, when no eye was fixed upon him, to taste the beverage, which he found had much the flavor of excellent Hollands. He was naturally a thirsty soul and was soon tempted to repeat the draught. One taste provoked another, and he reiterated
35 his visits to the flagon so often that at length his senses were

overpowered, his eyes swam in his head, his head gradually declined, and he fell into a deep sleep.

On waking, he found himself on the green knoll whence he had first seen the old man of the glen. He rubbed his eyes—it
5 was a bright, sunny morning. The birds were hopping and twittering among the bushes, and the eagle was wheeling aloft, and breasting the pure mountain breeze. "Surely," thought Rip, "I have not slept here all night." He recalled the occurrences before he fell asleep. The strange man with a keg
10 of liquor—the mountain ravine—the wild retreat among the rocks—the woebegone party at ninepins—the flagon—"Oh, that flagon! that wicked flagon!" thought Rip—"what excuse shall I make to Dame Van Winkle?"

He looked round for his gun, but in place of the clean, well-
15 oiled fowling-piece he found an old firelock lying by him, the barrel incrusted with rust, the lock falling off, and the stock worm eaten. He now suspected that the grave roisterers of the mountain had put a trick upon him, and, having dosed him with liquor, had robbed him of his gun. Wolf, too, had disappeared,
20 but he might have strayed away after a squirrel or partridge. He whistled after him and shouted his name, but all in vain; the echoes repeated his whistle and shout, but no dog was to be seen.

He determined to revisit the scene of the last evening's gambol,
25 and, if he met with any of the party, to demand his dog and gun. As he rose to walk, he found himself stiff in the joints and wanting in his usual activity. "These mountain beds do not agree with me," thought Rip, "and if this frolic should lay me up with a fit of the rheumatism, I shall have a blessed time with Dame Van Winkle."
30 With some difficulty he got down into the glen; he found the gully up which he and his companion had ascended the preceding evening; but to his astonishment a mountain stream was now foaming down it, leaping from rock to rock, and filling the glen with babbling murmurs. He, however, made shift to scramble
35 up its sides, working his toilsome way through thickets of birch,

sassafras, and witchhazel, and sometimes tripped up or entangled by the wild grapevines that twisted their coils or tendrils from tree to tree and spread a kind of network in his path.

At length he reached to where the ravine had opened through
5 the cliffs to the amphitheater, but no traces of such opening remained. The rocks presented a high, impenetrable wall, over which the torrent came tumbling in a sheet of feathery foam and fell into a broad, deep basin, black from the shadows of the surrounding forest. Here, then, poor Rip was brought to a
10 stand. He again called and whistled after his dog; he was only answered by the cawing of a flock of idle crows, sporting high in the air about a dry tree that overhung a sunny precipice, and who, secure in their elevation, seemed to look down and scoff at the poor man's perplexities. What was to be done? The morning
15 was passing away, and Rip felt famished for want of his breakfast. He grieved to give up his dog and gun; he dreaded to meet his wife, but it would not do to starve among the mountains. He shook his head, shouldered the rusty firelock, and, with a heart full of trouble and anxiety, turned his steps homeward.
20 As he approached the village, he met a number of people, but none whom he knew, which somewhat surprised him, for he had thought himself acquainted with everyone in the country round. Their dress, too, was of a different fashion from that to which he was accustomed. They all stared at him with equal
25 marks of surprise and, whenever they cast their eyes upon him, invariably stroked their chins. The constant recurrence of this gesture induced Rip, involuntarily, to do the same, when, to his astonishment, he found his beard had grown a foot long!

He had now entered the skirts of the village. A troop of
30 strange children ran at his heels, hooting after him and pointing at his gray beard. The dogs, too, not one of which he recognized for an old acquaintance, barked at him as he passed. The very village was altered; it was larger and more populous. There were rows of houses which he had never seen before, and those which
35 had been his familiar haunts had disappeared. Strange names

were over the doors—strange faces at the windows—everything
was strange. His mind now misgave him; he began to doubt
whether both he and the world around him were not bewitched.
Surely this was his native village, which he had left but the day
5 before. There stood the Kaatskill Mountains—there ran the silver
Hudson at a distance—there was every hill and dale precisely as
it had always been—Rip was sorely perplexed—"That flagon last
night," thought he, "has addled my poor head sadly!"

It was with some difficulty that he found the way to his
10 own house—which he approached with silent awe, expecting
every moment to hear the shrill voice of Dame Van Winkle. He
found the house gone to decay—the roof fallen in, the windows
shattered, and the doors off the hinges. A half-starved dog
that looked like Wolf was skulking about it. Rip called him by
15 name, but the cur snarled, showed his teeth, and passed on.
This was an unkind cut indeed—"My very dog," sighed poor Rip,
"has forgotten me!"

He entered the house, which, to tell the truth, Dame Van
Winkle had always kept in neat order. It was empty, forlorn,
20 and apparently abandoned. This desolateness overcame all his
connubial fears—he called loudly for his wife and children—the
lonely chambers rang for a moment with his voice and then
again all was silence.

He now hurried forth and hastened to his old resort, the
25 village inn—but it, too, was gone. A large, rickety wooden
building stood in its place, with great gaping windows, some of
them broken and mended with old hats and petticoats, and over
the door was painted, "The Union Hotel, by Jonathan Doolittle."
Instead of the great tree that used to shelter the quiet little
30 Dutch inn of yore, there now was reared a tall, naked pole, with
something on the top that looked like a red nightcap, and from
it was fluttering a flag on which was a singular assemblage of
stars and stripes—all this was strange and incomprehensible. He
recognized on the sign, however, the ruby face of King George,
35 under which he had smoked so many a peaceful pipe, but even

this was singularly metamorphosed. The red coat was changed for one of blue and buff, a sword was held in the hand instead of a scepter, the head was decorated with a cocked hat, and underneath was painted in large characters, General Washington.

5    There was, as usual, a crowd of folk about the door, but none that Rip recollected. The very character of the people seemed changed. There was a busy, bustling, disputatious tone about it, instead of the accustomed phlegm and drowsy tranquility. He looked in vain for the sage Nicholas Vedder, with his broad face, 10 double chin, and fair long pipe, uttering clouds of tobacco smoke instead of idle speeches, or Van Bummel, the schoolmaster, doling forth the contents of an ancient newspaper. In place of these, a lean, bilious-looking fellow, with his pockets full of handbills, was haranguing vehemently about rights of citizens—elections— 15 members of Congress—liberty—Bunker's Hill—heroes of seventy-six—and other words, which were a perfect Babylonish jargon to the bewildered Van Winkle.

The appearance of Rip, with his long, grizzled beard, his rusty fowling-piece, his uncouth dress, and an army of women 20 and children at his heels soon attracted the attention of the tavern politicians. They crowded round him, eyeing him from head to foot with great curiosity. The orator bustled up to him, and, drawing him partly aside, inquired on which side he voted. Rip stared in vacant stupidity. Another short but busy little 25 fellow pulled him by the arm, and, rising on tiptoe, inquired in his ear whether he was Federal or Democrat. Rip was equally at a loss to comprehend the question; when a knowing, self-important old gentleman in a sharp cocked hat made his way through the crowd, putting them to the right and left with his elbows as he 30 passed and planting himself before Van Winkle, with one arm akimbo, the other resting on his cane, his keen eyes and sharp hat penetrating, as it were, into his very soul, demanded in an austere tone what brought him to the election with a gun on his shoulder and a mob at his heels and whether he meant to 35 breed riot in the village. "Alas! gentlemen," cried Rip, somewhat dismayed, "I am a poor quiet man, a native of the place, and a loyal subject of the king, God bless him!"

Here a general shout burst from the bystanders—"A Tory! a Tory! a spy! a refugee! hustle him! away with him!" It was
5 with great difficulty that the self-important man in the cocked hat restored order, and, having assumed a tenfold austerity of brow, demanded again of the unknown culprit what he came there for and whom he was seeking. The poor man humbly assured him that he meant no harm, but merely came there
10 in search of some of his neighbors, who used to keep about the tavern.

"Well—who are they?—name them."

Rip bethought himself a moment and inquired, "Where's Nicholas Vedder?"

15 There was silence for a little while, when an old man replied, in a thin, piping voice: "Nicholas Vedder! why, he is dead and gone these eighteen years! There was a wooden tombstone in the churchyard that used to tell all about him, but that's rotten and gone, too."

20 "Where's Brom Dutcher?"

"Oh, he went off to the army in the beginning of the war; some say he was killed at the storming of Stony Point—others say he was drowned in a squall at the foot of Antony's Nose. I don't know—he never came back again."

25 "Where's Van Bummel, the schoolmaster?"

"He went off to the wars, too, was a great militia general, and is now in Congress."

Rip's heart died away at hearing of these sad changes in his home and friends and finding himself thus alone in the world.
30 Every answer puzzled him, too, by treating of such enormous lapses of time, and of matters which he could not understand: war—Congress—Stony Point. He had no courage to ask after any more friends, but cried out in despair, "Does nobody here know Rip Van Winkle?"

35 "Oh, Rip Van Winkle!" exclaimed two or three, "oh, to be sure!

that's Rip Van Winkle yonder, leaning against the tree."

Rip looked and beheld a precise counterpart of himself as he went up the mountain, apparently as lazy, and certainly as ragged. The poor fellow was now completely confounded. He
5 doubted his own identity and whether he was himself or another man. In the midst of his bewilderment, the man in the cocked hat demanded who he was and what was his name.

"God knows," exclaimed he, at his wits' end, "I'm not myself— I'm somebody else—that's me yonder—no—that's somebody else
10 got into my shoes—I was myself last night, but I fell asleep on the mountain, and they've changed my gun, and everything's changed, and I'm changed, and I can't tell what's my name, or who I am!"

The bystanders began now to look at each other, nod, wink
15 significantly, and tap their fingers against their foreheads. There was a whisper, also, about securing the gun and keeping the old fellow from doing mischief, at the very suggestion of which the self-important man in the cocked hat retired with some precipitation. At this critical moment a fresh, comely woman
20 pressed through the throng to get a peep at the gray-bearded man. She had a chubby child in her arms, which, frightened at his looks, began to cry. "Hush, Rip," cried she, "hush, you little fool; the old man won't hurt you." The name of the child, the air of the mother, the tone of her voice, all awakened a
25 train of recollections in his mind. "What is your name, my good woman?" asked he.

"Judith Gardenier."

"And your father's name?"

"Ah, poor man, Rip Van Winkle was his name, but it's twenty
30 years since he went away from home with his gun and never has been heard of since—his dog came home without him, but whether he shot himself or was carried away by the Indians, nobody can tell. I was then but a little girl."

Rip had but one question more to ask, and he put it with
35 a faltering voice:

"Where's your mother?"

"Oh, she, too, died but a short time since; she broke a blood vessel in a fit of passion at a New England peddler."

There was a drop of comfort, at least, in this intelligence.
5 The honest man could contain himself no longer. He caught his daughter and her child in his arms. "I am your father!" cried he—"Young Rip Van Winkle once—old Rip Van Winkle now! Does nobody know poor Rip Van Winkle?"

All stood amazed, until an old woman, tottering out from
10 among the crowd, put her hand to her brow and, peering under it in his face for a moment, exclaimed, "Sure enough, it is Rip Van Winkle—it is himself! Welcome home again, old neighbor —Why, where have you been these twenty long years?"

Rip's story was soon told, for the whole twenty years had
15 been to him but as one night. The neighbors stared when they heard it; some were seen to wink at each other and put their tongues in their cheeks; and the self-important man in the cocked hat, who, when the alarm was over, had returned to the fold, screwed down the corners of his mouth and shook
20 his head—upon which there was a general shaking of the head throughout the assemblage.

It was determined, however, to take the opinion of old Peter Vanderdonk, who was seen slowly advancing up the road. He was a descendant of the historian of that name, who wrote
25 one of the earliest accounts of the province. Peter was the most ancient inhabitant of the village and well versed in all the wonderful events and traditions of the neighborhood. He recollected Rip at once, and corroborated his story in the most satisfactory manner. He assured the company that it was a fact,
30 handed down from his ancestor, the historian, that the Kaatskill Mountains had always been haunted by strange beings. That it was affirmed that the great Hendrick Hudson, the first discoverer of the river and country, kept a kind of vigil there every twenty years, with his crew of the *Half Moon*, being permitted in this
35 way to revisit the scenes of his enterprise and keep a guardian

eye upon the river and the great city called by his name. That his father had once seen them in their old Dutch dresses playing at ninepins in a hollow of the mountain, and that he himself had heard, one summer afternoon, the sound of their balls like
5 distant peals of thunder.

To make a long story short, the company broke up and returned to the more important concerns of the election. Rip's daughter took him home to live with her; she had a snug, well-furnished house, and a stout, cheery farmer for a husband, whom
10 Rip recollected for one of the urchins that used to climb upon his back. As to Rip's son and heir, who was the ditto of himself, seen leaning against the tree, he was employed to work on the farm, but evinced an hereditary disposition to attend to anything else but his business.

15 Rip now resumed his old walks and habits; he soon found many of his former cronies, though all rather the worse for the wear and tear of time, and preferred making friends among the rising generation, with whom he soon grew into great favor.

Having nothing to do at home and being arrived at that happy
20 age when a man can be idle with impunity, he took his place once more on the bench at the inn door and was reverenced as one of the patriarchs of the village and a chronicle of the old times "before the war." It was some time before he could get into the regular track of gossip or could be made to comprehend
25 the strange events that had taken place during his torpor. How that there had been a revolutionary war—that the country had thrown off the yoke of old England—and that, instead of being a subject of His Majesty George the Third, he was now a free citizen of the United States. Rip, in fact, was no politician; the
30 changes of states and empires made but little impression on him, but there was one species of despotism under which he had long groaned, and that was—petticoat government. Happily that was at an end! He had got his neck out of the yoke of matrimony and could go in and out whenever he pleased, without dreading
35 the tyranny of Dame Van Winkle. Whenever her name was

mentioned, however, he shook his head, shrugged his shoulders, and cast up his eyes, which might pass either for an expression of resignation to his fate or joy at his deliverance. He used to tell his story to every stranger that arrived at Mr. Doolittle's hotel.
5 He was observed, at first, to vary on some points every time he told it, which was doubtless, owing to his having so recently awaked. It at last settled down precisely to the tale I have related, and not a man, woman, or child in the neighborhood but knew it by heart. Some always pretended to doubt the reality
10 of it and insisted that Rip had been out of his head and that this was one point on which he always remained flighty. The old Dutch inhabitants, however, almost universally gave it full credit. Even to this day they never hear a thunderstorm of a summer afternoon about the Kaatskill, but they say Hendrick
15 Hudson and his crew are at their game of ninepins, and it is a common wish of all henpecked husbands in the neighborhood, when life hangs heavy on their hands, that they might have a quieting draught out of Rip Van Winkle's flagon.


NOTES AND QUESTIONS

**Biography.** Washington Irving (1783-1859), often called "the father of American literature" and "the first American humorist," was born in New York City in the year in which the treaty of peace that ended the Revolutionary War was signed. In his boyhood he rambled over the city of New York, making excursions into the country, along the banks of the Hudson and over the Kaatskills. During these rambles he collected a great store of legends and tales which he later reproduced with inimitable humor in a number of short stories and a long book called *Knickerbockers History of New York*, one of the choicest pieces of burlesque in our literature. This and *The Sketch Book*, published ten years later, not only made Irving famous at home and in England, but proved that America was to take her place in literature among the nations of the world. *The Alhambra* and *The Life and Voyages of Columbus* were written after Irving's visit to Spain. His last work was *The Life of George Washington*, a tribute to the great man for whom he had been named. "Rip Van Winkle" is from *The Sketch Book*.

**Discussion.** 1. Where is the scene of this story laid? 2. What is the time? 3. Into what three parts does the story naturally divide? 4. Describe the hero of the story. 5. Where were the idle men of the village in the habit of meeting? 6. How were these meetings frequently broken up? 7. Where did Rip Van Winkle go to escape from his home? 8. Describe in your own words what he saw from his resting place high up in the mountain. 9. What was the time of day? 10. How does the mention of the shadows and solitude prepare you for what is to follow? 11. What does Wolf's behavior when Rip's name is called lead you to expect? 12. Why were you surprised at the appearance of the person who called to Rip? 13. Why did the author picture the players in old Dutch dress? What trick did the stranger play on Rip? 14. Describe Rip's awakening. 15. What difficulties did he meet in trying to return home by the way he had ascended the mountain? 16. What strange sights did he see when he entered the village? 17. How was the sign on the inn changed? 18. What does this tell you? 19. What questions did the "tavern politicians" ask Rip? 20. How did Rip make himself known to the villagers? 21. What legend corroborated Rip's story of the strange men on the mountain? 22. How is the interest of the story increased by the particular period which the author chose for Rip's sleep? 23. How much do the appearance and character of Rip's daughter add to the pleasure given by the story? 24. What do you think of the description of Rip's son? Why is this description given? 25. Make a list of passages that are particularly humorous. 26. In addition to amusing you with its humor, this selection has given you glimpses into early life in New York. Mention some features of this early life that interested you. 27. Find in the glossary the meaning of: descried; obsequious; patrimonial; alacrity; amphitheater; visage; impenetrable; connubial; austere; corroborated; evinced. 28. *Pronounce:* termagant; insuperable; patriarch; vehemently; august; alternative; unfrequented; gesture; disputatious; phlegm; refugee; draught.

### Phrases for Study

| | |
|---|---|
| domestic tribulation, **367**, 11 | gallows air, **369**, 17 |
| with impunity, **367**, 26 | reciprocated the sentiment, **371**, 2 |
| Tartar's lance, **367**, 31 | Babylonish jargon, **377**, 16 |

**Class Reading.** Make a list of descriptions to be read aloud in class.

**Outline for Testing Silent Reading.** Make an outline to guide you in telling the story.

**Library Reading.** Other stories from *The Sketch Book*.

## Evangeline: a Tale of Acadie

### Henry Wadsworth Longfellow

#### Prelude

This is the forest primeval. The murmuring pines and the
    hemlocks,
Bearded with moss, and in garments green, indistinct in the
    twilight,
Stand like Druids of eld, with voices sad and prophetic;
Stand like harpers hoar, with beards that rest on their bosoms.
5 Loud from its rocky caverns, the deep-voiced neighboring ocean
Speaks, and in accents disconsolate answers the wail of the
    forest.

   This is the forest primeval; but where are the hearts that
    beneath it
Leaped like the roe when he hears in the woodland the voice
    of the huntsman?
Where is the thatch-roofed village, the home of Acadian
    farmers—
10 Men whose lives glided on like rivers that water the woodlands,
Darkened by shadows of earth, but reflecting an image of
    heaven?
Waste are those pleasant farms, and the farmers forever
    departed!
Scattered like dust and leaves when the mighty blasts of
    October
Seize them, and whirl them aloft, and sprinkle them far o'er
    the ocean.
15 Naught but tradition remains of the beautiful village of Grand-
    Pré.

Ye who believe in affection that hopes, and endures, and
    is patient,
Ye who believe in the beauty and strength of woman's devotion,
List to the mournful tradition still sung by the pines of the
    forest;
List to a Tale of Love in Acadie, home of the happy.


Part the First


I

5 In the Acadian land, on the shores of the Basin of Minas,
Distant, secluded, still, the little village of Grand-Pré
Lay in the fruitful valley. Vast meadows stretched to the
    eastward,
Giving the village its name, and pasture to flocks without
    number.
Dikes, that the hands of the farmers had raised with labor
    incessant,
10 Shut out the turbulent tides; but at stated seasons the
    floodgates
Opened and welcomed the sea to wander at will o'er the
    meadows.
West and south there were fields of flax, and orchards and
    cornfields
Spreading afar and unfenced o'er the plain; and away to the
    northward
Blomidon rose, and the forest old; and aloft on the mountains
15 Sea-fogs pitched their tents; and mists from the mighty Atlantic
Looked on the happy valley, but ne'er from their station
    descended.
There, in the midst of its farms, reposed the Acadian village.
Strongly built were the houses, with frames of oak and of
    chestnut,

Such as the peasants of Normandy built in the reign of the
　　Henries.
Thatched were the roofs, with dormer-windows; and gables
　　projecting
Over the basement below protected and shaded the doorway.
There in the tranquil evenings of summer, when brightly the
　　sunset
5 Lighted the village street and gilded the vanes on the chimneys,
Matrons and maidens sat in snow-white caps and in kirtles
Scarlet and blue and green, with distaffs spinning the golden
Flax for the gossiping looms, whose noisy shuttles within doors
Mingled their sound with the whir of the wheels and the songs
　　of the maidens.
10 Solemnly down the street came the parish priest; and the
　　children
Paused in their play to kiss the hand he extended to bless them.
Reverend walked he among them; and up rose matrons and
　　maidens,
Hailing his slow approach with words of affectionate welcome.
Then came the laborers home from the field, and serenely the
　　sun sank
15 Down to his rest, and twilight prevailed. Anon from the belfry
Softly the Angelus sounded; and over the roofs of the village
Columns of pale blue smoke, like clouds of incense ascending,
Rose from a hundred hearths, the homes of peace and
　　contentment.
Thus dwelt together in love these simple Acadian farmers
20 Dwelt in the love of God and of man. Alike were they free from
Fear, that reigns with the tyrant, and envy, the vice of
　　republics.
Neither locks had they to their doors, nor bars to their
　　windows;
But their dwellings were open as day and the hearts of the
　　owners;
There the richest was poor, and the poorest lived in abundance.

Somewhat apart from the village, and nearer the Basin of
    Minas.
Benedict Bellefontaine, the wealthiest farmer of Grand-Pré,
Dwelt on his goodly acres; and with him, directing his
    household,
Gentle Evangeline lived, his child, and the pride of the village.
5 Stalwart and stately in form was the man of seventy winters;
Hearty and hale was he, an oak that is covered with snowflakes;
White as the snow were his locks, and his cheeks as brown as
    the oak-leaves.
Fair was she to behold, that maiden of seventeen summers;
Black were her eyes as the berry that grows on the thorn by
    the wayside;
10 Black, yet how softly they gleamed beneath the brown shade
    of her tresses!
Sweet was her breath as the breath of kine that feed in the
    meadows.
When in the harvest heat she bore to the reapers at noontide
Flagons of home-brewed ale, ah! fair in sooth was the maiden.
Fairer was she when, on Sunday morn, while the bell from its
    turret
15 Sprinkled with holy sounds the air, as the priest with his hyssop
Sprinkles the congregation, and scatters blessings upon them,
Down the long street she passed, with her chaplet of beads
    and her missal,
Wearing her Norman cap and her kirtle of blue, and the earrings
Brought in the olden time from France, and since, as an
    heirloom
20 Handed down from mother to child, through long generations.
But a celestial brightness—a more ethereal beauty—
Shone on her face and encircled her form when, after
    confession,
Homeward serenely she walked with God's benediction upon her.
When she had passed, it seemed like the ceasing of exquisite
    music.

Firmly builded with rafters of oak, the house of the farmer
Stood on the side of a hill commanding the sea; and a shady
Sycamore grew by the door, with a woodbine wreathing around
 it.
Rudely carved was the porch, with seats beneath; and a
 footpath
5 Led through an orchard wide, and disappeared in the meadow.
Under the sycamore-tree were hives overhung by a penthouse,
Such as the traveler sees in regions remote by the roadside,
Built o'er a box for the poor, or the blessed image of Mary.
Farther down, on the slope of the hill, was the well with its
 moss-grown
10 Bucket, fastened with iron, and near it a trough for the horses.
Shielding the house from storms, on the north, were the barns
 and the farmyard;
There stood the broad-wheeled wains and the antique plows
 and the harrows;
There were the folds for the sheep; and there, in his feathered
 seraglio,
Strutted the lordly turkey, and crowed the cock, with the
 selfsame
15 Voice that in ages of old had startled the penitent Peter.
Bursting with hay were the barns, themselves a village. In each
 one
Far o'er the gable projected a roof of thatch; and a staircase,
Under the sheltering eaves, led up to the odorous cornloft.
There too the dovecot stood, with its meek and innocent inmates
20 Murmuring ever of love; while above in the variant breezes
Numberless noisy weathercocks rattled and sang of mutation.

 Thus, at peace with God and the world, the farmer of Grand-
 Pré
Lived on his sunny farm; and Evangeline governed his
 household.
Many a youth, as he knelt in the church and opened his missal,

Fixed his eyes upon her as the saint of his deepest devotion;
Happy was he who might touch her hand or the hem of her
    garment!
Many a suitor came to her door, by the darkness befriended,
And, as he knocked and waited to hear the sound of her
    footsteps,
5 Knew not which beat the louder, his heart or the knocker of
    iron;
Or, at the joyous feast of the Patron Saint of the village,
Bolder grew, and pressed her hand in the dance as he whispered
Hurried words of love, that seemed a part of the music.
But among all who came young Gabriel only was welcome;
10 Gabriel Lajeunesse, the son of Basil the blacksmith,
Who was a mighty man in the village, and honored of all men;
For since the birth of time, throughout all ages and nations,
Has the craft of the smith been held in repute by the people.
Basil was Benedict's friend. Their children from earliest
    childhood
15 Grew up together as brother and sister; and Father Felician,
Priest and pedagogue both in the village, had taught them their
    letters
Out of the selfsame book, with the hymns of the church and
    the plain-song.
But when the hymn was sung, and the daily lesson completed,
Swiftly they hurried away to the forge of Basil the blacksmith.
20 There at the door they stood with wondering eyes to behold him
Take in his leathern lap the hoof of the horse as a plaything,
Nailing the shoe in its place; while near him the tire of the
    cartwheel
Lay like a fiery snake, coiled round in a circle of cinders.
Oft on autumnal eves, when without in the gathering darkness,
25 Bursting with light seemed the smithy, through every cranny
    and crevice,
Warm by the forge within they watched the laboring bellows;
And as its panting ceased, and the sparks expired in the ashes,

Merrily laughed, and said they were nuns going into the chapel.
Oft on sledges in winter, as swift as the swoop of the eagle,
Down the hillside bounding, they glided away o'er the meadow.
Oft in the barns they climbed to the populous nests on the
    rafters,
5 Seeking with eager eyes that wondrous stone which the swallow
Brings from the shore of the sea to restore the sight of its
    fledglings;
Lucky was he who found that stone in the nest of the swallow!
Thus passed a few swift years, and they no longer were children.
He was a valiant youth; and his face, like the face of the
    morning,
10 Gladdened the earth with its light, and ripened thought into
    action.
She was a woman now, with the heart and hopes of a woman.
"Sunshine of Saint Eulalie" she was called; for that was the
    sunshine
Which, as the farmers believed, would load their orchards with
    apples;
She too would bring to her husband's house delight and
    abundance,
15 Filling it full of love and the ruddy faces of children.

## II

Now had the season returned when the nights grow colder
    and longer,
And the retreating sun the sign of the Scorpion enters.
Birds of passage sailed through the leaden air, from the
    ice-bound,
Desolate northern bays to the shores of tropical islands.
20 Harvests were gathered in; and wild with the winds of
    September
Wrestled the trees of the forest, as Jacob of old with the angel.
All the signs foretold a winter long and inclement.

Bees, with prophetic instinct of want, had hoarded their honey
Till the hives overflowed; and the Indian hunters asserted
Cold would the winter be, for thick was the fur of the foxes.
Such was the advent of autumn. Then followed that beautiful
    season
5 Called by the pious Acadian peasants the Summer of All-Saints!
Filled was the air with a dreamy and magical light; and the
    landscape
Lay as if new-created in all the freshness of childhood.
Peace seemed to reign upon earth, and the restless heart of
    the ocean
Was for a moment consoled. All sounds were in harmony
    blended.
10 Voices of children at play, the crowing of cocks in the
    farmyards,
Whir of wings in the drowsy air, and the cooing of pigeons,
All were subdued and low as the murmurs of love, and the
    great sun
Looked with the eye of love through the golden vapors around
    him;
While, arrayed in its robes of russet and scarlet and yellow;
15 Bright with the sheen of the dew, each glittering tree of the
    forest
Flashed like the plane-tree the Persian adorned with mantles
    and jewels.

Now recommenced the reign of rest and affection and stillness.
Day with its burden and heat had departed, and twilight
    descending
Brought back the evening star to the sky, and the herds to the
    homestead.
20 Pawing the ground they came, and resting their necks on each
    other,
And with their nostrils distended inhaling the freshness of
    evening.

Foremost, bearing the bell, Evangeline's beautiful heifer,
Proud of her snow-white hide, and the ribbon that waved from
    her collar,
Quietly paced and slow, as if conscious of human affection.
Then came the shepherd back with his bleating flocks from the
    seaside,
5 Where was their favorite pasture. Behind them followed the
    watchdog,
Patient, full of importance, and grand in the pride of his
    instinct,
Walking from side to side with a lordly air, and superbly
Waving his bushy tail, and urging forward the stragglers;
Regent of flocks was he when the shepherd slept; their
    protector
10 When from the forest at night, through the starry silence, the
    wolves howled.
Late, with the rising moon, returned the wains from the
    marshes,
Laden with briny hay, that filled the air with its odor.
Cheerily neighed the steeds, with dew on their manes and their
    fetlocks,
While aloft on their shoulders the wooden and ponderous
    saddles,
15 Painted with brilliant dyes, and adorned with tassels of
    crimson,
Nodded in bright array, like hollyhocks heavy with blossoms.
Patiently stood the cows meanwhile, and yielded their udders
Unto the milkmaid's hand; whilst loud and in regular cadence
Into the sounding pails the foaming streamlets descended.
20 Lowing of cattle and peals of laughter were heard in the
    farmyard,
Echoed back by the barns. Anon they sank into stillness;
Heavily closed, with a jarring sound, the valves of the barn-
    doors,
Rattled the wooden bars, and all for a season was silent.

Indoors, warm by the wide-mouthed fireplace, idly the farmer
Sat in his elbow-chair, and watched how the flames and the
    smoke-wreaths
Struggled together like foes in a burning city. Behind him,
Nodding and mocking along the wall with gestures fantastic,
5 Darted his own huge shadow, and vanished away into darkness.
Faces, clumsily carved in oak, on the back of his armchair
Laughed in the flickering light, and the pewter plates on the
    dresser
Caught and reflected the flame, as shields of armies the sunshine.
Fragments of song the old man sang, and carols of Christmas,
10 Such as at home, in the olden time, his fathers before him
Sang in their Norman orchards and bright Burgundian vine
    yards.
Close at her father's side was the gentle Evangeline seated,
Spinning flax for the loom that stood in the corner behind her.
Silent awhile were its treadles, at rest was its diligent shuttle,
15 While the monotonous drone of the wheel, like the drone of
    a bagpipe,
Followed the old man's song, and united the fragments together.
As in a church, when the chant of the choir at intervals ceases,
Footfalls are heard in the aisles, or words of the priest at the
    altar,
So, in each pause of the song, with measured motion the clock
    clicked.

20   Thus as they sat, there were footsteps heard, and, suddenly
    lifted,
Sounded the wooden latch, and the door swung back on its
    hinges.
Benedict knew by the hobnailed shoes it was Basil the
    blacksmith,
And by her beating heart Evangeline knew who was with him.
"Welcome!" the farmer exclaimed, as their footsteps paused on
    the threshold,

"Welcome, Basil, my friend! Come, take thy place on the settle
Close by the chimney-side, which is always empty without thee;
Take from the shelf overhead thy pipe and the box of tobacco;
Never so much thyself art thou as when, through the curling
5 Smoke of the pipe or the forge, thy friendly and jovial face
    gleams
Round and red as the harvest moon through the mist of the
    marshes.
Then, with a smile of content, thus answered Basil the black-
    smith,
Taking with easy air the accustomed seat by the fireside:
"Benedict Bellefontaine, thou hast ever thy jest and thy ballad!
10 Ever in cheerfullest mood art thou when others are filled with
Gloomy forebodings of ill, and see only ruin before them.
Happy art thou, as if every day thou hadst picked up a
    horseshoe."
Pausing a moment, to take the pipe that Evangeline brought him,
And with a coal from the embers had lighted, he slowly
    continued:
15 "Four days now are passed since the English ships at their
    anchors
Ride in the Gaspereau's mouth, with their cannon pointed
    against us.
What their design may be is unknown; but all are commanded
On the morrow to meet in the church, where his Majesty's
    mandate
Will be proclaimed as law in the land. Alas! in the meantime
20 Many surmises of evil alarm the hearts of the people."
Then made answer the farmer: "Perhaps some friendlier
    purpose
Brings these ships to our shores. Perhaps the harvests in
    England
By the untimely rains or untimelier heat have been blighted,
And from our bursting barns they would feed their cattle and
    children."

"Not so thinketh the folk in the village," said warmly the black-
smith,
Shaking his head as in doubt; then, heaving a sigh, he
continued:
"Louisburg is not forgotten, nor Beau Séjour, nor Port Royal.
Many already have fled to the forest, and lurk on its outskirts,
5 Waiting with anxious hearts the dubious fate of tomorrow.
Arms have been taken from us, and warlike weapons of all
kinds;
Nothing is left but the blacksmith's sledge and scythe of the
mower."
Then with a pleasant smile made answer the jovial farmer:
"Safer are we unarmed, in the midst of our flocks and our
cornfields,
10 Safer within these peaceful dikes besieged by the ocean,
Than were our fathers in forts, besieged by the enemy's cannon.
Fear no evil, my friend; and tonight may no shadow of sorrow
Fall on this house and hearth; for this is the night of the
contract.
Built are the house and the barn. The merry lads of the village
15 Strongly have built them and well; and, breaking the glebe
round about them,
Filled the barn with hay, and the house with food for a
twelvemonth.
René Leblanc will be here anon, with his papers and inkhorn.
Shall we not then be glad, and rejoice in the joy of our children?"
As apart by the window she stood, with her hand in her lover's,
20 Blushing, Evangeline heard the words that her father had
spoken,
And, as they died on his lips, the worthy notary entered.

### III

Bent like a laboring oar that toils in the surf of the ocean,
Bent, but not broken, by age was the form of the notary public;
Shocks of yellow hair, like the silken floss of the maize, hung

Over his shoulders; his forehead was high; and glasses with
    horn bows
Sat astride on his nose, with a look of wisdom supernal.
Father of twenty children was he, and more than a hundred
Children's children rode on his knee, and heard his great watch
    tick.
5 Four long years in the times of the war had he languished a
    captive,
Suffering much in an old French fort as the friend of the
    English.
Now, though warier grown, without all guile or suspicion,
Ripe in wisdom was he, but patient, and simple, and childlike.
He was beloved by all, and most of all by the children;
10 For he told them tales of the Loup-garou in the forest,
And of the goblin that came in the night to water the horses,
And of the white Létiche, the ghost of a child who unchristened
Died, and was doomed to haunt unseen the chambers of
    children;
And how on Christmas eve the oxen talked in the stable,
15 And how the fever was cured by a spider shut up in a nutshell,
And of the marvelous powers of four-leaved clover and
    horseshoes,
With whatsoever else was writ in the lore of the village.
Then up rose from his seat by the fireside Basil the blacksmith,
Knocked from his pipe the ashes, and slowly extending his
    right hand,
20 "Father Leblanc," he exclaimed, "thou hast heard the talk in
    the village,
And, perchance, canst tell us some news of these ships and
    their errand."
Then with modest demeanor made answer the notary public:
"Gossip enough have I heard, in sooth, yet am never the wiser;
And what their errand may be I know not better than others.
25 Yet am I not of those who imagine some evil intention
Brings them here, for we are at peace; and why then molest us?"

"God's name!" shouted the hasty and somewhat irascible
    blacksmith;
"Must we in all things look for the how, and the why, and the
    wherefore?
Daily injustice is done, and might is the right of the strongest!"
But, without heeding his warmth, continued the notary public:
5 "Man is unjust, but God is just; and finally justice
Triumphs; and well I remember a story that often consoled me
When as a captive I lay in the old French fort at Port Royal."
This was the old man's favorite tale, and he loved to repeat it
When his neighbors complained that any injustice was done
    them.
10 "Once in an ancient city, whose name I no longer remember,
Raised aloft on a column, a brazen statue of Justice
Stood in the public square, upholding the scales in its left hand,
And in its right a sword, as an emblem that justice presided
Over the laws of the land, and the hearts and homes of the
    people.
15 Even the birds had built their nests in the scales of the balance,
Having no fear of the sword that flashed in the sunshine above
    them.
But in the course of time the laws of the land were corrupted;
Might took the place of right, and the weak were oppressed,
    and the mighty
Ruled with an iron rod. Then it chanced in a nobleman's palace
20 That a necklace of pearls was lost, and ere long a suspicion
Fell on an orphan girl who lived as maid in the household.
She, after form of trial condemned to die on the scaffold,
Patiently met her doom at the foot of the statue of Justice.
As to her Father in heaven her innocent spirit ascended,
25 Lo! o'er the city a tempest rose; and the bolts of the thunder
Smote the statue of bronze, and hurled in wrath from its left
    hand
Down on the pavement below the clattering scales of the
    balance,

And in the hollow thereof was found the nest of a magpie,
Into whose clay-built walls the necklace of pearls was inwoven."
Silenced, but not convinced, when the story was ended, the
    blacksmith
Stood like a man who fain would speak, but findeth no language;
5 All his thoughts were congealed into lines on his face, as the
    vapors
Freeze in fantastic shapes on the windowpanes in the winter.

    Then Evangeline lighted the brazen lamp on the table;
Filled, till it overflowed, the pewter tankard with home-brewed
Nut-brown ale, that was famed for its strength in the village
    of Grand-Pré,
10 While from his pocket the notary drew his papers and inkhorn,
Wrote with a steady hand the date and the age of the parties,
Naming the dower of the bride in flocks of sheep and in cattle.
Orderly all things proceeded, and duly and well were completed,
And the great seal of the law was set like a sun on the margin.
15 Then from his leathern pouch the farmer threw on the table
Three times the old man's fee in solid pieces of silver;
And the notary rising, and blessing the bride and the
    bridegroom,
Lifted aloft the tankard of ale and drank to their welfare.
Wiping the foam from his lip, he solemnly bowed and departed,
20 While in silence the others sat and mused by the fireside,
Till Evangeline brought the draught-board out of its corner.
Soon was the game begun. In friendly contention the old men
Laughed at each lucky hit, or unsuccessful maneuver;
Laughed when a man was crowned, or a breach was made in
    the king-row.
25 Meanwhile apart, in the twilight gloom of a window's embrasure,
Sat the lovers and whispered together, beholding the moon rise
Over the pallid sea and the silvery mist of the meadows.
Silently one by one, in the infinite meadows of heaven,
Blossomed the lovely stars, the forget-me-nots of the angels.

Thus was the evening passed. Anon the bell from the belfry
Rang out the hour of nine, the village curfew, and straightway
Rose the guests and departed; and silence reigned in the
household.
Many a farewell word and sweet good-night on the doorstep
5 Lingered long in Evangeline's heart, and filled it with gladness.
Carefully then were covered the embers that glowed on the
hearth-stone,
And on the oaken stairs resounded the tread of the farmer.
Soon with a soundless step the foot of Evangeline followed.
Up the staircase moved a luminous space in the darkness,
10 Lighted less by the lamp than the shining face of the maiden.
Silent she passed through the hall, and entered the door of
her chamber.
Simple that chamber was, with its curtains of white, and its
clothespress
Ample and high, on whose spacious shelves were carefully folded
Linen and woolen stuffs, by the hand of Evangeline woven.
15 This was the precious dower she would bring to her husband
in marriage,
Better than flocks and herds, being proofs of her skill as a
housewife.
Soon she extinguished her lamp, for the mellow and radiant
moonlight
Streamed through the windows, and lighted the room, till the
heart of the maiden
Swelled and obeyed its power, like the tremulous tides of the
ocean.
20 Ah! she was fair, exceeding fair to behold, as she stood with
Naked snow-white, feet on the gleaming floor of her chamber!
Little she dreamed that below, among the trees of the orchard,
Waited her lover, and watched for the gleam of her lamp and
her shadow.
Yet were her thoughts of him, and at times a feeling of sadness
25 Passed o'er her soul, as the sailing shade of clouds in the moonlight

Flitted across the floor and darkened the room for a moment.
And, as she gazed from the window, she saw serenely the moon pass
Forth from the folds of a cloud, and one star follow her foot steps,
As out of Abraham's tent young Ishmael wandered with Hagar.

## IV

5  Pleasantly rose next morn the sun on the village of Grand-Pré.
Pleasantly gleamed in the soft, sweet air the Basin of Minas,
Where the ships, with their wavering shadows, were riding at anchor.
Life had long been astir in the village, and clamorous labor
Knocked with its hundred hands at the golden gates of the morning.
10 Now from the country around, from the farms and neighboring hamlets,
Came in their holiday dresses the blithe Acadian peasants.
Many a glad good-morrow and jocund laugh from the young folk
Made the bright air brighter, as up from the numerous meadows,
Where no path could be seen but the track of wheels in the greensward,
15 Group after group appeared, and joined, or passed on the highway.
Long ere noon, in the village all sounds of labor were silenced.
Thronged were the streets with people; and noisy groups at the house-doors
Sat in the cheerful sun, and rejoiced and gossiped together.
Every house was an inn, where all were welcomed and feasted;
20 For with this simple people, who lived like brothers together,
All things were held in common, and what one had was another's.

Yet under Benedict's roof hospitality seemed more abundant,
For Evangeline stood among the guests of her father;
Bright was her face with smiles, and words of welcome and
    gladness
Fell from her beautiful lips, and blessed the cup as she gave it.

5    Under the open sky, in the odorous air of the orchard,
Bending with golden fruit, was spread the feast of betrothal.
There in the shade of the porch were the priest and the notary
    seated;
There good Benedict sat, and sturdy Basil the blacksmith.
Not far withdrawn from these, by the cider-press and the
    beehives,
10 Michael the fiddler was placed, with the gayest of hearts and
    of waistcoats.
Shadow and light from the leaves alternately played on his
    snow-white
Hair, as it waved in the wind; and the jolly face of the fiddler
Glowed like a living coal when the ashes are blown from the
    embers.
Gaily the old man sang to the vibrant sound of his fiddle,
15 *Tous les Bourgeois de Chartres*, and *Le Carillon de Dunkerque*,
And anon with his wooden shoes beat time to the music.
Merrily, merrily whirled the wheels of the dizzying dances
Under the orchard-trees and down the path to the meadows;
Old folk and young together, and children mingled among them.
20 Fairest of all the maids was Evangeline, Benedict's daughter!
Noblest of all the youths was Gabriel, son of the blacksmith.

    So passed the morning away. And lo! with a summons
    sonorous
Sounded the bell from its tower, and over the meadows a drum
    beat.
Thronged ere long was the church with men. Without, in the
    churchyard,

Waited the women. They stood by the graves, and hung on the
    headstones
Garlands of autumn leaves and evergreens fresh from the forest.
Then came the guard from the ships, and marching proudly
    among them
Entered the sacred portal. With loud and dissonant clangor
5 Echoed the sound of their brazen drums from coiling and
    casement
Echoed a moment only, and slowly the ponderous portal
Closed, and in silence the crowd awaited the will of the soldiers.
Then uprose their commander, and spake from the steps of
    the altar,
Holding aloft in his hands, with its seals, the royal commission.
10 "You are convened this day," he said, "by His Majesty's orders.
Clement and kind has he been; but how you have answered
    his kindness
Let your own hearts reply! To my natural make and my temper
Painful the task is I do, which to you I know must be grievous.
Yet must I bow and obey, and deliver the will of our monarch:
15 Namely, that all your lands, and dwellings, and cattle of all
    kinds
Forfeited be to the crown; and that you yourselves from this
    province
Be transported to other lands. God grant you may dwell there
Ever as faithful subjects, a happy and peaceable people!
Prisoners now I declare you, for such is His Majesty's pleasure!"
20 As, when the air is serene in the sultry solstice of summer,
Suddenly gathers a storm, and the deadly sting of the hailstone
Beats down the farmer's corn in the field, and shatters his
    windows,
Hiding the sun, and strewing the ground with thatch from the
    house-roofs,
Bellowing fly the herds, and seek to break their inclosures,
25 So on the hearts of the people descended the words of the
    speaker.

Silent a moment they stood in speechless wonder, and then rose
Louder and ever louder a wail of sorrow and anger;
And, by one impulse moved, they madly rushed to the doorway.
Vain was the hope of escape; and cries and fierce imprecations
5 Rang through the house of prayer; and high o'er the heads of
   the others
Rose, with his arms uplifted, the figure of Basil the blacksmith,
As, on a stormy sea, a spar is tossed by the billows.
Flushed was his face and distorted with passion; and wildly he
   shouted:
 "Down with the tyrants of England! We never have sworn them
   allegiance!
10 Death to these foreign soldiers who seize on our homes and
   our harvests!"
More he fain would have said, but the merciless hand of a soldier
Smote him upon the mouth, and dragged him down to the
   pavement.

   In the midst of the strife and tumult of angry contention,
Lo! the door of the chancel opened, and Father Felician
15 Entered, with serious mien, and ascended the steps of the altar.
Raising his reverend hand, with a gesture he awed into silence
All that clamorous throng; and thus he spake to his people;
Deep were his tones and solemn; in accents measured and
   mournful
Spake he, as, after the tocsin's alarum, distinctly the clock
   strikes.
20 "What is this that ye do, my children? What madness has seized
   you?
Forty years of my life have I labored among you, and taught
   you,
Not in word alone, but in deed, to love one another!
Is this the fruit of my toils, of my vigils and prayers and
   privations?
Have you so soon forgotten all lessons of love and forgiveness?

This is the house of the Prince of Peace, and would you
    profane it
Thus with violent deeds and hearts overflowing with hatred?
Lo! where the crucified Christ from his cross is gazing upon you!
See! in those sorrowful eyes what meekness and holy compassion!
5 Hark! how those lips still repeat the prayer, 'O Father, forgive
    them!'
Let us repeat that prayer in the hour when the wicked assail us;
Let us repeat it now, and say, 'O Father, forgive them!'"
Sank they, and sobs of contrition succeeded the passionate
    outbreak,
10 And they repeated his prayer, and said, "O Father, forgive
    them!"

    Then came the evening service. The tapers gleamed from the
    altar;
Fervent and deep was the voice of the priest, and the people
    responded,
Not with their lips alone, but their hearts; and the Ave Maria
Sang they, and fell on their knees; and their souls, with
    devotion translated,
15 Rose on the ardor of prayer, like Elijah ascending to heaven.

    Meanwhile had spread in the village the tidings of ill, and
    on all sides
Wandered, wailing, from house to house, the women and children.
Long at her father's door Evangeline stood, with her right hand
Shielding her eyes from the level rays of the sun, that, descending,
20 Lighted the village street with mysterious splendor and roofed
    each
Peasant's cottage with golden thatch, and emblazoned its
    windows.
Long within had been spread the snow-white cloth on the table;
There stood the wheaten loaf, and the honey fragrant with wild
    flowers;

There stood the tankard of ale, and the cheese fresh brought
    from the dairy;
And at the head of the board the great armchair of the farmer.
Thus did Evangeline wait at her father's door, as the sunset
Threw the long shadows of trees o'er the broad, ambrosial
    meadows.
5 Ah! on her spirit within a deeper shadow had fallen;
And from the fields of her soul a fragrance celestial ascended
Charity, meekness, love, and hope, and forgiveness, and patience!
Then, all forgetful of self, she wandered into the village,
Cheering with looks and words the disconsolate hearts of the
    women,
10 As o'er the darkening fields with lingering steps they departed,
Urged by their household cares, and the weary feet of their
    children.
Down sank the great red sun, and in golden, glimmering vapors
Veiled the light of his face, like the Prophet descending from
    Sinai.
Sweetly over the village the bell of the Angelus sounded.

15    Meanwhile, amid the gloom, by the church Evangeline lingered.
All was silent within; and in vain at the door and the windows
Stood she, and listened and looked, until, overcome by emotion.
"Gabriel!" cried she aloud with tremulous voice; but no answer
Came from the graves of the dead, nor the gloomier grave of
    the living.
20 Slowly at length she returned to the tenantless house of her
    father.
Smoldered the fire on the hearth; on the board stood the
    supper untasted.
Empty and drear was each room, and haunted with phantoms
    of terror.
Sadly echoed her step on the stair and the floor of her chamber.
In the dead of the night she heard the whispering rain fall
25 Loud on the withered leaves of the sycamore-tree by the window.

Keenly the lightning flashed; and the voice of the echoing
      thunder
Told her that God was in heaven, and governed the world he
      created!
Then she remembered the tale she had heard of the justice
      of Heaven;
Soothed was her troubled soul, and she peacefully slumbered
      till morning.

V

5    Four times the sun had risen and set; and now on the fifth day
Cheerily called the cock to the sleeping maids of the farmhouse.
Soon o'er the yellow fields, in silent and mournful procession,
Came from the neighboring hamlets and farms the Acadian
      women,
Driving in ponderous wains their household goods to the
      seashore,
10 Pausing and looking back to gaze once more on their dwellings,
Ere they were shut from sight by the winding road and the
      woodland.
Close at their sides their children ran, and urged on the oxen,
While in their little hands they clasped some fragments of
      play-things.

      Thus to the Gaspereau's mouth they hurried; and there on
      the sea-beach
15 Piled in confusion lay the household goods of the peasants.
All day long between the shore and the ships did the boats ply;
All day long the wains came laboring down from the village.
Late in the afternoon, when the sun was near to his setting,
Echoing far o'er the fields came the roll of drums from the
      churchyard.
20 Thither the women and children thronged.  On a sudden the
      church-doors

Opened, and forth came the guard, and marching in gloomy
    procession
Followed the long-imprisoned, but patient, Acadian farmers
Even as pilgrims, who journey afar from their homes and their
    country,
Sing as they go, and in singing forget they are weary and
    way-worn,
5 So with songs on their lips the Acadian peasants descended
Down from the church to the shore, amid their wives and their
    daughters.
Foremost the young men came; and, raising together their
    voices,
Sang they with tremulous lips a chant of the Catholic Missions:
"Sacred heart of the Savior! O inexhaustible fountain!
10 Fill our hearts this day with strength and submission and
    patience!"
Then the old men, as they marched, and the women that stood
    by the wayside
Joined in the sacred psalm; and the birds in the sunshine above
    them
Mingled their notes therewith, like voices of spirits departed.

Halfway down to the shore Evangeline waited in silence,
15 Not overcome with grief, but strong in the hour of affliction—
Calmly and sadly waited, until the procession approached her,
And she beheld the face of Gabriel pale with emotion.
Tears then filled her eyes, and eagerly running to meet him,
Clasped she his hands, and laid her head on his shoulder, and
    whispered—
20 "Gabriel! be of good cheer; for if we love one another
Nothing, in truth, can harm us, whatever mischances may
    happen!"
Smiling she spake these words; then suddenly paused, for her
    father
Saw she, slowly advancing. Alas! how changed was his aspect!

Gone was the glow from his cheek, and the fire from his eye;
    and his footstep
Heavier seemed with the weight of the weary heart in his bosom.
But with a smile and a sigh she clasped his neck and embraced
    him,
Speaking words of endearment where words of comfort availed
    not.
5 Thus to the Gaspereau's mouth moved on that mournful
    procession.

    There disorder prevailed, and the tumult and stir of
    embarking.
Busily plied the freighted boats; and in the confusion
Wives were torn from their husbands, and mothers, too late,
    saw their children
Left on the land, extending their arms, with wildest entreaties.
10 So unto separate ships were Basil and Gabriel carried,
While in despair on the shore Evangeline stood with her father.
Half the task was not done when the sun went down, and the
    twilight
Deepened and darkened around; and in haste the refluent ocean
Fled away from the shore, and left the line of the sand-beach
15 Covered with waifs of the tide, with kelp and the slippery
    seaweed.
Farther back in the midst of the household goods and the wagons,
Like to a gypsy camp, or a leaguer after a battle,
All escape cut off by the sea, and the sentinels near them,
Lay encamped for the night the houseless Acadian farmers.
20 Back to its nethermost caves retreated the bellowing ocean,
Dragging adown the beach the rattling pebbles, and leaving
Inland and far up the shore the stranded boats of the sailors.
Then, as the night descended, the herds returned from their
    pastures;
Sweet was the moist, still air with the odor of milk from their
    udders;

Lowing they waited, and long, at the well-known bars of the
  farmyard—
Waited and looked in vain for the voice and the hand of the
  milkmaid.
Silence reigned in the streets; from the church no Angelus
  sounded;
Rose no smoke from the roofs; and gleamed no lights from the
  windows.

5  But on the shores meanwhile the evening fires had been
    kindled,
Built of the drift-wood thrown on the sands from wrecks in
  the tempest.
Round them shapes of gloom and sorrowful faces were gathered,
Voices of women were heard, and of men, and the crying of
  children.
Onward from fire to fire, as from hearth to hearth in his parish,
10 Wandered the faithful priest, consoling and blessing and cheering,
Like unto shipwrecked Paul on Melita's desolate seashore.
Thus he approached the place where Evangeline sat with her
  father,
And in the flickering light beheld the face of the old man,
Haggard and hollow and wan, and without either thought or
  emotion,
15 E'en as the face of a clock from which the hands have been
    taken.
Vainly Evangeline strove with words and caresses to cheer him,
Vainly offered him food; yet he moved not, he looked not, he
  spake not,
But, with a vacant stare, ever gazed at the flickering firelight.
"Benedicite!" murmured the priest, in tones of compassion.
20 More he fain would have said, but his heart was full, and his
    accents
Faltered and paused on his lips, as the feet of a child on a
  threshold,

Hushed by the scene he beholds, and the awful presence of
    sorrow.
Silently, therefore, he laid his hand on the head of the maiden,
Raising his eyes full of tears to the silent stars that above them
Moved on their way, unperturbed by the wrongs and sorrows
    of mortals.
5 Then sat he down at her side, and they wept together in silence.

    Suddenly rose from the south a light, as in autumn the
    blood-red
Moon climbs the crystal walls of heaven, and o'er the horizon
Titan-like stretches its hundred hands upon mountain and
    meadow,
Seizing the rocks and the rivers, and piling huge shadows together.
10 Broader and ever broader it gleamed on the roofs of the village,
Gleamed on the sky and the sea, and the ships that lay in the
    roadstead.
Columns of shining smoke uprose, and flashes of flame were
Thrust through their folds and withdrawn, like the quivering
    hands of a martyr.
Then as the wind seized the gleeds and the burning thatch,
    and, uplifting,
15 Whirled them aloft through the air, at once from a hundred
    housetops
Started the sheeted smoke with flashes of flame intermingled.

    These things beheld in dismay the crowd on the shore and
    on shipboard.
Speechless at first they stood, then cried aloud in their anguish,
"We shall behold no more our homes in the village of Grand-Pré!"
20 Loud on a sudden the cocks began to crow in the farmyards,
Thinking the day had dawned; and anon the lowing of cattle
Came on the evening breeze, by the barking of dogs interrupted.
Then rose a sound of dread, such as startles the sleeping
    encampments

Far in the western prairies or forests that skirt the Nebraska.
When the wild horses affrighted sweep by with the speed of
    the whirlwind,
Or the loud bellowing herds of buffaloes rush to the river.
Such was the sound that arose on the night, as the herds and
    the horses
5 Broke through their folds and fences, and madly rushed o'er
    the meadows.

   Overwhelmed with the sight, yet speechless, the priest and
    the maiden
Gazed on the scene of terror that reddened and widened
    before them;
And as they turned at length to speak to their silent companion,
Lo! from his seat he had fallen, and stretched abroad on the
    seashore
10 Motionless lay his form, from which the soul had departed.
Slowly the priest uplifted the lifeless head; and the maiden
Knelt at her father's side, and wailed aloud in her terror.
Then in a swoon she sank, and lay with her head on his bosom.
Through the long night she lay in deep, oblivious slumber;
15 And when she woke from the trance, she beheld a multitude
    near her.
Faces of friends she beheld, that were mournfully gazing upon
    her,
Pallid, with tearful eyes, and looks of saddest compassion.
Still the blaze of the burning village illumined the landscape,
Reddened the sky overhead, and gleamed on the faces around her,
20 And like the day of doom it seemed to her wavering senses.
Then a familiar voice she heard, as it said to the people—
"Let us bury him here by the sea. When a happier season
Brings us again to our homes from the unknown land of our exile,
Then shall his sacred dust be piously laid in the churchyard."
25 Such were the words of the priest. And there in haste by the
    seaside,

Having the glare of the burning village for funeral torches,
But without bell or book, they buried the farmer of Grand-Pré.
And as the voice of the priest repeated the service of sorrow,
Lo! with a mournful sound like the voice of a vast congregation,
5 Solemnly answered the sea, and mingled its roar with the dirges.
'Twas the returning tide, that afar from the waste of the ocean,
With the first dawn of the day, came heaving and hurrying
    landward.
Then recommenced once more the stir and noise of embarking;
And with the ebb of that tide the ships sailed out of the harbor,
10 Leaving behind them the dead on the shore, and the village
    in ruins.

Part the Second

I

Many a weary year had passed since the burning of Grand-Pré,
When on the falling tide the freighted vessels departed,
Bearing a nation, with all its household goods, into exile,
Exile without an end, and without an example in story.
15 Far asunder, on separate coasts, the Acadians landed;
Scattered were they, like flakes of snow, when the wind from
    the northeast
Strikes aslant through the fogs that darken the Banks of New-
    foundland.
Friendless, homeless, hopeless, they wandered from city to city,
From the cold lakes of the North to sultry Southern savannas,
20 From the bleak shores of the sea to the lands where the Father
    of Waters
Seizes the hills in his hands, and drags them down to the ocean,
Deep in their sands to bury the scattered bones of the mammoth.
Friends they sought and homes; and many, despairing, heart-
    broken,
Asked of the earth but a grave, and no longer a friend nor a
    fireside.

Written their history stands on tablets of stone in the church-yards.
Long among them was seen a maiden who waited and wandered,
Lowly and meek in spirit, and patiently suffering all things.
Fair was she and young; but, alas! before her extended,
5 Dreary and vast and silent, the desert of life, and its pathway
Marked by the graves of those who had sorrowed and suffered
    before her,
Passions long extinguished, and hopes long dead and abandoned,
As the emigrant's way o'er the Western desert is marked by
Campfires long consumed, and bones that bleach in the sun-
    shine.
10 Something there was in her life incomplete, imperfect, unfinished;
As if a morning of June, with all its music and sunshine,
Suddenly paused in the sky, and fading, slowly descended
Into the east again, from whence it late had arisen.
Sometimes she lingered in towns, till, urged by the fever within
    her,
15 Urged by a restless longing, the hunger and thirst of the spirit,
She would commence again her endless search and endeavor;
Sometimes in churchyards strayed, and gazed on the crosses
    and tombstones;
Sat by some nameless grave, and thought that perhaps in its
    bosom
He was already at rest, and she longed to slumber beside him.
20 Sometimes a rumor, a hearsay, an inarticulate whisper,
Came with its airy hand to point and beckon her forward.
Sometimes she spake with those who had seen her beloved and
    known him,
But it was long ago, in some far-off place or forgotten.
"Gabriel Lajeunesse!" said others; "oh, yes! we have seen him.
25 He was with Basil the blacksmith, and both have gone to the
    prairies;
*Coureurs-des-bois* are they, and famous hunters and trappers."
"Gabriel Lajeunesse!" said others; "oh, yes! we have seen him.
He is a *voyageur* in the lowlands of Louisiana."

Then would they say, "Dear child! why dream and wait for him
    longer?
Are there not other youths as fair as Gabriel? others
Who have hearts as tender and true, and spirits as loyal?
Here is Baptiste Leblanc, the notary's son, who has loved thee
5 Many a tedious year; come, give him thy hand and be happy!
Thou art too fair to be left to braid St. Catherine's tresses."
Then would Evangeline answer, serenely but sadly, "I cannot!
Whither my heart has gone, there follows my hand, and not
    elsewhere.
For when the heart goes before, like a lamp, and illumines the
    pathway,
10 Many things are made clear that else lie hidden in darkness."
And thereupon the priest, her friend and father confessor,
Said, with a smile, "O daughter! thy God thus speaketh within
    thee!
Talk not of wasted affection; affection never was wasted;
If it enrich not the heart of another, its waters, returning
15 Back to their springs, like the rain, shall fill them full of refresh-
    ment;
That which the fountain sends forth returns again to the foun-
    tain.
Patience; accomplish thy labor; accomplish thy work of affec-
    tion!
Sorrow and silence are strong, and patient endurance is godlike.
Therefore accomplish thy labor of love, till the heart is made
    godlike,
20 Purified, strengthened, perfected, and rendered more worthy
    of heaven!"
Cheered by the good man's words, Evangeline labored and
    waited.
Still in her heart she heard the funeral dirge of the ocean,
But with its sound there was mingled a voice that whispered,
    "Despair not!"
Thus did that poor soul wander in want and cheerless discomfort,

Bleeding, barefooted, over the shards and thorns of existence.
Let me essay, O Muse! to follow the wanderer's footsteps—
Not through each devious path, each changeful year of existence;
But as a traveler follows a streamlet's course through the valley:
5 Far from its margin at times, and seeing the gleam of its water
Here and there, in some open space, and at intervals only;
Then drawing nearer its bank, through sylvan glooms that con-
    ceal it,
Though he behold it not, he can hear its continuous murmur;
Happy, at length, if he find a spot where it reaches an outlet.

## II

10    It was the month of May. Far down the Beautiful River,
Past the Ohio shore and past the mouth of the Wabash,
Into the golden stream of the broad and swift Mississippi,
Floated a cumbrous boat, that was rowed by Acadian boatmen.
It was a band of exile—a raft, as it were, from the shipwrecked
15 Nation, scattered along the coast, now floating together,
Bound by the bonds of a common belief and a common
    misfortune;
Men and women and children, who, guided by hope or by
    hear-say,
Sought for their kith and their kin among the few-acred farmers
On the Acadian coast, and the prairies of fair Opelousas.
20 With them Evangeline went, and her guide, the Father Felician.
Onward o'er sunken sands, through a wilderness somber with
    forests,
Day after day they glided adown the turbulent river;
Night after night, by their blazing fires, encamped on its borders.
Now through rushing chutes, among green islands, where
    plumelike
25 Cotton-trees nodded their shadowy crests, they swept with the
    current;
Then emerged into broad lagoons, where silvery sandbars

Lay in the stream, and along the wimpling waves of their margin,
Shining with snow-white plumes, large flocks of pelicans waded.
Level the landscape grew, and along the shores of the river,
Shaded by china-trees, in the midst of luxuriant gardens,
5 Stood the houses of planters, with Negro cabins and dovecots.
They were approaching the region where reigns perpetual
    summer,
Where through the Golden Coast, and groves of orange and
    citron,
Sweeps with majestic curve the river away to the eastward.
They, too, swerved from their course; and, entering the Bayou
    of Plaquemine,
10 Soon were lost in a maze of sluggish and devious waters,
Which, like a network of steel, extended in every direction.
Over their heads the towering and tenebrous boughs of the
    cypress
Met in a dusky arch, and trailing mosses in mid-air
Waved like banners that hang on the walls of ancient
    cathedrals.
15 Deathlike the silence seemed, and unbroken, save by the herons
Home to their roosts in the cedar-trees returning at sunset,
Or by the owl, as he greeted the moon with demoniac laughter.
Lovely the moonlight was as it glanced and gleamed on the
    water,
Gleamed on the columns of cypress and cedar sustaining the
    arches,
20 Down through whose broken vaults it fell as through chinks
    in a ruin.
Dreamlike, and indistinct, and strange were all things around
    them;
And o'er their spirits there came a feeling of wonder and
    sadness—
Strange forebodings of ill, unseen, and that cannot be compassed.
As, at the tramp of a horse's hoofs on the turf of the prairies,
25 Far in advance are closed the leaves of the shrinking mimosa,

So, at the hoof-beats of fate, with sad forebodings of evil
Shrinks and closes the heart, ere the stroke of doom has attained it.
But Evangeline's heart, was sustained by a vision that faintly
Floated before her eyes, and beckoned her on through the moonlight.
5 It was the thought of her brain that assumed the shape of a phantom.
Through those shadowy aisles had Gabriel wandered before her,
And every stroke of the oar now brought him nearer and nearer.

Then in his place, at the prow of the boat, rose one of the oarsmen,
And, as a signal sound, if others like them peradventure
10 Sailed on those gloomy and midnight streams, blew a blast on his bugle.
Wild through the dark colonnades and corridors leafy the blast rang,
Breaking the seal of silence and giving tongues to the forest.
Soundless above them the banners of moss just stirred to the music.
Multitudinous echoes awoke and died in the distance,
15 Over the watery floor, and beneath the reverberant branches;
But not a voice replied; no answer came from the darkness;
And when the echoes had ceased, like a sense of pain was the silence.
Then Evangeline slept; but the boatmen rowed through the midnight,
Silent at times, then singing familiar Canadian boat-songs,
20 Such as they sang of old on their own Acadian rivers;
And through the night were heard the mysterious sounds of the desert,
Far-off—indistinct—as of wave or wind in the forest,
Mixed with the whoop of the crane and the roar of the grim alligator.

Thus ere another noon they emerged from those shades; and
before them
Lay, in the golden sun, the lakes of the Atchafalaya.
Water-lilies in myriads rocked on the slight undulations
Made by the passing oars, and, resplendent in beauty, the lotus
5 Lifted her golden crown above the heads of the boatmen.
Faint was the air with the odorous breath of magnolia blossoms,
And with the heat of noon; and numberless sylvan islands,
Fragrant and thickly embowered with blossoming hedges of roses,
Near to whose shores they glided along, invited to slumber.
10 Soon by the fairest of these their weary oars were suspended.
Under the boughs of Wachita willows, that grew by the margin.
Safely their boat was moored; and scattered about on the
greensward,
Tired with their midnight toil, the weary travelers slumbered.
Over them vast and high extended the cope of a cedar.
15 Swinging from its great arms, the trumpet-flower and the
grapevine
Hung their ladder of ropes aloft like the ladder of Jacob,
On whose pendulous stairs the angels ascending, descending,
Were the swift humming birds, that flitted from blossom to
blossom.
Such was the vision Evangeline saw as she slumbered beneath it.
20 Filled was her heart with love, and the dawn of an opening
heaven
Lighted her soul in sleep with the glory of regions celestial.

Nearer and ever nearer, among the numberless islands,
Darted a light, swift boat, that sped away o'er the water,
Urged on its course by the sinewy arms of hunters and trappers.
25 Northward its prow was turned, to the land of the bison and
beaver.
At the helm sat a youth, with countenance thoughtful and
careworn.
Dark and neglected locks overshadowed his brow, and a sadness

Somewhat beyond his years on his face was legibly written.
Gabriel was it, who, weary with waiting, unhappy and restless,
Sought in the Western wilds oblivion of self and of sorrow.
Swiftly they glided along, close under the lee of the island,
5 But by the opposite bank, and behind a screen of palmettos;
So that they saw not the boat, where it lay concealed in the
willows;
And undisturbed by the dash of their oars, and unseen, were
the sleepers;
Angel of God was there none to awaken the slumbering maiden.
Swiftly they glided away, like the shade of a cloud on the prairie.
10 After the sound of their oars on the tholes had died in the
distance,
As from a magic trance the sleepers awoke, and the maiden
Said with a sigh to the friendly priest, "O Father Felician!
Something says in my heart that near me Gabriel wanders.
Is it a foolish dream, an idle and vague superstition?
15 Or has an angel passed, and revealed the truth to my spirit?"
Then, with a blush, she added, "Alas for my credulous fancy!
Unto ears like thine such words as these have no meaning."
But made answer the reverend man, and he smiled as he
answered:
"Daughter, thy words are not idle; nor are they to me without
meaning.
20 Feeling is deep and still; and the word that floats on the surface
Is as the tossing buoy that betrays where the anchor is hidden.
Therefore trust to thy heart, and to what the world calls illusions.
Gabriel truly is near thee; for not far away to the southward,
On the banks of the Teche, are the towns of St. Maur and St.
Martin.
25 There the long-wandering bride shall be given again to her
bridegroom,
There the long-absent pastor regain his flock and his sheepfold.
Beautiful is the land, with its prairies and forests of fruit-trees;
Under the feet a garden of flowers and the bluest of heavens

Bending above, and resting its dome on the walls of the forest.
They who dwell there have named it the Eden of Louisiana."

And with these words of cheer they arose and continued
their journey.
Softly the evening came. The sun from the western horizon
5 Like a magician extended his golden wand o'er the landscape;
Twinkling vapors arose; and sky and water and forest
Seemed all on fire at the touch, and melted and mingled together.
Hanging between two skies, a cloud with edges of silver,
Floated the boat, with its dripping oars, on the motionless water.
10 Filled was Evangeline's heart with inexpressible sweetness.
Touched by the magic spell, the sacred fountain of feeling
Glowed with the light of love, as the skies and waters around her.
Then from a neighboring thicket the mocking bird, wildest of
singers,
Swinging aloft on a willow spray that hung o'er the water,
15 Shook from his little throat such floods of delirious music,
That the whole air and the woods and the waves seemed silent
to listen.
Plaintive at first were the tones and sad; then soaring to madness
Seemed they to follow or guide the revel of frenzied Bacchantes.
Single notes were then heard, in sorrowful, low lamentation;
20 Till, having gathered them all, he flung them abroad in derision,
As when, after a storm, a gust of wind through the tree tops
Shakes down the rattling rain in a crystal shower on the
branches.
With such a prelude as this, and hearts that throbbed with
emotion,
Slowly they entered the Teche, where it flows through the
green Opelousas,
25 And, through the amber air, above the crest of the woodland,
Saw the column of smoke that arose from a neighboring dwelling;
Sounds of a horn they heard, and the distant lowing of cattle.

## III

Near to the bank of the river, o'ershadowed by oaks from
    whose branches
Garlands of Spanish moss and of mystic mistletoe flaunted,
Such as the Druids cut down with golden hatchets at yuletide,
Stood, secluded and still, the house of the herdsman.  A garden
5 Girded it round about with a belt of luxuriant blossoms,
Filling the air with fragrance.  The house itself was of timbers
Hewn from the cypress-tree, and carefully fitted together.
Large and low was the roof; and on slender columns supported,
Rose-wreathed, vine-encircled, a broad and spacious veranda,
10 Haunt of the humming-bird and the bee, extended around it.
At each end of the house, amid the flowers of the garden,
Stationed the dovecots were, as love's perpetual symbol,
Scenes of endless wooing, and endless contentions of rivals.
Silence reigned o'er the place.  The line of shadow and sunshine
15 Ran near the tops of the trees; but the house itself was in
    shadow,
And from its chimney-top, ascending and slowly expanding
Into the evening air, a thin blue column of smoke rose.
In the rear of the house, from the garden gate, ran a pathway
Through the great groves of oak to the skirts of the limitless
    prairie,
20 Into whose sea of flowers the sun was slowly descending.
Full in his track of light, like ships with shadowy canvas
Hanging loose from their spars in a motionless calm in the
    tropics,
Stood a cluster of trees, with tangled cordage of grapevines.

Just where the woodlands met the flowery surf of the prairie,
25 Mounted upon his horse, with Spanish saddle and stirrups,
Sat a herdsman, arrayed in gaiters and doublet of deerskin.
Broad and brown was the face that from under the Spanish
    sombrero

Gazed on the peaceful scene, with the lordly look of its master.
Round about him were numberless herds of kine that were
    grazing
Quietly in the meadows, and breathing the vapory freshness
That uprose from the river, and spread itself over the landscape
5 Slowly lifting the horn that hung at his side, and expanding
Fully his broad, deep chest he blew a blast, that resounded
Wildly and sweet and far, through the still, damp air of the
    evening.
Suddenly out of the grass the long white horns of the cattle
Rose like flakes of foam on the adverse currents of ocean.
10 Silent a moment they gazed, then bellowing rushed o'er the
    prairie,
And the whole mass became a cloud, a shade in the distance.
Then, as the herdsman turned to the house, through the gate
    of the garden
Saw he the forms of the priest and the maiden advancing to
    meet him.
Suddenly down from his horse he sprang in amazement, and
    forward
15 Rushed with extended arms and exclamations of wonder;
When they beheld his face, they recognized Basil the blacksmith.
Hearty his welcome was, as he led his guests to the garden.
There in an arbor of roses with endless question and answer
Gave they vent to their hearts, and renewed their friendly
    embraces,
20 Laughing and weeping by turns, or sitting silent and thoughtful.
Thoughtful, for Gabriel came not; and now dark doubts and
    misgivings
Stole o'er the maiden's heart, and Basil, somewhat embarrassed,
Broke the silence and said, "If you came by the Atchafalaya,
How have you nowhere encountered my Gabriel's boat on the
    bayous?"
25 Over Evangeline's face at the words of Basil a shade passed.
Tears came into her eyes, and she said, with a tremulous accent,

"Gone?  Is Gabriel gone?" and, concealing her face on his
    shoulder,
All her o'erburdened heart gave way, and she wept and lamented.
Then the good Basil said—and his voice grew blithe as he
    said it
"Be of good cheer, my child; it is only today he departed.
5 Foolish boy! he has left me alone with my herds and my horses.
Moody and restless grown, and tired and troubled, his spirit
Could no longer endure the calm of this quiet existence.
Thinking ever of thee, uncertain and sorrowful ever,
Ever silent, or speaking only of thee and his troubles,
10 He at length had become so tedious to men and to maidens,
Tedious even to me, that at length I bethought me, and sent him
Unto the town of Adayes to trade for mules with the Spaniards.
Thence he will follow the Indian trails to the Ozark Mountains,
Hunting for furs in the forests, on rivers trapping the beaver.
15 Therefore be of good cheer; we will follow the fugitive lover;
He is not far on his way, and the Fates and the streams are
    against him.
Up and away tomorrow, and through the red dew of the morning,
We will follow him fast, and bring him back to his prison."

Then glad voices were heard, and up from the banks of the
    river,
20 Borne aloft on his comrades' arms, came Michael the fiddler.
Long under Basil's roof had he lived, like a god on Olympus,
Having no other care than dispensing music to mortals.
Far renowned was he for his silver locks and his fiddle.
"Long live Michael," they cried, "our brave Acadian minstrel!"
25 As they bore him aloft in triumphal procession; and straightway
Father Felician advanced with Evangeline, greeting the old man
Kindly and oft, and recalling the past, while Basil, enraptured,
Hailed with hilarious joy his old companions and gossips,
Laughing loud and long, and embracing mothers and daughters.
30 Much they marveled to see the wealth of the *ci-devant* blacksmith

All his domains and his herds, and his patriarchal demeanor;
Much they marveled to hear his tales of the soil and the climate,
And of the prairies, whose numberless herds were his who
    would take them;
Each one thought in his heart that he, too, would go and do
    likewise.
5 Thus they ascended the steps, and, crossing the breezy veranda,
Entered the hall of the house, where already the supper of Basil
Waited his late return; and they rested and feasted together.

Over the joyous feast the sudden darkness descended.
10 All was silent without; and, illuming the landscape with silver,
Fair rose the dewy moon and the myriad stars; but within doors,
Brighter than these, shone the faces of friends in the glimmer-
    ing lamplight.
Then from his station aloft, at the head of the table, the herds-
    man
Poured forth his heart and his wine together in endless profusion.
Lighting his pipe, that was filled with sweet Natchitoches
    tobacco,
15 Thus he spake to his guests, who listened, and smiled as they
    listened:
"Welcome once more, my friends, who so long have been friend-
    less and homeless,
Welcome once more to a home, that is better perchance than
    the old one!
Here no hungry winter congeals our blood like the rivers;
Here no stony ground provokes the wrath of the farmer;
20 Smoothly the plowshare runs through the soil, as a keel
    through the water.
All the year round the orange-groves are in blossom; and grass
    grows
More in a single night than a whole Canadian summer.
Here, too, numberless herds run wild and unclaimed in the
    prairies;

Here, too, lands may be had for the asking, and forests of timber
With a few blows of the ax are hewn and framed into houses.
After your houses are built, and your fields are yellow with
    harvests,
No King George of England shall drive you away from your
    homesteads,
5 Burning your dwellings and barns, and stealing your farms and
    your cattle."
Speaking these words, he blew a wrathful cloud from his nostrils,
And his huge, brawny hand came thundering down on the table,
So that the guests all started; and Father Felician, astounded,
Suddenly paused, with a pinch of snuff halfway to his nostrils.
10 But the brave Basil resumed, and his words were milder and
    gayer:
"Only beware of the fever, my friends, beware of the fever!
For it is not like that of our cold Acadian climate,
Cured by wearing a spider hung around one's neck in a nutshell!"
Then there were voices heard at the door, and footsteps
    approaching
15 Sounded upon the stairs and the floor of the breezy veranda.
It was the neighboring Creoles and small Acadian planters,
Who had been summoned all to the house of Basil the herdsman.
Merry the meeting was of ancient comrades and neighbors.
Friend clasped friend in his arms; and they who before were
    as strangers,
20 Meeting in exile, became straightway as friends to each other,
Drawn by the gentle bond of a common country together.
But in the neighboring hall a strain of music, proceeding
From the accordant strings of Michael's melodious fiddle,
Broke up all further speech. Away, like children delighted,
25 All things forgotten beside, they gave themselves to the mad-
    dening
Whirl of the dizzy dance, as it swept and swayed to the music,
Dreamlike, with beaming eyes and the rush of fluttering gar-
    ments.

Meanwhile, apart, at the head of the hall, the priest and the herdsman
Sat, conversing together of past and present and future;
While Evangeline stood like one entranced, for within her
Olden memories rose, and loud in the midst of the music
5 Heard she the sound of the sea, and an irrepressible sadness
Came o'er her heart, and unseen she stole forth into the garden.
Beautiful was the night. Behind the black wall of the forest,
Tipping its summit with silver, arose the moon. On the river
Fell here and there through the branches a tremulous gleam of the moonlight,
10 Like the sweet thoughts of love on a darkened and devious spirit.
Nearer and round about her, the manifold flowers of the garden
Poured out their souls in odors, that were their prayers and confessions
Unto the night, as it went its way, like a silent Carthusian.
Fuller of fragrance than they, and as heavy with shadows and night-dews,
15 Hung the heart of the maiden. The calm and the magical moonlight
Seemed to inundate her soul with indefinable longings,
As, through the garden gate, beneath the brown shade of the oak-trees,
Passed she along the path to the edge of the measureless prairie.
Silent it lay, with a silvery haze upon it, and fireflies
20 Gleaming and floating away in mingled and infinite numbers.
Over her head the stars, the thoughts of God in the heavens,
Shone on the eyes of man, who had ceased to marvel and worship,
Save when a blazing comet was seen on the walls of that temple,
As if a hand had appeared and written upon them, "Upharsin."
25 And the soul of the maiden, between the stars and the fireflies,
Wandered alone, and she cried, "O Gabriel! O my beloved!
Art thou so near unto me, and yet I cannot behold thee?

Art thou so near unto me, and yet thy voice does not reach me?
Ah! how often thy feet have trod this path to the prairie!
Ah! how often thine eyes have looked on the woodlands around
me!
Ah! how often beneath this oak, returning from labor,
5 Thou hast lain down to rest, and to dream of me in thy slum-
bers!
When shall these eyes behold, these arms be folded about thee?"
Loud and sudden and near, the note of a whippoorwill sounded
Like a flute in the woods; and anon, through the neighboring
thickets,
Farther and farther away it floated and dropped into silence.
10 "Patience!" whispered the oaks from oracular caverns of darkness;
And, from the moonlight meadow, a sigh responded, "Tomorrow!"

Bright rose the sun next day; and all the flowers of the garden
Bathed his shining feet with their tears, and anointed his tresses
With the delicious balm that they bore in their vases of crystal.
15 "Farewell!" said the priest, as he stood at the shadowy threshold;
"See that you bring us the Prodigal Son from his fasting and
famine,
And, too, the Foolish Virgin, who slept when the bridegroom
was coming."
"Farewell!" answered the maiden, and smiling, with Basil
descended
Down to the river's brink, where the boatmen already were
waiting.
20 Thus beginning their journey with morning, and sunshine, and
gladness,
Swiftly they followed the flight of him who was speeding before
them,
Blown by the blast of fate like a dead leaf over the desert.
Not that day, nor the next, nor yet the day that succeeded,

Found they trace of his course, in lake or forest or river.
Nor, after many days, had they found him; but vague and
    uncertain
Rumors alone were their guides through a wild and desolate
    country;
Till, at the little inn of the Spanish town of Adayes,
5 Weary and worn, they alighted, and learned from the garrulous
    landlord
That on the day before, with horses and guides and companions,
Gabriel left the village, and took the road of the prairies.

## IV

    Far in the West there lies a desert land, where the mountains
Lift, through perpetual snows, their lofty and luminous summits.
10 Down from their jagged, deep ravines, where the gorge, like
    a gateway,
Opens a passage rude to the wheels of the emigrant's wagon,
Westward the Oregon flows and the Walleway and Owyhee.
Eastward, with devious course, among the Wind River Moun-
    tains,
Through the Sweetwater Valley precipitate leaps the Nebraska;
15 And to the south, from Fontaine-qui-bout and the Spanish
    Sierras,
Fretted with sands and rocks, and swept by the wind of the
    desert,
Numberless torrents, with ceaseless sound, descend to the ocean,
Like the great chords of a harp, in loud and solemn vibrations.
Spreading between these streams are the wondrous, beautiful
    prairies,
20 Billowy bays of grass ever rolling in shadow and sunshine,
Bright with luxuriant clusters of roses and purple amorphas.
Over them wander the buffalo herds, and the elk and the
    roebuck;
Over them wander the wolves, and herds of riderless horses;

Fires that blast and blight, and winds that are weary with
    travel;
Over them wander the scattered tribes of Ishmael's children,
Staining the desert with blood; and above their terrible war-
    trails
Circles and sails aloft, on pinions majestic, the vulture,
5 Like the implacable soul of a chieftain slaughtered in battle,
By invisible stairs ascending and scaling the heavens.
Here and there rise smokes from the camps of these savage
    marauders;
Here and there rise groves from the margins of swift-running
    rivers;
And the grim, taciturn bear, the anchorite monk of the desert,
10 Climbs down their dark ravines to dig for roots by the brookside;
And over all is the sky, the clear and crystalline heaven,
Like the protecting hand of God inverted above them.

Into this wonderful land, at the base of the Ozark Mountains,
Gabriel far had entered, with hunters and trappers behind him.
15 Day after day, with their Indian guides, the maiden and Basil
Followed his flying steps, and thought each day to o'ertake him.
Sometimes they saw, or thought they saw, the smoke of his
    camp fire
Rise in the morning air from the distant plain; but at nightfall,
When they had reached the place, they found only embers and
    ashes.
20 And, though their hearts were sad at times and their bodies
    were weary,
Hope still guided them on, as the magic Fata Morgana
Showed them her lakes of light, that retreated and vanished
    before them.

Once, as they sat by their evening fire, there silently entered
Into the little camp an Indian woman, whose features
25 Wore deep traces of sorrow, and patience as great as her sorrow.

She was a Shawnee woman returning home to her people,
From the far-off hunting grounds of the cruel Comanches,
Where her Canadian husband, a *coureur-des-bois*, had been
     murdered.
Touched were their hearts at her story, and warmest and
     friendliest welcome
5 Gave they, with words of cheer, and she sat and feasted among
     them
On the buffalo-meat and the venison cooked on the embers.
But when their meal was done, and Basil and all his companions,
Worn with the long day's march and the chase of the deer and
     the bison,
Stretched themselves on the ground, and slept where the
     quivering firelight
10 Flashed on their swarthy cheeks, and their forms wrapped up
     in their blankets,
Then at the door of Evangeline's tent she sat and repeated
Slowly, with soft, low voice and the charm of her Indian accent,
All the tale of her love, with its pleasures, and pains, and
     reverses.
Much Evangeline wept at the tale, and to know that another
15 Hapless heart like her own had loved and had been disappointed.
Moved to the depths of her soul by pity and woman's
     compassion,
Yet in her sorrow pleased that one who had suffered was near her,
She in turn related her love and all its disasters.
Mute with wonder the Shawnee sat, and when she had ended,
20 Still was mute; but at length, as if a mysterious horror
Passed through her brain, she spake, and repeated the tale of
     the Mowis;
Mowis, the bridegroom of snow, who won and wedded a maiden,
But, when the morning came, arose and passed from the wigwam,
Fading and melting away and dissolving into the sunshine,
25 Till she beheld him no more, though she followed far into the
     forest.

Then, in those sweet, low tones, that seemed like a weird
    incantation,
Told she the tale of the fair Lilinau, who was wooed by a
    phantom,
That, through the pines o'er her father's lodge, in the hush of
    the twilight
Breathed like the evening wind, and whispered love to the
    maiden,
5 Till she followed his green and waving plume through the forest,
And nevermore returned, nor was seen again by her people.
Silent with wonder and strange surprise, Evangeline listened
To the soft flow of her magical words, till the region around her
Seemed like enchanted ground, and her swarthy guest the
    enchantress.
10 Slowly over the tops of the Ozark Mountains the moon rose,
Lighting the little tent, and with a mysterious splendor
Touching the somber leaves, and embracing and filling the
    woodland.
With a delicious sound the brook rushed by, and the branches
Swayed and sighed overhead in scarcely audible whispers.
15 Filled with the thoughts of love was Evangeline's heart, but a
    secret,
Subtle sense crept in of pain and indefinite terror,
As the cold, poisonous snake creeps into the nest of the swallow.
It was no earthly fear. A breath from the region of spirits
Seemed to float in the air of night; and she felt for a moment
20 That, like the Indian maid, she, too, was pursuing a phantom.
And with this thought she slept, and the fear and the phantom
    had vanished.

    Early upon the morrow the march was resumed, and the
    Shawnee
Said, as they journeyed along—"On the western slope of these
    mountains
Dwells in his little village the Black Robe chief of the Mission.

Much he teaches the people, and tells them of Mary and Jesus;
Loud laugh their hearts with joy, and weep with pain, as they
    hear him."
Then, with a sudden and secret emotion, Evangeline answered,
"Let us go to the Mission, for there good tidings await us!"
5 Thither they turned their steeds; and behind a spur of the
    mountains,
Just as the sun went down, they heard a murmur of voices,
And in a meadow green and broad, by the bank of a river,
Saw the tents of the Christians, the tents of the Jesuit Mission.
Under a towering oak, that stood in the midst of the village,
10 Knelt the Black Robe chief with his children. A crucifix
    fastened
High on the trunk of the tree, and overshadowed by grapevines,
Looked with its agonized face on the multitude kneeling
    beneath it.
This was their rural chapel. Aloft, through the intricate arches
Of its aerial roof, arose the chant of their vespers,
15 Mingling its notes with the soft susurrus and sighs of the
    branches.
Silent, with heads uncovered, the travelers, nearer approaching,
Knelt on the swarded floor, and joined in the evening devotions.
But when the service was done, and the benediction had fallen
Forth from the hands of the priest, like seed from the hands
    of the sower,
20 Slowly the reverend man advanced to the strangers, and bade
    them
Welcome; and when they replied, he smiled with benignant
    expression,
Hearing the homelike sounds of his mother tongue in the forest,
And, with words of kindness, conducted them into his wigwam.
There upon mats and skins they reposed, and on cakes of the
    maize-ear
25 Feasted, and slaked their thirst from the water-gourd of the
    teacher.

Soon was their story told; and the priest with solemnity
    answered:
"Not six suns have risen and set since Gabriel, seated
On this mat by my side, where now the maiden reposes,
Told me this same sad tale; then arose and continued his
    journey!"
5 Soft was the voice of the priest, and he spake with an accent
    of kindness;
But on Evangeline's heart fell his words as in winter the snow
    flakes
Fall into some lone nest from which the birds have departed.
"Far to the north he has gone," continued the priest; "but in
    autumn,
When the chase is done, will return again to the Mission."
10 Then Evangeline said, and her voice was meek and submissive,
"Let me remain with thee, for my soul is sad and afflicted."
So seemed it wise and well unto all; and betimes on the morrow,
Mounting his Mexican steed, with his Indian guides and
    companions,
Homeward Basil returned, and Evangeline stayed at the Mission.

15    Slowly, slowly, slowly the days succeeded each other—
Days and weeks and months; and the fields of maize that were
    springing
Green from the ground when a stranger she came, now waving
    above her,
Lifted their slender shafts, with leaves interlacing, and forming
Cloisters for mendicant crows and granaries pillaged by squirrels.
20 Then in the golden weather the maize was husked, and the
    maidens
Blushed at each blood-red ear, for that betokened a lover,
But at the crooked laughed, and called it a thief in the cornfield.
Even the blood-red ear to Evangeline brought not her lover.
"Patience!" the priest would say, "have faith, and thy prayer will
    be answered!

Look at this delicate plant that lifts its head from the meadow,
See how its leaves all point to the north, as true as the magnet;
It is the compass-flower, that the finger of God has suspended
Here on its fragile stalk to direct the traveler's journey
5 Over the sea-like, pathless, limitless waste of the desert.
Such in the soul of man is faith.  The blossoms of passion,
Gay and luxuriant flowers, are brighter and fuller of fragrance,
But they beguile us and lead us astray, and their odor is deadly.
Only this humble plant can guide us here, and hereafter
10 Crown us with asphodel flowers, that are wet with the dews
     of nepenthe."

So came the autumn, and passed, and the winter—yet Gabriel
     came not;
Blossomed the opening spring, and the notes of the robin and
     bluebird
Sounded sweet upon wold and in wood, yet Gabriel came not.
But on the breath of the summer winds a rumor was wafted
15 Sweeter than song of bird, or hue or odor of blossom.
Far to the north and east, it said, in the Michigan forests,
Gabriel had his lodge by the banks of the Saginaw River.
And, with returning guides, that sought the lakes of St. Lawrence,
Saying a sad farewell, Evangeline went from the Mission.
20 When over weary ways, by long and perilous marches,
She had attained at length the depths of the Michigan forests,
Found she the hunter's lodge deserted and fallen to ruin!

Thus did the long sad years glide on, and in seasons andplaces
Divers and distant far was seen the wandering maiden:
25 Now in the Tents of Grace of the meek Moravian Missions,
Now in the noisy camps and the battlefields of the army.
Now in secluded hamlets, in towns and populous cities.
Like a phantom she came, and passed away unremembered.
Fair was she and young when in hope began the long journey;
30 Faded was she and old when in disappointment it ended.

Each succeeding year stole something away from her beauty,
Leaving behind it, broader and deeper, the gloom and the shadow.
Then there appeared and spread faint streaks of gray o'er her
    forehead,
Dawn of another life, that broke o'er her earthly horizon,
5 As in the eastern sky the first faint streaks of the morning.

V

In that delightful land which is washed by the Delaware's
    waters,
Guarding in sylvan shades the name of Penn the apostle,
Stands on the banks of its beautiful stream the city he founded.
There all the air is balm, and the peach is the emblem of beauty,
10 And the streets still reecho the names of the trees of the forest,
As if they fain would appease the Dryads whose haunts they
    molested.
There from the troubled sea had Evangeline landed, an exile,
Finding among the children of Penn a home and a country.
There old René Leblanc had died; and when he departed,
15 Saw at his side only one of all his hundred descendants.
Something at least there was in the friendly streets of the city,
Something that spake to her heart, and made her no longer a
    stranger;
And her ear was pleased with the Thee and Thou of the Quakers,
For it recalled the past, the old Acadian country,
20 Where all men were equal, and all were brothers and sisters.
So, when the fruitless search, the disappointed endeavor,
Ended, to recommence no more upon earth, uncomplaining,
Thither, as leaves to the light, were turned her thoughts and
    her footsteps.
As from a mountain's top the rainy mists of the morning
25 Roll away, and afar we behold the landscape below us,
Sun-illumined, with shining rivers and cities and hamlets,
So fell the mists from her mind, and she saw the world far
    below her,

Dark no longer, but all illumined with love; and the pathway
Which she had climbed so far, lying smooth and fair in the
        distance.
Gabriel was not forgotten.  Within her heart was his image,
Clothed in the beauty of love and youth, as last she beheld him,
5 Only more beautiful made by his deathlike silence and absence.
Into her thoughts of him time entered not, for it was not.
Over him years had no power; he was not changed, but
        transfigured;
He had become to her heart as one who is dead, and not absent;
Patience and abnegation of self, and devotion to others,
10 This was the lesson a life of trial and sorrow had taught her.
So was her love diffused, but, like to some odorous spices,
Suffered no waste nor loss, though filling the air with aroma.
Other hope had she none, nor wish in life, but to follow,
Meekly with reverent steps, the sacred feet of her Savior.
15 Thus many years she lived as a Sister of Mercy; frequenting
Lonely and wretched roofs in the crowded lanes of the city,
Where distress and want concealed themselves from the sunlight,
Where disease and sorrow in garrets languished neglected.
Night after night when the world was asleep, as the watchman
        repeated
20 Loud, through the gusty streets, that all was well in the city,
High at some lonely window he saw the light of her taper.
Day after day, in the gray of the dawn, as slow through the
        suburbs
Plodded the German farmer, with flowers and fruits for the
        market,
Met he that meek, pale face, returning home from its watchings.

25    Then it came to pass that a pestilence fell on that city,
Presaged by wondrous signs, and mostly by flocks of wild
        pigeons,
Darkening the sun in their flight, with naught in their craws
        but an acorn;

And, as the tides of the sea arise in the month of September,
Flooding some silver stream, till it spreads to a lake in the
    meadow,
So death flooded life, and, o'erflowing its natural margin,
Spread to a brackish lake the silver stream of existence.
5 Wealth had no power to bribe, nor beauty to charm, the
    oppressor;
But all perished alike beneath the scourge of his anger;
Only, alas! the poor, who had neither friends nor attendants,
Crept away to die in the almshouse, home of the homeless.
Then in the suburbs it stood, in the midst of meadows and
    woodlands;
10 Now the city surrounds it; but still, with its gateway and wicket
Meek, in the midst of splendor, its humble walls seem to echo
Softly the words of the Lord: "The poor you always have with
    you."
Thither, by night and by day, came the Sister of Mercy. The
    dying
Looked up into her face, and thought, indeed, to behold there
15 Gleams of celestial light encircle her forehead with splendor,
Such as the artist paints o'er the brows of saints and apostles,
Or such as hangs by night o'er a city seen at a distance.
Unto their eyes it seemed the lamps of the city celestial,
Into whose shining gates erelong their spirits would enter.

20     Thus, on a Sabbath morn, through the streets, deserted and
    silent,
Wending her quiet way, she entered the door of the almshouse.
Sweet on the summer air was the odor of flowers in the
    garden,
And she paused on her way to gather the fairest among them,
That the dying once more might rejoice in their fragrance and
    beauty.
25 Then, as she mounted the stairs to the corridors, cooled by the
    east-wind,

Distant and soft on her ear fell the chimes from the belfry of
    Christ Church,
While intermingled with these, across the meadows were wafted
Sounds of psalms, that were sung by the Swedes in their
    church at Wicaco.
Soft as descending wings fell the calm of the hour on her spirit;
5 Something within her said, "At length thy trials are ended";
And, with light in her looks, she entered the chambers of sickness.
Noiselessly moved about the assiduous, careful attendants,
Moistening the feverish lip and the aching brow, and in silence
Closing the sightless eyes of the dead, and concealing their faces,
10 Where on their pallets they lay, like drifts of snow by the
    roadside.
Many a languid head, upraised as Evangeline entered,
Turned on its pillow of pain to gaze while she passed, for her
    presence
Fell on their hearts like a ray of the sun on the walls of a prison.
And, as she looked around, she saw how Death, the consoler,
15 Laying his hand upon many a heart, had healed it forever.
Many familiar forms had disappeared in the night time;
Vacant their places were, or filled already by strangers.

    Suddenly, as if arrested by fear or a feeling of wonder,
Still she stood, with her colorless lips apart, while a shudder
20 Ran through her frame, and, forgotten, the flowerets dropped
    from her fingers,
And from her eyes and cheeks the light and bloom of the
    morning.
Then there escaped from her lips a cry of such terrible anguish,
That the dying heard it, and started up from their pillows.
On the pallet before her was stretched the form of an old man.
25 Long, and thin, and gray were the locks that shaded his temples;
But, as he lay in the morning light, his face for a moment
Seemed to assume once more the forms of its earlier manhood;
So are wont to be changed the faces of those who are dying.

Hot and red on his lips still burned the flush of the fever,
As if life, like the Hebrew, with blood had besprinkled its portals,
That the Angel of Death might see the sign, and pass over.
Motionless, senseless, dying, he lay, and his spirit exhausted
5 Seemed to be sinking down through infinite depths in the
    darkness,
Darkness of slumber and death, forever sinking and sinking.
Then through those realms of shade, in multiplied reverberations,
Heard he that cry of pain, and through the hush that succeeded
Whispered a gentle voice, in accents tender and saintlike,
10 "Gabriel! O my beloved!" and died away into silence.
Then he beheld, in a dream, once more the home of his childhood:
Green Acadian meadows, with sylvan rivers among them,
Village, and mountain, and woodlands; and, walking under their
    shadow,
As in the days of her youth, Evangeline rose in his vision.
15 Tears came into his eyes; and as slowly he lifted his eyelids,
Vanished the vision away, but Evangeline knelt by his bedside.
Vainly he strove to whisper her name, for the accents
    unuttered
Died on his lips, and their motion revealed what his tongue
    would have spoken.
Vainly he strove to rise; and Evangeline, kneeling beside him,
20 Kissed his dying lips, and laid his head on her bosom.
Sweet was the light of his eyes; but it suddenly sank into
    darkness,
As when a lamp is blown out by a gust of wind at a casement.

All was ended now, the hope, and the fear, and the sorrow,
All the aching of heart, the restless, unsatisfied longing,
25 All the dull, deep pain, and constant anguish of patience!
And, as she pressed once more the lifeless head to her bosom,
Meekly she bowed her own, and murmured, "Father, I thank
    thee!"

Still stands the forest primeval; but far away from its shadow,
Side by side, in their nameless graves, the lovers are sleeping.
Under the humble walls of the little Catholic churchyard,
In the heart of the city, they lie, unknown and unnoticed.
5 Daily the tides of life go ebbing and flowing beside them:
Thousands of throbbing hearts, where theirs are at rest and
      forever;
Thousands of aching brains, where theirs no longer are busy;
Thousands of toiling hands, where theirs have ceased from
      their labors;
Thousands of weary feet, where theirs have completed their
      journey!

10      Still stands the forest, primeval; but under the shade of its
      branches
Dwells another race, with other customs and language.
Only along the shore of the mournful and misty Atlantic
Linger a few Acadian peasants, whose fathers from exile
Wandered back to their native land to die in its bosom.
15 In the fisherman's cot the wheel and the loom are still busy;
Maidens still wear their Norman caps and their kirtles of home
      spun,
And by the evening fire repeat Evangeline's story,
While from its rocky caverns the deep-voiced, neighboring ocean
Speaks, and in accents disconsolate answers the wail of the
      forest.

NOTES AND QUESTIONS

For **Biography** see page 138.

**Historical Note.** The conflict for supremacy between the French and
the English is a part of the early history of Nova Scotia, which was called
Acadie by the French. The Acadians were French in their blood and in their
sympathies, though the English were from time to time in authority over
the country. At one time the English demanded an oath of allegiance from
the Acadians. This they refused to take unless it should be so modified as
to exempt them from bearing arms against France. It was finally decided

to remove the Acadians from the country, scattering them throughout the American colonies. Accordingly, they were driven on board the English transports, and three thousand of them were sent out of the country (1755). In the confusion, families and friends were separated, in many cases never to meet again. Longfellow based his poem upon a legend that sprang from this exile.

It is interesting to note that a bronze statue of "Evangeline" was unveiled on July 29, 1920, at Grand Pré, Nova Scotia. The statue represents Evangeline about to leave her native land, her face turned slightly backward in a sorrowful manner.

**Discussion.** 1. Into what parts is the poem divided? 2. With what does Part the First deal? Part the Second? 3. What purpose does the prelude serve? 4. What may have given rise to the comparison of the trees to harpers? 5. What tells us that the mood of the ocean is in sympathy with the melancholy of the forest? 6. To what are the lives of the farmers compared? 7. Upon whom does the poet call to listen to his story?

Part the First. (I) 1. What does Longfellow mean when he says that vast meadows gave the village its name? 2. In what sense was the richest in Acadie poor? 3. Find lines that describe Evangeline's father. 4. Find lines that describe Evangeline. 5. How has the "craft of the smith" been regarded from earliest times? How can you account for this? (II) 6. What do we call that "beautiful season" which the Acadians called the "Summer of All-Saints"? 7. What pictures make up the evening scene? (III) 8. How was the betrothal celebrated? 9. What forebodings were expressed? (IV) 10. What proclamation was made at the church? 11. How was it received by the Acadians? 12. How did Evangeline try to help the women and children? (V) 13. What happened when the time came for entering the boats? 14. What was done to the homes that the Acadians had left? 15. What caused the death of Evangeline's father? 16. Find in the glossary the meaning of: (1) ethereal; mutation; (II) regent; glebe; notary; (III) irascible; congealed; (IV) jocund; vibrant; dissonant; convened; solstice; imprecations; (V) refluent; kelp; unperturbed; gleeds; oblivious. 17. *Pronounce:* prelude; (I) hearth; heirloom; exquisite; (III) warier; (IV) sonorous; clement; mien; contrition. (For "Phrases" see p. 442.)

Part the Second. (I) 1. Where did the Acadians land? 2. What did the exiles do in the strange country? 3. Find the words with which the priest comforted Evangeline. 4. How does the poet say he will follow Evangeline's footsteps? (II) 5. Who accompanied Evangeline and the priest on their journey down the Mississippi? 6. What thought sustained Evangeline on this voyage? 7. What vision came to her? (III) 8. Describe the meeting with Basil. 9. Find lines in which Basil contrasts his new home with the

old.  10. Why was it that Evangeline's party failed to see Gabriel's boat?
(IV) 11. Where did Evangeline seek for Gabriel as the years passed?  12. How
did her appearance change as time went on?  (V) 13. What had her life of
sorrow taught her?  14. What did her loving heart lead her to do?  15. Where
did her work as a Sister of Mercy take her?  16. How had the priest's words
come true?  17. Contrast the conduct of Evangeline in the time of pestilence
with that of Prince Prospero in Poe's story "The Masque of the Red Death."
18. What helped Evangeline to recognize Gabriel?  19. What reasons for
thankfulness did she have?  20. What words of the good priest may have
come to her mind at this time?  21. This is a tale of devotion showing the
beauty and holiness of affection "that hopes and endures and is patient";
it also teaches certain facts about early American history.  Which of these
values do you think the poet wished to impress upon us?  22. The poem
has the "twofold province" about which you read in the "Introduction" on
pages 336 and 337; can you show that this is true?  23. This poem consists
of a series of descriptions, each forming a beautiful picture; make a list of
these scenes and place a star before those that you can see most distinctly.
24. What did you learn from the "Introduction" on page 337 about the value
of literature as a supplement to your history?  How has this poem added
to your understanding of the wild, unsettled regions of early America?
25. If you have seen "Evangeline" in motion pictures tell how the film story
differed from the poem story.  26. Find in the glossary the meaning of:
(I) inarticulate; shards; devious; (II) multitudinous; (III) hilarious; accordant;
inundate; oracular; (IV) incantation; cloisters; mendicant; (V) abnegation;
diffused; assiduous.  27. *Pronounce:* (II) tenebrous; demoniac; buoy;
(IV) implacable; taciturn; subtle; (V) presaged.


## Phrases for Study

reign of the Henries, **386**, 1

envy, the vice..., **386**, 21

penitent Peter, **388**, 15

held in repute, **389**, 13

ripened thought...**390**, 10

sign of the Scorpion, **390**, 17

birds of passage, **390**, 18

plane-tree...adorned, **391**, 16

royal commission, **402**, 9

natural make, **402**, 12

tocsin's alarum. **403**, 19

with devotion translated, **404**, 14

Prophet descending...**405**, 13

shipwrecked Paul, **409**, 11

adverse currents, **422**, 9

Foolish Virgin, **427**, 17

Ishmael's children, **429**, 2

like the Hebrew, **439**, 2


**Library Reading.**  *The Last of the Mohicans*, Cooper.

**Suggestions for Theme Topics.** Contrast the advantages of living in your home region with living in some other section of our country, as Basil contrasted the advantages of Louisiana over Canada.

**A Suggested Problem.** Dramatize selected scenes from this poem, or prepare a program for a "Longfellow Day."

---

# THE GRAY CHAMPION*

## NATHANIEL HAWTHORNE

There was once a time when New England groaned under the actual pressure of heavier wrongs than those threatened ones which brought on the Revolution. James II, the bigoted successor of Charles the Voluptuous, had annulled the charters of
5 all the colonies and sent a harsh and unprincipled soldier to take away our liberties and endanger our religion. The administration of Sir Edmund Andros lacked scarcely a single characteristic of tyranny: a governor and council holding office from the king, and wholly independent of the country; laws made and taxes
10 levied without concurrence of the people, immediate or by their representatives; the rights of private citizens violated, and the titles of all landed property declared void; the voice of complaint stifled by restrictions on the press; and, finally, disaffection overawed by the first band of mercenary troops that
15 ever marched on our free soil. For two years our ancestors were kept in sullen submission by that filial love which had invariably secured their allegiance to the mother country, whether its head chanced to be a Parliament, protector, or monarch. Till these

---

*See Silent and Oral Reading, page 13.

evil times, however, such allegiance had been merely nominal, and the colonists had ruled themselves, enjoying far more freedom than is even yet the privilege of the native subjects of Great Britain.

5 At length a rumor reached our shores that the Prince of Orange had ventured on an enterprise the success of which would be the triumph of civil and religious rights and the salvation of New England. It was but a doubtful whisper; it might be false, or the attempt might fail; and, in either case, 10 the man that stirred against King James would lose his head. Still, the intelligence produced a marked effect. The people smiled mysteriously in the streets and threw bold glances at their oppressors; while, far and wide, there was a subdued and silent agitation, as if the slightest signal would rouse the 15 whole land from its sluggish despondency. Aware of their danger, the rulers resolved to avert it by an imposing display of strength, and perhaps to confirm their despotism by yet harsher measures. One afternoon in April, 1689, Sir Edmund Andros and his favorite councilors, being warm with wine, assembled 20 the redcoats of the Governor's Guard and made their appearance in the streets of Boston. The sun was near setting when the march commenced.

The roll of the drum, at that unquiet crisis, seemed to go through the streets, less as the martial music of the soldiers than 25 as a muster-call to the inhabitants themselves. A multitude, by various avenues, assembled in King Street, which was destined to be the scene, nearly a century afterwards, of another encounter between the troops of Britain and a people struggling against her tyranny. Though more than sixty years had elapsed since 30 the Pilgrims came, this crowd of their descendants still showed the strong and somber features of their character, perhaps more strikingly in such a stern emergency than on happier occasions. There was the sober garb, the general severity of mien, the gloomy but undismayed expression, the scriptural forms of 35 speech, and the confidence in Heaven's blessing on a righteous

cause, which would have marked a band of the original Puritans when threatened by some peril of the wilderness. Indeed, it was not yet time for the old spirit to be extinct, since there were men in the street, that day, who had worshiped there beneath
5 the trees, before a house was reared to the God for whom they had become exiles. Old soldiers of the Parliament were here, too, smiling grimly at the thought that their aged arms might strike another blow against the house of Stuart. Here, also, were the veterans of King Philip's War, who had burned villages
10 and slaughtered young and old, with pious fierceness, while the godly souls throughout the land were helping them with prayer. Several ministers were scattered among the crowd, which, unlike all other mobs, regarded them with such reverence as if there were sanctity in their very garments. These holy men exerted
15 their influence to quiet the people, but not to disperse them. Meantime, the purpose of the governor, in disturbing the peace of the town at a period when the slightest commotion might throw the country into a ferment, was almost the universal subject of inquiry, and variously explained:

20 "Satan will strike his master stroke presently," cried some, "because he knoweth that his time is short. All our godly pastors are to be dragged to prison! We shall see them at a Smithfield fire in King Street!"

Hereupon the people of each parish gathered closer round
25 their minister, who looked calmly upward and assumed a more apostolic dignity, as well befitted a candidate for the highest honor of his profession, the crown of martyrdom. It was actually fancied, at that period, that New England might have a John Rogers of her own, to take the place of that worthy in the
30 Primer.

"We are all to be massacred," cried others.

Neither was this rumor wholly discredited, although the wiser class believed the governor's object somewhat less atrocious. His predecessor under the old charter, Bradstreet, a venerable
35 companion of the first settlers, was known to be in town. There

were grounds for conjecturing that Sir Edmund Andros intended, at once, to strike terror, by a parade of military force, and to confound the opposite faction by possessing himself of their chief.

5 "Stand firm for the old charter, Governor!" shouted the crowd, seizing upon the idea. "The good old Governor Bradstreet!"

While this cry was at the loudest, the people were surprised by the well-known figure of Governor Bradstreet himself, a patriarch of nearly ninety, who appeared on the elevated steps
10 of a door, and, with characteristic mildness, besought them to submit to the constituted authorities.

"My children," concluded this venerable person, "do nothing rashly. Cry not aloud, but pray for the welfare of New England, and expect patiently what the Lord will do in this matter!"

15 The event was soon to be decided. All this time the roll of the drum had been approaching through Cornhill, louder and deeper, till with reverberations from house to house, and the regular tramp of martial footsteps, it burst into the street. A double rank of soldiers made their appearance, occupying the
20 whole breadth of the passage, with shouldered matchlocks and matches burning, so as to present a row of fires in the dusk. Their steady march was like the progress of a machine that would roll irresistibly over everything in its way. Next, moving slowly, with a confused clatter of hoofs on the pavement, rode a party of
25 mounted gentlemen, the central figure being Sir Edmund Andros, elderly, but erect and soldier-like. Those around him were his favorite councilors and the bitterest foes of New England. At his right hand rode Edward Randolph, our archenemy, that "blasted wretch," as Cotton Mather calls him, who achieved the
30 downfall of our ancient government and was followed with a sensible curse through life and to his grave. On the other side was Bullivant, scattering jests and mockery as he rode along. Dudley came behind, with a downcast look, dreading, as well he might, to meet the indignant gaze of the people, who beheld
35 him, their only countryman by birth, among the oppressors of

his native land. The captain of a frigate in the harbor, and two or three civil officers under the Crown were also there. But the figure which most attracted the public eye, and stirred up the deepest feeling, was the Episcopal clergyman of King's Chapel,
5 riding haughtily among the magistrates in his priestly vestments, the fitting representative of prelacy and persecution, the union of church and state, and all those abominations which had driven the Puritans to the wilderness. Another guard of soldiers, in double rank, brought up the rear.
10 The whole scene was a picture of the condition of New England and its moral, the deformity of any government that does not grow out of the nature of things and the character of the people. On one side, the religious multitude, with their sad visages and dark attire, and on the other, the group of
15 despotic rulers, all magnificently clad, flushed with wine, proud of unjust authority, and scoffing at the universal groan. And the mercenary soldiers, waiting but the word to deluge the street with blood, showed the only means by which obedience could be secured.
20 "O Lord of Hosts," cried a voice among the crowd, "provide a champion for thy people!"

This ejaculation was loudly uttered and served as a herald's cry to introduce a remarkable personage. The crowd had rolled back, and were now huddled together nearly at the extremity
25 of the street, while the soldiers had advanced no more than a third of its length. The intervening space was empty—a paved solitude, between lofty edifices, which threw almost a twilight shadow over it. Suddenly, there was seen the figure of an ancient man, who seemed to have emerged from among the
30 people and was walking by himself along the center of the street to confront the armed band. He wore the old Puritan dress, a dark cloak and a steeple-crowned hat, in the fashion of at least fifty years before, with a heavy sword upon his thigh, but a staff in his hand to assist the tremulous gait of age.
35 When at some distance from the multitude, the old man

turned slowly round, displaying a face of antique majesty,
rendered doubly venerable by the hoary beard that descended
on his breast. He made a gesture at once of encouragement and
warning, then turned again and resumed his way.

5      "Who is this gray patriarch?" asked the young men of their
sires.

"Who is this venerable brother?" asked the old men among
themselves.

But none could make reply. The fathers of the people, those
10 of fourscore years and upwards, were disturbed, deeming it
strange that they should forget one of such evident authority,
whom they must have known in their early days, the associate
of Winthrop and all the old councilors, giving laws and making
prayers and leading them against the savage. The elderly men
15 ought to have remembered him, too, with locks as gray in their
youth as their own were now. And the young! How could he
have passed so utterly from their memories—that hoary sire, the
relic of long-departed times, whose awful benediction had surely
been bestowed on their uncovered heads in childhood?

20      "Whence did he come? What is his purpose? Who can this
old man be?" whispered the wondering crowd.

Meanwhile, the venerable stranger, staff in hand, was pursuing his solitary walk along the center of the street. As he drew
near the advancing soldiers, and as the roll of their drum came
25 full upon his ear, the old man raised himself to a loftier mien,
while the decrepitude of age seemed to fall from his shoulders,
leaving him in gray but unbroken dignity. Now, he marched
onward with a warrior's step, keeping time to the military
music. Thus the aged form advanced on one side, and the
30 whole parade of soldiers and magistrates on the other, till,
when scarcely twenty yards remained between, the old man
grasped his staff by the middle, and held it before him like a
leader's truncheon.

"Stand!" cried he.

35      The eye, the face, and attitude of command, the solemn,

yet warlike peal of that voice, fit either to rule a host in the
battlefield or be raised to God in prayer, were irresistible. At the
old man's word and outstretched arm, the roll of the drum was
hushed at once, and the advancing line stood still. A tremulous
5 enthusiasm seized upon the multitude. That stately form,
combining the leader and the saint, so gray, so dimly seen, in
such an ancient garb, could only belong to some old champion of
the righteous cause, whom the oppressor's drum had summoned
from his grave. They raised a shout of awe and exultation, and
10 looked for the deliverance of New England.

The governor and the gentlemen of his party, perceiving
themselves brought to an unexpected stand, rode hastily forward,
as if they would have pressed their snorting and affrighted
horses right against the hoary apparition. He, however, blenched
15 not a step, but glancing his severe eye round the group, which
half encompassed him, at last bent it sternly on Sir Edmund
Andros. One would have thought that the dark old man was
chief ruler there, and the governor and council, with soldiers at
their back, representing the whole power and authority of the
20 Crown, had no alternative but obedience.

"What does this old fellow here?" cried Edward Randolph,
fiercely. "On, Sir Edmund! Bid the soldiers forward, and give
the dotard the same choice that you give all his countrymen—to
stand aside or be trampled on!"

25 "Nay, nay, let us show respect to the good grandsire," said
Bullivant, laughing. "See you not, he is some old roundheaded
dignitary, who hath lain asleep these thirty years and knows
nothing of the change of times? Doubtless, he thinks to put us
down with a proclamation in Old Noll's name!"

30 "Are you mad, old man?" demanded Sir Edmund Andros in
loud and harsh tones. "How dare you stay the march of King
James's governor?"

"I have stayed the march of a king himself, ere now," replied
the gray figure with stern composure. "I am here, Sir Governor,
35 because the cry of an oppressed people hath disturbed me in my

secret place, and beseeching this favor earnestly of the Lord, it
was vouchsafed me to appear once again on earth, in the good
old cause of his saints. And what speak ye of James? There is no
longer a tyrant on the throne of England, and by tomorrow noon
5 his name shall be a byword in this very street, where ye would
make it a word of terror. Back, thou that wast a governor, back!
With this night thy power is ended—tomorrow, the prison!—back,
lest I foretell the scaffold!"

The people had been drawing nearer and nearer and drink-
10 ing in the words of their champion, who spoke in accents long
disused, like one unaccustomed to converse, except with the
dead of many years ago. But his voice stirred their souls. They
confronted the soldiers, not wholly without arms and ready to
convert the very stones of the street into deadly weapons. Sir
15 Edmund Andros looked at the old man; then he cast his hard
and cruel eye over the multitude and beheld them burning
with that lurid wrath so difficult to kindle or to quench, and
again he fixed his gaze on the aged form, which stood obscurely
in an open space, where neither friend nor foe had thrust
20 himself. What were his thoughts, he uttered no word which
might discover. But whether the oppressor were overawed
by the Gray Champion's look or perceived his peril in the
threatening attitude of the people, it is certain that he gave
back and ordered his soldiers to commence a slow and guarded
25 retreat. Before another sunset, the governor, and all that
rode so proudly, with him, were prisoners, and long ere it was
known that James had abdicated, King William was proclaimed
throughout New England.

But where was the Gray Champion? Some reported that
30 when the troops had gone from King Street and the people
were thronging tumultuously in their rear, Bradstreet, the
aged governor, was seen to embrace a form more aged than his
own. Others soberly affirmed that, while they marveled at the
venerable grandeur of his aspect, the old man had faded from
35 their eyes, melting slowly into the hues of twilight, till, where

he stood, there was an empty space.  But all agreed that the
hoary shape was gone.  The men of that generation watched
for his reappearance, in sunshine and in twilight, but never saw
him more, nor knew when his funeral passed, nor where his
5 gravestone was.

And who was the Gray Champion?  Perhaps his name might
be found in the records of that stern Court of Justice which
passed a sentence, too mighty for the age, but glorious in all
after times, for its humbling lesson to the monarch and its
10 high example to the subject.  I have heard that whenever the
descendants of the Puritans are to show the spirit of their sires,
the old man appears again.  When eighty years had passed,
he walked once more in King Street.  Five years later, in the
twilight of an April morning, he stood on the green, beside the
15 meeting house, at Lexington, where now the obelisk of granite,
with a slab of slate inlaid, commemorates the first fallen of the
Revolution.  And when our fathers were toiling at the breastwork
on Bunker's Hill, all through that night the old warrior walked
his rounds.  Long, long may it be ere he comes again!  His
20 hour is one of darkness and adversity and peril.  But should
domestic tyranny oppress us, or the invader's step pollute our
soil, still may the Gray Champion come, for he is the type of
New England's hereditary spirit, and his shadowy march, on the
eve of danger, must ever be the pledge that New England's sons
25 will vindicate their ancestry.

## NOTES AND QUESTIONS

**Biography.** Nathaniel Hawthorne (1804-1864), the first great American
writer of prose romance, was born in Salem, Massachusetts.  He graduated
from Bowdoin College in the class with Longfellow and Franklin Pierce, who
became president.  Hawthorne held positions in the customhouse, and, for
a time, represented the United States as consul in England, but his interest
always lay in writing.  He was a master of the short story as a means for
interpreting character, particularly the character of the Puritan founders of
New England.  He popularized New England history in the form of stories,

such as those in *Grandfather's Chair*. He wrote also legends of colonial times, which portray the stern methods of Governor Endicott, or tell a humorous story of the pine tree shillings, or recount the weird story of the champion who defied Governor Andros. But besides these legends, he wrote stories of lovers who sought vainly for happiness, and tales of a great stone face on the mountain side, or of the strange search for a precious gem, and what these things signified. Somewhat longer than these tales—*Twice-Told Tales* he called them, from which "The Gray Champion" is taken—are his romances, such as *The Scarlet Letter*, *Mosses from an Old Manse*, and *The House of the Seven Gables*.

**Historical Note.** A tradition handed down from the time of King Philip's War gave Hawthorne the suggestion for this story. In the attack made upon the village of Hadley, Massachusetts, by the Indians in 1675 a venerable man of stately form and with flowing white beard suddenly appeared among the panic-stricken villagers, took command, and helped them put the savages to flight. Then he disappeared as suddenly as he had come. In their wonder, not knowing where he had come from or where he had gone, many believed he had been sent from Heaven to deliver them.

Their defender was William Goffe, who had been an officer in Cromwell's army and a member of the court which condemned Charles I to death. (Read the reference to this court in the story, page 451, lines 6-10.) Goffe was a Puritan, a man of deep religious feeling, whose acts had been governed by the desire to secure for his countrymen their liberties. When Charles II succeeded to the English throne, Goffe fled to New England to escape the king's vengeance. Officers were sent across the ocean in pursuit of him. For this reason he lived in hiding, his name and identity being known only to friends who aided and protected him. He had many narrow escapes, but was never captured. From his hiding place he saw the Indians stealing upon the people of Hadley and went forth to battle against them. After living in exile for the rest of his life, he died about 1679.

In this story, Hawthorne altered facts to suit his purpose, making the Gray Champion appear at the time of the Boston Insurrection, in 1689. In this year James II, who had succeeded his brother, Charles II, was dethroned and fled from his kingdom, and his son-in-law, William III, Prince of Orange, was made king of England.

The Gray Champion is made to typify the spirit of liberty—that spirit which animated Goffe as a Puritan soldier under Cromwell and which sent the Pilgrims and Puritans forth to find a home in the New World.

**Discussion.** 1. Note that part of the story which pictures the conditions of New England under Andros. 2. What were the wrongs under which the people suffered? 3. Did they submit willingly? 4. What rumor gave them hope of a return of "civil and religious rights"? 5. How did this rumor affect the governor and his councilors? 6. Why was the guard assembled? 7. What effect upon the people had its appearance at this time? 8. What does Hawthorne call this scene in the street? 9. What does he say is its "moral"? 10. Who came to have the advantage, the governor and his soldiers or the people? 11. Find all that accounts for the champion and his sudden appearance. 12. What great cause did he come to champion? 13. What cause were Andros and his soldiers supporting? 14. Who was victorious? 15. Tell briefly the main incident. 16. Give your opinion as to Hawthorne's purpose in writing this story. 17. Read "The Short Story," page 106 and see if you can find the four parts of this story. 18. Show how this story, though based upon a legend, is the kind of literature mentioned in the "Introduction," page 337, that supplements your knowledge of history. 19. In the "Introduction" to "Part III," on page 256, you read a discussion of the "Eternal Spirit of Freedom." What similar ideas did you gain from reading "The Gray Champion"? 20. Find in the glossary the meaning of: concurrence; filial; extinct; confound; constituted; archenemy; sensible; blenched; abdicated; obelisk. 21. *Pronounce:* inquiry; apostolic; predecessor; truncheon; dotard.

### Phrases for Study

annulled the charters, **443**, 4
civil and religious, **444**, 7
house of Stuart, **445**, 8
prelacy and persecution, **447**, 6

roundheaded dignitary, **449**, 26
domestic tyranny, **451**, 21
vindicate their ancestry, **451**, 25

**Class Reading.** Select passages to be read aloud in class.

**Outline for Testing Silent Reading.** Make an outline to guide you in telling the story.

**Library Reading.** The "Introduction" on page 338 tells you that the more selections you read like the ones given in this part of your book the better you will understand America. Such reading may well include other stories from *Twice-Told Tales*, such as "The May-Pole of Merry Mount," "Legends of the Province House," "The Gentle Boy," "Sights from the Steeple"; also *The Hoosier Schoolmaster*, Eggleston; *Northwestern Fights and Fighters*, Brady; *The Story of Tonty*, Catherwood; *Cadet Days*, King; *The Pilot*, Cooper.

### The Deacon's Masterpiece

#### A Logical Story

#### Oliver Wendell Holmes

Have you heard of the wonderful one-hoss shay
That was built in such a logical way
It ran a hundred years to a day,
And then, of a sudden, it—ah, but stay,
5 I'll tell you what happened without delay,
Scaring the parson into fits,
Frightening people out of their wits—
Have you ever heard of that, I say?

Seventeen hundred and fifty-five.
10 *Georgius Secundus* was then alive
Snuffy old drone from the German hive,
That was the year when Lisbon-town

Saw the earth open and gulp her down,
And Braddock's army was done so brown,
Left without a scalp to its crown.
It was on the terrible Earthquake-day
5 That the Deacon finished the one-hoss shay.

Now in building of chaises, I tell you what,
There is always *somewhere* a weakest spot—
In hub, tire, felloe, in spring or thill,
In panel, or crossbar, or floor, or sill,
10 In screw, bolt, thoroughbrace—lurking, still,
Find it somewhere you must and will—
Above or below, or within or without—
And that's the reason, beyond a doubt,
A chaise *breaks down*, but doesn't *wear out.*

15 But the Deacon swore (as Deacons do,
With an "I dew vum," or an "I tell *yeou*")
He would build one shay to beat the taown
'N' the keounty 'n' all the kentry raoun';
It should be so built that it couldn' break daown.
20 —"Fur," said the Deacon, "t's mighty plain
Thut the weakes' place mus' Stan' the strain;
'N' the way t' fix it, uz I maintain, is only jest
T' make that place uz strong uz the rest."

So the Deacon inquired of the village folk
25 Where he could find the strongest oak,
That couldn't be split nor bent nor broke
That was for spokes and floor and sills;
He sent for lancewood to make the thrills;
The crossbars were ash, from the straightest trees,
30 The panels of white-wood, that cuts like cheese,
But lasts like iron for things like these;
The hubs of logs from the "Settler's ellum"—

Last of its timber—they couldn't sell 'em;
Never an ax had seen their chips;
And the wedges flew from between their lips,
Their blunt ends frizzled like celery-tips;
5 Step and prop-iron, bolt and screw,
Spring, tire, axle, and linchpin too,
Steel of the finest, bright and blue;
Thoroughbrace, bison skin, thick and wide;
Boot, top, dasher, from tough old hide
10 Found in the pit when the tanner died.
That was the way he "put her through."
"There!" said the Deacon, "naow she'll dew."

Do! I tell you, I rather guess
She was a wonder, and nothing less!
15 Colts grew horses, beards turned gray,
Deacon and deaconness dropped away,
Children and grandchildren—where were they?
But there stood the stout old one-hoss shay
As fresh as on Lisbon-earthquake-day!

20 Eighteen Hundred—it came and found
The Deacon's masterpiece strong and sound.
Eighteen hundred increased by ten—
"Hahnsum kerridge" they called it then.
Eighteen hundred and twenty came—
25 Running as usual; much the same.
Thirty and forty at last arrive,
And then came fifty, and FIFTY-FIVE.

Little of all we value here
Wakes on the morn of its hundredth year
30 Without both feeling and looking queer.
In fact, there's nothing that keeps its youth,
So far as I know, but a tree and truth.

(This is a moral that runs at large;
Take it.—You're welcome.—No extra charge.)

First of November, the Earthquake-day—
There are traces of age in the one-hoss shay,
5 A general flavor of mild decay,
But nothing local, as one may say.
There couldn't be—for the Deacon's art
Had made it so like in every part
That there wasn't a chance for one to start.
10 For the wheels were just as strong as the thills,
And the floor was just as strong as the sills,
And the panels just as strong as the floor,
And the whippletree neither less nor more,
And the back-crossbar as strong as the fore,
15 And spring and axle and hub *encore*.
And yet, as a whole, it is past a doubt
In another hour it will be *worn out!*

First of November, fifty-five!
This morning the parson takes a drive.
20 Now, small boys, get out of the way!
Here comes the wonderful one-hoss shay,
Drawn by a rat-tailed, ewe-necked bay.
"Huddup!" said the parson.—Off went they.
The parson was working his Sunday's text—
25 Had got to *fifthly*, and stopped perplexed
At what the—Moses—was coming next.
All at once the horse stood still,
Close by the meet'n'-house on the hill.

First a shiver, and then a thrill.
30 Then something decidedly like a spill—
And the parson was sitting upon a rock,
At half-past nine by the meet'n'-house clock—

Just the hour of the Earthquake shock!
What do you think the parson found,
When he got up and stared around?
The poor old chaise in a heap or mound,
5 As if it had been to the mill and ground.
You see, of course, if you're not a dunce,
How it went to pieces all at once—
All at once, and nothing first—
Just as bubbles do when they burst.

10 End of the wonderful one-hoss shay.
Logic is logic. That's all I say.

NOTES AND QUESTIONS

For **Biography** see page 322.

**Discussion.** 1. What is a chaise? 2. Explain the allusion to Lisbon.
3. What is meant by "Braddock's army"? 4. Of what besides chaises is
the statement in the second line of the third stanza true? 5. What did
the deacon determine to do? 6. Find the words that tell how the deacon
thought this could be done. 7. What woods were used in making the chaise?
8. Find the lines in which the poet mentions the only things that keep
their youth. 9. What happened on the morning of the hundredth year of
the "shay's" life? 10. Explain how the chaise went "to pieces all at once."
11. Have you ever heard of a carriage or coach that lasted one hundred
years? 12. Which is it that is funny, the thought that the chaise lasted one
hundred years, or the thought that it "went to pieces all at once"? 13. Did
you ever hear of such a happening? Do you think the poet ever heard of
such an occurrence? 14. Find lines in which the humor is furnished by
the poet's manner of telling the incident. 15. *Pronounce:* ellum; hahnsum;
encore.

**Class Reading.** Bring to class and read the selection by Holmes that
you think is his funniest.

**A Suggested Problem.** Make a program for a "Holmes Day" celebration in your school. Holmes was a member of the famous Harvard class of
1829, which held annual reunions as long as any of its members were able to
attend. In 1889, at the sixtieth anniversary, ten of the fifty-nine classmates
were still living. At these class reunions everyone looked to Holmes for
the anniversary poem; some of these anniversary poems are: "Bill and Joe"

(1851); "The Boys" (1859); "Lines" (1860); "The Smiling Listener" (1871); "The Archbishop of Gil Blas" (1879); and "After the Curfew" (1889). Some of the more interesting of these class poems, together with other selections by Holmes found or suggested in this book, will furnish material for an interesting program.

**Suggestions for Theme Topics.** 1. Present-day "newspaper fun." 2. A proposed exhibit of humorous clippings from newspapers. 3. A plan for making a collection of the best cartoons for "Cartoon Day" in your school.

## The Ballad of the Oysterman

### Oliver Wendell Holmes

It was a tall young Oysterman lives by the riverside.
His shop was just upon the bank; his boat was on the tide.
The daughter of a fisherman, that was so straight and slim,
Lived over on the other bank, right opposite to him.

5 It was the pensive Oysterman that saw a lovely maid
Upon a moonlight evening, a-sitting in the shade;
He saw her wave a handkerchief, as much as if to say,
"I'm wide awake, young Oysterman, and all the folks away."

Then up arose the Oysterman, and to himself said he,
10 "I guess I'll leave the skiff at home, for fear that folks should
    see;
I read it in the story book, that, for to kiss his dear,
Leander swam the Hellespont—and I will swim this here."

And he has leaped into the waves, and crossed the shining stream,
And he has clambered up the bank, all in the moonlight gleam;

Oh, there are kisses sweet as dew, and words as soft as rain—
But they have heard her father's steps, and in he leaps again!

Out spoke the ancient fisherman: "Oh, what was that, my
    daughter?"
"'Twas nothing but a pebble, sir, I threw into the water."
5 "And what is that, pray tell me, love, that paddles off so fast?"
"It's nothing but a porpoise, sir, that's been a-swimming past."

Out spoke the ancient fisherman: "Now bring me my harpoon!
I'll get into my fishing boat, and fix the fellow soon."
Down fell the pretty innocent, as falls a snow-white lamb;
10 Her hair drooped round her pallid cheeks, like seaweed on a clam.

Alas for those two loving ones! she waked not from her swound,
And he was taken with the cramp, and in the waves was
    drowned;
But Fate has metamorphosed them, in pity of their woe,
And now they keep an oyster shop for mermaids down below.

## NOTES AND QUESTIONS

For **Biography** see page 322.

**Discussion.** 1. This poem is a parody on the old ballads, that is, it mimics the style of these ballads in such a way as to make it absurd. In what respects does it resemble the early ballads you have read? In what ways does it differ? 2. What is the story of Leander and the Hellespont? 3. What expression used by the oysterman makes his resolve to swim across the river ludicrous, instead of heroic? 4. To what does the poet compare the pale face of the girl with the hair falling around it? 5. To what might he have compared it if he had wished to rouse your sympathy?

**Library Reading.** "The Broomstick Train," "The September Gale," and prose selections by Holmes: "My Hunt After the Captain," "The Physiology of Walking," "The Three Johns" (from Chapter III of *The Autocrat of the Breakfast-Table*).

# New England Weather

### Mark Twain

There is a sumptuous variety about the New England weather that compels the stranger's admiration—and regret. The weather is always doing something there; always attending strictly to business; always getting up new designs and trying them on
5 the people to see how they will go. But it gets through more business in spring than in any other season. In the spring I have counted one hundred thirty-six different kinds of weather within four and twenty hours. It was I who made the fame and fortune of the man who had that marvelous collection of weather on
10 exhibition at the Centennial, which so astounded the foreigners. He was going to travel around the world and get specimens from all climes. I said, "Don't do it; just come to New England on a favorable spring day." I told him what we could do in the way of style, variety, and quantity. Well, he came, and he made his
15 collection in four days. As to variety, he confessed that he got hundreds of kinds of weather that he had never heard of before. And as to quantity, after he had picked out and discarded all that was blemished in any way, he not only had weather enough, but
20 weather to spare, weather to hire out, weather to sell, weather to deposit, weather to invest, and weather to give to the poor.

Old Probabilities has a mighty reputation for accurate prophecy and thoroughly deserves it. You take up the paper and observe how crisply and confidently he checks off what today's
25 weather is going to be on the Pacific, down South, in the Middle States, in the Wisconsin region. See him sail along in the joy and pride of his power till he gets to New England, and then see his tail drop. He doesn't know what the weather is going to be in New England. Well, he mulls over it, and by and by he
30 gets out something like this: "Probable northeast to southwest

winds, varying to the southward and westward and eastward
and points between; high and low barometer, swapping around
from place to place; probable areas of rain, snow, hail, and
drought, succeeded or preceded by earthquakes with thunder
5 and lightning." Then he jots down this postscript from his
wandering mind to cover accidents: "But it is possible that the
program may be wholly changed in the meantime." Yes, one of
the brightest gems in the New England weather is the dazzling
uncertainty of it. There is certain to be plenty of weather, a
10 perfect grand review, but you never can tell which end of the
procession is going to move first. You fix up for the drought;
you leave your umbrella in the house and sally out with your
sprinkling pot, and two to one you are drowned. You make up
your mind that an earthquake is due; you stand from under and
15 take hold of something to steady yourself, and the first thing
you know you are struck by lightning.

But, after all, there are at least two or three things about
that weather (or, if you please, the effects produced by it)
which we residents would not like to part with. If we hadn't our
20 bewitching autumn foliage, we should still have to credit the
weather with one feature which compensates for all its bullying
vagaries—the ice storm. Every bough and twig is strung with
ice beads, frozen dewdrops, and the whole tree sparkles cold
and white like the Shah of Persia's diamond plume. Then the
25 wind waves the branches, and the sun comes out and turns all
those myriads of beads and drops to prisms that glow and burn
and flash with all manner of colored fires, which change and
change again, with inconceivable rapidity, from blue to red, from
red to green, and green to gold. The tree becomes a spraying
30 fountain, a very explosion of dazzling jewels, and it stands there
the acme, the climax, the supremest possibility in art or nature,
of bewildering, intoxicating, intolerable magnificence. One
cannot make the words too strong. Month after month I lay up
hate and grudge against the New England weather, but when
35 the ice storm comes at last, I say: "There, I forgive you now;

the books are square between us; you don't owe me a cent;
your little faults and foibles count for nothing; you are the most
enchanting weather in the world."

## NOTES AND QUESTIONS

**Biography.** Samuel Langhorne Clemens (1835-1910), better known
by his pen name, "Mark Twain," is America's greatest humorous writer. He
was born in the village of Florida, Missouri, and at the age of four years
moved with his parents to the town of Hannibal, where he later became a
printer and then a pilot on a Mississippi steamboat. His next venture was
in a mining camp, and although he found only a very small amount
of gold, his experiences in the West furnish the basis of some of his most
popular stories. As a newspaper reporter he chose the pen name, Mark
Twain, an old river expression meaning the mark that registers two (twain)
fathoms of water. He traveled through Europe and the Holy Land, paying
his expenses by means of a series of letters describing his trip, written
for a San Francisco newspaper. Mark Twain was for a time part owner
and associate editor of the *Buffalo Express*, but the investment was not
profitable. In his later years he spent much of his time on the lecture
platform. His most popular books are: *Tom Sawyer*, *Huckleberry Finn*,
*Roughing It*, *The Innocents Abroad*, and *The Prince and the Pauper.*

**Discussion.** 1. What do you know to be true of the New England
climate? What has the author done to this well-known fact to produce the
humor of this selection? 2. Who is meant by "Old Probabilities"? 3. In what
way does the weather forecast for New England, as outlined by the author,
differ from forecasts you read in the daily papers? 4. Why does the author
predict earthquakes for New England? 5. In what part of the selection do
you think the writer is in earnest? 6. Find the lines that describe the effect
of the sun upon the ice-covered trees. 7. What does this description tell
you about the author's powers of observation? 8. For what does he say this
beautiful sight atones? 9. How does the author make his story humorous?
Find particularly good examples of his humor. 10. Find in the glossary the
meaning of: Centennial; vagaries.

**Class Reading.** Bring to class and read some humorous selections
from recent issues of *Life*, or other magazines devoted to humor.

**Library Reading.** *Huckleberry Finn*, Mark Twain; *The Boy's Life
of Mark Twain*, Paine.

## THE RANSOM OF RED CHIEF

### O. HENRY

It looked like a good thing, but wait till I tell you. We were down south, in Alabama—Bill Driscoll and myself—when this kidnapping idea struck us. It was, as Bill afterwards expressed it, "during a moment of temporary mental apparition," but we 5 didn't find that out till later.

There was a town down there, as flat as a flannel cake, and called Summit, of course. It contained inhabitants of as undeleterious and self-satisfied a class of peasantry as ever clustered around a Maypole.

10 Bill and me had a joint capital of about six hundred dollars, and we needed just two thousand dollars more to pull off a town-lot scheme in western Illinois. We talked it over on the front steps of the hotel. Philoprogenitiveness, says we, is strong in semi-rural communities; therefore, and for other reasons, a 15 kidnapping project ought to do better there than in the radius of newspapers that send reporters out in plain clothes to stir up talk about such things. We knew that Summit couldn't get after us with anything stronger than constables and, maybe, some lackadaisical bloodhounds and a diatribe or two in the *Weekly* 20 *Farmers' Budget*. So it looked good.

We selected for our victim the only child of a prominent citizen named Ebenezer Dorset. The father was respectable and tight, a mortgage fancier and a stern, upright collection-plate passer and forecloser. The kid was a boy of ten, with bas-relief 25 freckles and hair the color of the cover of the magazine you buy at the news stand when you want to catch a train. Bill and me figured that Ebenezer would melt down for a ransom of two thousand dollars to a cent. But wait till I tell you.

About two miles from Summit was a little mountain covered

*See Silent and Oral Reading, page 13.

with a dense cedar brake. On the rear elevation of this mountain was a cave. There we stored provisions.

One evening after sundown, we drove in a buggy past old Dorset's house. The kid was in the street throwing rocks at a
5 kitten on the opposite fence.

"Hey, little boy!" says Bill, "would you like to have a bag of candy and a nice ride?"

The boy catches Bill neatly in the eye with a piece of brick.

That boy put up a fight like a welterweight cinnamon bear,
10 but at last we got him down in the bottom of the buggy and drove away. We took him up to the cave, and I hitched the horse in the cedar brake. After dark I drove the buggy to the little village, three miles away, where we had hired it, and walked back to the mountain.

15 Bill was pasting court-plaster over the scratches and bruises on his features. There was a fire burning behind the big rock at the entrance of the cave, and the boy was watching a pot of boiling coffee, with two buzzard tail feathers stuck in his red hair. He points a stick at me when I come up, and says:

20 "Ha! cursed paleface, do you dare to enter the camp of Red Chief, the terror of the plains?"

"He's all right now," says Bill, rolling up his trousers and examining some bruises on his shins. "We're playing Indian. We're making Buffalo Bill's show look like magic-lantern views
25 of Palestine in the town hall. I'm Old Hank the Trapper, Red Chief's captive, and I'm to be scalped at daybreak. By Geronimo! that kid can kick hard."

Yes, sir, that boy seemed to be having the time of his life. The fun of camping out in a cave had made him forget that he was a
30 captive himself. He immediately christened me Snake-eye the Spy and announced that when his braves returned from the warpath I was to be broiled at the stake at the rising of the sun.

Then we had supper, and he filled his mouth full of bacon and bread and gravy, and began to talk. He made a during-dinner
35 speech something like this:

"I like this fine. I never camped out before, but I had a pet 'possum once, and I was nine last birthday. I hate to go to school. Rats ate up sixteen of Jimmy Talbot's aunt's speckled hen's eggs. Are there any real Indians in these woods? I want
5 some more gravy. Does the trees moving make the wind blow? We have five puppies. What makes your nose so red, Hank? My father has lots of money. Are the stars hot? I whipped Ed Walker twice, Saturday. I don't like girls. You dassent catch toads unless with a string. Do oxen make any noise?
10 Why are oranges round? Have you got beds to sleep on in this cave? Amos Murray has got six toes. A parrot can talk, but a monkey or a fish can't. How many does it take to make twelve?"

Every few minutes he would remember that he was a pesky
15 redskin and pick up his stick rifle and tiptoe to the mouth of the cave to rubber for the scouts of the hated paleface. Now and then he would let out a war whoop that made Old Hank the Trapper shiver. That boy had Bill terrorized from the start.

"Red Chief," says I to the kid, "would you like to go home?"
20     "Aw, what for?" says he. "I don't have any fun at home. I hate to go to school. I like to camp out. You won't take me back home again, Snake-eye, will you?"

"Not right away," says I. "We'll stay here in the cave a while."
25     "All right!" says he. "That'll be fine. I never had such fun in all my life."

We went to bed about eleven o'clock. We spread down some wide blankets and quilts and put Red Chief between us. We weren't afraid he'd run away. He kept us awake for three hours,
30 jumping up and reaching for his rifle and screeching: "Hist! pard," in mine and Bill's ears, as the fancied crackle of a twig or the rustle of a leaf revealed to his young imagination the stealthy approach of the outlaw band. At last I fell into a troubled sleep and dreamed that I had been kidnapped and chained to a tree
35 by a ferocious pirate with red hair.

Just at daybreak, I was awakened by a series of awful
screams from Bill. They weren't yells, or howls, or shouts, or
whoops, or yawps, such as you'd expect from a manly set of
vocal organs—they were simply indecent, terrifying, humiliating
5 screams, such as women emit when they see ghosts or caterpil-
lars. It's an awful thing to hear a strong, desperate, fat man
scream incontinently in a cave at daybreak.

I jumped up to see what the matter was. Red Chief was
sitting on Bill's chest with one hand twined in Bill's hair. In the
10 other he had the sharp case knife we used for slicing bacon, and
he was industriously and realistically trying to take Bill's scalp,
according to the sentence that had been pronounced upon him
the evening before.

I got the knife away from the kid and made him lie down
15 again. But, from that moment, Bill's spirit was broken. He
lay down on his side of the bed, but he never closed an eye
again in sleep as long as that boy was with us. I dozed off for
a while, but along toward sunup I remembered that Red Chief
had said I was to be burned at the stake at the rising of the
20 sun. I wasn't nervous or afraid, but I sat up and lit my pipe and
leaned against a rock.

"What you getting up so soon for, Sam?" asked Bill.

"Me?" says I. "Oh, I got a kind of a pain in my shoulder. I
thought sitting up would rest it."

25    "You're a liar!" says Bill. "You're afraid. You was to be burned
at sunrise, and you was afraid he'd do it. And he would, too,
if he could find a match. Ain't it awful, Sam? Do you think
anybody will pay out money to get a little imp like that back
home?"

30    "Sure," said I. "A rowdy kid like that is just the kind that
parents dote on. Now, you and the Chief get up and cook breakfast,
while I go up on the top of this mountain and reconnoiter."

I went up on the peak of the little mountain and ran my eye
over the contiguous vicinity. Over toward Summit I expected to
35 see the sturdy yeomanry of the village armed with scythes and

pitchforks beating the countryside for the dastardly kidnappers.
But what I saw was a peaceful landscape dotted with one man
plowing with a dun mule. Nobody was dragging the creek, no
couriers dashed hither and yon, bringing tidings of no news to
5 the distracted parents. There was a sylvan attitude of somnolent
sleepiness pervading that section of the external outward surface
of Alabama that lay exposed to my view. "Perhaps," says I to
myself, "it has not yet been discovered that the wolves have
borne away the tender lambkin from the fold. Heaven help the
10 wolves!" says I, and I went down the mountain to breakfast.

When I got to the cave I found Bill backed up against the
side of it, breathing hard, and the boy threatening to smash him
with a rock half as big as a coconut.

"He put a red-hot boiled potato down my back," explained
15 Bill, "and then mashed it with his foot, and I boxed his ears.
Have you got a gun about you, Sam?"

I took the rock away from the boy and kind of patched up
the argument. "I'll fix you," says the kid to Bill. "No man ever
yet struck the Red Chief but what he got paid for it. You better
20 beware!"

After breakfast the kid takes a piece of leather with strings
wrapped around it out of his pocket and goes outside the cave
unwinding it.

"What's he up to now?" says Bill, anxiously. "You don't think
25 he'll run away, do you, Sam?"

"No fear of it," says I. "He don't seem to be much of a home-
body. But we've got to fix up some plan about the ransom.
There don't seem to be much excitement around Summit on
account of his disappearance, but maybe they haven't realized
30 yet that he's gone. His folks may think he's spending the night
with Aunt Jane or one of the neighbors. Anyhow, he'll be missed
today. Tonight we must get a message to his father demanding
the two thousand dollars for his return."

Just then we heard a kind of war whoop, such as David
35 might have emitted when he knocked out the champion Goliath.

It was a sling that Red Chief had pulled out of his pocket, and he was whirling it around his head.

I dodged, and heard a heavy thud and a kind of a sigh from Bill, like one a horse gives out when you take his saddle off. A
5 niggerhead rock the size of an egg had caught Bill just behind his left ear. He loosened himself all over and fell in the fire across the frying pan of hot water for washing the dishes. I dragged him out and poured cold water on his head for half an hour.

10 By and by, Bill sits up and feels behind his ear and says, "Sam, do you know who my favorite Biblical character is?"

"Take it easy," says I. "You'll come to your senses presently."

"King Herod," says he. "You won't go away and leave me
15 here alone, will you, Sam?"

I went out and caught that boy and shook him until his freckles rattled.

"If you don't behave," says I, "I'll take you straight home. Now, are you going to be good, or not?"

20 "I was only funning," says he sullenly. "I didn't mean to hurt Old Hank. But what did he hit me for? I'll behave, Snake-eye, if you won't send me home, and if you'll let me play the Black Scout today."

"I don't know the game," says, I. "That's for you and Mr.
25 Bill to decide. He's your playmate for the day. I'm going away for a while, on business. Now, you come in and make friends with him and say you are sorry for hurting him, or home you go, at once."

I made him and Bill shake hands, and then I took Bill aside
30 and told him I was going to Poplar Cove, a little village three miles from the cave, and find out what I could about how the kidnapping had been regarded in Summit. Also, I thought it best to send a peremptory letter to old man Dorset that day, demanding the ransom and dictating how it should be paid.

35 "You know, Sam," says Bill, "I've stood by you without batting

an eye in earthquake, fire, and flood—in poker games, dynamite outrages, police raids, train robberies, and cyclones. I never lost my nerve yet till we kidnapped that two-legged skyrocket of a kid. He's got me going. You won't leave me long with him,
5 will you, Sam?"

"I'll be back sometime this afternoon," says I. "You must keep the boy amused and quiet till I return. And now we'll write the letter to old Dorset."

Bill and I got paper and pencil and worked on the letter
10 while Red Chief, with a blanket wrapped around him, strutted up and down, guarding the mouth of the cave. Bill begged me tearfully to make the ransom fifteen hundred dollars instead of two thousand. "I ain't attempting," says he, "to decry the celebrated moral aspect of parental affection, but we're dealing
15 with humans, and it ain't human for anybody to give up two thousand dollars for that forty-pound chunk of freckled wildcat. I'm willing to take a chance at fifteen hundred dollars. You can charge the difference up to me."

So, to relieve Bill, I acceded, and we collaborated a letter
20 that ran this way:

Ebenezer Dorset, Esq.:

We have your boy concealed in a place far from Summit. It is useless for you or the most skillful detectives to attempt to find him. Absolutely the only terms on which you can have him restored to you are these: We
25 demand fifteen hundred dollars in large bills for his return; the money to be left at midnight tonight at the same spot and in the same box as your reply—as hereinafter described. If you agree to these terms, send your answer in writing by a solitary messenger tonight at half-past eight o'clock. After crossing Owl Creek, on the road to Poplar Cove, there are three large
30 trees about a hundred yards apart, close to the fence of the wheat field on the right-hand side. At the bottom of the fence post, opposite the third tree, will be found a small pasteboard box.

The messenger will place the answer in this box and return immediately to Summit.
35     If you attempt any treachery or fail to comply with our demand as stated, you will never see your boy again.

If you pay the money as demanded, he will be returned to you safe and well within three hours. These terms are final, and if you do not accede to them, no further communication will be attempted.

Two Desperate Men.

5    I addressed this letter to Dorset and put it in my pocket. As I was about to start, the kid comes up to me and says:

"Aw, Snake-eye, you said I could play the Black Scout while you was gone."

"Play it, of course," says I. "Mr. Bill will play with you. What 10 kind of a game is it?"

"I'm the Black Scout," says Red Chief, "and I have to ride to the stockade to warn the settlers that the Indians are coming. I'm tired of playing Indian myself. I want to be the Black Scout."

15    "All right," says I. "It sounds harmless to me. I guess Mr. Bill will help you foil the pesky savages."

"What am I to do?" asks Bill, looking at the kid suspiciously.

"You are the hoss," says Black Scout. "Get down on your hands and knees. How can I ride to the stockade without a 20 hoss?"

"You'd better keep him interested," said I, "till we get the scheme going. Loosen up."

Bill gets down on his all fours, and a look comes in his eyes like a rabbit's when you catch it in a trap.

25    "How far is it to the stockade, kid?" he asks, in a husky manner of voice.

"Ninety miles," says the Black Scout. "And you have to hump yourself to get there on time. Whoa, now!"

The Black Scout jumps on Bill's back and digs his heels in 30 his side.

"For Heaven's sake," says Bill, "hurry back, Sam, as soon as you can. I wish we hadn't made the ransom more than a thousand. Say, you quit kicking me, or I'll get up and warm you good."

35    I walked over to Poplar Cove and sat around the post office

and store, talking with the chawbacons that come in to trade.
One whiskerando says that he hears Summit is all upset on
account of Elder Ebenezer Dorset's boy having been lost or
stolen. That was all I wanted to know. I bought some smoking
5 tobacco, referred casually to the price of black-eyed peas, posted
my letter surreptitiously, and came away. The postmaster said
the mail carrier would come by in an hour to take the mail on
to Summit.

When I got back to the cave Bill and the boy were not to be
10 found. I explored the vicinity of the cave and risked a yodel or
two, but there was no response. So I lighted my pipe and sat
down on a mossy bank to await developments.

In about half an hour I heard the bushes rustle, and Bill
wabbled out into the little glade in front of the cave. Behind
15 him was the kid, stepping softly like a scout, with a broad grin
on his face. Bill stopped, took off his hat, and wiped his face
with a red handkerchief. The kid stopped about eight feet
behind him.

"Sam," says Bill, "I suppose you'll think I'm a renegade, but I
20 couldn't help it. I'm a grown person with masculine proclivities
and habits of self-defense, but there is a time when all systems
of egotism and predominance fail. The boy is gone. I have sent
him home. All is off. There was martyrs in old times," goes
on Bill, "that suffered death rather than give up the particular
25 graft they enjoyed. None of 'em ever was subjugated to such
supernatural tortures as I have been. I tried to be faithful to our
articles of depredation, but there came a limit."

"What's the trouble, Bill?" I asks him.

"I was rode," says Bill, "the ninety miles to the stockade,
30 not barring an inch. Then when the settlers was rescued, I was
given oats. Sand ain't a palatable substitute. And then, for
an hour I had to try to explain to him why there was nothin'
in holes, how a road can run both ways, and what makes the
grass green. I tell you, Sam, a human can only stand so much.
35 I takes him by the neck of his clothes and drags him down the

mountain. On the way he kicks my legs black-and-blue from the knees down, and I've got two or three bites on my thumb and hand cauterized."

"But he's gone"—continues Bill—"gone home. I showed him
5 the road to Summit and kicked him about eight feet nearer there at one kick. I'm sorry we lose the ransom, but it was either that or Bill Driscoll to the madhouse."

"Bill," says I, "there isn't any heart disease in your family, is there?"

10 "No," says Bill, "nothing chronic except malaria and accidents. Why?"

"Then you might turn around," says I, "and have a look behind you."

Bill turns and sees the boy and loses his complexion and
15 sits down plump on the ground and begins to pluck aimlessly at grass and little sticks. For an hour I was afraid for his mind. And then I told him that my scheme was to put the whole job through immediately and that we would get the ransom and be off with it by midnight if old Dorset fell in with our proposition.
20 So Bill braced up enough to give the kid a weak sort of a smile and a promise to play the Russian in a Japanese war with him as soon as he felt a little better.

I had a scheme for collecting that ransom without danger of being caught by counterplots that ought to commend itself to
25 professional kidnappers. The tree under which the answer was to be left—and the money later on—was close to the road fence with big, bare fields on all sides. If a gang of constables should be watching for anyone to come for the note they could see him a long way off crossing the fields or in the road. But no sirree!
30 At half-past eight I was up in that tree as well hidden as a tree toad, waiting for the messenger to arrive.

Exactly on time, a half-grown boy rides up the road on a bicycle, locates the pasteboard box at the foot of the fence post, slips a folded piece of paper into it, and pedals away again back
35 toward Summit.

I waited an hour and then concluded the thing was square.
I slid down the tree, got the note, slipped along the fence till I
struck the woods, and was back at the cave in another half an
hour. I opened the note, got near the lantern, and read it to
5 Bill. It was written with a pen in a crabbed hand, and the sum
and substance of it was this:

Two Desperate Men.

Gentlemen: I received your letter today by post, in regard to the
ransom you ask for the return of my son. I think you are a little high in
10 your demands, and I hereby make you a counter-proposition, which I am
inclined to believe you will accept. You bring Johnny home and pay me
two hundred and fifty dollars in cash, and I agree to take him off your
hands. You had better come at night, for the neighbors believe he is lost,
and I couldn't be responsible for what they would do to anybody they saw
15 bringing him back.

Very respectfully,
Ebenezer Dorset.

"Great pirates of Penzance!" says I, "of all the impudent—"
But I glanced at Bill and hesitated. He had the most appeal-
20 ing look in his eyes I ever saw on the face of a dumb or a talking
brute.

"Sam," says he, "what's two hundred and fifty dollars, after
all? We've got the money. One more night of this kid will send
me to a bed in Bedlam. Besides being a thorough gentleman,
25 I think Mr. Dorset is a spendthrift for making us such a liberal
offer. You ain't going to let the chance go, are you?"

"Tell you the truth, Bill," says I, "this little he ewe lamb has
somewhat got on my nerves, too. Well take him home, pay the
ransom, and make our getaway."

30 We took him home that night. We got him to go by telling
him that his father had bought a silver-mounted rifle and a
pair of moccasins for him, and we were going to hunt bears
the next day.

It was just twelve o'clock when we knocked at Ebenezer's

front door. Just at the moment when I should have been abstracting the fifteen hundred dollars from the box under the tree, according to the original proposition, Bill was counting out two hundred and fifty dollars into Dorset's hand.

5     When the kid found out we were going to leave him at home he started up a howl like a calliope and fastened himself as tight as a leech to Bill's leg. His father peeled him away gradually, like a porous plaster.

"How long can you hold him?" asks Bill.

10     "I'm not so strong as I used to be," says old Dorset, "but I think I can promise you ten minutes."

"Enough," says Bill. "In ten minutes I shall cross the Central, Southern, and Middle Western States, and be legging it trippingly for the Canadian border."

15     And, as dark as it was, and as fat as Bill was, and as good a runner as I am, he was a good mile and a half out of Summit before I could catch up with him.

## NOTES AND QUESTIONS

**Biography.** William Sidney Porter (1862-1910), better known by his pen name, O. Henry, was born in Greensboro, North Carolina. As a child he read widely and showed a natural gift for sketching. While a mere boy, he went to Texas, where he spent two years on a sheep ranch. He became a reporter for the *Daily Post* of Houston, Texas, and later wrote extensively for the leading magazines. In 1902 he went to New York City to live, and from that time on he devoted himself almost exclusively to short story writing. O. Henry holds a prominent place among the world's great short story writers. Among his well known books are *Whirligigs*, from which this story is taken, *Heart of the West*, portraying life in Texas, and *The Four Million*. His stories are mainly drawn from real situations, and they picture the various types found in American life. They are noted for the surprises that characterize their endings and for their human sympathy.

**Discussion.** 1. Show that this is a typical short story. 2. What is the climax? 3. Can you think of an outcome that would furnish greater surprise than the proposals contained in Dorset's letter? 4. Find examples of comic exaggeration. 5. What other selection by this author have you read? 6. What did you learn in the "Introduction," pages 337 and 338, about the value to America of the spirit of laughter and good humor? What evidence do you find in newspapers and magazines that humor plays a prominent part in American thought today? 7. Find in the glossary the meaning of: apparition; diatribe; welterweight; incontinently; surreptitiously; renegade; counter-proposition. 8. *Pronounce:* bas-relief; reconnoiter; contiguous; somnolent; casually; palatable.

### Phrases for Study

| | |
|---|---|
| mental apparition, **464**, 4 | King Herod, **469**, 14 |
| mortgage fancier, **464**, 23 | articles of depredation, **472**, 27 |

**Class Reading.** Make a list of passages containing good examples of humor to be read aloud in class.

**Outline for Testing Silent Reading.** Make an outline to guide you in telling the story.

**Library Reading.** Other stories from *Whirligigs*.

**Newspaper Reading.** Bring to class and read the best example of a humorous short story you can find in a newspaper or a magazine.

# AMERICAN WORKERS AND THEIR WORK

## Work: A Song of Triumph

### Angela Morgan

Work!
Thank God for the might of it,
The ardor, the urge, the delight of it—
Work that springs from the heart's desire,
5 Setting the brain and the soul on fire—
Oh, what is so good as the heat of it,
And what is so glad as the beat of it,
And what is so kind as the stern command,
Challenging brain and heart and hand?

10 Work!
Thank God for the pride of it,
For the beautiful, conquering tide of it,
Sweeping the life in its furious flood,
Thrilling the arteries, cleansing the blood,
15 Mastering stupor and dull despair,

Moving the dreamer to do and dare.
Oh, what is so good as the urge of it,
And what is so glad as the surge of it,
And what is so strong as the summons deep,
5 Rousing the torpid soul from sleep?

Work!
Thank God for the pace of it,
For the terrible, keen, swift race of it;
Fiery steeds in full control,
10 Nostrils a-quiver to greet the goal.
Speeding the energies faster, faster,
Work, the Power that drives behind,
Guiding the purposes, taming the mind,
Holding the runaway wishes back,
15 Reining the will to one steady track,
Triumphing over disaster.
Oh, what is so good as the pain of it,
And what is so great as the gain of it?
And what is so kind as the cruel goad,
20 Forcing us on through the rugged road?

Work!
Thank God for the swing of it,
For the clamoring, hammering ring of it,
Passion of labor daily hurled
25 On the mighty anvils of the world.
Oh, what is so fierce as the flame of it?
And what is so huge as the aim of it?
Thundering on through dearth and doubt,
Calling the plan of the Maker out.
30 Work, the Titan; Work, the friend,
Shaping the earth to a glorious end,
Draining the swamps and blasting the hills,
Doing whatever the Spirit wills—

Rending a continent apart,
To answer the dream of the Master heart.
Thank God for a world where none may shirk—
Thank God for the splendor of work!

## NOTES AND QUESTIONS

**Biography.** Angela Morgan was born in New England, spent most of her childhood in the Middle West, and in her youth entered upon a career in journalism. Her warm sympathy for the industrial worker and her keen interest in social reforms make her a poet of the people. Some of her best known poems are "Wood Hath a Soul" and "Open the Gates" in *Forward March!* and "Today," and "Kinship" in *The Hour Has Struck*, from which "Work: A Song of Triumph" is taken.

**Discussion.** 1. To what is work compared in the first stanza? 2. What is meant by the "stern command" which challenges "brain and heart and hand"? 3. What does work do to stupor and despair? What does work do for the dreamer? 4. Read the third stanza so that you feel the swift pace of the horses to which your purpose, your mind, and your will are compared. 5. Who is the driver? 6. What is meant by the expression "runaway wishes"? 7. How does work hold them back? 8. What is meant by "reining the will"? 9. What may the goad be which forces us on? 10. To what is work compared in the first part of the fourth stanza? 11. Who were the Titans? 12. Why are swamps drained? 13. When is it necessary to blast hills? 14. The making of what great canals may be described as "rending a continent apart"? 15. What other great achievements can you mention as the result of man's work? 16. Why should everyone do his part of the world's work? 17. In the "Introduction" on page 338 what is said to be the secret of our national prosperity? What is said about the need for cooperation? Point out lines in this poem that express somewhat the same ideas. 18. Find in the glossary the meaning of: torpid; taming; goad.

**Library Reading.** "The Telephone Directory" and "The Power Plant," Braley (in *Songs of a Workaday World*); *Famous Leaders of Industry,* Wildman; *Heroes of Progress*, Morris; *Modern Americans*, Sanford and Owen; *The Silver Horde*, Beach; *Pictures of the Wonder of Work*, Pennell; the magazine *The World's Work;* Biography of Angela Morgan, *The Review of Reviews* for April, 1919.

## PETE OF THE STEEL MILLS*

HERSCHEL S. HALL                    .

It was a very black and a very dirty street down which I made my way that November morning at half-past five. There was no paving, there was no sidewalk, there were no lights. Rain had been falling for several days, and I waded through seas of
5 mud and sloshed through lakes of water. There were men in front of me and men behind me, all plodding along through the muck and mire, just as I was plodding along, their tin lunch pails rattling as mine was rattling. Some of us were going to work, some of us were going to look for work—the steel mills
10 lay somewhere in the darkness ahead of us.

We who were not so fortunate as to possess a magical piece of brass, the showing of which to a uniformed guard at the steel mills' gate would cause the door to swing open, waited outside in the street, where we milled about in the mud, not unlike a
15 herd of uneasy cattle. It was cold out there. A north wind, blowing straight in from the lake, whipped our faces and hands and penetrated our none-too-heavy clothing.

"I wisht I had a job in there!" said a shivering man at my side, who had been doing some inspecting through a knothole
20 in the high fence. "You got a job there?" he asked, glancing at my pail. I told him I had been promised work and had been ordered to report.

"You're lucky to get a job, and you want to freeze on to it. Jobs ain't to be any too plentiful this winter, and if this war
25 stops—good-night! I've been comin' here every mornin' for two weeks, but I can't get took. I reckon I'm kind o' small for most of the work in there." He began to kick his muddy shoes against the fence and to blow upon his hands. "Winter's comin'," he sighed.

---

*See Silent and Oral Reading, page 13.

A whistle blew, a gate swung open, and a mob of men poured out into the street—the night shift going off duty. Their faces looked haggard and deathly pale in the sickly glare of the pale blue arcs above us.

5     "Night-work's no good," said the small man at my side. "But you got to do it if you're goin' to work in the mills."

A man with a Turkish towel thrown loosely about his neck came out of the gate and looked critically at the job hunters. He came up to me. "What's yer name?" he demanded. I told
10 him. "Come on!" he grunted.

We stopped before the uniformed guard, who wrote my name on a card, punched the card, and gave it to me. "Come on!" again grunted the man with the towel. I followed my guide into the yard, over railroad tracks, past great piles of scrap iron
15 and pig metal, through clouds of steam and smoke, and into a long, black building where engines whistled, bells clanged, and electric cranes rumbled and rattled overhead. We skirted a mighty pit filled with molten slag, and the hot air and stifling fumes blowing from it struck me in the face and staggered me.
20 We crept between giant ladles, in whose depths I could hear the banging of hammers and the shouting of men. We passed beneath a huge trough through which a white, seething river of steel was rushing. I shrank back in terror as the sound of the roaring flood fell upon my ears, but the man with the towel,
25 who was walking briskly in front of me, looked over his shoulder and grunted, "Come on!"

Through a long, hot tunnel and past black, curving flues, down which I saw red arms of flame reaching, we made our way. We came to an iron stairway, climbed it, and stepped out upon a
30 steel floor into the open hearth. "Come on!" growled my guide, and we walked down the steel floor, scattered over which I saw groups of men at work in front of big, house-like furnaces out of whose cavernous mouths white tongues of flame were leaping. The men worked naked to the waist, or stripped to
35 overalls and undershirt, and, watching them, I began to wonder

if I had chosen wisely in seeking and accepting employment in this inferno.

"Put yer pail there. Hang yer coat there. Set down there. I'll tell the boss ye're here." And the man with the towel went
5 away.

I was sitting opposite one of the furnaces, a square, squat structure of yellow brick built to hold seventy-five tons of steel. There were three doors on the front wall, each door having a round opening in the center, the "peephole." Out through these
10 peepholes poured shafts of light so white and dazzling they pained the eye they struck. They were as the glaring orbs of some gigantic uncouth monster, and as I looked down the long line of furnaces and saw the three fiery eyes burning in each, the effect through the dark, smoke-laden atmosphere was
15 grotesquely weird.

I watched a man who worked at one of the doors of the furnace nearest me. He had thrust a bar of iron through the peephole and was jabbing and prying at some object inside. Every ounce of his strength he was putting into his efforts.
20 I could hear him grunt as he pulled and pushed, and I saw the perspiration dripping from his face and naked arms. He withdrew the bar—the end that had been inside the door came out as white and as pliable as a hank of taffy—and dropped it to the floor. He shouted some command to an invisible person, and
25 the door rose slowly and quietly, disclosing to me a great, snow-white cavern in whose depths bubbled and boiled a seething lake of steel.

With a quick movement of his hand the workman dropped a pair of dark-colored spectacles before his eyes, and his arms
30 went up before his face to shield it from the withering blast that poured out through the open door. There he stood, silhouetted against that piercing light, stooping and peering, tiptoeing and bending, cringing and twisting, as he tried to examine something back in the furnace. Then with another shout he caused the
35 door to slip down into its place.

He came walking across the floor to where I sat and stopped in front of me. The sweat in great drops fell from his blistered face, ran in tiny rivulets from his arms and hands, and splashed on the iron floor. He trembled, he gasped for breath, and I 5 thought he was going to sink down from pure exhaustion, when, to my surprise, he deliberately winked at me.

"Ought never to have left the farm, ought we? Eh, Buddy?" he said with a sweaty chuckle. And that was my introduction to Pete, the best open-hearth man I ever knew, a good fellow, 10 clean and honest.

"Mike, put this guy to wheeling in manganese," said a voice behind me, and I turned and saw the boss. "Eighteen hundred at Number Four and twenty-two hundred at Number Six."

"Get that wheelbarrer over yender and foller me," instructed 15 Mike, a little, old, white-haired Irishman who was, as I learned afterward, called "maid of all work" about the plant. I picked up the heavy iron wheelbarrow and trundled it after him, out through a runway to a detached building where the various alloys and refractories used in steel-making were kept.

20 "Now, then, you load your wheelbarrer up with this here ma'ganese and weigh it over on them scales yender, and then wheel it in and put it behind Number Four," Mike told me.

"Why is manganese put into steel?" I asked Pete on one of my trips past his furnace.

25 "It settles it, toughens it up, and makes it so it'll roll," he answered.

A few days later I asked one of the chemists about the plant the same question. "It absorbs the occluded gases in the molten steel, hardens it, and imparts the properties of ductility and 30 malleability," was his reply. I preferred Pete's elucidation.

All day I trundled the iron wheelbarrow back and forth along the iron floor, wheeling in manganese. I watched the powerful electric cranes at work picking up the heavy boxes of material and dumping their contents into the furnaces. I watched the 35 tapping of the "heats," when the dams holding in the boiling

lakes would be broken down and the fiery floods would go rushing and roaring into the ladles, these to be whisked away to the ingot molds. And I watched the men at work, saw the strain they were under, saw the risks they took, and wondered if, after
5 a few days, I could be doing what they were doing.

"It is all very interesting," I said to Pete, as I stood near him, waiting for a crane to pass by.

He grinned. "Uh-huh ! But you'll get over it. 'Bout tomorrow mornin', when your clock goes rattlety-bang and you look to see
10 what's up and find it's five o'clock, you'll not be thinkin' it so interestin', oh, no! Let's see your hands." He laughed when he saw the blisters the handles of the wheelbarrow had developed.

Pete was right. When my alarm clock awakened me next morning and I started to get out of bed I groaned in agony.
15 Every muscle of my body ached. I fancied my joints creaked as I sat on the edge of the couch vainly endeavoring to get them to working freely and easily. The breakfast bell rang twice, but hurry I could not.

"You'll be late to work! The others have gone!" called the
20 landlady. I managed to creak downstairs. My pail was packed and she had tied up an extra lunch in a newspaper. "You can't stop to eat, if you want to get to work on time," she said. "Your breakfast is in this paper—eat it when you get to the mills."

I stumbled away in the darkness, groaning and gasping, and
25 found my way to the black and dirty street. The mud was frozen hard now, and the pools of water were ice covered, and my heavy working shoes thumped and bumped along the dismal road in a remarkably noisy manner.

The number of job hunters was larger this morning. Among
30 them I saw the small man who could not "get took," and again he was peeking wishfully through the knothole in the fence.

"You're on, eh?" he said when he spied me. "I wisht I was. Say, you haven't got a dime you could spare a feller, have you?" I discovered a dime.

35        I showed my brass check—a timekeeper had given me one

the day before, Number 1266—to the uniformed watchman. He waved me on, and I entered the gate just as the whistle blew. A minute later and I would have been docked a half-hour.

Mike, "maid of all work," took me in hand as soon as I came
5 on the floor and proceeded to give me a few pointers. "I kept me eye on ye all day yestiddy, and ye fair disgoosted me with the way ye cavorted round with the Irish buggy. As though ye wanted to do it all the first day! Now, ye're on a twelve-hour turn here, and ye ain't expected to work like a fool. Ye want
10 to learn to spell. (Mike wasn't referring to my orthographic shortcomings.) Ye'll get in bad with the boss if he sees ye chinnin' with Pete. He don't like Pete, and Pete don't like him, and I don't blame Pete. The boss is solid bone from the collar button up. He has brainstorms. Watch out for 'em."
15 I followed much of Mike's advice. All that day I trundled the wheelbarrow, but I made an easier day of it, and no one objected to my work. And as the days ran by I found my muscles toughening, and I could hear the alarm-bell at five in the morning without feeling compelled to squander several valuable minutes
20 in wishing I had been born rich.

For two weeks I worked every day at wheeling in materials for the furnaces. Then for one week I worked with the "maid of all work," sweeping the floors and keeping the place "righted up," as he called it. Then I "pulled doors" for a while; I "ran tests"
25 to the laboratory; I "brought stores"; I was general-utility man. Then one day, when a workman dropped a piece of pig-iron on his foot and was sent to the hospital, I was put on "second helping."

By good luck I was sent to Pete's furnace. Pete and I by this
30 time were great cronies. Many a chat we had had, back behind his furnace, hidden from the prying eyes of the boss. I found Mike was right—it was just as well to keep out of his sight. I soon discovered that he did not like Pete. In numberless mean and petty ways did he harass the man, trying to make him do something
35 that would give him an excuse to discharge him. But Pete was

naturally slow to anger, and with admirable strength he kept his feelings under control.

I was working nights now, every other week. The small man at the gate—he had finally "got took" and was laboring in 5 the yard gang—who had told me that "night work is no good" knew what he was talking about. I found night work absolutely "no good." The small hours of the night are the terror of the night worker.

To be aroused by a screaming whistle above your head at 10 two o'clock in the morning; to seize a shovel and run to the open door of a white-hot furnace and there in its blistering heat to shovel in heavy ore and crushed limestone rock until every stitch of clothing on your body is soaked with perspiration; to stagger away with pulses thumping, and drop down upon a bench, 15 only to be ordered out into a nipping winter air to raise or lower a gas valve—this is the kind of work the poet did not have in mind when he wrote about "Toil that ennobles!" I doubt whether he or any other poet ever heard of this two-o'clock-in-the-morning toil.

20     When the "heat" was ready to tap I would dig out the "taphole." Another "second helper" would assist me in this work. The taphole, an opening in the center and lower part of the back wall of the furnace, is about a foot in diameter and three in length. It is closed with magnesite and dolomite when the 25 furnace is charged. Digging this filling out is dangerous work; the steel is likely to break out and burn the men who work there. When we had removed the dolomite from the hole I would notify the boss. A long, heavy bar was thrust through the peephole in the middle door, and a dozen men would "Ye-ho! Ye-ho!" back 30 and forth on the bar until it broke through the fused bank of magnesite into the taphole. Then the lake of steel would pour out through a runner into the ladle.

This tapping a "heat" is a magnificent and startling sight to the newcomer. I stood fascinated when I beheld it the first time. 35 A lake of seventy-five or eighty tons of sun-white steel, bursting

out of furnace bounds and rushing through the runner, a raging river, is a terrifying spectacle. The eye aches as it watches it; the body shrinks away from the burning heat it throws far out on all sides; the imagination runs riot as the seething flood roils
5 and boils in the ladle.

Sometimes when we had had a particularly hard spell of work and were dead beat with fatigue and exhaustion, then Pete might be expected to put his well-known question: "Ought to have stayed on the farm, oughtn't we? Hey, buddy?"
10 The foolish question, and his comical way of asking it, always made me laugh. Seeing that Pete had once been a farm laborer, the remark does not appear so silly, after all. It was his way of comparing two kinds of work; it was his favorite stock jest. I know farm work, too, from pigs to potatoes, and I do not believe
15 there is any kind of farm work known, ten hours of which would equal thirty minutes of "splashing" on an open-hearth furnace, in muscle-tearing, nerve-racking, back-breaking, sweat-bringing effort.

Pete and I were working on Number Three furnace, the
20 latest type and the "fastest" of any in the group. Its monthly output was three or four hundred tons more than that of any other. It belonged to Pete by rights—he was the oldest man on the floor, and he was regarded by all the other furnace men as the best "first helper" in the plant. No other "first helper"
25 watched his roof so carefully as did he. No other could get as many heats "from a roof" as did he. For every three hundred and fifty heats tapped from a furnace before the furnace required a new roof, the company gave the "first helper" a bonus of fifty dollars. This was to encourage them to watch their furnaces
30 closely, to see that the gas did not "touch" the roofs.

One morning Pete and I were notified that we were transferred to Number Ten, the oldest, the slowest, and hardest furnace to work of any. "Bulger" Lewis, a Welshman, a bosom friend of the boss, was to take Number Three. Pete would lose
35 the bonus money due in thirty days.

"What's this for?" he demanded of the boss.

"Because you don't watch your furnace!" snarled the boss in reply. "You've touched that roof! There are icicles on it right now!"

5      Pete walked over to the air valves, jerked the lever, and threw up the middle door. "Show me an icicle in there!" he cried. "I'll give you five hundred dollars for every one you point out!"

"Lower that door!" roared the boss. "And get down to
10  Number Ten! Or go get your time, if you prefer!"

Pete was silent for a moment. Then he threw up his head and laughed. Going to his locker, he took out his lunch pail and started for Number Ten.

"I rather think I am goin' to take a trip back to Minnesota
15  pretty soon—to see the folks, you know," he said to me that afternoon.

Number Ten melted "soft" that day, and Pete could not get the heat hot. We pigged steadily for two hours, but it remained cold and dead. We were played out when, about four o'clock,
20  the boss came up.

"Why don't you get that heat out?" he demanded. "You've been ten hours on it already!" Pete made no reply. "Where's a test bar?" He shoved the test bar into the bath, moved it slowly back and forth, and withdrew it. "She's hot now! Take
25  her out!"

Pete looked at the end of the bar. It was ragged, not bitten off clean as it would have been had the temperature of the bath been right. "She's a long way from bein' hot," he said, pointing at the test bar.

30      "Don't you dispute me!" roared the boss. "If I say she's hot, she's hot! If I tell you to take her out, you take her out!"

We took out the heat. And a miserable mess there was. It was so cold it froze up in the taphole, it froze up in the runner, it froze up in the ladle. The entire heat was lost. It was an
35  angry crew of men that worked with sledges, bars, and picks,

cleaning up the mess. I was sorry the boss could not know how much that bunch of men loved him.

I saw him approaching Pete; I saw him shaking his clenched fist; I heard an ugly word; the lie was passed, a blow was struck, 5 and the long-expected fight was on.

Out on the smooth iron floor, in the glare of the furnace flames—someone had hoisted the three doors to the top—the two enemies fought it out. They were giants in build, both of them, muscled and thewed like gladiators. It was a brutal, 10 savage exhibition. Finally, the boss reeled, dropped to his knees, swayed back and forth, and went down.

Pete, having floored the boss, took a bath, changed his clothes, shook hands all round, and came seeking me. "Well, buddy, I'm off," he chuckled, peeping at me from a chink in 15 his swollen face. "Like as not I'll be shuckin' punkins up in Minnesota this time next week. Oh, no use my tryin' to stick it out here—you can't stay here, you know, when you've had a go with the boss. So long!"

I did not go to work the next day, nor the next. I was 20 deliberating whether I would go back at all, the morning of the third day, when the "maid of all work" came looking for me. "Pete wants you to come to work," he announced.

"Pete?" I said, wondering what he meant.

"You said it! Pete's boss now!"

25       "No!"

"Yes! Oh, the super, he ain't blind, he ain't! He knowed what was goin' on, he did, and it didn't take him long to fix him when he'd heerd the peticlars. I'll tell Pete you'll be comin' along soon." And Mike departed.

30       I went back and resumed my old position on Number Three, with John Yakabowski, a Pole. Yakabowski was an exceptionally able furnace man and an agreeable fellow workman. There was great rejoicing all over the plant because our old boss was out, and there was general satisfaction over Pete's appointment 35 to his place. This feeling among the men was soon reflected

in the output of the furnaces—our tonnage showed a steady increase.

Pete was nervous and ill at ease for a few weeks. To assume the responsibilities that go with the foremanship of an open-
5 hearth plant the size of that one was almost too much for him. He was afraid he would make some mistake that would show him to be unworthy of the trust the superintendent had placed in him.

"No education—that's where I'm weak!" he said to me in one of
10 our confidential chats. "Can't write, can't figger, can't talk—don't know nothin'! It's embarrassin'! The super tells me to use two thousand of manganese on a hundred-and-fifty-thousand-pound charge. That's easy—I just tell a hunky to wheel in two thousand. But s'pose that lunk-head out in them scales goes wrong, and
15 charges in a hundred and sixty-five thousand pounds and doesn't tell me until ten minutes before we're ready to tap—how am I goin' to figger out how much more manganese to put in? Or when the chief clerk writes me a nice letter, requestin' a state-ment showin' how many of my men have more than ten children,
20 how many of 'em can read the Declaration of Independence, and how many of 'em eat oatmeal for breakfast, why, I'm up against it, I tell you! No education! I reckon I ought never to've left the farm. Hey, buddy?"

I understood Pete's gentle hint, and I took care of his clerical
25 work, writing what few letters he had to send out, making up his statements, doing his calculating, and so forth.

Six months passed. Pete had "made good." The manage-ment was highly pleased with him as a melter. Success had come to me, too, in a modest way—I had been given a fur-
30 nace—I was now a "first helper." It was about the time I took the furnace that I began to notice a falling off in the number of requests from Pete for assistance. I thought little of it, supposing that he was getting his work done by one of the weighers. But one night when there was a lull in operations and
35 I went down to his office to have a chat with him, I found him

seated at his little desk poring over an arithmetic. Scattered about in front of him were a number of sheets of paper covered with figures. He looked up at me and grinned in a rather shamefaced manner.

5 "Oh, that's it, is it?" I said. "Now I understand why I am no longer of any use to the boss!"

"Well, I just had to do somethin'," he laughed. "Couldn't afford to go right on bein' an ignoramus all the time."

"Are you studying it out alone?"

10 "You bet I ain't. I'd never get there if I was! I've got a teacher, a private teacher. Swell, eh? He comes every other night, when I'm workin' days, and every other afternoon, when I'm workin' nights. Gee, but I'm a bonehead! He's told me so a dozen times, but the other day he said he thought I was 15 softenin' up a bit."

Good old Pete! I left him that night with my admiration for the man increased a hundred times.

Another six months passed, six months of hard, grinding, wearing toil, and yet a six months I look back upon with genuine 20 pleasure. I now had the swing of the work and it came easy; conditions about the plant under Pete's supervision were ideal; I was making progress in the work I had adopted; we were making good money. Then came the black day.

How quickly it happened! I had tapped my furnace, and the 25 last of the heat had run into the ladle. "Hoist away!" I heard Pete shout to the crane man. The humming sound of the crane motors getting into action came to my ears. I took a look at my roof, threw in a shovelful of spar, turned on the gas, and walked toward the rear of the furnace. The giant crane was groaning 30 and whining as it slowly lifted its eighty-ton burden from the pit where the ladle stood. It was then five or six feet above the pit's bottom. Pete was leaning over the railing of the platform directly in front of the rising ladle.

Suddenly something snapped up there among the shafts 35 and cables. I saw two men in the crane cab go swarming up the escape ladder. I saw the ladle drop as a broken cable went flying out of a sheave. A great white wave of steel washed over the ladle's rim, and another, and another.

5 Down upon a shallow pool of water that a leaking hose had formed, the steel was splashed, and as it struck, the explosion came. I was blown from my feet and rolled along the floor. The air was filled with bits of fiery steel, slag, brick, and debris of all kinds. I crawled to shelter behind a column and there beat out the flames that were burning my clothing in a half-dozen places. 10 Then, groping through the pall of dust and smoke that choked the building, I went to look for Pete.

Near the place where I had seen him standing when the ladle fell I found him. Two workmen, who had been crouching behind a wall when the explosion came, and were unhurt, were 15 tearing his burning clothes from his seared and blackened body. Somebody brought a blanket, and we wrapped it about him. We doubted if he lived, but as we carried him back I noted he was trying to speak, and stooping, I caught the words: "Ought never to have left the farm, ought we? Hey, buddy?"

20 That was the last time I ever heard Pete speak. That was the last time I ever saw him alive.

Two o'clock in the morning. Sitting at the little desk where I found Pete that night poring over his arithmetic, I have been writing down my early experiences in the open hearth. Here 25 comes Yakabowski with a test. I know exactly what he will say: "Had I better give her a dose of ore?" Two o'clock in the morning! The small man at the gate was right: Nightwork is no good!

I was mistaken; Yakabowski doesn't ask his customary ques-30 tion. He looks at me curiously. "You don't look good, boss," he says. "You sick, maybe?"

Yes, I'm sick—I always am at two o'clock in the morning, when I'm on the night shift. I stretch, I yawn, I shudder.

"Ought never to have left the farm, ought we? Hey, Yak-35 abowski?" I say to the big Pole.

## NOTES AND QUESTIONS

**Biography.** Herschel S. Hall (1874-1921), a writer of short stories and novels, was born in Indiana, but spent most of his life in Ohio. His firsthand knowledge of work in the steel mills made his descriptions of great value. Mr. Hall is the author of *Steel Preferred*, and he was a frequent contributor to many magazines. This story appeared in *Scribner's Magazine* for April, 1919.

**Discussion.** 1. Notice how the author makes the story seem real by vivid pictures; by the conversation of the men; by making clear the difficulty of the work, amidst the heat and the noise, through describing the effects they produce; find examples of these devices. 2. What do you admire most in Pete's conduct? 3. What do you learn from this story about the work in the steel mills? 4. Make a list of humorous passages. 5. Does the language of the workers seem suited to the speakers? 6. What did Mike mean when he advised the author "to learn to spell"? 7. Find the lines on page 486 where the author speaks humorously about the poet's idea of work. Do you think the author would seriously doubt the truth of Angela Morgan's poem "Work: A Song of Triumph"? 8. How is the heroism of toil shown in this story? 9. What were you told in "Literature and Life," pages 19 and 20, about literature as a source of learning the "facts of life"? How does this story give you a clearer idea of the "facts of life" in a great steel mill than you could gain from your geography or from an encyclopedia? 10. Find in the glossary the meaning of: alloys; ductility; malleability; elucidation; fused; bonus. 11. *Pronounce:* orthographic; laboratory; harass; admirable; ignoramus; genuine; debris; column.

**Outline for Testing Silent Reading.** Tell the story, following this outline: (a) Outside the steel mills; (b) The open hearth with its long line of furnaces; (c) The workers—the "small man," Pete and his favorite jest, Mike and his advice; (d) Night work; (e) Pete and the boss; (f) Pete as foreman; (g) Pete's education; (h) The accident.

**Library Reading.** *Steel Preferred*, Hall.

**Newspaper Reading**. Bring to class and read the most interesting account you can find in a newspaper or magazine, telling about conditions of work in some industry such as mining, fishery, etc.

**A Suggested Problem.** Find out by a personal visit all you can about the way some industry or business is carried on (for example, some local store, or your father's business) and report to the class. Illustrate your talk, if possible, by pictures or blackboard drawings.

## THE THINKER

### BERTON BRALEY

Back of the beating hammer
By which the steel is wrought,
Back of the workshop's clamor
The seeker may find the Thought,
5 The Thought that is ever master
Of iron and steam and steel,
That rises above disaster
And tramples it under heel!

The drudge may fret and tinker
10 Or labor with dusty blows,
But back of him stands the Thinker,
The clear-eyed man who Knows;
For into each plow or saber,
Each piece and part and whole,
15 Must go the Brains and Labor,
Which give the work a soul!

Back of the motors humming,
Back of the belts that sing,
Back of the hammers drumming,
20 Back of the cranes that swing,
There is the eye which scans them,
Watching through stress and strain,
There is the Mind which plans them—
Back of the brawn, the Brain!

25 Might of the roaring boiler,
Force of the engine's thrust,
Strength of the sweating toiler,
Greatly in these we trust.

But back of them stands the Schemer,
The Thinker who drives things through;
Back of the job—the Dreamer
Who's making the dream come true!

## NOTES AND QUESTIONS

**Biography.** Berton Braley (1882-1966), poet and journalist, was a native of Wisconsin, and graduated from the University of Wisconsin in 1905. He served on the staff of *The Evening Mail*, New York, and was for a time associate editor of the magazine *Puck*. During World War One, Mr. Braley was a special correspondent in France and England. He was a frequent contributor to the leading magazines and newspapers. Among his published works are: *Songs of a Workaday World; A Banjo at Armageddon; In Camp and Trench.*

**Discussion.** 1. What is the theme of the poem? 2. What is the relation of the planner to the worker? 3. What confidence does the poet express in the worker? In the "Dreamer"? 4. What does the poet mean when he says that the brain is back of the brawn? 5. Show that the poem is a plea for the cooperation that is discussed in the "Introduction" on page 338.

**Class Reading.** Read the poem aloud to bring out the meaning and the rhythm; bring to class and read other poems from *Songs of a Workaday World* that particularly interest you.

## THE WAY TO WEALTH

### BENJAMIN FRANKLIN

Courteous Reader: I have heard that nothing gives an author so great pleasure as to find his works respectfully quoted by others. Judge, then, how much I must have been gratified by an incident I am going to relate to you.

5    I stopped my horse, lately, where a great number of people were collected at an auction of merchants' goods. The hour of the sale not being come, they were conversing on the badness

of the times, and one of the company called to a plain, clean old man with white locks: "Pray, Father Abraham, what think you of the times? Will not these heavy taxes quite ruin the country? How shall we ever be able to pay them? What would
5 you advise us to do?"

Father Abraham stood up and replied: "If you would have my advice, I will give it to you in short; for 'a word to the wise is enough,' as Poor Richard says." They joined in desiring him to speak his mind, and, gathering around him, he proceeded as
10 follows: "Friends," said he, "the taxes are indeed very heavy, and if those laid on by the government were the only ones we had to pay, we might more easily discharge them, but we have many others, and much more grievous to some of us.

"We are taxed twice as much by our idleness, three times
15 as much by our pride, and four times as much by our folly, and of these taxes the commissioners cannot ease or deliver us by allowing an abatement. However, let us hearken to good advice, and something may be done for us. 'Heaven helps them that help themselves,' as Poor Richard says.

20 "It would be thought a hard government that should tax its people one tenth part of their time to be employed in its service, but idleness taxes many of us much more; sloth, by bringing on diseases, absolutely shortens life. 'Sloth, like rust, consumes faster than labor wears; while the used key is always bright,'
25 as Poor Richard says. How much more than is necessary do we spend in sleep! forgetting that 'the sleeping fox catches no poultry,' and that there will be sleeping enough in the grave.

"'Lost time is never found again, and what we call time enough always proves little enough.' Let us, then, be up and
30 doing, and doing to the purpose; so by diligence shall we do more with less perplexity. 'Drive thy business, and let not that drive thee' and 'early to bed and early to rise makes a man healthy, wealthy, and wise,' as Poor Richard says.

"So, what signifies wishing and hoping for better times? We
35 may make these times better if we bestir ourselves. 'Industry

need not wish, and he that lives upon hopes will die fasting.'
'There are no gains without pains; then help hands, for I have
no lands.' 'He that hath a trade hath an estate, and he that hath
a calling hath an office of profit and honor'; but then the trade
5 must be worked at, and the calling well followed, or neither
the estate nor the office will enable us to pay our taxes. Work
while it is called today, for you know not how much you may
be hindered tomorrow. 'One today is worth two tomorrows,' as
Poor Richard says, and further, 'Never leave that till tomorrow
10 which you can do today.'

"If you were a servant, would you not be ashamed that a
good master should catch you idle? Are you, then, your own
master? Be ashamed to catch yourself idle, when there is so
much to be done for yourself, your family, and your country.
15 It is true, there is much to be done, and perhaps you are weak-
handed, but stick to it steadily, and you will see great effects,
for 'constant dropping wears away stones,' and 'little strokes
fell great oaks.'

"But with our industry we must likewise be steady, settled,
20 and careful, and oversee our own affairs with our own eyes, and
not trust too much to others, for, as Poor Richard says, 'Three
removes are as bad as a fire'; and again, 'Keep thy shop, and thy
shop will keep thee'; and again, 'If you would have your business
done, go; if not, send'; and again, 'The eye of the master will do
25 more work than both his hands'; and again, 'Want of care does
us more damage than want of knowledge.'

"So much for industry, my friends, and attention to one's own
business, but to these we must add frugality, if we would make
our industry more certainly successful. A man may, if he knows
30 not how to save as he gets, keep his nose to the grindstone
all his life, and die not worth a groat at last. 'If you would be
wealthy, think of saving as well as of getting.'

"Away with your expensive follies, and you will not then
have so much cause to complain of hard times, heavy taxes, and
35 chargeable families, for 'what maintains one vice would bring up

two children.' Beware of little expenses. 'Many a little makes a mickle'; 'A small leak will sink a great ship.' Here you are all got together at this sale of fineries and knick knacks. You call them goods, but if you do not take care, they will prove
5 evils to some of you.

"You expect they will be sold cheap, and perhaps they may be, for less than cost, but if you have no occasion for them, they must be dear to you. Remember what Poor Richard says: 'Buy what thou hast no need of, and ere long thou shalt sell
10 thy necessaries.' 'Silks, satins, scarlet, and velvets put out the kitchen fire.' These are not the necessaries of life; they can scarcely be called the conveniences; and yet, only because they look pretty, how many want to have them!

"By these and other extravagances, the greatest are reduced
15 to poverty and forced to borrow of those whom they formerly despised, but who, through industry and frugality, have maintained their standing. 'If you would know the value of money, go and try to borrow some, for he that goes a-borrowing goes a-sorrowing,' and, indeed, so does he that lends to such people,
20 when he goes to get it again.

"It is as truly folly for the poor to ape the rich as for the frog to swell in order to equal the ox. After all, this pride of appearance cannot promote health, nor ease pain; it makes no increase of merit in the person; it creates envy; it hastens
25 misfortunes.

"But what madness it must be to run in debt for superfluities! Think what you do when you run in debt: you give to another power over your liberty. If you cannot pay at the time, you will be ashamed to see your creditor; you will be in fear when
30 you speak to him; you will make poor, pitiful, sneaking excuses, and by degrees come to lose your veracity, and sink into base, downright lying, for 'The second vice is lying, the first is running in debt,' as Poor Richard says, and again, 'Lying rides upon debt's back.'

35     "This doctrine, my friends, is reason and wisdom, but industry,

and frugality, and prudence may all be blasted without the
blessing of Heaven.  Therefore ask that blessing humbly, and be
not uncharitable to those that at present seem to want it, but
comfort and help them."

5     The old gentleman ended his harangue.  The people heard
it, and approved the doctrine, and immediately practiced the
contrary, just as if it had been a common sermon, for the auction
opened, and they began to buy extravagantly.  I found the good
man had thoroughly studied my almanac and digested all I had
10 dropped on these topics during the course of twenty-five years.
The frequent mention he made of me must have tired anyone
else, but my vanity was wonderfully delighted with it, though I
was conscious that not a tenth part of the wisdom was my own
which he ascribed to me, but rather the gleanings that I had
15 made of the sense of all ages and nations.

However, I resolved to be the better for the echo of it, and,
although I had at first determined to buy the stuff for a new
coat, I went away resolved to wear my old one a little longer.
Reader, if thou wilt do the same, thy profit will be as great
20 as mine.

## NOTES AND QUESTIONS

**Biography.**  Benjamin Franklin (1706-1790) was born in Boston, the
youngest son of a large family.  At the age of ten he began to work for
his father, a tallow chandler and soap boiler.  Two years later he was
apprenticed to his brother James, who was a printer.  Although Benjamin
Franklin received very little education in school, he was constantly reading
and studying.  When he was seventeen years old he went to Philadelphia
and soon was established as a successful printer and proprietor of a
newspaper.

In 1736 he entered political life and from that time held many positions
of public trust.  He went as envoy to England and to France, in which latter
place he was exceedingly popular.  It is said that Benjamin Franklin was the
only man whose name was attached to the Declaration of Independence, the
Constitution, the Treaty of Peace with England, and the Treaty of Alliance
with France.  Probably no native of this country ever ranked higher in the
estimation of European thinkers and statesmen.  In 1732 Franklin began the

publication of *Poor Richard's Almanac* under the name Richard Saunders. This proved extremely popular, and in 1758, when the last edition was issued, Franklin gathered together, in "Father Abraham's Speech," the best of the maxims which had appeared in the almanac. These maxims had been thought out by Franklin during his own years of thrift and hard work.

**Discussion.** 1. What question led to this speech by Father Abraham? 2. What taxes besides government taxes does he say we pay? 3. How much does idleness tax people? 4. What is better than wishing for better times? 5. Against what practices do these maxims warn us? 6. What habits or virtues do they advise us to acquire? 7. Can you explain how Benjamin Franklin helped his country by publishing these maxims? 8. With which of the maxims are you familiar? What ones will you learn today? Which one will help you most? 9. What was done to encourage thrift during the World Wars? 10. Find in the glossary the meaning of: abatement; sloth; diligence; ape; superfluities; veracity; doctrine; harangue; ascribed; gleanings.

**Library Reading.** *Autobiography*, Franklin.

**Suggestions for Theme Topics.** 1. What I know about thrift stamps. 2. Other thrift measures in use during the World Wars.

---

## A Message to Garcia*

### Elbert Hubbard

In all this Cuban business there is one man stands out on the horizon of my memory like Mars at perihelion. When war broke out between Spain and the United States it was very necessary to communicate quickly with the leader of the insurgents. Garcia
5 was somewhere in the mountain fastnesses of Cuba—no one knew where. No mail or telegraph message could reach him. The president must secure his cooperation, and quickly.

What to do!

Someone said to the president, "There's a fellow by the name
10 of Rowan will find Garcia for you, if anybody can."

Rowan was sent for and given a letter to be delivered to Garcia.

---

*See Silent and Oral Reading, page 13.

How "the fellow by the name of Rowan" took the letter, sealed it up in an oilskin pouch, strapped it over his heart, in four days landed by night off the coast of Cuba from an open boat, disappeared into the jungle, and in three weeks, came out on 5 the other side of the island, having traversed a hostile country on foot, and delivered his letter to Garcia—are things I have no special desire to tell in detail now. The point I wish to make is this: McKinley gave Rowan a letter to be delivered to Garcia; Rowan took the letter and did not ask, "Where is he at?" 10 By the Eternal! there is a man whose form should be cast in deathless bronze and the statue placed in every college in the land! It is not book learning young men need, nor instruction about this or that, but a stiffening of the vertebrae that will cause them to be loyal to a trust, to act promptly, 15 concentrate their energies: do the thing—"Carry a message to Garcia."

General Garcia is dead now, but there are other Garcias.

No man who has endeavored to carry out an enterprise wherein many hands were needed, but has been well-nigh 20 appalled at times by the imbecility of the average man the inability or unwillingness to concentrate on a thing and do it.

Slipshod assistance, foolish inattention, dowdy indifference, and half-hearted work seem the rule, and no man succeeds, unless, by hook or crook or threat, he forces or bribes other 25 men to assist him, or mayhap, God in his goodness performs a miracle and sends him an Angel of Light for an assistant. You, reader, put this matter to a test: You are sitting now in your office—six clerks are within call. Summon any one and make this request: "Please look in the encyclopedia and make a brief 30 memorandum of Correggio."

Will the clerk quietly say, "Yes, sir," and go to the task?

On your life he will not! He will look at you out of a fishy eye and ask one or more of the following questions:

Who was he?

35    Which encyclopedia?

Where is the encyclopedia?

Was I hired for that?

Don't you mean Bismarck?

What's the matter with Charlie doing it?

5   Is he dead?

Is there any hurry?

Shall I bring you the book and let you look it up for yourself?

What do you want to know for?

And I will lay you ten to one that after you have answered
10 the questions and explained how to find the information and
why you want it, the clerk will go off and get one of the other
clerks to help him try to find Garcia—and then come back and
tell you there is no such man. Of course I may lose my bet, but
according to the Law of Average, I will not.

15    Now if you are wise you will not bother to explain to your
"assistant" that Correggio is indexed under the C's, not in the
K's, but you will smile sweetly and say, "Never mind" and go
look it up yourself.

The dread of "getting the bounce" Saturday night holds many
20 a worker to his place. Advertise for a stenographer, and nine
out of ten who apply can neither spell nor punctuate—and do
not think it necessary to.

Can such a one write a letter to Garcia?

"You see that bookkeeper?" said a foreman to me in a large
25 factory.

"Yes; what about him?"

"Well, he's a fine accountant, but if I'd send him uptown on
an errand, he might accomplish the errand all right, and on the
other hand, might stop on the way, and when he got to Main
30 Street would forget what he had been sent for."

Can such a man be entrusted to carry a message to Garcia?

We have recently been hearing much maudlin sympathy
expressed for the "downtrodden denizens of the sweatshop" and
the "homeless wanderer searching for honest employment," and
35 with it all often go many hard words for the men in power.

Nothing is said about the employer who grows old before his time in a vain attempt to get frowsy ne'er-do-wells to do intelligent work and his long, patient striving with "help" that does nothing but loaf when his back is turned. In every store
5 and factory there is a constant weeding-out process going on. The employer is constantly sending away "help" that have shown their incapacity to further the interests of the business, and others are being taken on.

No matter how good times are, this sorting continues, only if
10 times are hard and work is scarce, the sorting is done finer— but out and forever out the incompetent and unworthy go. It is the survival of the fittest. Self-interest prompts every employer to keep the best—those who can carry a message to Garcia.

I know one man of really brilliant parts who has not the
15 ability to manage a business of his own, and yet who is absolutely worthless to anyone else, because he carries with him constantly the insane suspicion that his employer is oppressing or intending to oppress him. He cannot give orders, and he will not receive them. Should a message be given him to take to Garcia, his
20 answer would probably be, "Take it yourself!"

Tonight this man walks the streets looking for work, the wind whistling through his threadbare coat. No one who knows him dare employ him, for he is a regular firebrand of discontent.

Of course I know that one so morally deformed is no less
25 to be pitied than a physical cripple, but in our pitying, let us drop a tear, too, for the men who are striving to carry on a great enterprise, whose working hours are not limited by the whistle, and whose hair is fast turning white through the struggle to hold in line dowdy indifference, slipshod imbecility, and the
30 heartless ingratitude which, but for their enterprise, would be both hungry and homeless.

Have I put the matter too strongly? Possibly I have, but when all the world has gone a-slumming I wish to speak a word of sympathy for the man who succeeds—the man who,
35 against great odds, has directed the efforts of others, and

having succeeded, finds there's nothing in it—nothing but bare board and clothes. I have carried a dinner pail and worked for day's wages, and I have also been an employer of labor, and I know there is something to be said on both sides. There is no
5 excellence, *per se*, in poverty; rags are no recommendation; and all employers are not rapacious and high-handed, any more than all poor men are virtuous.

My heart goes out to the man who does his work when the "boss" is away, as well as when he is at home. And the man who,
10 when given a letter for Garcia, quietly takes the missive, without asking any idiotic questions, and with no lurking intention of chucking it into the nearest sewer, or of doing aught else but delivering it, never gets "laid off." Civilization is one long, anxious search for just such individuals. Anything such a man asks shall
15 be granted. His kind is so rare that no employer can afford to let him go. He is wanted in every city, town, and village—in every office, shop, store, and factory.

The world cries out for such; he is needed, and needed badly—the man who can carry A MESSAGE TO GARCIA.

## NOTES AND QUESTIONS

**Biographical and Historical Note.** Elbert Hubbard (1859-1915), a native of Bloomington, Illinois, was an author and lecturer, his message being the joy of work well done. He founded the Roycroft Shop, in East Aurora, New York, which is devoted to the making of fine editions of books. Mr. Hubbard was one of the ill-fated passengers on board the *Lusitania* when it was sunk during World War One.

The author tells us that this "literary trifle," "A Message to Garcia," was written February 22, 1899, after supper, in a single hour, and after a particularly trying day. It was suggested to him by a discussion, over the teacups, of the Spanish-American War, his son maintaining that Rowan was the real hero of the war. The day after "A Message to Garcia" was published, the New York Central Railway ordered reprints of it, distributing over a million copies among its employees. The story has been translated into all written languages, and the author estimated that during his lifetime, "Thanks to a series of lucky accidents," forty million copies had been printed.

Garcia (1836-1898) was a Cuban patriot who gave valuable aid to the American forces during the Spanish-American War. At the close of the war he was made chief of a commission to discuss with President McKinley the future of Cuba. Andrew Rowan (1857-1943), a West Point graduate, was promoted to the office of lieutenant colonel of the United States army for the service described in this sketch.

**Discussion.** 1. Discuss whether or not, in your opinion, the author is too hard on "help." 2. Why do you think the New York Central Railway distributed copies among its employees? 3. What resolve might you well make after reading "A Message to Garcia"? 4. Are you one of the "Rowans" in your school? 5. How does Rowan's devotion differ from that of the hero in the "Incident of the French Camp"? 6. Which is of more value to a country, devotion to a cause or to a leader? 7. What other story on efficiency in work have you read? 8. Point out sentences in this selection that show the author's belief in the importance of the cooperation discussed in the "Introduction" on page 338. 9. Find in the glossary the meaning of: insurgents; traversed; vertebrae; appalled; imbecility; memorandum; accountant; maudlin; denizens; missive. 10. *Pronounce:* horizon; encyclopedia; rapacious.

## Phrases for Study

| | |
|---|---|
| Cuban business, **500**, 1 | regular firebrand, **503**, 23 |
| Law of Average, **502**, 14 | world has gone a-slumming, **503**, 33 |
| weeding-out process, **503**, 5 | *per se*, **504**, 5 |
| survival of the fittest, **503**, 12 | |

**Class Reading.** Make a list of passages to be read aloud in class.

**Questions for Testing Silent Reading.** Make a list of questions to bring out the main thought of the story.

**Magazine Reading.** Make a report in class on the most interesting article, on efficiency and faithfulness to duty, that you have read in *The American Magazine*, *The World's Work*, or in any other periodical.

# THE BUILDING OF THE SHIP

HENRY WADSWORTH LONGFELLOW

"Build me straight, O worthy Master!
   Stanch and strong, a goodly vessel,
That shall laugh at all disaster,
   And with wave and whirlwind wrestle!"

5 The merchant's word
Delighted the Master heard;
For his heart was in his work, and the heart
Giveth grace unto every Art.
A quiet smile played round his lips,
10 As the eddies and dimples of the tide
Play round the bows of ships
That steadily at anchor ride.
And with a voice that was full of glee,
He answered, "Ere long we will launch
15 A vessel as goodly, and strong, and stanch
As ever weathered a wintry sea!"

And first with nicest skill and art,
Perfect and finished in every part,
A little model the Master wrought,
20 Which should be to the larger plan          ·
What the child is to the man,
Its counterpart in miniature;
That with a hand more swift and sure
The greater labor might be brought
25 To answer to his inward thought.
And as he labored, his mind ran o'er
The various ships that were built of yore,

And above them all, and strangest of all,
Towered the Great Harry, crank and tall,
Whose picture was hanging on the wall,
With bows and stern raised high in air,
5 And balconies hanging here and there,
And signal lanterns and flags afloat,
And eight round towers, like those that frown
From some old castle, looking down
Upon the drawbridge and the moat;
10 And he said, with a smile, "Our ship, I wis,
Shall be of another form than this!"

It was of another form, indeed;
Built for freight, and yet for speed,
A beautiful and gallant craft;
15 Broad in the beam, that the stress of the blast,
Pressing down upon sail and mast,
Might not the sharp bows overwhelm;
Broad in the beam, but sloping aft
With graceful curve and slow degrees,
20 That she might be docile to the helm,
And that the currents of parted seas,
Closing behind, with mighty force,
Might aid and not impede her course.

In the shipyard stood the Master,
25    With the model of the vessel,
That should laugh at all disaster,
   And with wave and whirlwind wrestle!

Covering many a rood of ground,
Lay the timber piled around;
30 Timber of chestnut, and elm, and oak,
And scattered here and there, with these,
The knarred and crooked cedar knees,
Brought from regions far away,

From Pascagoula's sunny bay,
And the banks of the roaring Roanoke!
Ah! what a wondrous thing it is
To note how many wheels of toil
5 One thought, one word, can set in motion!
There's not a ship that sails the ocean,
But every climate, every soil,
Must bring its tribute, great or small,
And help to build the wooden wall!

10 The sun was rising o'er the sea,
And long the level shadows lay,
As if they, too, the beams would be
Of some great, airy argosy,
Framed and launched in a single day;
15 That silent architect, the sun,
Had hewn and laid them every one,
Ere the work of man was yet begun
Beside the Master, when he spoke,
A youth, against an anchor leaning,
20 Listened, to catch his slightest meaning.
Only the long waves, as they broke
In ripples on the pebbly beach,
Interrupted the old man's speech.

Beautiful they were, in sooth,
25 The old man and the fiery youth!
The old man, in whose busy brain
Many a ship that sailed the main
Was modeled o'er and o'er again;
The fiery youth, who was to be
30 The heir of his dexterity,
The heir of his house and his daughter's hand,
When he had built and launched from land
What the elder head had planned.

"Thus," said he, "will we build this ship!
Lay square the blocks upon the slip,
And follow well this plan of mine.
Choose the timbers with greatest care;
5 Of all that is unsound beware;
For only what is sound and strong
To this vessel shall belong.
Cedar of Maine and Georgia pine
Here together shall combine;
10 A goodly frame, and a goodly fame,
And the Union be her name!
For the day that gives her to the sea
Shall give my daughter unto thee!"

The Master's word
15 Enraptured the young man heard;
And as he turned his face aside,
With a look of joy and a thrill of pride,
Standing before
Her father's door,
20 He saw the form of his promised bride.
The sun shone on her golden hair,
And her cheek was glowing fresh and fair,
With the breath of morn and the soft sea air.
Like a beauteous barge was she,
25 Still at rest on the sandy beach,
Just beyond the billow's reach;
But he
Was the restless, seething, stormy sea!

Ah, how skillful grows the hand
30 That obeyeth Love's command!
It is the heart, and not the brain,
That to the highest doth attain,
And he who followeth Love's behest
Far excelleth all the rest!

Thus with the rising of the sun
Was the noble task begun,
And soon throughout the shipyard's bounds
Were heard the intermingled sounds
5 Of axes and of mallets, plied
With vigorous arms on every side;
Plied so deftly and so well
That, ere the shadows of evening fell,
The keel of oak for a noble ship,
10 Scarfed and bolted, straight and strong,
Was lying ready, and stretched along
The blocks, well placed upon the slip.
Happy, thrice happy, every one
Who sees his labor well begun,
15 And not perplexed and multiplied,
By idly waiting for time and tide!

And when the hot, long day was o'er,
The young man at the Master's door
Sat with the maiden calm and still,
20 And within the porch, a little more
Removed beyond the evening chill,
The father sat, and told them tales
Of wrecks in the great September gales.
Of pirates upon the Spanish Main,
25 And ships that never came back again,
The chance and change of a sailor's life,
Want and plenty, rest and strife,
His roving fancy, like the wind,
That nothing can stay and nothing can bind,
30 And the magic charm of foreign lands,
With shadows of palms, and shining sands,
Where the tumbling surf,
O'er the coral reefs of Madagascar,
Washes the feet of the swarthy Lascar,

As he lies alone and asleep on the turf.
And the trembling maiden held her, breath
At the tales of that awful, pitiless sea,
With all its terror and mystery;
5 The dim, dark sea, so like unto Death,
That divides and yet unites mankind!
And whenever the old man paused, a gleam
From the bowl of his pipe would awhile illume
The silent group in the twilight gloom,
10 And thoughtful faces, as in a dream;
And for a moment one might mark
What had been hidden by the dark,
That the head of the maiden lay at rest
Tenderly, on the young man's breast!

15 Day by day the vessel grew,
With timbers fashioned strong and true,
Stemson and keelson and sternson-knee,
Till, framed with perfect symmetry,
A skeleton ship rose up to view!
20 And around the bows and along the side
The heavy hammers and mallets plied,
Till, after many a week, at length,
Wonderful for form and strength,
Sublime in its enormous bulk,
25 Loomed aloft the shadowy hulk!
And around it columns of smoke, upwreathing,
Rose from the boiling, bubbling, seething
Caldron, that glowed,
And overflowed
30 With the black tar, heated for the sheathing.
And amid the clamors
Of clattering hammers,
He who listened heard now and then
The song of the Master and his men:

"Build me straight, O worthy Master,
 Stanch and strong, a goodly vessel,
That shall laugh at all disaster,
 And with wave and whirlwind wrestle!"


5 With oaken brace and copper band
Lay the rudder on the sand,
That, like a thought, should have control
Over the movement of the whole;
And near it the anchor, whose giant hand
10 Would reach down and grapple with the land,
And immovable and fast
Hold the great ship against the bellowing blast!
And at the bows an image stood,
By a cunning artist carved in wood,
15 With robes of white, that far behind
Seemed to be fluttering in the wind.
It was not shaped in a classic mold,
Not like a nymph or goddess of old,
Or Naiad rising from the water,
20 But modeled from the Master's daughter.
On many a dreary and misty night
'Twill be seen by the rays of the signal light,
Speeding along through the rain and the dark
Like a ghost in its snow-white sark,
25 The pilot of some phantom bark,
Guiding the vessel, in its flight,
By a path none other knows aright!


Behold, at last,
Each tall and tapering mast
30 Is swung into its place;
Shrouds and stays
Holding it firm and fast!

Long ago,
In the deer-haunted forests of Maine,
When upon mountain and plain
Lay the snow,
5 They fell—those lordly pines!
Those grand, majestic pines!
'Mid shouts—and cheers
The jaded steers,
Panting beneath the goad,
10 Dragged down the weary, winding road
Those captive kings so straight and tall,
To be shorn of their streaming hair,
And, naked and bare,
To feel the stress and the strain
15 Of the wind and the reeling main,
Whose roar
Would remind them for evermore
Of their native forests they should not see again.

And everywhere
20 The slender, graceful spars
Poise aloft in the air,
And at the masthead,
White, blue, and red,
A flag unrolls the Stripes and Stars.
25 Ah! when the wanderer, lonely, friendless,
In foreign harbors shall behold
That flag unrolled,
'Twill be as a friendly hand
Stretched out from his native land,
30 Filling his heart with memories sweet and endless!

All is finished! and at length
Has come the bridal day
Of beauty and of strength.

Today the vessel shall be launched!
With fleecy clouds the sky is blanched,
And o'er the bay,
Slowly, in all his splendors dight,
5 The great sun rises to behold the sight.

The ocean old,
Centuries old,
Strong as youth, and as uncontrolled,
Paces restless to and fro,
10 Up and down the sands of gold,
His beating heart is not at rest;
And far and wide,
With ceaseless flow,
His beard of snow
15 Heaves with the heaving of his breast.
He waits impatient for his bride.
There she stands,
With her foot upon the sands,
Decked with flags and streamers gay,
20 In honor of her marriage day,
Her snow-white signals fluttering, blending,
Round her like a veil descending,
Ready to be
The bride of the gray old sea.

25 On the deck another bride
Is standing by her lover's side.
Shadows from the flags and shrouds.
Like the shadows cast by clouds,
Broken by many a sunny fleck,
30 Fall around them on the deck.

The prayer is said,
The service read,
The joyous bridegroom bows his head;

And in tears the good old Master
Shakes the brown hand of his son,
Kisses his daughter's glowing cheek
In silence, for he cannot speak,
5 And ever faster
Down his own the tears begin to run.
The worthy pastor—
The shepherd of that wandering flock
That has the ocean for its wold,
10 That has the vessel for its fold,
Leaping ever from rock to rock—
Spake, with accents mild and clear,
Words of warning, words of cheer,
But tedious to the bridegroom's ear.
15 He knew the chart
Of the sailor's heart,
All its pleasures and its griefs,
All its shallows and rocky reefs,
All those secret currents, that flow
20 With such resistless undertow
And lift and drift, with terrible force,
The will from its moorings and its course.
Therefore he spake, and thus said he:

"Like unto ships far off at sea,
25 Outward or homeward bound, are we,
Before, behind, and all around,
Floats and swings the horizon's bound,
Seems at its distant rim to rise
And climb the crystal wall of the skies,
30 And then again to turn and sink,
As if we could slide from its outer brink.
Ah! it is not the sea,
It is not the sea that sinks and shelves,
But ourselves

That rock and rise
With endless and uneasy motion,
Now touching the very skies,
Now sinking into the depths of ocean.
5 Ah! if our souls but poise and swing
Like the compass in its brazen ring,
Ever level and ever true
To the toil and the task we have to do,
We shall sail securely, and safely reach
10 The Fortunate Isles, on whose shining beach
The sights we see and the sounds we hear
Will be those of joy and not of fear!"

Then the Master,
With a gesture of command,
15 Waved his hand;
And at the word,
Loud and sudden there was heard,
All around them and below,
The sound of hammers, blow on blow,
20 Knocking away the shores and spurs.
And see! she stirs!
She starts—she moves—she seems to feel
The thrill of life along her keel,
And, spurning with her foot the ground.
25 With one exulting, joyous bound,
She leaps into the ocean's arms!

And lo! from the assembled crowd
There rose a shout, prolonged and loud,
That to the ocean seemed to say,
30 "Take her, O bridegroom, old and gray,
Take her to thy protecting arms,
With all her youth and all her charms!"
How beautiful she is! How fair

She lies within those arms, that press
Her form with many a soft caress
Of tenderness and watchful care!
Sail forth into the sea, O ship!
5 Through wind and wave, right onward steer!
The moistened eye, the trembling lip,
Are not the signs of doubt or fear.

Sail forth into the sea of life,
O gentle, loving, trusting wife,
10 And safe from all adversity
Upon the bosom of that sea
Thy comings and thy goings be!
For gentleness and love and trust
Prevail o'er angry wave and gust;
15 And in the wreck of noble lives
Something immortal still survives

Thou, too, sail on, O Ship of State!
Sail on, O Union, strong and great!
Humanity with all its fears,
20 With all the hopes of future years,
Is hanging breathless on thy fate!
We know what Master laid thy keel,
What Workman wrought thy ribs of steel,
Who made each mast, and sail, and rope,
25 What anvils rang, what hammers beat,
In what a forge and what a heat
Were shaped the anchors of thy hope!
Fear not each sudden sound and shock;
'Tis of the wave and not the rock;
30 'Tis but the flapping of the sail,
And not a rent made by the gale!
In spite of rock and tempest's roar,
In spite of false lights on the shore,

Sail on, nor fear to breast the sea!
Our hearts, our hopes, are all with thee,
Our hearts, our hopes, our prayers, our tears,
Our faith triumphant o'er our fears,  .
5 Are all with thee—are all with thee!

## NOTES AND QUESTIONS

For **Biography** see page 138.

**Discussion.** 1. What two stories run side by side in this poem? 2. Who is represented as speaking lines 1 to 4 on page 506? To whom are these words addressed? 3. What is the story of the "Great Harry"? 4. What trees are mentioned as furnishing timber for the vessel? 5. What comparison do the long level shadows of the early morning bring to the mind of the poet? 6. What is the significance of having Maine cedar and Georgia pine help to build a vessel that is to be called the *Union*? 7. Find the lines in which the poet first compares the master's daughter to a ship. 8. To what does the poet compare the rudder of the ship? To what does he compare the anchor? To what does he compare the pines that were felled to make the masts? 9. Find lines that describe the flag at the masthead. 10. What two brides does the poet show us? 11. Find lines in which he addresses the ship that has been launched. 12. Find lines addressed to the girl who has become the wife of the shipbuilder. 13. Find the lines addressed to the "Ship of State." 14. What lines on page 508 suggest the need of cooperation? Compare the thought in lines 20 to 22, page 517, with what Webster says in the last paragraph of "The American Experiment." 15. How many of the terms used by the poet in describing the building of the ship are familiar to you? 16. Where or how did you learn the ones you know? How did Longfellow learn so much about ships? 17. Perhaps these lines from his poem, "My Lost Youth," will help you to understand how it was possible for Longfellow to write so understandingly and lovingly about a ship:

I remember the black wharves and the slips.
    And the sea-tides tossing free,
And Spanish sailors with bearded lips,
And the beauty and mystery of the ships,
    And the magic of the sea.

18. Point out lines in the poem that express some of the same ideas about work that you read in the "Introduction" on page 338. 19. A cantata for this poem, prepared by Henry C. Lahee, was published by Oliver Ditson Company, Boston. 20. Find in the glossary the meaning of: argosy; behest; Naiad; sark. 21. *Pronounce:* stanch; miniature.

**Suggestions for Theme Topics.** 1. What I know about shipbuilding in America during the World Wars. 2. Some advantages that come to a country that has a large fleet of merchant ships.

**Library Reading.** *Our Industrial Victory*, Schwab; "Ships for the Seven Seas," Graves (in the *National Geographic Magazine*, September, 1918); "Cargoes," Masefield (in *Collected Poems*).

### Phrases for Study

giveth grace unto every Art, **506**, 8

answer to his inward thought, **506**, 25

docile to the helm, **507**, 20

parted seas, **507**, 21

heir of his dexterity, **508**, 30

scarfed and bolted, **510**, 10

Spanish Main, **510**, 24

shaped in a classic mold, **512**, 17

shorn of their streaming hair, **513**, 12

Ship of State, **517**, 17

A REVIEW

"Literature and Life in the Homeland" is the general subject of "Part IV"; under what three headings is the subject treated? How do the selections in the group called "American Scenes and Legends" help you to understand what America means and how her present grows out of the past? In the "Introduction," page 335, you read that in one sense literature knows no time or place, yet in another sense it reflects the life and ideals of a particular time and a definite people. Does the poem "Snow-Bound" picture scenes of pioneer America merely or has it also qualities that belong to all time? What quality in Evangeline makes her a heroine not merely of colonial times, but of all time? What is there in "The Gray Champion" that belongs to all time? In what sense is this story a part of American history? What quality do we recognize in Rip Van Winkle that we find also in ourselves in a greater or less degree? How does this recognition affect our sympathy for Rip? How do the descriptions of American scenes by Lanier, Whittier, Irving, Longfellow, and Hawthorne differ from those found in your geography?

Humor is said to be one of our American characteristics; name some well-known humorists of our national literature. Which of these names are represented in the group called "American Literature of Lighter Vein"? Bring to class some interesting bits of humor from *Life* or from other magazines devoted to humor. In Irving's time, and even in that of Holmes, pictures were not widely used to furnish humor for the readers of newspapers and magazines; name some present-day cartoonists and the well-known characters they have created. Discuss in class different kinds of cartoons: (a) those that drive home a truth in the form of a joke; (b) those that are clever; (c) those that are merely silly. Bring to class illustrations of these kinds of cartoons. Make a collection for "Cartoon Day" in your school.

Which of the selections that picture America at work did you find most interesting? Which selection in this group made you feel the joy of work? Which selection emphasized the importance of efficiency in work? Which selection shows the relation of the worker to the planner? What different kinds of workers did you learn about in your library reading suggested in "Part IV"? What occupations particularly interest you? What selections broadened your sympathies for the worker? How has *The Readers' Guide to Periodical Literature* helped you to find magazine articles describing different kinds of industries?

What quotations from memory can you make from this year's reading? Compare your list of quotations with those of your classmates; what quotations do you find most often on these lists? What is your method of memorizing? Tell briefly some interesting facts that you learned about forms of literature—the lyric, the ballad, and the short story. What short story writers have you become acquainted with in this book? What contemporary poets? What book reviews given during the year interested you most? What discussions growing out of "Suggestions for Theme Topics" were most profitable? What "Suggested Problems" were most interesting? What progress in silent reading—speed and comprehension—have you made?

And now that you have come to the end of your book you may well ask yourself, "What are the benefits I have gained from my reading?" It is the earnest hope of the authors that you have been helped to observe nature; to delight in noble literature; to appreciate the highest forms of wit and humor; to have sympathy for all sorts and conditions of men; to take satisfaction in work well done; to be kind to all; and to love home and country. For these are the things that this book and others of the series have aimed to foster in you for your individual happiness and for the well-being of all with whom you associate.

# GLOSSARY

a as in m<u>a</u>t    ə as in b<u>a</u>nana    ä as in f<u>a</u>ther    Ø as in s<u>i</u>de
e as in b<u>e</u>d    ər as in f<u>ur</u>th<u>er</u>    aů as in l<u>ou</u>d    ŋ as in si<u>ng</u>
i as in t<u>i</u>p    ā as in d<u>ay</u>    ē as in n<u>ee</u>d    ō as in sn<u>ow</u>
ȯ as in s<u>aw</u>    ȯi as in c<u>oin</u>    ü as in r<u>u</u>le    ů as in p<u>u</u>ll
   ᵊ as in eat<u>e</u>n    <u>th</u> as in hea<u>th</u>er

**a bate ment** (ə-bāt-mənt) decrease
**ab by** ('a-bē) monastery; castle
**ab di cat ed** ('ab-di-kā-təd) given up the throne
**ab hor** (əb-'hȯr) hate
**ab ject** ('ab-jekt) humble
**ab ne ga tion** (ab-ni-'gā-shən) giving up all thought
**aboard, laid** went onto
**Abraham...Ishmael...Hagar** ('ā-brə-ham; 'ish-mā-əl; 'hā-gär) *see* Genesis XXI:9-20
**Abrahams** pictures of Abraham
**a breast** (ə-'brest) side by side
**ab sti nence** ('ab-stə-nənts) going without
**ab stract ing** (ab-'strak-tiŋ) sneaking
**A by dos** (ə-'bØ-dəs)
**a byss** (ə-'bis) immeasurable space; deep gulf; sea
**A ca di a** (ə-'kā-dē-ə) former name of Nova Scotia
**A ca die** (ä-kä-'dē) *see* Acadia
**ac ced ed** (ak-'sē-dəd) agreed
**ac cor dant** (ə-'kȯr-dᵊnt) harmonious
**accountant** one who makes financial statements
**ac me** ('ak-mē) perfection
**ac qui es cence** (a-kwē-'e-sᵊnts) agreement
**ad a mant** ('a-də-mənt) hardest stone
**A day es** ('ä-dā-ēz)
**ad dled** ('a-dᵊld) confused

523

**ad dress** (ə-'dres) formal speech
**ad her ent** (ad-'hir-ənt) supporter
**Ad ju tant** ('a-jə-tənt) officer through whom the Commander receives communications and gives orders
**ad mi ra ble** ('ad-mə-rə-bəl) praiseworthy
**Adonis** dandy. Adonis, in mythology, was a beautiful youth beloved by the goddess Venus
**ad vent** ('ad-vent) beginning
**ad ver sary** ('ad-vər-ser-ē) foe; opponent
**ad verse currents** streams that flow different ways
**ad ver si ty** (ad-'vər-sə-tē) misfortune
**ad vo ca cy** ('ad-və-kə-sē) behalf
**ae ri al** ('ar-ē-əl) airy
**Aer shot** ('är-skȯt) town in Belgium
**af fa bil i ty** (a-fə-'bi-lə-tē) friendliness
**af front** (ə-'frənt) insult
**affronted** offended
**aft** ('aft) toward the stern
**ag gres sor** (ə-'gre-sər) enemy
**a ghast** (ə-'gast) horrified
**ag i tat ed** ('a-jə-tā-təd) blown; excited
**a gog** (ə-'gäg) eager
**Ai denn** ('ā-dən) paradise
**Aix** ('āks) city in France
**alac ri ty** (ə-'la-krə-tē) willingness
**al der** (ȯl-dər) tree which grows in moist ground
**A li Ba ba** (a-lē; 'bä-bə)
**alien** ('ā-lē-ən) foreigner
**alien ate** ('ā-lē-ə-nāt) separate
**Al la hu** ('ä-lə-hü) Allah
**al le giance** (ə-'lē-jənts) loyalty
**al lit er a tion** (ə-li-tə-'rā-shən) repetition of the same letter or sound at the beginning of successive words
**al loys** ('a-lȯiz) combinations of metals
**all per va sive** (pər-'vā-siv) universal
**al lu sion** (ə-'lü-zhən) reference
**al ly** (ə-'lꞮ) friend; aid
**al mond** ('äl-mənd)
**alms house** ('älmz-haȯs) poorhouse
**al oe** ('a-lō) plant which blossoms when it is one hundred years old

**alp** mountains in general

**al ter na tive** (ȯl-'tər-nə-tiv) choice

**a lu mi num** (ə-'lü-mə-nəm) very lightweight metal, silver-colored

**a main** (ə-'mān) at full speed

**am a ranth** ('a-mə-ranth) an imaginary flower which never fades

**am bro si al** (am-'brō-zhəl) beautiful

**ami a ble** ('ā-mē-ə-bəl) lovely

**am i ca ble** ('a-mi-kə-bəl) friendly; peaceful

**Am o noo suck** (am-ō-'nü-sək)

**a mor phas** (ə-'mȯr-fəs) the amorpha, a flowering plant

**a move or two** "the ways of the world"

**am phi the ater** ('amp-fə-thē-ə-tər) a circular building with seats gradually higher toward the back; in the large central open space, called the arena, the Romans had their gladiatorial contests

**A mun** ('ä-mün) one of the Egyptian gods, represented as a ram with curling horns

**anat o my** (ə-'na-tə-mē) study of the human body

**an cho rite monk** ('aŋ-kə-rȯt) one bound by a vow to live in solitude

**anew** (ə-'nü) again

**Angel of the backward look** angel that records our lives

**An ge lus** ('an-jə-ləs) bell calling the people to evening prayer

**Anglo-Saxon divinity of Spring** Eoster, worshiped by the Early English as the goddess who brought back life to the earth

**an ni hi la tion** (ə-nØ-ə-'lā-shən) total destruction

**an nulled the charters** (ə-'nəld) taken away the legal writing which allowed certain rights

**a non** (ə-'nän) soon; immediately

**a non y mous** (ə-'nä-nə-məs) nameless

**answer to his inward thought** correspond to his idea of what he wished to be

**an tag o nis tic** (an-ta-gə-'nis-tik) strongly opposed

**an ti dote** ('an-ti-dōt) a remedy to counteract the effects of something taken, or applied, by mistake

**ape** ('āp) imitate

**Ap ol lo ni us** (a-pə-'lō-nē-əs) ancient Roman philosopher who lived at the time of Christ and was said to be able to converse with birds and animals

**ap o plec tic op u lence** (a-pə-'plek-tik; 'ä-pyə-lənts) overflowing riches

**ap os tol ic** (a-pə-'stä-lik) spiritual

**ap palled** (ə-'pȯld) horrified
**ap pa ri tion** (a-pə-'ri-shən) ghost
**ap pel la tion** (a-pə-'lā-shən) name
**ap praised** (ə-'prāzd) priced
**ap pre hen sion** (a-pri-'hen-shən) fear
**ap pren tice** (ə-'pren-təs) helper who is learning the business; apprenticed, taught a trade while working; 'prentice, young man learning his trade
**ap prise** (ə-'prØz) inform
**ap pro ba tion** (a-prə-'bā-shən) approval
**apt ly** ('apt-lē) fittingly
**Ar ab** ('ar-əb) Arabian
**ar a besque** (ar-ə-'besk) in geometric design
**arched** made an arch over
**arch-enemy** worst enemy
**a re na** (ə-'rē-nə) *see* amphitheater
**Ar go nauts** ('är-gə-nȯts) sailors on the Argo who went in search of the Golden Fleece. *See* a mythology
**ar go sy** ('är-gə-sē) airy; imaginary vessel made of sunbeams
**Ariel-airy ease** ('ar-ē-əl) with the light movements of Ariel, a spirit of the air, in Shakespeare's *The Tempest*
**ar is toc ra cy** (ar-ə-'stä-krə-sē) more fortunate classes in society which have riches, power, education, etc.
**a ro ma** (ə-'rō-mə) fragrance
**ar o mat ic** (ar-ə-'ma-tik) fragrant; strong scented
**artful** coquettish; artful dog, mind, a clever fellow, you may be sure
**articles of dep re da tion** (de-prə-'dā-shən) agreement to kidnap
**ar ti cu la tion** (är-ti-kyə-'lā-shən) careful sounding of consonants
**ar ti fice** ('är-tə-fəs) unnatural covering; trick
**as cribed to me** (ə-'skrØbd) said was mine
**a skance** (ə-'skants) sideways
**as pho del** ('as-fə-dəl) in Greek mythology, a flower associated with the underworld and the dead
**as pi ra tions** (as-pə-'rā-shənz) ambitions
**as pire** (ə-'spØr) fly upward; hope to reach
**as si du i ty** (a-sə-'dü-ə-tē) industry
**as sid u ous** (ə-'sij-wəs) devoted
**as sign** (ə-'sØn) representative
**as suage** (ə-'swāj) relieve
**as sump tions** (ə-'səmp-shənz) boldness

**Atchaf a laya** (ə-cha-fə-'lǿ-ə) bayou which is an outlet of the Red and the Mississippi rivers

**at his famous best** as fast as it was possible for him

**attained the extremity** walked through to the opposite side

**attunes his pipe anew** begins singing again

**au gust** (ȯ-'gəst) dignified

**au re ole** ('ȯr-ē-ōl) circle of light around the head, i.e., a halo

**aus tere** (ȯ-'stir) severe; **austerity** severity

**avail** (ə-'vāl) have power to hold me back; help

**av a lanche** ('a-və-lanch) ice, snow, or land sliding down a mountainside.

**av a rice** ('a-və-rəs) greediness

**av a tar** ('a-və-tär) symbol

**A ve Ma ri a** (ä-vā-mə-'rē-ə)

**aye and a non** ('ǿ; ə-'nän) constantly

**az ure** ('a-zhər) clear blue

**Babylonish jargon** (ba-bə-'lō-nish; 'jär-gən) confusion; Genesis XI:1-10

**bac cha nal** ('ba-kə-n³l) a drunken merry-maker; Bacchanals, the followers of Bacchus, the god of wine

**bac chan tes** (bə-'kants) riotous merry-makers

**bale ful** ('bāl-fəl) gloomy

**bal let dancer** ('ba-lā) toe-dancer

**balm** something delightful or soothing

**balm in Gil e ad** ('gi-lē-əd) relief from pain, in heaven

**Bap tiste**

**bar** prevent

**bar bar ic** (bär-'bar-ik) vivid and striking (as used by primitive peoples)

**bard** professional poet and singer

**barge** ('bärj) small, graceful sailboat

**bar rack** ('bar-ək) of the soldier's lodgings

**Basin of Mi nas** ('mi-nəs) Eastern arm of Bay of Fundy

**bas re lief** ('bä-ri-'lēf) standing out from the rest of his face

**bast ed been** ('bās-təd) had water poured over them as a roast has

**bat tal ions** (bə-'tal-yənz) crowds

**bay** reddish-brown horse

**bay ou** ('bǿ-ü) inlet from the Gulf of Mexico, lake, or large river, sometimes sluggish; of Plaquemine, town in Louisiana

**beam** widest part

**Beau Sejour** (bō; sā-'zhür) town in Acadia, attacked by the British in 1745

**Beautiful River** Ohio River

**be dight** (bi-'dØt) decorated

**Bedlam** ('bed-ləm) insane asylum in London

**beetling** jutting out into the street

**be guile** (bi-'gØl) spend; deceive; beguile you from, make you forget; beguiling, coaxing

**be hest** (bi-'hest) command

**be lie, did** (bi-'lØ) acted in a manner opposite to

**Belle Fontaine** (bel-ə-fän-'tān)

**Bel loy en San terre** (bel-'wä-än-són-'tär)

**Bel shaz zars** (bel-'sha-zərz) pictures of Belshazzar, last king of Babylon

**belted half the horizon** extended half-way along the skyline

**Ben e dic i te** (ben-ā-'dēs-i-tā) bless you

**be nev o lence** (bə-'nev-lənts) kindness; organ of, heart

**be nig nant** (bi-'nig-nənt) kind

**be nig ni ty** (bi-'nig-nə-tē) kindness

**be parties to** assist in telling

**be reave ment** (bi-'rēv-mənt) sorrow

**be tro thal** (bi-'trō-thəl) engagement

**bid defiance to contagion** live without fear of the disease

**big no ni a** (big-'nō-nē-ə) a kind of tropical vine which bears flowers

**big ot ry** ('bi-gə-trē) narrow mindedness

**birds of passage** birds going south for the winter

**bishop** wine and fruit juices

**bi zarre** (bə-'zär) unusual

**blanched** ('blancht) grew pale; pale; whitened

**blank verse** poetry with rhythm but no rhyme

**blas phe mous** ('blas-fə-məs) indecent

**blenched** ('blencht) hesitated

**Blom i don** ('bläm-i-dən) a mountain

**blooms, leafless** the blossoms come before the leaves in the spring

**bluff headland** high, steep bank

**Board of Trade** the committee having charge of commerce

**"bob"** slang for shilling

**bodiced zone** waist encircled with a wide girdle

**bole** ('bōl) trunk

**bonnet and plume**  tam o'shanter with a large feather for decoration
**bo nus**  ('bō-nəs)  extra pay
**boon**  ('bün)  favor
**bootless**  idle
**border**  region between England and Scotland
**bor ough**  ('bər-ō)  village
**Bourbon scepter**  the rule of the Bourbons, a French family, members
    of which became tyrannical rulers in France, Spain, and Italy
**bow**  ('baù)  front part of a ship
**Bow doin**  ('bō-dᵊn)  in Brunswick, Maine
**bows**  ('bōwz)  U-shaped pieces about the necks of oxen, fastened to
    the yoke brace, pair
**brackish**  ('bra-kish)  salt-water
**Braddock's army**  men under General Braddock, defeated by the
    French and Indians, 1755
**Brains of Labor**  genius of invention, organization, etc., which is the
    great force back of all labor
**brake**  thicket
**brant**  ('brant)  kind of wild duck
**brawn**  ('brón)  roasted meat; physical strength
**bra zier**  ('brā-zhər)  pan for burning coals
**breach**  opening
**breeches**  ('brē-chəz)
**brewing on a large scale**  cooking in large quantities with clouds
    of steam
**brig ands**  ('bri-gandz)  highwaymen
**Brig id**  ('bri-jəd)  Saint Brigid, patroness of Ireland (453-523)
**broad-girthed**  large and fat
**brooch**  ('brōch)  pin
**brood ing**  ('brü-diŋ)  thoughtful
**buck**  dashing young fellow
**bucking**  leaping
**buffcoat**  close, leather coat
**buffer**  protection to lessen the shock
**buffoon**  (bə-'fün)  clown
**Bunker Hill**  a famous battle of the early Revolutionary days (June
    17, 1775)
**buoy**  ('bü-ē)  object kept afloat on the water to mark something below
    the surface
**bur gess**  ('bər-jəs)  citizen

**burlesque** (bər-'lesk) caricature

**burning Sappho** ('sa-fō) Greek lyric poetess of intense feeling (600 B.C.)

**bus kins** ('bəs-kənz) high boots

**but all except their sun, is set** the greatness they have been famous for is now gone

**butte** ('byüt) hill

**but ting** ('bə-tiŋ) pushing

**butts** ('bəts) handle ends

**by common consent** unanimously

**cables** ropes and chains

**cadence** ('kād-ᵊns) rhythm

**Cains and Abels** pictures of Cain and Abel, sons of Adam and Eve; *See* Genesis IV

**caldron** ('kȯl-drən) kettle

**calender** one who presses cloth between rollers to glaze it

**Cal i ban** ('ka-lə-ban) an ugly creature, half man, half monster, in Shakespeare's *The Tempest*

**cal li o pe** (kə-'lῑ-ə-pē) a musical instrument with steam whistles

**Camden Town** a suburb of London

**"came down" handsomely** did a generous thing (a pun)

**can de la brum** (kan-də-'lä-brəm) large ornamental branched candlestick

**can dor** ('kan-dər) frankness

**can is ters** ('ka-nə-stərz) cases for coffee and tea

**Can no bie Lee** ('kan-ə-bē) rising ground in southern Scotland

**cant** ('kant) hypocritical preaching

**can ta ta** (kən-'tä-tə) musical accompaniment

**ca pa cious** (kə-'pā-shəs) roomy; broad

**ca pi tal** ('ka-pə-tᵊl) attractive

**ca pi ta list** ('ka-pə-tᵊl-ist) a possessor and controller of money

**cap sule** ('kap-səl) small cylindrical-shaped case

**car a coled** ('kar-ə-kōld) turned

**cardinal** a high officer in the Catholic church

**ca reer ing** (ka-'ri-riŋ) running

**car ri on** ('kar-ē-ən) dead body

**Car thu sian** (kär-'thü-zhən) one of the order of monks whose rigid vows compel almost absolute silence

**Ca sa Gui di** ('kä-sə; 'gwē-dē)

**case ment** ('kās-mənt) window opening on hinges from one side

**cas tel la ted** ('kas-tə-lā-təd) built like a castle, with towers and ramparts

**castes** ('kasts) different ranks of society

**cas u al ly** ('kazh-wə-lē) carelessly

**catch** a round

**cath o lic** ('kath-lik) universal

**caus tic** ('kȯs-tik) sharp

**cau ter ized** ('kȯ-tə-rØzd) burned to prevent infection

**cav al cade** (ka-vəl-'kād) horseback procession

**Ca wein** (kā-'wØn)

**Ce dra** ('sē-drə) a river

**celebrated herd in the poem** *see* Wordsworth's poem "March"

**ce les tial** (sə-'les-chəl) divine

**cen ser** ('sen-sər) vessel for perfumes or to burn incense in

**Cen ten ni al** (sen-'te-nē-əl) 100th anniversary of 1776; centennial birthday, 100th anniversary

**certain flight** straight, sure path

**ces sa tion** (se-'sā-shən) stopping

**C'est toi, c'est toi, Marcel! Mon frere comme je suis heureuse** ('sā 'twä mär-'sel mō 'frer 'kem 'zhə 'swē zər-'rüz)

**chafed ocean-side** ('chāft) wave-washed shore

**chaf finch** ('cha-finch) common European song bird

**chaise** ('shāz) light carriage; chaise and pair, carriage and two horses

**Chal de an plain** (kal-'dē-ən) wide, uncultivated stretches of land in Chaldea, an ancient country of Asia

**cha lised** ('cha-ləst) cup shaped

**Chalk ley's journal** ('chȯk-lēz) the incident was retold from the *Journal of Thomas Chalkley* (1675-1741), a traveling Quaker preacher

**chambered cell** roomlike part of the shell

**chan cel** ('chan-səl) the part of the church reserved for the ministers or priests

**change ling** ('chānj-liŋ) child supposed to have been changed, by fairies, for another

**'Change, upon** in the Royal Exchange, the center of London commerce

**chap let** ('chap-lət) rosary

**character** standing

**chargeable** burdensome

**charger** horse

**Charles the Voluptuous** (və-'ləp-chə-wəs)  Charles II of England (1630-1685), who cared only for pleasure

**char wo man** ('chär-wu-mən)  woman hired by the day to clean

**chasm** ('ka-zᵊm)  deep break in the earth

**chaunt** ('chȯnt)  song of praise

**cheapens his array**  makes his plumage look dull and faded

**Cheapside**  street in London

**Cher so nese** ('kər-sə-nēz)  Eastern Greece

**chi val rous** ('shi-vəl-rəs)  valiant

**Chris ti na, Fort** (kris-'tē-nə)

**chro nic** ('krä-nik)  habitual

**chro ni cle** ('krä-ni-kəl)  living record

**chub**  a kind of fish

**ci de vant** ('sē-də-'vän)  former

**cir cuit** ('sər-kət)  journeys from hour to hour

**civil and religious**  both of citizenship and of the church

**claim his toll** ('tōl)  seize his share, and kill for food

**clap boards** ('kla-bȯrdz)  extra boards to keep out rain, shingles

**cla ret** ('klar-ət)  purplish red

**clar i on** ('klar-ē-ən)  clear and loud, like a trumpet

**clean-winged**  swept clean with a turkey's wing

**clem ent** ('kle-mənt)  indulgent

**clois ter** ('klȯi-stər)  covered outdoor passage lined with columns

**clout ed** ('klau̇-təd)  patched

**Co che cho** (kō-'chē-kō)

**coil**  chain; trouble

**col lab o rat ed** (kə-'la-bə-rā-təd)  wrote together

**col league** ('kä-lēg)  associate

**col on nades** (kä-lē-'nādz)  series of columns of trees

**Columbian Plains**  in Western Canada

**Columkill**  Saint Columba, an Irish missionary to Scotland in the sixth century

**col umn** ('kä-ləm)  pillar

**Co man ches** (kə-'man-chēz)  warlike Indian tribe

**come ly** ('kəm-lē)  good-looking

**comforter**  long, knitted scarf

**commonplace**  likenesses

**communing** (kə-'myü-niŋ)  having personal relations

**com pact** (käm-'pakt)  crowded together

**com pass** ('käm-pəs)  range

**compassed** controlled
**compass flower** plant with leaves which indicate the points of the compass
**com pen sate** ('käm-pən-sāt) make up
**com pe tence** ('käm-pə-təns) wealth
**com pe tent** ('käm-pə-tənt) good
**composed** at rest
**com pound** ('käm-paúnd) mixture
**com pre hen sive** (käm-pri-'hend-siv) extensive; comprehensive ocean, vast extent
**con ceived** (kən-'sēvd) begun
**con cep tion** (kən-'sep-shən) design; idea
**con cur rence** (kən-'kər-əns) agreement
**con curs with their movements** (kən-'kərz) assists in their undertakings
**con demn** (kən-'dem) criticize
**con de scen sion** (kän-di-'sen-chən) friendliness as though they were equals
**con duce** (kən-'düs) lead
**con du cive** (kən-'dü-siv) helpful
**con fis ca ted** ('kän-fə-skä-təd) seized
**con fla gra tion** ('kän-flə-'grā-shən) fire
**con found** (kən-'faúnd) confuse
**con gealed** (kən-'jēld) hardened; congealed into, shown in
**con i cal** ('kä-ni-kəl) cone shaped
**con jec ture** (kən-'jek-chər) infer; think
**con nu bi al** (kə-'nü-bē-əl) matrimonial
**con scious ness** ('kän-chəs-nəs) knowledge
**con se cra tion** ('kän-sə-'krā-shən) giving up in a noble manner
**constituted** lawful—here, English
**con sum ma tion** (kän-sə-'mä-shən) bringing to a perfect close
**contemplation of theorists** ('thē-ə-rists) attention of those who merely think about it and do not put their ideas into practice
**con tem po ra ry** (kən-'tem-pə-rer-ē) of the present day
**con tig u ous** (kən-'ti-gyə-wəs) adjoining
**con tri tion** (kən-'tri-shən) repentance
**con tro ver sy** ('kän-trə-vər-sē) dispute
**con vened** (kən-'vēnd) called together
**conventional standards of greatness** the way the majority of people decide whether a man is great or not

**con vert**  (kän-'vərt)  change
**co op er at ion**  (kō-ä-pə-'rā-shən)  help
**cope**  ('kōp)  canopy
**co pi ous**  ('kō-pē-əs)  many
**copper**  wash-boiler; kettle
**cor al reefs**  ('kȯr-əl)  skeletons of certain small sea animals have been
    deposited through the ages and form islands
**Corner for the Rustic Muse**  column of contributed poetry
**Cornland**  farmland, in general
**cor po ra tion**  (kȯr-pə-'rā-shən)  legislative body
**cor ral**  (kə-'ral)  an enclosure for confining animals
**Cor reg gi o**  (kə-'re-jē-ō)  Italian artist
**cor rob o ra ted**  (kə-'rä-bə-rā-təd)  admitted the truth of
**corrupt**  spoiled; dishonest; corrupted, changed from good to bad;
    corruption, dishonesty
**corse let**  ('kȯr-slət)  armor
**Cos ta Ri ca's everglades**  (kȯs-tä-'rē-kə)  swamps of Costa Rica, a
    republic in Central America
**Cotton Mather**  American clergyman (1663-1728)
**couch ant**  ('kau̇-chənt)  squatting
**cou lee**  ('kü-lē)  bed of a dried-up stream
**coun ter feit**  ('kau̇nt-ər-fit)  pretend
**counterplots**  schemes to defeat him
**counter-proposition**  proposal  in answer to your own
**cou reurs des bois**  (kü-'rər-dä-bwä)  French or French and Indian
    hunters and traders of western North America, especially Canada
**court i er**  ('kōr-tē-ər)  attendant on a king, queen, or prince
**cov ert ly**  ('kō-vərt-lē)  secretly
**cov et ous**  ('kə-və-təs)  greedy
**coy o te**  ('kø-ō-tē)  prairie wolf
**crane**  iron hook for supporting kettles over a fire; machine for handling
    great weights
**crank**  top heavy, a fault of ships of that time
**cran nied**  ('kra-nēd)  having crevices
**cra vat**  (krə-'vat)  necktie
**crav en**  ('krā-vən)  coward
**craw**  crop
**cre den tials**  (kri-'den-chəlz)  letters of recommendation
**cred i tor**  ('kre-di-tər)  the one to whom you owe money
**cre du li ty**  (kri-'dü-lə-tē)  willingness to believe

**creed of caste** belief that one must remain in the class into which one was born

**Creeks** ('krēks) Indians who went from Georgia beyond the Mississippi in 1826

**Cre ole** ('krē-ōl) person of Spanish or French descent brought up in a colonial possession

**cring ing** ('krin-jiŋ) shrinking

**croup** ('krüp) back of the horse

**crown** English coin, ordinarily worth about $1.20 [1921]

**cru sade** (krü-'sād) fight for American ideals

**crypt** ('kript) hiding place

**crys tal line** ('kris-tə-lən) uncloudy

**Cuban business** Spanish-American war, 1898, to free Cuba from Spanish misrule

**cumberless** free

**cum brous** ('kəm-brəs) clumsy

**cunning-warded** carefully guarded

**cu po la** ('kyü-pə-lə) peaked structure

**cur few** ('kər-fyü) a bell signalling people to retire to their homes

**cut lass** ('kət-ləs) short, heavy sword

**cy press tree** ('sØ-prəs) tree used as a symbol of mourning

**daft** foolish

**das tard** ('das-tərd) coward

**daunt ed** ('dȯn-təd) scared

**daunt less** ('dȯnt-ləs) brave

**daws** ('dȯz) jackdaws, birds noted for stealing

**deal forms** benches made of pine

**dearth** ('dərth) want

**de bris** (də-'brē) ruins; rubbish

**de cant er** (di-'kan-tər) glass bottle

**de ceased** (di-'sēst) dead

**dec i sive** (di-'sØ-siv) clear

**de co ra of mere fashion** (dā-'kȯ-rə) the style of the times

**de co rum** (dē-'kȯr-əm) idea of what was proper; dignity

**decrepitude** (di-'kre-pə-tüd) feebleness

**de cry** (di-'krØ) undervalue

**def er ence** ('de-fə-rəns) respect

**de fi ance** (di-'fØ-əns) challenge

**de file** (di-'fØl) narrow pass

**deflowered**  opened out; killed
**deformity**  (di-'fór-mə-tē)  wrong form
**deftly**  cleverly
**de gen er ate**  (di-'jen-ə-rāt)  sink dishonored
**deg ra da tion**  (də-gra-'dā-shən)  gradual process of becoming worse
**deigned**  ('dānd)  kindly consented
**delegated power**  ('de-li-gā-təd)  power of one to act or vote for others, with their permission
**de li ri ous**  (di-'lir-ē-əs)  wildly happy
**De los**  ('dē-läs)  island southeast of Greece
**dem a gogue**  ('de-mə-gäg)  leader who has the confidence of the people but who has not their welfare at heart
**de mean or**  (di-'mē-nər)  bearing
**De me tri us**  (di-'mē-trē-əs)
**dem o cra cy**  (di-'mä-krə-sē)  a government by the people
**de mo ni ac**  (di-'mō-nē-ak)  wicked
**den i zens**  ('de-nə-zənz)  workers
**de pend ed**  (di-'pen-dəd)  hung
**de pict**  (di-'pikt)  picture
**de ploy ing**  (di-'plói-iŋ)  enlarging
**de pop u la ted**  (dē-'pä-pyə-lā-təd)  deprived of inhabitants
**de rived**  (di-'rØvd)  received; born
**de scried**  (di-'skrØd)  made out
**desert**  ('de-zərt)  lonely; sandy waste
**desert's highest born**  the proudest and most intelligent of the desert animals
**destined end**  ('des-tənd)  end nature intended for him
**de tract**  (di-'trakt)  take away (their honor)
**de vice**  (di-'vØs)  trick
**de vi ous**  ('di-vē-əs)  winding; restless
**dev o tee**  (de-və-'tē)  very religious person
**dew drop**  ('dü-dräp)
**dexterously**  ('dek-strə-əs-lē)  skillfully
**di a tribe**  ('dØ-ə-trØb)  article of abuse
**dif fuse**  (di-'fyüz)  spread; diffused, given to many instead of to only one; diffusion, spreading
**dight**  ('dØt)  decked
**di lap i dat ed**  (də-'la-pə-dā-təd)  old and worn-out looking
**diligence**  perseverance

**dim i nu tion** (di-mə-'nü-shən) lessening
**dimpling valleys** fertile, rolling ground
**dip** candle
**dirge** ('dərg) funeral song
**dirges of his Hope** death songs of his last hope
**dis af fec tion** (di-sə-'fek-shən) hostility
**dis ci plined intellect** ('di-sə-plənd) well-trained mind
**dis con cert** (dis-kən-'sərt) confusion
**dis coun te nanc ing** (dis-'kaùn-tᵊn-ən(t)-siŋ) discouraging
**dis course** ('dis-kōrs) speech
**dis cred i ted** (dis-'krə-də-təd) disbelieved
**dis gorged** (dis-'gȯrjd) threw out
**dis mant ling** (dis-'mant-liŋ) removing its guns, and then selling
**dis mem ber ed** (dis-'mem-bərd) separate
**dis pelled** (di-'speld) driven away
**dis perse** (di-'spərs) send away
**dis pu ta tious** (dis-pyù-'tā-shəs) argumentative
**dis si pat ed, been** ('di-sə-pā-təd) disappeared
**dis sol u tion** (di-sə-'lü-shən) complete breaking down
**dis so nant** ('di-sə-nənt) discordant
**distant** unsociable
**ditto** image
**di vers** ('d∅-vərs) many; different
**di ver si fied** (də-'vər-sə-f∅d) various
**divert** (də-'vərt) turn; diverted, amused
**di vine** (də-'v∅n) foretell; guess
**doc ile to the helm** ('dä-səl) easily steered
**doc trine** ('däk-trən) lesson
**doff** remove
**dog days** hottest part of the summer
**dog ged** ('dȯ-gəd) stubborn
**domestic trib u la tion** (tri-byə-'lā-shən) matrimonial troubles
**domestic tyranny** ('tir-ə-nē) an enemy to democracy in our coun-
    try
**dom i cile** ('dä-mə-s∅l) home; here, wagon
**dom i nant** ('dä-mə-nənt) impressive
**Don Juan** ('dän-hwän)
**dot age** ('dō-tij) foolish affection
**dot ard** ('dō-tərd) old idiot
**doub let** ('dəb-lət) close-fitting coat

**dow er** ('daủ-ər) treasure; gift, wealth, or property which a bride brings to her husband; dowering, supporting; dowerless, without any money or property to bring to her husband

**draught** ('draft) drink

**draught-board** ('draft) checker board

**dread** ('dred) dreadful

**drought** ('draủt) dryness

**Druids of eld** ancient order of Celts who held trees sacred

**Dryad** ('drØ-ad) wood nymph

**du bi ous** ('dü-bē-əs) uncertain

**duc til i ty** (dək-'ti-lə-tē) imparts "makes it so it'll roll"

**Duf feld** ('də-felt) town in Belgium

**dug out** ('dəg-aủt) cave where the soldiers lived

**du ly** ('dü-lē) conscientiously

**Du val** (dü-'väl)


**Earthquake day** *see* Lisbon

**Ec cen tric** (ik-'sen-trik) peculiar

**ec sta sy** ('ek-stə-sē) happy outburst; great joy

**Eden never lost, charm which** love

**ed i fice** ('e-də-fəs) a house

**ef fi ca cious** (e-fə-'kā-shəs) efficient

**ef fi ca cy** ('e-fi-kə-se) power

**eg lan tine** ('e-glən-tØn) the sweetbrier

**e go tism** ('ē-gə-ti-zəm) conceit

**e jac u la tion** (i-ja-kyə-'lā-shən) exclamation

**eke** ('ēk) also

**elements** noise of the wind, etc.

**elfin** fairy

**e lic i ted** (i-'li-sə-təd) drew the information

**"el lum"** dialect for elm

**Ellwood, Thomas** Quaker author of an epic poem of the life of David

**elm-tree** ('elm)

**e lu ci da tion** (i-lü-sə-'dā-shən) explanation

**Elysian Fields** (i-'li-zhən) the Greeks' name for paradise; they believed the soul would be forced to wander about through eternity unless the body was buried

**em a na tion** (e-mə-'na-shən) gift

**em bar go** (im-'bär-gō) obstruction

**embattled** armed

**em bel lish ments** (im-'be-lish-mənts) decorations
**em bod i ment** (im-'bä-di-mənt) example
**em bra sure** (im-'brā-zhər) wall opening
**e merge** (i-'mərj) appear
**em i nence** ('e-mə-nəns) height
**e mit ted** (ē-'mi-təd) uttered
**em pow er ed** (im-'paú-ərd) given the power
**en am eled** (i-'na-məld) glossy
**en am ored** (i-'na-mərd) much in love
**en com pass** (in-'kem-pəs) surround
**en core** ('än-kōr) besides
**en cy clo pe di a** (in-sØ-klə-'pē-dē-ə) book of information for reference
**ends will change** future will be different
**en gross es you** (in-'grō-səs) occupies all your thought and time
**en join** (in-'jóin) require; enjoined, commanded
**en kind leth** (in-'kin-də-ləth) inspires
**en voy** ('en-vói) representative
**envy the vice of republics** in a country where all people are politically equal, some are likely to dislike those who have more money or intelligence then they
**e rad i cat ed** (i-'ra-də-kā-təd) removed
**Erze roum** (erz-'rüm) a division of Turkey
**Esq., esquire** title of courtesy
**es say** ('e-sā) attempt
**es say** (e-'sā) to try
**es sence** ('e-sᵊns) soul
**eternal summer** summer all the year round
**e the re al** (i-'thir-ē-əl) spiritual
**ethereal minstrel** celestial singer
**eu lo gy** ('yü-lə-jē) oration of praise
**even** ('ē-vᵊn) evening
**ever-during** constant
**e vinced** (i-'vinst) clearly showed
**ev o lu tions** (e-və-'lü-shənz) dancing
**ewe-necked** ('yü) with a hollowed-out, thin neck
**ex al ta tion** (eg-zól-'tā-shən) glorifying; intense emotion
**ex cheq uer** ('eks-che-kər) purse
**ex e cra ble** ('ek-si-krə-bəl) shocking
**ex e cu tor** (ig-'ze-kyə-tər) person appointed to carry out the provi-

sions of a will

**ex em pli fy** (ig-'zem-plə-fØ) illustrate

**Ex pe di tion a ry** (ek-spə-'di-shə-ner-ē) sent from one country to another

**ex pos tu la tions** (ik-späs-chə-'lā-shənz) protests

**ex qui site** (ek-'skwi-zət) perfect

**extent of its compass** length of range, from high notes to low

**ex tinct** (ik-'stiŋkt) dead

**ex trav a gance** (ik-'stra-vi-gənts) absurdity

**ex trem i ty** (ik-'stre-mə-tē) farthest part; worst place he could think of

**ex u ber ant fertility** (ig-'zü-bə-rənt) great richness

**ex ul ta tion** (ek-səl-'tā-shən) delight

**Fabre** ('fäbrᵊ)

**fabric of social order** organization of humanity

**facetious** (fə-'sē-shəs) agreeable

**fac ile** ('fa-səl) easy

**fac il i ty** (fə-'si-lə-tē) readiness

**fac tion** ('fak-shən) party politics

**fac tious** ('fak-shəs) own selfish

**fain** ('fān) forced; gladly; fain for, eager to

**Fal co Star len** ('fal-kō; stär-lən)

**familiar of men** companion of people

**familiars** intimate friends

**Fan euil Hall** ('fan-yəl)

**fan tas tic** (fan-'tas-tik) extraordinary; queer

**far thing** ('fär-thiŋ) fourth of an English penny, half cent in our money [1921]

**fastnesses** strongholds

**fatal sisters** three Fates of Greek mythology, who were believed to decide the course of men's lives

**Fa ta Mor ga na** (fä-tə; mȯr-'gä-nə) a mirage, that is, an appearance which seems real but actually is not

**fate of a nation** future happiness of the land

**Father of Waters** Mississippi River

**fath om** ('fa-thəm) six feet

**fay** ('fā) fairy

**fe al ty** ('fēl-tē) loyalty

**Federal or Democrat** the names of the political parties of that time

**feign** ('fān) imitate; like to imagine
**feint** ('fānt) pretense; trick
**Fe lic ian** (fi-'li-shən)
**fe lic i ty** (fi-'li-sə-tē) happiness
**fell** marsh; fierce
**fel loe** ('fel-ō) wooden rim of a wheel
**fer ment** ('fər-ment) tumult
**fer ret** ('fer-ət) sharp—like a ferret's teeth
**fete** ('fāt) festival
**fet lock** ('fet-läk) the tuft of hair on a horse's foot
**fet tered** ('fe-tərd) bound with chains; fettered race, enslaved people
**feu dal or military principle** ('fyü-dᵊl) system which requires people to remain in the class in which they were born, or that which keeps them under their ruler's military power
**fictitious** (fik-'ti-shəs) artificial
**filberts** nuts
**fil i al** ('fi-lē-əl) of a son or daughter
**filled the chains** had fallen into the "chains" or rigging along the sides
**Fi na le** (fə-'na-lē) end; last part
**finished talent** natural ability developed to its highest point
**firelock** old-fashioned gun
**fire-winged by martyrdom** many early Quakers suffered death, by burning, because of their religious beliefs
**fir ma ment** ('fər-mə-mənt) heavens
**five-and-sixpence** five shillings and sixpence = $1.32 [1921]
**flag-bird** French flag, flying in the air
**fla gon** ('fla-gən) a large drinking vessel
**flake** ('flāk) bunch
**flam ing** ('flām-iŋ) set on fire by the enemy
**flat heresy** ('her-ə-sē) absolute disloyalty
**flaunt ing** ('flȯn-tiŋ) insolent
**Flemish pictures** pictures which treat simple subjects lovingly and in detail. Rembrandt's works are good examples of this school
**Fleu rette** (flü-'ret)
**fluc tu ate** ('flək-chə-wāt) changed
**flue** ('flü) pipe
**foal** ('fōl) colt
**foc sle** ('fōk-səl) forecastle, fore part of upper deck

**foi ble**  ('fòi-bəl)  weakness
**foil**  ('fòil)  outwit
**folded**  ('fōl-dəd)  put in their enclosure for the night
**fo li age**  ('fō-lē-ij)
**Fontaine-qui-bout**  (fän-'tän-ke-bü)
**Foolish Virgin**  *see* Matthew XXV:1-13
**for age**  ('fòr-ij)  food, usually for animals
**for bear**  (fòr-'bar)  stop
**forbearance**  patience
**for bears**  (fòr-'barz)  ancestors
**fore bod ing**  (fōr-'bō-diŋ)  terrifying
**forecloser**  man who forces his debtors to give up their property if
    they have no money
**fore head**  ('for-həd)
**for sworn**  (fòr-'swōrn)  forsaken
**for that**  because
**forwardness**  preparation
**fouled the scuppers**  filled the holes used to let water run off the
    decks
**fourscore**  eighty
**fowler**  hunter
**frail tenant**  the nautilus, a shellfish
**Franks**  other European powers
**fraught**  ('fròt)  burdened
**fray**  ('frā)  fight
**fre quent ing**  ('frē-kwən-tiŋ)  visiting often
**from tent to tent**  from grave to grave
**from zone to zone**  from north to south
**fron tier**  (frən-'tir)  farthest part of settled territory
**front let**  ('frənt-lət)  forehead
**fru gal i ty**  (frü-'ga-lə-tē)  thrift
**fume**  ('fyüm)  rage
**funeral-pile**  the Romans burned their dead on wooden piles
**furze**  ('ferz)  evergreen shrubs
**fused**  ('fyüzd)  melted solidly together
**fu tile**  ('fyü-t³l)  powerless

**Gael's blood**  ('gālz)  fighting blood of the brave Irishmen of old
**gain say**  (gān-'sā)  contradict
**gal lant**  ('ga-lənt)  brave young lover

**gal le on** ('ga-lē-ən) ancient sailing vessel
**gal liard** ('gal-yərd) a dance by two
**gal li-gas kins** (ga-li-'gas-kənz) loose breeches
**Gallipoli** (ga-'li-pə-lē)
**gallows air, with a** as though he were about to be hung
**Gam bi a** ('gam-bē-ə) river in Africa. The quoted line is from "The African Chief" by Mrs. Sarah Wentworth Morton, in a school book of Whittier's
**gam bol** ('gam-bəl) prank; frisk about; party
**garb** ('gärb) clothing
**Garcia** (gär-'sē-ə)
**garden-girt** surrounded by gardens
**gar goyle** ('gär-góil) a queerly carved, ugly, stone animal head
**gar ri son** ('gar-ə-sən) body of troops; arms
**gar ru lous** ('gar-ə-ləs) talkative
**Gas per eau** ('gas-pər-ō)
**Gate of Da mas cus** (də-'mas-kəs) in "Bedreddin Hassin," from *The Arabian Nights*
**Gates of Hercules** Gibraltar
**gaud y** ('gȯ-dē) showy
**gauge** ('gāj) measure
**gen i al** (je-nyel) comfortable
**ge nii** ('jē-nē) supernatural being in *The Arabian Nights*
**Gen i us** ('jēn-yəs) spirit
**gentlemen of the free-and-easy sort** those who are not easily alarmed
**gen u ine** ('jen-yə-wən) real
**ge o met ric signs** (jē-ə-'me-trik) patterns in regular designs
**Georg ius Se cun dus** ('jōr-jəs; sē-'kən-dəs) George II, king of England (1727-1760), was born in Germany
**Ger o ni mo** (jə-'rä-nə-mō) a chief of the Apache Indians
**ges ture** ('jes-chər) movement
**ghast ly wan** ('gast-lē; wän) deathly pale
**Ghent** ('gent) a city in Belgium, one hundred miles from Aix
**ghosts of shores** the slightest trace of land
**gigantic** (j∅-'gan-tik) most; hardest
**gills** ('gilz) loose flap of red skin under beak
**gird ed** ('gər-dəd) bound
**giveth grace unto every art** makes all work delightful
**glad i a tors** ('gla-dē-a-tərz) those who fought with weapons for the

amusement of the Roman public

**glam our** ('gla-mər) charm

**glean ings** ('glē-niŋz) collections

**glebe** ('glēb) ground

**glee** ('glē) song in parts

**gleeds** ('glēdz) burning coals

**glistened at her noon** she was still youthful in middle life

**gloaming** ('glō-miŋ) twilight

**Glorious Revolution** the people of England revolted against their king, James II, because he wished to rule without their aid

**goad** ('gōd) whip; necessity which acts as a whip

**golden quest** pursuit of wealth; the reference is to the story of Jason and the golden fleece

**Go li ath** (gə-'lØ-əth) the giant killed by David with a sling. *See* I Samuel XVII

**Goody** woman

**Goth ic** ('gä-thik) of Gothic architecture a beautiful and dignified style of medieval architecture distinguished especially by its pointed arches

**gra da tion** (grā-'dā-shən)blending of notes

**gra na ry** ('grā-nə-rē) storehouse for grain

**Grand-Pré** (grän-'prā) French for *great prairie*

**gra tis** ('gra-təs) for nothing

**Gray A zores** ('ā-zōrz) distant islands. The Azores are west of Spain in the Atlantic Ocean

**Great Harry** first warship of the British navy, built in 1488

**great plot** play taking place on "the great stage of the Nation's history"

**gren a dier** (grən-ə-'dir) a member of a special regiment or corps

**grip ing** ('gri-piŋ) painful

**grist-mill** mill for grinding grain

**grizzled** gray

**groat** ('grōt) old English coin worth two cents in our money

**grog** ('gräg) mixture of liquor and water unsweetened

**groom** servant

**gro tesque** (grō-'tesk) very queer

**guile** ('gØl) deceit; guileless, innocent

**guinea** ('gi-nē) an English gold coin no longer in use worth about $5.11 [1921]

**guise** ('gØz) manner; appearance

**gun da low** ('gən-də-lō) variant of *gondola,* a flat-bottomed boat

**ha bil i ments** (hə-'bi-lə-mənts) clothing

**hab i ta tion** (ha-bə-'tā-shən) home

**hag gard** ('ha-gərd) dreary; tired-out

**"hahnsum"** ('han-səm) *handsome,* good looking

**hake** ('hāk) fish related to the cod

**half a crown** about sixty cents [1921]

**half-a-quar tern of ig nit ed brandy** ('kwȯr-tərn; ig-'n∅-təd) half a gill of brandy which had been lighted and burned for a few seconds

**half-re cum bent** (ri-'kəm-bənt) half-lying, half-sitting

**hal low** ('ha-lō) make holy

**hap less** ('ha-pləs) unfortunate

**ha rangue** (hə-'raŋ) speech; haranguing, giving a speech

**har ass** (hə-'ras) annoy

**ha rem** ('har-əm) here, hens. The wives of a Turk are called his harem

**harmonious madness** a burst of inspired poetry

**har row** ('har-ō) agricultural implement to level plowed land

**har ry** ('har-ē) attack; follow

**haunts** ('hȯntz) homes

**haut boy** ('hō-bȯi) a musical wind instrument

**haz ard ing** ('ha-zər-diŋ) risking

**hearth** ('härth) fireplaces

**Heathen Nine** nine Muses of Greek mythology, patrons of the fine arts

**heath er** ('he-thər) small blossoming evergreen shrubs

**he carries weight** he is weighted down heavily as a handicap, as race horses sometimes are

**heif er** ('he-fər) young cow

**heir loom** ('ar-lüm) inherited gift

**heir of his dex ter i ty** ('ar; dek-'ster-ə-tē) one who would inherit one's skill

**held in re pute** (ri-'pyüt) considered honorable

**Hel i con** ('he-lə-kän) a mountain in central Greece

**helmsman** man who steers

**her e sy** ('her-ə-sē) disloyalty

**Her mes** ('hər-mēz) famous Egyptian philosopher

**Her mia** ('hər-mi-ə)

**Her na ni** (ər-'nä-nē) an opera by Verdi, the Italian composer

**high divide** ridge of high ground between two drainage areas

**hi la rious** (hi-'lar-ē-əs) laughing and talking
**hoar** ('hōr) white with age
**hoard ing** ('hōr-diŋ) being saved
**hob** projection on a fireplace to warm things on
**hobbling** tying the legs so that the horses could not run away
**Hollands** strong, alcoholic drink
**hol ster** ('hōl-stər) pistol case
**hom age** ('ä-mij) respect
**ho ri zon** (hə-'rØ-zⁿn) skyline; landscape: top
**horny** calloused
**hostage from the future took** gained what would help him in time to come
**house of Stuart** Scotch and English royal family to which Charles II, James II, and William III belonged
**housings** saddle cover and trimmings
**hue and cry** loud outcry with which law-breakers were anciently pursued
**humility** (hyü-'mi-lə-tē) humbleness
**Hy me ne al** (hØ-mə-'nē-əl) for a wedding
**hy pothe sis** (hØ-'pä-thə-səs) supposition
**hys sop** ('hi-səp) sprinkler for holy water

**id i om** ('i-dē-əm) phrasing
**i dyl** ('i-dᵊl) poem of rustic life
**idyl lic ease** (Ø-'di-lik) carefree life in the country
**ig no ble** (ig-'nō-bəl) undignified
**ig no min i ous ly** (ig-nə-'mi-nē-əs-lē) dishonored and disgraced
**ig no ra mus** (ig-nə-'rä-məs) an ignorant person
**il lim it a ble** (il-'li-mə-tə-bəl) boundless; absolute
**il lus tri ous** (i-'ləs-trē-əs) remarkable
**im be cil i ty** (im-bə-'si-lə-tē) stupidity
**immortality** life beyond the grave
**imparted** given
**im pend ing** (im-'pen-diŋ) overhanging
**im pen e tra ble** (im-'pe-nə-trə-bəl) dark which could not be seen through; which he could not get over
**im per cep ti bly** (im-pər-'sep-tə-blē) gradually
**im pet u os i ty** (im-pe-chə-'wä-sə-tē) impatience; impetuous, impatient
**im pla ca ble** (im-'pla-kə-bəl) unsatisfied

**im por tu nate** (im-'pór-chə-nət) insistent
**im pos tor** (im-'päs-tər) pretender
**im pos ture** (im-'päs-chər) trickery
**im po tent** ('im-pə-tənt) helpless
**im pre ca tion** (im-pri-'kā-shən) curse
**im pro pri e ty** (im-prə-'pr∅-ə-tē) improper behavior
**improvident** (im-'prä-və-dənt) thoughtless of the future
**im pro vi sa to ri** (im-'prä-və-zə-'tōr-ē) those who compose and sing, or recite, short poems
**in ad e quate to** (i-'na-di-kwət) unable to meet
**in ar tic u late** (i-när-'ti-kyə-lət) indistinct
**in au di ble** (i-'nó-də-bəl) which would not be heard
**inborn certainty** ('ser-tᵊn-tē) perfect sureness
**in cal cu la ble** (in-'kal-kya-lə-bəl) priceless
**in can ta tion** (in-kan-'tā-shən) magic chant
**in ca pac i ty** (in-kə-'pa-sə-tē) inability
**incessant** constant (dropping of the sands in the hourglass)
**in cle ment** (in-'klε-mənt) severe
**in co her ent** (in-kō-'hir-ənt) which could not be understood
**in con stan cy** (in-'kän-stənt-sē) unfaithfulness
**in con ti nent ly** (in-'känt-tᵊn-ənt-lē) uncontrollably
**in cred i ble** (in-'kre-də-bəl) unbelievable
**in cred u lous** (in-'kre-jə-ləs) doubtful
**in dict ing** (in-'d∅-tiŋ) using as a charge of arrest
**indispensable** (in-di-'spen-sə-bəl) absolutely necessary
**in di vid u al is tic** (in-də-vij-wə-'lis-tik) personal
**in do lent** ('in-də-lənt) even-tempered
**in dom i ta ble** ('in-dä-mə-tə-bəl) untamable
**in ev i ta ble** (i-'ne-və-tə-bəl) unavoidable
**in ex o ra ble** (i-'nek-sə-rə-bəl) unrelenting
**in ex pli ca ble** (i-nik-'spli-kə-bəl) inexplainable
**in fal li ble** (in-'fa-lə-bəl) sure
**in fa mous** ('in-fə-məs) shameful
**infernal atmosphere** breeze from the lower regions; inferno, hot region
**infractions** (in-'frak-shənz) breaks
**in got** ('in-gət) a bar of metal
**in gress nor e gress** ('in-grəs; 'ē-grəs) entrance nor departure
**inimitable** (i-'ni-mə-tə-bəl) matchless
**i ni ti a tive** (i-'ni-shə-tiv) leadership

**in merry pin** in a jolly mood
**innocent of books** whose knowledge had not come from reading
**in quir y** (in-'kwȮr-ē) curiosity
**in sid i ous ly** (in-'si-dē-əs-lē) treacherously
**in sin u ate** (in-'sin-yə-wāt) suggest
**in stan ta ne ous** (int-stən-'tā-nē-əs) immediate
**in stinct** (in-'stiŋkt) feeling
**in su per a ble** (in-'sü-pə-rə-bəl) incurable
**in sur gents** (in-'sər-jənts) rebels
**in tan gi ble power** (in-'tan-jə-bəl) a power not defined or necessarily legal, but very strong
**in ter cedes** (in-tər-'sēdz) pleads with
**in ter course** ('in-tər-kōrs) experience
**in ter lude** ('in-tər-lüd) short poem making a break in the longer one
**in ter me di ate** (in-tər-'mē-dē-ət) gradual
**in ter ven tion** (in-tər-'ven-shən) influence
**in ti ma tion** (in-tə-'mā-shən) suggestion
**in tol er able** (in-'tä-lə-rə-bəl) hardly to be stood
**into the air's embrace** straight over the open space
**in tri cate** ('in-tri-kət) many perplexing
**in trigue** (in-'trēg) plotting
**in un date** ('i-nən-dāt) flood; inundated, flooded
**in vet er ate an tip i thies** (in-'ve-tə-rət; an-'ti-pə-thēz) incurable; inveterate antipathies, long-standing hatreds
**in vol un tar i ly** (in-vä-lən-'ter-ə-lē) without thinking
**inward light** religious beliefs
**i ras ci ble** (i-'ra-sə-bəl) hot-tempered
**i rised** ('Ø-rəst) colored
**i ron-mon ger y** ('Ø-ərn 'mən-gə-rē) general name for all articles made of iron
**ir rep a ra ble** (i-'re-pə-rə-bəl) beyond repair; not to be prevented
**ir re sist i ble** (ir-i-'zis-tə-bəl) overpowering
**ir res o lu tion** (i-re-zə-'lü-shən) hesitation
**Ish ma el's children** ('ish-mā-əl) Indians who, like Ishmael, "lived in the wilderness" and were archers. *See* Genesis XXI:20
**Islands of the Blest** imaginary islands in the Atlantic where the favorites of the gods went after death
**Is ling ton** ('iz-liŋ-tən) a section of London
**i so lat ed** ('Ø-sə-lā-təd) shut off

**jack boots** ('jak-büts) large knee-boots
**Jacob, ladder of** *see* Genesis XXVIII:12; Jacob of old, *see* Genesis XXXII
**jad ed steers** ('jā-dəd) exhausted oxen
**jan gling** ('jaŋ-gliŋ) quarreling
**jer kin** ('jər-kən) jacket
**jes sa mine** ('jes-mən) climbing shrub with fragrant yellow flowers; jasmine
**Jes u it** ('je-zú-ət) Catholic order of the Society of Jesus
**Joaquin** (wä-'kēn)
**joc und** ('jä-kənd) merry
**Joe Miller** an English comedian
**John Rogers** a religious martyr
**Jolly Roger** the black banner of pirates
**journalist** magazine or newspaper writer
**jun to** ('jən-tō) association
**Jupiter** chief of the gods

**keel** ('kel) ridge on bottom of a boat
**keel son** ('kel-sən) strengthening structure above the keel, which *see*
**kelp** ('kelp) seaweed
**kenned** ('kend) knew
**khan** ('kän) resting place for caravans
**kindred points** far-distant places that are alike
**kine** ('kØn) cows
**King Herod** king of Judea, who slew all children under two years of age. *See* Matthew II:16
**kir tle** ('kər-tᵊl) jacket and upper skirt attached to it
**knave** ('nāv) rascal
**knees** natural bends of wood selected to fit angles in frame of ship
**knocker** a more or less decorated metal door fixture which took the place of a doorbell
**knolls** ('nōlz) small round bills
**Koor dis tan** (kür-də-'stän) region formerly partly in Turkey and partly in Persia
**Kur ro glou** (kər-ə-'glü)
**Ky rat** ('kē-rät)

**lab o ra to ry** ('la-brə-tōr-ē) workroom for chemical experiments
**lack a dai si cal** (la-kə-'dā-zi-kəl) languid

**laggard in love**  unworthy suitor
**lagoon**  small shallow arm of a large body of water
**La Illah illa Allah**  there is no God except Allah
**La jeunesse**  (lä-zhü-'nəs)
**lan guor**  ('laŋ-gər)  dullness
**Lannes**  ('län)
**La oc o ön**  (lä-'ä-kə-wän)  Trojan priest of Apollo who with his two
  sons was killed by serpents coiling about them
**laps ing**  ('lap-siŋ)  gently splashing
**Las car swarthy**  ('las-kər)  dark-skinned East Indian sailor
**la tent**  ('lä-t∘nt)  hidden
**Latin fraud**  Italian treachery.  Greece knew she could not depend
  upon Italy
**laughed a pitiless laugh**  ('läft)  was almost unbearably hot
**lav ing**  ('lä-viŋ)  dipping into the water
**Law of Average, according to the**  there is as much chance that one
  will be right as there is that one will be wrong
**lay**  ('lā)  song
**lea**  ('lē)  meadow
**lea guer**  ('lē-gər)  camp of a besieging army
**league, with**  ('lēg)  with an understanding
**Le an der**  (lē-'an-dər)  in Greek legend, the lover of Hero, whom he
  swam the Hellespont (modern Dardanelles) to visit each night. One
  night her light, by which he was guided, went out, and he perished.
  When Hero discovered his body on shore, she killed herself
**Le blanc**  (lə-'blónk)
**Le Carillon de Dunkerque**  ('kar-ə-län; 'dan-kərk)  The Chimes of
  Dunkirk
**ledgers**  account books
**lee**  ('lē)  the side protected from the wind; protection
**le gend**  ('le-jənd)  a story coming down from the past
**le gion**  ('lē-jən)  multitude; too many to count
**Le tiche**  ('lə-tish)
**Leuc tra**  ('lük-trə)  where the Boeotians, to which people Spartacus's
  ancestors belonged, defeated the Spartans, another Greek people
**Lexington and Concord**  the scene of the first bloodshed of the
  Revolution
**like the Hebrew**  *see* Exodus XII:21,30
**Li lin au**  (li-'lin-aủ)
**lim pid**  ('lim-pəd)  clear

**linchpin** pin to hold wheel on
**linking fancy unto fancy** imagining one thing after another
**links** torches
**linnet** small singing-bird
**Lis bon** ('liz-bən) city of Portugal which had an earthquake in 1755
**lis some** ('li-səm) graceful
**lists** knightly contests
**lithe** ('lØth) graceful
**littered** ('li-tərd) spread down straw, hay, etc., as bedding for animals
**little rel e van cy bore** ('re-lə-vən-sē) had little to do with the matter asked about
**li ve ry** ('li-və-rē) citizens of London; uniform
**livid** ('li-ved) grayish; pale
**local discriminations** (dis-kri-mə-'nā-shənz) loyalty to one's state or city
**Loch in var** (lók-ən-'vär)
**logical heirs** rightful successors
**lol ling** ('lä-liŋ) lounging
**loon** large fish-eating bird
**looping** winding over
**looted** robbed
**lore** ('lōr) learning
**Louisburg** French fort on Cape Breton, captured by the English in 1745, in the war between France and England
**Loup-garou** (lü-gə-'rü) a person who has been changed into a wolf
**loved her love** a game with words beginning with letters of the alphabet
**love-knot** bow of ribbon as a token of love
**low er ing** ('laü-ər-iŋ) gloomy
**low-vaulted past** outgrown habit of life
**lu mi nous** ('lü-mə-nəs) bright
**lures made** invited me
**lu rid** ('lür-əd) stern
**lus trous** ('ləs-trəs) shining
**lyre** ('lØr) harp-like musical instrument
**Lys an der** (lØ-'san-dər)

**Mad a gas car** (ma-də-'gas-kər) island off the east coast of Africa
**magnesite and dolomite** ('mag-nə-sØt; 'dō-lə-mØt) kinds of rock used

in the making of steel

**mail of Calvin's creed**  strict belief of John Calvin, French religious reformer

**main**  ('mān)  ocean

**maize**  ('māz)  corn

**mal a dy**  ('ma-lə-dē)  trouble

**mal heureux**  (mal-hú-'rü)  French for *unhappy man*

**mal le a bil i ty**  (ma-lē-ə-'bi-lə-tē)  *see* ductility; malleable, yielding

**Mal ta**  (mȯl-tə)  British island in the Mediterranean Sea

**Mammon's vilest dust**  money; Mammon is the god of riches

**Mammoth**  large, elephant-like animal, which no longer exists

**man date**  ('man-dāt)  order

**ma neu ver**  (mə-'nü-vər)  plan to outwit the other player; act

**man ga nese**  ('man-gə-nēz)  hard, brittle, grayish white metal tinged with red

**man i fold**  ('ma-nə-fōld)  many

**manslaughter**  killing a person

**Mar a thon**  ('mar-ə-thän)  a plain in Attica, Greece, where the Greeks won a great victory over the Persians

**ma raud ers**  (ma-'rȯ-dərz)  plundering bands

**marge**  ('märj)  poetic for *margin*

**mar quis**  (mär-'kēz)  a title of nobility

**Marshal**  commander

**mar tial**  ('mär-shəl)  warlike

**masquerade li cense was unlimited**  ('l∅-sənz)  people had been allowed to wear any kind of costume they chose

**matchlock**  an old-fashioned gun

**material**  actual; worldly

**ma te ri al is tic**  (mə-tir-ē-ə-'lis-tik)  fonder of things than of ideals

**mat in**  ('ma-tᵊn)  morning song

**ma tron**  ('mā-trən)  married woman

**ma ture**  (mə-'tùr)  careful

**maud lin**  ('mȯd-lən)  silly and sentimental

**max im**  ('mak-səm)  principle

**Mc Greg or**  (mə-'kgər-gər)  Sir Gregor McGregor, who tried in 1822 to establish a colony in Costa Rica

**measure lead**  have a dance

**Mech eln**  ('me-keln)  town in Belgium

**medium**  means; medium of the plank, the captives of the pirates were blindfolded and compelled to walk off a plank into the sea

**meet** fitting

**Melita** ('me-lə-tə or me-'lē-tə) *see* shipwrecked Paul

**mem o ran dum** (me-mə-'ran-dəm) record; account; sketch

**me mo ri al** (mə-'mōr-ē-əl) Lincoln's birthplace, a log cabin near Hodgensville, Kentucky, was presented to the nation in 1916

**Mem phre ma gog** (mem-fri-'mā-gäg) lake in Vermont and Canada

**men ace** ('me-nəs) threat

**men di cant** ('men-di-kənt) begging

**men in nations** all the countries which were under Persian power

**mental ap pa ri tion** (a-pə-'ri-shən) Bill means mental **aberration** (a-bə-'rā-shən) confusion of mind

**mer ce na ry troops** ('mər-sᵊn-er-ē) soldiers paid to fight for a country not their own

**merciless a creditor in his successor** as cruel a man to owe money to in Scrooge's place

**met a mor phosed** (me-tə-'mór-fōzd) changed

**me te or, hoary** ('mē-tē-ər) strange white appearance in the sky— snow

**meter** ('mē-tər) about 3¼ feet

**metes** ('mēts) goals

**mick le** ('mi-kəl) great deal

**Middlesex** ('mi-dᵊl-seks) county in northeastern Massachusetts

**mien** ('mēn) manner

**mi gra tion** (mØ-'grā-shən) trip

**Mil ti a des** (mil-'tØ-ə-dēz) famous Athenian general and statesman

**mimic flame** reflected glow

**mi mo sa** (mə-'mō-sə) very sensitive tropical shrub

**minded** noticed

**min i a ture** ('mi-nē-ə-chùr) a small scale

**minister** messenger

**mi rage** (mə-'räzh) dream of the future

**mired** ('mØrd) stuck fast

**misanthropic** (mi-sᵊn-'thrä-pik) gloomy looking

**mis cel la ne ous tatters** (mi-sə-'lā-nē-əs) many different kinds of rags

**mis con ceive** (mis-kən-'sēv) misunderstand

**mis sal** ('mi-səl) book of religious service of the Catholic church

**mis sile** ('mi-səl) weapon

**missive** ('mi-siv) letter

**Mis so lon ghi** ('mi-sə-loŋ-gē)

**Missouri Bad Lands**  section of country that produces almost no vegetation

**moat** ('mōt) ditch of water around castle for protection

**mob violence**  gaining what he wants by organized force—strikes, etc.

**mo du la tions** (mä-jə-'lā-shənz) tones

**molten slag**  melted waste matter

**mon a mi** (mō-na-'mē) my friend

**mon grel** ('män-grəl) dog of mixed breed

**mon o graph** ('mä-nə-graf) written account of a single life

**mo not o nous** (mə-'nä-tᵊn-əs) unchanging; tiresome

**moor** ('mur) stretch of waste land; sandy marsh

**Mo ra vi an** (mə-'rä-vē-ən) of the United Brethren

**morning-star**  the brightest star of the morning

**mo rose** (mə-'rōs) ill-tempered; sullen

**mortgage fancier** ('mor-gij) one who takes pleasure in lending money as some enjoy pets

**motley-braided** ('mät-lē) made of rags of different colors

**mounting the breach**  boldly rising to the occasion

**Mo wis** ('mō-wis)

**Mo zart** ('mōt-särt) Austrian composer and pianist (1756-1791)

**mulled** ('məld) sweetened and spiced

**mulls**  meditates

**mul ti tu di nous** (məl-tə-'tüd-nəs) thousands of

**mumbled**  chewed

**mum mer** ('mə-mər) masker

**mu nif i** (myù-'ni-fi) he was going to say munificence—generosity

**must wander**  *see* Elysian Fields

**mu ta tion** (myü-'tā-shən) changes in the weather

**mutual consideration**  joint thought

**myr i ad** ('mir-ē-əd) great number; numberless

**Mystic**  river in Connecticut


**Na iad** ('nā-əd) water nymph

**Natch i toch es** (natch-ə-'tōch-ēz)

**natural make**  own disposition

**natural se quence** ('sē-kwəns) logical order of events, cause followed by result

**Nature's lyceum** (l∅-'sē-əm) school of the outdoor world

**Nebraska** Platte River

**neck or naught** no matter what happened

**ne gus** ('nē-gəs) a beverage containing wine

**ne pen the** (nə-'pen-thē) a drink producing forgetfulness of pain

**Ne ther by clan** ('ne-thər-bē) Netherby was the name of the ancestor from whom they were descended

**nethermost** lowest

**newt** ('nüt) a small, lizard like animal

**night-encampment** the cemetery

**Night's Plutonian shore** the borderland of Hades, ruled over by Pluto

**night-wind of the Past, borne on the** handed down in story

**Ni lus** ('nØ-ləs) Latin for *Nile*

**nom i nal** ('nä-mə-nᵊl) in name, not in actual practice

**Nor folk Biffins** ('nór-fək) apples from Norfolkshire, England

**Norman cap** cap worn in Normandy, which has square corners turned back from the face

**no ta ry** ('nō-tə-rē) a public officer who writes, or is witness to, legal papers

**nothing loath** no reluctance

**Nu mid i an** (nù-'mi-dē-ən) from Numidia, ancient country of North Africa

**nup tials** ('nəp-shəlz) marriage

**nur tured** ('nər-chərd) carefully tended


**oath of allegiance** solemn promise of loyalty

**o bei sance** (ō-'bē-səns) bow or other sign of respect

**ob e lisk** ('ä-bə-lisk) four-sided tapering monument

**O be ron** ('ō-bə-rän)

**ob liq u ity of moral or mental vision** (ō-'bli-kwə-tē) false ideas of right and wrong

**ob liv i ous** (ə-'bli-vē-əs) forgetting everything; oblivion, forgetfulness

**ob scene** (äb-'sēn) indecent

**ob se qui ous** (əb-'sē-kwē-əs) excessively humble

**oc clud ed** (ə-'klü-dəd) which it contains

**oc cult** (ə-'kəlt) mysterious

**of credit and renown** trusted and well known

**of fal** ('ó-fəl) rubbish

**offices** services

**of high mark** extraordinary

**Old Noll** ('nol) Oliver Cromwell

**Old Probabilities** nickname for chief of office furnishing weather reports

**O lym pus** (ə-'lim-pəs) mountain in Greece, believed by the ancient Greeks to be the home of the gods

**om i nous** ('ä-mə-nəs) threatening

**one burden bore** had one set expression

**o paque** (ō-'pāk) which could not be seen through

**Op e lou sas** (ó-pə-'lü-səs) Louisiana town

**open-hearth** one of the processes of making steel

**oppressive** burdened down

**o rac u lar** (ó-'ra-kyə-lər) like an oracle. Oracles used to utter their prophecies from the depths of eaves

**orbs** ('órbz) eyes

**Or fah** ('ór-fə)

**orthographic** (ór-thə-'gra-fik) spelling

**ost ler** ('äs-lər) stableman

**Ourcq** ('ürk)

**outgrown shell** the body which the soul has freed itself from

**out-Her o ded Herod** ('her-ə-dəd) was worse than anyone could have imagined. The character of Herod in the old-time plays was always greatly exaggerated

**O wy hee** (ō-'wØ-hē) branch of the Snake River; the region is a mountainous and desert portion of Idaho

**pa geant** ('pā-jent) exhibition

**painful Se wel's ancient tome** ('sü-əlz) William Sewel's history of the Quakers and their sufferings

**pal at a ble** ('pa-lə-tə-bəl) agreeable tasting

**pal imp sest** ('pa-ləmp-sest) parchment which has been used several times, erased and rewritten

**pall** ('pōl) covering

**pal la di um** (pə-'lā-dē-əm) safeguard

**Pal las** ('pa-las) one of the names of Athena, goddess of wisdom

**pal let** ('pa-lət) poor, small bed

**pal lid** ('pa-ləd) pale colored; pale

**pal met to** (pal-'me-tō) palm tree

**pal pa ble** ('pal-pə-bəl) heavy and close

**pan o ram ic** (pa-ne-'ra-mik) with one scene after another in succession

**par a pets** ('par-ə-pəts) railings around the roof

**pard like** leopard like

**Par lia ment** ('pär-lə-mənt)  law-making body in England corresponding to our Congress

**parted seas**  the ocean, divided by the prow into two parts

**parties**  people whose contract he was writing—a legal term

**Pas ca gou la**  (pas-kə-'gü-lə)  river in Mississippi

**passion**  sin; evil ambition; anger

**passionless**  uninterested

**pa tri arch**  ('pā-trē-ärk)  veteran

**Patrick**  Saint Patrick, patron saint of Ireland

**pat ri mo ni al**  (pa-trə-'mō-nē-əl)  inherited from his father

**pa tri ot**  ('pā-trē-ət)  one who loves his or her country

**pawn bro kers**  ('pȯn-brō-kərz)  money lenders, where people may use personal property as security

**ped a gogue**  ('pe-de-gäg)  teacher

**ped ant**  ('pe-dᵊnt)  one who lays too much stress on book learning

**pe des tri an**  (pə-'des-trē-ən)  walking

**peer**  ('pir)  equal

**pel li cle**  ('pe-li-kəl)  tiny film of ice

**pen ance**  ('pe-nəns)  punishment

**pen du lous**  ('pen-jə-ləs)  hanging

**pen du lous excrescence**  ('pen-jə-ləs; ik-'skre-ᵊns)  wart hanging

**pen i tent Peter**  ('pe-nə-tənt)  *see* Matthew, XXVI:75-76

**Penn the Apostle**  (ə-'pä-səl)  William Penn, the great Quaker who founded Pennsylvania

**penthouse**  overhanging; roof

**pe remp to ry**  ('pə-remp-tə-rē)  forceful

**per force**  (pər-'fōrs)  necessarily

**per i he li on**  (per-ə-'hēl-yən)  the spot nearest the horizon, so that it shows most plainly

**per me a ting**  ('per-mē-ā-tiŋ)  far reaching

**per se**  ('pər-sā)  in itself

**per se vere**  (pər-sə-'vir)  keep on

**Persian's grave**  Marathon, where the Persians were defeated by the Greeks

**per verse**  (pər-'vərs)  wrongly

**per ver sion**  (pər-'vər-zhən)  disgrace

**pestilent**  annoying

**pet ri fac tion**  (pe-trə-'fak-shən)  hardened stone (referring both to its actual material and its uninviting atmosphere)

**Pe tru chi o's Kate**  (pə-'trü-ki-ōz)  the scolding wife of Petruchio in

Shakespeare's *The Taming of the Shrew*

**phan tasm** ('fan-ta-zəm) ghostliness

**Pha raoh's daughters** ('fer-ōz) pictures of Pharaoh's daughter, who found Moses in the bulrushes. *See* Exodus II:1-10

**phe nom en on** (fi-'nä-mə-nän) extraordinary occurrence

**phil o mel** ('fi-lə-mel) nightingale

**phil o pro gen i tive ness** (fi-lə-prō-'je-nə-tov-nəs) love for one's own children

**phil o soph i cal principles, on** (fə-'la-sə-fi-kəl) from sound reasoning; philosopher, thinker

**phlegm** ('flem) calmness

**Phoe bus** ('fē-bəs) Apollo, the god of the sun. He was supposed to have been born on the island of Delos

**pilgrim** traveler

**pil laged** ('pi-lidj) robbed

**Pin dus-born A rax es** ('pin-dəs; ə-'rak-sēz) now the Arta, a river famous in Greek mythology, which rises in the Pindus mountains

**pin ion** ('pin-yən) wing; pinioned, held

**piping** playing a tune

**pi quan cy** ('pē-kən-sē) smartness

**pique** ('pēk) spur

**Pi sa's leaning miracle** ('pē-zə) tower in Pisa, Italy, which leans to one side

**Pis cat a qua** (pi-'ska-tə-kwȯ) river forming the boundary line between Maine and New Hampshire

**pith** soundness

**plac id** ('pla-səd) peaceful looking

**plain tive** ('plān-tiv) pathetic

**plaited mail** very strong armor

**plaiting** ('plā-tiŋ) braiding

**plane-tree the Persian adorned** Xerxes, King of Persia, decorated a certain plane-tree (sycamore) that he admired, with silks and jewels

**plash y** ('pla-shē) wet

**Plenty's horn** large curving horn overflowing with fruits, etc., carried by Plenty, symbol of abundance

**pli a ble** ('plØ-ə-bəl) bendable

**pli ant and mal le a ble** ('plØ-ə-bəl; 'ma-lē-ə-bəl) easily handled and adaptable

**plied** ('plØd) worked at

**plume** ('plüm) pride
**plundered** mussed
**poet laureate** ('lór-ē-āt) office, with title of same name, given a poet by king of England. His duty is to write poems on historical events
**poi lu** (pwäl-'yü) French soldier
**political unity** one government for the entire country, North and South
**polity** ('pä-lə-tē) state
**pol lu tion** (pə-'lü-shən) something unclean
**pom mel** ('pə-məl) pound
**pomp** ('pämp) wealth
**Poor Law** law for the relief of the poor
**Poor Richard** the name Franklin assumed in *Poor Richard's Almanac*
**pop ul ace** ('pä-pyə-ləs) the common people
**por tent** ('pór-tent) sign
**portentous** (pór-'ten-təs) a thing full of meaning
**porter** ale; one who carries bundles
**Port Royal** town in Nova Scotia, now called Annapolis, captured by the English in 1710
**possessed of a demon** under the control of an evil spirit
**postboy** driver
**pos tern** ('pōs-tərn) gate
**posting down** riding at full speed
**po tent** ('pō-tᵊnt) powerful
**Poul ter ers shop** ('pol-tər-ərz) where fowls are sold
**pound** British money, about five dollars [1921]
**praetor** ('prē-tər) public officer
**prairie schooner** ('skü-nər) canvas-covered wagon used for travel across the western plains
**prec e dent** (pri-'sē-dᵊnt) custom established by the action
**pre cepts** ('prē-septs) lessons
**pre cincts** ('prē-siŋkts) walls
**pre cip i tate** (pri-'si-pə-tət) very fast; precipitation, haste
**pre cip i ta tion** (pri-si-pə-'tā-shən) rash haste
**pred e ces sor, his** ('pre-də-sə-sər) governor who held office before him
**pre dic a ment** ('pri-di-kə-mənt) difficulty
**pre dom i nant** (pri-'dä-mə-nənt) in authority; predominance, authority

**prel ac y and persecution** ('pre-lə-sē) power of the church to rule and to punish

**prel ude** ('pre-lüd) introduction

**pre ma ture ly** (prē-mə-'tür-lē) before expected

**pre pos ter ous** (pri-'päs-tə-rəs) absurd

**pre saged** ('pre-sijd) foretold

**press** newspaper or other publication

**pre tense** ('prē-tens) show

**pretensions** (pri-'ten-chənz) claims

**prev a lent** ('pre-və-lənt) common

**prhyme** ('pr∅m) best part of

**Prhymer** the first reader of the early colonists, much of its subject matter was religious

**pri me val** (pr∅-'mē-vəl) that reminded one of the time when the world was new and uncivilized; primeval forest, forest whose trees have never been cut by man

**prim ing** ('pr∅-miŋ) ammunition

**Prince of Orange** a Holland nobleman who became William III of England

**prisms** ('pri-zəmz) crystals

**privacy of glorious light, etc.** you are all alone, having flown too high for other birds to follow you

**pro cliv i ties** (prō-'kli-və-tēz) tendencies

**procuring** (prə-'kyür-iŋ) management

**Pro di gal Son** ('prä-di-gəl) *see* St. Luke XV:11-32

**prodigies** ('prä-də-jēz) wonderful feats

**pro di gious ly** (prə-'di-jəs-lē) astonishingly

**prof fer** ('prä-fər) offer

**pro fuse** (prō-'fyüs) many; abundant

**prone** ('prōn) downcast

**prop a gat ed in succession** ('prä-pə-gā-təd) taken up by one after another

**Prophet descending from Sinai** ('s∅-n∅) Moses; *see* Exodus XXXIV

**Prophet's rod** *see* Exodus VII

**proposition** belief

**pro pri e ty** (prə-'pr∅-ə-tē) decency

**pros trate** ('prä-strāt) powerless; prostrates principalities, overcomes tyranny

**province** proper uses; purpose

**pro vin cial** (prə-'vin-chəl) for one section alone

**prying day** ('prø-iŋ) daylight that reveals everything
**pseu do nym** ('sü-d³n-im) pen name
**purpling plain** twilight landscape

**quaff** ('kwäf) drink; quaffed off, drank
**Queen of Leb an on** ('lə-bə-nən) Lady Hester Stanhope, an eccentric Englishwoman with whom Harriet Livermore, "the half-welcome guest," lived for a time in Syria, where Lady Stanhope was leader of some half-civilized tribes. They both believed in the second coming of Christ in their lifetimes
**Queens of She ba** ('shē-bə) pictures of the Queen of Sheba, an ancient country in southern Arabia; *see* I Kings, X
**quer u lous** ('kwer-ə-ləs) complaining
**quidding** tobacco chewing

**rabble** crowds of common people
**radius** region
**rail** make fun of
**rak ish** ('rā-kish) dashing
**ral lied** ('ra-lēd) joked
**rank** overgrown
**ra pa cious** (rə-'pā-shəs) greedy
**ra pi er** ('rā-pē-ər) sword
**rapture** burst of joyous song
**Rat is bon** ('rat-is-bon) a town in Germany
**reach the dust-cloud** overtake the long trail of dust left behind Kyrat
**read the destiny for others** *see* far enough ahead, as president of the United States, to judge what are the best courses to follow
**re as sur ance** (rē-ə-'shúr-əns) comfort
**re ces ses** ('rē-se-səs) far corners
**re cip ro cat ed the sentiment** (ri-'si-prə-kā-təd) returned the feeling
**rec la ma tion** (re-klə-'mā-shən) reformation
**recompensed** ('re-kəm-penst) rewarded
**rec on noi ter** (rē-kə-'nói-tər) explore
**re dress** (ri-'dres) relief
**red streamer** sunrise glow
**ref lu ent** ('re-flü-ənt) receding, as the tide flows back to the sea
**re frac to ries** ('ri-frak-tə-rēz) materials which form a glaze

**refractory** ('ri-frak-tə-rē) unmanageable; obstinate

**ref u gee** (re-fyù-'jē) one who flees for safety; man in hiding because of his political beliefs

**re fuse** ('re-fyüs) cast off

**re gent** ('rē-jənt) one who takes the place of the rightful ruler—here, of the shepherd

**regular firebrand of discontent** person who always stirs up trouble wherever he goes

**reigning the will to** keeping all the energies directed toward

**reign of the Henries** last half of the sixteenth century. The Henries were French kings

**re it er at ed** (rē-'i-tə-rā-təd) repeated

**re mon strat ed** ('re-mən-strā-təd) protested

**ren dez vous** ('rän-di-vü) a meeting by appointment

**ren e gade** ('re-ni-gād) deserter

**Re ne Le blanc** ('rə-nā; lə-'blon)

**rent** broken

**repeater** small spring which makes a watch strike the time

**re plet ed** (ri-'ple-təd) oversatisfied

**re pute** (ri-'pyüt) respect

**re sid u a ry leg a tee** (ri-'zi-jə-wer-ē; le-gə-'tē) heir to what is left after provisions of the will are carried out

**re signed** (rē-'sØnd) submissive

**re sort** (ri-'zòrt) go; hiding

**re source** ('rē-sōrs) means of help

**res pite** ('res-pət) rest

**re ten tive of** (ri-'ten-tiv) similar to

**retort** quick reply, severe or witty, intended to quiet the person addressed

**rev el ers** ('re-və-lərz) merry-makers

**rev els** ('re-vəlz) frolics

**re ver ber a tions** (ri-vər-bə-'rā-shənz) echoes

**rev er ie** ('re-və-rē) daydream

**revoke** cancel; remove

**Reyhan** ('rā-ən)

**rho do ra** (rō-'dōr-ə) New England plant

**ricks** stacks protected from wet by some covering

**rime** short, white, stiff hair that suggested frost

**ripened thought into action** influenced others to carry out the good deeds they were thinking of

**roan** ('rōn) chestnut horse

**Ro a noke** ('rō-ə-nōk) river in Virginia and North Carolina

**Robin Crusoe** Robinson Crusoe, the hero of Defoe's famous story of that name. He had a slave named Friday and a parrot

**ro bust** ('rō-bəst) strong

**roe** ('rō) a kind of deer

**roisterer** ('rói-stər-ər) merry-maker

**rood** ('rüd) 40 square rods

**Rouge Bouquet** (rüzh; 'bü-kā)

**roundheaded dignitary** Puritan who revolted, under Oliver Cromwell, against Charles I in 1649. The Puritans wore their hair cut close as opposed to the royalists' long curls

**Rou shan** ('rü-shän)

**royal commission** king's order

**rub i cund** ('rü-bi-kənd) red faced

**ruf fi an** ('rə-fē-ən) rascal

**rumor reached our shores** the rumor that the Prince of Orange was to be put in power in place of James II

**runaway wishes** desires we should not give in to

**running such a rig** engaging in such a frolic

**rural de i ties** ('dē-ə-tēz) gods and goddesses of the farm

**rus tic meal** simple country meal

**ruth less ly** ('rüth-ləs-lē) pitilessly

**sa ber** ('sā-bər) sword

**sac ri fice** ('sa-krə-fØs) offering of unselfishness

**sa ga cious** (sə-'gā-shəs) wise

**sages** ('sā-jəz) wise people

**Saint Dunstan** English monk of the 10th century who was tempted at his forge by an evil spirit, whose nose he seized with his red-hot tongs

**Saint Eu la le** (sän; u-la-lē)

**Sal a mis** ('sa-lə-məs) ancient city of Cyprus

**Salis bur y** ('sólz-ber-ē) town in Massachusetts

**Salm on** ('sa-mən)

**salts** sailors

**Sa mi an** ('sā-mē-ən)

**samp** porridge made of Indian corn coarsely ground and browned

**sampler** piece of needlework which shows one's skill in sewing

**sark** ('särk) drapery

**sa ti ety** (sə -'tØ-ə-tē) weariness

**Sa to ry** ('sä-tō-rē)

**sa van na** (sə-'va-nə) subtropical, treeless grassy plain

**sa vor** ('sā-vər) flavor; odor

**scab bard** ('ska-bərd) case for sword

**scarfed and bolted** fitted together and screwed

**scarred** full of shell holes

**schooner** ('skü-nər) two-masted vessel, having fore-and-aft rig, the large sail being on the after mast; **schooner-rigged** (*see above*)

**scourge** ('skərj) curse

**scouring** searching

**screw** miser

**Scriptural forms** use of *thee, thou,* etc.

**scrup ul ous in imputing motives to** ('skrü-pyə-ləs) careful in suspecting

**scru ti nize** ('skrü-tᵊn-Øz) investigate

**scut tled** ('skə-tᵊld) filled with holes

**sectional** between two places, races, or classes

**seed that's spread** ideas which grow as they are spread

**self-ac cu sa to ry** (a-'kyü-zə-tōr-ē) blaming themselves

**sensible** aware; causing bodily injury

**sep ul chers** ('sə-pəl-kərs) gravelike piles

**seraglio** (sə-'ral-yō) former official palace of the Turkish sultan

**ser a phim** ('ser-ə-fim) angels

**ses ter ces** ('ses-tər-sēz) the sesterce was a silver coin

**Seventh Day** there was on foot a movement to close on Sundays the public bake-shops, where the poor, whose houses contained fireplaces but no ovens, had much of their cooking (especially Sunday dinner) done at a small cost

**shaft** monument; steel bar

**shagbark** rough-barked, nut-bearing hickory tree

**shah** ('shä) ruler

**shape and shadow** life

**shaped in a classic mold** made to look like a Greek statue

**shards** sharp stones

**share** metal part of plow which cuts the ground

**Shaw nee** (shȯ-'nē) one of the tribe of Algonquins

**shay** for *chaise,* carriage

**sheen** shining; brilliance

**sheer** turn; absolute; straight up

**Sheik** ('shēk) Arab chief
**Shelley, Percy Bysshe** ('bish)
**Ship of State** the government
**shipwrecked Paul** the apostle Paul was shipwrecked off the coast of the island of Melita (now Malta) in the Mediterranean
**shores** supports
**shorn of their streaming hair, be** have their foliage cut off
**shrapnel** ('shrap-nᵊl) explosive shell
**shrew** ('shrü) a scold
**shrine** protection for a sacred relic. The little log house is placed within a granite shelter
**shroud** drapery; shrouds, ropes leading from the masthead
**si dled** ('si-dᵊld) moved sidewise
**Sie na's saint** (sē-'ə-näz) St. Catherine of Siena was noted for her sanctity and her wonderful visions
**Si er ra** (sē-'er-ə) range of mountains
**significant** full of meaning
**sign of the Scorpion** the Scorpion is a constellation which the sun enters about October 23
**sil hou ette** (si-lə-'wet) outline; shadow; silhouetted, outlined in black
**sill** timber on bottom of carriage
**sylvan** forest-covered; countrylike; sylvan glooms, forest darkness
**silver sphere** moon
**sim i le** ('si-mə-lē) comparison
**sin ews** ('sin-yüz) muscles; sinewy, strong
**singular** queer; unusual
**singularity** strangeness
**si ren** ('si-rən) sea-nymph
**"Sir Roger de Coverly"** ('kə-vər-lē) a dance like the Virginia reel
**skipper** master of a vessel; here, teacher. *See* Chalkley
**Sky ros** ('skē-rós)
**slacker** looser
**sleek est** ('slē-kəst) smoothest
**slip** platform on which ships are built
**sloth** ('slóth) laziness
**Smithfield** section of London where martyrs suffered death by burning
**smithy** blacksmith shop
**Smyr na** ('smər-nə) town in Turkey

**soar, but never roam**  rise, but always return

**social the o rists**  ('thē-ə-rists)  those who study people in their relations to one another

**sol em nized**  ('sä-ləm-nØzd)  honored

**so lic i tude**  (sə-'li-sə-tüd)  anxiety

**solstice of summer**  ('sōl-stəs)  one of the times when the sun is farthest from the equator—June 21

**Sol way**  ('säl-wā)  Solway Firth, noted for its swift tides

**som bre ro**  (səm-'brer-ō)  kind of broad-brimmed hat

**som no lent**  ('säm-nə-lənt)  drowsy

**son of the road**  one who lived out-of-doors; a highwayman

**so no rous**  (sə-'nōr-əs)  resounding

**sor did**  ('sȯr-dəd)  unidealistic; selfish

**sou brette**  (sü-'bret)  frivolous young woman of the stage—here, a singer

**soul's de bat a ble land**  (di-'bā-tə-bəl)  province of right and wrong

**sov er eign**  ('sä-vrən)  important

**sow the world with**  scatter over the earth

**Spanish Main**  Caribbean Sea

**spar**  ('spär)  mast; mineral substance

**Spartans**  ('spär-t⁹nz)  a people of ancient Greece famous for their bravery and endurance

**spe cies**  ('spē-shēz)  kinds; type

**spectral**  ghostly

**sphere**  circle of activity

**spher ule**  ('sfir-ül)  little sphere-shaped particle

**spon ta ne ous com bus tion**  (spän-'tā-nē-əs; kəm-'bəs-chən)  fire caused by chemical action within a substance

**spouse**  ('spaüs)  wife

**spume-flakes**  ('spyüm)  froth

**spurned Arabian plains**  rushed over the wide deserts of Arabia

**spurs**  timbers which hold the ship

**squab**  ('skwäb)  short and fat

**stable**  lasting

**stagnant-blooded**  lazy

**stal wart**  ('stȯl-wərt)  strong and brave

**stanch**  ('stȯnch)  steadfast

**stan chion**  ('stan-chən)  of stalls

**standard of values**  ideal to judge people's actions by

**stars . . . cypress trees** *see* cypress tree

**state** great importance

**stature** ('sta-chər) height

**stave** musical term, meaning staff. *A Christmas Carol* is therefore divided into staves rather than chapters

**stays** supports

**stay spur** stop using the spur; slow-up

**St. Catherine** St. Catherine was vowed to a single life; to braid her tresses is to remain unmarried

**steeped in** filled with; soaked

**stem son** ('stem-sən) piece of curved timber on the bow of a ship's frame

**stern son-knee** ('stərn-sən) end of a keelson, which *see*

**St. Fran çois** (san; frän-swä) St. Francis River, in Canada

**stir rups** ('stər-əps) foot supports hanging from saddle

**St. Michael** ('mi-kəl) in the Bible, the leader of the entire host of angels

**stock** wooden handle

**stock and store** supply of words

**stodg y** ('stä-jē) settled in their ways

**Stony Point** fort on the Hudson River captured by the British, and retaken by Americans in 1779

**stop-gap** temporary stoppage

**strait waistcoat** binding jacket for insane

**stu ar ti a** (stü-'är-shə) shrub with large single flowers

**stubborn right abide, my** acknowledge my power today

**Stuy ve sant** ('stØ-və-sənt)

**subjugated** he means *subjected*

**submits its processes** depends upon for its development

**sub sis tence** (səb-'sis-təns) a living

**substance** wealth

**sub tle** ('sə-tᵊl) mysterious; subtly, mysteriously

**sub vert** (səb-'vərt) destroy

**suf fuse** (sə-'fyüs) overspread

**suite** ('swēt) number of adjoining rooms

**Sultan's Groom** a hunchback who sought the princess's hand. *See The Arabian Nights*

**Summer of All-Saints** Indian summer

**sump tu ous** ('səmp-shə-wəs) luxurious

**sunder, in** into parts

**Su ni um** ('sü-ni-üm) a rocky headland on the extreme south of Attica, now Cape Colonna

**super** superintendent

**su perb** (sù-'pərb) beautifully formed

**su per flu i ties** (sü-pər-'flü-ə-tēz) things you do not need

**su per nal** ('sù-'pər-n°l) heavenly

**supernatural, the** strange happenings

**supplication** entreaty

**sur cease** ('sər-sēs) forgetfulness

**surge** ('serj) waves

**sur plus population** ('sər-pləs) number of unnecessary people

**sur rep ti tious ly** (sər-əp-'ti-shəs-lē) in a stealthy manner

**survival of the fittest** selection and preservation of those who are the most able. This theory was worked out by Charles Darwin, nineteenth century scientist

**sus cep ti ble** (sə-'sep-tə-bəl) possible to be developed into

**sustain its role** ('rōl) act the part it was dressed to represent

**su sur rus** (sù-'sər-əs) whispering

**swain** ('swān) young fellow

**swales** ('swālz) small valleys

**swan-like, let me sing and die** the swan was supposed to sing musically just before its death

**swar ded** ('swòr-dəd) grassy

**swarth y** ('swòr-thē) dark colored

**swath** ('swäth) line of grass already cut

**sweep** road; long pole attached to post, for lowering and raising a bucket

**Sweet-water valley** *see* Nebraska

**swound** ('swaùnd) swoon or faint

**symbol of re gen er ate nature** (ri-'je-nə-rāt) sign of new-born life

**sym pho ny** ('sim-fə-nē) music

**tac it ly** ('ta-sət-lē) silently

**tac i turn** ('ta-sə-tərn) silent

**taffrail** rail around a ship's stern, or poop

**take a final stand** make one last effort to exist

**take six bars** jump as high as he can

**tallow-chandler** maker of tallow candles

**taming the mind** controlling willfulness

**tan gi ble** ('tan-jə-bəl) real
**tangled ram** *see* Genesis XXI:1-13
**tap** quality
**tap es tries** ('ta-pə-strēz) heavy curtains and hangings
**Tartar's lance** long spear carried by Tartars, fierce horsemen of Asia
**taw ny** ('tȯ-nē) yellow; tawny mound, brown outline
**Ta yg e tus** (tā-'ij-ə-təs) mountain in Greece
**teal** ('tēl) river duck
**Teche** ('tesh) river in Louisiana
**te di ous** ('tē-dē-əs) long
**tendril** slender, coiling attachment to the stern
**ten e brous** ('te-nə-brəs) gloomy
**Tents of Grace** translation of the name given by the Moravians to
    their mission
**termagant** ('tər-mə-gənt) quarreling
**ter res tri al** (tə-'res-trē-əl) of the map of the world. The celestial
    globe shows heavenly bodies
**terse** ('tərs) brief
**Ther mop y lae** (thər-'mä-pə-lē) *see* "Historical Note," page 265
**Theseus** ('thē-süs)
**the time-of-day** whatever might happen during the day
**thewed** ('thüd) built
**thill** either of the two shafts between which a horse is hitched
**thin atmosphere** the higher up in the air, the thinner the air
    becomes
**tholes** supports to which the oars are fastened in rowing
**thoroughbrace** leather strap used as a spring
**thrall** ('thrȯl) in slavery
**threadbare** shabby
**threading** making his way carefully
**thyme** ('tØm) a fragrant plant
**tier** ('tir) layer
**Time's burst of dawn** beginning of the greatest period in history
**Tit an** ('tØ-tᵊn) *see* Titan-like
**Ti ta ni a** (tØ-'tān-ē-ə) queen of the fairies
**Titan-like** like the fabled giants, Titans, who lived at the beginning
    of the world
**toc sin's a la rum** ('täk-sənz; ə-'lär-əm) warning signal
**to learn to spell** learn to work and rest by turns
**tol er a ble** ('tä-lə-rə-bəl) moderate; tolerably, fairly

**ton nage** ('tə-nij) weight in tons
**tor pid** ('tȯr-pəd) stupid
**torpor** heavy sleep
**Tory** man on the king's side in the Revolution
**Total Abstinence Principle** rule of going without alcoholic liquor; here, having nothing to do with spirits
**to the manner born** who had been born to fill that very place in life
**to the quick** till they were sore
**Tous les Bour geois de Chartres** (tü-lā-'bür-zhwä-də-shärt) all the people of Charters
**trainband captain** captain of a company of trained citizen-soldiers
**tram mels pen dent** ('tra-məls; 'pen-dənt) iron hooks to hang kettles over a fire
**tran quil** ('traŋ-kwəl) calm; tranquillity, peace
**transfigured** beautifully changed in appearance; become a spiritual being
**tran sient** ('tran-sē-ənt) temporary
**tran si tion very foreign** (tran-'si-shən) change in a trend of thought which was not customary
**tran si to ry** ('tran-sə-tōr-ē) brief
**trans mute** (trans-'myüt) change
**transports** raptures
**trav ail** (trə-'vāl) work and suffering
**tra versed** ('tra-vərst) crossed
**Treadmill** a form of prison discipline
**Treb i zond** ('tre-bə-zänd) one of the former divisions of Turkey
**trem u lous** ('trem-yə-ləs) shaky; tremulousness, fright
**trice** ('trȯs) instant
**trim** a condition
**tri pod** ('trȯ-päd) three-legged stand
**Tripolitan** (tri-'pä-lə-tᵊn) of Tripoli
**Tri ton** ('trȯ-tᵊn) a sea-god
**Truce of God** an attempt of the Church in the middle ages to lessen the evils of private warfare
**trun cheon** ('trən-chən) staff of command
**try the strength of gold** test the real power of wealth
**tucker** front in her dress
**tu mul tu ous** (tü-'məl-chə-wəs) wild
**tu nic** ('tü-nik) long, loose garment

**tur bu lent** ('tər-byə-lənt) rushing
**turnpike men** keepers of the gate where a toll, or tax, had to be paid
**twelfth-cakes** cakes made for Twelfth Night, the 12th night after Christmas

**u biq ui tous** (yü-'bi-kwə-təs) who were everywhere at once
**u na nim i ty** (yü-nə-'ni-mə-tē) congeniality
**unbartered** not bought
**unbeholden** unseen
**unbodied joy** spirit of happiness
**unconstrained de mea nor** (di-'mē-nər) happy, informal conduct
**unconventional** different from most people
**un couth** (ən-'küth) rude; terrible
**un del e te ri ous** (ən-de-lə-'ti-rē-əs) harmless
**undulating** ('ən-jə-lā-tiŋ) rolling; undulations, waves
**un fre quent ed** (ən-frē-'kwen-təd) rarely visited
**unhallowed** (ən-'ha-lōd) unworthy
**un im ped ed** (ən-im-'pē-dəd) without hindrance
**United States' security** several of the states had just refused to be responsible for their bonds, thus weakening United States' credit abroad
**un per turbed** (ən-pər-'tərbd) untroubled
**un pre med i tat ed art** (ən-prē-'me-də-tā-təd) beautiful singing which comes so natural to you
**unprofaned** sacred
**un scrup u lous** (ən-'skrü-pyə-ləs) unprincipled
**unseasonable allusions** unsuitable remarks
**unshadowed main** the ocean which has nothing on it to cast a shadow
**unstable** unfixed; constantly changing
**U phar sin** (yü-'fär-sən) *see* Daniel V:1-3; The blazing comet reminds Evangeline of God's power as the handwriting upon the wall reminded Belshazzar
**up roar i ous** (əp-'rōr-ē-əs) noisy and confused
**u sur pa tion** (yü-sər-'pā-shən) striking out entirely instead of by amending

**va ga ries** ('vā-gə-rēz) fickleness
**Valentine...Orson** characters in a legend of the time of Char-

lemagne

**va lid i ty** (və-'li-də-tē) truth

**vanes** ('vānz) weather vanes to show which way the wind was blowing

**vans** ('vanz) wings

**various communions of our Christian faith** different branches of the Christian church

**veered** ('vird) turned

**ve he ment ly** ('vē-ə-mənt-lē) furiously

**ven due** ('ven-dü) auction

**ve ner a ble** ('ve-nə-rə-bəl) worthy old

**vent** express; expression

**venturing** boasting

**veracity** (və-'ra-sə-tē) truthfulness

**Ver dun** (vər-'dən) town in France

**verge** ('vərj) edge

**ver i est** ('ver-ē-əst) worst

**ver nal** ('vər-nªl) spring

**ver te brae** ('vər-tə-brā) plural of vertebra, a bone of the spinal column

**very, the** even the

**ves tal** ('ves-tªl) everlasting; the vestal virgins were young maidens who continually tended the sacred fires of Vesta, goddess of the hearth

**ves tige** ('ves-tij) trace

**vestments** robes

**vi brant** ('v∅-brənt) throbbing

**victorious eagles** the figure of an eagle was the Roman emblem. It was mounted on a tall staff and carried in front of the troops

**vig il** ('vi-jəl) watch; vigilant watchful

**vin di cate their ancestry** be loyal to the ideals of their forefathers

**virago** (və-'rä-gō) quarrelsome woman

**virgins** *see* vestal

**vis age** ('vi-zij) face

**vision of life and death** Roushan Beg alive, yet so near death

**visitation** visit

**vis ta** ('vis-tə) view; vistaed, arranged in two rows through which a view is seen

**vit al** ('v∅-tªl) powerful; vitality, power

**vixen** ('vik-sən) ill-tempered woman

**voiceless shore** shore on which the songs of liberty no longer are heard

**void** without having had any effect; illegal

**voi là** ('vwä-lä) there he is!

**vol ley** ('vä-lē) outburst

**Vol tur nus** (väl-'túr-nō) a river, now spelled *Volturno*

**vo lup tu ous** (və-'ləp-chə-wəs) luxurious

**vo tive stone** ('vō-tiv) a monument sacred to them

**vouchsafed** (vaúch-'säft) permitted

**voy a geur** (vói-ə-'zhər) one who transports goods to and from stations for fur companies

**vul ture** ('vəl-chər) large, eaglelike, flesh-eating bird

**waifs of** things left by

**wains** ('wānz) wagons

**Walk er** slang term meaning "You don't mean it!"

**Wa le way** ('wä-lə-wā) branch of the Columbia river

**wan ing** ('wā-niŋ) passing; fading

**wan ton** ('wón-t²n) playful

**Ward** officer of the ward, one of the divisions of London

**warded** protected

**wa ri er** ('war-ē-ər) more cautious; warily, cautiously

**water-gourd** ('gōrd) pumpkinlike fruit hollowed out and dried to drink from

**wayward** self-willed

**weary year** months when I am an unimportant person

**weeding-out process** getting rid of inefficient employees

**weld** melt together so they could never be opened

**welterweight** medium weight

**Westminster Abbey** ('west-min-stər) famous church in London. It is the chief burial place of Great Britain's distinguished men and contains memorials to many noted foreigners

**what odds** what does it matter

**what the knowing ones call "nuts"** what people who know call the easiest thing in the world

**where to have him** how to annoy him

**whims** ('hwimz) notions

**whippletree** swinging bar to which part of a harness is fastened

**White of Selborne's** Gilbert White, who wrote *A Natural History of Selborne,* the district in England in which he was born

**whitethroat** European warbler
**Wi ca co** (wi-'kä-kō)
**wielder** user
**wim pling** ('wim-pliŋ) rippling
**Wind-river Mountains** part of the Rockies in Wyoming
**Winthrop, John** Governor of Massachusetts Colony (1588-1649)
**wire fence still is not** where no fences have been built
**wis** ('wis) think
**withal** (wi-'thȯl) besides; also
**with devotion translated** carried away by religious enthusiasm; for Elijah, *see* II Kings, XI
**with im pu ni ty** (im-'pyü-nə-tē) without punishment
**wold** ('wōld) plain; pasture
**wolfish** starved
**wont** ('wȯnt) accustomed
**wordy** in words (as opposed to the snowball)
**world has gone a-slumming** people are on the side of the poor
**world kings** governments whose power is controlled by one man
**worldling** one unused to simple life
**worthies** great men
**wreathed horn** the sea-god, Triton, blew a trumpet, made from a spiral seashell, to raise or calm the sea
**wrest** ('rest) to obtain by force
**writhed** ('rθthd) twisted
**wrought** ('rȯd) made; worked; wrought me her shadowy self to hold, cast a shadow for me to mirror; wrought its ghost, cast its shadow

**Xer xes** ('zərk-sēz) king of Persia (486-465 B. C.)

**Ya ka bow ski** (yä-kä-'bau̇-ski)
**yellow Tiber** the sands in the riverbed made the water appear yellow
**yeoman** ('yō-mən) farmer
**Yp si lan ti's Mai note Greeks** (ip-sə-'lan-tēz; 'mi-nōt) revolutionary cavalry recruited by Ypsilanti, Greek patriot from Maina, to fight against Turkey
**Yu kon** ('yü-kän) valley of the Yukon, in Alaska
**Yus souf** ('yə-səf)

**zeal** enthusiasm
**zeph yr** ('ze-fər) gentle breeze

# *Books Available from*
## Lost Classics Book Company
### American History
*Stories of Great Americans for Little Americans*..Edward Eggleston
*A First Book in American History* ...................... Edward Eggleston
*A History of the United States and Its People*....... Edward Eggleston
### Biography
*The Life of Kit Carson*........................................................Edward Ellis
### English Grammar
*Primary Language Lessons* ..................................................Emma Serl
*Intermediate Language Lessons*.................................... Emma Serl
*(Teacher's Guides available for each reader in this series)*
### Elson Readers Series
Complete Set ......................William Elson, Lura Runkel, Christine Keck
*The Elson Readers: Primer*.......................William Elson, Lura Runkel
*The Elson Readers: Book One* ...................William Elson, Lura Runkel
*The Elson Readers: Book Two* ...................William Elson, Lura Runkel
*The Elson Readers: Book Three* ..................................... William Elson
*The Elson Readers: Book Four* ...................................... William Elson
*The Elson Readers: Book Five* ..............William Elson, Christine Keck
*The Elson Readers: Book Six* ................William Elson, Christine Keck
*The Elson Readers: Book Seven*...........William Elson, Christine Keck
*The Elson Readers: Book Eight*.............William Elson, Christine Keck
*(Teacher's Guides available for each reader in this series)*
### Historical Fiction
*With Lee in Virginia* ..............................................G. A. Henty
*A Tale of the Western Plains* .......................................... G. A. Henty
*The Young Carthaginian*..................................................G. A. Henty
*In the Heart of the Rockies* ....................................................G. A. Henty
*For the Temple* .......................................................G. A. Henty
*A Knight of the White Cross* ...............................................G. A. Henty
*The Minute Boys of Lexington*......................... Edward Stratemeyer
*The Minute Boys of Bunker Hill*....................... Edward Stratemeyer
*Hope and Have* ............................................................ Oliver Optic
*Taken by the Enemy*, First in *The Blue and the Gray Series*...............Oliver Optic
*Within the Enemy's Lines*, Second in *The Blue and the Gray Series* ..Oliver Optic
*On the Blockade*, Third in *The Blue and the Gray Series*.....................Oliver Optic
*Stand by the Union*, Fourth in *The Blue and the Gray Series*..............Oliver Optic
*Fighting for the Right*, Fifth in *The Blue and the Gray Series*............Oliver Optic
*A Victorious Union*, Sixth and Final in *The Blue and the Gray Series*.....Oliver Optic
*Mary of Plymouth* ...............................................................James Otis

**For more information visit us at: http://www.lostclassicsbooks.com**

Made in the USA
Lexington, KY
14 April 2018